OF REALMS AND CHAOS

THE COVETED: VOL. II

BREA LAMB

For every soul who saw their fear and fought it with rage. May you always face your evils and win.

Trigger Warning:

This novel contains depictions of sexual assault, violence, gore, strong language, death, abuse, suicidal thoughts and actions, depression, and other heavy themes that might be difficult for some readers. Discretion is advised.

WELCOME TO THE WORLD OF THE COVETED

EOFORHILD

Demon Realm

HAVEN

PIKE

FOREST OF
TRAGEDIES

SOPHISTES

CLAUD

ELPIS

KRATOS

DUNAMIS

THE
ROYAL
CITY

ANDREIA

YENTAIN

EROS

GRISHEL

THE
SEA OF
AKIV

THE MIST

MORTAL REALM

BETOVERE

Fae Realm

ISLE READER

TOMORROW LANDS

READER RIVER

YESTERDAY LANDS

SLE ELEMENT

AIR LANDS

FIRE LANDS

THE CAPITAL

SINGLE LANDS

GOLDEN GUARD BASE

MULTIPLE LANDS

WATER LANDS

EARTH LANDS

ISLE SHIFTER

ISLE HEALER

N

W   E

S

MORTAL REALM

BEHMAN

SELK

The IBIDEM SEA

JORE

ELDOR PEAKS

XALIE

TAKORT

RAZC

TEMPLE
OF THE
GODS

CALESS

VESTEER

GANDRY

H

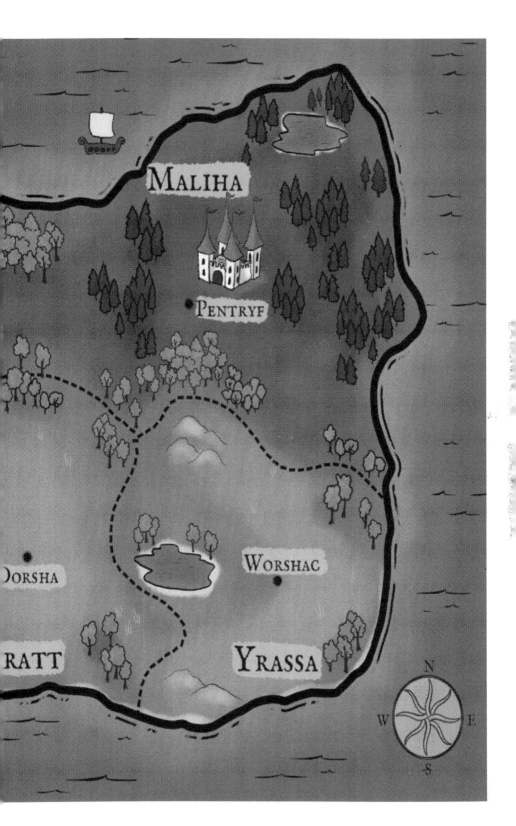

PRONUNCIATION GUIDE

Adbeel: Add-buh-hail

Alemthian: Uh-lem-the-in

Andreia: On-drey-uh

Asher: Ash-er

Asta: Ah-s-tuh

Augustu: Uh-gus-too

Ayad: Eye-ed

Behman: Bay-men

Bellamy: Bell-uh-me

Betovere: Bet-O-veer

Bhatt: Buh-ah-t

Bhesaj: Beh-saw-j

Braviarte: Brah-vee-ar-tey

Bronagh: Bro-nuh

Caless: Cuh-less

Calista: Cuh-lee-stuh

Claud: Claw-d

Cyprus: Sigh-prus

Dalistori: Dah-leh-store-E

Damon: Day-mun

Daniox: Dawn-wuah

Davina: Duh-vee-nuh

Demis: Deh-me-s

Dorsha: Door-shuh

Druj: D-roo-juh

Dunamis: Doo-nuh-miss

Elpis: El-pus

Engle: Aye-n-gull

Eoforhild: U-for-hill-d

Eros: Air-O-s

Farai: Fair-eye

Gandry: G-an-dree

Genevieve: Jen-eh-vee-v

Graham: Gr-am

Grishel: G-re-shell

Harligold: Har-leh-gold

Henry: Hen-ree

Heratt: Her-at

Herberto: Air-bear-tow

Ignazio: Eye-na-see-O

Iniko: In-E-co

Ishani: E-shaw-nee

Isolda: is-ole-duh

Jasper: Jas-pur

Jesre: Jess-ray

Jonah: Jo-nuh

Jore: Juh-or

Judson: Juh-d-son

Kafele: Kah-fey-lay

Karys: Care-is

Kratos: Cray-tow-z

Kyoufu: Kee-oh-foo

Lara: Lah-ruh

Lawrence: Lor-ence

Lazarev: L-ah-zuh-re-v

Lian: Lee-en

Likho: Lee-k-ho

Luca: Loo-cuh

Malcolm: Mal-k-um

Maliha: Muh-lee-uh

Maybel: May-bell

Mia: Me-uh

Mordicai: Moor-de-k-eye

Mounbetton: Mon-bet-tun

Nayab: Nay-eb

Nicola: Nee-co-lah

Noe: No-ee

Nyla: N-eye-luh

Odilia: Oh-dill-E-uh

O'Malley: O-mal-lee

Padon: Puh-d-on

Papatonis: pah-puh-tone-is

Paula: Paw-luh

Pentryf: Pen-t-riff

Pike: P-eye-k

Pino: Pee-n-yo

Prie: Puh-ree

Ranbir: Run-beer

Raymonds: Ray-mun-d-s

Razc: R-ah-z-k

Revanche: Rey-vah-n-ch

Salvatore: Sal-vuh-tor

Samell: Sah-mell

Selassie: Seh-lah-see

Selkans: Sel-k-en-s

Shah: Sh-aw

Shamay: Shuh-may

Sipho: S-eye-f-oh

Sophistes: So-fee-st-es

Stassi: S-tah-see

Stella: S-tell-uh

Sterling: Stir-ling

Takort: Tuh-core-t

Theon: Th-E-on

Tish: T-ish

Trint: T-rin-t

Tristana: Tris-tah-nuh

Ulu: Oo-loo

Venturae: Ven-ter-aye

Vesteer: Veh-s-tear

Windsor: Wind-soar

Winona: Why-no-nuh

Worshac: War-shack

Xalie: Zay-lee

Xavier: Ex-ay-vee-er

Yarrow: Yahr-r-oh

Yentain: Yen-t-A-n

Youxia: Yo-shaw

Yrassa: Ear-ah-suh

Zaib: Zay-buh

Zohar: Z-oh-hawr

GLOSSARY

Afriktor: Omniscient creature that lives in the Forest of Tragedies, created by the God of Death and Creation.

Air: Element sub-faction with the ability to wield Air power (i.e. create wind).

Betovere: Also known as Fae Realm, made up of five islands that are inhabited by the fae species.

Dalistori: A feline-like creature with the ability to alter its size, created by the God of Death and Creation.

Earth: Element sub-faction with the ability to wield Earth power (i.e. grow flowers).

Element: Faction of fae with the ability to wield elements.

Ending: Term used by fae that means death. It is believed that the fae will sense when Eternity calls them home, and that is when they will choose to pass on.

Eoforhild: Also known as the Demon Realm, this is the continent that the demon species reside on.

Eternity: The sentient place that fae power comes from, as well as the higher power they pray to and believe their souls return to after death.

Faction: Term used to group together fae with similar powers (i.e. Readers or Shifters).

Fae Council: Group of fae who aid the King of the Fae Realm with decision making.

Fetch: A dream-walking creature with the power to track magical signatures, created by the God of Death and Creation.

Fire: Element sub-faction with the ability to wield Fire power (i.e. create a flame).

Healer: Faction of fae with the ability to heal.

Honey Tongue: Ability to influence beings with the sound of one's voice.

Lady/Lord: The title bestowed on demons who reside over one of the five territories in Eoforhild.

Magic: General term for abilities that are thought to be bestowed by gods, wielded most notably by demons.

Moon: Ability to wield the raw magic from the moon (i.e. wield shadows).

Mortal: General term for the humans who do not live indefinitely.

Multiple: Shifter sub-faction with the ability to alter their appearance in indefinite ways, though they can only maintain that form for a short period of time.

Navalom: Creature that lives in the Forest of Tragedies and feasts on memories.

Oracle: Term for a being who can see both the past and the future without touching a being. This ability is rare and believed to only be possessed by fae.

Power: The general term for abilities gifted by Eternity, wielded by fae.

Prime: Member of the fae council who is in charge of particular specialties that are needed to maintain the Fae Realm (i.e. trade or coin). They live in The Capital.

Reader: Faction of fae with the ability to read the past or future.

Royal Court: Members of the fae council who are the strongest in their respective sub-faction. They are chosen to represent said sub-faction and live in The Capital (ie. Royal Healer or Royal Fire).

Shifter: Faction of fae with the ability to alter their physical appearance.

Single: Shifter sub-faction that can alter their appearance into one chosen form for an unlimited amount of time (i.e. wolf or panther).

Siren: Water folk with the ability to have legs on land and a large fin underwater. Can lure their prey with their singing.

Sub-faction: Term used to represent fae who wield the same power.

Sun: Ability to wield the raw magic from the sun (i.e. wield light).

Tomorrow: Reader sub-faction with the ability to read the future of anyone they touch.

Warden: Title bestowed on the second strongest member of each sub-faction. They rule over their respective lands.

Water: Element sub-faction with the ability to wield Water power (i.e. create waves).

Whisp: Creature that can turn their body into various forms, such as black mist, bubbles, etc.

Wraith: Creature with the ability to blend into their surroundings, their form fading and turning them nearly invisible. Often called ghosts by the fae, though they are living beings.

Yesterday: Reader sub-faction with the ability to read the past of anyone they touch.

Youngling: The fae and demon equivalent to a child.

BEFORE WE BEGIN,
LET US FIRST REFRESH...

Following over two centuries of being brainwashed, manipulated, and abused, Asher Daniox had become a blank canvas—existing for the sole purpose of allowing others to paint her into anyone they wished. But when her wedding came to a bloody end, Asher was stolen away by the very male she had been told was her sworn enemy—The Elemental. After spending months with Bellamy and his Trusted, she slowly but surely fell in love with the demon prince, and perhaps even crafted a family of her own along the way.

Facing loss, terror, life-altering realizations, and an uncertain future, we last saw our wayward princess riding off to the capital of the Demon Realm, The Royal City. There, she and Bellamy would meet with King Adbeel Ayad. What Asher did not realize was that her dashing prince, whom she had just proclaimed her undying love for, was lying to her in more ways than one. You see, Bellamy was not a demon at all. Rather, he was a fae. A fae who had bore witness to his and Asher's future play out in Reader River. With the two vowing to tell each other the difficult truths and each harboring their own goals, the ending of the lovers' tale seemed to be heading quickly towards a cliff's edge.

We open our story just like that, with two beings that are desperately in love and the knowledge that on a nearby shore, an orange-haired queen plots revenge.

ACT I
~ TO LOVE ~

PROLOGUE

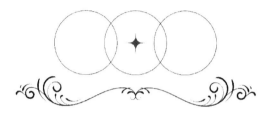

Long ago, far longer than most remember, the Demon Realm known as Eoforhild had a family upon its throne. King Adbeel Ayad and Queen Solei Ayad had two younglings, a son and a daughter. An inseparable pair in their youth, Malcolm and Zaib loved each other dearly, just as all who met them did—though, that was true for every Honey Tongue.

Zaib in particular had an affinity for captivating the masses. As she grew and matured, the demon princess would find a passion for diplomacy. Many believed that, despite being the younger of the two, it was she who should be named heir.

Like most rivalries, the fight between the prince and princess began and ended with jealousy. With support for the princess growing, and his own wavering, Malcolm found himself in a precarious position. For how could he give up his claim to the throne he had been born to sit upon?

No, that simply would not do.

So when the royal family awoke one night to the cataclysmic shattering of the nearby Fae Realm known as Betovere, the prince did nothing. He merely waited, knowing his sister well enough to anticipate her next move. He had been correct in his assumptions.

The princess, so dedicated to peace and unification, offered to act as an emissary. She would travel to Betovere and form an alliance. It was her belief that uniting could prevent conflict in the future and, perhaps, change the world for the better.

King Adbeel disagreed vehemently. Pointless, he called it. Let them attack, let them start a war they could not win. What did it matter to them? Malcolm agreed. If not because war was a chance to prove himself, then simply because he enjoyed watching his sister lose.

Watching her embarrass herself with failure.

Years passed, then decades, then centuries, and the princess remained persistent. The attacks from Betovere were harsh, and many from both sides lost their lives in battle. The fae were far stronger than King Adbeel had believed, especially with their restricted breeding. Bloodlines remained pure, and the new fae born were stronger.

After three centuries had come and gone, the years growing bloodier and more uncertain, the king finally agreed. Zaib would take a team of highly skilled demons to Betovere to negotiate peace. Treaties would be signed, allegiances formed, and Eoforhild would be better for it.

What the princess did not account for was the strength of jealousy—of feuding. She did not consider how far her beloved brother would go to secure his claim.

That was, until he slit her throat.

CHAPTER ONE

ASHER

The palace was something out of a fairytale.

As we drew closer, I could see that vines grew up the walls, painting the white and gray with tangled strokes of green. Lilies of the valley sprouted throughout the vast expanse of grass that covered the hillside leading to the towering gray gates. Large windows sporadically lined the structure, giving small glimpses of the interior.

I wondered how something as beautiful as this city could exist when the world around it was so ugly.

Bellamy remained silent beside me, our horses nearly touching as we rode up the path to whatever future he had so carefully cultivated. My own lies and hidden plans hung heavy in my mind, reminding me that I would be a hypocrite to hold his against him.

I would leave soon, prepared to fight the fae royals who had raised me, who had betrayed their realm and their ward. The crown and the kingdom would never be the same. I would make sure of that. Overthrowing them was our only hope of stopping the coming war between demons and fae before it started—before it decimated both realms and dragged the mortals down too.

Around us, the residents of The Royal City smiled and waved at their prince, not even the coming twilight stopping them from being outside and enjoying one another's company. Younglings roamed the crowd. Joy radiated from them all, uplifting my own mood.

Would it ever not surprise me to see beings of all kinds gathered around, freely mingling? And would there ever be a time that the small voice in my head did not deem it wrong or dangerous?

Many stopped to stare at their prince, some of the younger ones chasing Bellamy—throwing flowers his way and requesting he give them a show. The prince obliged, sending flowers of black flame into the air. For one of the younglings, he offered a small whirlpool of water into her hand, laughing as it burst when he released it. Then the wind came, fluttering in our hair and ruffling our clothes. When vines lifted off houses and danced with the tiniest little male, cheers erupted. The others argued over who would get a turn next, pushing and shoving their way to the crown prince of Eoforhild.

A few of the grown demons seemed weary of me, as if they could sense that there was something off about my appearance. They were right to be afraid, right to cower. I *was* dangerous. But I did not wish hurt upon them. In fact, I wished to see them live a life without war threatening their peace.

One demon in particular seemed to stare straight into my soul. It was as if she was unable to take her eyes from my face, her brows furrowed in concentration. She looked rather young, about the same age as Mia or Ignazio—Nicola's father. Intense gaze aside, it was her mind that set off my warning bells.

It cannot be her. She has long been rumored dead. No, this must be someone else. But why then, would she be with the prince? Why would she be here otherwise?

From that point on, I stared forward, ignoring them all. It seemed I was deceased. At least, according to demon gossip.

Well, stares were better than being stoned—a definite positive.

Quicker than I had been ready for, we approached the gates of the palace that housed King Adbeel Ayad, the leader of the demons. Unsure what to suspect, I allowed my power to wander, tasting the air and the minds that occupied the area. Two guards stood at attention, wearing light blue uniforms with the demon sigil in black, white, and silver at the center. It was the clothing form of the tapestry that hung in Henry's chambers back in Haven, a sign of the Sun's deep love for his realm.

Both guards were on high alert, eyes darting between Bellamy and I as if they were attempting to decipher what he could possibly be doing with me. I tried not to take it as an insult…and failed. My chin tilted up faintly, a gesture that I hoped would make me seem more regal and confident, though it was just as likely that it made me look foolish.

"Open the gates, now," Bellamy ordered the two guards. A mere moment passed before the gates were spreading apart, groaning loudly, as if they were not often used.

We urged our horses forward, both blue-clad demons watching me closely. I fought off the urge to stick my tongue out at the one who glared slightly. Their job was to maintain the safety of King Adbeel, and I could not fault them for doing simply that.

Blue and gray stones made up the courtyard beyond the gates, looking as if a beautiful storm was attempting to overtake a bright, clear sky. White stone arches lined the outer walls, creating a covered area to roam beneath. Beyond that, the castle stretched at least six stories high, the top seeming to touch the clouds overhead. Those same green vines crawled up the stone, like claws gripping the looming structure.

A large blue flag with the demon sigil flew on each pointed tower, as well as many within the courtyard itself. A square of the brightest green grass lined with multicolored rocks sat in the center. Randomly placed were patches of dirt that housed large trees whose branches and leaves reached towards the ground, as if weeping at the beauty of it all.

Bellamy still had that smile plastered on his face, dimples on full display. He quickly dismounted his horse, practically leaping off, his eagerness contagious. A stable hand ran to retrieve the reins. I watched as she offered Bellamy a swift curtsy and a small smile. He tilted his head down, a gesture no fae royal would have ever granted anyone in Betovere. Her scarlet blush made me smile.

That charming bastard.

Then he was making his way to me, lifting his arms to aid my own dismount. For no reason other than stubbornness, I attempted to slide myself off the other side, but Bellamy was there before my feet could hit the ground, catching me amidst a cloud of black shadows. The smell of cinnamon and smoke was heavy in the air, and I wondered to myself how anyone could live like this.

How did one survive love? It seemed desperate to take over my every thought, to throw out my inhibitions and bring me to my knees in submission. A position I would gladly spend all day in for the prince in front of me.

It had been one day since we admitted our love for one another, and already I was losing my gods damned mind.

"If you keep looking at me like that, Princess, I will be forced to take you here in the courtyard," Bellamy rasped into my ear, sending a shiver down my spine.

"I did not take you for an exhibitionist," I remarked, smirking up at the demon.

He laughed, a deep sound that heated me to my core. "For you, I would be anything."

His sly grin was the only warning I got before his lips were on mine, the heat of his tongue tracing the seam of my mouth with fervor, like an attempt to memorize it.

Eagerly, I opened, tasting the rich flavor of the neem twig he had used that morning to clean his teeth. Moments passed, and he was lifting me up, my legs wrapping around his waist as he carried me through the palace doors.

A rough cough sounded from the left, and we quickly parted to see an amused blue-clad guard watching us. Bellamy chuckled, but I hastily wiggled myself out of his hold and stepped away.

I was so used to hiding, to feeling an overwhelming amount of guilt for sneaking around with The Capital guards and visiting vendors, that being open about my affections terrified me, and I did not know how to take this last leap into the beginning of my new life. Into my future.

Fortunately for me, the demon prince was far from dismayed. Bellamy grabbed me by the arm, grip firm as he tugged my body into his. His other hand moved to my throat, a ringed thumb pressing under my chin to tilt my face up.

Then he devoured me once more, tongues and teeth clashing, his hunger never quite satiated. Bellamy's hand traveled up my bicep, which had become far more toned in our weeks of traveling and training, and then began sliding at a tantalizingly slow pace down my back. At the base of my spine, those wicked fingers just grazing the top of my trousers, he pulled away.

"You are too incredible to continue hiding. Your mind, your heart, your soul—they are rare and beautiful and worthy of being seen. Do not hide, Princess. Do not cower. Bless the world with yourself, and watch as we all fall to our knees before you," he whispered, placing a kiss to each of my cheeks. Then he pecked my forehead, my chin, my nose. Finally, he offered a soft kiss to my lips, so much love poured into it that tears pricked my eyes.

I nodded, unwilling to speak for fear of falling into a fit of sobs. I had never felt so loved, so unconditionally treasured. If he was aware of the effect he had on me, Bellamy did not show it. He merely smiled, his dimples poking holes into his cheeks.

The guard in blue was not afraid to watch us, to bear witness to our affections. It seemed no one was, the demons walking around clearly unbothered but not uninterested. Servants were bustling about and courtiers were conversing, all eyes flitting our way every so often.

Do not hide. Do not cower.

Our hands entwined as we followed the guard through the palace, weaving past brilliant white corridors that were decorated with paintings. Some I recognized as Bellamy's work, while others I could tell were not. It was as if his pulled my eye, begging me to notice the way the brush strokes moved, the play on colors, the often eerie look of doom and sorrow. Beside me, Bellamy said nothing, not even sparing his art a glance.

Greenery was everywhere, the air tasting clean and fresh from the abundance of plants. I took note of the lilies of the valley, so many that I wondered if they held significance to the residents of The Royal City, to the king, or if they were just a favored local flower.

Gorgeous blue runners lined every hallway with differing patterns woven into them in silver, white, and black. The bleached wooden floors below are a perfect complement to the colors. Crystal chandeliers sat above, reflecting rainbows from the demon light in a similar way to the one above Bellamy's piano forte in Haven. The thought of the all-white room with the stunning black piano at the center brought a soft smile to my face. Maybe one day I would be able to play it again.

Light blue accents had been added anywhere they could be, flowing seamlessly with the white walls and abundance of plant life. Seeing the decorations that represented the pride of their realm was astonishing. Somehow, King Adbeel managed to showcase his love for Eoforhild without overindulging in the colors, choosing instead to sprinkle them gracefully.

Every demon we passed had the same breathtaking light blue tied into their outfits in one way or another. A startling sight, seeing as only the royals and the guards were allowed to wear gold in The Capital. The color of the fae sigil, of the palace and the center island itself, was reserved for those with a crown atop their heads. Here, it was worn by all who wanted to show their love for the realm that saw them come into this world and would one day watch them leave it.

Here, it was unifying.

"Your Highness, it is so wonderful to see you back home once more." The female who spoke, her voice deep and soothing, was standing directly ahead of us.

She wore a sky blue gown that traveled tightly down her body, highlighting her every curve, the train at least five feet long. It was the type of extravagance one might see at a ball rather than casually walking through a corridor. Her hair was a blonde so light it was almost white, eyes nearly the shade of honey. They reminded me of Sipho's. Yet on this demon, they held anger rather than curiosity. Like revenge left to boil, her golden eyes stirred with heat.

"Revanche, how are you?" Bellamy responded, his voice curt. I noted the way this female eyed Bellamy, as if she might kiss him—or perhaps eat him.

A far cry from how her eyes scrutinized me. Her thoughts, somehow both loud and flat, projected my way.

Who does this little tart think she is, walking into the palace on Prince Bellamy's arm? She is not even pretty. Look at her ragged hair. Probably found her in a brothel and cannot shake her.

I simply could not help myself.

"Actually, Ree—can I call you Ree? Who am I kidding, of course I can. Anyways, Ree, he found me in a palace. Though a brothel does sound fabulous right about now. In fact, Prince Bellamy and I were just discussing exhibitionism. I am known to be quite shy, but for you, lovely Ree, I can make an exception," I said, voice of sugar and ice.

The female blanched, but I did not see what she did after that because I turned and pulled Bell down by his tunic, bringing our lips together.

Either Bellamy was not fond of Revanche, or he simply did not care, because he met my kiss with full force. His tongue was on mine for mere moments before he began tracing his way down my neck with his lips, hand holding my chin up. Still, I managed a quick wink to the now raging female before us.

Bellamy stopped his slow torture, bringing his mouth to my ear, whispering to me in a voice of gravel and lust, "I am not done with you, wicked creature."

I looked at him, truly taking him in. His dark waves were exceptionally unruly from the ride here but also from my hands finding their way into them. His cheeks were tinted red, from excitement or embarrassment I did not know. But it was the adoration I saw in his face that made me feel like the only female in existence, leaving me too stunned to speak.

"Where is the king, Revanche?" he asked the female, his eyes never leaving mine.

For a moment, I could have sworn a bit of black swirled in his irises, like ink spilling into blue waters. With a blink it was gone, and I was suddenly not sure I had seen it at all.

"King Adbeel is away. If that was where you were headed, it might be best to think of something else to do. Father needed his help in Andreia," she responded, still seething. Then she looked my way, a smirk on her face. "My father is Judson Garnier, Lord of Andreia."

Her pride at her father's title truly rounded out her character, telling me everything I needed to know about her. I desperately wanted to tell her that I was a princess, that I was The Manipulator, that I was Bellamy's lover. Anything to rile her. Instead, I nodded, smiling.

"Well, that is fine. It gives me time to show Ash around," Bellamy said with a broad, dimpled smile on his face. "If you will excuse us, Revanche."

"Wait!" she exclaimed, putting her hand on his chest to stop him. I quietly raged at the sight of her hands on him. Touching what was so clearly *mine.* "I have missed you, Bellamy. I see you have brought a friend, but what of me? What of the time we spent together? Does the agreement between our fathers mean nothing to you?"

At that, Bellamy's eyes widened, peering my way in a panic. He looked as if he might take me and run or beg on his knees. I rolled my eyes, pressing past Bellamy's simmering wall of fire and into his mind. Where he was obviously expecting me to be.

I am not some jealous fool, Bellamy. I do not care that you slept with this female, though I am interested in this agreement. But for the love of Eternity, put the poor thing out of her misery.

"Revanche, this is Asher. She is not a mere friend. She is the love of my life and the female I plan on spending the rest of my existence with. There will be no other, regardless of our fathers' desire for us to be wed someday. Now, if you will excuse us, I would like to show Asher the palace I grew up in. Please do not disturb us again."

With that, Bellamy grabbed my hand and began walking us down the corridor. One final look at Revanche had me nearly bursting into laughter. Her jaw was practically hanging on the floor, eyes bulging and tan skin flushed. She had her hands balled into tight fists at her sides, and there was a murderous tone to her thoughts. I smirked, turning away from her.

"That was incredibly sexy, Elemental," I said, poking him in the ribs as we wove through the palace.

He laughed, tugging my body to his. One arm was wrapped casually around my shoulders, and I found myself subconsciously reaching my hand up to hold his at my shoulder.

Strange and unsettling, that was what this peace and comfort was. Never had I felt this carefree, and I wondered when it would all come crashing down. Though, in truth, I knew when.

"Where are you taking me?" I asked, trying to shake the awful thought from my mind. There was no use in ruminating on what would be. That only served to steal away the small piece of happiness I had cultivated.

Bellamy's smile grew infinitely wider, his excitement seeping from him. He was practically bouncing as we continued down the many halls, the sun creeping down the sky, casting a vibrant yellow-orange hue to the white walls.

"Somewhere you will love," he responded.

I scoffed, hating not knowing. My power pressed out, testing his mental shield to see if it was still purposefully weakened. Sadly, it was not, the black flames nearly lighting fire to my mind.

Just as I was considering ways I might force the information out of him, we paused in front of a set of blue double doors, the demon sigil proudly etched into them in their signature colors.

I quirked a brow at him, waiting for some sort of explanation, but Bellamy just laughed once more, opening the doors and revealing what was inside.

I gasped, nearly falling to my knees in tears of joy.

"This, Princess, is the royal library."

CHAPTER TWO

BELLAMY

There were very few things in life that I knew with absolute certainty.

One, the sun would rise again. I knew this because it did every day. With each nightmare that plagued me in the evenings, the sun was there, dawn coming to chase away the beasts in my head. I woke up, and the sun did too.

Two, I would die one day. It was not until a year ago that I realized how soon death would knock on my door. But that was inevitable, right? We all died. The difference was that not all of us lived.

Which brought me to the third thing that I knew without a shadow of a doubt. Asher was my life. She was the gift given to an undeserving, wicked being. She was *my* Eternity.

Looking at her never felt real, as if she were a mirage that would disappear upon closer inspection.

I could still recall the first time I ever laid my eyes on her. Not the time Pino had shown me visions of the wonderful and short future we would have, but the real experience of seeing her.

It had been days after I brought Pino to Eoforhild. I had panicked upon hearing his many prophecies. The past, present, and future that needed to merge to create the only possible outcome that would see the world survive. It was...overwhelming, to say the least. But when I finally left my chambers in Haven after painting so much of what I had seen in Reader River, I portaled to Betovere—to The Capital. I had to wait nearly four hours before she finally emerged.

It was a gloriously sunny day, and she wore the most hideous gold gown. It sucked into her waist so tightly that I swore it was impossible she was breathing. The layers and flare of the skirt had to have been suffocating as well, especially in the heat of early spring. But as she walked by herself through the green grass, the sun beating down on her tan skin and glowing in her gray eyes, I could not imagine a more beautiful female. A more beautiful *anything*.

That day was the first of my true life. The first day I took a breath and wanted more. She revived me after an existence stuck in purgatory. No star would ever burn as bright, no water would ever be as deep, no fire would ever feel as warm, no darkness would ever be as all-consuming as my love for her.

After two centuries of never feeling as if I belonged, I had finally found my home.

Now, as I watched her browse through the shelves upon shelves of books within the palace library, I could not fathom how life could possibly be this right. Especially when war loomed, threatening to burn the world to dust.

Yet there she stood, the picture of serenity amidst the mahogany shelves built from floor to ceiling. They lined the walls and housed the thousands of books the royal family had collected over time. A family that I was not technically part of.

But Asher, she could be my family, just as my Trusted were. Those idiots, with all their nagging and foul mouths and ferocious souls, they were what I had cherished the most all these years. Adding Asher to the dynamic had felt natural.

Not having her with me had been the most painful torture, one that had led me to paint and repaint my chambers until I had to move into new ones. To hide away from such a dark space.

Now I was left wondering what would happen when I told her all that Pino had prophesied, all that he had shown me of the past. Those truths would change everything, and I was not eager to watch this joy crumble.

"When I was young, the scholars had to lock me in here and force me to study," I said to her. She turned, her face lit up with a smile that threatened to steal my breath away.

Gods she was beautiful.

"Oh really? Sounds about right," she retorted, her stormy-gray eyes scrunched in amusement. "You are a bit dimwitted."

"I chose to hone *other* skills," I responded, my tongue sliding across my lips as I slowly took her in from head to toe.

I heard her swallow, the tempo of her heart loud in my ears as it sped. Her face did not show any sign of nerves or lust. No, Asher was used to playing a part, to hiding all she felt.

"However, I did find that books were excellent hiding places." My words piqued her interest, her brows raising.

I waved my hand, motioning for her to follow. Many days had been spent locked in this room—so many that I knew it like the back of my hand. It was not long before I was at the shelf I needed, pulling out a book with a faded green spine and a title no longer legible.

The ceiling stretched nearly four stories high, the wooden shelves built to reach the very top. Ladders and stairs were not nearly as useful as magic to the many scholars who maintained the royal library. But the magic that had been infused within me did not manifest like that of other Moons. I could not wield the shadows like Noe, only able to merge it with my flames or portal with it. So I had settled on easily accessible shelves those many years ago.

Asher was impatiently waiting, her ever curious mind paving the way for a rare moment of eagerness. She did not smile enough. I would have to work on that, to show her what happiness could be like if she allowed herself to feel it.

Books smelled horrid. They were boring and dusty, and I so loathed being confined to these four walls in my youth.

Who wanted to read about wars past when we were constantly on the brink of one? Who wanted to read about the gods when they never answered my prayers anyways? Who wanted to read about smut when there was always a willing female to fuck?

Perhaps I had been wrong. Asher's love for reading, her eagerness to escape from a world she felt so lost and alone in, made sense. Though what I had done with the books instead had brought me my own version of escape.

"You did not do that to a book," Asher said with a gasp. I chuckled, grabbing the small vial from inside the pages I had jaggedly hollowed out with a dagger many years prior. "Stupid demon, you vandalized it!"

Her smack stung against my arm, but the giggles that filled the room made me think she was not quite as mad as she was attempting to portray herself. I smiled at her, a wicked and mischievous raise of my lips.

"I needed something to pass the time, and this right here did an astonishingly fine job of keeping Henry and I distracted from our studies."

That perked her up, gray eyes widening as she stepped closer and inspected the teardrop-shaped vile of lavender colored liquid.

"What is it?" she asked.

"It was something Henry and I had cooked up after many failed attempts. If you drink it, you lose all inhibitions. It brings euphoria and energy to the surface while masking fear and nerves," I said, eyeing her to gauge her reaction.

Asher did not disappoint. Her mouth dropped open, and a book fell from her hands. For a moment she remained that way, frozen in shock and disbelief, then she burst into laughter. The melodic sound of her full and unencumbered amusement, the view of her throat when her head tilted back, made something low within me stir.

She was driving me mad.

I had not been this horny since that one time Henry and I had spent a week straight in a shady Eros brothel. In fact, the very concoction in my hand had single-handedly helped us work through the predicament of an odd number of female entertainers. I silently chuckled at the memory of us settling on sharing the odd one out.

None of them compared to Asher though. To the way the Sun magic glinted off her large eyes and full lips. To the curve of her neck and the sultry sound of her voice. To the way she commanded every room she walked into. She made me want to fall to my knees and pray to her.

"Books are good for something it seems," I said, my voice hoarse from my frantic thoughts.

"You would be surprised what you can find in a book, Your Highness," she responded.

Her hand moved to her chest, fingers slowly grazing the black fighting leathers and lingering just above her full breasts. I swallowed, salivating as she let her hand trace her curves.

"Like what?" I asked, not trying to hide the way my voice deepened in yearning.

With calculated slowness, she began backing away from me. A groan escaped my mouth when I watched her hand disappear behind her back then heard the sound of buttons popping free.

She would be the death of me.

With immense effort, I maintained her pace, stalking her like a predator hunting its prey. Yes, that was what I was. Because, when the game ended, I would devour her.

"Well, I once read this tantalizing book where the male tied the female to a bed. Glorious descriptions, if I do say. I especially enjoyed the vivid way the writer described how the ropes chafed as the female climaxed." Her fingers slipped under her leather trousers, and I lost all control.

I ran at her, dipping low to pick her up with one hand and roughly tug her hair to bring her lips to my own with the other.

She smelled of vanilla from her bath that morning and tasted like the mint leaves she constantly chewed. Everything about her was intoxicating in a way that no mead or wine could ever compete with. She was delicious and addicting and *mine*.

Her arms were around my neck, hands in my hair. Setting her down on a large table I distinctly recalled once passing out drunk on, I pressed her down until her back thudded against the dark wood.

Taking her this time was different. It had been an unbearably slow burn of need that led up to the first time I was inside of her. Even when I had her a second and third time last night, it was surreal. A year of dreaming about what I would do to her when I had her in my arms had made me sloppy and desperate.

Now, with her beneath me on the table, I could show her what I truly had to offer. I could give her anything and everything and watch as she unraveled from the pleasure of it all.

I broke off our kiss, pressing my hand to her chest when she tried to follow me as I stood up straight. Her bottom lip jutted out, pouting like a youngling who did not get their way.

With deftness that seemed to take her off guard, I ripped her leathers over her head, tossing the top and then moving to pull off her shoes before yanking off her trousers in one clean motion. She gasped, but it was I who was left speechless. Her naked body was luminous, olive skin glowing in the demon light above. The chandelier reflected small rainbows over her body, like she was covered in thousands of tiny diamonds. Her brown curls were fanned around her, already somewhat knotted from my tugging on them.

I drank her in like a dehydrated male in the desert. That was where I felt I was these days, living in a constant state of desire—eager for a taste of her.

With no explanation, I began backing up to the many windows on the nearest wall. Her brows scrunched as I threw open the sky-blue curtains, giving us a view of the setting sun as it met the horizon. It bathed her in orange and pink, the rainbows from the chandelier mixing and making her look like a goddess in the flesh. Like Asta as she descended The Above. Fitting, as she too had stolen the heart of demon royalty.

"I want to see all of you. Every minute detail. I want to learn you, to study you. I want the shape of your body to be burned into my mind—my soul. And, once I have seen it all, I want to lick every inch of you," I rasped.

Asher's inhaled gasp was delicious. A sound that could undo me as swiftly as my hand. She remained laying down, watching while I untied the ropes that secured the curtains back and kept each as I went.

When I had four of the silver ties, I began my slow stalk towards her once more, each step sending her heart racing faster—her breaths coming harder. I could not read minds, but I knew what Asher was thinking—felt the lust and desire radiating from her. She filled the room with it, making my head swim and my cock throb.

At the end of the table, I stopped, peering down at the way the light reflected between her thighs and highlighted how tauntingly wet she was.

Unable to help myself, I took my finger and slowly grazed it up her core. Her back arched, breasts bouncing and throat vibrating as she moaned. Her eyes found mine as I sucked on my finger, tasting her. Savoring her.

I winked, then moved to the side of the table where her head was. She gazed at the bulge in my leathers, and I felt my own cheeks heat at the intensity of that stare.

"Not yet, Princess," I whispered to her, leaning down to place a kiss on her lips.

Instead of standing back up, I grabbed her hand and yanked it towards the corner of the table. She let out a yelp, and it took everything in me not to laugh at her baffled expression.

Then I began tying the rope around her wrist. The confusion made way for pure need as she realized what I was doing.

When I had made a tight enough knot, remembering her comment about the pleasure of the rope rubbing, I leaned the rest of the way down and secured the rope to the leg of the table. I repeated this with her other wrist then slowly moved towards her legs, tying her ankles too.

One look at my handy work nearly had me losing my control. She was glorious, arms and legs spread so no part of her was hidden from me. Between her thighs she remained wet and hot, calling to me like a beacon in the night.

"Such a long journey we had, Princess. Are you as hungry as I am?" I asked as I leaned forward, placing my palms on the table.

She looked at my face for but a moment before her eyes found my trousers. Found my cock. I growled, an animal hunger taking over.

"Starved," was her only response.

Then I was on her, my mouth sinking between her legs and desperately lapping up the results of her desire. She wiggled and jerked, indecent and erotic moans leaving her lips in irregular intervals. I reached down and tightened the ropes with the ends I had left free, having figured I would need to adjust later on.

Now she was pinned, but it seemed the bite of pain had only turned her on further. As if to prove those thoughts correct, she gasped in pleasure. Further encouraged, I slipped two of my fingers inside of her and gave a slight shake of my head. Arching my fingers as I added a third, I leaned in further and devoured her. She tasted like nothing I had ever experienced before, a sweet and salty concoction that had liquid beading in my trousers.

I continued my ministrations, rasping praise against her as she writhed and bucked on the table—encouraging her to come for me, to give me what I wanted.

And she did.

Asher let out a beautiful scream of pleasure, orgasming onto my tongue and pulling on the ropes so hard that I knew she would have bruises. But she did not seem to care. No, Asher was not finished in the slightest.

"More, demon. Give me more," she ordered, her voice taking on that haunting tone of The Manipulator.

With my shield of black flames down, I was unable to fight off the order. But I did not want to. No, I would never deny her, never dream of doing so. Not now, when I knew that she loved me. That she was *mine*.

"Yes, Your Highness," I said, slowly unbuttoning my trousers and letting them fall before tugging my shirt off in one swift motion.

I grabbed onto my hard cock, pumping as I made my way back to the head of the table. She smirked, but I could see the way she eyed me, the hunger in her gaze.

When I reached her, she opened her mouth—impatient as ever. I thought about teasing her, considered how I could draw this out, but Asher was fast.

In my mouth, Bellamy. Put it in my mouth, now.

With her silent orders ringing in my head, I shoved myself down her throat, listening as she gagged when I was halfway in. I nearly pulled out, but then she adjusted, beginning to work me inside of her mouth with alternating sucks and licks and taking me deeper with every thrust I offered.

When her teeth grazed me, I hissed in pleasure, pounding harder. She moaned, the vibration sending me into a frenzy. I could see how wet she still was, the way she glittered in the light begging me to take her.

I ripped myself out, bending down to loosen the ties at her wrists before making my way to her legs and untying her ankles. When both were undone, I tied them together, forcing her legs to remain tightly shut. Then I pulled her as far as the ropes around her wrists would allow, her ass nearly hanging off the edge.

Bound ankles in hand, I straightened her legs, resting her feet on my chest. And, just as her eyes met mine, I thrust the entirety of my length inside of her. She bit back a cry, arms ripping on the silver ropes, but they did not budge.

"Come on, Princess. Scream for me. Say my name." And then I began pounding into her, holding her legs to anchor her to me.

Filthy curses mingled with my name, and once or twice I heard her mention Eternity. She was *my* Eternity. My salvation. And every thrust, every sound that slipped past her lips, had my orgasm building, rising like a steep mountain peak.

"Do you like taking all of me, beautiful creature?" I asked her, thrusting harder.

She nodded, a messy and violent movement that sent her hair flying. I smirked, watching as she lost control—as I made her come utterly undone.

"Then say it. Tell me how much you love feeling my cock inside of you. Tell me how desperately you need it. Let me hear that pretty mouth sing, Princess," I ordered.

"Someone might hear," she gasped between her heaving breaths, my own breath hitching at the sight as I enjoyed the view of her losing all thought. Seeing pure freedom find her as I pumped harder and faster, the lightness something she never seemed to be able to hold onto.

Soon she would have it, not just beneath me but within herself. Freedom was hers now, and I knew she would change the world with it.

"Let them hear. Let them walk in and witness the way I claim you. Let them watch as I worship you. Let them see all they desire but cannot have," I said, feeling her climax build as she tightened around me. I nearly came. Nearly.

What I did not say aloud, was how I would gouge their eyes from their sockets as I watched my release drip from inside of her.

Asher gave in, screaming my name and straining against the ropes as her back arched up. She was a divine offering, a gift worth more than all the gold in Betovere. This female was molded by the gods for me as I was for her.

As a reward for the beautiful way my name left her lips, my thumb began working between her thighs, stroking her softly and quickly. I watched shamelessly as my fingers sent shaking spasms to her legs, my other hand gripping her bound ankles tighter.

Then she was shattering beneath me again, the feel of her soaking my cock forcing me over that edge as well. Together we finished, orgasms rushing through our bodies and leaving us both trembling. My body felt heavy, entirely spent, as I stood above her. And I could not help but silently beg to Stella to spare my life. To give me more time with my stormy-eyed princess.

Slowly, I untied the ropes until she was free once more. She did not sit up though, instead remaining slumped on the wooden table. I picked her up, our lips meeting in a delicate kiss as I portaled us into my chambers.

Setting her down on the bed, I rushed to my bathing chambers to grab a rag. My powers flared to life, seeking water to dampen the cloth. I watched a small stream of it float through the window, soaking the fabric. Then I was back in my chambers, making my way to Asher. She was lying back on the bed, her smile soft and her eyes half closed.

I made quick work of cleaning the two of us before I laid down beside her. When she curled up into me, her head against my chest and an arm over my stomach, I smiled too. Without thinking, my own hand drifted to her hair, massaging gently.

Taking care of her in this way—in any way she would let me—was comforting. Asher made me feel as if I had finally found my place. Like perhaps I was no longer split in two, both sides warring with the other to return to where they belong. Instead, I was whole, my entire being seeking her as if she were the center of my universe.

As her breathing slowed, I whispered three words that did not feel like nearly enough. Maybe no words would ever exist that could explain the way I felt for her.

"I love you."

CHAPTER THREE

ASHER

Nowhere. That was where I was. Nowhere, yet everywhere. This place—full of darkness and light, nothing and everything—felt as if it might bury me in its depths. As if it might never let me leave.

Was it my mind? Was I in my mind?

"Interesting that you assume such a place exists within you, my love."

What a strange voice. It echoed across the space as if Eternity itself spoke to me. But it was not Eternity. No, I had heard this voice before. How many times had I replayed it in my mind? The embodiment of death, ice cold and disorienting. The very voice that had once told me I was doomed to a lifetime of loneliness, that Bellamy would sooner cut off my head than love me.

"I was right, by the way. He doesn't love you. He will never love you. Not like you deserve to be loved," the voice said.

I turned, and there it was, a mere handful of steps away.

The fae-like creature was just as I remembered, hauntingly beautiful and wholly terrifying. Its ears still pointed outwards, pale skin showing a blue blush rather than red. Startlingly white eyes stared as I assessed it, trying to find any differences. The only noticeable change was the shorter hair, which had been messily cropped—the purple strands pointing every which way.

"You cut your hair," I noted. I did not know why I said something so pointless, but the creature laughed, a sharp melody that made me want to hum a low tune to balance it.

"I did," it said, face suddenly pinched in discomfort. Had I said something wrong? The war within its face ended just as quickly as it began, and it spoke once more. "I thought maybe you preferred this style."

That roused me from my confused state. Why would this thing care what I *preferred*? Who was this? Where was I?

So many thoughts and questions swarmed me, like bees to a hive. I needed to escape. This space that had once appeared to stretch on forever now felt too small, too constricting. My urgency felt far away, like it was not within me, but sat heavily in the air instead. That fear was important, though, because I would die here if I did not get out.

"You won't die, my love. Please, allow me to answer your questions. I'm not like that foolish prince. I will tell you anything you wish to know," it said, reaching out towards me but not quite grazing my skin. I did not fail to notice how it refrained from touching me.

"Who are you?" I asked after a moment of hesitation.

The being allowed its gaze to roam down my body, leisurely taking me in. I followed the action, tilting my head down and noting the black slip dress I was wearing. Where had I gotten this? If the creature had dressed me, I would—well, I guess I did not know what I would do.

26

Though it was so very beyond what I normally would have felt, I recognized the resignation slowly building inside of me. The acceptance.

My eyes flew up, squinting at the creature. Once again, I observed how the being in front of me acted as if there was a battle raging within it that it struggled to win. The creature's hand abruptly fell back to its side, thick muscles tensing.

Its clothes were different too. This time, rather than whimsical yet horrifying black robes, the creature wore a plain tunic with the sleeves rolled up to the elbow and tight-fitting trousers. Boots remained unlaced on its feet, a bow strapped to its back. All black.

"My name is Padon," it said. "*He,* Asher, not *it.*"

"Sorry," I offered, my brow pinched in confusion. "How do you know my name? And how can you hear my thoughts?"

"I first sensed you not long after your magic manifested, around five years following your birth, but I have been waiting for you for many millennia. Finding you on your wretched world isn't quite as easy as merely sensing you, it seems."

Well that was interesting. But before I could ask a new question, he pressed on.

"I'm privy to your thoughts because, while this is not *your* mind, it is *mine.* Now, I do apologize for my haste, but there are important things for us to discuss, and little time to do so."

I nodded, complacent and agreeable and so contrary to how I normally was. Padon chuckled, the sound reverberating in my bones, in my very soul. Without thought, I joined in, my laugh echoing across the space that was both empty and full.

His eyes lit up at my enthusiasm, and then he was against me, our breathing uneven, working in opposition to one another. So different to how in sync Bellamy and I always were.

"Don't think of him. Not when you're with me," he growled. His irises seemed to fade to black, the white hidden behind shadows.

I froze, eyes wide as fear fought its way to me through the sludge of tranquility. But, for some reason that I could not understand, my body and mind refused the emotion. As if nothing but curiosity could hold me.

"I apologize, my love. I have a bit of a temper to me, but for you, I'll work on it."

Padon leaned down, brushing a piece of my hair behind my ear and stroking the ruined tip. He was tall, similar in height to Henry and maybe two inches taller than B—another male I knew.

"Good. That was so good, Asher. You learn quickly."

His finger met the underside of my chin, skin cold as ice, and my head was tilted up until our eyes met. The breath whooshed out of me as if I had been hit in the stomach. I knew him. Somehow.

Had he visited me before that night near the Forest of Tragedies?

Padon smiled, those too-white teeth flashing quickly before he leaned in. I thought he might kiss me, but it was as if my body could not move to get away. There was no dodging the affection, no running from the creature before me.

Cold lips met the skin above my brow, and I felt myself relax. Whether it was due to the fact that I was not being forcibly kissed or the ease and comfort his presence brought me, I was not sure. The latter was what finally brought a modicum of fear into my being, though it was gone as quickly as it came.

"You say love as if you did not warn me against allowing others into my heart mere months ago," I said, the trepidation leaving me in favor of amusement. Something was wrong, horribly so. Yet those feelings of terror and distrust that had guided me since leaving The Capital seemed just out of reach.

"Well, honestly, the goal was to get you away from the princeling. You deserve more than him. I'm no mere prince, though. I'm an emperor, a god in comparison to beings like him. You were born to be even more—to rule over worlds and creatures of all kinds. To bring them all to their knees. You were born to be *mine*," he said, his voice full of eagerness.

When I looked up, I could not help the words that left my mouth. "Why does everyone seem to think I am theirs? I am *no one's* but my own," I growled, my anger at long last finding me.

There I was.

I pushed away, putting space between us. My body nearly crumpled against the onslaught of emotions, of autonomy, that filled me. The space around me shuddered, fading slightly, and a weight could be felt pressing down on my stomach, not heavily, but enough for me to notice. As if I were being held.

My power came back to me, slowly at first, then all at once. I could sense Padon there, his confusion and love and obsession, as images of me filled his mind. Not the space that we stood in, but his actual mind—where his thoughts swirled with me. Me. Me. Me. Me. Me.

Padon let out a heavy sigh then, like a youngling who had their toy taken away for misbehaving.

"It seems we have run out of time, but you'll understand soon. I promise, my love. One day, not long from now, this will all make sense." Padon faded to nothing in front of my eyes as he finished speaking.

He appeared out of thin air once more, directly in front of me—our lips grazing ever so faintly. It was a shock to my system, the way he felt against me. He tasted of death, of life, of the universe itself—so cold he burned. Before I could push away again, Padon was gone, and for a moment, I was there alone, witnessing his vision for the future play out in front of my eyes.

An image of him and me, eternally mated. We sat atop ashen thrones, each of us wearing crowns of silver that looked sharp enough to cut flesh. In front of us, thousands upon thousands of fae-like creatures bowed.

A triumphant smile graced my lips as, together, Padon and I raised Bellamy's decapitated head in victory.

"Soon, my love."

***

Screams filled the air as I jolted up.

Someone was in danger. Someone needed me.

My arms flailed, reaching for my dagger—for something to protect myself with. To protect everyone with.

The weight on my stomach tightened, and in my ear, a husky voice whispered, "I am here, Princess. I have you."

Bellamy.

A nightmare—just a nightmare. My imagination was so horribly talented when it came to conjuring terror to wreak havoc in my mind. Still, it had felt so real.

A look down revealed it was his arm around me. I was naked, my clothes likely left behind in the library, but my amethyst necklace still rested just below my collarbones, the silver wiring wrapping it tightly. On instinct, my hand reached up and grasped it.

Bellamy's hand encircled my own, his thumb rubbing the jagged stone as he sat up with me.

"He will always be with you, Princess. Just as you will always be with him." He spoke those words with such conviction that I had no other choice but to nod. "Would you like to talk about it?"

I knew he was referencing my nightmare, but I was not eager to tell him about it. Guilt ate at me for dreaming of a creature so vile, the way his lips caressed mine nearly sending me into a panic once more.

It was not real. How could it have been?

Still, I was sure I would never forget the way Bellamy's head looked in my hand or the smile on my face as I held it.

"Do demons feel the call of Eternity?" I asked, avoiding his question entirely.

I could not talk about what I had seen. What was worse, I could not shake the eerie feeling that Bellamy might not survive me. But if I knew he would end up in Eternity, would hear it beckoning him home one day in the very distant future and *choose* his Ending, then perhaps I would not be so prone to this fear. Or inclined to imagine him in that foreign world with his head dangling between my fingers.

Bellamy hesitated, as if he was contemplating the right way to phrase his answer, and maybe he was. There was no denying that he still held many secrets, ones which I would not know until I met his king—his father.

I did not assume that something as simple as the afterlife would be one of them though.

"Demons believe that, upon death, one's magic and soul returns to the home of the gods. That is why we burn the bodies of the fallen. We do not wish to banish them to a lifetime of wandering a world they have left behind, so we release them to The Above. However, demons and fae age differently—vastly so. Demons can, and do, live for thousands of years, but there is a limit to life. The oldest demon I have met was just over two millennia. From what I understand of the death of a demon, there is no call from the ethers when it is one's time to pass. Demons just cease to exist within this plane."

It was not the answer I was hoping for. Yet it was exactly the answer I should have expected. Smooth and somewhat vague, not presenting any true answers or reassuring me that he might live long enough to see me end this war before it begins. Long enough to allow me to find him once more. Any future we might have will be far away, a distant thought that might materialize if given time. Though, in his defense, I asked an equally ambiguous and dismissive question.

"What do *you* believe?" I asked, mustering up the courage I would need for the answer.

This time, he did not pause, did not need a moment to think through his answer.

"I believe in you. I believe that this life is far greater than anything that might occur after because *here* I have you. Here, I possess the only thing that will ever matter." He paused, his hand letting go of my necklace to lie flat on my chest. "Your heart."

That very heart began beating at a ferocious pace, feeling as if it might leap from my chest.

Stupid, sappy demon.

I leaned into his warmth, placing a kiss to his lips. There was a desperation to the love I felt for him, one that had grown in the last few months but had heightened since I realized that this small pocket of time might be all we ever possessed.

I needed him like I needed air, and there was only so long I could go before my lungs gave out.

How he always managed to say the right thing, I was not sure. Perhaps it was the magic of his ancestor, Asta, whose spoken words could convince masses to comply. Or maybe he was secretly a poet. His paintings were the perfect example of his affinity towards the arts, so I would not be surprised if he were.

I could easily picture him hiding in a dark room while writing sonnets about how annoying Henry could be and the art of ripping hearts from the chests of one's enemies. Or how much he adores whoever discovered kohl. Composing the music for that one would have to be my job, as I also owed thanks to that individual. There were not many things that could beat the way his eyes looked when lined with black.

Bellamy was quick to deepen the kiss, his tongue hot against mine. One hand cupped my cheek while his other slowly trailing up my leg. When his fingertips hit my inner thigh, a low moan slipped from between my lips. He continued to tease, drawing designs on my skin that I could not quite decipher—like I was his newest canvas, ready to be made into something beautiful by him.

Of course, the demon had grander thoughts.

"Wait here," he whispered against my lips. I groaned, reaching for him as if I could force his body to remain in the bed, but he was up before I could latch on to him.

His ivory skin glowed in the morning sunlight that streamed through the many windows gracing the far wall. Every inch of him was made up of hard muscles, his back dotted with freckles and covered in those strange tattoos. He was glorious, his body far more magnificent than any painter could dream of creating.

As he disappeared through a far door, I found my eyes roaming over the room. I had not taken it in before, but it struck me how stunning it was in that moment. Dazzling, but so utterly opposite of The Elemental.

The walls were a startling white shade, bright and beautiful and blank. The sheets below me were made of a bright blue silk, as light as the sky on a clear summer day. All around the room was furniture in the same blue shade, covered in intricate designs that held the remaining three colors in the demon sigil. Plant life thrived, vines crawling up the walls and wrapping themselves around the ceiling. Rather than looking unkempt, the plants appeared intentional, like a form of decoration that brought fresh air and earthy smells.

If these were Bellamy's chambers, they were nothing like who I knew him to be—nothing like the foreboding castle I had gotten lost in many times during my stay in Haven.

Bellamy came back into the room then, carrying a blank canvas and an easel. I blanched, quickly yanking the silk sheets over my naked body. He merely chuckled and set the easel down near the center of the room, placing the canvas upon it.

My eyes tracked his every movement, watching as he went to a white desk in the corner farthest from the enormous bed I lay on. His hands moved with practiced efficiency, opening drawers and pulling out various vials of paint.

At one point, the demon turned around, lifting a brown and a yellow up. One of his eyes scrunched closed as he held the colors out, looking as if he were pointing them at me. Then he turned once more, sifting through them all until he had everything he needed. Piling his supplies into a wooden container, Bellamy grabbed a stool and dragged it across the room. He perched atop it in front of his easel, then he flashed me a wicked smirk, eyes alight with the heat of his own arousal.

"Will you let me paint you, Princess? Will you allow me the honor to commit you to memory—to immortalize you with the stroke of my brush?" Oh, he knew how his words sounded, what the innuendo did to me.

How could I think when he sat there completely naked and hard as steel? I wanted to melt, to beg for him. To do anything but lay on the bed nude and allow him to paint every one of my flaws.

"Where will you hang such a scandalous piece? The throne room?" I asked sarcastically, the panic inside me causing my head to swim. I needed time to figure out how to get out of this without showing him how foolishly insecure I was feeling at the mere thought of it.

The demon simply tilted his head to the side in that frustrating way he always did, waiting for me to lower the sheet.

I would rather be splayed out on a table in front of him a thousand times over than feel his keen eyes on me as he paints every soft curve and imperfection of my body. Being vulnerable in that way, allowing him the chance to see more of my inadequacies in startling clarity, was something I could not do.

I was not taught to show weakness. Not raised to be anything but a golden statue to be viewed and used, fitting into whatever space those around me needed. Always hiding every imperfection so no one could see the truths within them.

"Am I so horribly boring that you need paint to act as foreplay?" I asked, trying my hand at more humor.

Something had to give. Something had to get him away from that damn paint. At my words, Bellamy stiffened. I saw the moment his excitement faded to concern, the second his anger began to simmer.

"It seems I have not made myself clear, Asher. So let me say it plainly now."

Bellamy stood, his black waves a mess and his piercing eyes trained on me. He looked like a beast ready to hunt, and I was his next meal.

His feet were slow, the pace daunting. I swallowed, clutching the sheets closer to my body. What would he say? That he already knows I am not ideal? That he is not stupid, so clearly he is aware of my faults? I was not sure that would make me feel better at all.

"No part of you is less than perfect to me. No curve or freckle or tangle. There is nothing that you can show me that will leave me feeling anything less than obsessed with you."

He was mere feet away now, a hunger in his gaze that had my stomach doing flips. I could handle this, our bodies coming together in a rush of passion and lust. This was easy in comparison to thinking of the fine details he might add to a painting.

"I will have all of you, Ash. Every part of you is mine, and I love it all. There will be no hiding, no fear, and no hesitation. Not with me. *Never* with me. You will remember my words because I will remind you every day for the rest of my life." The words were practically a growl, his deep and heavy drawl slowing in pace.

Then he was at the bed, leaning down with his palms on either side of my hips. His lips met mine only briefly before a gust of cold air hit my body. I screeched, clawing at the receding cover with horror.

"I will have *all* of you. Now, pose for me like a good princess."

With that, he was gone, dragging the sheet along with him as he made his way back to the stool. I could feel every roll, every indent and blemish. Every reminder of what I would never be. Everything that he

35

was now looking at with his artist's eye. I wanted to crawl into a hole, to dig myself a grave and never see the light of day again.

"Lay down horizontally across the bed and close your eyes," Bellamy rasped as he sat down on his stool once more, unfazed by his own nudity. For once, I immediately did as I was told, shutting my eyes tightly as I shifted on the bed. "Relax. Breathe. Just focus on the sound of my voice."

I nodded, trying to loosen up my limbs, to release the tension that had built up in my body from the moment he entered with that canvas and easel in tow. I draped one hand above my head, marginally hanging off the bed, and the other rested near my collarbone.

Breathe. Relax.

"Have I ever told you about the way your eyes sparkle when you look at me?" he asked.

I huffed in annoyance at his self-importance, though he was technically right. I did enjoy the sight of him.

"No? Well have I told you about the way your head falls back when you laugh? Or the indecent sway of your hips as you walk?"

I was not sure what he was doing, but his comments made me feel lighter somehow. As if the words, mixed with the soothing and tantalizing sound of his voice, grounded me. I shook my head, keeping my eyes closed tightly.

"Huh, I really thought I would have mentioned that at some point. I know I must have described in great detail the way your thighs feel when I lift you in my arms, how my hands mold around them as if they are a lifeline. Or the delicious way your breasts rub against my chest. Now, *that* I had to have mentioned."

I chuckled at his tone but refused to open my eyes for fear of his scrutinizing gaze.

"Or this, right here," he said, the sound of a brush scraping the canvas causing my jaw to clench. "The spot just below your belly button. I love this spot. The way you writhe beneath me when I kiss here, how you moan in pleasure. It's addictive."

Tension seeped from my body, flowing out of me like the water of a river rushing past a broken dam.

My eyes opened.

He loved it.

My stomach. The same part of me that the castle seamstress had loathed, had complained about making accommodations in my clothing for. The part of me that Mia feared Sterling would hate.

Bellamy loved it.

Our gazes met, my gray staring into his blue, neither of us daring to so much as blink. Bellamy was the first to break eye contact, licking his lips as he turned to the canvas.

We continued that way, him sharing every detail of my body that he adored and me staring at him, until he announced we needed a water break. Ever the wicked demon, he gave me a sultry kiss, forced me to drink, and then left me once more to continue his work.

He announced the completion of the painting by loudly moaning at it as he leaned back, looking quite pleased with himself. I noted how hard he was once again, how he casually stroked himself as he admired his work. It made my cheeks heat and my mind go blank.

I had no idea how long had passed, but based on the ache of my body, it must have been hours. I sat up fully, moving to get a look at the finished art—which only made me vaguely uneasy now that I saw just how much he liked looking at it.

"What do you think you are doing?" he asked.

I startled at his words, falling back onto the bed with my brows furrowed.

"I want to see what all the fuss is about. It better be exquisite," I responded.

"No, that is not how this is going to work, Princess. My brush painted the canvas, and while that dries, my tongue will paint *you*."

There was no time to hesitate or argue because Bellamy appeared before me in a cloud of black, scooping me from the bed. We portaled again, the pain becoming far less noticeable the more we did so.

I burst into laughter as we landed in a full tub, water flying over the sides and splashing onto the floor. It was ice cold, but the demon instantly began warming it, his body heating quickly. I laughed again at his antics as well as the cold.

Bellamy devoured my amusement, his tongue beginning the slow and glorious torment of painting me. He tasted his way down my throat, paying expert attention to the place where my neck met my shoulder. I groaned, my head falling back as his teeth grazed just above my collarbone. I wanted to bottle this feeling and save it for when I would one day be starved of him.

"I thought you could not portal in Dunamis," I breathed out the words, my mind trying to fight against the storm of lust that was invading it. Bellamy's chuckle rumbled against my ribs before he peeked up at me through his thick lashes.

"No, I said that we could not portal *into* Dunamis, but once we are past the wards we can portal within the territory and out of it. Honestly though, I would have found a way to stall us even if we could have portaled straight to the castle. Anything to have even a moment more of your time before the world falls apart, beautiful creature." I meant to speak, to say something snarky in return, but then his mouth taunted me once more.

True to his word, that wicked tongue of his brushed teasing strokes over every inch of my skin. When he bit down on that area just below my belly button, I did exactly what he said I would. I writhed below him, moaning out his name.

He lifted me onto a ledge that connected the comically large white tub to the wall opposite the many windows, where the light blue curtains were drawn open to reveal the day.

They sure did enjoy sunlight and scenic views in this castle. And there was no denying that the sight was beautiful. The ocean was a stunning teal color, the sky above clear of clouds. More vines poked through the windows, letting in a chilly breeze.

I hummed at the feel of his lips as he kissed his way up my leg, the water below him growing warmer the higher he got. I felt something slide across my shoulder and looked down to see a vine slowly creeping up my arm. When it wrapped around my neck, I gasped, the pressure causing heat to travel down to my core.

With perfect timing, Bellamy's mouth found my center. His first lick was slow and agonizing, like he wanted to draw out my pleasure for as long as he possibly could. So I lifted my hips, pressing myself further into his face. A growl erupted from his chest, then he was bringing my legs over his shoulders and hooking his arms around my thighs, utterly consuming me.

Every shake of his head and slip of his tongue inside of me had me climbing higher, his name leaving my lips in lust-filled screams.

Tighter and tighter he held me, until I knew that I would bruise under his grasp, while the vine remained hugging my throat like a necklace that I never wanted to take off, adding to my growing pleasure. When two of Bellamy's fingers thrust inside of me, I fell back against the wall, grabbing onto his hair as if I would drown without him anchoring me.

"Fuck me, Bellamy. Fuck me now," I demanded, needing him to be inside of me when I fell off the edge.

As if he could hear my thoughts, the prince shot up out of the water, our lips crashing together in a violent kiss.

Separating our lips, leaving me with the salty taste of myself on my tongue, the prince flipped me. He wrapped my hair around his fist and pressed my torso down until my chest was flush with the ledge. I moaned at the mere idea of what he was about to do to me as Bellamy leaned down, his lips caressing the side of my face.

"Spread your legs, Princess. I want to watch as you take all of me," he whispered, placing a kiss on the jagged top of my ear.

I did as I was told, listening with satisfaction as he shouted praise to me within his mind. Then he was shoving himself inside, filling me up until I swore no more could fit. The angle was delicious, stealing my breath and muddling my mind. Then he was grabbing my wrists, holding them behind me with one hand while the other still gripped my hair.

His first slide out of me was slow, as if he were testing the way it affected me. I did not hold back, groaning at the loss of him and gasping out when he pressed back in. As if that was all the confirmation he needed, Bellamy quickened his pace, his thrusts bruising in their force. With each thrust, he hit that spot inside of me, the one that made my knees shake and my vision swim.

"I love you," he proclaimed, the words a raspy growl. "I will love you until my final breath and long after."

The sound of his voice and the declaration he made was euphoric, so much so that I could not help the mumbled three words from leaving my own lips over and over again. He let go of my hair, opting to dig his fingers into my hip as he sped up, the sound of our skin slapping and the water sloshing mingled with our gasped affection.

The vine tightened around my neck, Bellamy's grip on my wrists tugging until I was hovering over the ledge. For a moment, it felt like the plant was pulsing. Then Bellamy's grasp tightened, pulling my attention to him. "Now, Asher. Come for me now."

The erotic way he ordered my release sent me plunging over the edge, the pleasure of my orgasm causing me to tighten around him. Bellamy's hand gently set me down and the vine let me go as I came down from the high of his touch. Hot lips placed tender kisses to my back while he pulled me to a standing position, hands on my hips as he spun me to face him.

"Breathe, Ash." His voice had the exact opposite effect in that moment.

Slowly, he turned us, walking backwards until it was he who sat upon the ledge. For a moment, he leisurely trailed kisses south of my lips, taking his time as he pecked and nipped and sucked. His fingertips met my thighs, lazily tracing circles closer and closer to my center. Every one of my nerve endings was aflame as my back arched for even a semblance of his skin on mine.

Then his fingers arrived at their destination and my head flew back on a gasp of pleasure. "Break time is over, Princess."

I caught sight of his smirk, a single dimple popping into existence on his left cheek. Those blue irises were nearly black, the desire darkening them as he openly stared at his fingers working me. His hardened member twitched when I called out his name, the three syllables a prayer of sorts. Groaning, he tugged me forward, both hands moving to my hips once more to guide my knees onto the ledge. I hovered above him for only a moment until he forced me down onto him. Without missing a beat, he began lifting and lowering me, taking full control once more. I screamed out, unable to stop myself as he drove me to the madness that was this bliss, my nails digging into his shoulders like an anchor seeking purchase.

I felt as he shattered, the pulse of him within me and my name on his lips eliciting a deep moan from somewhere low in my throat.

Madness, that was what it felt like to love and be loved. My mind was consumed by him and everything he gave me. The pleasure, the trust, the freedom. I could lose myself in this—in Bellamy.

Perhaps I already had.

CHAPTER FOUR

ASHER

"We do not have to worry about an accident, just so you know."

I cringed at my word choice, silently chastising myself for making a perfectly joyous brunch awkward. Maybe I could run. How fast could he be with all that muscle weighing him down?

"An accident?" Bellamy inquired after he swallowed his eggs. His furrowed brow and pursed lips made me wish to find an early grave. Anything to get away from the growing embarrassment.

My eyes darted to the blue doors at the end of the enormous wooden table. I could make that, but where would I go from there? I could jump out a window. I bet Bellamy would find a nice place to bury me.

"Why do you look as if you want to fling yourself off a cliff?" he asked, a smirk lighting up his face.

Shoving a pastry into my mouth for moral support, I chewed while I considered that. A cliff would work too. Though jumping out of one of those windows would mean also jumping off a cliff, so really I could do both.

No, the demon would stop me. I covered my eyes with my hands, hoping I could hide from my own embarrassment since a quick death was out of the question.

"Ash?" His voice—soft and sweet—had a smile to it, I could tell just by the sound. Slowly, I lowered my hands from my face. "What do you mean by 'an accident'?"

I eyed him. Stalling, truthfully. He looked devastatingly handsome today, as per usual.

After our bath, he had gotten us dressed in a matching set of clothes. His blue tunic had silver accents, the long sleeves rolled up his arms to show the tattoos below. On his bottom half he wore black trousers, simple in comparison to the intricate detailing of his top.

He had offered me a stunning dress in the same blue. It was loose and flowy, the silver ropes on my shoulders that acted as straps making me blush in memory of our library excursions. It parted, the material splitting so high up my thighs that it was not far from where the fabric sat low on my back. After he had slipped the dress up my body, Bellamy had gotten on his knees to slowly tie the silver sandals up my legs, the straps ending just above my calves.

Being tended to by him felt even more intimate than kissing him sometimes.

The final touch was a silver sheath, which he strapped to my thigh with tantalizingly soft caresses that turned to swipes of his tongue and lips that left me gripping his hair and screaming his name.

Once I was fully dressed, he had braided my curls and even added kohl to my eyes after I complimented his. He was always quick to take care of me, to show me his love through actions just as often as he did through words.

I would not mind a tiny him one day, perhaps a couple hundred years from now. But how could I explain to Bellamy that I might never be able to give him that, even if we did find our way back to one another?

With an audible gulp, my eyes locked on one of the many demons that stood at attention. He followed my gaze, staring down each guard before waving his hand at them.

"Leave us, please."

They shuffled out quickly, not hesitating to follow the command of their prince. Bellamy merely watched me, his eyes narrowed as if he were trying to determine what I had been meaning to say without needing to ask me again.

"I cannot conceive," I blurted out after the guards were all gone.

It hurt to say aloud, to admit such a thing. Fae younglings were a rarity, and they were deeply loved. Bellamy had told Revanche yesterday that he wanted to spend the rest of his life with me. Would that still be true if he found out that I was likely never going to give him younglings?

After I leave him to take my kingdom, he might not want me anyways. I supposed it did not matter if this bothered him when I would do far worse.

"Xavier and Mia had been angry following Sipho's death. At me, at him, at themselves. They called me reckless and said they could not risk me conceiving a youngling due to my stupidity. After a night in my low level room—"

Bellamy cut me off with a growl, his anger thick and heavy in the room. Tension crawled up my spine, leaving me unsure of how to proceed. I swiped a mint leaf off the small silver dish just past my plate, popping it into my mouth and anxiously chewing it. Neither of us enjoyed talking about the royals, though we somehow always managed to bring them into conversations.

"I awoke to find Mia there. She was stroking my hair and humming to me. It was the first kind thing she had done for me since Sipho's death, and it made me feel as if things might get better with time. Xavier had said it was my fault, and I believed him. My anger felt misplaced—wrong, even. Though I did not forgive them, I also was unwilling to show that when it seemed wrong to feel such a thing."

I sighed, readying to tell him something that would change the way he viewed me. The way he pictured his future.

"It was then she explained that she had found a way for Tish to make me infertile, just until I was wed and needed to produce an heir. None of them clarified how it worked, and I never asked, which means I cannot bear children. So no accidents will occur. It is impossible," I finished, exhaling a deep and painful breath.

Younglings were not something I wanted right now, or anytime soon, but I had always pictured being a mother one day. I was unsure what Bellamy wanted for his future other than he wanted to be more than a husband or a father or a soldier. That he wanted to be *someone* rather than just anyone. And I understood that, down to my core. Did that mean though that he did not ever want those things? Or did he simply mean he wanted to accomplish more in his life than only those things?

"Ash, I am sorry that happened to you. That you were violated in such a way."

Broken, his voice sounded so broken, but I shook my head, trying to stop the tears and explain why this was probably for the best.

"Honestly, it is okay. I do not want younglings in the near future, and I am not sure if someone like me should conceive anyways. Wanting to be a mother and deserving to be one are two vastly different things."

Bellamy shot out of his chair, causing it to scratch across the wood floors and topple backwards. He did not seem to care as he made his way to me, rage causing his pupils to grow and overtake the stunning blue that I so loved.

My eyes went wide, mind reeling and unsure what to do as he stormed over to me. Was he that mad at me?

Bellamy pulled my chair out from under the table, twisting me around and then placing his hands on either arm rest. He leaned in, the smell of him intoxicating enough to mask the fear I felt for a moment.

"Do not ever act as if you are undeserving of what you want in life. Do not ever say that the things they did to you, what they stole from you, was okay. That the loss and pain and tragedies you suffered are not a big deal. That it is all fine. None of that is *fine.*"

No, it was not. I did agree. But what I would not say to him, or anyone, was that I still remembered the happy times. The moments when Mia would braid my hair as I played the pianoforte or when she would wake me up in the night to go lay in the gardens and look at the stars. Or the ones when Xavier would sneak me cookies beneath the dinner table and play pranks on the guards with me. That I missed those small pockets of joy more than anything. Some days, the pain had felt worth it, because their love had felt endless.

Hating them would make everything easier, but life was not easy.

"Are you mad at me?" I asked, my voice small and quiet—nervous for his answer.

Bellamy flashed me a stunned face, as if he could not believe I would ask such a thing. That was because he had a father who loved him, who stood up for him and cared for him. He did not understand the pain that came with my situation.

To be isolated and alone save for the couple who raised you. To suffer at their hands and be supposedly loved by them within the same breath. To then learn that every bit of that was fake, that you were a pawn and a fool and everything that you fought so hard not to be. I knew now that every move they had made was calculated and false, which perhaps made it all worse, because now I feared that no love came without pain.

Ignoring the good to assume someone is evil does no one justice. It only makes the reality more painful when it hits you in the face and reminds you of the truth. No one was truly good or evil.

"No, Princess, I am not mad. I would never be angry with you for struggling after the trauma you endured. I love you—so much more than you understand," he said, placing a finger below my chin to tilt my head up.

Our eyes met, the sheer power of his love bringing me to tears. I found myself once again wondering how anyone survived such a feeling.

"I mean, are you mad because of my inadequacies? I am not some delicate princess who is simply feeling down. I am broken and torn and a mess of a being. I know nothing of the world—I am both dangerous and terrified, and there is no part of me that is worthy of you. I cannot give you an heir or a life of joy. I am not...*whole.*"

Hearing the words slip from my lips made me realize just how pathetic they sounded. How did such a perfect evening lead to a morning like this? I felt exposed and raw, as if I were stripped bare and then skinned until my very soul was displayed.

Bellamy stood there for a moment, watching the tears fall from my eyes as I silently cried. I wished I was not letting my emotions get the best of me. I used to be so much better at hiding it all.

"I know that no amount of times I say this will convince you of something you do not believe, but you are not inadequate. You are more than I ever dreamed I would have." When I did not immediately respond, he sighed.

"Can we talk about something less horrid? There are too many feelings, too much weighing down on me. I just want to be happy and enjoy your company." I meant every word, but we both knew I was also avoiding something that I would one day have to face.

"Okay, Princess. Okay." He placed a kiss on my forehead, lingering for a minute. He pulled away suddenly as his eyes lit up and a smile spread across his face. "Come. Let me show you something."

With that, he stood up straight, reaching a hand out to me. I took it without thinking, my cheeks still wet from the grief of what could have been in another life. What should have been.

"Are you going to pretend to show me the library again so you can fuck me?" I asked, a small chuckle leaving my lips despite my morose mood.

Bellamy laughed too, shaking his head as he lifted me up. He wiped away a stray tear with his thumb, a ring grazing my skin and sending shivers down my back.

"I would like to think that I am taking you somewhere even better, but that might be because I plan to be inside of you in every room of this castle," he whispered into my ear.

I gasped, and then the familiar pull of portaling tore at my body. It was unnatural, portaling. Like fighting the universe.

"How lazy are you demons? We could have walked," I said, both of us laughing and smiling at the other as our feet found solid ground.

"Take a look around and tell me if you still wish we would have made the long walk here."

My body was turned, and then I was facing a room similar to the others—white walls and driftwood floors, blue rugs and white furniture with gorgeous silver designs. The windows were enormous with curtains matching the sky beyond. Three massive blue sofas sat in a U-shape with small white tables placed where they met, arranged facing a white brick fireplace off to the left.

None of that was why Bellamy brought me there though. No, the reason we stood in that doorway was sitting off to the right, light from the open window shining on it and making it look as if it were aglow.

A large, silver pianoforte was there, the matching bench with a light blue cushion practically begging for me to take a seat.

I had not played since that moment in Haven when I felt as if my life was ending. When I was alone and scared and unaware of the dangers that awaited me back home in the Fae Realm—in Betovere. Bellamy had walked in then, and I had simply left. Our relationship was different now, but I still felt just as broken.

Bellamy led me to the bench, taking my hand as I sat down before moving to the side and leaning forward with his elbows atop the shiny surface. My breath hitched at the beauty of it. Chandeliers hung above us, identical to the others I had seen within this palace and Bellamy's Haven residence. They bathed the room in demon light, the Sun magic doing what it did best—highlighting beautiful things.

They lit Bellamy's face up and cast him in a magnificent glow of colors, the rainbow on his cheeks sending my heart into a sprint. The piano was also alight, silver mixed with the colors making it look like a rare gemstone.

I could weep at the sight of it.

There was something freeing about this moment. Perhaps it was the difference in my mental state or even the way the wind felt like it was calling to me as it blew through an open window. Maybe it was the high of being able to make my own choices. Every moment from now would be my own to dictate and mold. Mine.

With my back straight and the memory of Henry telling me that I sat like I had a stick up my ass bringing a smile to my face, I began to play.

Unlike the last time I was able to pour my heart into the keys, this time my fingers found a more triumphant rhythm. There was excitement and beauty to the melody, a distinct sense of rightness as it built.

My hands flew, my heart racing right along with them. I was not able to focus on Bellamy, to look his way or attempt to hear his thoughts. All I could do was think of the journey that had led me here. The painful and devastating parts seemed smaller in the wake of the laughter and warmth and love I had found. Though they still hurt, there was no denying that I had at long last discovered my place in this world.

OF REALMS AND CHAOS

With that realization, I slowed to a soft close. I left my hands there, hovering over the keys as I breathed in deeply. Everything would move quickly from here. King Adbeel would come, and I would meet with him and then deny them my aid. When the arguing that was sure to ensue ended, I would have Bellamy take me home, and I would win my crown. All that would happen was enough to convince me that I deserved these small moments of peace.

"Beautiful," Bellamy whispered from his place to the right, his eyes alight with more emotion than I was capable of understanding. He smiled, walking over to me and beginning to rub small circles on my back. I sighed, leaning into his touch, and was glad for his anchoring presence.

"Such a compliment coming from an artist. Truly, I am blushing, Your Highness."

He snorted at my sarcasm, flicking my nose. "It would have been rude of me to say you were off-key at the start." I gasped, fighting back the laugh that I knew he was hoping for with his remark. Especially since I had definitely not been off-key. I was never off. Not when I was in my right mind, at least. "Not all of us can be perfect, but I love you all the same."

Looking up at him made my heart stutter—his chiseled jaw and high cheekbones mixed with the glow of his blue eyes and the part of his full lips. It was like seeing a god in the flesh. He was far too flawless for his own good.

Clearly that big ego had grown from years of well-deserved praise.

I wondered if anyone outside of his Trusted knew that he was even more stunning on the inside. His love for, and dedication to, the family he had made; the way he fought for not only his realm, but all of them; even his patience and heart were something beyond that of many in The Capital. This male was so worthy of the joy that lit his eyes now.

"Well, the painting of me was shaky and unimpressive, so I guess neither of us are perfect." The painting of me was actually stunning, annoyingly so. Stupid, cocky, talented demon.

Bellamy offered me his hand with a deep chuckle, smiling as if the world had been laid at his feet when I took it. Together we walked through the palace, which mirrored the world outside with its blue skies and white clouds. Though there was no snow on the ground, the air was still quite chilly, and I found that the farther down we went, the colder I got.

By the time we arrived at the arched doors that would lead us out, I was shivering. Bellamy said nothing, opting to simply call upon my silver cloak—the darkness wrapping around me like a blanket before disappearing to reveal the silver fabric. He reached behind me and pulled the hood up, placing a soft peck to my lips before calling to his own cloak as well.

"Where are we going?" I asked. My curiosity moved to the forefront of my mind now that I was not as uncomfortably cold, my free hand clasping the button at my neck.

A blue-clad guard opened the doors for us, a soft breeze hitting my face that smelled of pine and jasmine. Bellamy dipped his head in thanks, and oddly enough, I found myself doing the same. Strange how easily one could change.

"Since we have decided to have a joyous day, I want you to meet one of the happiest little creatures I have ever encountered." He said it with a sense of eagerness that made me nervous. Anyone who had Bellamy this excited was someone to be slightly terrified of.

We walked in silence through the courtyard and down the large hill. It was steeper on foot, and I found that my legs were still sore from riding for weeks on end.

Quiet moments like these were dangerous, because they allowed the mind to wander. It was all too easy to think of King Adbeel, to wonder when Bellamy would send word to him that he should return to The Royal City. Despite my desire to live in this small piece of happiness, I knew that time was not on our side. Xavier and Mia would not wait forever, especially now that we—I—had slaughtered their demon search party. Meeting the king and returning to Betovere was far too important to let it go undiscussed.

"When will your father return?" I asked Bellamy, attempting nonchalance and failing miserably.

He quirked a brow as he peered down at me, clearly debating what he wanted to say and choosing his words carefully. More pretty lies, but I knew I would have my answers soon enough. I was always good at being patient, at waiting for the right time. Growing up a princess taught me that patience was a virtue one could not live without.

"Tomorrow. I will send for him tomorrow. Give me one more day with you where we can enjoy this—us." He grabbed onto my hand, pulling it up to his chest.

I knew that whatever it was he needed to say in front of his king was monumental. More than likely, my power—magic—whatever it was—sat in the center of it all.

One day. I could wait that long.

Nodding, I continued on, allowing him to keep ahold of my hand as we walked. We remained that way until we reached the white and brown cottages along the cobblestone path. It was even more stunning at midday, the sun beating down on the little imperfections that made these places homes.

The area was far less congested now, likely because many had gone off to work and learn. To exist. Empty, but still full. That was how this place felt. As if it were made with enough love to last through those quieter moments.

My mind wandered, thinking of all the beauty I had seen since we arrived last night. The buildings, the landscape, even the demons were all uniquely magnificent.

I thought back to the many I had seen along the way to the library last night, Revanche standing out amongst them. She was stunning, but her personality could use some work.

"You and Revanche were engaged?" I asked, trying to sound casual despite my interest. I had no right to be angry since I was engaged when we first met. In fact, my engagement technically never ended.

Would one consider that to be infidelity?

Before I could further panic over my tragic love life, Bellamy responded, "That is debatable. Revanche is barely ninety years, but her entire life has been dedicated to becoming queen. I am half convinced that Judson conceived her simply to marry me." His voice was not shaky, and his face showed no sign of nerves, but I could feel his unease at the topic.

"And the agreement between your fathers?"

He looked at me then, his face far more serious than I imagined the conversation warranted. The furrow of his brow and purse of his lips filled the air around us with an odd sense of anger as well, as if this topic was one best left alone. Yet he continued.

"King Adbeel felt marrying Revanche would help with my reputation of violence and promiscuity. Not to mention that it would not hurt to have heirs being born with the Ayad name and the Garnier bloodline. I will not lie, we had many...encounters, but the king was aware I never intended to marry her."

King, not father. How often had I heard Bellamy call King Adbeel his father? Once? Never? I was unsure. I had no personal experience in familial interactions, but Nicola, Farai, and Jasper never called their fathers by their first names. Was Bellamy's relationship with his own so strained that he could not even bring himself to acknowledge his parentage out loud?

Despite my everlasting curiosity, I dropped the topic, allowing the silence to once more consume us as we wove through the homes.

Bellamy brought us to a stop at one of the brown cottages, the vines wrapping the structure like a warm embrace. The door was a creamy white—a small pair of sandals left at the base of it, as if a youngling had carelessly kicked them off on their way inside.

I smiled at that, the idea of such peace existing. This world took so often and with little regard for those it stole from. Younglings deserved joy, as we all did, and it was nice to know that someone had that somewhere.

When the door swung open, I was met with a pair of wide brown eyes. The female stood before us, her long brown skirt and loose white top billowing in the wind that pushed through the open doorway. Her hair was also brown, cropped short to her head. She had high cheekbones and thin lips, her eyes taking up so much of her face that she looked eternally youthful—like a child or a youngling.

"Bronagh, I am so glad we caught you before you left," Bellamy said.

He leaned down to pull the small female into him. The embrace was tender, almost familial. Her lips spread into one of the widest smiles I had ever seen, bordering on unsettling in its appearance. A chill snaked up my back causing the hairs on my arms to rise. Something was not right, clearly, but Bellamy seemed more than comfortable in her presence. So when her melodic voice, soft and enchanting, welcomed us both inside, I followed him through the doorway.

Bronagh's home was warm and inviting, the mismatched furniture and woodsy smell creating a comforting atmosphere. The soft, yellow glow of the candles was unexpected, as I had yet to see any area lit by anything other than demon light. Yet she had them everywhere, wax coating the counters and tables and even the floor in some places.

One thing was noticeably absent: toys. There was no sign of a youngling's presence other than the shoes on the doorstep.

"What brings you here today, Bell?" she asked, her tone affectionate in the way a mother's was to their child. I looked between the two, suddenly realizing that I was not aware of how they knew one another.

In that moment, it was hard not to wonder who Bellamy's mother was. I had never asked before. Not because I was not curious, but because I had not thought it was my place seeing as he had not brought it up in conversation—had not even hinted at a mother at all. But now, with so much between us and an uncertain future, was Bellamy introducing me to her?

With impressive speed, my palms began to sweat.

"There is news on Betovere that I figured you would be interested in hearing," he said, lifting his shoulders as if the topic were no more than small talk.

Neither Bronagh nor I were fooled.

"Well, how considerate of you. And I am sure this beautiful female beside you has absolutely nothing to do with your visit today?" she said, eyebrows raised and arms crossed.

I could not stop the laugh that slipped from my lips at her sarcasm. Bronagh practically lit up at my amusement, flashing that same too-large grin and winking at me. Bellamy smiled too, his own chuckles echoing through the home.

"You got me. I was being honest about Betovere though, things are not well. I believe you will be called back to base sooner rather than later," he said.

No one could deny the way that the air seemed to charge, a furious and sorrowful mood settling in between us all. They scared me, the emotions pouring off of the female. Every instinct told me to run, to cower—to get as far from her as I possibly could. Without thought, I stepped closer to Bellamy, our hands touching ever so gently.

"This is Asher. She is my—"

And then Bellamy hit the floor. His hand gripping his chest, and his scream piercing in its volume.

Bronagh and I both dropped to our knees, clutching at him and begging him to speak. To say anything. To tell us how to help.

Ten agonizing seconds passed before Bellamy's wide eyes met mine. I knew then what had happened. Pino had told us, and we were foolish to think we could be prepared. More than that, it would explain the horror on his face and the pain in his eyes.

Bellamy could feel his wards shattering.

"They are attacking."

CHAPTER FIVE

ASHER

Chaos. That was the only word that came to mind as we portaled into Haven.

We landed in the middle of the town square, a beautiful stone fountain in the center pouring bloody water like whimsical gore. My heart lurched at the sight of the white houses that now bore streaks of red, hundreds of previously unsuspecting fae leaving those homes behind to fight or run for their lives. With The Mist to the north and the warded Forest of Tragedies to the south, the inhabitants of Haven would have nowhere to run.

A fierce rage built inside of me as the Golden Guard—the formal title for the fae forces—tore through unarmed males, females, and even younglings.

OF REALMS AND CHAOS

I would kill them all. I would torture and maim them. I would rip them apart limb from limb.

My feet moved before my brain had fully processed the scene in front of me. My flimsy dress was catching in the wind, slowing me down as it wrapped around my legs. But there had been no time to change, no time to do anything other than grab our weapons. Now I was running at a nearby guard that had a female on her knees in front of him, smirking at her ripped dress and exposed breasts. She cried, begging for mercy, and he *laughed*.

I swung my sword, cutting through flesh and bone—shattering his skull and slicing his eye in half. He fell, screaming on the ground before lying limp seconds later.

To my left, a guard was using her power to shove seawater down the throat of a fae who had been darting for the forest. He writhed on the ground, his body convulsing as he struggled to resist the water that was being forced into his lungs. I grabbed onto her mind, shattering it quickly before moving on.

Not enough. *Never* enough.

Once more, I was on the move, running through the crowd of panicked fae. A great shake of the cobblestones at my feet had me struggling to remain upright. The ground was splitting beneath us, dirt and grass and stone ripping up and flying in all directions. A chunk landed in my eye before I could duck my head, forcing me to quickly rub at it until I could see again, the burn nothing compared to the inferno of my fury.

Still, that small moment of hesitation was nearly enough to have my stomach sliced open by a female with claws as long as my forearm. I dodged her at the last second, her talons ripping open my thigh instead. She fell to my power before she could send another strike my way.

The bloody fountain water was lifting, racing towards Winona as she fought off a particularly large Shifter who had taken on the body of a wolf. I stopped, wanting to help her—to warn her. Anything.

Just as I opened my mouth to scream, a great beast with leathery gray skin and a horn atop its snout charged into me. The impact sent me flying through the air, landing with a horrible crack on a patch of dirt. I had no time to appreciate the flowers around me, no time to consider that this likely had been beautiful hours ago—the culmination of someone's sweat and tears and hard work. All I could think was that the pain in my hand was nauseating, that the screaming fae needed my help. That this was all my fault.

I forced myself up into a sitting position, noting that two of my fingers sat at odd angles and were bleeding profusely. I had no idea how to help myself. That was the problem with living in a palace with a Royal Healer, I never needed to know how to provide a quick fix for an injury.

With my dagger in one hand and my power poised to compensate for the mangled digits on the other, I stood once more. The Shifter who had attacked me stared my way, prepared to pounce. I smiled, a wicked raise of my lips that bared my teeth.

"Hello, you hideous little creature. Tell me, do you think you can snap my neck before I turn your brain to mush?" I taunted over the screams. The Shifter let out a vicious snarl, snapping their head up as if demonstrating how it would spear me. "Well then, tiny, may the best fae win."

Not a second passed before the Shifter charged, tilting their chin down and running headfirst my way. I dove into their mind, opting to stay still and watch the dread light up their face as I forced them to stop mere inches from me. When we were nose to snout, I smirked, looking into those hazel eyes and speaking into its mind.

Kill the Golden Guard, beasty.

And then it was off, diving through the crowd and barreling into golden armor. My voice had been that of The Manipulator, and she was to be obeyed.

With the battle still raging on, I ducked down near one of the white houses, closing my eyes and trying to focus on the minds around me. It was no use though. I could avoid taking down Bellamy and his

Trusted, but I did not know the minds of the fae from Haven. Without time to dig into their thoughts and memories, I would not be able to decipher friend from foe.

Which meant one at a time.

Pushing to my feet, the fingers on my right hand still dripping red, I watched as Bellamy swirled his hands, the wind around him picking up. My braid whipped across my face, leaving me temporarily without sight. I shoved it back just in time to see Bellamy form a vortex of wind around himself. He stood there, the eye of a storm ready to tear apart all who came in his path.

"Lian!" he shouted, catching the attention of the Air not far from him. She paused to look back, her sword still inside of a guard's neck. "Catch."

He twisted his hand higher, then flicked it forward, as if swatting away a pesky bug. Lian ripped her sword free of the female's neck and threw up her hands, catching the tornado like a youngling catching a ball. She held it airborne for a moment before sweeping her arms to her left and releasing her grip. The wind went careening towards the golden ships in the bay, shattering a quarter of them upon impact.

Bellamy maintained his momentum, stomping his foot to the ground and fragmenting it in a perfect sphere around him. Two guards lost their balance and fell into the large cracks, piercing screams echoing behind them. The Elemental laughed as they dropped, reaching his arms out to lift water from the sea.

His hands rose, both water and earth moving to the sky. When the winds came back ten-fold, Bellamy brought the three together with a loud smack of his hands. As the whirlwind of elements formed, the prince snapped and fire caught. With what must have been an immense amount of energy, he threw his arms forward, the storm of all four elements ripping apart the remaining boats.

I gasped at the sight of his power, the extent to which he could destroy. Then I smiled in glee, turning on the stunned Golden Guards. Six of them were in my sight, all frozen in fear after Bellamy's display.

My turn.

I slashed through their minds like steel on skin, grabbing hold with bloody claws. They all cried out in agony, clutching their skulls as if they could dig me out like a weed. Unfortunately for them, I was far more stubborn. With a little focus, I could sense their abilities. Two Multiples, a Fire, and an Earth. Useful.

Their bodies shook as I scraped my way down their minds, and I pictured snipping their free will like dead hair. Watching the emotions leave their faces brought a level of satisfaction that had me smiling as I ordered them to take down their own.

Before they had even left my side, I was once more jumping into the battle. Winona was alight, her Sun magic nearly singeing the end of my braid as she spun and beheaded a guard. Beside her, Ranbir had his hands splayed out, palms facing the ground. I paused just long enough to watch as he leached the color from the grass below him in thin lines, making his way to unsuspecting guards. Slowly, bodies began to collapse, life drained from them.

Dagger in my good hand, I began the dance once more—my balance off, but my adrenaline making up for it. From the water, Calista led sirens to land, the fierce screams coming from the entirely nude creatures sending a handful of Golden Guards running. I continued on, not able to see Noe, Henry, or Cyprus in the fray.

After three more bodies fell from my hand and power, I felt a familiar mind wink into existence nearby.

My head whipped to the right, where I caught sight of her tangerine hair. In that moment, time seemed to freeze. The breath caught in my throat, heart racing to an unsteady beat. There was no sound, no fighting, just gray eyes staring into blue ones.

Mia was here. She was here, and she was looking right at me.

I had not seen her since she looked on in terror as Bellamy snatched me from my own wedding. Since she held her hands to a wounded Sterling, saving the mortal prince who had violently assaulted me. Since I found out she had been slowly poisoning me, using me just like everyone else. Since I learned that she was killing her own subjects.

She wore a flowing golden gown, the nearly sheer fabric so light that it blew in the breeze. Her orange hair was loose, the length now to her collar bones. Everything about her was so different than it always had been, as if this fae in front of me was not the same one that had raised me. Yet it was not her who had changed, but me instead. My perception of her and all that she was. My mindset and beliefs. My *heart*.

Pink lips tilted into a smile. Did she think she won? Was she enjoying the sight of me so enraged? She had never cared for my temper, but now it gave her an advantage.

At least, she thought it did.

I began moving before I had made the decision to do so, my feet carrying me towards the female who had been like a mother to me. Who had beaten me down and nearly destroyed me. After I took a handful of steps, Mia dropped her hands to the ground, her eyes never leaving mine.

Slowly, too slowly, I screamed out a warning. The ground shook, and branches the size of tree trunks broke through the dirt and grass, through stone and brick, stabbing chests and wrapping around necks.

Mia was careless with her power, taking out both the fae of Haven and the fae of the Golden Guard. I watched on in horror as she killed by the masses, bodies being torn apart regardless of age or allegiance. Only the sirens, who dove for the water, made it out. The deaths were quick and many. A small form, the youngling no more than five years, was slumped down nearby, and my sorrow heated into an inferno of fury.

She laughed, standing upright. "Come, Asher darling. Let the Guard take care of these filthy creatures."

Her voice was as beautiful as ever—her body and face full of harsh lines, making her look like the queen she was born to become. She clearly had not considered that I would deign to warn the fae of her oncoming attack. Or perhaps she thought I had been trying to save the Guard. There were many who had hesitated, who seemed to wish that they were not being forced to take the lives of their own. For them, I still would not show mercy.

Mia did not know that though. Over the last couple of months, I had changed, enough so that she no longer knew me at all. I was not the princess she had molded me into. I was not The Manipulator Xavier had trained me to become. I was Asher, and I was free.

I pushed out my power, meeting a golden garden of resistance and blocking my path to her mind. No matter, this was what I had been practicing day and night for. I could take her down even without my powers.

I would never concede. I would fight until my final breath and then rage from the Underworld where I knew my blackened soul belonged.

I would win.

A loud scream of fury came from my back, halting me in my pursuit. Turning, I watched as Bellamy, his body hidden beneath scorching black flames, ran at us. Behind him lay the bodies of every Golden Guard and every Haven inhabitant.

She had killed them all.

The Trusted remained, the group of them gathered in a circle. Only Cyprus and Luca were missing, the two of them likely still in Betovere. Ranbir was on the ground with his hands to the dirt and his jaw tense as he put everything he had into stopping the queen's attack.

Mia began sprouting vines with thorns and red flowers that had teeth, using her power in an attempt to keep Bellamy back as she walked towards me. But he pressed on, burning through the leaves and slicing branches in half with powerful gusts of wind. I watched as the queen's face faltered, a rare crack in her mask of cool confidence.

"Asher, my flower, we must go now," she said, grabbing hold of my bad hand and tugging me back towards the water. I howled in pain, but she did not seem to notice.

On the edge of the sand stood a male with dark mahogany hair and tanned skin, looking uncomfortably familiar though I was unable to put my finger on why.

I pulled with all my might, trying to free myself from her hold on me, but the queen was far stronger than I realized. She tightened her grasp until the agony nearly consumed me. Despite that, I still struggled in her grip, imagining what it would mean to be dragged back to Betovere— picturing a new golden wedding aisle and Sterling waiting at the end of it. Picturing more and more fae bodies falling at my feet on a wooden stage.

The panic came in full force, and then I was shouting, searching her mind for any way in. For a single chance to break her before she broke me. Mia seemed to finally notice my resistance, and she paused momentarily, leaving Bellamy to fight through a particularly nasty patch of thorned roses.

"Asher, we do not have time for this. They are all gone, so you cannot save them. No fae is worth your life. We must leave immediately," she said, her voice a rush of anxiety and determination.

That was when I realized that Mia had not tried to harm me. In fact, she had taken great care to hurt everyone *but* me. The look in her eyes, one of relief and fear, made me think that she was under the impression she was rescuing me. Mia thought me in danger, and that meant she would kill anyone in her way if I did not kill her first.

I finally pushed away from her, ducking under a branch to put distance between us. She stared at me, mouth agape and eyes bulging. I had never—not once—seen Mia quite this stunned, not even as she watched me being taken from my wedding. That had been terror. This was pure shock. The raise of her brows and slackening of her shoulders was the opposite of the Mia I knew.

Was it foolish that it hurt me to see her this way?

Bellamy made it to me then, his hand immediately resting on my lower back—nearly scorching me through the ripped dress. At the sight of him touching me, Mia's face lit up in fury. She lifted an arm, and a vine thicker than rope shot out of the ground. I watched in horror as it wrapped around Winona's leg, causing her to fall. The vine dragged her away from Ranbir, who had still been working to wither the other plants, her nails digging into the dirt and pulling chunks of grass free. He screamed as he dove for her, but the weeds suddenly grew larger, entrapping every one of Bellamy's Trusted.

Ranbir's screams did not die out. Instead, they became louder—hoarser—with every foot closer Winona got to Mia. He fought, throwing his power out with the type of strength that I had not realized he had, killing every plant within a fifteen-foot radius. But Mia was faster, more brutal. Each dead plant had three sprouting in its wake. Escaping quickly became impossible for all of them.

What seemed to be hours were mere seconds. One moment, Winona was beside the love of her life, her husband and soulmate, then she was suddenly beside the fae queen, vines covering every inch of her body below the neck. Bellamy and I froze, too afraid that moving would mean risking Winona's life.

"Now then, let us not be imprudent. Release the princess, Elemental. Do that, and I will not kill you all where you stand," Mia said, her voice dripping with authority.

Winona remained silent, her face stoic. She would not cry. Nor would she beg. It was not in her nature to do so. A faint glow emitted from her, but as the vines tightened around her, those Sun powers faded into nothing. She gave a curt shake of her head, eyes trained on her prince.

Noe screamed from behind me as she fought against the vines with her shadows, slashing and tearing one only for two to replace it. Each of Bellamy's Trusted projected thoughts of terror and fury as they did the same.

I felt my body begin to shake as I took a slow step forward, my power still pressing into the gilded flowers that shielded Mia's mind. All I needed was one chance, and I could save them. I might not have saved the innocent fae of Haven, I might have failed them entirely, but I could prevent the death of the male I loved and the family I had found.

I took a second step and then Bellamy was grabbing my arm, pulling me into him. My back hit his chest, and for once, I could sense all of his feelings, hear many of his thoughts. He pictured watching Mia take me away, the soul-crushing loss of me, and he could not stomach it. Not even to save his friends. His family.

"Touch her, and I will rip your heart from your chest and feed it to your plants," he seethed.

Mia growled, a deep sound I would have never thought could come from her whimsical and usually soothing voice. Winona let out a faint gasp as the vines tightened, and I could not stop myself from reaching out a hand in her direction, prepared to save her in any way possible.

"Please, Mia, do not do this. Do not hurt them. I beg you! Just let them go," I said, the words pouring out of me with such speed that they became muddled.

The queen heard though because the look of realization on her face was obvious. My mistake was not silently going with her when I had the chance; I understood that then. Now she knew what side I had chosen, and it was not hers.

Her eyes flicked between Bellamy and I, eventually settling on him as he moved to push me behind him. I wrapped my arm in his, trying and failing to reclaim my position in the front. No one but I deserved Mia's wrath, and no one but I would kill her.

"I see. It seems you have let them taint you, little love. An unfortunate turn of events. Which means you have forced my hand." As if her propensity for the dramatics won out, Mia tightened her hand, forming a fist. The vines slithered up Winona's neck like snakes, suffocating her.

I dropped to my knees, listening as Ranbir begged for Mia to take him instead, watching as the queen smiled his way. Bellamy refused to let me go, falling to the ground with me.

"Spare her, please! Take me, I will go with you! Please, do not hurt her!"

Mia would not, could not, hear reason.

"No, Ash!" Winona rasped, wiggling against the vines, her face gaining a moderately purple hue. A breeze came, blowing the scent of lilacs my way. The scent of Mia. I raged against Bellamy's hold, needing to get to Winona.

He suddenly got to his feet, flames lighting his arms. He ran at Mia, throwing balls of fire that left her dodging and sending piles of sand to compensate. Plant life continued to attack the Trusted, forcing them to fight for their lives while Winona's remained so clearly at risk. For a moment, Bellamy and Mia remained in a deadly battle, his sword of fire only barely grazing her cheek to draw first blood. But Mia was as strong as she was smart. One of the strongest Earth's to grace the Fae Realm, in fact. And she would not yield.

He continued to gain the upper hand, tearing through her plants and leaping over branches. Every time she would rip the ground apart, he would stitch it back together. A growl of frustration left her lips when he combated her barely formed strike of sand, and all at once, thorned vines were barreling towards me. I gasped, shoving at her mental shields with all of my strength, but it was as if they were fortified with a second consciousness somehow.

Bellamy screamed, throwing a wall of scorching fire in front of me. It was too late by the time we both realized what Mia had done, the distraction she had utilized, as one of those vines speared through his shoulder, sending him flying backwards.

Suddenly, I too was standing, raising my dagger to her. The queen giggled as if the sight of me doing such a thing was a joke. Smaller vines reached up, wrapping around my wrists and ankles. Holding me still. Horrifying defeat consumed me as, with a great shove, I tried and failed to break through her mental shields.

"Take this as a lesson, you traitorous little thing. The more you love, the more you stand to lose. And I vow to be the one ripping it all away from you. Come home or watch as everything you love withers before you."

"I love you," Winona said to her husband, just as Mia conjured a thorned dagger and swiped it across the Sun's neck. Mia let her fall, and then the mahogany-haired male was by her side, smiling as Winona hit the ground with a fleshy thud.

Ranbir—always so soft spoken, so controlled—screamed out, breaking down before us. He fought viciously against the vines, but he was no match for Mia.

"Not my wife, please! Please, not my wife! Not her! Please, not my wife!" Over and over again he chanted the same words, and sometime in that span of a handful of seconds, I wormed my way past Mia's shields. Past the strange black that sat behind them, now no more than a mist, as if it were distracted.

I could kill her, end it all. She would fight it, but I would be triumphant. Yet, in that second, I faltered. Was it fear that stopped me from crushing her mind? Love?

My single instant of hesitation—a horrible lapse in judgment—was all it took. Blowing a kiss and offering a wink, the male held onto Mia, black shadows engulfing them. Leaving nothing but their scent and the bodies around us.

Ranbir, now free after finally killing off the plants, darted to Winona's side, his hands alight with his healing power. I knew, though, that she was gone. That so many were gone. Because of *me*. Because I could not simply kill Mia when I had the chance.

I was not the only one thinking so. In Ranbir's mind, he too hated my lack of action. He too knew that I could have stopped her. He too placed the blame on me.

The others rushed to the fallen Sun, crowding her body and shouting through their tears. Her green hair was just as blood soaked as Ranbir's white top, her throat ripped open wide.

Bellamy was nearby, holding a hand to his torn shoulder while he bent over a body that was so mangled and bloody it was nearly unrecognizable. Yet I knew just by the shredded velvet clothes and the wrinkled tan skin that it was Pino.

The prince closed the Oracle's remaining eyelid then slowly made his way to Winona. I stayed rooted in place and watched on as Bellamy fell to his knees beside Ranbir, placing one shaking arm around his mourning friend and his free hand on Winona's forever still face.

"May they return to Eternity," I whispered without intending to, my ears ringing and my eyesight fogging.

His sobs were the last thing I heard before I began running. I could not be there, could not listen to Bellamy's grief. Could not see the gore that I helped create. Could not listen to Ranbir's mental or physical voice as he prayed for his wife to return. His other half. His world.

My feet took me all the way to Bellamy's home, the castle of night and blood—a name so fitting for the recent tragedy. It had sustained some damage, mostly walls and windows shattered, but there was no actual carnage here.

The second I made it through the entrance, my feet took me up. Up. Up until I was in front of a set of doors I had only seen once. I shoved them open, walking into an all-white room with a dazzling chandelier. In the center lay a black pianoforte, small red designs painted onto it.

Beautiful. So incredibly beautiful. Too beautiful.

I turned and promptly vomited, the images of the small dead bodies, Winona's gasping breaths, and Ranbir's raw screams bombarding me. My leg poured blood onto the white floors, and my sick stained the walls. Still, the only thing I could think was that this death, this brokenness, this disaster, was my fault. I brought horror upon this sweet and unsuspecting place.

All of it was enough to send me down a spiral.

With my throat on fire, my fingers throbbing, and my stomach twisted, I took the stool in front of the instrument and threw it against the wall. The white quartz chipped but held steady, wood from the seat splintering off in pieces. I grabbed the largest chunk of the chair, and with an unbearable amount of anger and self-loathing, I began smashing the pianoforte.

CHAPTER SIX

ASHER

Perhaps I would always be haunted by the smell of burning bodies.

CHAPTER SEVEN

BELLAMY

What were goodbyes if not the end?

ACT II
~ TO LEAD ~

CHAPTER EIGHT

ASHER

It had been one month since I had chai.

What a foolish thing, to hide behind lies and boats and bottles of mead. To pretend one is anything other than the monster they were born to be. To whisper to oneself that life is made of pain and joy and the molding of the two—that fault and failure are a balance of success and triumph.

For so long, I had done that. Convinced myself that I could recover from every misstep, that my mistakes would be redeemed by my fight to save a broken world. Up until that very moment, I had drowned my mind in liquor and pain and planning.

Yet as I looked down on my fingers, now whole once more save for the small scars that stood out in stark contrast to my olive skin, I realized how wrong I had been.

The nausea in my stomach came not only from the rocking ship as waves barreled into it, but also from the recollection of the dead and hollow look in Ranbir's eyes as he had fixed these very fingers. The gasp he had made when he later healed my bleeding arms.

No, I had not had chai in quite some time. How could I when memories of Ranbir's smiling face and Winona's soft touch plagued the taste of those spices?

"Hey, little brat, are you still sulking about being cut off?"

I sighed, looking up to meet Henry's moss green eyes, his orange hair at startling odds with the dull blue-gray water and the faded wood surrounding us. Stubble littered his tan face, growing out now that he no longer had Winona to cut it. A part of me wondered if he refused to do so because he could not bring himself to have such an act be done by anyone but the green-haired Sun.

He was staring down at me, a smirk on his freckled face despite the clear concern that pinched his brow.

It seemed I had taken to drinking too much, and pumpkin, here, was not impressed.

"Do not look at me like I am some fragile addict who is constantly five seconds away from offing themself," I hissed.

"Are you not?"

At that precise moment, a wave smashed into the boat with enough force to set me off balance, and my stomach decided that it was not willing to contain the bread and coffee from earlier. I clutched for the edge, leaning over and vomiting.

Henry's hands found my body, holding up my hair and rubbing soothing circles on my back. When I stopped heaving, I wiped my mouth, gasping for fresh air and picturing solid ground.

At least this time I was not puking up rum.

"At least this time you are not puking up mead."

Or mead. Maybe I did have a problem.

I could throw myself from the boat. A swifter death than hurling up my insides.

Probably should not think that way when I just argued about my sanity and will to live.

"Come on, we need to train. You have not picked up a weapon since Ha—" Henry stuttered to a stop, his breath hitching at what he almost said.

What none of us would say.

Haven. The beautiful place of safety and acceptance, a sanctuary for fae who escaped the rule of tyrants. All dead now. Just like Pino. Just like Winona. Dead not only because of a wicked queen's fight for power, but also because of a stupid princess's selfish desire for freedom.

"I have not been in the mood, obviously," I said, grabbing the edge and making my way down the ship towards our shared cabin. He would push until I agreed, so I might as well collect my weapons while we argue. I was nothing if not a multitasker.

"Unfortunately, we do not have the time to cater to your moods. This will be more dangerous than the journey through Eoforhild. We not only have to survive, but we have to win these beings over. We cannot do that with weak form and smelly breath," he chastised.

"I am sure that is what all the females say to you," I spit. It was immature, but I was in a particularly foul state of mind.

He chuckled, a deep laugh that made me stop in my tracks. A façade, that was what it was. We were close enough to not pretend with one another, yet we still hid. Him behind smiles and teasing, me behind scowls and sarcasm.

Neither of us were okay, far from it. When I turned to say that to his face, I froze. Those green eyes bore into me, so expressive that I did not need the power of mind manipulation to know he was just as ashamed and concerned as I was. Just as broken.

"Fine, we can train. You are right. There is no room for mistakes." With that, we continued moving forward inch by inch, me holding onto the edge and him walking with his hands in his trouser pockets. I nearly tripped him just to get the haughty look off of his face.

By the time we were back in our cabin, I was practically crawling, desperate for stability and stillness. I had never been at sea before this, and I was suddenly very sure that I would have died long before I reached The Mist had I gone with my original plan of escape those many months ago in Haven.

With the ache in my chest at the memory of that once beautiful place and the horrific thought of bloody white floors and rasping breaths, I promptly dove for the bed. Maybe a second of rest would stop me from vomiting all over the floors?

Henry and I had to share, doing our best to stay inconspicuous as we traveled. He was easily the worst bedmate in history, taking up well over half the bed and snoring so loudly it reverberated off the walls.

A male as tall as him truly could not fit anywhere, but watching him duck under the door frame and scrunch onto the bed beside me was a reminder of why he probably also hated traveling by sea. We made quite the duo.

"Listen, I am here if you want to talk. I am not sure how many more times I can say that before you understand I mean it. For the sake of time, I will assume that it is infinite and you are about to turn me down, so how about we cut to the good part and I teach you dagger throwing?"

I turned, prepared to give my best rebuttal, but a piece of paper wrapped around a pen smacked me in the face, bouncing and hitting him too. A spark of excitement flitted through me as I grabbed it, untying the yarn and opening the note.

I can think of quite a few things I can do with a candle that would change your mind, Princess.

A gasp left my lips before I could stop it, my thighs clenching together out of instinct. Wicked demon.

Bellamy had a tendency to send me inappropriate messages at the most inconvenient of times, the worst being when I was so drunk that I responded to his mention of his extensive sailing experience by saying that I was very interested in what his tongue could do while steering a ship.

"You know, his flirting could use some work. Imagine if you misinterpreted that and thought he was threatening to shove a lit candle up your—"

"Okay, okay, enough of that. Get up. We have training to do," I said, chuckling despite myself.

Henry was always good at that, finding humor in awful situations and making me smile when all I wanted to do was cry. He reminded me of Nicola, so sure of himself and who he was that he could find joy and meaning in anything.

My heart ached for Nicola, for the danger she might be in due to me. I had begged Bellamy to rescue her, Farai, and Jasper. Pleaded for him to save them before I killed them, because I knew it would be my hands their blood would stain if Mia chose to punish me by harming them. Because life without them would be empty and incomplete.

Everyone had been vehemently against going to them—Henry most of all. He had said it was not worth the risk of his kind, his realm. A fight sparked between him and Bellamy, leading to a verbal sparring that outdid all of my grandest arguments with The Elemental.

OF REALMS AND CHAOS

Bellamy had agreed, I could tell by the way he fought with words of love rather than words of strategy.

"She cannot help us if she is consumed with worry for her friends!"

"If she or any of us go after them, then the trap will spring and we will play right into their hands!"

"So you expect her to do nothing? You expect me to watch as she withers and crumbles in front of us?"

"If it were anyone else, you would not hesitate to do so!"

Henry had been right, of course. I could do nothing for them if I were not alive. He had also laid bare a truth Bellamy had been hesitant to acknowledge: there was nothing the prince would not do for me. We all knew it, but it was during that argument—when his response had been storming away rather than denying the truth—that had made us all distinctly aware of the extent. Aware of just how much he would sacrifice for me.

It was unnerving. Unsettling. Uncalled for.

And I was unworthy.

So instead, I did my best not to think of my friends, to find distractions in mead and plotting and complaining. Apparently, now I would find those distractions in training. Which made sense, as our journey was not a vacation or a time for sightseeing. There was purpose to this choice, one that would alter the outcome of the war that we now understood was inevitable.

A sad and unfortunate truth that left all of us on edge as we concocted a plan that was simultaneously ludicrous and undeniably brilliant.

It was my idea, after all.

"Ash?" Henry's voice pulled me out of my thoughts, his hands gripping either side of my face to bring my gaze to his.

I blinked. Once, twice, three times.

My mind rarely turned off these days. Though, thankfully, Bellamy had taught his Trusted well. It was rare for their mental shields to slip. Henry's in particular was strong, a wall of bright white light that felt as if it burned through my power. So it was only my own thoughts that plagued me.

"Sorry," I said with a sigh. I got up, snatching my dagger off of the bedside table on my way towards the cabin door. I doubted it would work for throwing, but I felt grounded when it was in my hand. It had not glowed since Haven, no matter what I did to it, as if only death could please the runes enough to light up.

Henry did not mention my aloof state again, opting to grab my hand and lead me quickly out of our cabin. Slow, that was what he often called me. This ship had made walking especially difficult, so he was prone to drag me around and ignore my nausea in favor of arriving places quicker.

I could not wait to never step foot on one of these wretched things again.

We stopped once so I could dive for the edge, dry heaving as my body attempted to find anything to expel from my empty stomach. Henry huffed but once again held my hair, mumbling under his breath about how horribly embarrassing I was.

"Ah yes, I am a poor excuse for a sailor. Remind me to find a new dream, as being a pirate is officially off the list." There was very little bite to my tone, but I rolled my eyes and squared my shoulders all the same.

"Dramatic as always."

When we found an open spot on the deck that would allow us to train, Henry opened his faded brown jacket to reveal multiple black straps and sheaths covering his body, cinching the thin white tunic and highlighting the thick muscles of his chest. Daggers, smaller and sharper than my own, sat poised for dealing death. Each of them had blue hilts, the same stunning color of the demon sigil.

He grabbed one, freeing it of its confines and placing the tip against his finger. The sharp metal glinted in the morning light, the beauty lethal and violent and strangely alluring.

"First lesson of the day, little brat. We all must face death eventually, but it is what we do when we stare into its wicked eyes that defines our fate. I do not believe in choiceless lives and moments of chance. You see an obstacle, and you overcome it. You hear the call of your end, and you deny it," Henry said, pointing the dagger at my chest. "You, Asher, will not lose. You will not concede. You *will not die*. Now, repeat that."

I sighed, rolling my eyes. There was something about a demon demanding me to repeat an oath to live that really got on my nerves.

"I will not lose, concede, or die. Can we move on now?" I asked, batting the dagger away. I felt the blade slice through my skin, blood welling on my hand.

It was impossible to deny how good it felt, the bite of pain. More than that, the idea of a beautiful new scar to tell the story of where I had been was enticing, addicting.

My olive skin now bore evidence of the afriktor attack, the demon fight, the battle of Haven, and all of the many sparring sessions that had left me bleeding. This would be a wonderful new addition.

Quickly, I slid my hand across my black trousers, the blood smearing away, as Henry watched me with keen eyes that always saw more than I wanted him to.

"Ash," he said, the soft whisper of his voice making my heart ache. His dagger slowly lowered, the concern he felt evident in the furrow of his brows and the downturn of his lips.

Silence was my friend in situations like these. I could not talk about the way I felt, could not explain the pain when a lifetime of experiences and rules had taught me to hide it.

So I did the only rational thing I could.

I punched him in the face.

My fist connected with his cheek with a resounding crack, his head flinging backwards upon impact. Pain rippled from my knuckles up to my elbow, not nearly as bad as when I first hit Bellamy those many months ago but still enough to leave me gritting my teeth.

"I should have seen that coming," Henry chuckled, touching a finger to the cut on his cheek. He smiled, his white teeth shining and his eyes crinkling at the corners.

With as much speed as I could muster, I grabbed my dagger, slicing towards his unprotected midsection. The Sun barely jumped back in time, my blade singing through the air like a song of death and retribution and fear. So much fear. Fear of the unknown, the known, and every question that sat in between the two.

Henry was on me in a second, beating me down with two of the smaller daggers, overpowering me. I was sloppy and angry, not to mention that the act of sparring was overwhelming.

A part of me thought of how easy it would be to simply not pull back, to throw myself in the line of one of his vicious strikes and allow death to have me. If only to finally know peace.

That part of me was loud, but I fought against it in the same way I fought Henry—with desperate maneuvers and careless aim.

Henry soon ditched his blades, as if he knew just how badly I was losing to myself. Fists raised and body tense, he pressed forward, swinging at me. I pushed out my power, seeking a foothold that would allow me to hear his thoughts. He winced when I attacked, clawing at his shield with the type of despair and ferocity that could bury entire realms.

It was then that he dove for me, one thick arm wrapping around my waist while his other elbow struck my wrist with enough force to send my dagger flying across the deck. My legs collapsed from under me, my back hitting the floor. Henry's hand flew up to my head to protect it from the fall.

85

I laid there, trying to catch my breath and looking into his knowing green eyes, and the fight left me swiftly. In its place, the sorrow I had been working to drown with distractions and vices quickly took root.

Henry's warm hand met my cheek, cradling it with the tenderness I imagined a brother might have for a sister—the love of family. That one touch sent me over the edge, tears spilling from my eyes and my body shaking. I sobbed into Henry's chest as he rolled us over and pulled me into him.

"I know, Ash. I know," he murmured against my head, placing a kiss to my hair.

In the near distance, I heard a male call above the crashing waves, "Land ahead!"

Henry leaned down, whispering into my ear, "Welcome to the Mortal Realm, little brat. Time to get to work."

CHAPTER NINE

BELLAMY

She still had not responded.

Any rational male would assume that she was busy or, perhaps, that she did not want to talk.

I had never pretended I was rational, not in the slightest.

Pacing the length of the war room, I dutifully imagined all of the horrible scenarios that might have led to her silence. An hour—a full hour! Anything could have taken her in that time. Demons, fae, mortals, the sea.

For fucks sake, she could have taken herself.

Despite my consistent attempts not to do so, I thought of that day in Haven again. I remembered the way we had sobbed over Winona's lifeless body, the way I held a screaming Ranbir as Henry and Cyprus

OF REALMS AND CHAOS

lifted his soulmate off the ground—needing to prepare her to return to The Above. Then I recalled my realization that Asher was missing, a feeling of dread that had left me gasping for air.

I had gone into a panic, convinced that the queen—my cursed *mother*—had taken the love of my life. That she had somehow found a way back and discreetly abducted Ash without my knowledge.

Somehow, the truth was far worse.

Without a word, I had left the group, frantically searching for her. Begging whatever high being that was out there that she was alive and still in Haven. It had taken far too long to contemplate searching my manor. So long that by the time I had torn apart the first floor, I could already smell the blood.

From there, it had not been hard to follow the scent—her scent. She was on the floor amidst shattered pieces of the pianoforte. Red soaked the white room, painting it in the type of gore usually only depicted in war scenes.

Her eyes had been closed, arms slashed so deeply that no amount of magic in her veins could save her. She would not heal from it on her own.

My feet had taken me to her so fast that I had slipped in the liquid, hitting the ground hard enough to startle her back into consciousness. Her gray eyes held the type of brokenness that rarely could be mended, the whimper that left her lips a weak version of the piercing cry I knew she wanted to emit.

I crawled to her, tears streaming down my face as I begged for help, screamed for it. I had ripped my shirt off, shredding it to tie around her wounds. It was unsanitary and sloppy, but it was all I could do to staunch the blood flow. It was then that Asher's anger shone through, the fury that I had not noticed in my own attempt to find in her the sorrow I had felt.

"Do not touch me!" she roared with impressive volume, trying to pull her arms from my grasp. I held on, forcing her to allow me to tighten the fabric around her forearms. She too began to sob, the fight in her weakening with every second. **"Please, Bell. Please let me die. Let me do what I can to save you all. Please do not make me live when all I do is bring death. Do not force me to be the reason more die."**

I held her, forever haunted by her pleas for death. Her hair was matted with mud and blood, her once stunning blue gown shredded and stained. The kohl on her lids had smeared down, darkening her under eyes in a way that resembled a long-dead corpse. What a fitting image, to see her shattered that way—a perfect mirror of her clearly broken soul.

I hated myself for it, for contributing to the pain she now felt with startling force. More than that, I hated my parents. I hated the fae king and queen who had raised her in my place, who had abused and used her for so long that she now knew no peace. That she now would rather sacrifice herself than live and suffer at their hands.

Ranbir, Lian, and Henry had found us like that. Asher unmoving, barely breathing. Me rocking us, pleading for her to hold on, to not leave me, to give me a chance to make this world worthy of her.

"Bell?"

The sound of Noe's voice cut me out of my trance, the painful memory gone but never far away. My eyes came back into focus, and apparently, I had stopped pacing at some point, leaving me standing in the middle of the war room, unmoving.

The war council members were all staring at me as if I had gone mad. Quite honestly, I had. That was the problem with finding something you loved. Suddenly, the things that you did out of obligation and duty seemed far less important.

"Sorry, what were you saying?"

Noe shook her head, the disappointment and frustration she so clearly felt pinching her face. Lian seemed far more inclined to pity me, as if the sight of a bloody Asher in my arms as I screamed and cried brought her back to the loss of Yuza.

I would never forget that moment either. The way Lian clung to Yuza's body, the way she stroked the blonde's hair and repeatedly chanted that she was going to be okay. I had sat a few feet from her, waiting, trying not to scare her any more than she already was.

Hours had passed before she finally allowed me to portal the two of them to Eoforhild. By then I had already concocted a plan, and we landed on the beach of what would one day be Haven. What would one day be a graveyard for more than just Yuza.

So it made sense that the sight of Asher and I would bring back harsh memories of the very event that left Lian forever changed. Only three days after I rescued her, she asked me to teach her how to defend herself. How to never allow herself to be a victim again. Which was how a fae from the Air Lands would end up becoming a captain in the demon army and my swordmaster.

Now, as she stared at me with unashamed sympathy, I felt the weight of my own death and how it would affect Asher. How much I would need to fix before I left her. Though I knew in my heart that I would always be with her, that she would never be alone again, I also knew that she would suffer immensely. I needed to be strong enough to leave this world a place worthy of her.

With that in mind, I shook my head, as if clearing it of the thoughts that plagued me. Then I squared my shoulders and walked up to the center table, where a wooden model of Alemthian resided, all three realms that made up our world recreated in stunning clarity.

I was a prince, a general, a force of nature.

A fucking idiot, yes, but also a greatly feared being.

And now I needed to plan a way to win this war. Something I was born to do, something I was conceived to accomplish. Though I would win it for a different side than I had been made to support. Or maybe I would find a way to leave every realm intact, to win it for the innocents that Asher was so desperate to protect.

"Damon, tell me about the attacks," I said, looking from the replica to the silver-haired demon across the way.

Damon was one of my chief strategists and my lieutenant general. Having Henry absent meant I needed my other seven captains and Damon to be present during this discussion, Noe joining as my spymaster as well.

A cold chill blew in through an open window, the early months of spring not enough to prevent the mountainous area of Sophistes from showing us discomfort over hospitality. The northeastern territory of Eoforhild was notorious for having colder weather, but this particular portion of Lady Timea's lands was especially cruel. Still, this was the heart of the demon military, with above and underground facilities situated between the peaks to act as a base. For many, this was where they lived all year, a home of sorts. Even the cold could not sway them to leave Pike.

Over the last eighty years, I had been slowly building our army back to what it once was. As a newly appointed general, I was keen to prove myself, prepared to be as ruthless as needed to show that I deserved the leadership role. I spent decades recruiting, remaking, and restructuring the military so that we would be ready to take down the fae.

However, it was Lian's blood curdling screams and the way she constantly rocked back and forth at night that made me truly ready to fight in another Great War. The previous one had lasted over five hundred years, only stopping when Adbeel had lost his son and daughter—his wife gone not long after.

He knew then that the war was not worth the lives of someone's children, parents, or partners. It was a realization that came far too late, but one that was widely supported among the demons of Eoforhild. Still, I knew that it was Zaib, his late daughter, that made him end the violence. That, and his wife's pleas.

More than that, he allowed refugees of all kinds to find safety in Eoforhild. Faeries and wraiths and banshees, even fae when I asked to create Haven. When I found purpose in a world that seemed to want nothing but my death and sorrow. When I stumbled upon the truth that lay behind the pointed ears and pretty power.

I had told Asher that I went to Betovere because I needed to connect with that portion of myself, which was not a lie, but a piece of me desired to see the parts that so many demons had said were wrong. To understand their hate and finally feel it as well. Little did I know that I would not hate the fae, but instead would loathe and curse my own parents.

Not that I had previously liked them. Adbeel himself had been the one to cut down Asher's family—had taken me and never looked back— and he had told me at an early age that my parents had not once attempted to get me back. Not once even asked.

"They are growing far more vicious. Since the first attack, we have had three villages laid to waste. One in northeast Eros, one in the western mountains of Elpis, and the final attack being in central Kratos yesterday."

Damon's voice was steady, his dark eyes focused and full of rage. He, like everyone at the table, was prepared to fight. I nodded, encouraging him to continue and staring down at the five islands to the east of our realm. The five islands that were home to hundreds of thousands of unsuspecting and innocent creatures.

As I stood there listening to Damon describe the horrific attacks the fae were laying on Eoforhild through the use of a traitor demon, I knew that I was not like the male who had raised me. Because I would not prevent the war to save the realm. No, I would burn the entire thing to the ground to save Asher. And that made me the most dangerous thing anyone would face.

"Clearly, the demon that is working with them is strong. I saw him portal ten ships past The Mist, each full of Golden Guard. They are able to strike anywhere at any time because of him. Which means we have a target," I said, pointing my finger at The Capital. The tiny island was the center of Betovere and the home to the royals. "The demon clung to the fae queen like a male begging the gods to be spared from death. It was obsessive, the way he followed her. I cannot imagine he would be willing to live apart from her."

Along with the leaders of my military force, the five members of the war council were present. Each of them were brutal and dangerous warriors that had fought in the Great War. Their advice had never been utilized before now because I did not need suggestions of invading and conquering. Now, I took them gladly—greedily. I was desperate.

"So we lay waste to The Capital," Marjorie said, her face stoic and calm despite the rage that simmered in her fierce brown eyes. Her scarlet hair was full of intricate braids swaying in the next gust of wind that came through the window, but she did not shiver. Her dark skin did not pebble. No, she drew warmth from that fury.

"Precisely. I have been there more times than I can count. Their defenses are weak, their guards sloppy. The forest at their southern border is rarely patrolled, especially with the lake—"

"Perhaps there are better options," Finnick said, cutting me off mid-sentence. I clenched my teeth, attempting not to argue with the eldest member of the war council—or remind him of whom he bowed to.

The group of us all looked to him at once, but it was me he stared at, his gaze alight with vengeance and violence. Merely looking at him told me I would not like his idea. In fact, it sent waves of nausea through me.

"What, pray tell, would these so-called better options be?"

My voice was full of pent-up rage and fear, the rasp dangerously close to a growl. Finnick, despite his history of success upon the battlefield and the centuries of life he had lived beyond me, flinched. It took an immense amount of self-control not to flash a smug grin his way.

"The fae royals want their ward—their princess. While I would not dare suggest sending her back to become their weapon—"

"As you should not," Lian hissed, Noe shaking with anger beside her. I did not move, did not remove my eyes from his. If I did, I might separate his head from his neck.

"—I would suggest that we rid ourselves of her while simultaneously sending a message." The group went silent, eerily so. We all waited, hanging on to his every word. Waiting for him to dig his own grave. "Imagine the blow it would be to the fae if we returned their princess to them in bloody pieces. If we spit on them by taking their greatest advantage out of the equation? If we—"

Finnick did not have the opportunity to continue. I lunged for him, knocking over a small table that had held refreshments, wine and glass hitting the floor with a crash only moments before the gray-haired demon did.

I was atop him, my hands around his neck as I smashed his head down onto the hard stone below. Once, twice, three times, I shoved him into the ground, his skull cracking upon the final blow. He wailed in agony, the pain likely excruciating.

Not enough. Never enough.

My hand lit up in black flames, the fire somehow both hot and cold. Finnick's screams amplified as I shoved my hand into his chest, ripping free his heart with ease.

Abruptly, the male went silent, his eyes and mouth opened wide in terror. I stood, holding his still beating heart in my hand—blood dripping to the ground to mix with the glass and wine below. With great satisfaction, I leaned down and spit on his corpse. Then I turned to face the still-silent group. Horror filled the eyes of all but Noe, Lian, and Damon. It had been a long time since I had acted so unstable.

I squeezed his heart one final time before slamming it onto the model of Alemthian, blood splattering all of our faces. Noe cursed while Lian scoffed in protest, but the rest of the council flinched and remained silent. I slowly moved my eyes across all of them, making sure they each saw my coming threat for the truth it was.

"I will paint the world in blood before I allow anyone to touch the princess—*my* princess. She will be your queen, at my side for the remainder of my life. And, when the day comes that the late Queen Solei's obsidian crown rests upon her head, you will all bow down to Asher Daniox."

CHAPTER TEN

STASSI

Something could be said for the way these creatures lived and fought and loved. A madness that I would never be able to understand, and a chaos so beautiful that it captivated me.

My magic hummed here. I could feel the way it built up, the strength of it far surpassing anything I had ever experienced before. It was as if this world was full of sin and virtue, ripe with it. Their bellies had consumed so much lust and hatred, so much joy and innocence, that they were bloated with it all, leaking it into the air as they breathed and laughed.

I felt drunk on the sensations of it all; a high I wanted to continue bathing in.

Sadly, I had work to do.

Lying was beneath me, so if I was being honest with myself, I had taken my time looking for them. I knew *he* wouldn't be happy, nor would he feel I was being fair.

Yet how couldn't I explore this place where I found strength like never before? I was so used to being the weakest of us all, never fitting into the mold that had been crafted for me.

Yes. I could get used to this.

The fae were a particularly interesting breed. They claimed that this *power* of theirs came from Eternity, a blessing of sorts. Knowing how the demons came into their magic, I was not quick to dismiss the idea. Their strange abilities couldn't be explained with magic, so why not suggest it was a gift from the one thing no one knew a single fact about?

It was logically illogical. I liked it.

From across the room a crash sounded, screams following not far behind. Ah, yes, perfect timing. The male who had been thrown to the ground was begging now, the other male above him raining punches down and flinging blood everywhere.

So very exciting.

"Please, Edmund, I am sorry! You know I would never try to touch Kay that way. I do not know what came over me!" the one on the ground screeched, his voice broken and muffled as he choked.

He might not know, but *I* did.

I laughed, the sound soft in comparison to the hectic voices filling the tavern. Edmund didn't stop, didn't show mercy. Didn't hesitate to pummel the male below him until he was a mess of flesh and bone and blood.

Dead. Excellent.

Magic engulfed me, almost painful in its intensity. I stood, though the weight of it threatened to bring me to my knees. No one looked my way, the entire room staring on as my magic left Edmund—his face blanching at the sight of his dead friend below him. The friend that I had convinced to act on his colorful thoughts about Kay, Edmund's wife.

Fun, such fun.

Making my way out of the tavern, I wove through groups of fae attempting to find the source of the commotion. The air outside was foul, burning my nose and making me sneeze, but the atmosphere was euphoric. Everywhere around me were sinful and virtuous minds, mingling to make a dangerous cocktail that might leave me too intoxicated to continue my search.

I took a deep breath of the nasty air then pushed on. Demons were here at some point, I could feel it, as if the magic itself was calling my name. There was no knowing if these were the right demons, but anything was a start when finding her was so heinously difficult.

Asher. Such a nice name. Blessing, that was what it meant. Unfortunately for her she seemed to be less of a blessing and more of a curse if the stories around here were true.

In fact, I heard from many that she was closer to a plague than a benediction. I had a feeling that I would love her. Like calls to like, after all.

"Well, hello there, beautiful. Can I help you find what you are looking for?" The male was stout, smaller than most around him.

His hair was so short that it nearly showed his scalp, the color of it a muddy brown to match his eyes. He was a kind soul, one that likely did not belong with those surrounding him. Waters. That was what these fae called themselves, if I remembered correctly. They were far less irritable than the Fires I had visited before, though it was never hard to get them riled up. Not for me, that was.

"Why, yes, you can help me," I said with a smile, flashing my too-white teeth. The male suddenly looked unsettled, as if for a moment he saw behind my mask.

That was, until I flicked back my hair, the pink hue of my locks shining in the afternoon sun. The dress I wore was simple, a thin silk slip that reached mid-calf. The sleeveless garment left little to the imagination, even with my cloak overtop. That was what I wanted, what I craved. Any temptation for those around me, anything to feed my magic.

They made it all too easy, males and females both flocking towards me like pigs to the slaughter. This male, with his pure intentions and kind thoughts, was no exception. His eyes wandered as I put my hands behind my back and squared my shoulders, my breasts pushing forward and my cloak falling back.

"Wh-what can I do for you?" He cleared his throat, shaking his head before he looked back up to my pink eyes. There it was again, that flash of uncertainty. I was quite scary, admittedly.

"Where would one find passage to Eoforhild?" I asked, feeding into his sin, tempting him with the greatness that came with being wicked.

The male stared at me with a confused frown. Had I misspoke? Did I feed too much magic into him?

"I am sorry, miss, but I do not know of a place with that name. Is it in the Mortal Realm?" he inquired, his eyes briefly falling back down and then shooting up once more.

The Mortal Realm? They separated by realms rather than kingdoms now? That was surely a new development. Not that I had been here before, but I knew enough from what the others said.

"I apologize, I must have misheard the name. I'm trying to find a port that has ships sailing for the demon lands."

My biggest mistake yet. In the days I had been here, enjoying myself rather than gleaning any information I could, no one mentioned the demons. I should have understood that meant strain, fear, distrust, *hatred.*

The male reared back, his eyes wide and his mouth open. For a moment in time, I witnessed what it was to truly feel terror, to know dread like one knows a lover—intimately and wholly.

"Listen here, I do not know what sick joke you are playing or what you stand to gain from it, but I suggest you rethink your plans." His voice lost the sweet and considerate tone, taking on a harsh edge that left spit flying from his mouth.

How could I have possibly been so offensive that it warranted that reaction?

"I apologize, I didn't mean to—"

"No, you need to go back to whichever isle you come from and never step foot in the Water Lands again. We do not take well to those who wish to spread fear for the sake of a laugh."

I nearly giggled at his rage, the likes of which was so pathetic that I couldn't even attempt to take him seriously. That was, until he began to pull water from a nearby stream. This outfit was far too delicate, and my hair was far too perfect, to let that water hit me.

With a quick flick of my hand, I pulled the sinful thoughts of every fae in the area to the forefront of their minds. Some were all too easy to influence, their hopes and dreams and tantalizing wants already in line with their evil nature.

Fae came together in dire embraces, some stripping naked before they even found someone to take them. Others let their fists speak instead, fights breaking out and shouts splitting the air. I watched as two attacked another, stealing handfuls of coins.

Arguments ensued, a female nearby taking off what looked to be a ring and throwing it in the face of a male who stared open-mouthed at her. Water flew everywhere, the weaker fae losing ground in their fights and the desperate ones falling to the grass. The sounds of wet skin slapping together was nearly as loud as the screams.

Soon, all of the Water Lands, as that fae called this place, would erupt into a cacophony of vices being explored.

I reveled in it, my gaze trained on the fae who was now once more looking at me with lust—the longing for me evident. I allowed my magic to flow free, my eyes changing, waves of pink setting me aglow. He fell to his knees, the addictive mixture of fear and desire a beautiful thing.

I had always been beautiful. No one could deny that. Nor did they wish to. My face and body were a means to an end, luring in those I might use. This world, though, was different. The way the fae felt was stronger, more evident. It had to be overwhelming to feel so much so often. Tragically so. As strong-willed as I was, I didn't imagine I would fare well living a life such as theirs.

I bent down, bringing myself eye-level with the male in front of me once more. He was entranced, my beauty and magic otherworldly to these creatures.

"Are you a goddess?" he asked, his voice nearly a whine with the exertion it took to speak through the onslaught of need that filled him more fully the closer I got. I continued pressing out on the area, my magic slipping into every fae it could find. The more I pushed, the stronger I became.

"Don't tell me you believe in gods when Eternity sings to this place—blesses it with gifts beyond understanding. In your veins flows something previously unheard of. Don't spite what lies above simply because I'm other."

He nodded. His mouth dropped open to drool as I leaned farther forward, my dress falling from my skin to expose my bare chest.

Too easy. These beings were so delightfully foul.

"Now, tell me how to get to the land of the demons, to their realm," I ordered, placing a single finger under his chin—the pink glow lighting up his pale skin.

He moaned, feeling the magic seep into his body. What felt good to him felt euphoric to me. There was no sweeter sensation than that of sin or virtue, and as it exploded around us, I thought I might combust as well. Every fiber of my being fought to embrace that, to revel in what I had created, but I had a task.

"There is no way there. The Mist—it protects their realm, blocks us from it. No one would seek to go anyways. They are evil." I ran my finger down his neck, letting my nail dig into his skin lightly. He jerked below my touch, his eyes closing and head lulling back. "Please, more."

I did so love when they begged.

"What is The Mist?" I asked, letting my caresses drift lower. His breathing came in heavy pants, his moans louder. I did not have much longer, the poor thing was clearly deprived.

"We do not know. No one does. It is some kind of black magic, filled with creatures that consume the flesh of anyone who dares to pass through."

Inconvenient. That meant there was no inconspicuous way for me to go about finding them. I would need to get creative. I doubted their maps would have information on a realm they so clearly feared.

A part of me grew excited at the knowledge that far more sinister creatures walked this world. My magic pulsed, the madness around me soaring upwards, threatening to burn in their too-bright sun. Time was running out, along with my fun.

I stopped my finger just shy of the bulge within the fae's trousers, causing him to groan. He began begging again, reaching up to touch and grab me. My hand shot out, latching around his throat before his filthy hands could stain my dress.

"Thank you for your help, dear. But it seems you have exceeded your usefulness." With a squeeze of my hand, I snapped the male's neck, the light fading from his eyes and the husk losing its appeal. There was nothing to gain from the dead. They were empty of what satiated my hunger.

I expertly dodged the gore and bodily fluids that flung through the air as I walked on, trying to determine exactly where I would go next. I had searched every isle but one, which meant she was likely with the demons still. He had been right, naturally.

How would I get there when I did not know exactly where there was? What a quandary.

Decisions, decisions.

I imagined that I could search that final isle before exploring my options. Even better, I also needed to inspect the home of the fae rulers. Now that would be fun.

He could not blame me for being thorough. There was no proof she had remained in the lands of the demons. How could I claim to have searched for her if I simply skipped over two islands?

No, that would not do. Continuing on was in the best interest of my mission. At least, that was what my excuse would be.

Quickly, I scrawled out a missive, just a brief update on what I had found—or, well, not found. While I knew I would have to check in soon, I also knew that, as impatient as he was, there was a part of him that wanted me to have the joy this world offered. We felt such things so rarely that it was imperative we took advantage of the opportunities put before us. Still, he would grow angry eventually.

Groaning, I sent off my note, hoping it would satisfy him for a while. Lifting a hand, I twirled it and welcomed my magic home. Some came back while other bits of it dissipated in the air. Just like that, the fae were free of my clutches. Still, they continued on, slowing but not stopping. That was the thing about giving in to your worst impulses—your darkest desires—once you started, it was hard to stop.

Like the fae, I found myself uninterested in ceasing now that I had begun.

CHAPTER ELEVEN

ASHER

This becomes more and more boring each time.

Henry tried and failed to hide his laugh as I spoke into his mind.

The male—*man*—in front of us stared at Henry for a moment. His perplexed expression and seemingly confused thoughts lasted all of three seconds before he returned his stare to me. When vile fantasies started to swarm through his mind, I ground my teeth, attempting to hold myself back.

Truly, it was my fault. I should not have admitted I was bored. Karma had me there.

Still, he was nauseating to listen to. Or, well, bear witness to was more like it. I could only make out the conjured images. Which was what made this so increasingly repetitive.

The male spoke then, his speech foreign to me. He had a smooth voice, the words blending together with such speed that I struggled to fathom how anyone could understand what he was saying. Henry did though.

Every once in a while, the demon would nod, scowl, or hum. Very rarely did he respond in kind, mostly opting for silence unless speaking was required of him. Hiding his accent was not something Henry would be able to accomplish for long, but it was best that no one suspected who—or what—we were.

I had not known before that the mortals did not speak the common tongue—that each of the six kingdoms spoke six separate languages. Henry had explained to me that only those of noble birth were required to speak the language of the gods, though others chose to learn. Incidentally, this was also the language of both the fae and the demons, who had once not only been civil but close allies.

That was an interesting part of fae history that had not been told correctly. In Academy, younglings learned of how we had attempted to teach the demons our ways, to nurture them with good and prevent their evil roots from taking hold. We learned to speak as they did, allowing the language of The Old Ones to fade. We granted them access to our lands, traded with them, even taught them how to manage their magic. Still, they had turned on us, slaughtering any power-wielder they could and eating the raw flesh of their victims. Our past was broken, missing pieces and confusing at best, but we had all known of the wicked creatures to the west that threatened our realm.

Henry had contradicted that. Many demons remembered the time before the splitting of Betovere. They were privy to the knowledge that fae and demons and creatures of all kinds had been united once, thus the reason highborn demons were taught all six languages of the Mortal Realm.

Which begged the question: what happened to the memories of the fae and the mortals?

No one knew, not even Bellamy. With Pino gone, his soul free to return to Eternity, there was likely no way to find out.

"We have our answer then," Henry whispered to me as he offered the man three gold coins. The mortal's eyes lit up in astonishment, then a triumphant smile split his face. With his payment in hand, he left us be.

Henry grabbed my arm, tugging me up from my seat and out of the tavern. He was testy this evening, though so was I. We had been in the Mortal Realm for three days with no luck.

Our first day here, we had felt hopeful. The maps were exquisitely detailed, allowing us the opportunity to portal without the fear of ending up in the sea or someone's home or the center of a volcano. That meant we could go to any of the kingdoms in a moment's notice, find what we were looking for, then continue on with our journey. No longer would we spend weeks on the back of a horse or the deck of a ship.

That was, until we realized how little the people of the Mortal Realm knew. Their rumors and tales gave us no results. We would wander into wooded areas or deserted homes and find nothing, just as empty handed as before.

The first day, we decided it was just poor luck. The second, we began to suspect that we were in for a much more difficult excursion than we originally thought. Today, however, we awoke with an astonishing sense of defeat.

As we made our way into the early fall air, the residual pollen from summer's blooms burning my nose while we walked, I readied for bad news. I was fully prepared for Henry to tell me what I already suspected— there was nothing to find in the Kingdom of Behman.

We stopped not far from the inn, hiding from the afternoon sun under the canopy of a tree. This kingdom was full of trees, even along the coast. They were everywhere, as if forests had taken control of every piece of the land and the inhabitants had decided to simply build around it.

Green grass spread for miles, only interrupted by the dirt roads that were a result of carriages permanently destroying the plant life. Henry had not dressed for the weather, his top so thin that the white was nearly transparent. His brown trousers clung to him and tucked into his black boots that reached mid-calf. His fiery hair nearly passed his chin now, the stubble on his face closer to a beard.

"We have a lead," he said, a reluctant smile spreading across his face as he released my arm. "This is it. I can feel it."

I froze, unsure if I heard him right. For a moment, I simply stared at him, wondering if he was being hopeful simply for the sake of my sanity or because he genuinely believed that this was going to be our first success. When he did not break under my gaze, I decided that this just might be a good day after all.

"Where is it?" I asked, suddenly far more energetic than I had been in a while. Without realizing it, I began to bounce on the balls of my feet, thinking of how much this could change the tide of the coming war.

We did it. We finally did it.

"Here in Behman—just as we suspected. Although, I think we were wrong about what it is based on the description that man gave. Either way, we will know as soon as we portal there. There is a small range of mountains just north of here called the Eldor Peaks. All of the signs are there, but if we want to make it before the sun falls, then we have to go now. I want to portal just outside of the range to make sure we have a safe landing."

I nodded, eagerly grabbing onto his hand and leaning up on my toes.

Henry pulled out the map that had been in his satchel, giving my hand a squeeze before letting it go to open up the folded paper. His eyes roamed over it for a moment before he took a deep breath. His fingers gripped the map harder, wrinkling the edges.

I wanted to reassure him that it would be alright and this was the breakthrough we needed. More than that, I wanted to promise we would survive. As someone who did not quite enjoy being lied to, though, I decided against it.

Instead, I took deep breaths as well, focusing my mind for the task ahead. It was imperative that I steeled my heart and mind. No longer could I wallow and suffer in sadness. It was my duty to save this world. I could feel it in my bones. I had to take my despair and morph it into the flint that would light a fire within my soul.

Being a savior did not mean living a life of joy and love. No, it was a path paved with blood and death and loss. And it was not until this precise moment that I realized just how much more I would sacrifice to make sure Alemthian survived the coming war in one piece. I would maim and burn and kill for that future.

Henry took my hand once more, a hopeful smile lifting his lips one last time before we portaled.

The ground was uncomfortably hard in comparison to the grass we had once stood upon. When Henry called the range small, he had been grossly under exaggerating. The gray stone before us loomed above, two of the mountains reaching up to kiss the clouds like a lost lover. The air here was cooler, an unsettling stillness to it that made goosebumps coat my skin.

The man had been right. We had found what we were searching for.

Henry and I were tasked with securing allies in not only the mortals but also the magical creatures that had sought refuge in the Mortal Realm. Over the course of the last few days, we had been searching for one creature in particular, the dalistori.

"Can you feel it?" I asked Henry, hoping he realized just how successful—and dangerous—a situation we had found ourselves in.

Stories told us that we would face evil like the world had never seen. A beast larger than a cottage with razor sharp teeth and a love for the blood of men. It had consumed hundreds of unsuspecting or unwise mortals that found themselves within its vicinity in recent years. There was no surviving it according to legends. Which was the very reason we were here. Either risk our own deaths now or face the very real possibility that Eoforhild would fall.

"I feel it," he answered, his heavy drawl a whisper in the wind. "The nearby village was evacuated when a group of men tried to scale these mountains. Those who chose to remain, the prideful and disbelieving, were slaughtered. Hundreds reduced to fat and flesh. Food for flies and wild animals."

I blanched at his words, the image bringing back memories of Haven painted in gore to my mind.

My nerves got the best of me when a sharp crack sounded to our left. I jumped, smacking into Henry's side. The Sun careened forward, his arms grabbing onto me and sending us both to the ground. We hit the rocky terrain hard, pained groans replacing comprehensible words momentarily.

"Watch where you are going!" he shouted once he caught his breath, knocking me off of him and onto the ground. I gasped, my outrage palpable.

"You were the one who knocked us over!" My bristling earned me nothing more than a glare as he stood, dusting off his trousers and not so much as offering me a hand up.

"Sorry that gravity exists," he mumbled, straightening up to his full height. With a moan of annoyance, I smacked the ground and proceeded to stand as well.

"Gravity is for the weak. Learn to fly or move over." Before he could think of a retort, a rock fell from somewhere ahead. The sound of stone hitting stone left both of us holding our breath. After a moment, we finally looked at one another. Henry's eyes were wide, as if he were pleading for some sort of reassurance.

Sadly, I had none. Lifting my hands and shrugging my shoulders, I silently conveyed that I, in fact, had no fucking clue.

"Could be a ghost," he whispered, eyes darting away from me to look around.

"Could be Luca," I offered in the spirit of being delusional.

"It is not Luca." His chiding tone had me leveling him with a look of disbelief, because how was what I said any less likely than a ghost? "Maybe it is friendly."

"It mutilated two men last week. It is likely even less friendly than I am, and I have to fight the urge to castrate you daily." A gasp of horror left his lips at my words, and I had to bite back the laugh that threatened to escape me.

"Oh, shut up and go," he ordered, pointing in the direction of the sound.

"You go!"

"No, you go!"

In the end, I was the one who took the first step forward, sending my power out to search for any creature that might be prepared to brutally slaughter us. For the dalistori.

Something was there, though it was more of an afterthought. Like a feeling of hollowness that differed from the empty feeling of the non-sentient world. A blank spot where there should have been something more.

It is here. We need to head east.

Henry did not flinch when I spoke into his mind. He was used to the silent form of communication by now. With a stiff nod and a heavy breath, I began moving, the Sun on my heels.

The deeper we wove between the daunting mountains, the more my skin seemed to crawl. With the sun creeping closer to the horizon, we sped up. We had wasted far too much time at that tavern, relying on my ability despite my clear inadequacy when it came to interpreting the foreign tongue. Now we had to rush, my feet slipping on uneven rocks and Henry's hands shaking with nerves as he took the lead.

"Are you sure you sensed it here?" Henry whispered as he turned to face me. I nodded, trying to conjure the words that would explain the feeling of such a thing. Before I could, another voice came, the haunting sound of it echoing like a melody of death.

"Yes, she did sense me here."

Whipping my head in the direction of the voice, I caught sight of a pair of yellow eyes about five feet above our heads. The dalistori was nothing at all like the legends and rumors had suggested. What was described as a man-eating monster ten times the size of its prey was actually far less sinister in appearance.

"I see that my food has come hunting me for once. What an exciting turn of events. Do tell me why the two of you have traveled so far just to die." Even the gravely and deep voice of the dalistori seemed less foreboding when paired with the form of it. I clenched my teeth together, determined not to voice my thoughts and struggling immensely.

It was just so…*adorable.*

"A cat?" Henry said, baffled. That was all it took for me to lose every one of my senses. I moved forward, desperately wanting to touch the silky gray fur of the feline creature above.

"I am not some domesticated pet!" it screeched, its tail and the fur on its back reaching up, but it did not attack.

It was small, barely larger than an average cat. It had wide, circular eyes the color of the setting sun behind us—a deep yellow that was nearly gold. Pointed ears stuck out of the top of its head, the inside of them the same soft pink as its little button nose.

"You are so cute," I said, stopping at the rock face and looking up. A smile broke across my lips as the tiny fangs of the creature caught the light. I knew that it was supposed to be a horrifying and murderous thing, but nothing other than delight filled me. Raising a hand, I clicked my tongue, trying my best to get the supposed dalistori to come down.

"Stop, creature, or face my wrath!" it shouted, stepping forward.

I did laugh then. Henry remained silent, a look of confusion on his face, though his eyes still held that fear.

"Wrath would be a wonderful name. Do you like that name, sweets? Or do you already have one?" I cooed as I climbed onto a higher rock, bringing our faces level.

The dalistori did not move, though it eyed me like it was going to eat my hand. Or my heart. Oddly enough, that only made it more endearing. As a particularly anger-driven being, I liked the solace a fellow furious little thing could bring me.

"Do not call me sweets, you inferior female. I should rip your tongue from your mouth for daring to speak to me that way!" With a smile, I reached up and slowly brought my hand towards its head.

"What about Violence? Or maybe Chaos?" My fingers reached its fur, the softness of it making my chest warm. Raven, a council member's daughter, had a cat that I had been permitted to cuddle once and I recalled being jealous of her luck. I had never been allowed a pet.

It growled, teeth bared and eyes in slits. I could not fully feel its mind, but I knew there were murderous intentions within it.

"No, I think Wrath is the best of them." Yes, I would call it Wrath.

Unfortunately, the dalistori did not seem to like that name as much as I did. It scowled at me, those eyes unsettling to say the least. Still, I continued to scratch it.

"You pesky little—oh, that is nice." I smiled wider, my fingers grazing the top of its head. "No, not there. Behind my ear. Yes, that is the spot," it said, that voice making the hairs on my arms raise.

From behind, I could hear Henry approaching us. Anxiety and fear radiated from him, his mental shields down and his thoughts a mess.

"You are psychotic. That thing is going to murder you!" he said quietly, tone sharp. I knew that I was likely scaring him, but there was something about the dalistori that called to me. Like it belonged with me.

Wrath ignored Henry entirely, leaning farther into my hand and humming softly.

"We did come here for a reason, actually." It opened its eyes at my words, recoiling faintly. I frowned, already missing the warmth of its fur. "We have heard stories of your kind. None of them pleasant, but all of them confirm to us that your help could be something that saves many lives."

This time, the dalistori backed away fully, hissing. Henry let out a soft gasp behind me as the creature grew larger. The demon rushed to me, putting a hand on my waist and trying to pull me down. I remained on top of the rock, unwilling to run.

The dalistori's silky gray fur had turned thick and coarse, its fangs lengthening until they were the size of my forearm. A smile split the creature's face, the edges of its mouth nearly touching its ears. The expression mixed with the yellow eyes was a horrifying sight, one born of the Underworld.

When it stopped growing, it had far surpassed even Henry's height, towering over us. Still, I knew from legends that it had not reached even half of its full size. The hiss turned to an echoing growl that made my stomach churn and my hands shake, the vibration of it rattling my bones and knocking Henry back, forcing him to unwrap his arm from around me.

Whether it was out of stubbornness or determination, I did not know, but I remained still, not daring to step back. My hands dug into divots within the rocks in front of my chest, holding on and keeping my gaze forward. The dalistori lowered its head, bringing those yellow eyes down to meet mine.

"What makes you believe me to be a creature that cares for life? I will gladly eat thousands of living things and not bat an eye."

Nodding, I pondered that statement. It was not the idea of helping us that bothered it, rather the assumption that it would want to save lives. I could work with that.

"Well, in saving lives, you will also get to slaughter many others. Though, ideally, we can stop the war before too many innocents are lost."

The creature—Wrath—for its part, merely stared. No emotion showed on its face. No feelings radiated from its mind.

"Tell me, have you ever tasted a queen?" I asked, dusting lint that was not there off of my shoulder. Calm. I was calm. No terror could find me. I was The Manipulator—one of the most feared beings in existence. I would not cower.

My words had the desired effect on the creature, causing it to pause and regard me with a squinted gaze. I watched as it wiggled its hazardous claws, the curve of them perfect for gutting. It seemed that the kitty was not quite so sweet. My power swelled inside of me, itching for a fight that I did not want.

"Now *that* is a proposition," it said. I watched as it slowly shrunk back down to the size of a large cat, though small enough to hold. Strange how I seemed to recoil at the idea of hurting such a vicious beast. Perhaps that was part of what made it so dangerous. "Do tell how you expect to find me a queen to feast on."

Henry began shouting into his mind, the prodding at my power a bothersome feeling that I did not have time for. We had one chance at this, only one.

"The fae have their sights set on war, likely hoping they will one day rule over all. I am sure you recall, or at least are aware of, the way they eradicated any and all magical beings that were within their realm during The Great War. Imagine what they would do if they had control over all three realms. How do you think you would fare against a world such as that? I wager we would all be in danger."

Wrath stared, listening but not showing any signs that it was agreeing with what I was saying. My hands began to sweat, the fear trying to take over. I swallowed it down, refusing to submit.

"Now, imagine how great it would feel to eat the heart of the fae queen, the one who would sentence you to death for simply existing. I could give you that. If you help the demons in the coming war, you could have both the king and the queen. Even better, you can keep your freedom without the fear of death chasing you wherever you go."

The speech was flimsy, and I knew it was not particularly enticing to a creature that seemed capable of defending itself without trouble. Hopefully royal blood tasted better than most.

"I am *born* of death, stupid girl."

I waved a hand in dismissal, not remotely understanding what it meant and unwilling to show that.

Wrath stilled, head tilting to the side. I held my breath, thinking of how much help it would be to have this beast on our side when the fae attacked. A part of me wondered how many innocents would perish simply because their king and queen told them they had to fight. That part also could not help but hope that some miracle would come and prevent the war—in the ways I had previously dreamed of doing.

That way of thinking would not do me any good though.

"Do you not fear that I will turn on you? That I will eat you here and now?" it asked. Without hesitation, I shrugged, offering up an indifference that—Eternity willing—made me appear stronger.

"I have suffered at the hands of pretty creatures my entire life. A bit more pain would be nothing new. But hear me when I say this, I will not make it easy, and you will not walk away unscathed." Probably not true, but I imagined that confidence would carry me farther than terror.

Wrath laughed, the sound horrifying. It rang in my ears, a rough and menacing cackle that sent shivers down my spine. It was far too cute for the menacing sounds it made.

Clearly, I had finally overstepped. Should I apologize? Offer more scratches?

"Brave of you. I do not think that I have ever been threatened in such a way, let alone believed it." I let out a breath, the surprise rushing through me. It laughed again, this time a far less scream-inducing sound. "Fine, I shall keep you. Not because I particularly like you, nor do I care about saving lives. But because my own life lacks entertainment, and you seem to be in abundance of it. Especially if the blood of my enemies is involved."

I whooped in exclamation, swiping it up into my arms when it approached and rubbed against me. I had done it. I could not believe it, but I had.

"Sure thing, Wrath, let's go."

I had not felt this level of joy in quite some time. Wrath was right. This was an exciting turn of events. How strange that we had walked into these mountains believing that we would die here, and instead, we were walking away with the sweetest little—

"That thing is not coming with us!" Henry shouted, jogging after me as I began retracing our path. "We need to portal it to Bell and let him figure out what to do with it!"

Like the dalistori, I ignored the demon's pessimism, the smile on my face impossibly large. "We did it, Henry! Let's just be happy and get back to the inn. Then, we will figure out what comes next."

"Absolutely not. It. Is. Not. Coming." Oh he was livid.

"I am not an *it*. I am a *him*. Though I do believe I like the idea of having a name. You, too, may call me Wrath. And I will go where I please, which at the moment is wherever this female is." Wrath curled farther into my body, nuzzling that sweet little head into my neck. It took me a moment to realize that he was smelling me.

His mind still felt odd, as if it were the hole left in an unfinished puzzle—something that should be there but was not. Something that was missing, somehow.

BREA LAMB

I decided there was no harm in trying to use my power on him.

Can you hear me, angry little one?

Wrath ceased his sniffing, his body going rigid. I took that as a yes. He leaned back, those yellow eyes meeting mine with a curious and suspicious light in them.

Strange thing you are, female.

"You can call me Asher," I offered. Wrath took one last look at me, an inquisitive and calculating stare that made me wonder if he also felt that odd connection we seemed to have with one another.

"Ash!" Henry shouted, grabbing onto my shoulder and spinning me around. I shook off his hand, beginning to lose my temper. Wrath was not pleased by it either.

"Do not touch my creature, you gangly fool, or I shall end you with a thousand cuts! I shall feast on your innards and sacrifice your still-pulsing heart to the great God of Death and Creation! I shall—"

"He is so cute," I said, cutting off his monologue and scratching under his chin. Hoping that would be the last interruption, I began walking again.

"He just threatened to murder me!"

I turned, my hand stilling as I glared at Henry. For someone who was supposedly attempting to save his realm, the Sun sure was doing a poor job of winning over those who could help.

"Did I tell you that you could stop scratching me?" Wrath said, slapping my face with his paw—his claws nearly breaking my skin. I huffed and turned my glare to him before complying.

I continued petting him, making impeccable timing on the journey back now that I was not scared senseless. Still, I hoped that Henry would concede soon and portal us to our next stop. We had a long way to go.

Henry was not wrong; we had decided to portal any magical creature that agreed to help us straight to Bellamy. The plan was that he would remain with the military, readying for possible attacks, as well as find a place for any creatures we could convince to aid our cause.

The prince had yet to send word that any attacks beyond the one at Haven had occurred, but I had a sneaking suspicion that he would not tell me if he could help it.

Months ago, I had dreamed of a love that would be all-consuming. Having someone who cherished me beyond anything else had seemed romantic. Now, I feared what Bellamy might risk for me.

Whatever secrets he withheld on our journey to Dunamis had been important enough to involve the king, which meant time had likely been of the essence. Still, he slowed us down, giving me time to heal and, likely, also hoping I would love him like he loved me. That sort of love was dangerous. It would not only overwhelm and devour us but the entire world too. And a part of me believed that Bellamy would gladly watch it all fall if it meant I was safe.

"Is that thing behind us not a demon? Why are we walking when we could simply portal?" Wrath asked, the annoyance in his tone clear.

He leapt from my arms, his body growing in size slightly just before he stretched. I stymied a laugh when he yawned and pawed the ground, the movement so cat-like that for a moment I forgot he was a deadly creature with a taste for blood.

"The only place I am portaling you is to Eoforhild or the Underworld, you psychotic little—"

"Your first mistake, orange one, was believing that I would mind returning home to my god. Furthermore, I believe it is *you* who needs *me*. So stop your pouting and portal us to wherever you two were headed next, then explain this likely horrendously idiotic plan you have concocted."

Now I really did laugh. Henry grunted, his arms crossing as he glared daggers at Wrath—who flashed his razor-sharp teeth in return. Suddenly, I felt as if this adventure of ours would not be quite as awful as I had first thought.

CHAPTER TWELVE

ASHER

Could a fae die from annoyance?

"Will the two of you *please* shut up before I rip off the rest of my ears?" I shouted, cutting off Henry and Wrath as they bickered.

Do not murder them. Do not murder them. Do not murder them.

Henry had put up his strongest mental shields, but I was not above shattering them if need be. Something—anything—to get them to stop.

"Perhaps if we simply got rid of the spare, our journey would be far easier," Wrath said, his voice calm despite the haunting fury within his words.

Henry bristled, his Sun magic lighting up his hands—the color of it blinding in its intensity. A deep growl crawled its way up Wrath's throat, the dalistori challenging the demon.

Absolutely ridiculous, the both of them. Briefly, I wondered how far I could get on my own, but that thought was quickly squashed by the glaring fact that I was in no way capable of doing any of this alone.

"Do not think I will hesitate to cook you, kitty." Henry stood, his fists clenched so tightly they shook with the force. Oh, what I would give for the peace and quiet I had in The Capital. Why I had once loathed such a thing was beyond me.

"Do not think I will hesitate to eat you raw, mortal."

I watched on as Wrath's form grew, a warning to Henry of the danger he was in. Pumpkin's anger was so prominent that veins began to bulge in his head, his freckled face burning scarlet. If they were not so irritating, I might have laughed.

"I am no mortal, you overgrown rat!" Now he was screaming. Why must he scream?

Rolling over on the bed, I brought the quilt over my head and pressed out my power. Everyone was listening, quite literally the entirety of the inn. These walls were far too thin and my temper far too short for this.

"When you stand next to a deathless being such as myself, then you are a mortal in comparison, fool."

That was it.

I took my foot and promptly kicked Wrath, sending him flying into Henry. They collided with a loud smack, the two of them falling to the floor in a tangled heap. With a rage that turned my vision red, I tossed the quilt to the side and flung myself off the bed.

"How *dare* you!" Wrath hissed.

Not in the mood to hear either of their voices, I latched onto their minds. I had quickly learned that Wrath's consciousness was there in that hollow space, even if it did not feel as though it was. Like the afriktor, I could not manipulate him in quite the same way I could a fae or a demon.

Unfortunately for him, I was a quick study. I threw my power into them both, letting it shove its way to what nearly felt like their souls. Bodies seizing, the two looked at me with horror.

"I said, shut up!"

They both stared up at me as I towered over them, a looming presence that promised only pain and death. The things I had to do to be heard were utterly absurd.

"A day. That is how long you have been bickering. A full day of me listening to your pointless fights when we should have been deciding where to go next."

Pressing further, my power hummed, enthusiastic about this new experience. I had never gone so deeply into a creature's mind, burrowed myself into the very core of something in such a way. The darker side of myself, The Manipulator I kept hidden away, urged me to kill them for their insolence and end my suffering. Despite my love for Henry and my quickly growing affection for Wrath, I had to fight back against those urges.

"Now, I would never dare tell you that you are not allowed to disagree. Honestly, you can rip each other apart if you would like, but do it when we have successfully formed alliances with these mortal kingdoms and—ideally—found a horrifying and deadly creature or two."

With that, I released them, listening as they gasped for air. Had I been halting their breathing? If so, it was not intentional. I considered saying that, but their gazes left me and moved to each other, the silent jabs vexing enough to stop me from apologizing.

How had I surrounded myself with imbeciles *again?*

Ignoring the demon and the dalistori the best I could, I reached over and snatched the rolled map off the bed, making my way to the table.

Our room at this inn was far nicer than the others we had chosen. It had a bed large enough for both Wrath and I to sleep in, though the scratchy, dingy yellow quilt and the stained pillows were not the best. The lighting was dull, only a single small window and one nearly spent candle offering sanctuary from the darkness.

Unless you were a Sun, then you would probably juggle balls of light for the fun of annoying a sleeping dalistori.

A sofa that barely held three-quarters of Henry's body sat in the far-right corner, sporting violently red cushions with what looked to be burn marks atop worn wood. Henry had been particularly floored when Wrath claimed the bed alongside me, which meant that he now had to resort to curling up on the sofa. I offered him the bed with the dalistori, but that led to him nearly ripping my head off too.

Opposite of it was the table, wood also worn but more of a yellow hue rather than the cherry color of the sofa. The ground below our feet creaked, chunks missing from the planks. I had tripped twice already, nearly shattering my ankle the second time.

A long, long night and day it had been. Sighing, I contemplated our next move.

Behman was the smallest of the six kingdoms, sitting at the northern tip of the continent. Each kingdom had a capital city at the very center, home of the royal family that sat atop the throne. In Behman, that city was called Jore.

Unrolling the map, I grabbed onto four small rocks, using them to hold down the corners. The mortals had an affinity for detail, that much was clear. Though they lacked the level of wealth and resources that the demons and fae had in abundance, they made up for it in innovation. Every aspect of the map in front of us showed that.

Villages and cities were surrounded by dirt roads, connecting them for better accessibility. Brothels, markets, inns, and all types of businesses littered the map, marked with what I assumed was immaculate precision. If we had the desire, we could very easily get from this small coastal village of Takort to the overly large city of Jore without magic.

Time was limited, though. Sightseeing and gallivanting about was not ideal or even realistic. We needed to convince Queen Shah that we were a worthy investment and a reasonable risk. I would be staking my claim as the rightful ruler of Betovere—preparing to end the tyranny of the Mounbetton's.

Every word we said, every move we made, every promise we gave would need to be tirelessly calculated and flawlessly executed. There was no room for mistakes anymore. Our only hope of minimizing casualties was having enough support to force the fae royals to pause.

Yet how could we convince foreign kingdoms to stand by our side? To possibly fight in a revolution that had nothing to do with them? This would not be a simple conversation. It would be us begging them to potentially send their people to the slaughter.

We were out of our depth, dreadfully unprepared, and only seconds away from the palace gates if we portaled there.

I tried to think of all the training I had gone through, the hours upon hours spent at that table listening to the royal court argue and bicker.

Xavier's voice resonated in my mind, telling me to remember my strengths—to assess what I did and did not know, to listen and learn.

The fae king was brilliant at that. He would ascertain a solution simply by bearing witness to the situation. Not a day had gone by without him etching the makings of a monarch into my mind—my soul. Mia, too, had prepared me for a future of sitting on a throne and ruling an entire realm. They might not have loved me, but they had made sure I would be a great leader.

No matter my failings, I had been raised to be a queen. It was my destiny.

Henry and Wrath had remained silent, taking up my flanks as I stared down at the map, my fists bunched and mind reeling. After another minute passed in silence, Wrath jumped atop the table, his head cocked to the side as he, too, took in the sight of Jore to the north of Takort.

"What do we know about Shah?" I asked, my eyes still trained on the city.

Henry's low timbre sounded from my left, "She is twenty-nine years of age, widowed two years ago when her king consort died of a mortal disease that attacks the lungs, a dedicated philanthropist, and loved dearly by her people. Nothing that I can think of would be valuable when we go to see her."

I nodded, remembering all of that from when we first planned out our route through the Mortal Realm.

"Oh, one interesting fact I learned yesterday: she changed her family crest when she came into power about seven years ago. What used to be a green and yellow snake wrapped around a sword is now a crowned raven in red and purple. I thought that was strange," Henry added nonchalantly.

His words pulled me out of my trance, my head jerking towards him. A young widow, an even younger queen. She had come into power early on, likely married not long after. Following the death of the monarchs before her, she changed her family crest. Those were sacred symbols to the fae, and seemingly the demons as well.

That was the important part. If the mortals cared even half as much as we did about sigils, then what she did was likely unheard of.

What I would have given to alter the fae crest, to get rid of the gold and make something new. Something that represented my strength and resilience, that highlighted the change I would bring to the realm.

"Was the marriage arranged? How old was her king consort when he passed? Has she remarried?"

Henry looked surprised by my line of questioning, as if I was asking the wrong ones. Every part of my mind was racing with thoughts and plans and strategies, each coming together as the information came in.

Wrath stayed silent, his yellow eyes focused on me with an intensity that was impossible to miss. Over the last day, he had studied me that way, like I was a problem to be solved—one that had baffled him from the start. His gray fur was silky, body small, and long tail swishing back and forth. Calm, for now.

"Yes, seventy-one, and no," Henry answered, drawing my attention back to him. "Why?"

A mortal queen who lived a life of rules and expectations, never making choices for herself. She wed who she was told, the man older than she and doubtfully her first choice. Two years after the death of her husband, she still had not remarried. Why would she when being unwed meant freedom?

Not so different from a fae princess who suffered in the same way.

"What is the significance of the raven?" I prodded, earning an eye roll from the Sun. One thing about Henry was that he maintained a short leash on his emotions. If he was happy, sad, angry, annoyed, he showed it.

A horrible courtier he would make.

When I refused to fall victim to his displeasure, he huffed out a breath and answered.

"Well, to the demons it means intelligence and insight. We view it as a symbol for wisdom."

I nodded, feeling the resolve form within me.

"The fae think similarly. We believe the creature represents prophecy and transformation—the belief in oneself and the ability to morph into something better. What a leap, to a raven from a snake. A cunning and chaotic thing, ever changing and shedding to fit a new mold.

Even the colors are vastly different. Green and yellow to red and purple, a sign of power, femininity, and royalty," I mused.

The kingdom of Behman was not only the smallest but also the poorest. Their ports were closest to Eoforhild, the waters far enough from The Mist that there was no true danger. Still, the red hue on the horizon was enough to make them nearly deserted, few ships willing to dock there.

Henry and I had portaled to Betovere, the two of us disguised so we could board a ship headed to Maliha, the kingdom that Sterling's family ruled over. I had briefly seen Isle Healer, but in my grief and drunkenness, I had not cared to take in the sights around me. The moment we landed in Maliha, we portaled to Behman and got to work. Even in that small glimpse of Isle Healer and Maliha, it was clear how Behman struggled.

The residents were thin, their eyes sunken in, clothes stained and ripped. Every aspect of life within this kingdom seemed dull and painful, the only thing bringing some semblance of joy and health being the obscene amount of trees and greenery.

Why would a new queen—one who had watched her kingdom fall victim to poverty through no fault of her own—want to keep a sigil crafted and worshiped by ancestors who let her throne crumble? Why would a woman who spent her life being told who to marry and what to say and how to dress want to serve under the cunning snake and violent sword?

"Ash, can you please tell me what is going on in that terrifying head of yours?" Henry asked, his voice a sharp plea.

Wrath, who had questioned me extensively after we portaled to the inn yesterday, seemed to catch on before Henry did. The dalistori knew quite a bit about why we were fighting against the fae. Though I left out much of my personal suffering, I imagined he had come to his own conclusions about my life and relationship with Mia and Xavier.

"You think she will rally to your cause because she, too, has lived a choiceless life." Wrath's voice hung in the air, that haunting tone taking on a sense of finality as it echoed through the silence. I wondered if he, like the afriktor, knew more than a normal creature. If he had a sense of what was to come.

Henry knew then where my thoughts had gone, the plan I was concocting. Whether or not he understood after two centuries of being loved by a mother and father who adored him—albeit in strange and rather violent ways—I did not know, but the look on his face seemed to say that he would follow my lead on this. That he trusted me.

"Shah gaining the crown was a unique opportunity. She had the chance to start fresh and mold the kingdom into something new, something she viewed as better. Yet she was still wed to a man she likely had no interest in but who probably had quite a bit of interest in her and that crown. It is hard to make big changes when your consort is an old man with little desire to alter a system that stands to benefit him. Those who gain from an oppressive system care not for those who will suffer beneath it. Yet Shah seems to want change. Her people love her and talk highly of her. How many of them mentioned her when we spoke to them? At least two from what you have told me."

Nodding, Henry brought a finger to his chin, seeming to contemplate what I said. I waited patiently for him to chime in, to confirm what I knew in my heart was true.

"Yes, they do. She hosts balls to raise coin for the needy and drastically reduced her consumption to donate as well. The first woman we spoke to said that Shah had opened up a sort of shelter for women in need, specifically those who have been victims of a man. She is a spearhead for programs that feed the hungry and clothe the poor."

"She is a dreamer," I whispered, thinking back to that night months ago when Bellamy had first come to me during one of my nightmares. Recalling his words and my pessimistic beliefs.

Even now—with the loss of Winona, Pino, and the residents of Haven—I thought of the world as a place too dark to hope for light, myself too wicked for dreaming, but maybe enough people with influence and control could make something better.

Maybe I had been wrong.

Looking up, I ran over to my satchel, digging through it until I found the pencil with Bellamy's note still wrapped safely around it. He would sense me touching it, prepared to whisk it back to him the second I let it go.

I am eating with Noe, Luca, Cyprus, and Lian. They are arguing about strategy and dessert, and all I can think is that your sarcastic jibes would make this far more entertaining.

I miss you.

The words upon the page made my heart ache. I missed him too, more than I ever thought I would. But his constant questioning and refusal to simply let me be had been tiring, and this distance helped. Though he still pestered me with endless questions, I had a reprieve from the fear in his eyes. The terror I had placed in him with my own stupidity.

After we had discussed Wrath, he had tried to pry by asking how I felt, if I needed anything, what I had eaten, and so on. Each inquiry was more desperate than the last, the paper torn from how hard he had pressed and how quickly he had written.

What I needed was not to be coddled but to be given the opportunity to make amends for my gross failures. For the lives lost because of me. Sometimes I wondered if Bellamy understood just how poisonous I was. To him, to his family, to his realm. I had apologized over and over again, but he simply repeated the same thing each time.

"It is not me you need to apologize to, Asher. I am not mad at you. None of us are. The one who deserves the apology that is constantly on the tip of your tongue, is *you.*"

It had taken me a while to understand what he meant by that. But now, as I began writing the note to him and preparing to meet with a woman who just might have the same self-hatred in her soul as I did, I think I finally understood.

Who loathed me more than I did? Who had been more spiteful, more cruel to me than I had to myself?

Not Mia or Xavier or Sterling. Not anyone.

And perhaps that is what happens when you are born in a castle of flame and earth, bound by the heat of fury and the suffocation of inadequacy. Love becomes a violent storm of self-sacrifice. You ponder what you could have done better, why you had not been good enough, where you would be without those that hurt you, and how you might fix what you had broken. And in the end, those that harmed you are not the true evil. You are.

Which was why, despite what he thought, Bellamy and the others did deserve an apology. One that could not be given through words, but rather actions.

If I wanted to show Shah why we deserved her support, then I would have to allow her to view the shattered pieces of my heart and soul, to give her access to parts of me that even I did not fully know or understand.

Could I do such a thing? Give a stranger the means to tear me apart? It would not take much, especially in the eyes of Betovere whose subjects already feared me. Thinking me weak would do me no favors.

Before I could doubt myself, I scribbled on the note and hastily wrapped it back around the pencil. I tossed it into the air, watching as it disappeared in a puff of black shadows.

Well, I have been watching a cat and a pumpkin fight. Needless to say, I miss you too.

Now that I have properly buttered you up, I need a favor.

"What are you planning?" Wrath asked, his yellow eyes bright in the light of Henry's Sun magic. I looked at him, that same feeling of familiarity within me.

Henry made his way to us, plopping down on the bed beside me, his foot swinging towards Wrath and shoving him back. The dalistori growled, a low sound that shook the walls, then moved to my other side.

My body hit the bed between the two, the exhaustion weighing me down. I knew I needed to tell them where my head was at, but I felt that if I spoke aloud, it would all crumble. That the plans I desperately hoped would work, would then fall apart in the same way everything in my life always had.

And what I feared above all else was failure. If I did not succeed with this first queen, I might not have it in me to continue on. I felt like a tower of cards, only one small gust of wind away from crashing down. Fighting the urge to give up, to watch the world burn and let myself finally burn with it, was the hardest thing I had ever done.

As always, Bellamy stopped the panic from gaining a foothold within me. The pencil puffed back into existence, somehow smacking Henry in the face. Wrath snickered as he cuddled further into my side, his head resting on my stomach.

Henry did not bother to pick up the pencil, opting to lift it off of his face with a tendril of light and send it my way with a soft toss. I caught it, rolling my eyes.

Lazy demon.

Do not pretend that I am not going to give you anything you ask for. I am nothing if not consistent in my utter obsession with you, wicked creature.

My eyes crinkled as an involuntary smile overtook my face. I tried to fight it, wishing I could pretend like he did not have my whole heart in the palm of his hand. It would be less terrifying, make me less weak, prevent all of the many things Mia warned me against.

No. Following the orders and will of a female who brutally abused and used me my entire life was far more dangerous than allowing myself the small pocket of love and peace Bellamy brought.

Do you remember the red dress? The one you bought me from Pino's stall in

My hand stilled, the thought cut off by the now-painful memory.

Quickly, I scratched out the last four words, a tear splashing the paper. When I finished, I rolled the paper around the pencil, securing it with the leather band before tossing it in the air and watching it disappear.

The Tomorrow's laugh echoed through my head, the utter joy he had felt upon hearing me compliment his brilliance now a scalding picture in my mind.

Then, the thought of his prophecy crossed my mind for the first time in what felt like years. What had he said, again? He called my magic a force—I remembered that. And he had mentioned something about salvation, about worlds colliding and love defeating vengeance.

More than any of his other words, I recalled the horrifying way he had told me that my reign would be the end. That fire would light the realms ablaze.

This time, when the pencil reappeared, I caught it, ready for the way his words would ground me, secure me, protect me.

Henry and Wrath both watched with keen eyes as I unrolled the paper and read what Bellamy wrote. As always, he found a way to drag up the corners of my mouth, forcing me to smile through the pain.

I would sooner forget my own name than the way you looked in that dress. Be ready to catch.

CHAPTER THIRTEEN

BELLAMY

Sweat stung my eyes as I swung, my sword slicing through the neck of a particularly talented Air. She was brilliant, which meant she was absolutely lethal.

Every gust of wind or vortex of air had sent our soldiers flying, some of them being ripped to shreds in the process. Even worse, she was capable of slicing through bone, the speed of the air making it as sharp as a blade. When she reached for her throat, desperately trying to staunch the blood, all I could think was one thing: what a waste.

Diving, I barely dodged a chunk of rock. The move cost me precious seconds, forcing me to remain on the ground and roll away from a bubble of water that threatened to trap me. Stopping as my back hit the ground, I caught the water, fighting against the Element who still held control of it. In the end, I won, shoving it back at the crowd of gold-clad soldiers and freezing it when it hit their bodies.

So painfully wasteful. This battle—this war—brought nothing but death and destruction, and for what? I would not pretend like the power in my bones and the magic in my veins did not hum at the scent of death around me. My mind and heart knew better though. The potential and life being lost were not worth it.

With that thought at the forefront of my mind, I decided it was time to end the battle before any more of my demons fell. I stretched my hands out, black fire shooting in both directions and effectively cutting off the bulk of the charging enemy. For now.

"Fall back!" I shouted, the order echoing across the open valley, calling onto every element and taking out the gold-clad soldiers who remained on our side of the fire.

Damon did not need to be told twice, his sky-blue armor a beacon as he lifted his sword to the air. His shadows shot skyward. They swirled, mixing with the soft white clouds to form three rings—the edges just barely intertwined. With the sigil above us, the demons began their steady push back towards the rolling hills of green grass and vibrant pink trees. Damon remained by my side for a moment longer, spearing his shadows through the final two fae, before I gave him a slight nod. I watched as he ran towards our army, the soldiers reflecting the light in their silver armor while he seemed to blend with the sky in his blue.

As the fae began to spray water at and attempt to manipulate the fire blocking them, I took slow and measured breaths. So long, it had been so long since I allowed myself this freedom to release the so-called blessings within me. Among other things, it was a fine line to walk. Losing myself now to the high of retribution and death would not make me any more fit to guide us through this war, despite what the war council thought.

First to break through was a Water, his golden armor melting in some areas. He charged me, the scream that left his mouth a throaty and broken sound. Like many of the others, he was desperate. For vengeance, for safety, for a life outside of such gore. They were not evil creatures that fought their way to me. No, they were as innocent as the ones that ran for their lives behind me.

The next to break through was another Fire, her anger palpable even through the golden helmet that covered her face. Dropping the wall of flames, I took one final moment to beg Eternity, the gods, anything that would listen to help us stop this war.

Silence met me like an old friend, the constant reminder that there was nothing and no one that would save us from this mess.

My black armor lit up, the charcoal flames licking at the air around me and tasting the sweet tang of fear. I leaned my head back, taking in a decisive breath of fresh air. When my head snapped forward, I welcomed the rage that burned inside of me. This would end now, with no help from any higher power.

As the fae closed in on me, I was the god.

With a guttural roar, I thrust my hands into the air, immediately bringing them down and smashing them into the grass below my feet.

A great shudder racked through the valley as the Water approached me. He stopped, eyes wide through the opening in his helmet. They were a watery brown, similar to the mud to which he would soon return.

"You might want to run," I said, unable to stop the smirk that lifted my cheek. There was no denying how good it felt as the magic and power simultaneously left my body.

The grass split then, sucking in screaming fae as they unknowingly ran to their deaths—to me. Geysers of molten rock flew up into the air, raining the mighty wrath of the Underworld down upon the golden soldiers. With as much control as I could manage, I willed it to continue forward, a river of destruction rushing at the fae as they ran for their lives.

Conjuring a sword of black flames, I quickly jumped to my feet and severed the head of the Water, ending him before the lava could.

Then I was running too, my flames finding their mark in the holes between the golden plates protecting the fae.

When they realized I was coming, the Shifters took on new forms, their bodies reshaping themselves into far more dangerous creatures. With a twist of my finger, I built up a cyclone of air around me, reminding the world that I was the eye of the storm. I sent it careening towards a larger group, watching as it tore them to bloody pieces that scattered across the open valley.

Screams rang through the air, a melody of pain that left me dancing across the grass, every parry or thrust in time with the beat.

I was no hero. I had always known that. Perhaps it was better because, while a hero might spare them—might attempt to save those that were innocent, I would kill them all to secure Asher's safety. Her future.

A final roar of fury left my lips as I threw my hands forward, fire catching at the tips of my fingers and scorching every inch of the land before me. The screams came to a crescendo, the armor doing nothing to stop the flames from burning them all alive—especially with the lava still at their backs. I hummed in time to the piercing wails, relishing in the way it felt to end those responsible for the deaths of my soldiers and civilians, despite knowing it was wrong.

Even the Waters and Fires were not fast enough, their power failing them in their final moments. What a sad thing, to discover that what makes you special, what you had been told your entire life made you better than any other being in existence, did nothing to save you in the end.

Slowly, I lowered my hands, my breath heavy and heart pounding. I had expended more than I should, and I felt that hollowness inside of my chest. Oh yes, I would pay for this later.

It was at that moment that a sharp pain pinched my side. I looked down, finding a dagger shoved through a small gap in my sparkling black armor.

Good aim.

Then everything went black.

***

Before Asher, I had always imagined myself dying alone on a battlefield. Sometimes, I had even wondered if it would come down to her and I facing off.

I had heard of her, the princess of the fae who could control minds. Adbeel and I had spent many years contemplating what exactly she was and how she had come to be.

Knowing what we did about her parents at the time, we had come to the conclusion that she was likely infused in a similar way I had been. A memory sparked at the thought.

"There is something sinister in that female's veins," Adbeel said, his brow furrowed as he read the latest report.

Princess Asher Daniox, The Manipulator, had killed four fae the week prior—two sets of couples who had decided to fraternize outside of their faction. What a selfish and wicked law, to restrict who one could find love in.

"We need to kill her, Adbeel. We cannot allow her to continue on. If we do, they will sic her on us one day, and when that time comes, the demons will not survive her."

Just as my parents before me, I was without sympathy. I had begged and begged Adbeel to let me simply kill her, to end the fae's poison before she became our own. She had been vulnerable, cooped up in that comfy palace. Yet he had refused time and time again. Zaib never would have wanted the demons to attack, he would argue, insisting that his late daughter's desire for peace was anything but horrifyingly stupid.

Which it was. Zaib's ridiculous wish to maintain the peace was what led to the death of her and her brother, Malcolm. Adbeel had fallen into a fit of rage at their demise, preparing his armies to sail and portal into Betovere. Readying for war.

It was in that time, with the loss of her son and daughter so fresh and that of her beloved subjects eminent, that Queen Solei broke. Adbeel had only told me the story once, the horrific details spared. But it was not hard to understand what led to her sudden death.

The last thing she had ever asked Adbeel was to end the violence, to stop the fighting—for Zaib.

And stop he did.

As he had held her limp body in his arms, his fit of grief and fury sending raw magic shooting into the air, Adbeel did the impossible. Some scholars believed her Moon magic and his Sun magic merged somehow, bursting free of them and surrounding the realm like a wall.

The Mist.

It was an extraordinary and unfathomable form of magic, one that nobody was capable of understanding, let alone replicating. More than that, it was a promise to his late wife, an apology to his dead son and daughter, and a gift to his living subjects.

No more war. No more loss. No more suffering.

Then he found me, wrath incarnate, a plague to a king who had lost so much. I was everything he had once been and everything he had fought to no longer be.

Which was why he had forbidden me from taking our armies to Betovere, convinced that nothing good would come from attacking. He feared the loss that came from action in the same way I feared the loss that came from inaction. We were at a stalemate, neither willing to budge.

The attack on Claud, a village that resided on a small hill above a sprawling valley, was my tipping point. No longer would I allow us to remain complacent, waiting for their attacks and simply fighting back. Defensive approaches were not working, not anymore.

I tore through Judson's estate, glaring at each of the guards that attempted to stop me, a storm raining pure rage down upon the unsuspecting residents of Yentain. They all wore the signature silver of Eoforhild but with violet stitching rather than blue, signaling that they hailed from Andreia. The whole gods forsaken manor was the same violet color, to the point that it bordered on the gaudiness of the fae royals' love for gold.

When I finally reached the meeting room, still clad in my bloody armor from that morning, I found Engle guarding the stupid purple doors. I attempted to sidestep him, not in the mood for whatever he had to say this time. Of course, he stepped with me, a smirk on his face.

I was not in the mood. After Noe had come back for me and brought me to Ranbir to be healed from the stab wound to my side, I could do nothing but simmer in my rage like a pot ready to boil over.

Breathe in. Breathe out.

"You look quite worn out today, Bellamy," he said, his laugh loud as he once again blocked my way.

Breathe in. Breathe out.

"What? No comment or retort? Is poor Belly angry that his little pet is not with him?" Ah, Revanche must have told him about Asher.

I let loose a sigh of annoyance when he backed into the doors, pressing himself to the wood and concealing the silver handles. I was not in the right frame of mind for this verbal sparring. Nor was I ever in a good enough place mentally to be near Engle for more than a few moments at a time.

Henry, Engle, and I had all grown up together. Henry as the Lady of Kratos' son, Engle as the Lord of Andreia's son, and myself as the crown prince of Eoforhild were all pushed into friendship from youth. I was the youngest, Henry a few decades older than me and Engle about a century older than him. From the moment I had mastered my power, around nineteen years after my birth, we had been trained and taught together.

For a while, it was fine. Things had been smooth, and we really did all get along well enough. There were many good memories from those early years. So many that I had struggled with the idea of not being his friend when I realized he no longer even liked me. Not only was I a rather angry and hateful thing, but by the time I reached half a century, I had grown in power immensely. I was a force of nature, someone most feared but many still revered. At the center of attention in every circumstance, was me.

Engle did not like that.

"Move," I said between clenched teeth, trying to remain calm while my magic and power fought to escape me.

Killing him would be so easy, like smearing an insect across the ground or wiping a spill from a table. He was a pest—a poisonous one. Like his father and sister, Engle was power-hungry and manipulative, which was a danger to any monarch.

I wanted to smash his face into a rock.

"Oh, the big bad Bellamy told me to move. I am shaking in my boots. Please, My Prince, do not harm me." His tone was mocking, both hands reaching up to rest on his cheeks in false fear.

For a moment, I wondered what life would have been like if Engle had not been so competitive. Would he be one of my captains too? Would he be at my side instead of in my way, prepared to yell at our superiors—our fathers? Perhaps I could still appeal to that side of him.

"Engle, this is ridiculous. We have the same desire—to keep the demons safe from the enemy. I need to get into that room so that I can protect Eoforhild. Please, let me pass," I said, my tone soft and friendly.

Long gone was the violent and uncontrolled Bellamy. I was different now. Not only for myself and my realm but for Asher. She deserved better than a maniac with a taste for blood. Today was a misstep, but a reasonable one. We needed to fight back, and I had. Even so, I could be civil with this demon, my once comrade.

"You know what? You are right. We should all be putting feuds and discomfort aside to rid ourselves of the enemy," Engle said, a small smile lifting his cheeks.

I nodded with a smile of my own, eager to simply move on from the petty rivalry. When I breathed a sigh of relief and attempted to step forward, Engle moved with me, that smile morphing into a wicked thing. He reached out, grabbing onto my arm and digging his fingers into my flesh. I froze, forcing myself not to move. If I did, all I would do was kill the fucker.

Engle leaned in, his lips nearly grazing my pointed ears, the very things that marked me as so clearly other.

"*You* are the enemy, fae filth. Do not for a moment believe that we accept you—that we *want* you—as our prince. Do not for a moment believe that we will not revolt the instant Adbeel puts his obsidian crown upon your wretched head. One day, you will get what is coming to you. When that day comes, know that it will be me who rips your heart from your chest."

Breathe in. Breathe out.

It meant nothing. He meant nothing. They had accepted me. Most of them, that was. I was enough. I had to be enough.

"And Revanche told me about that fae princess of yours. She sounded quite ravishing. Fear not, I will take good care of her when you return to the gods, *My Prince*."

What happened next was a blur. One second Engle was beside me, his foul breath in my ear and fingers wrapped around my arm. Then the next, the Moon was on the ground, my fists pounding into his face over and over *and over* again.

The thuds of my knuckles connecting to his skull and then his skull smashing into the marble below rang through the violet hall—the beat of war.

"Come for me. Just try it. I will burn every last one of you to dust," I said between punches, Engle's blood staining the velvet purple tunic he wore. It splashed up, hitting my cheeks and my obsidian armor and mixing with the filthy fae blood he so despised.

I paused, wanting to make sure that he heard every word I said. Wanting to relish in the way they tasted coming from my lips. Engle did not open his eyes, both of them bloody and swollen, but I knew that he was listening. I ran my finger across one of his ears, slowly tracing the curve of it, then I leaned in, letting my breath hit his skin in the same way his had hit mine.

"Know this. If you touch a single hair on Asher's head, I will peel off your nails and feed them to you. After, I will cut your limbs off one by one with a rusted and dull knife. When you are begging for death and the loss of blood is slowly driving you mad, I will have my *filthy fae* Healer seal your wounds and nail you to your hideous violet door. Then, just to remind you which of us is stronger—which of us *matters more*—I will place that obsidian crown atop my head and carve her name into your fucking chest."

Just as I finished my threat, the doors behind us swung open. I turned, glaring up at King Adbeel and Lord Judson and taking in their faces full of stunned horror. With all the grace of a crowned prince, I stood, dusting off the bloody shoulders of my armor.

"Remember who you are, Engle, for there are many who would kill to remind you." At that, I pivoted and marched into the meeting room.

So much for no longer being violent and uncontrolled.

Behind me, I heard Judson's voice raise to a shout, his dramatics exhausting.

"Are you going to let that psychopath get away with this, Adbeel? He is out of control, a danger to the realm! Look at my son's face!"

With very little care for Judson or Engle's feelings, I dropped myself into one of the violet seats, the relief of the heavily cushioned chair pulling a groan from my lips. At least Judson's tackiness did not prevent comfort.

"The male is fine. He should not start what he cannot finish," Adbeel said with a sigh. I laughed, loud and unencumbered, knowing it would help little. "Now, take him to see a medic."

I heard the loud huff of anger that came from Judson then the sound of Adbeel reentering the meeting room. Looking over my shoulder, I watched Adbeel begin to close the door, stopping just before it clicked shut.

He leaned out, his voice quiet and lethal, the younger version of the demon king coming out to play. "You too ought to remember your place, Lord Judson. That tongue better recall how to say My King or, perhaps, it should be removed."

This time, I stifled my laugh as Adbeel slammed the door shut, rattling the paintings on the walls.

"He started it," I said, smiling up at the male who raised me.

Adbeel Ayad was not a young male, but he was a formidable one. He stood tall, the two of us about eye-to-eye when next to one another. Where my skin was pale as ivory, his was a deep brown, kissed by the sun and wrinkling softly at his dark eyes and full mouth. His beard was neatly trimmed, sculpted to end an inch or so below his chin. Thick mahogany curls graced the top of his head, just short enough to not touch his shoulders. Built like any warrior and as graceful as any monarch, Adbeel was everything a realm could wish for in a ruler.

Those nearly black eyes were the same color as every member of the Ayad line, the portraits of his late family showing that the color had indeed passed on to the younglings he had hoped would rule. Life had not been kind to this king though, and instead a blue-eyed fae would take over his realm.

It was with that thought at the forefront of my mind that I noticed just how tired Adbeel looked. Which meant little grace for his "psychotic" ward. Bracing myself for the scolding of a lifetime, I straightened my back and squared my shoulders.

"Must we do this again, Bell? For so long, you have found outlets for that fire inside of you, and now after decades of peace, you decide to return to your horrid ways?" he said.

Oh, how I loathed that tone—one of a disappointed father speaking to a son, to a youngling. Despite never once calling me son, he had always treated me like one. Praise and punishment, teaching and guiding, it had all fallen onto Adbeel. Unfortunately for him, I was not a fan of being parented.

"You heard what he said. Whispers do not hide words from demon ears. Was I supposed to simply allow him to say those things about me? About her?" I asked, just as tired as he was.

Adbeel took in my disheveled appearance. I pictured the crusted blood, bruised cheek, and dented armor that he was seeing now. In comparison to his black form-fitting top and light blue vest, I must have looked a mess.

I hoped the velvet below me stained.

The king pulled out the chair beside me, sitting down with stiff limbs. An argument was brewing, and we both knew it. The only question left was who would break first.

After minutes passed in silence, Adbeel decided he would.

"Why her, Bellamy? There are so many females in Eoforhild, Revanche aside. We already deal with the demons dismissing your title, taking a fae bride will not help you any. She does not belong here, and protecting her will bring war to our doorstep." He reached out, grabbing onto one of my hands and squeezing softly. The words made me tense, but the gesture calmed me, a painful contrast.

"If Solei had been fae, would you let the world tell you that she was unworthy of your hand?" I asked, doing my best to appeal to his emotions rather than allow my own to take over.

He ripped his hand away, standing up so quickly that the table shook. As he began to pace, I thought over what I could say that would convince him to allow us to bring the fight to Betovere when he was so intent on the opposite.

"You know I would have fought tooth and nail to keep her at my side, no matter what blood ran through her veins. Still, you are facing a predicament that is the fault of yourself. I told you that we were to leave her be, yet you went and stole her from our oldest enemies. Then, you bed her and expect the demons of your realm to bow down at her feet? This future you see, one which revolves around a female with something so clearly wicked in her veins, is not realistic. We must think like rulers, not like horny soldiers!"

With each sentence, his voice grew louder, reaching a shout so brash that I could hear the pattering of feet as servants and residents ran from the sound of their angry king. Tragic, the fear that he held over the demons but did not use. Such power with so little desire to utilize it. Monarchs should not rule over their realm without justice and kindness, but too much of such a sweet thing would rot the teeth.

"This visit is not about Asher or her right to be here. I came to talk about Betovere. They attempted to lay siege on Claud. We lost thirty-four civilians and twelve soldiers, as well as the village itself. Ninety-one demons remain wounded, most receiving treatment in the surrounding cities and villages. You have to see that we cannot remain on the defense, Adbeel. It is killing us to do so."

Adbeel stopped, his shoulders tensing at my words. That was only one attack. The others had left even more wounded, even more dead. So many lost forever because we were not willing to take control of the inevitable war.

"You act as if I am not doing everything I can to protect the realm!" Adbeel's shouts were punctuated with the raise of his hands, cutting through the air as if to silence any doubts within his own mind. "I have set up wards. I have widened The Mist. I am here in Andreia to make sure the Lords and Ladies are prepared for anything that might come their way. Everything that can be done—that should be done—is occurring as we speak. I am handling it in the only way that I can."

"No, you are not! We sit back and allow innocents to die for our crimes, Adbeel! An entire village of fae that I promised sanctuary and a good life are gone. Mia rained the Underworld down upon them. My fae, my friends, my *family*. They bleed and suffer because we are not showing the Mounbetton's that the demons should be feared rather than spit on." My jaw strained and my head pounded as I spoke—the words barelling into my mind as if they hoped to end me with brute force. "Let me take my army to The Capital. Let me lay waste to the gold palace that saw the death of your son and daughter. Let me do this, not only for the realm or for you but for me. I deserve vengeance. I deserve their blood!"

"You *deserve* nothing, foolish male! Those fae who you will slaughter in order to get to the parents who abandoned you are just as innocent as the demons who cower in your presence! This war will not win you the crown you are so desperate to earn nor will it heal your broken soul. Accept that sometimes violence is not the answer. Understand that attacking now means only more death. We will strengthen our defenses, deploy our units across the realm, and remain vigilant. Send Noe to Betovere. Have her find and eliminate the traitor. That I will allow. That we can do. What we will not do is portal into a hostile area and send our subjects to the slaughter so that you can get what you think you are owed!"

Anger vibrated through me, my body shaking so viciously that my teeth chattered and my stomach churned. He would never understand what it meant to be unloved, but what I could not accept was that he did not clearly see how much loss we would suffer if we chose his route. The plan he laid out would buy us time, but only so much. Death would still wash over Eoforhild, and I refused to sit by and let it.

I smacked the table, the purple wood burning beneath my touch. With a finger in his face and fury in my eyes, I looked at the demon king, knowing that my next words would be my last to him for the foreseeable future.

"You will regret this when your lakes run red and your sky rains embers."

Then, I portaled away, the force of time and space threatening to rip apart my body in the same way Adbeel had shredded my heart.

I appeared in an all-too-familiar room, the walls black and floors red. A bed in the center that was big enough to fit my entire family—the one I had found and formed on my own. On the desk to my right were vials and plants and papers full of healing remedies. To my left sat a vanity, cosmetics, and jewelry neatly organized on top of the shiny black marble. She had always found a way to make even her clutter appear beautiful, decorating the world with her joy and love and life. It seemed so horribly dull now, like her Sun magic had stolen light from us all when it returned to Stella in the Above—or wherever demons truly went to rest.

With trembling fingers, I picked up one of the gold bracelets that I had given her for Star Festival one year. The diamonds on it still sparkled, gleaming in the fading light from the window and casting rainbows onto the ceiling. I saw the tear splash against the black vanity before I realized that I was crying.

As if the first tear had brought the dam crashing down, I fell into a fit of sobs. With a resounding thud, my knees hit the ground, legs giving out. Suddenly I was fully shaking, not from anger but from sorrow. Clinging to the bracelet, I let the rest of my body hit the floor, my forehead against the cold marble.

"I miss you," I whispered, speaking to no one and nothing but the dust in the air of my dead friend's chambers. "Ranbir is a mess. He has been hiding away in the infirmary in Pike, not speaking other than when required. He does not eat or sleep, does not smile. You left, and you took him with you. I think you took a small part of all of us."

Silence enveloped me, as heavy as the world that rested upon our shoulders—mine and Asher's. No answer would come.

"She tried to kill herself. You died, and we broke, and she thought us all better off without her. You died, and we were not ready to say goodbye. You died, Nona. I need you, but you are gone. You died."

Winona died, and more would fall if we did not do something.

My resolve was building, or perhaps it was crumbling. They felt so similar these days. Before I could marinate in the sadness, I felt the tug that told me someone had touched an item I had laced with my essence. I stilled, waiting for the feeling to go away, the pull ceasing and telling me whoever it was had let go. There were so few things that I had allowed my trace to remain on, which meant that this was likely Asher.

She had not responded after I sent her a note last night. Her communication was stilted, often full of hidden pain and rage. Henry was quick to fill me in on how she was doing, but we both knew she was skilled at masking how she felt. If she looked sad, then that meant she was slowly dying inside—the pain eating her alive.

I sensed her let go and immediately called onto my shadows to fetch the pencil and paper, the feeling of relief at expelling more of that poisonous magic lasting mere seconds. I opened my hand just in time for those shadows to turn solid, the pencil dropping into my palm.

Hastily, eagerly, I opened up the note. Chuckling at her words despite myself, I quickly scribbled back a response and sent it her way. Pocketing Winona's bracelet, I stood once more, the tears still slowly crawling down my cheeks.

"I will take care of him—of all of us—just like you did. I will seek retribution for what they did to you, and I will find a way to make the world bright once more. Rest knowing our family will have joy again someday."

With a final pat to her vanity, I left Ranbir and Winona's chambers in Haven, portaling to the space another fallen friend had once held.

Pino's chambers were a disaster, cloth and paper and needles spread over every surface. The mess reminded me of the visions he had once shown me, a cyclone of so much happening at once. My chest tightened at the sight of the journal on his desk, still open to a drawing of a female shaped much like Ash, her curves decorated in what could only be described as liquid obsidian—the black accented with flecks of silver and gold. The gown was low-cut and form-fitting, dragging at least three feet behind. It was sleeveless, a cape-like piece of fabric attached to the back to trail behind the wearer in the same way the train did.

A smile lifted my cheeks. She would have looked beautiful in it— the same female who currently wrote to me, the feel of her holding the pencil sending a tingling sensation from the tips of my fingers to my toes.

Gently, I picked up the journal, skipping back to the last marked page. It was a large chunk of writing, looking as if it had been scribbled in a rush.

Your magic is a force, a strength previously unheard of and ever-reaching. As you find the light and dark, you shall see that they will guide you if you dare heed their call. When you do, a prince you will lose, a prince you will gain, and a king you will hold. And when the moon paints the sky red, retribution will light fire to the realms. As promised by the true queen who defied her false destiny, when two worlds collide and history repeats, from it will come the salvation. From it, love will defeat vengeance. But, if you fear what you do not know or do not understand, you might find yourself dead before you have even lived. And so the world will fall not far behind. No matter the choice you make, your reign will be the end.

I read it once, twice, three times before I truly understood it.

His prophecy, the one that had made Asher realize she had not been in the Fire Lands so long ago. This was not just for designing and doodling, this was also the place he recorded his prophecies and visions.

Just then, Asher let go, finished writing her response. I called onto it, snatching it from the shadows. I read her note then the prophecy then her note once more before tucking it into the journal.

Adbeel was wrong.

I *deserved* the chance to make this world better for Asher.

CHAPTER FOURTEEN

ASHER

Comfort was an interesting concept. Where one might be content in a flowing red gown, another might be appalled by the idea of formal wear.

Henry was the latter.

He and Wrath both had mixed feelings about approaching Queen Shah tonight. Neither was as confident as I was that we could secure an alliance with her, though we all knew that—as Bellamy once said—desperation could get you anywhere.

We were more than desperate. Henry had let slip that Eoforhild was sustaining attacks, Bellamy leading his forces into flooded cities and razed villages. Males, females, and younglings were all dying left and right, the Golden Guard decimating everything in their wake.

Finding alliances was more important than ever. The fae had far more soldiers than the demons did. Our—their—ranking system automatically enlisted fae within certain rankings. The sweet spot were those who did not have deep enough wells of power to be in diplomatic positions, but had more power than should go to "waste" doing jobs that did not require their abilities at all.

Though it was cumbersome, invasive, and borderline dictatorial, it did make for a rather pristine realm. The demons were different in that sense. They did not force enlistment—nor did they choose what one would spend their life doing. In that, there was peace but also danger.

By now, I knew that there was a better way to rule, but that nagging voice in my head said that those simple things could damn an entire realm.

While Henry continued to fuss with his lapels, I walked over to Wrath, my dress dragging on the floor behind me.

Pino had made drastic changes to it since that moment all those months ago that I had tried it on in his clothing stall. Gone were the short, sheer sleeves. They were replaced instead with tight-fitting, wrist-length sleeves. The front still plunged, but now there was a thin piece of sheer fabric the exact color of my skin connecting the split material, tiny jewels that looked suspiciously close to diamonds dotting it.

Wrath watched me approach, his mind still a hollow space despite the obvious gleam in his eye that suggested he was plotting. Just as we all were.

"Hello, Strange One."

Would his voice ever sound less foreboding?

"Hello, Wrathy." I laughed as the dalistori seemed to cringe, obviously not a fan of the nickname. With a soft nudge, I scooted into the spot next to him on the sofa. He let out a soft purr when I began scratching behind his ears, the feel of his fur in this form so much like silk that I found myself jealous.

"That is a ridiculous thing to call me. Do not do it again," he threatened just before cuddling further into me. I scoffed as I noticed the little gray pieces of hair already sticking to my dress.

"Why are you here, Wrath?" A question that had been heavy on my mind since the high wore off from his agreement to join us.

He seemed to think that over, his small head tilting to one side. The movement confirmed what I already assumed: Wrath had not simply wanted entertainment or the taste of royal blood.

"Do you not feel it?" He sat up, his gray fur standing on edge and yellow eyes wide. My own skin grew cold, a chill clawing up my spine. I heard Henry stop his pacing, the tell-tale sign that he was listening.

"Feel what?" I asked, feigning ignorance.

"It is like my soul calls to yours. I belong here, with you, in this moment. I know it. I was made to follow you, of that I am certain. I am yours to command. Just as you belong to us all now."

I had no idea what to say to that. There was no doubt that I too felt the pull, but for him to say he was mine to command? That seemed excessive. I was one being, no more worthy of his allegiance than Henry or Bellamy or any of the others ready to sacrifice their lives for a future without violence and mass murder.

"You are special, Strange One." His breathy murmur was barely audible, but I heard it, practically felt it in my soul. How often had Mia told me that I was special? Not in the way a mother says to their youngling, but in the same knowing way Wrath just had.

"Wrath, what am I?" I inquired, careful with the way I worded something so delicate when Henry was clearly listening.

The dalistori peered up at me for a moment before licking a paw. I waited, watching as his small pink tongue repeatedly cleaned the same patch of gray fur. After a minute, I huffed out an annoyed breath, causing Wrath to roll his eyes in return.

"Are you not fae, Asher?" he asked, his tone bored.

"I do not know. In my worst nightmares, I am a curse sent from the Underworld to destroy us all. A Tomorrow once prophesied that I would be the end, that the world would burn. Sometimes, I wonder if I was named Ash because even my parents knew that I would leave the world covered in it."

"No, Strange One, you will not see the world end. You will see it remade," Wrath said, his tone far gentler than I had yet heard it.

Henry's mental walls of light fell then, his thoughts bursting free of their confines as my power—magic—whatever it was—called to him.

Without thought, I tugged on a memory that seemed to come to the front of his mind. It was of Bellamy frantically painting a canvas that nearly covered the entire wall. The red and black coloring of the room led me to assume that they had been in Haven, likely the art studio Bellamy had mentioned in his castle-like manor.

He was screaming, the paint flying across the walls and floors and staining the surfaces. The assortment of shades brought the bleak colors into stunning light, a rainbow of more emotions than I thought one being could feel. Henry ran to him, ripping at his shoulders and trying to get the prince to snap out of what appeared to be a panic attack.

It was then that Bellamy turned with tears rushing down his face.

I had not fully entered the memory, choosing to reside on the surface instead. I could not feel what Henry had, barely able to hear what Bellamy uttered next.

"She left, Henry. She left, and I ruined everything. I just sentenced us all to death."

Henry seemed to be murmuring something placating, trying to calm down the broken demon in front of him. Bellamy would not listen though, his body jerking away from Henry's grasp.

He turned away once more, his back hunched forward. His next words were even harder to make out, a mere whisper. The tone, soft and filled with pain, threatened to stop my heart.

"We need her. I need her. How can I live without her? How can I *die* without her?"

I gasped, my consciousness leaving Henry's mind with a violent jolt. He looked just as off-balance as I felt, his eyes wide and hands braced on the back of one of the rickety wooden chairs.

"Henry," I said between aching breaths, my chest heaving like it might explode from the force of air coming in and out of it. When the Sun's green eyes looked away from me, his mouth pressed into a line, I stood. "What was that?"

"You really should contemplate not being so horribly inconsiderate of one's privacy." The words were nonchalant, but the break in his voice and slight shake to his hands suggested anything but indifference.

Wrath remained seated, his head cocked to the side as he watched us battle over something he had not seen.

Lucky him.

"Well, demon, are you going to answer her?" he asked, his tail swishing back and forth in what appeared to be delight—those golden eyes alight with his namesake. Of course, he would be considering this an opportunity to harm Henry.

"Mind your business, cat!" Henry yelled, pointing at the dalistori with barely tempered panic and rage. Wrath's body began to grow, a low growl climbing up his throat and rattling the flimsy walls.

"For Eternity's sake, just tell me! We do not have time for this. Nor can I afford to be in a panic about Bell when we meet Shah." My words seemed to slice through the tension in the air, both creatures backing down.

As usual, Wrath was relatively quick to calm, his body shrinking back down before he curled up in a ball and closed his eyes. If only everyone were that easy to order around.

Henry, on the other hand, began pacing again—his mental shields back up though flimsy. I forced myself not to peek, to allow him the opportunity to collect his thoughts before explaining the memory. He had been right about one thing: I had a horrible tendency to cross those boundaries.

After another minute or so, Henry took a deep breath, a hand flying up to his orange hair and ruffling it. Nervousness was such a rare emotion for him, but twice in two days I had seen him shaken this way. It was disconcerting. Before I could remind him that we were on a schedule, he stopped moving and faced me.

"Bellamy has not explained anything to me in detail, but on more than one occasion, he has suggested that—" He paused, taking in another deep breath and shutting his eyes tightly before continuing, "that without you, our world will end."

I gasped, unable to speak. My gaze flew to Wrath, who now had his eyes open with those eerie yellow irises trained on me. The look on his feline face was knowing, as if he had been aware before of this ridiculous theory.

"No matter the choice you make, your reign will be the end."

That was what Pino had said. Never had he insinuated that I was any sort of savior though I had fought these last few months to be. But how could they say that it was me or nothing? That if I did not save the world, no one would?

It was all too much, too confusing, too heavy.

For two hundred years, I have suffered from others leading my life and forcing me to follow, never giving me answers beyond the bare minimum that I needed to complete their dirty work. To accomplish their goals. Even then, it was not always the truth offered.

Now, here I stood, still not knowing anything but being told I was somehow supposed to save the world or else it would fall.

That was not troubling and terrifying at all.

"We do not have time for this. You want me to save this damn world? Then fix your fucking lapels and portal us to Jore." Henry flinched at my words, but Wrath merely chuckled as he stretched, his tiny back arching and front claws digging into the old cushion to create small holes.

Such a cute and horrifying thing you are.

Such a strange creature you are, oh great savior of the world.

I rolled my eyes at the dalistori's sarcasm, secretly thankful for the small respite after that heavy conversation. I would ask Bellamy tomorrow, after I could also promise allies. Perhaps that would be enough to convince him I deserved answers.

Henry was flattening his lapels, his face flushed in what I assumed was either fear or embarrassment. When he looked up, his emerald gaze meeting my stormy one, I realized with a sigh that it was neither. The stupid demon was angry.

"Apologies for raising my voice, pumpkin. It will probably happen again before the world inevitably ends," I joked, watching the corner of his mouth briefly twitch upwards.

There he was.

I thought of Bellamy then, of the broken way he had spoken in Henry's mind. I wondered if I could be enough to save our world—to save him. Without any reason to do so other than visions of a future not guaranteed, Bellamy had placed an immeasurable amount of faith in me. He had convinced himself that I was everything.

Sometimes, I thought he could be right, that maybe I could be enough if I only tried harder. Other times, I feared how badly it would hurt him when I undoubtedly failed. He loved me too much, too hard.

Horrifying—that was what being loved was. Because I had never amounted to what those around me thought I would. Every step along the way, I stumbled and fell, always clawing up a pedestal I would never reach the top of. Perhaps he knew that, too, and that was why he never spoke those things aloud to me. Why he still held so many secrets.

"Okay, time to go," Henry said, his voice back to that steady and sure tone he usually maintained.

I nodded, leaning down to briefly place a kiss on Wrath's head—which he promptly wiped away with a paw, his annoyed huff making me laugh. The dalistori looked up at me, those yellow eyes sharing all the growing affection and dedication that he would not speak again.

Briefly, I wondered if, when all was said and done, Wrath would be willing to follow me to Betovere.

Then, Henry's hand was on mine, our fingers threading together as the light of the sun embraced us—the warmth ripping apart our bodies and stitching us back together.

We appeared in what I assumed was Jore, a castle made of worn gray stone kissing the clouds above. I gasped out at the way the trees had overtaken the area, grass and leaves and foliage nearly suffocating the structure.

Looking at the way the moss seemed to consume the stone, how thorns protruded from bushes of long-dead roses, I wanted to cry. This was not the same cohesive beauty that the vines in The Royal City had with the Ayad palace. No, this was tragic. A display of long-forgotten hope and painful loss. Only the large, wooden doors remained clear, as if someone had hacked away at the growth to make an arched hole.

The air felt thick with starvation and desperation, a blend of hopelessness that tainted the atmosphere. I slowly began to open that golden gate in my mind, chopping away at every barrier I had put up to block out the minds around me. As I did, a cacophony of voices found me, so many feelings and thoughts and memories flooding my mind. The orchestra of it took over my senses, the overarching tone of the melody one that permeated my heart with despair.

Despite the horror of how quickly beauty can fade to brokenness, I found myself comforted by the fact that I had been right about Shah. Something inside of me reached out, seeking solace from the soul within that had been left behind to rebuild a kingdom that had previously given her no love.

For all the good it seemed she had done, Shah was still plagued with self-hatred and pain. Her mind was easy to find, the commanding presence it held clear. I listened intently to her thoughts as she spoke.

Of course, he thinks himself right. Of course, he doubts my judgment. Two years have passed with solely me atop the throne, nearly eight hundred days of slowly growing peace and stability, and yet he continues to suggest me weak.

Even though I had absolutely no insight into the situation, I still found myself bristling. I fought back the urge to shatter the mind of the stupid male—man—beside Queen Shah, knowing it would be of little help.

Instead, I caressed Shah's mind, humming a soothing tone to her. Her mind stilled, body relaxing.

"Are you ready?" I asked Henry, squeezing his hand. Our sweat mingled together, the nerves neither of us were willing to admit tacky on our skin.

Henry nodded, squaring his shoulders. I breathed out and tried to expel the anxiety from my body. This would be a delicate moment. I needed Shah to fear me, but I also needed her to understand me. There was a fine line to be walked, and I could not so much as stumble.

"Here we go." My words seemed to echo in the air, a chilling declaration.

I closed my eyes and let my power grab onto Shah, her mind seeming to flinch away from me. Her thoughts raced, terror causing her to bend over at the waist. I maintained my hold, not squeezing any tighter or loosening my hold—just remaining still.

Hello, Shah, Queen of Behman.

Shah let out a fierce scream. I felt the pain that came from her clawing at her head, and I wondered if I were being just a bit too theatrical.

Remain calm, Your Majesty.

She stilled, her heartbeat slowing. A part of me, one that seemed to constantly be seeking a foothold at the forefront of my mind, questioned why we could not simply force the mortals to join our cause.

I had to take another long, deep inhale of air and remind myself that allies forcibly found were allies easily lost. That making someone possibly march to their death was wrong.

I mean you no harm. I simply wish for an audience with you. Please, do let me in.

I did not force her, did not push. I, instead, loosened my hold. My power slunk away from her, the feel of it fully returning to me like reuniting with a lover.

Henry and I waited, my chest rising and falling in quick, rapid movements. Hopefully, I was not too threatening. At least if I was too kind, I could always be firmer—that would be an easy task.

"Do you think she will allow us entrance?" Henry asked, his voice a whisper on the wind.

Nothing would make me happier than to say yes, to reassure him that we would succeed tonight. Yet I could not bring myself to do so. Not when I was so unsure of what lay ahead. Instead, I turned my head, smiling up at him.

"If not, we could always fight our way in. As you said, I need the practice." He laughed, his face tilting up to the cloud-filled sky, the orange and pink shades of the setting sun lighting up his freckled face. "Plus, their blood will blend with the dress."

A hand went to my arm, pushing me to the side. I laughed too and shoved him in return with far more force than he had used on me. He stumbled backwards, nearly falling down into the overgrown bushes just off the barely there path. I burst into a fit of cackles, the sound sharp and everything that I had been trained to be the opposite of. It was freeing, becoming exactly what Mia had never wanted me to be.

I briefly pondered if a day would ever come that I did not think of her.

Before those thoughts could find purchase, the wooden arch began to fall, slowly making its way to the ground. Henry and I froze for a moment, the stunned look on his face likely mirroring my own. Then we were up, both of us rushing back to make room for what I now knew was a gate. When it was fully lowered, hitting the ground with an earth-shaking thud, a small man stepped into the open archway.

He was a stout man, looking as if he might barely reach my chin. His hair was white, the top of his head bare, exposing his brown scalp. The long-sleeved tunic and trousers he wore were purple with red stitching, a red raven taking flight on the left side of his chest.

Could mortals see as well as fae and demons? The question hit me so suddenly, so fiercely, that I realized I had very little knowledge of mortals. I had never had the chance to ask Sterling, not only because he was exhausting to be around, but because he never seemed to want to talk about those aspects of his life. The only time I could think of was when he rambled nonsense while asking me to travel the world with him. Even around Farai, Jasper, and Kafele, he seemed set on reinventing himself, as if the moment he stepped onto The Capital's soil he had been made new.

"Identify yourselves," the man commanded, his voice a rich tenor. He had the same accent as other mortals of Behman, his rendition of the common tongue rolling and quick.

Henry took a step forward, his right shoulder crossing in front of me infinitesimally as his left hand went to the hilt of his sword. I recalled the way he and the others had spilled blood in Bellamy's open wound months ago, their vows to protect me ringing through The Forest of Tragedies. Perhaps that disgusting practice held more weight than I had previously suspected.

What none of them seemed to understand was that I did not need protection. I was far stronger than any of them, far more powerful.

The only ones who needed protection were those who crossed my path. I would see to that.

I shoved past Henry, taking several steps forward to ensure the mortal could see me. It was time I finally let the world know who I really was.

"I am Asher Daniox, The Manipulator. The rightful ruler of Betovere"—debatable—"and I come to seek an audience with your queen."

With that, I bowed low at the waist, my eyes trained on the overgrown grass below my feet.

For a few moments, I was met with only the sounds of the insects that invaded these lands, the man's silence both terrifying and enraging. My breaths halted, holding in that fury.

Something deep inside of my chest seemed to stir, encouraging me to simply end him and storm my way through the castle. I desperately wanted to. Failure was not an option—at least, not for me.

"Queen Shah will see you. Follow me." The moment I heard his steps begin to retreat, I straightened, blowing out that breath I had been holding.

"Took him long enough," I grumbled, much to Henry's delight.

The Sun beside me shoved both hands into the pockets of his trousers, the scrunching of his shoulders causing the lapels on his jacket to go askew once more. A groan left my lips as he flashed me a smile and started walking forward, a skip to his step that was far too nonchalant for how dire the situation was.

Begrudgingly, I followed behind him rather than stepping up to his side. Tiny gray hairs still littered my red dress, woven in so deeply that I had to pick them out as we walked. With my attention focused downwards, I did not realize how drastically the scenery changed until Henry's shocked gasp cut through the silence.

My head flew up, the haunting imagery stopping me in my tracks. The archway opened up to a desolate courtyard, the gray stones—cracked and stained with what appeared to be blood—towered above us on the left and right. It seemed to be a long, rectangular-shaped entrance to the castle ahead. Less foliage had taken up residence here, but there were more than enough burned flags and broken weapons to clutter the space.

It looks like a graveyard.

Henry's mental voice was loud, a startled shout. His outer demeanor was much the same. His wide eyes and faintly parted lips told anyone watching everything they needed to know about him.

I forced my expression to be the opposite, to hold in every fear and horrible thought. To not let the images of bodies crumpling onto wooden stages and younglings covered in blood in front of white cottages affect me. Every rusted sword and burnt piece of cloth threatened to drag me into the sea of despair that I had been fighting against for two hundred years.

Not today.

I would not let it win.

The man ahead of us, who had not bothered to slow down or even introduce himself, continued walking on as if nothing were amiss. Perhaps it was not. None of this looked new, nor did it appear that Queen Shah had her sights set on cleaning it up any time soon.

I reached out to Henry, grabbing his hand and tugging him forward at a faster pace. Gone was the childlike charm that had him smiling moments ago, but I would not let him stumble.

Keep your eyes forward. Think of nothing. Do not let yourself be vulnerable here. Not yet. Walk.

His hand tightened within mine, the grip almost painful. I did not care though, not if it meant he had heard and would heed my warning. With every ounce of strength I possessed, I forced myself to stare straight ahead at the true entrance to the castle.

Similar to the gate behind us, the double doors ahead were a faded and splintered wood, entirely plain and bleak—a lifeless rendering of the hollowness that can come with royalty.

It was quite the opposite of the ostentatious castle that Xavier and Mia resided in at this very moment. What a tragedy, to bear witness to the beauty given to the cruel and the pain given to the kind.

If there were any gods out there, then they were no friends of mine.

The man stopped at the doors, pulling them open with a strained heave. His breath caught, the rise and fall of his shoulders speeding up. Mortals were weaker. I knew that much.

Unless they were in a violent rage and their future wife was nearby, prepared to provoke them.

No. Not the right time to think of something like that.

A faint golden glow could be seen from the entryway as we grew near. When the man finally had the doors open fully, a slight sheen of sweat adorning his face, Henry and I got our first real glimpse of what life for Shah was like.

In comparison to the exterior, the inside of the castle was far more grand. Not the same extravagance most royals would deem necessary for their residence, but also not an eerie shrine to war and loss either.

The floors were a bold green that reminded me of Winona's hair, though the shade was not nearly as beautiful as hers had been.

The walls, on the other hand, were a dreadful yellow. Not the shade of the sun or the center of a daisy. Nothing alluring like that. This was far more vibrant; so bright that it stung my eyes to look at for too long.

Color notwithstanding, the shine and life of the inside was spectacular. Oil paintings sporting an assortment of sceneries graced the yellow walls and red roses in purple vases sat atop pristine wooden tables barely big enough to hold them. The ceiling stretched up to the top floor. A staircase hugged the wall to our right, wrapping up to the very top— landings on each level allowing for access to whatever rooms residents lived within.

What I assumed was the foyer opened up straight ahead to a long hallway. The man continued forward, glancing back at us briefly before rolling his eyes and marching on, his shoulders squared and aura insufferably haughty.

Since I had long since abandoned my morals in favor of assuaging my curiosity, I allowed myself to take a peek into the pompous fool's head.

...cursed creature. An abomination to our world, walking among us like she belongs anywhere other than the Underworld with her wicked—

Horribly unoriginal.

We continued following the imbecile through the winding hallways, heading towards the top of a grand green staircase. The marble reflected the glow of the yellow chandeliers above us, holding candles dripping wax as they burned. Something about the room below called to me, making my heart flutter and my soul ache.

Eager to see what was so special about it, I picked up my pace, earning a huff from the mortal man as he was forced to speed up too. The stairs grew wider the lower they went, the lush yellow runner leading us down to a ballroom that spanned the entire lower portion of the castle. The walls in this room were a dark red, the glossy paint looking fresh. A purple dais sat at the far end of the room, a golden throne atop it with— who I imagined was—Queen Shah draped comfortably upon it.

But it was not Shah or Henry or even the throne room that caught my eye, leaving me frozen at the top of the staircase. I felt as if all the air had been stolen from my lungs, like there was nothing and no one but the male at the foot of the stairs.

There he stood, regal and foreboding. He sported a sky-blue set of trousers and jacket, the tunic below black and partially unbuttoned to reveal those vein-like tattoos. His charcoal waves were as messy as ever but a bit longer now. A thin dusting of hair graced his cheeks, the shadow of a beard making him look even more fearsome and stripping him of the boyish quality that had once stood in stark contrast to his handsome face.

The male watched me with a predatory gaze, those icy eyes wide and full lips parted. He looked both stunned and smug, as if he had been told he were right about something important despite not believing he would be.

I gripped onto the flowing red fabric of my dress, begging the stupid gods to at least not let me fall as I made my way down the stairs. Each step of my black heels sent a loud clicking sound echoing across the room, which had gone utterly silent at our arrival. Still, I could not bring myself to see or hear anything but him.

Bellamy.

CHAPTER FIFTEEN

STASSI

This Eternity-forsaken place was covered in too much light and heat.

Few things made me miss Shamay—very few. This searing heat, though, did. I thought of the constant darkness of home, the way our many moons seemed to always seek our attention. Even our sun was different, the teal of it vastly more beautiful than the horrid yellowish white of this world.

As I ground my body on top of the male below me, I wondered if the sticky mess between my thighs was sweat or come. I wouldn't be surprised. None of them had impressed me in the bedroom as of yet, but I had to do *something* while looking for the female.

My hair stuck to my exposed back, the thin cotton dress I had adorned that morning now discarded on the ground beside the bed. The dress had covered far too much skin, and the black color of the fabric seemed to call to the heat. To my surprise, it was far shorter than what the fae in these lands wore.

Actually, they did have some use.

Releasing my magic, I called to the male below me, seeking out every sinful thought he had ever possessed. He froze below me, his eyes rolling to the back of his head, his nearly black skin losing its glow as he turned ice cold. Oops, was that too much? I continued to bounce myself atop him, his cock not quite filling me the way I had hoped.

Truthfully, the way his cold skin slapped against my scorching flesh felt wonderful. It was nearly enough relief to convince me to let him stay that way, but I needed him to participate. Pulling some of that magic back, the pink glow faded as I stilled for a moment, waiting for him to come to. His lids were closed, body shaking below mine, and then those chocolate eyes were flaring wide, seeking out answers to a question he was not smart enough to ask.

My melodic laugh filled the room as I ran a finger down his toned chest, the muscles flinching at my touch. His cock twitched inside of me, just barely grazing that spot I needed him to reach. I moaned, grinding atop him. With less force, I let my magic crawl into him, practically begging for that roughness he enjoyed in the bedroom.

The very same rough sex that had his previous lover in tears. He feared that part of himself now, viewed it as wrong and evil. Sinful.

Everything that I wanted was in there if only he would set it free. My magic hit its mark, finding a foothold inside of that wicked nature. Then he was flipping us, his long, black hair fanning over me. The curls tickled at my skin, but I didn't mind—not now as he was lifting my legs, securing them over his shoulders. He was on his knees, my lower half hovering over the bed as he quickly shoved himself back inside of me.

His thrusts were brutal and quick, the grip he had on my thighs digging into me with bruising force. I cried out at the ecstasy it brought me, the magic in my chest humming as he lost control. The fiercer he got, the stronger I became, and it was just as delicious as the feeling of my impending orgasm.

A loud smack echoed across the room, the sting on my breast telling me I was finally making the progress I needed with him. He moaned, the sound so guttural that I feared he might be close to finishing.

"Don't come, or I will slit your throat," I hissed out, allowing my lips to contort in a menacing sneer. He froze for a moment, the terror on his face clear, but my glare brought him back to the moment.

With a deftness that I had not been aware these mortals possessed, he ripped himself free of me and grabbed me by the throat with a firm grip. He wrenched me up, shoving his tongue into my mouth as his other hand stroked between my legs—both rubbing and pinching at my clit.

The grip on my neck tightened, constricting my airway, and I found myself soaring towards that peak, preparing to jump off the edge. My breaths halted, the lack of oxygen a heady feeling that made my vision swim.

Just as I was about to finish, my release a beautiful sight in the near distance, the male stopped. He shoved me back onto the bed, the force of it knocking the air right back into my waiting lungs. I gasped out, my magic still being steadily fed by him. Before I could even begin to catch my breath, the male flipped me onto my stomach, immediately grabbing my hips and lifting my backside into the air.

His mouth was on me in seconds, far more skilled than his cock. Teeth latched on to the skin of my hip at the same time one of his hands made stinging contact with my center, my cry of pain an encouraging sound. That pain was followed by immediate pleasure as he brought his mouth lower, soothing the throbbing bundle of nerves with his tongue and sucking it into his mouth.

Without thought, I began grinding further into his face, my hands digging into the quilt below. His responding growl vibrated into me, ripping a moan from my lips. After a moment, I felt his tongue glide from my front all the way up to my lower back, a delicious act that it seemed

BREA LAMB

his previous lover was also not a fan of. I, on the other hand, was pleased when I felt his thumb press into my ass just as his cock thrusted back into my core.

Finally!

"Fuck, yes, baby. Just like that. Take me inside of you," he said, his voice rough with lust. I shoved myself farther back, forcing more of his finger inside of me—the biting pain making me throw my head back.

Something interesting for once. What a lucky find on my part.

I slowly drew back my magic, hoping that he would be so far gone to those sinful desires that he would no longer need me to feed into them. His pace didn't change as I did so; in fact, it seemed as if he was more enthralled without my magic inside of him.

Giving no warning, the male pulled out, once more stopping just as my orgasm was nearing, the edging a taunt I would soon grow tired of. I didn't complain though, not when I felt his cock shove into my ass with little remorse. I cried out, the sting bringing tears to my eyes. The male grabbed me by the throat again, using it as leverage to pull me into his thrusts—the speed and force just as painful as the way he seemed to be splitting me open.

If he weren't mediocre in size, at best, I might have actually ripped.

One of my falling tears hit his skin, and the realization sent a spark of frenzy through him. He liked dishing out that pain, liked the hurt he could inflict. I liked it too.

With no more words left to be said, he tightened his hold, cutting off my airway once more as he forced my back to arch further. My breasts bounced, the sound of them slapping into one another nearly as loud as the sound of him slamming into me. His mouth found my neck, teeth and tongue attacking the skin there with fervor until I was—finally—falling off that edge I had been walking. I screamed out in pleasure, the sound seeming to force him over as well. Our orgasms sent violent spasms

169

through us, both of us shaking from the exertion, my magic erupting in waves of pink.

He let me go, my body hitting the bed with a final, resounding thud. I felt his hands go to my ass, spreading me apart. Another moan escaped his lips at the sight, sending an unpleasant wave of annoyance through me.

"That was the best sex of my life," he rasped, his finger slowly pumping in and out of me, playing with his own release. I rolled over, looking up at his handsome face, drenched in sweat. He smiled, full lips parting to reveal brilliantly white teeth. As he leaned down, prepared to kiss me and likely start anew, I reached up and promptly snapped his neck.

"It was ordinary," I said as his body landed atop mine. I shoved off the corpse, vexed that it even touched me once more. "And that is me being generous."

Making my way off the bed, I let my feet step atop the male's dead body, whistling as I headed to his attached bathing chamber. It was small, the brown walls and metal tub far too plain for my liking. But there was a bucket of water, which was enough to make me giddy with joy.

Cleaning myself up, I enjoyed the feel of the magic inside of my chest, growing stronger every day I was in this foreign world. Still, the increase of magic would quickly grow boring if I didn't find more appealing things to play with.

I made my way back to the bed, passing by the male's body without a second look. My dress was still on the floor, and I quickly picked it up, slipping the now-wrinkled fabric over my head. Any idiot would know that I didn't belong here simply by paying a modicum of attention, so the dress was of little worry.

The house was stifling, pushing me to get out before the horrid smell stuck to my skin. I wondered if that past lover of his would find him. Perhaps she would feel less disgusted by this so-called home. Briefly, I stopped at the door to slide my feet into the soft white slippers that were quickly turning brown from the dirt. Then I wrenched it open, letting the wood hit the wall with a loud thud.

The moment my body stepped through the doorway of the hut-like structure, the scorching air enveloped me. I groaned, instantly irritated. Taking a path through the dry and insect-infested lands of what the fae called Isle Healer, I tried to ponder what I should do next.

Another unsuccessful excursion. He'd be livid with my update, but what was I to do? There was some sort of barrier protecting the lands, and I had no map of Eoforhild to help me.

My eyes darted around, taking in what was actually a fairly beautiful place. If it hadn't been for the heat, I would enjoy the sprawling landscape, crops stretching for miles. It was relatively flat, only small hills rolling here and there to break up the even land. Fae here were kind and chatty, always interested in speaking to one another even if it hindered their day. There was far less sin here, but the virtue was immense, plentiful in its intoxication.

Still, the hot air was too much. I needed out.

My hand slipped into the small pocket of my dress, pulling out the only item I carried—a map of Betovere.

Unfolding it, I eyed the general location I had found myself in today, reading off the name. Rafferty. Sadly for them, the fae of Rafferty would soon find a murder on their hands.

Fortunately for me, I was headed elsewhere.

My eyes found The Capital, the depictions of gold an alluring sight. So much wealth, so much beauty. Despite knowing Asher was not there, I still felt the need to look around. He would like anything of hers that I could find, so I'd make sure to swipe something she had left behind.

A shout came from nearby, drawing my attention. I made my way through the homes, weaving between small gardens and wells that seemed randomly placed. My eyes caught movement, and I ducked down as I saw what the commotion was about.

OF REALMS AND CHAOS

Four little ones stood gathered in a circle, a fifth smaller youngling in the center. Quiet laughter came from three of them as the biggest reached forward and shoved the smallest. Sadly, my magic did not grow with these actions, and perhaps that was because sin was not something youths fully understood. There was enough of it within them though that a small wave of my hand had the larger one gasping in surprise, her hands reaching down for the tiny male on the ground. When she had helped him up fully, the other three moved forward, dusting off his dirty clothes and drying his wet cheeks.

The tiny male was stunned, his eyes wide as the four little bullies profusely apologized.

And, because I am me and couldn't help myself, I laughed maniacally as I heightened that youngling's hatred. I watched as the small fae jumped onto the big one, bringing her to the ground and pummeling her relentlessly. The three onlookers fled, screaming words like "help" and "crazy."

Yes, run like the little cowards you are.

Once the small male was noticeably growing tired, I stole the sin, offering him enough virtue to encourage him to heal the worthless youth beneath him. She twitched and groaned, and then she was somewhat whole again, though disgusting in all the blood and dirt.

My work done and my mood much improved, I straightened the map again. With one more look to the golden palace, I closed my eyes and made a choice.

CHAPTER SIXTEEN

BELLAMY

Surely this was a dream.

It had to be, because there was no reality in which I should be gifted with a sight as magnificent as Asher descending the stairs in that dress. She was more beautiful than any painting, her red dress fitting to every curve and hollow of her body, her eyes alight with more joy than I had seen in them since our time in The Royal City. Perhaps even before then.

Maybe I was vain for thinking so, but I could not resist the idea that it was the sight of me waiting for her that brought that smile to her red lips. The color was a perfect match to her dress, the kohl that lined her eyelids coming out to a sharp point on the outer edges. She had rouge on her cheeks, the pink tint growing darker with each step she took my way.

Even with it all, I knew the allure was simply *her*. That biting humor of hers was always quick to remind others to remain humble. The way she demanded attention, authority coating her and dripping at the flick of her wrist or blink of her eye. Every kind and considerate thought she had. The way she seemed to gravitate towards aiding others. Her magic—the pure power of it enough to bring anyone to their knees. She was Eternity incarnate, a goddess walking among us.

Her exceptional temper and hesitancy to trust were endearing as well. No part of her was anything less than immaculate. Nothing other than perfect, for me, for Eoforhild, and for all of Alemthian. Asher was our savior, even if she did not know it.

I only wished she could see her own greatness, could sense that magic inside of her and see it for what it was—the answer.

As she closed the distance between us, her eyes glassy, I considered what I needed to give her to ensure she always had that smile—that joy.

The world. I would give her the world if I could.

But, as soon as it came, it vanished, replaced by a soft downturn of her lips and scrutinizing eyes. The novelty of my appearance had clearly worn off, and now, it was questions that filled her mind.

One moment, she was walking to me like a beacon in the night, and the next, she was right there—a breath away. I reached out my hand, and she placed hers into it without hesitation.

"Hello, Princess," I whispered.

"Hello, demon," she offered back through upturned lips.

Perhaps it was the high of being reminded that Asher chose me—that she was *mine*—which led me to snake my arms around her waist, spinning her around. Her melodic laughs filled the throne room, her head falling back and hair fanning out.

When I stopped, I made sure to tug her body even closer to mine, breathing her in. Asher smelled like vanilla and mint and the sun itself.

She pulled away, those big gray eyes boring into me, searching for answers. So many secrets I have kept from her, all wishing to be shared. I wanted to, so badly. She deserved that much, at least. But I could still hear the haunting way that Pino had warned me not to tell her until I could have the audience I needed, none of whom was more important than Adbeel. If he met her, he would understand. He would finally take action. I knew it.

"Okay, love birds, we do have company," Henry said from behind us, his drawl casual. I turned, catching a glimpse of the smile that he attempted to hide with a roll of his eyes.

She is not doing well.

That was what Henry had said three days ago in a letter, telling me all about how badly she was suffering. I would help her. We would find allies and win the war. I would leave her with a castle and a throne and a better life.

Together, with aid, we could do this. She could be happy.

"I think it is you that is considered company, seeing as you are in *my* home." The accent was quick and rolling, just as all residents of Behman. But the regal way she spoke the common tongue was what made her voice stand out above all others.

I released Asher from my hold, swiping my thumb across her cheek, before I turned to face the queen that we were supposed to be impressing.

She had not been too difficult when I first arrived. Unlike Asher and Henry, I had portaled straight into her castle, causing quite the scene in her throne room. Although in their defense, it had to be fairly scary for smoke-like shadows to appear out of nowhere, a male walking out as if he is death itself.

Shah had ordered her guards to halt, watching as I lifted my hands up, showing I was unarmed. Then, just for the flair of it, I had lit every wall sconce in the throne room, the hideous yellows and greens of the staircase nauseating under the firelight. Screams had rent the air, reminding me of the sweet sound of the fae at Asher's so-called wedding. Oh, how I reveled in the fear that my parents had held in their eyes as well as the sound of my dagger cutting into that heinous mortal boy.

"Queen Shah," I said, turning to face her as I bowed low.

She was wearing a gown made of purple silk, the fabric hugging every wide curve of her body and showing off what had once been sold away to a man three times her age. Despite being a couple of inches shorter than me, Shah held herself with the sort of confidence that made it seem as if she were towering over us all. Her liberation seemed to remind her of her worth, and she showed that now with her proud stance and commanding aura. As if she were screaming to us all that she was a ruler who deserved the crown atop her head.

Red bangles clinked together—at least ten bracelets stacked on each of her wrists. Her crown was gold, the intricate twists and curls of it reaching up towards the ceiling, meeting in a single point at the center.

None of that was what truly made her eye-catching though. No, it was Shah's tattoos that drew attention. Her dark skin was covered in Behman tongue and images and seemingly random line work. None of it was unintentional. I had learned of the tradition of tattooing within this kingdom. Their desire to collect their victories, losses, and everything in between upon their skin, like memories that could not be forgotten.

When I was younger, I had promised myself that, if I ever found a way to get this stolen magic out of my body, I would cover my newly clean skin in my story. As Asher leaned into me, her presence soothing my troubled mind, I wondered if the gods or Eternity would be kind enough to allow me the opportunity to have our story written upon my skin before I die.

"Prince Bellamy," Shah said, her smile taunting. I did not miss how she refused to bow, just as she had when I first arrived. Such a thing did not bother me when I could not care less about a crown or a title or a gesture of acknowledgement.

Asher moved forward, dipping into a low curtsy and holding herself there. Sometimes I forgot that Asher had been ingrained with matters of diplomacy and ruling, every aspect of her life preparing her to be queen. She was made for this, and that fact shone as she waited on steady legs.

"Queen Shah, it is a pleasure to meet you," she said, her face still to the floor.

Shah stared at her, brown eyes wide as she took in everything that was Asher Daniox. It *was* a lot. To be so near Asher meant feeling that pulse of her magic, the demanding nature of it forcing one to submit. When Shah dipped into an equally low curtsy, I nearly let out a mad cackle, but I pursed my lips and covered my mouth, resisting the urge. My eyes flicked over to Henry, who also seemed to be on the verge of a fit of laughter.

The queen's advisor, Lord Callahan, glared at us from her left. In the hour or so that I had been at Castle Jore, Callahan had screamed at me twice, called me a beast, threatened my life, and scowled at least fifty times. Entertaining did not even begin to describe him. That permanent crease between his brows and downturn of his thin lips was absolutely hilarious.

Asher and Shah both stood, the two of them momentarily frozen as their eyes locked.

"You threatened me," Shah said, her face stony but voice amused.

My eyes went wide, darting to Asher in surprise. I was aware that she had entered the queen's mind the moment Shah screamed out, her nails digging into her scalp. But she had *threatened* her? That seemed so unlike the Asher who was set on choice and peace. Had something gone wrong?

"Well, that is an exaggeration, Your Majesty. I merely told you I wanted an audience," Asher countered, a small shrug lifting her shoulders.

On the outside, she seemed comfortable, completely unfazed by the situation. Inside, I knew she was likely near panicking at the thought of failure.

Luckily for us, Asher rarely did so.

"It felt like you were squeezing my brain!" Shah exclaimed, a baffled laugh following.

Asher smirked, her eyes alight with a small piece of that mischief she used to sport so often in Betovere. Watching her back then had been both painful and intoxicating. She was hurting and trapped, but she was also far more carefree, the feeling of security she held allowing her to play pranks on her friends and sneak out at night and practice her pianoforte for hours on end. I had a sinking feeling that I would never get to see that Asher again, not in this life at least.

"Technicalities." The wave of Asher's hand and her growing smile seemed to bring a sense of ease to the room, everyone's shoulders relaxing a fraction.

"Well, since you went to all the trouble to come here and even dressed in Behman red, would you like to join us for dinner as we discuss whatever it is that you so desperately need to speak with me about?" Shah was being far nicer to Ash than she had been to me, but there was still a hardness to her face that her soft tone could not mask. She did not trust us in the slightest.

All five of us, followed closely by a group of guards in purple and red armor, made our way to a long table at the opposite end of the throne room, the single golden throne a daunting presence at our backs. The red table—so dark it was nearly black—looked large enough to seat dozens, but only six places were set, one more than we technically needed.

I paused, my head tilting to the side as I considered that. There was to be another guest. But who? Of course, it had likely been discovered that there were immortal beings within Behman, but had anyone realized that Henry was a demon? Or that Asher was the fae princess?

Clicking sounded to my right, the classic sound of heels meeting the floor. My head whipped around, catching the brown-eyed gaze of a woman. Her hair was like spun gold, the curls thick and bordering on unruly. Her pale skin had a slight blush to it, as if being in this room made her nervous. Still, her posture was impeccable, her head high and chin raised as she made her way to us. She wore the forest green and navy blue of Maliha, the gown a puff of tulle and silk that skated across the tile below. At her brow was a golden diadem, the diamonds on it bright in the light of the flames.

"Genevieve," Asher said with a gasp to my left.

This was the soon-to-be queen of Maliha, then—Sterling's older sister.

Fury filled me at the realization, threatening to burst free and take my magic with it. This disgusting mortal family, which had been the root of so many of my problems, deserved to feel that rage. King Lawrence and Queen Paula raised one monster, the likelihood of the golden heir apparent heading our way being just as evil was high.

"I do apologize for being late, friend. I had quite a lot of dress to attempt to slip into." Her voice was bright, as if her hair had claimed the sun and that light poured out of her in rays. She had the same heavy accent that all from Maliha had, like her tongue was too large for her mouth, though she spoke the common tongue so well that it was faint in comparison to most in her lands.

"It is not a problem at all. I have saved you a seat by my side," Shah said, patting the back of the violet chair to her left, directly across from Asher.

Genevieve closed the remaining distance quickly and gracefully, gently taking her seat. Asher went rigid at my side, her hands balled into fists on her lap. I reached over, gripping both of her hands in one of my own and offering a small squeeze of reassurance. Based on her blank stare and pin-straight back, Asher would not relax any time soon.

"Introductions are in order, it seems. This is Genevieve Windsor, Heir Apparent to the kingdom of Maliha. I believe," Shah said, turning to look Asher in the eye, "you are engaged to her brother."

Henry growled at my side, the sound rumbling the dishes on the table as his Sun magic faintly leaked from his hands. I felt my own body shake as I stared at the princess, holding myself in my chair with sheer will alone.

Killing her would send the wrong message—not only to the mortals, but to the demons and the fae as well. We could not allow ourselves to be the evil that others deemed us.

It did not slip my attention that I was as hypocritical as they came.

Genevieve's brown eyes never left Asher's gray ones—the two females squaring off, both so clearly on edge. Lord Callahan cleared his throat, as if that small sound would quell the growing tension within the room. Genevieve flicked her steely gaze towards him, and I watched with reluctant amusement as the prickly man scrunched back into his seat.

Then she looked my way, and all hints of delight faded.

"Ah yes, and this is Bellamy Ayad, Prince of the Demon Realm," Shah said rather dismissively. I did not miss the shake in her voice as she said the word demon.

Genevieve's eyes openly roamed over me, her pink tongue darting out to lick her blue painted lips—the color matching the line of cosmetics on her lids. If Asher had not been schooled in diplomacy, she probably would have combusted on the spot, but—unfortunately for us all—she had been. So, instead of ripping the mortal girl to pieces, Asher simply latched onto my hand with startling force, her nails digging into my skin.

"Believe it or not, I have heard some rather enticing rumors about The Elemental. The most exciting being about what wicked things you can do with that power in your veins. Tell me, is it true that you once made a woman reach completion with only water?" Genevieve's taunting did not hit the mark she was aiming for, because Asher remained firmly planted in her chair, though I could hear the way her teeth ground together.

Instead, the Princess of Maliha's mocks left Henry hunching forward, his laughs echoing across the vaulted violet ceilings. Asher snorted beside me, the aura of her magic pressing into me. Whatever she was stealing from the minds around her, it had to be comical.

Genevieve rested her glare on Henry next, her lips turning down in a frown as she watched the Sun catch his breath. He reached a finger up to swipe away a stray tear, his laughter slowly dying out.

"Sorry, I heard something funny and could not help myself," Henry said, not caring to elaborate further.

"Well, that is quite rude," Genevieve stated with a scrunch of her button nose.

I rolled my eyes, not interested in hearing her somehow play the victim during this strange dinner. "You just inquired about my sex life and openly flirted with me in front of my—" I cut myself off, not knowing exactly what to refer to Asher as. Would she be upset if I said she was my future queen? My lover? My wife-to-be? My reason for existing?

Genevieve's gaze lit up with excitement, something sneaky in the brown depths that I had not seen before.

You just played right into her hand. She can spin this in her favor, Bell. She will make me out to be a liar and a fool—an unfaithful wife. If it were just Shah, it would be different, but this is Sterling's sister.

Bristling at her mental tone, I crossed my arms and offered a curt nod to Ash, letting her know that I was going to play the part of a good little prince. Well, I would *try*.

"It is very nice to meet you, Genevieve. I am afraid I have not heard much about you from…Sterling. What brings you to Behman?"

Genevieve's eyes formed slits, her thin lips taking on a sort of pout and her face flaming. Since she already knew what Asher was to me, I let a toothy smile loose on her, leaning over to absently twirl one of

Asher's loose curls. It was more than likely that I was annoying Ash, but oh was it fun.

"I am visiting my close friend, not that it is any of your concern. Though I am quite eager to hear all about whatever it is you are here for. Especially since you are supposedly with my brother as we speak."

That had me tensing, Asher's brown hair slipping from my fingers. Henry, ever the open book, let out a soft gasp. Daring a look at Asher, I found her face as blank as ever, nothing in those eyes but boredom.

"Yes, I am also curious, Princess Asher. Is there a reason you have brought demons to my doorstep?" Queen Shah's question was not filled with the same malice that Princess Genevieve's was, but I could still sense that fear and distrust in the darting of her eyes and uneven beat of her heart.

None of them had filled me in on exactly what their plan was to win over Shah, but I knew that Asher felt fairly confident that this would be a successful night. Genevieve threw off the balance of her plan, but I had a feeling Asher could still manage this.

My princess, gods bless her, offered Shah a soft smile, her hands releasing mine and absentmindedly straightening the red fabric on her lap. Sparing a glance at Henry, I noted how he too watched Asher's hands, his brows pinched.

"I am sure you have heard about the coming conflict between the fae and the demons," Asher said.

Queen Shah's eyes went wide, Callahan coughing beside her. Servants came out then, carrying trays of what appeared to be some sort of meat and potato dish, the scent of gravy heavy in the air. Our cups were filled to the brim with wine, the color of it the same red as the table. Before Asher could drink hers, I swiped it, sniffing at the liquid. Not poisoned. At least, not with one I could scent.

Asher gasped when I lifted the cup to my lips, aiming to take a sip of hers first. I was planning to make sure that if one of us were to die tonight, it would be the least important of the two, but Henry snatched the glass from me, causing a splash of it to hit the table.

His eyes met Asher's, and then she nodded. Witnessing how close the two of them had become these last few months was hard, but seeing how that had somehow grown into silent conversations and inside jokes made me hopeful that she was slowly healing.

And, I will admit, it also made my fucking skin crawl.

"Do drink up, Genevieve. I would not want you to become parched as you listen to my tale." Her voice was clear, the haunting tone of her magic demanding obedience as Henry held out the cup to Genevieve. Callahan seemed to shrivel at the sound of it, Shah also noticeably shrinking into her chair.

Genevieve snatched Asher's cup without hesitation, a blank look in her eyes as she dumped back well over half of the glass. Everyone waited, no one daring to breathe while we watched for any signs of poison. When a full minute had passed without Genevieve so much as wincing, we decided it was worth the risk and began partaking, Henry digging into his food with a passion.

Under her breath, I heard Genevieve murmur "pig" and choked on my wine. She was not wrong. I took another long sip of the sweetest wine I had ever tasted, a sort of cherry flavor there in its depths.

"I will not play coy, we need your assistance for what is to—"

Shah cut in before Asher could continue. "We? Who does that consist of, *Princess* Asher? Your kind, or theirs?" she said with a tone of ice, her head nodding towards Henry and I. This time, I had to physically restrain Henry, pressing my hand into his leg to keep him seated.

"Do not interfere. Trust her to accomplish what she came here to do," I whispered to him, the words too low and quick for the mortals to hear.

Henry bristled, crossing his arms over his chest and slouching back into his chair much like I had minutes ago. Genevieve watched him as he did, those keen eyes seeing too much.

"If you would let me finish, Your Majesty, then you would know that I mean both. There is no world in which a war does not spell doom for every creature of Alemthian. The fae royals seek to conquer. They want power above all else, and they will not stop with the Demon Realm. Do not think neutrality will save you." The three mortals all stiffened— their faces betraying their nerves, just as their elevated heart rates did.

Lord Callahan was the first to break free from the spell of Asher's words. He shook his balding head, his glare boring into the fae princess.

"We have no qualms with the Fae Realm, nor do we plan on creating conflict when it is not needed. Perhaps you have mistaken our silence for neutrality, but we do not stand in the middle. We are firmly on the side of the fae, who seek to rid the world of the demons. Let them return to the Underworld. We care not if—"

"When my crown sits atop your head, then you may speak for the kingdom over which I rule. Until then, do shut up, Lord Callahan," Shah said, cutting Callahan off mid-sentence. Asher's answering smile was a thing of divine beauty, the darkness lurking beneath calling to that which hid within me. "That being said, I fail to see how you think I can help you, even if I wanted to. With my limited resources and starving soldiers, I imagine I would be of little aid, especially when Maliha's forces march with the Fae Realm."

Surprise filled me at her words, especially since she did not outright deny us. Asher seemed equally surprised, but her baffled expression was trained on Genevieve rather than Shah. Whatever Shah's words had triggered in the Heir Apparent, it must have been intriguing to silence Asher when she was so clearly winning.

Genevieve blanched, her skin so flushed that she looked sickly. I cocked my head to the side, assessing the stare-down between the two. What were Genevieve's goals? She would sit on a throne one day, but did she understand what most kings and queens did not—that you cannot rule over a dead kingdom?

"Did you know that the Mounbettons are not my parents?" Asher asked the mortals, her eyes tracing over each of them. All three shook their heads silently, their faces once more stony. "I assumed as much. My parents were murdered. For the longest time, I believed that demons had done that. That they had killed my family and the fae prince. When I was told that demons cut my ears to send a message, that they let me live as a warning—or perhaps an accident—I believed it."

Wincing internally, I willed my face to remain blank. Now was not the time for Asher to know the truth of how her parents died. One day, when I had both her and Adbeel in the same room, I would let him tell her what befell her family that day.

"Imagine my surprise when I learned that the two fae that I had loved with every fiber of my being—that I had lied and killed and suffered for—were not honest with me about how my parents died. Worse, they had told me false stories of demons attacking our fae, slaughtering en masse over the years."

If what Asher said surprised the queen, she did not show it. In fact, Shah seemed eerily stoic as she listened. Genevieve, too, was taking the story in stride, acting as if the words were not of importance—or maybe they were simply ones she had already heard.

"Tell me, do you know what it is like to be lied to your whole life? To learn that the beings you had looked at like parents had forced you to kill innocents under the guise of treachery and protecting the masses? I do. I know that feeling intimately. Just as I know what it feels like to be beaten unconscious and then to wake up and see a smile upon the face of the one who made you bleed, listening to them say they love you as if it had all been for your own good. I know what it is like to believe those things, to blame yourself and wish you had not provoked such a punishment." Asher stuttered then, her voice catching as a single tear streamed down her face.

Shah finally began to show emotion, her brown eyes watering and breathing ragged. Genevieve's eyes went wide, her lips quivering as she listened despite the clear effort she was putting in to prevent the reaction. To my right, Henry seethed, his fury second only to my own at the broken sound of Asher sharing her story.

"Yet I know worse still. My great love was named Sipho. He was everything I had ever wanted in a lover: kind, brilliant, honest, brave. There was nothing he would not have given me or done for me. The last time I saw him, he was burning alive, Xavier Mounbetton's flames stealing away his life. Do you know what it is like to hear the desperate screams of your soulmate? To bear witness to the way the flesh you had once kissed and touched and worshiped melted off? To smell the boiling of blood and burning of hair that you dreamed your younglings—children—might someday have? I do."

She paused, letting her tears stream down her face. Three times now, Asher had told that story. One she had held close to her for nearly two centuries, never letting herself think of it if she could resist, let alone share it with others. Now, as she shook through her growing sobs, Asher stood up, letting those emotions rise to her advantage. Letting Sipho's death mean something more.

"For some reason, I think you thoroughly understand such feelings, Queen Shah. Something tells me that the nightmares that haunt my sleep also plague yours. Why is it that a queen of barely two decades married a man well into his seventieth year? Why is it that a queen with enough love in her heart for her kingdom that she is willing to give away her riches was so eager to alter the sigil that had represented it for centuries?"

Callahan shot up from his seat beside Genevieve, his chair flying backwards and crashing to the floor. Both hands smacked onto the table, cups of wine teetering back and forth, threatening to spill.

"How dare you speak on matters you know nothing about, you wretched girl!" he shouted.

As if I could not resist—as if my soul itself forced me—I stood too, towering over the man who I had watched undermine both females who held titles far surpassing his. Fire erupted from the wall sconces, flames shooting so high they nearly singed the vaulted ceilings. The wine in our cups rose, and the ground at our feet shook. I willed the wind to come to me, the sound of it barreling into the stone walls of the castle deafening.

"Funny, I do not recall the future queen of Betovere granting you permission to speak." I let my black flames burst to life at the tip of my pointer finger, flashing Callahan a wide smile. "Have you ever smelled the scent of a burning tongue?"

He froze, violently shaking his head back and forth. Speechless, for once.

"Would you like to?" I asked with glee.

Callahan shouted, his terror contorting his face. Genevieve also looked horrified, her body shaking as she held onto her chair with a vice-like grip. If Shah felt fear, she did not portray it, her eyes still locked onto Asher's. The two of them stared at one another, not even so much as flinching at what was happening around them.

I stopped, letting every ounce of my magic and power fade from the room. The silence that followed was somehow louder than the sound of the screaming. Genevieve was visibly distressed, her body still convulsing. Callahan had turned a green hue, as if he were on the verge of being sick.

"Well, that was a strange way of not interfering," Henry said from my side, his laugh ripping through the quiet.

I rolled my eyes, my smile fading into a small smirk. "It seems I have reduced myself to a territorial lackey, though I cannot say I mind when the reward is so *delicious*." My eyes remained on Genevieve's as I spoke, not wanting to miss the moment her mind registered what I was saying.

The princess bristled, her cheeks gaining back their pink hue in record timing. "You are all psychotic!"

I laughed then, not able to stop the amusement that had slowly built up inside of me. Henry looked at me, and then he, too, burst into a fit of laughter. As I fell back in my seat, I leaned my elbow onto Henry's broad shoulder, laughing harder when I saw a tear slip down his cheek.

Genevieve and Callahan seemed to grow angrier, both of them sitting straight once more now that the latter had retrieved his chair. But it was not them who spoke next. No, it was Shah.

"Well then, Queen Asher, it looks like we have a deal."

CHAPTER SEVENTEEN

ASHER

Shah was stunning. Not just because of her bright smile and intricate tattoos, but because of her soul. For so long, I had hated my gifts, thinking them a curse—a plague. But when Shah's thoughts had screamed out, my power flocking to her like a starving animal seeing food for the first time, I realized how much of a blessing they could be.

While everything went downhill around us, I listened as Shah shared memories and stories of her past. I bore witness to the pain inflicted upon her—both mentally and physically—by her late husband. At a speed that nearly left me lost in her mind, we had sailed through her memories, watching as she grew and matured. Witnessing the increasing panic in her words and thoughts as her parents fell sicker. Feeling the dread weighing heavier and heavier on her heart the days leading up to her wedding.

Shah, as formidable as she seemed beside me at dinner, had been too scared to do anything other than listen. When her parents died days after her wedding to a manipulative and violent lord, she allowed herself to be meek, malleable. Every day for eleven years, she felt more and more of herself being chipped away.

Until one day, she snapped.

I would not tell anyone that Shah had murdered her husband, because she did not deserve to be punished for doling out retribution that was more than deserved. Watching him choke and sputter and whip his hands out as she suffocated him with his own pillow was so satisfying that I nearly pulled out of her mind and jumped with joy.

But then, disaster struck.

The attack started in the middle of the night, nine days after Queen Shah had announced she would not be taking a new consort.

When she awoke to people slaughtering her guards en masse and burning the Behman flag, Shah had been terrified. But she had refused to be weak any longer. Her rabid and desperate screams had rang through the then pristine courtyard as she swung her father's sword.

The first man she cut down had brought her to tears.

The eighth brought her to her knees.

And when the sun rose the next morning—shining light on the gore-filled courtyard—so did the Queen of Behman.

The next day, with a dislocated shoulder, a sliced thigh, and a vengeful heart, Shah changed the sigil that had represented her home for centuries.

Now, as I walked through her castle, I noted how most of the rooms were still that horrible yellow and green combination. Did it bother her to see signs of what had once been but would never be again? Did she still feel the horrid chill of Lord Starsh, his foul breath and sharp words and heavy hands haunting her as she walked her own halls?

I know I had. I used to think that it was the lack of decoration in the palace of The Capital that made it feel like anything but home. Now though, I wonder if it was my body taking note of something my mind had not—that place would never be anything other than a gilded prison.

Was it the same for Shah?

When we strategized tomorrow, I would have to fight the urge to ask her. The three of us continued through the halls, making our way to the rooms Shah offered us for the night. Bellamy led the way, already having been to the rooms earlier. Wrath would be furious when he realized that we were not coming back tonight.

"You have some serious explaining to do, Daniox," Henry said from my side. I laughed as he nudged me, the weight that had been on my chest since I first decided we would come here finally lifting.

I did it.

Just as I was about to tell them both to mind their business, seeing as Shah's story was not mine to tell, a voice that made my nerves skyrocket and my power buzz inside my chest sounded behind us.

"What kind of trickery have you used to sway Shah?" Genevieve was angry by the tone of her words, the volume of her voice slowly increasing as she spoke. "You wretched little monster! First, you steal my brother away from us, and now, you want to attempt to lead the only considerate and honest ruler in the Mortal Realm to her death? Have you not ruined enough of the world yet?"

Her finger was inches from my face, the two of us standing at the same height. Princess Genevieve Windsor was as imposing as she was glamorous. The scowl on her face seemed permanent, though even that did not affect her perfectly painted on cosmetics. Golden curls fanned out from her head, each ringlet silky and soft.

She reminded me so much of Sterling I thought I might be sick. Even the brown of her eyes was that same lovely chocolate color of his.

Just looking into them for a moment sent waves of pain through my abdomen, the grimy feel of hands exploring my body making me tense.

Or perhaps it was her words that made my teeth grind and tears prick my eyes. They stung because they were far more accurate than she realized. I had ruined so much, had been the thief of countless lives. The acid in her tone was deserved.

One thing I would not stand for, was her attempting to make her brother out as the victim. I was many things, but Sterling Windsor's abuser was not one of them.

"Oh, your wonderful, innocent brother. The very one who beat me to near death and threatened to rape me on our wedding night. Truly, what a prize. So glad I *stole* him."

Surprise flitted across her face as she stumbled back. Briefly, I wondered what Sterling had been like before he arrived in Betovere last summer. Just as quickly as the curiosity came, it faded away, my anger at the family rising quickly. Genevieve recovered fast too, that scowl pinching her beautiful face once more.

"Yes, you seem to be quite traumatized. Tell me, did my brother's supposed abuse lead you to the cock of a demon, or had you already been fucking The Elemental before then? What a way to heal, beneath the body of a murderer. Then again, I guess you have killed just as many innocents—"

Henry's hands lit up, the startling white of his Sun magic burning my eyes. Genevieve squealed as Henry approached her, his anger tangible through his magic.

"How dare you speak to her like that, you inferior mortal! You are lucky to be in her presence, lucky to meet someone as brave as she is!" His shouts drew the attention of four guards clad in the same navy and forest greens as Genevieve. They hastily came our way, unsheathing their swords as they ran.

I grabbed onto Henry's arm, yanking him back from the princess, who was somehow both terrified and furious—emotions permeating the air.

As the guards flanked her, I felt the presence of their minds, the overwhelming sense of terror too much after listening to the hateful—and undeniably true—words Genevieve had thrown my way.

Bellamy's hand found my other one, and then we were portaling, my feet moving from the green tile to an ornate yellow rug. With a violent tug, I ripped my hands out of theirs, turning away from them. I took deep breaths, trying to calm my growing anxiety and never-ending dread.

What would we do if Genevieve contacted the remaining kingdoms? There was no way we could convince them to ally with us if she spewed poison into their ears first. Something had to be done about her.

"Henry," I said through heavy breaths, my hands wrapped around my chest as if I could contain the panic. The Sun bent down slightly, his green eyes meeting mine. I hated what I needed to say to him, especially after he had defended me that way. "Take a breather, get washed up, then go find Princess Genevieve. We have risked everything by treating her with disrespect. Each of us will apologize, beginning with you."

Henry's jaw went slack as he stared at me, baffled by my order. But I could not think like a disgruntled or wronged princess. If I wanted to be a queen, I needed to act like one. Which meant swallowing my pride and apologizing to that bitch.

"Go. I have her," Bellamy whispered from somewhere behind me. With that, Henry offered a curt nod and straightened, stomping to a pair of doors that looked to be the yellow color of moldy cheese. He yanked them open and slammed them closed behind him, the paintings rattling and the green curtains swaying.

The moment I heard Henry's retreating footsteps fade, I fell to the floor, my body hunching over as I shook. For every success, two failures found me. Behman would side with Eoforhild, but at the cost of many lives. Genevieve had not been wrong about that, nor had she spoken falsely when she accused me of murder. I was a creature that tormented the dreams of mortals across this realm, stories of me reaching far and wide. No matter how much good I brought to the world, the evil within me would always outweigh it.

Bellamy slowly made his way around me, stopping once his shiny, black shoes were in my line of sight. When he gently lowered himself to the floor, his knees nearly touching mine, I had to fight against collapsing.

I could not fail him, not now when I had cost him so much.

Waiting for him to speak my thoughts was agonizing, because I knew that he was thinking the same thing. He had to be.

"Tell me what you need to feel safe," he whispered, his raspy voice soft. Taken aback, I peered up at him. What I expected to be hateful condemnation was actually loving sympathy, those emotions suddenly projecting my way, his shouted thoughts pushing out my own.

Whatever you need, Ash, I will give it to you. I will steal the stars from the sky and hang them on your neck. I will melt every spec of gold in The Capital and forge something new. I will battle entire armies and lay their swords at your feet. I will do anything for you, if only you let me.

A single tear ran down my cheek, the only one I would let fall. I could not afford sobs of inadequacy and self-hatred right now. Preparing for the meeting tomorrow was what my mind needed to focus on, if I could just clear it. If I could just convince myself that I was capable of accomplishing more than ruination.

I do not know who I am, Bellamy. Everyone thinks something different of me. Wrath deemed me a savior, Genevieve called me a murderer, some think me a monster. I fear I am worse than all of those things. What if I am a curse?

It felt oddly comforting to speak the words, even if not aloud. *Especially* because it was not aloud. In fact, my near constant use of my power these days had been relieving, too. But nothing could soothe the ache of knowing what I was. Pino had said I would be the end, and every day I grew more convinced he was right.

"It seems you have forgotten, so let me remind you." Bellamy's words were less gentle now, the sturdiness of them more forceful than he usually was with me.

His fingers met my skin, reaching under my arms and lifting me to a standing position. Then one of his hands was at my back, straightening my spine as the other lifted my chin. When he slid behind me, he slowly turned my body to face away from the double doors. My knees shook as I took in the room. It was large, the two windows on the far wall closed off with heavy yellow curtains that matched the rug below our feet with green embroidered snakes creeping up to the ceiling.

To our right was a huge, four-poster bed. The wood was dark brown with bright green curtains offering privacy on all four sides, a large brick fireplace nestled in the corner. To the left was an armoire made of the same dark wood, its massive presence taking up every inch of the wall that the small desk beside it did not. Between the two windows ahead was a mirror that reached at least a foot above Bellamy's head, the width of it nearly twice my size.

The Elemental loomed behind me, his presence demanding, as if I could look at nothing but him in our reflection. His head was turned down, inspecting me as I watched him. It was oddly thrilling standing here this way, witnessing the heated looks the prince gave me.

"What do you see, Ash?" he asked, his sultry rasp sending chills down my spine. Slowly, he slid his fingers up my arms, the featherlight touch a heady feeling.

Gazing at myself, I tried to find the answers he was looking for, but I could not fathom what he saw in me that was so special.

I was pretty, that was not something I would deny. My long brown waves—which had begun to take on more of a curl in my time away from The Capital—cascaded down my back, ending at the base of my spine. My heart-shaped face and big gray eyes fit well with my full lips and tan skin. Despite what the seamstress in The Capital said about my body—and what I myself thought of it—the roundness was highlighted in a beautiful way tonight. The red fabric was perfectly fitted, forming a second skin. The dip between my breasts glittered with the diamond-like gems. Pino was good at making anyone and everyone look stunning, not that he would ever get the chance to do so again.

My heart stuttered in my chest, the pain of that loss so strange when I had known him for such a short time. Still, it did hurt to know that he would never breathe again. That none of the residents of Haven would breathe again. That Winona would not breathe again.

That was one thing I could not understand, especially as I looked at myself now. Why take away such kind souls and let my blackened one see another day?

"Not much," I finally responded, nothing else coming to mind. Bellamy tsked, his fingers brushing my hair behind my mutilated ears. He had always loved them, though I could not begin to understand why.

"You are so very wrong, Princess." Then his hands were sliding down my back, unbuttoning my dress as they went. I gasped as his warm fingers met my cold skin, the way he maintained eye contact with me as he did so wickedly erotic. "In that mirror is a female brave enough to stand up to those who sought to abuse and belittle her. She is strong enough to fight back against those who wish harm upon her realm. She is kind, though also humble enough to not realize it. She is smart and cunning, always solving problems before they occur. That female is a leader, a warrior, a *survivor.*"

As he spoke, Bellamy let his fingers explore my exposed back, gliding across the skin with teasing strokes. When his hand slid up to my shoulders, tugging the material off, he brought his mouth down. The first scorching press of his lips to my flesh was impossibly satisfying, as if the teasing touches had electrified me. Every swipe of his tongue and graze of his teeth threatened to pull a moan from my lips, melting my core. When my chin tilted up at the pleasure of his tongue on my neck, Bellamy reached around and gripped my jaw. He forced my head back down with his tight hold, making me watch as he tasted me.

When he spoke next, it was against my skin.

"I have dreamed of you for so long, probably even longer than I realized. My wishes and prayers, every ounce of my faith, was directed towards you. I did not only want you. I *needed* you. Now here you are, so close, yet so far. I see it in you, that obsession with being a hero—a savior. Believe me, I think you one too. But now I feel it stealing you away, taking what little time we have."

His speech was tainted with lust, but the words still held weight. They still cut deep, the honesty of them sending pain to my chest, leaving my heart aching and sore. I wanted to deny it, to pretend like I did not place redemption over him—over everyone. But did I deserve any of them if I let the world fall apart?

"If I fail to save us all, then how can I live with myself? How can you love me if I am the evil that I seem destined to be?" I asked, my voice cracking.

One of his hands skated across my peaked nipple, the quick touch making my back arch. Still, I watched, his other hand holding my head firmly in place. When he cupped my breast, his raspy moan vibrating against my neck, I thought I might implode from so many warring emotions.

"You do not ever have to be anything other than yourself with me. My love is not contingent on your success. In fact, I would gladly watch the world burn if it meant you were at my side while it did."

Just as I was about to scold him, to call him a liar and tell him to never say things like that, his hand plummeted. His wicked fingers went past my stomach and immediately between my thighs, finding that sensitive spot with perfect accuracy.

Without thought, I reached up and wrapped my hands behind his neck, the pleasure of his touch leaving me aching for more. He was meticulous, so thorough that I was gasping for breath not long after he began.

"Do you know how often I have touched myself to the image of you? How desperately I crave you? How many times I have come to the memory of my name on your lips? I am sure of few things, Asher. But you, I will always be certain of."

Those fingers plunged into me then, ripping a cry of ecstasy from my lips. With startling force, I realized just how dangerous we were. Our love was made of both honey and venom, a sickly sweet poison that would kill us long before we were satiated.

In and out his fingers went, curving into me despite the tight fabric. As if he could read my thoughts, Bellamy pulled his hands away, quickly tugging down the dress. It put up a valiant fight, sticking to my now scorching body like it never wished to part from me, but Bellamy succeeded. When it was all the way off, he forced me to step out, then tossed the red garment to the side.

I stood in front of the mirror, wearing only my necklace and my heeled shoes. A growl clawed its way up Bellamy's throat as he began the tantalizing task of undressing himself. First to go were his shoes and jacket. He put far less care into preserving his clothing, the black shirt making a slight ripping sound when he pulled it over his head. With him faintly to the side of me, I could see the bulge in his trousers, straining in a way that looked almost painful. If he noticed, he did not say, opting to simply tug off the bottoms and his undergarments in one fell swoop.

Then we were both bare to each other, the image reflected back causing butterflies to take flight in my stomach. He was handsome in a way that many would never see, let alone achieve. No painting would ever be able to depict his raw beauty, which stemmed from his heart in the same way those tattoos of his did.

Pale muscled arms wrapped around me, tracing nonchalant circles across my tan skin. When he brushed over my stomach, slowing down at that spot where it jutted out, I felt my nerves rise. No matter how many times he had told me that he loved every curve, I would likely always fear his rejection.

Yet Bellamy did not flinch or stray. Those icy eyes of his seemed to melt while he watched us in the mirror, his erection growing impossibly larger as it pressed into my back. I moaned when his fingertips pinched at one of my peaked nipples, once more teasing me in the best way.

"Touch yourself, Princess," he whispered into my ear, never ceasing his own movements. Pressing a kiss to the jagged tops, he wrapped one arm more firmly around me, holding my body still from just below my breasts. Then his other hand found my throat, wrapping around it with enough pressure to wrench a gasp from my lips.

Fear did not hold weight in my sex life. Seeking out my pleasure had always been a secret, but it had never been scary. The repercussions, yes. But the act itself? No. I had spent quite a bit of time learning, sampling males from each faction. Once, Nicola and I even had a drunken tryst with a guard. Even my most adventurous moments now seemed tame in comparison to what Bellamy's imagination conjured, though. Still, I would not balk at this challenge.

With the same tantalizing slowness that he had used, I began sliding my hands down my neck. His breathing sped up as I let my fingers drag across my breasts, the feel of it blowing on my ear lighting every nerve on fire. Or perhaps that was Bellamy himself, the heat of his Fire power warming me from the back.

By the time I reached that throbbing spot between my thighs, both of us were practically panting. Bellamy watched my hand as I started to rub firm circles, but I never took my gaze from him. His eyes were heavy, his head still bent down to rest just above my left ear. That hand around my throat tightened vaguely when I dipped my fingers inside of myself, his deep growl paired with the stretch nearly undoing me.

"Do you like watching me?" I asked him, my voice a husky whisper.

At my words, he groaned, and I could not stop the smirk that lifted one side of my lips. Grabbing onto his hand that wrapped around my waist, I dragged it down, stroking myself with his fingers. His sharp hiss mixed with my moan to create a stunning symphony of lust and need.

"Do you feel how wet I am?" He nodded, his tongue darting out to lick his full lips. Knowing that big head of his was inflating, I gleefully smiled and said, "No one knows how to do it like me, it seems."

For a moment, he froze, his eyes wide and mouth open. When my words seemed to register fully, his gaze narrowed. Suddenly, my feet were in the air. I let out a heinous screech of surprise as he brought us both to the ground. My knees hit the rug first, and then he pushed me forward, forcing my breasts and arms down. His hands gripped my hips as he placed a knee on either side of my legs.

Every movement was riddled with need, his reflection not allowing him to hide the desperation there. The hunger.

"So, you think you can take care of yourself better than I can?" he asked. I meant to say something sarcastic, but then I felt him tease my entrance with the head of his member, gliding it up and down. "Does that mean you do not need me anymore, Princess?"

As if to really emphasize how truly wonderful he was at pleasing me, Bellamy stopped sliding himself to quickly slap my backside. I moaned letting my forehead hit the floor, breaking the unspoken rule to not look away.

Hands gripped my hair, pulling until my eyes were once more focused on the two of us. "Watch."

Bellamy's pale skin practically glowed beside my brown, his freckles and tattoos standing out in stark contrast. My gaze lingered on every rippling muscle, his biceps and abs flexing as he tensed behind me. To spite him, I shoved past his mental walls, extinguishing his black flames before he could think to fortify them.

You could use a tan, demon.

Bellamy shoved inside me, my body eagerly making room for the intrusion. I gasped, the pleasure after being taunted making my head swim. Stupid demon did know how to make every second count.

A hand remained tangled in my hair, the other digging into my hip as he thrusted into me, the relentless pace euphoric. He was not gentle tonight, not when he had a point to prove. And as the sounds of our bodies joining filled the room, my eyes fighting against the euphoria to remain open, I said the one thing my mind could conjure.

"I love you."

His head flew back, exposing his throat. Just as the pleasure claimed me, his name leaving my lips in a cry of ecstasy, I watched Bellamy's tattoos *move*. They crept further up his neck, like snakes slinking across the ground. My eyes won then, finally squeezing tight as wave after wave of bliss washed through me, the orgasm leaving me a shaking and gasping mess.

Upon realizing I had come, Bellamy sped up, his hips thrusting harder. I opened my eyes right as he finished, his own screams drowned out by the roar of the fire coming to life in the previously unlit fireplace. The flames were black, shooting upwards with violent force. For a heartbeat, I feared that Bellamy would burn the castle to the ground, but then they disappeared as quickly as they were conjured. He crumpled, his arms grabbing me at the last second to flip us.

We both laid there, my head on his chest and his lips pressed to my hair, as we caught our breath. After a moment of silence, I looked up at him, inspecting his tattoos. They were no longer moving, the very tips now barely grazing his collarbones again. I wanted to ask, but my fear of an answer I would not like won out against my curiosity.

A flash of white appeared just to my left, saving me from having to say anything. Orange hair obstructed my vision before a pair of green eyes met mine.

"It is terribly rude of you to have sex in someone else's home," Henry said.

CHAPTER EIGHTEEN

ASHER

Bellamy quickly covered Henry's eyes to hide my body, his annoyed huff somehow sounding menacing.

"Oh, please, like we have not had a naked female between us before." Henry's words earned him a smack to the back of the head, and then I was covered in shadows, the inky blackness turning heavy before my silver cloak met my skin. "Besides, I am sure I will have you both in my bed at some point in our lives. I am way too attractive to resist."

This time it was me who reached up and slapped the back of the Sun's head, causing him to lean forward with a grunt. He muttered something along the lines of "assholes" before standing up.

"Well, I am off to grovel at the feet of a bitchy mortal. When you dream of me naked tonight, little brat, remember that my cock is proportionate to my exceptionally large body."

I burst into laughter at Henry's words, which earned an angry growl from Bellamy—a muscle in his jaw ticking.

"Seeing as I am privy to how you look in skin-tight leather, I think it is safe to say there is nothing there that is of particular interest to me," I teased, watching as his hand met his chest with his mouth agape in false horror. Bellamy was all too eager to chime in, speaking before Henry could respond.

"As Henry said, we are both intimately aware of what the other's body looks like, and I can confirm that his size is just as unimpressive as his technique. The females had loads of complaints at the end." With that, Henry rolled his eyes and stormed out, Bellamy and I laughing as he did.

We remained wrapped up in each other for a few moments before Bellamy forced me up to clean off. He led us to a bathing chamber, the yellow door matching the walls so perfectly that I had not noticed it before. The greens and yellows were nauseating, so I closed my eyes and let Bellamy take over—giggled when he tickled my feet after removing my shoes. As he washed me off, the two of us soaking in water he had conjured and heated, I drifted off into a rest far more peaceful than I deserved.

***

"I feel as though it should be considered taboo to only open your mind to me after you fuck that abomination."

I felt the scream tear free of me before I heard it, the ear-splitting sound not so much as reverberating off of the nothingness.

I whipped my head back and forth, trying to gain my bearings. Truly, there is only so much a fae can take before they lose their mind, and I feared I was on the cusp as I frantically tried to understand where I was.

After a moment, my mind focused, and I realized that I was once more in that strange space I had dreamed of before. Which meant that the voice had been...

"Hello, Padon."

A content sigh escaped him, as if there were no place more blissful than here.

I turned, facing the direction his voice had come from. He stood nearby in the endless space, which was once more both light and dark— nothing and everything. His outfit this time was more intricate, regal even. He wore all black, the long-sleeve shirt held together by gold buttons. The swirls of gold and silver that crawled up the tight-fitting trousers and shirt formed some sort of strange image I could not decipher. Atop his head, that purple hair still chopped messily, was the same sharp and jagged crown from last time.

"My name on your lips is even more delicious than I imagined."

Ignoring the creature, I looked down, trying to assess what I was wearing. The same black slip, its silk shining in a light that was both there and not. "You could at least dress me in something less scandalous," I said nonchalantly, my shoulders lifting into a shrug.

Padon chuckled, an eerie sound that seemed to dig into my bones. When his feet began moving, the space between us quickly closing, I realized just how menacing his presence truly was. Padon stopped in front of me, his height forcing me to tilt my head back. A smile lifted the corners of his mouth, chilling in its perfection. Watching as he reached a hand out to me, I noted the blue blush spreading quickly across his nearly translucent skin. His fingers were ice cold against my cheek, the drag of them across my face and over my ear so strangely familiar.

"I'm sorry this was done to you. You deserved better." As he spoke, Padon seemed to trace the shape of a fae ear, fixing what was ruined.

I flinched away from the contact, needing space from him. Why did he bring me here? What did he want with me?

"You know what I want, Asher. Deep down, you know." I wanted to rip my hair out at his insinuation—at the thought of one more creature trying to use me.

A toy, that was what I was. A thing to pass around and be played with until I no longer pleased my owner. How fitting, to be disposable in such a way when I could not seem to get rid of myself. Maybe I would get lucky and Padon would do it for me. Prevent the world from ending by simply ending me.

If only it were that easy.

"That's quite the bleak turn your thoughts took. Is there a reason you're so upset?" he inquired, one of his purple brows raising. His eyes were still a bright white as they assessed me, practically glowing. I began walking away from him, heading in no particular direction seeing as the never-ending space appeared to act as a sort of prison.

"Do you not already know? It seems like you have more access to the mind than I do." At that, I froze, even my breathing halting momentarily. The mind. Padon had manipulation powers—magic—whatever it was, he had it too. "You are like me."

That terrifying and infuriating laugh came again, the sound like a beacon, trying to grab me and pull me into him. I wanted to hate this creature, if only for the things he said about Bellamy.

"Unfortunately, I don't have the same magic you do. What you possess is something else entirely. I can wait for you to open yourself to me, for your magic to call to me and then answer. The reason I know what you're thinking is because you're practically speaking those thoughts into my mind. You are in control here. Mostly."

I shook my head, as if I could empty it of those words. I had not called to him. There was no way I could seek out what I did not know or understand.

"Perhaps if you spent less time stalking females who want nothing to do with you, then you would be able to come up with a more convincing lie." It was an immature thing to say, like a youngling stomping their foot and insulting someone to get a rise from them. Even worse was that it only seemed to encourage the creature.

"You have such an addictive presence, has anyone ever told you that? I feel as if I could spend an eternity with you and it would still never be enough." His cool breath hit my ear as he spoke, the feeling causing goosebumps to rise on my skin. "I fear that no food or water will ever satisfy me again now that I have tasted the air which you breathe."

Scoffing at his obsessive behavior, I stepped away from his body, resisting the gravity of it that attempted to force me to him. He had far more control than he was willing to admit, and we both knew it.

"What do you want me for? A slave? A whore? Is that why you hate Bellamy so much?" My questions were pointed, full of building rage and dread that threatened to swallow me whole. Not that I would balk from living in a chasm of misery when my own mind seemed to be just as horrifying.

"You are no one's whore. Don't ever say that again." The threat in his voice was obvious, a source of tension I had not realized was there before. Did he care about me? "Of course I do, you foolish female. I care more than any other living being, including your prince who you seem so set on loving. I can sense your apprehension with him, the lies you know he tells and the secrets you know he keeps. Despite that, you don't even attempt to find answers. It's a pity and a waste of your potential."

Red-hot fury filled me, and suddenly, I was facing him, my fist swinging. But he dodged my blow easily, moving just out of reach before grabbing onto my hand. Without thinking about the consequences, I dove into his mind, seeking a foothold as I ripped my fingers out of his grasp. The walls there were strong, like gray bricks stacked on top of one another to prevent entry.

Only more aggravated now, I shoved him with both of my hands and stormed away. Stubbornness ate at my mind, leaving my breaths heavy and my vision swimming. Instead of continuing forward, I spun, quickly facing back towards Padon. His answering smile was playful, his eyes alight and hands in the pockets of his trousers.

"You know nothing about me or him. And what do you expect me to do?" I asked, readying for a fight. I did not even know who this male really was, and still, I was fearless as I closed the distance that I had been so desperate for before. We were toe-to-toe, neither of us so much as flinching at the contact.

"I *expect* you to use all of that magic you have been gifted. I *expect* you to take what you want rather than waiting for it to be given."

For a moment, his eyes flicked down to my lips, but just as quickly, they were up once more, boring into mine. I wanted to gouge them from the sockets. I wanted to show him how powerful I could be.

"He has mental walls as strong as yours!"

"Then break them." A shrug and an eye roll, then he was still again. As if it were that easy.

"I cannot do that to him—I *will* not do that to him. I love him." Why was I telling him this? Why was I entertaining him?

My words, or maybe my thoughts, finally ruffled him. He bristled, white eyes a burning inferno. The fear that I had not felt before engulfed me. I backed up, but Padon followed, matching each of my steps. Reaching out, he grabbed either side of my face, his hands so large they seemed to cradle my entire head.

"Then break *him.*" I froze, not ready to accept that this creature, whatever he was, meant every threat he wished upon Bellamy. Upon the love of my life. "Loving a mortal is pointless. All it will bring you is heartache."

None of his words made sense, now more than ever. My mind felt like a cyclone of emotions—all of the feelings I tried so hard to hold back fighting their way to the surface. My head shook of its own accord, denying the male's words.

"He is not mortal. We are not."

"Slow aging isn't the same as undying, my love. They are a watered-down version of what a true immortal is. You, I can make *more*. I can give you strength beyond your wildest imagination. With my help you will never die, never fall. That thing tells you that he will burn the world for you? Well I will end it with a mere flick of my wrist. For you, I will destroy all of those beings who hated, judged, and belittled you. Any place full of creatures who see you as a monster rather than the salvation you are deserves the doom I will wreak upon it."

"Gods! Why do all of you think I need the world to be ended for me? Why do you think that I want that? There is no reality in which I wish doom upon a world full of innocents. All you both want is to spare me, but I cannot be spared! I *am* a monster. The only ones who need sparing are those I endanger. How do you not see that?"

"You are not. All who have made you believe so shall find themselves suffering slow and painful deaths." Again, a shrug. Whatever he was offering, the delusional male thought he could make good on it.

"Oh, so you will just murder all of my enemies?" I asked sarcastically, the burning cold of his fingers stinging as I attempted to break free of his grasp.

"Do you want me to?" His face drew closer, his desire for not only me but death as well, apparent. It radiated off of him in waves, pressing into my skin and igniting that bloodlust I so desperately tried to hide.

There was a hidden meaning to his question, and I knew that, if I told him yes, he would go farther than just my enemies. Without a shadow of a doubt, I knew Bellamy's body would lay at my feet if I allowed this creature any free rein.

"No. I do not believe you would stop at two fae royals." A smile lifted his cheeks, not quite meeting his eyes. Both thumbs slid back and forth across my skin, the casual touch seeming absentminded.

One day I would cut those thumbs off and shove them up his ass.

"Good girl." With that, he leaned in and placed a gentle kiss to my lips. Faster than before, I attacked, this time opting to lift my knee into his groin and hoping it hurt him just as badly as it had hurt Sterling. Though touching him felt odd in this place—far away and distant.

Satisfaction filled my chest when he released me with a grunt of pain, bending over at the waist. I knelt, bringing my mouth to his ear. "I am no mere girl. Mortal girls are weaker and quick to die. If I were so small, the world that rests upon my shoulders would have crushed me long ago."

When I stood, so did Padon, his throaty chuckles filling the space—his mind, apparently. "That is a good thing, Asher."

"One might think so, but the mortals live a different way." How could I explain what I had learned in such a brief time within the Mortal Realm? "They love harder and move faster, desperately seeking success. Their time is limited in ways I cannot fathom, so they are braver and kinder. Forgetting and forgiving is practically second nature to them because they cannot waste what little life they have. I envy them that. But if I wish to save Alemthian, then I must be *more*."

And maybe, when I become more, I will be able to dig out the self-hatred that had been buried inside of me. Perhaps when I save Alemthian, I will finally feel as if I deserve to walk upon its soil. If I am lucky, that future will exist and I will live.

"It's far easier to destroy than it is to mend. Take my hand, Asher, and we can start over. Together we can rebuild that world into something far more fit for you." With that, he reached out said hand, which I promptly ignored in favor of a scowl.

"What world are you from, if not this one? Will you tell me that?" I watched as his hand fell, stretching out at his side before closing into a fist. A glare that would likely bring anyone not as stupid as me to tears was leveled my way.

"No. Figure that out on your own. If you want answers, then find them. Stop waiting for someone to give what you can take." Padon crossed his arms, the muscles beneath straining against the black and gold sleeves.

Showoff.

"Does keeping things from me not make you just like the male you so often criticize?" Circling him, I smiled, knowing that he would have to follow my movements if he wanted to maintain his oh-so-threatening gaze. He wanted to play games? Then I would set the rules. Padon began to spin right along with me, as though he was ready to follow them.

"Trusting that you are strong enough to get what you want isn't the same as lying to you in hopes you never discover the truth."

Fair enough.

"Will you at least tell me what you are? Or do I have to figure that out by myself as well?"

Padon came to me with a speed too fast to track, cutting off my path and snatching my hand. "Let me show you."

With that, the area around us changed, morphing into something real and tangible. We stood in a throne room of sorts. The marble floors below our feet shone back a morphed reflection of us, the matching gray walls and vaulted ceilings making the room seem endless. Crystal chandeliers hung from the ceiling, each boasting multiple tiers and burning candles. Through the wall of towering windows to my left, a bright blue-green hue tinted the sky. Violent and ground-shaking screeches sounded from somewhere beyond, mixing with what could only be described as beating wings.

My eyes flicked over to the imposing gray throne on the far wall. It was atop a storm-colored dais, the stairs leading up to it the same shining marble as the floors. Padon appeared then, materializing on the throne with all the comfort of a long-standing ruler.

"I am an emperor, a conqueror of worlds. Just as you will be." With a snap of his fingers, a second, identical throne popped into existence beside his. I gasped as I felt a strange tingle across my skin. Looking down, I watched the black slip morph into something new.

Dark branches and leaves snaked up my body, the design so impossibly similar to a tree that my jaw went slack. Sections remained missing, exposing my light brown flesh below in far too many places. Sheer black sleeves suddenly began to cover my arms, the wispy and flowing fabric adorned with diamonds in a similar way to how my red dress had been.

"That's why others seek you out. They sense that greatness within you. Despite the way they fear it, they also desire it. As you can see, I have all the magic I need, so I don't covet you for the same reasons they do. All I want is *you*. No one else will ever do that, not even your precious prince. If not me, then you risk a life of loneliness and mediocrity."

A single blink, and then I was beside him, sitting on that matching throne. He reached up, grabbing onto his crown and pulling it off. As he placed the symbol of his reign atop my head, he whispered something that made my teeth grind.

"There is no limit to what I can give you, Asher. All I ask is that you love me."

He would not manipulate me. There was no longer time for me to wallow and let others use that as a weapon. I would turn that sadness and fear and self-hatred into anger. I would let my fury burn as hot as the sun, allowing it to consume and scorch and scar me.

Shooting up from my seat, I whirled on him, hoping that every ounce of the wicked thing within me was finding its way to the forefront—ready to bear its teeth and flash its claws.

"I will not be your *anything*. I am no one's but my own, and I will not be used ever again. If they think me evil, then let them."

When I lifted my hands, quickly slashing them out in a downward strike, the image around us crumbled. Padon had only a moment to shout my name before the dream was over, and suddenly, I was letting out a piercing scream of terror and fury, the yellow and green room in Jore back once more.

Bellamy sat beside me, his eyes full of emotions I could not read after giving so much of my power to the dream. Magic—that was what Padon had called it. And he was not the only one.

The prince's hand was hovering in the air, as if he were unsure whether or not he could touch me. Scooting away from him, I breathed deeply and tried to focus my mind.

My whole body shook, the weight of my dream and Padon's determination and the universe itself bearing down on my chest. The endless burden of it tried to crush my heart, my spirit, my *soul*. I felt it there, but I was stronger than I knew, and perhaps I could fight.

Magic or not, it was time to stop holding back. Soon everyone would know what it was like to witness the wrath of a desperate and angry princess.

I was coming for any who stood in my way, and no amount of preparation would save them now.

CHAPTER NINETEEN

ASHER

"Do you want to talk about it?" Bellamy's question came after nearly an hour of allowing me space to process. He had filled yet another bath, adding lavender and vanilla after heating it up then carefully placed me into it. I sighed, knowing that he would soon ask questions I was not sure I could answer.

"No." Not if I could help it. His jaw tensed, the muscles there twitching as his anger momentarily snuck through that fiery shield of his. I would have laughed if it was not so ridiculous.

"We need to discuss this, Asher. You cannot simply pretend you are okay." His words left me bristling, any attempt at composure failing before it could be executed. How could I explain that I would drown if I wallowed in the sorrow? In the pain? I no longer had the capacity to float within my emotions. It was swim or die.

Briefly, my mind flashed back to the moment he had found me in his piano room, the sound of him hitting the floor jarring me awake. I had been so upset with him for finding me because I knew then what I still know now—the world was better off without me in it. But if I were going to stay, then I needed to move forward rather than remain stagnant.

"Why ask a question if you are only willing to accept one answer?" From his spot on the floor beside the porcelain tub, Bellamy fumbled on his words.

I knew he meant well, he always did. Whatever Pino showed Bellamy had been promising because he seemed to think I was his future.

One thing Nicola had always told me was that the future was forever changing—there was no assurance in the visions of a Tomorrow. Even those of the Yesterdays were unreliable, as they were through the eyes of whoever's past it was—whoever the Reader touched. Pino had been different, of course, his ability to see both past and present something my mind could not even comprehend, but that did not mean his visions were a guarantee.

Bellamy knew this, yet still, he seemed determined to make me the center of his world, regardless of how unworthy I was of such a thing.

"Tell me, are your secrets somehow less damning than mine? Is the fact that you have refused to be completely honest with me since the day we met not just as horrible as my choice not to detail out my nightmares and feelings?" It was a low blow, but I was not finished, and for some reason I felt that the fire below my feet had to burn brighter or I would harden into a block of ice. The water around me even seemed colder now, as if threatening to freeze over if I did not push harder.

"I thought you understood that there was a right time to explain it all. If I give you all of the answers you want right now, then I risk—"

"I do not care about what you have seen! Why must you neglect the present for a future that might never come to pass? I cannot wait around for you to deign to give me answers, Bellamy. I am not some pet who sits and stays until you are ready to walk me. I lived two centuries of lies and manipulation, I cannot do that again!" My angry hand gestures caused waves in the tub, some of the water escaping and splashing onto Bellamy. He did not seem to care though. Instead, his eyes stayed focused on mine, refusing to break contact. Never one to back down from a challenge of will, I stared right back.

"Choose what you say carefully, Ash, because there is no antidote for the poison of a few words. They often kill faster than a blade." Without thought, I stood, even more water sloshing over the edge. Bellamy rose to his feet as well, the way he looked down on me necessary but still infuriating.

We were on the cusp of something dangerous. I knew it, and so did he. It was a hazard to fight when tension already coiled in my stomach like a knot, but I could not stop myself from squaring my shoulders and clenching my teeth.

I felt it then, the tug to take what I wanted from his mind. To force him into honesty.

"Then break *him*."

A chill crawled up my spine as Padon's words echoed through my mind. Break him. Break him. Break him. *Break. Him.*

On instinct, my arms wrapped around me, trying to contain the bloodlust, the pain, all of it. There was always another path, another choice. Yes, I would sacrifice many things, but Bellamy was not one of them. I did not need him, nor did I need anyone. He was not the sun, the center of my universe keeping me in orbit. But I did want him. His love and hope and strength, I *wanted* those things.

"I am sorry, but I need something, Bell. Anything. All I ask for is one truth, which I promise to give in return." Could an ultimatum be spoken without threat? Without being explicitly said? If so, I had given one just then. It was in the roughness of my tone and the widening of my eyes as I continued to stare up at him, not even my shivers from the cold enough to deter me.

Deep breaths lifted his chest, the slow and heavy movements speaking volumes on just how close to the edge he was too. Ever since losing so many in Haven, we had both been teetering on a cliff littered with shards of glass. We were forced to choose the path forward, excruciating and long, or the path down, less painful but also fatal.

That was the problem. Tragedy always seemed so close by, like a pest constantly flying past our ears. No matter how many times we swatted it away, it came right back.

With loss, grief, anger, and lies between us, tragedy was not far away. I felt that sorrow of knowing I was going to lose something in that moment. Bellamy loved me in ways I could not fathom, possibly ways I could never love him in return, but everyone had their limits. As I waited with bated breath, the dread settled within me. I prepared myself for the punishment—or worse, the goodbye.

To my surprise, Bellamy did not hit me or yell at me or even walk away. Instead, he sighed before stepping into the water, his body still without clothes from our time together earlier in the night. His arms wrapped around me, pulling us down until we were both sitting, somewhat submerged and limbs tangled. A reminder that perhaps love did not always come with pain—that Bellamy had never been the royals, and he never would be.

When his hands grabbed either side of my face, warm and right and so different from Padon's touch, I felt a tear slide down my cheek. The part of me that still sounded like Mia chastised me for my constant crying.

"Be strong, do not feel deeply or allow others to see your weakness," Mia used to say.

It seemed that I was only capable of the opposite these days. I tried to harden myself again, to remember that anger, but then Bellamy leaned in and shattered every defense I had. With a kiss on my forehead, then my chin, then both of my cheeks, and finally my nose, he soothed me.

"When we first heard about you, King Adbeel and I had assumed you were infused with foreign magic at birth. Some type that we had never seen before, from a creature we knew nothing of. There was something so odd about Eternity gracing you with a power that was previously unheard of. Why you? Why then? Why at all? None of it made sense, and we feared what lengths the fae would go to in the hopes of conquering."

I stilled, too stunned to even breathe. Every word felt like a stab to my chest, tiny pieces of iron shredding through me. Bellamy's eyes searched mine, as if desperate for a reprieve from the honesty. There was so much fear there within their icy depths, so many layers of hardened water beneath that all other feelings were distorted and far away.

"Infused into me? Is that even possible? I have never heard of something like that before." Questions swirled through my mind, each begging to be acknowledged and answered.

But it was when Bellamy's eyes flitted down to the now-writhing tattoos crawling their way up his hands that something within me clicked.

Bellamy never called King Adbeel Ayad his father. He never wielded his shadows in the same way that Noe did, the magic always manifesting through his fae power or when portaling. The tattoos were like veins, as if something dark flowed through his blood. He never said "we" when referencing demons.

Our discussion about the afterlife had consisted of him telling me what demons believe, not what he believes. His ears, his power, his emotions riling up his magic, the way he seemed to always separate himself from demonkind. Slowly, cautiously, I brought my fingers to his tattoos—no, his *magic*. I was sure of it then.

Bellamy was not demon at all.

"They forced magic into my veins not long after I was born. It nearly killed me. Pino showed me. I watched visions of myself screaming and convulsing, looking for all the world as if I was being tortured. When my tiny body finally settled, Moon magic started attacking me from the inside, like poison in my veins. The demon who had worked with my parents placed a ward on my heart, ancient magic that protected me from being consumed by that which did not belong." Pausing, he grabbed my fingers, stilling them. I looked on as his eyes scrunched closed, a muscle ticking in his jaw. "Adbeel thinks that is why I developed an affinity to all four elements. His running assumption is that my power tried to balance out the magic, to combat it. Or maybe it was Eternity giving me a fighting chance." His hands shook against mine, the truth sitting between us like a tangible being.

An urge to soothe him—to make sense of something so horrid and settle that pain I felt steadily tainting the air—came to me. I nearly choked on the force of it, the taste sour in my mouth. Every ounce of anger melted away, my heart only capable of breaking now. When he let go of my hands, backing up slightly, I quickly followed him. Wide blue eyes stared at me as I climbed onto his lap, so many versions of a single apology on the tip of my tongue.

Smoothing his wild black waves down, the hair becoming damp, I brought my forehead to his. Bellamy lost so much in such a short amount of time, two beings who had been like family to him as well as an entire village of fae that he had saved.

For the first time, I wondered if Bellamy felt guilt similar to mine. Over a month had passed of me wallowing in my own feelings, not considering the fact that he likely suffered in the same way. After focusing so much on his grief and sorrow, I realized now that I had overlooked the regret and accountability he likely suffocated on.

"I am so sorry, Bellamy." His shoulders fell, body slumping forward. Leaning on me, I realized. "I love you—not because of or despite where you come from, but for who you are. I know I can be difficult, that sometimes I am unfair to you, and I will not pretend that it is okay. I do know, though, that you deserve all the love in the world."

And when I grabbed him, pulling him into an embrace, I decided that I would do better—*be* better. He wrapped his arms around me, the tightness of the hold oddly comforting.

"I see you, all of you, and I am not afraid," I whispered, my lips gently grazing his bare shoulder.

I wanted to know more—to understand how Bellamy came to be under Adbeel's care, where his parents were now, what he thought my magic was, if they suspected that Mia and Xavier had done it after my parents' deaths or…if my parents had done this to me.

But right now, while I basked in the presence of the male I loved and who loved me, all I could do was trust him with a truth too. As we both sat in the space where mistakes and remorse collided, I spoke.

"They are not always nightmares. Sometimes, I am visi—"

"You wretched little thing, I cannot believe you were going to leave me in that poor excuse for an inn while you slept in this—albeit hideous—castle!"

Bellamy and I both startled at the sudden presence beside us, the eerie voice a chilling sound that had us separating. Or perhaps the cold was from the water which Bellamy had instantly iced with his power.

Wrath sat perched on the side of the tub, looking incredibly bored. His soft fur and swishing tail were a strange contrast to his yellow eyes, but I was used to it by now, seeing as the tiny menace had not left my side for the last two days. Bellamy had only ever heard of the dalistori through notes though, so his instant wariness and confusion was not surprising.

"Twice we have been walked in on tonight. That might not seem like a lot to you, Wrathy, but it is quite strange that two creatures who are not Bellamy have seen me nude in a matter of hours."

In front of me, Bellamy stared open-mouthed at Wrath, who briefly glared at me for the nickname before licking his paw casually. Stifling my growing laugh, I reached over to a nearby wooden rack and snatched one of the green towels.

"It seems this conversation will have to wait."

"Yes, it seems so." Bellamy's growled words were followed by a vicious glare towards Wrath. The dalistori rolled his eyes in return. I chuckled, leaning into Bellamy in the hopes that only he would hear what I was about to say.

"Just so you know, I am still calling you 'demon'. If only because you have a knack for tempting me in a way only wicked things can," I whispered into his ear, offering him a kiss to his lips after. He groaned, but I slid free of him before he could get ahold of me. Then I stood, wrapping the towel around my body and exiting the tub.

"Disgusting." Wrath's bored and annoyed response towards my statement was all it took to send Bellamy into a mood, his loud huff and shaking of his towel telling me he was not a fan. He and Henry were about to have an incredible bonding experience.

I laughed, enjoying the small break from the everlasting intensity that filled my life. My feet slid on the ground, the cold making my teeth chatter. Leave it to me to skip over spring and summer by going South.

Heading back over to my red dress, a piece of gold fabric shone in my peripheral. I froze, not wanting to make eye contact with whatever garment sat atop the large bed.

Please say that is not for me.

Bellamy cocked his head to the side, the yellow towel around his hips low enough to show that indecent V shape as well as the magic below his veins. If magic had been infused into me, then why did I not have the same lines? Why did I not suffer the same pain he had?

Or maybe I did and I simply do not remember. Perhaps whoever did that to me had perfected it by the time I was ready. Could that be why I constantly felt my manipulation abilities, like they were something distinctly other?

Before he could make it to the bed, Bellamy froze, his eyes wide and darting back and forth, as if he were searching for something. A moment later, and his palm was up, shadows twirling around it until a pencil wrapped with paper appeared. Despite knowing that this would mean goodbye, I watched him open it with pointless hope.

"Shit. Fuck!" The prince looked at me, his stare burning. Yes, he would leave now with so many truths left unspoken. Once again, the universe was creating a fissure between us, and perhaps that was the biggest sign of what would come.

"Go. I understand. Write when you can, but focus on what is important." I silently prayed to Eternity that I looked somewhat believable in my conviction.

Appearing unconvinced, Bellamy sighed. Then, as if not able to help himself, he closed the distance between us, both of his hands releasing his towel to cup my face. Our lips met, and the world ceased to exist. There was only Bellamy and I and this moment. A kiss like this could kill, could starve, could heal. It was charging, like a storm building up in the sky, the energy so all-encompassing that everyone in the area could surely feel it. My arms wrapped around his neck, red dress still in one hand while the other gripped the black mess of waves at the back of his head.

When the shadows enveloped him, pulling him away from me, Bellamy muttered one final sentiment.

"I love you."

And then he was gone, only Wrath and I remaining.

Bellamy never said goodbye, and I wondered if that was because he feared what it implied. An ending of sorts. A confirmed period at the close of a sentence. Something final. In my chest, my *magic* stirred, as did my growing panic. Stuffing down those feelings, I did everything I could to remind myself of the decades of training I had been given on proper expressions. I was not a youngling. I could manage my emotions.

With a deep breath, I dropped the red dress and walked over to the bed. A floor-length golden gown was there, the silk thin. The designer had gathered parts, creating small folds on each side of the waist. The small straps, nearly as narrow as a needle, were black, as were the silk slippers beside it.

My heart picked up, a bit of sweat beading on my neck despite the way my body shook from the cold. Bellamy's black flames still roared in the fireplace from when he had lit it upon my waking, but they felt more like ice than fire—the strange searing heat like a cold burn as it kissed my skin.

The dress was beautiful, though not as incredible as what Pino had crafted time and time again. But could I wear it? What would it feel like for anything gold to grace my skin? If I did, was that conceding to Mia and Xavier? Would they metaphorically win?

Subconsciously, I started chewing on my lip, tearing at the skin there and likely making my mouth look horrid. Mia had always hated that. She said beauty was a female's strongest weapon and that, when cultivated, one could conquer with their looks alone. My lips took from my beauty, stole it away and left me with a face empty save for the imperfections once hidden beneath.

In the last couple of months, I had sealed away all that was taught to me in my two hundred years of being a ward to Mia and Xavier. It felt easy to gild those ideas, beliefs, and rules, imprisoning them. But sometimes, I felt that gold seeping into other parts of my mind.

It was Wrath's bored expression and confused eyes as he jumped onto the bed and got comfortable that made me realize I already knew the answer to my own question.

Yes, I cared. Even if it was stupid, even if it was dramatic, I cared about what putting gold on my body meant. And I could not do it.

Shaking my head, I backed away from the dress.

"Is this some sort of test? What am I expected to do? *Wear* that?" When I hit the wall, I felt the tremors begin, once more looking far weaker than I wanted. Not again. I could not break apart and show so many feelings—so much pain. What would they think of me if I broke down over a *dress?* "It is hideous, and I will not put it on."

Wrath looked far more concerned than before, his hair standing on edge and body growing. With as much dignity as I could muster when acting like a fool, I tightened my towel and proceeded to run out of the room. Cheeks heated and heart racing, I stumbled forward in the halls, opening every unlocked door in a desperate attempt to find Henry.

But after scaling a set of yellow stairs and rushing through yet another hallway, I found myself in front of a set of faded green double doors, the handles a strange brassy color. I ripped them open, not hesitating to dive into the unlit room. I could not search any longer, could not do anything other than fall to the floor in a fit of sobs.

My knees hit first, quickly followed by my free hand. The tears tore through my body, crashing waves of betrayal in a sea of remembered pain.

Bellamy was gone, likely throwing himself into harm's way to protect innocents with the remainder of his Trusted. Nicola, Farai, and Jasper were surrounded by vipers with golden scales. Winona and Pino were fucking *dead*.

And I could not breathe.

How many times would I die upon a floor until it finally stuck? Eternity might bless the world yet and end me now. What an embarrassing way to break, at the hands of silk and past hurts, nearly naked on the floor of someone else's home.

Even with the knowledge that anyone could have seen me running through the halls in only a towel, I still could not do anything but gasp for air and feel everything. With the last dregs of my strength, I let my mental gates open and tried to pull in any emotion outside of my own.

To my surprise, there was a mind not far away, full of curiosity and empathy.

Shah.

I looked up, grasping at my throat as I did, and there she was. Atop a seat built just below a wide window, which provided a beautiful view of the star-filled sky and vast expanse of trees, sat the Queen of Behman. Despite the sight, her eyes remained trained on me, the dark depths of them lit by the moon and so extensive they seemed endless. It was terrifying how much I saw inside of them.

Her thoughts raced—her mind just as full as that gaze.

Why was I there? What was wrong with me? What should she do? Was it a panic attack? Was someone hurting me?

On and on, question after question until I forced that stupid golden gate closed, watching it slam and locking it tight. Then I shook my head, my damp hair whipping back and forth as I tried to rid myself of everything. Tears still quickly fell down my cheeks, the salty taste of them drying out my mouth.

How should I explain that I was drowning above water? Suffocating on a color that had smothered me my entire life?

Shah stood, coming into clearer view the closer she got. Whatever this room was, she knew it well to be walking so gracefully in the dark. And as if our nearness made her realize exactly what was happening, she sighed, finally speaking to me.

"Breathe, Asher. You must breathe through it, or those demons—pardon my term—will eat you alive." Her voice sounded far away, like words shouted down a tunnel.

My soul felt weak and dim, like a candle nearly snuffed out, burning on a spent wick. What I would give to simply stop. To take this aching pain in my chest and pounding beat in my head and shut it all off.

"Asher, you cannot let yourself fall. You are a queen. You are a survivor. Do not let them win." And then Shah's arms were around me, her larger build and height allowing her to embrace me fully. She smelled divine, like lemon and lavender, both invigorating and lulling. This would not be a horrible place to die, in the arms of someone who understood. "You will not die."

Had I said that out loud? What a ridiculous thing to say. She probably thought me mad. Maybe I was. Perhaps whatever evil magic was inside of me was slowly stripping me of my sanity now that it had taken so much of my conscience.

"Breathe." Shah's voice was soft, her accent as soothing as the hand that stroked my hair.

Just then, so eerily similar to how it had on sentencing days, rain began to fall. The sound of it hitting the castle drowned out my mental voice, allowing me a lull long enough to take in a desperate breath of air, the first full one since Bellamy had left. Had that been minutes ago? Or hours?

Shah shushed me, her hand moving down to rub circles on my back as my sobs slowed. Through each breath, I told myself to morph the sorrow into something else, just as I promised I would when on Padon's throne.

Turn it into rage. Turn it into vengeance. Anything other than the gaping hole of torment and sadness in my chest.

And so I did.

CHAPTER TWENTY

BELLAMY

The most interesting thing about war was choosing which side to fight for. Whichever one picked would say more about who they were than any misdeed or act of service. Laying down one's life for a cause was something that took absolute conviction.

Well, normally it did.

Perhaps that was why portaling into a battle zone did not spark the kind of hatred it should. Because, as I landed in Grishel, I was met with the sight of fae warriors forced to fight for a cause—a realm—they likely did not fully believe in. Led by royals who cared little that they sent many of them to die today.

Hot air met my face, my armor still dirty from the battle yesterday, leaving the scent of warming blood to fester. The desert of Grishel was not a friendly place to those who were foreign to its scorching weather. Like the gold-clad soldiers ahead, I was not built for the heat. It made me slower than normal, a feeling that unsettled me as I portaled once more, landing in the center of the fray.

One thing that was immediately clear was that our side was losing. This was the largest battalion Betovere had sent, at least a thousand soldiers fighting under the fae banner.

Over the years, I had learned that my fae powers could be conjured from nothing, just like an Element. However, it took more out of me to create something from nothing, rather than utilize what was around me. Which was why, as I crafted shards of ice, my chest burned. Hundreds of them rose into the air, aiming for the waiting second line of defense in the distance.

Calling to the wind, I willed the ice to fly. At first, the fae there did not notice, all bearing witness to the fight that they smugly thought they would win. It was not until a shouted warning came from the single soldier that stood slightly ahead that they realized what was coming for them.

Many attempted to raise their shields, the thick golden protection far too heavy to lift in time. Ice tore through flesh, my aim true as over half of them fell with frozen weapons embedded into their faces.

And then I was moving once more, my sword of inky flames burning through armor and bone.

Noe appeared at my side momentarily, whips of hardened shadow wrapping around necks and beheading soldiers. She was strong, her magic able to form tangible objects in ways that many could not. Her father had cultivated and abused it in the hopes of forging his own weapon. But now, she wielded herself, not allowing anyone to control her ever again.

Her screams of fury were loud as she watched a Shifter rip off the arm of a demon, the female shrieking in agony before the fae sunk its teeth into her face. When Noe jumped onto the panther's back, digging her fingers into its fur like claws and forcing her Moon magic into it, I let out a wicked and throaty chuckle. The Shifter was dead before it hit the ground.

The moment of distraction cost me, a blade skimming across my cheek before I could dodge it fully. My helmetless head reared back, the pain making me hiss through my teeth. I knew I forgot something.

An arrow found its new home in the fae's eye just as I lifted my sword. For a moment she remained standing with her mouth agape, but then she crumpled, her body limp. I turned, seeing Lian behind me and feeling the rush of her Air power rumple my hair. She had dropped her bow, opting to use wind to send the arrows careening, never missing. She attributed her power to her uncanny ability to wield weapons, but I knew the truth. It was pure fury and dedication that got her where she was.

Instead of allowing myself to be distracted again, I summoned my flames, further deepening that inner ache as I brought a second sword to the air. Kicking my foot into the chest of a Golden Guard, the force of my blow sent him flying into one of his comrades. A nearby demon bent down, shoving a dagger into each of their foreheads.

Without hesitation, I moved on, cutting them down as quickly as I could. There was only so much I could manage with my fae abilities when my soldiers were in such close proximity to my enemies, which left me utilizing my sword far more than normal. Still, I pushed forward, dodging shadows, light, water, air, fire, and earth. Shifters also littered the space, most of them Multiples that could take on any form they would like. The benefit to that was their waning energy, the power it took to shift limiting them.

After slicing through seven more soldiers, I came to an abrupt halt at the sight of a familiar face. One I should not know. One that would not know me.

Farai Sibanda.

His dual-toned skin was just as striking as his white eyes, the frenzy within them palpable. As the scorching sun lit up the ivory parts of his face, making the distinction between the dark brown portions starker, the image of Asher's smile as she told me how much she adored the

Shifter and his ethereal beauty came to me. I wondered if, perhaps, one day Asher would forgive me for this cruelty. For stealing away a friend she had described with such detail to me in a Fire Lands cave.

I watched him now, his eyes frantically searching the sea of bodies as if he were seeking something—or someone—in particular. He looked up at me when I stepped towards him, and he raised his sword. When I braced myself, ready to end the life of a male who had cared for my soulmate, the fae stopped. The world stilled as we stared at one another, Farai's eyes wide in recognition. And then I remembered that he had been there during the ball—he had seen me.

"She is safe." I feared my shout would not be heard over the sounds of battle raging around us, but somehow, he heard. Farai seemed to think over my words, contemplating what he would do next if the furrowing of his brow and darting of his eyes was any indication.

Then I did something truly stupid. Something I could only blame on my foolish and obsessive heart.

I closed the distance between us, grabbed his arm, and portaled the Shifter away. When we landed in the dungeons of Pike, Farai fell to the ground, heaving violently.

"The pain of portaling will pass. I will be back for you soon." He looked up at me in growing horror as shadows curled around me, the sight probably startling for someone who had never bore witness to Moon magic in action this way.

My feet moved from gray stone to orange sand, and I knew that even if I had done wrong by my realm, I had done right by Asher.

With Farai safe, I joined the fight once more, my back somehow meeting Damon's as we fought off a perfectly paired group of Elements. They each used their power at just the right time, so in sync with one another that Damon and I were only able to defend ourselves in the beginning. When the Water summoned far more than he could handle on his own, I latched onto the opportunity, stealing it from the air.

"Duck, now!" Damon did not hesitate to follow the command, falling to the ground as I heated the water into a searing steam, shoving my hands forward and spinning in a circle. The water burned all four of them, bubbling the skin on their faces and hands. Their melting flesh permeated the air with a nauseating smell, especially as the sun bore down on us with unrelenting heat.

As the fae fell in agony, their screams mixing with those in battle and making my teeth grind, my eyes locked on a lone figure in the distance. Even without my fae sight I would have known him. He was so uncannily similar to me that it was like looking in a mirror, a reflection staring back at me.

Xavier Mounbetton kept a slow pace as he made his way to the battlefield, his shoulder-length black hair waving in the breeze, the color and waves the same as mine—as was the dimple on his cheek that appeared with his smile.

My resentment grew at the sight of him, at his grace and strength, at our likeness. Every bit of my sense left me, and I portaled again, the shadows bringing me mere feet away from my father.

King Xavier's armor was not gold, but instead black with a golden shield on his chest that had the symbol of Eternity engraved into the center. His pale skin was taking on a pink hue, likely from the sun, though he would probably heal faster than he would burn.

His steps stilled when he noticed me, head cocking to the side. Just as mine did. I ground my teeth together at the sight.

"Well, she was right. We were foolish not to see it before." His voice was deep, our accents mercifully different—nurture winning against nature. We were so close that I could make out the brown of his eyes, amusement crinkling them at the corners.

"I do not believe your inability to recognize me makes the list of your top ten idiocies, perhaps not even the top twenty." Despite the pride I knew was there lurking beneath the calm facade, Xavier did not take my bait. Instead, his smile broadened.

"My son, you turned out so handsome. Tell me, what does Asher think of your looks? Does she find them...familiar?" All of my stoicism threatened to retreat at the sound of her name on his lips. I wanted to cut his tongue from his mouth so he could never again utter those two syllables. Then I would cut off his hands, penance for putting them on her time after time.

Patience tried and failed to win out, my body lighting up in flames—his flames. But Xavier moved quickly and without remorse, stealing them from my body and tripling them. With a wink, he formed the fire into a ball and threw it into the battle. I screamed, trying to call the flames back to me. Before I could, Xavier jumped onto me, shoving my face into the sand over and over. Grains of it filled my mouth and nose, and I was forced to push him off of me with a violent gust of wind.

My eyes burned from the tiny grains that seemed to slice into them, that pain worse than my aching throat and running nose. I willed water to rush out of them, flushing out the sand. When the burning stopped and my vision did not immediately return, panic almost loomed, threatening to overtake me. But the healing began, my fae heritage coming in handy as the battle before me slowly came back into view.

Fae and demons alike shouted as their bodies caught flame, the fire burning all it touched. I forced myself to my feet, stumbling at the dizziness that came from my head wound.

They needed my help. I had to move. I had to get to them. I had to—

This time, Xavier's body barreled into mine so hard we flipped over one another, both of us hitting the sand hard enough to knock the wind from our lungs. Gasping, we looked at each other, neither of us willing to walk away until the other was dead.

Digging my fingers into the desert below, I closed my eyes and demanded obedience. A tremor came, small at first, then large enough to knock soldiers down. Damon did not hesitate, shadows surging towards the cloudless sky, crafting the demon sigil in the air. Screams of retreat echoed across the blazing terrain, those who could portal grabbing as many as they could in flashes of light and shadow—white and black.

The fae soldiers yelled, trying to make chase, cutting down as many as they could. My focus went back to Xavier, who was staring at the shifting sand below him. This time, it was I who smiled, watching with delight as the ground beneath him began to part.

"Goodbye, father. May Eternity damn you to the Underworld where you belong."

He shouted, begging for someone to help. The remainder of the fae lined up in the distance charged forward, coming towards me. The group making chase halted, a commanding voice demanding they turn around and save their king.

Perhaps this was the future Pino had seen, maybe Asher would find my dead body here and sob over it. If my time had come, then at least I was able to take Xavier down with me. I thought of all the times he beat Asher into unconsciousness, each instance where he belittled her, and I roared with fury.

But just as he was about to sink fully, his screams becoming muffled by the sand, a puff of black appeared in the hole, a demon walking out of it. His mahogany hair and black eyes were the very same as that of the male whose painting hung on Adbeel's wall in his office.

"Malcolm?" The baffled question came out as a whisper, my eyes growing wide. The lost prince, the one I had assumed was killed by the same royals who had slaughtered the lost princess. The very princess whose death Pino had shown me over a year ago. How had I not noticed it was him in Haven?

Malcom looked up, flashing me a smile before he grabbed onto Xavier and disappeared in another burst of shadows. The demon prince, the true one, just rescued our enemy.

But I did not have time to think, not when every single gold-clad soldier charged me, the mass of warriors quickly closing in. My mind swam with too much knowledge, too many secrets invading my senses.

"Cover your ears, My Prince." Whipping around, I saw Bronagh, her furious gaze trained on the soldiers coming from the North. I did as she said, pressing my hands to my ears and willing a bubble of air to pocket me, acting as a sort of sound barrier.

I knew what was coming.

When the female opened her mouth and let out a piercing wail, not even my power could save me from nearly fainting from the sound. Her Sun magic lit up her eyes, the last of her light she possessed after losing Isa—after her magic morphed into something new and strange, the death of her daughter too great to bear.

As the banshee screamed, the sound shredded through the ears of the coming fae, every single one of them falling to the ground and convulsing. When their heads began bursting, blood and brain matter flying into the sky before raining back down, I reinforced my air shield. The scream still found its way through, bringing me to my knees and causing my vision to fade to black.

When her screams stopped, I knew that the last of the fae were dead. My shield dropped, the well of power in my chest aching for more, more, more. The silence was startling, emphasizing how hollow death had made the world. Not knowing how long we had before either of us fainted, I grabbed Bronagh's leg and willed us to Pike.

We landed in a heap, both of us hitting the stone floor of the infirmary with a painful thud. Screams of the injured made me wince, my still-ringing ears dripping blood.

"I am so sorry, Bell. I did not know what to do when I realized you were not retreating." I shook my head, trying to assuage some of Bronagh's guilt, but not able to form words just yet. She had saved my life, and I was more than grateful.

"Ranbir, I found him!" Noe's voice was far too loud and far too close, nearly making me heave with the pain. But soon, cold hands were on my ears, the pain intensifying before it ebbed, my entire body going limp as the Healing power filled me.

When Ranbir was done, Lian shoved her way towards me, leaning down and slapping me across the face. It stung, the force of it snapping my head to the right. A hush filled the room, even most of the sounds of pain fading at the sight of their prince being smacked.

"You fucking idiot! Winona would kill you herself if she knew what you did. How dare you. What do you think Asher would do if she found out we left you for dead on a battlefield? Do you think she would survive your death, you moronic prick?" Her tone was full of far more emotion than she likely wanted, the fury not masking the fear and sadness that threatened to break free.

If only she knew that I was dead either way.

"I deserved that," I said with a groan of pain. Cyprus laughed from his position against the wall, a cut on his forehead slowly bleeding. Luca was beside him, as he always was, but his face was far more serious. He shook it, glaring my way. "Family is supposed to love unconditionally. This feels much more like barely tempered hatred."

Lian let out a noise that sounded close to a growl, standing up straight again. "They often go hand-in-hand."

When she offered me help up, I took it, the ache in my body pulling a groan up my throat. Ranbir had begun working on Bronagh, though not much could be done for magic depletion other than rest. I turned to what remained of my Trusted, trying to catch all of their gazes.

"We help the medics where we can and then meet in the dungeons in an hour." They all seemed confused but, after realizing how serious I was, nodded and got to work.

Time passed far quicker than expected, the bells chiming at the top of every hour signaling that three had passed rather than one. But the medics needed aid desperately, and they always insisted that the soldiers had a higher chance of survival if I was there to encourage them.

When we finished, the seven of us made our way down the winding stairs to the bottom floor, dark and dank and a form of torture in itself. I led the way, taking them to the final cell, gripping the iron bars as

I approached. Farai sat on the cot, armor still on but helmet removed. His white hair matched his eyes, both glowing in the light of the distant Sun magic.

"What the fuck is that?" Noe's words came out as both angry and confused, her voice startling Farai. He stood, hand on his sword and eyes roaming over our group. I imagined he was quite scared, though he did not tremble.

"His name is Farai, and he is not to be harmed," I ordered, my voice firm.

Lian scoffed, her annoyance at the sight of a fae guard likely there to mask her growing rage. The kind that stemmed from loss.

Farai bristled, moving closer to the bars, his narrowed eyes scrutinizing us. "Where is she, demon?"

Though I expected him to ask and was prepared with an answer, it was Luca who spoke up, his voice surprisingly soft. "She is not here."

The Shifter did not back down, his growing upset putting everyone on edge. Luca and Cyprus likely knew of Asher's friends, as they were tasked with watching over her. But Noe, Lian, Damon, and Ranbir probably did not recall the name, as Asher had kept much to herself.

It was her way.

"They have not announced her absence, so how is it you are aware she is not still in The Capital?" Cyprus asked, suspicion heavy in his tone. The Shifter leaned from one foot to the other, his face full of sorrow.

"King Xavier told me before we came with that creature. He said that if I saw Asher, I was to approach her and rescue her. I was the only one told about her supposed abduction." Noe and Lian both seemed to realize at the same time who this fae was, their jaws going slack as they stared at him.

Luca leaned towards Ranbir and Damon, giving them a whispered explanation, hasty and frank. Noe moved for the lock, grabbing it as if she were going to free the fae, but Lian quickly slapped her hand away, scowling up at the Moon.

"What is wrong with you? Just because he is Ash's friend does not mean he is any less of a liability. Bell should not have brought him here in the first place."

The two of them argued back and forth, tossing insults at each other and me, though I paid them no mind. Farai and I were both staring the other down, my head subconsciously tilting to the side as I thought through what he had said. The suspicion that was undoubtedly there. Something we could use to our advantage.

"You do not believe the story told to you by the royals." Not a question, but a statement. I uttered it with enough conviction to silence everyone, all eyes moving to the fae behind the bars. For a moment, he did not speak, his gaze feeling as if it might burn right through me. But then, he answered.

"I believe Ash was held captive by them long before she was taken by you."

***

"Do we tell him?" Noe seemed the most inclined to inform Adbeel about Malcolm, her heart winning out just as it had in her argument to release Farai. She won the latter, securing Farai his own chambers and a promise to see Asher soon as long as he complied.

The others were on edge at the thought of him being there, but I tried to remind them that it was no different than the fae rescued in Haven. Farai did not trust the royals, nor did he support them. He bore witness to Asher's mistreatment for years, though it was clear that he did not know the extent of her abuse.

"We must tread lightly. This is going to be upsetting for King Adbeel. Malcolm and Zaib have been believed to be dead for hundreds of years. To find out that his son not only survived but betrayed his crown?

That would devastate anyone." Luca's reasoning was sound, as it normally was.

"Hold on. Do we actually think telling him is a good idea? He is already refusing to allow us to take an offensive approach. Why would he change his mind just to fight his son? Sure, Bellamy has been like a son to him, and for all Alemthian knows, he is, but this is Adbeel's *blood*. I doubt he will let that go."

Doing my best not to flinch at Lian's words, I eyed Damon from across the way. But his eyes were trained on Noe, as usual. Poor male was never going to get over what happened between them.

Noe, with her golden-brown hair and cat-like hazel eyes, was predatorial and daunting to most, but to Damon, she was a force he desperately wished to submit to. He saw her in a way many before had not, and for that, I appreciated him. In fact, it was Noe who encouraged me to welcome him into our circle decades ago. But Noe would always turn down his advances, always tell him no, always draw that line after the last time. And Damon would never cross it.

For all her strength, Noe was also broken in a way I understood. She did not trust love or romantic relationships, nor did she envy or desire them. I could not fault her in that, not after the abuse she had suffered at the hands of her father—the one man in the world who was biologically meant to love her but did not. His warm blood on my hands and gasping gurgle in my ears was euphoric, as well as far too short-lived.

So I did not wish for her to submit to Damon, or anyone for that matter. Noe was happy as she was, and if the others understood that loneliness and being without a partner were two different things, then they would stop encouraging Damon.

"What do you think, Bellamy?" Cyprus was the embodiment of a neutral party as he spoke, his voice a monotone of perpetual impartiality. It was difficult to pretend as though I was not prepared to ignore it all and simply kill the filthy traitor.

"I think that it would be far easier to burn the entire world and start anew. I do not care for scheming or politics, and yet I constantly find myself at the center of both." So easy to say in front of those I trusted with my entire being, but never something I would admit to anyone else. My greatest fault was that I was selfish and angry, I was too quick to fight and too slow to talk. And that was why Haven had been so good for me, a way to fight with kindness and peace rather than fists and blood. But Haven was gone now, the fae royals had seen to that.

"Seeing as killing off all of the innocents that Asher is trying to save would likely make her upset, I do not see you going that route." Noe's eyes were narrowed, her gaze accusatory. She knew me far too well.

"She is also one of the hottest females I have ever seen, so if you mess things up with her you would be a fool," Lian added, much to my dismay. Noe reached around Damon, offering a high five to the Air. I glared at them both, wishing that I could be anywhere but here. When Cyprus nodded, I nearly lost it, my fists clenching so tight that I felt my nails dig into my skin.

Something inside of me needed to give, to bend before I snapped. I thought spending time with Asher would have instilled at least a modicum of peace within me, but our fight and her tears and that stupid fucking gold dress had only put me more on edge. Then the battle, my father, the burnout, Farai, Malcolm. It was all too much.

"I will tell Adbeel, and hopefully it sways him to fight. They turned his own son against him, so retribution should be his. Now, we must force him to claim it."

CHAPTER TWENTY-ONE

STASSI

I was wrong. The fae were fascinating.

The king and queen were the most exciting creatures I had encountered on this planet, both of them so full of sin that I was practically drowning in it.

Watching the queen was proving to be more entertaining, her constant fury thick in the air around her as flowers grew from her skin. She made her way through her golden castle, the likes of which I had never seen and desperately envied, each of her steps shaking the ground as she ripped the still forming buds from her arms. If there had been anything gracing the walls, it surely would have fallen.

Beside her walked a mortal man, if his ears were any indication. He did not wear gold, instead sporting navy blue trousers with the small collar of the matching top raised and a few buttons undone to expose his hairless chest. Perhaps man was a little too generous—this was a mere boy.

His golden curls were bright under the light of the flames, such a contrast to his dark eyes. He was small, not that much taller than me, which was saying something. The queen beside him towered his height, her shoulder-length orange hair swaying with her violent steps. I followed them, waiting to hear the name I was looking for. But when the queen finally spoke, it had nothing to do with Asher.

"Try to not ruin everything this time. Recall your place, and know I can send you right back the moment you cease to be useful to me." With a final glare of her icy blue eyes, the fae queen shoved the blonde boy and made her way down the hallway to the left.

Oh wonderful, I did love the taste of ferocity strong enough to kill. Such a delicious sin. Yet it wasn't anger that tempted his sinful nature, it was the sweet tang of vengeance.

Naturally, I followed.

Golden boy was fast for a mortal, turning corners with the kind of determination that suggested he was prepared to truly ruin someone's day. And because of that, he was going to make mine abundantly better.

The tap of his black shoes and the racing beat of his heart were soon the only things that led me to him as he quickly moved through the palace. Which likely meant the sneaky thing didn't want to be caught. My ears led me to the top of a set of soot-colored stairs, the odd and out-of-place color further piquing my curiosity and bringing a smile to my face.

As I descended, a putrid smell invaded my senses, immediately making my eyes water and my nose burn. Could one lose sight from a smell? If so, this would surely do it. Despite how horrific the scent was, what it came from was enough to leave me practically hopping down the stairs, the smile on my face likely far more maniacal than beautiful.

This was the scent of torture that kissed my magic, a feisty hello.

Though the lack of screams wasn't promising, I still picked up my pace, turning corners based on the scent and the sound of the mortal. When the cells came into view, I halted, taking a few steps back. A single wooden door was there, a small rectangle cut out at the top. The space was too small for even a child to escape through, barely big enough to let in a modicum of light, but three metal bars still secured it. Something about it felt familiar, as if a piece of home was there.

As eager as I was to watch the mortal in action, my inquisitive nature would not let me ignore this sense of knowing. Approaching slowly, I made my way to the door, both unremarkable and intriguing. Fingers reaching for the wood, I hissed at the contact, the door ripping my magic from my veins.

Biting down on my tongue to avoid cursing from the pain, I reared back, cradling my fingers. A siphon spell, there was a siphon spell on the fucking door. What wicked little creature would use such a thing?

He would not like this, not one bit. Because there was only one female I knew of that would need to be restrained in such a way, and any pain inflicted on her would likely lead to dismemberment at the hands of a *very* angry male. Yes, I would need to tell him, even if I wasn't positive that this had been a prison built for Asher. With a sigh of annoyance, I scowled at the door and hastily made my way back towards the cells.

The golden boy was crouching down in front of a cell on the left, his full lips lifted in a sneer. His elbows rested on his knees, back hunched as he whispered.

"No, I agree. But it would take you breaking free for that to happen. So it seems I will get to stay a while longer." I risked getting closer as the boy's greasy voice invaded the air, his sinful nature making my chest hum the closer I got.

But when I allowed myself to get within fifteen feet of the mortal, I realized it was not the sin in the dungeons that brought the euphoric feel of overwhelming magic, it was virtue.

"We will see how long you last here, among creatures you do not belong beside." The male within had a deep voice, the accent smooth and heavy, different than that of the fae. Interesting. "Speaking of which, did you know I saw a youngling taller than you when I first arrived?"

My hand flew to my mouth, stifling a cackle. The boy bristled, standing up and squaring his shoulders. His body was shaking, the fury within prominent as his skin reddened. An odd sense of tension enveloped the dungeons, my magic reaching out for the sin that poured off of the mortal like a rushing river.

Distraction was a foolish thing, always mucking up everything. And in my moment of it, I unknowingly leaned my hand on a loose section of the wall, a chunk of the ashlar breaking free and falling to the ground. The audible smack of stone on stone echoed through the hall of cells, causing the golden boy to look in my direction. I leaned into the wall, hoping I wouldn't blow my cover so soon and miss out on whatever fun could be found here.

"You got lucky this time. But know that the next time I spill your filthy blood, I will make sure you know your place." Hearing him repeat the same words the queen had said to him told me all I needed to know about his motives. The boy didn't hate the prisoner. He hated himself. Being a magicless creature among those blessed by Eternity would do that.

Storming away, the boy didn't so much as look my direction as he passed, too angry and nervous to do anything but hastily make his exit. I smiled, eager to taste more of that mortal sin. Perhaps I would make a trip to the Mortal Realm before heading to Asher in Eoforhild.

First, I simply had to meet whoever the fae royals deemed dangerous and valuable enough to lock up rather than execute. With far less carefulness, I made my way to the cell, allowing my shoes to click against the stone floors now that I knew I was free of being caught. A sharp intake of breath came from behind the bars—a sign that whoever was in there had much more fear than they allowed the mortal to see.

I put little thought into my decision to grab hold of the bars and lean in, letting the call of my magic guide me instead. He was delicious in a way I hadn't felt yet on this world. Tilting my head to the side, I took in the male against the far wall.

His hair was thick and dark, matted with dirt and blood. The skin on display through the ripped clothing, bare feet, and slack face was ghostly pale, his eyes a dull and lifeless brown. It was as if he had been below ground for so long that all the color within him had fled, the darkness scaring away the vibrance. His jaw was strong, arms still corded in muscle despite the clear malnutrition his body was experiencing.

Beneath the dirt and grime, it was clear that the male was handsome—at least, he had been before getting thrown into a dungeon. When he copied me, leaning his head to the right, I let out a laugh. If only he knew what kind of creature had just stumbled across him. His growing smirk sent a jolt of sin into the atmosphere, but it was his virtue that still won out, the genuine kindness and love for his realm so potent that I could not stifle the moan that left my lips.

Standing, the male slowly made his way towards me, his height forcing me to raise my gaze in order to maintain eye contact. His own stare roamed over me, likely taking in the soft yellow of my dress, which ended at my mid-thigh. It was a far more appropriate piece, hiding my cleavage and shoulders, but the beauty of it was in tempting others to find out what was underneath.

My hair was left loose, the pink tint far more alluring than most other colors. In fact, the male reached out and grabbed a strand, his boldness making my heart race in enthusiasm. Yes, he would be a fun toy indeed.

"Hello, lovely. What brings you to my humble abode?" He released my hair to gesture with open arms at the cell around him, a smile on his face. That deep voice of his was rich, though it could not hide the despair and desperation he felt. The brokenness in his eyes was far too obvious to do so.

"Boredom." Shrugging, I leaned forward, resting my head on the edge of an iron bar, openly taking him in once more. Now was the moment I would find out if he was worth my time. "Entertain me."

A laugh came from his lips, the baffled sound matching his wide eyes. But instead of obeying, the male slowly walked backwards until he made contact with the far wall once more. He crossed his arms, smiling broadly still. A new energy filled the stale air, something igniting within him that almost made me steal him away.

"Set me free, and I will entertain you for days on end." The sultry tone he used paired wonderfully with his words, a promise I was far too inclined to take. The only problem that came with having desire was the potential for disappointment.

"Bargaining, are we?" I asked, pacing back and forth. Letting my fingers drag across the bars, I maintained eye contact, the smile on my face never faltering. "I highly doubt you can keep up with me for more than an hour."

If my insult offended him, he didn't show it, undeterred in his pursuit. For freedom or me was the question.

Dark spots stained his tunic, which I imagined was once white. The black trousers he wore were riddled with holes, the entirety of his person covered in filth—though he didn't seem injured. Not physically at least.

The male approached me once more, taking measured steps as he crossed the cell. I paused my movement, drinking him in. It was like watching prey approach a predator, and I was eager to get my fill. Basking in the way my magic ignited around him, I didn't pay attention to his nearness. When a finger lifted my chin, the two of us staring at one another, I made the decision to go against my better judgment and waste a little more time.

"I look forward to proving you wrong, sugar."

My core heated at the mere thought. I would need to clean him first, but I had a feeling the kind of reckless fun we could have together would be the best I had on this planet.

"There isn't an ounce of sugar in me, unfortunately."

He leaned in, our lips grazing ever so slightly through the bars. My chest fluttered with the swell of magic, that overwhelming sense of power consuming me the closer I got to taking what I wanted.

"Even better. I have always had a craving for spice."

Pink light lit up my body, my magic bursting from me. He didn't move back, though he did flinch. I smiled, letting my magic slowly slink into him. Sampling.

"You will likely regret this, handsome."

CHAPTER TWENTY-TWO

ASHER

After I had completely broken down in Shah's arms, the two of us decided that it was time we stop letting others control our lives. We both wanted a world in which our nightmares faded and our dreams came true. In order to secure this future, we had to work together.

Without much thought, I took the lead in plotting ways Eoforhild could aid Behman, especially when they were sending their people to fight in a war that was not their own. Over the last hour, Shah and I discussed strategies, alliances, potential enemies, and everything in between. Most importantly, we calculated ways in which we could maintain the safety of the forces she would rally for Eoforhild. The numbers were small, but I knew better than anyone that a single soul could alter the future.

"We will keep your forces behind the demons, acting as a sort of last defense. I cannot promise they will not die, but I can give my word that I will fight to my death to protect them." Hoping my words conveyed the honesty within my heart, I wiped my hands on my gown.

Shah had offered me a stunning violet piece, the lavender lace work on top of the cotton adding dimension that mirrored Nicola's favored dresses. The amount of material was both overdone and impossibly comforting. There was a sense of peace that came with the weight of the fabric attempting to anchor me in place, even the tight bodice was oddly grounding. It reminded me of the good that I needed to fight for, the parts of Betovere that not only needed, but *deserved* to be saved.

Hardening my heart was not as difficult as I thought, not when I had so much to be furious about. So I let it consume me, that red-hot rage within, the very temper that Mia chastised me for time and time again. It propelled my mind forward, helping me gain enough speed to make the alliance with Behman work.

"I will not force anyone to join, but even those willing might not be ready to die. So it means a lot to me that you are prepared to protect them." Shah was wearing a similar gown, though hers seemed to be thinner, less flamboyant in its size.

Three cups of coffee in, I came up with a system in which Eoforhild could portal ships of supplies to Behman as payment. When the agreed upon debt was paid, then the demons would continue to trade with the mortals of Behman, as well as any other kingdom that brought their banners to our cause. Shocked was an understatement for how Shah reacted to the offer. She was stunned into silence for a few minutes, which prompted me to admit I did not necessarily have the authority to make the agreement. We had fetched Henry, as well as Wrath, and now the two of them sat nearby.

Henry had not made contact with Bellamy, but he was confident the prince would be willing to accept the terms of the alliance. The captain in Henry took over as Shah and I discussed placement of her soldiers, his presence suddenly moving from the background to my side.

OF REALMS AND CHAOS

"Yes, that would be safest in theory, but the fae are smart and strong. They can take out a hundred soldiers in the blink of an eye, and I fear they might target your party for what their rulers will view as treachery."

Having not thought of that, I sat down, trying to reform a plan in my head that would lead to the least loss of life. But that was the hardest part because there would be loss of life no matter what. Innocent fae forced to fight and die, demons wielding swords to save their realm, and mortals battling for something better.

Unless...

"Okay, so then we train together. Portal any man and woman willing to fight into Eoforhild and teach them. Merge them into our ranks, mask them. That ensures they are not targeted, makes them more equipped to fight, and presents us as a united front."

Both queen and captain seemed to contemplate my plan, their faces pinched. Wrath remained silent at my back, but I could practically feel him there, the excitement in his mind loud.

"Hear me out. What is the best outcome of this war?"

Without hesitation, Henry answered, "Eoforhild is victorious."

I sighed, pinching the bridge of my nose. "Let me rephrase. What is the best outcome of this war for *everyone?*"

Wrath chuckled, the sound making Henry jump. A near silent spew of curses left his lips, but then Shah spoke, cutting him off from his tirade.

"We are all victorious." Hands to her lips and brow still furrowed, it seemed Shah was picturing that world, how we could achieve such a thing.

With a sigh, I turned around, walking over to Wrath. He was seated on a small sofa, curled up and tracking us. Scooting next to him on the green velvet, I absently scratched behind his ears as I thought.

248

The idea of fighting against my own kind again made my stomach churn. If Bellamy was right, then I was fae, but there was something *other* inside of me. Even if I had no fae blood in my veins, even if I was the horrifying creature from the Underworld that many thought me to be, I would still want safety for the realm that raised me.

Yes, ideally, all would survive this.

"If we have a big enough army, then maybe we can get them to pause long enough for me to challenge Mia. Xavier taught me a lot about politics, but he also schooled me on war and universal laws. I was brought up on strategies and winning plays, reared for a position of power. Because of that, I know that to decline a direct challenge from an enemy will be seen as weakness. She would never allow it, not when she has been hiding away her power for centuries in order to showcase it in a display of triumph. It will be too good of an opportunity to pass up, and she thinks me weak-willed enough to pull my hits."

More than that, I knew what it was like to be desperate to prove yourself—to need the acceptance of those around you in a way that was all-consuming. Mia wanted the respect afforded to a supreme ruler, and she would do anything to gain that, even risk her life for the chance to slaughter me in front of thousands. Once, I was something to mold and craft—a toy—but now, I was the enemy that needed to be silenced.

"Is she right?" Shah's question held no hint of animosity or hostility, but it still sank deep into my chest, piercing through my already shredded heart. What Shah did not know was that I had suffered the consequences of doing so once before.

The blood-soaked soil of Haven was proof of that.

Henry stilled, his green eyes taking on a haunted look before moving to me. His plum tunic and black trousers were tight-fitting, the tops of his low-cut boots showing due to the pants being too small. Shah was unfazed by Henry's open caution, casually leaning forward against the wooden table in the center of the meeting room, her dark eyes never leaving mine.

"I want to say no, but I cannot deny that I have failed to stand up to her for two hundred years." My voice wavered, tears pricking my eyes. Wrath snuggled further into me, so out of character for the dalistori. Though I only knew him for a few days, I was confident in the fact that the creature cared little for the feelings of others.

Before the sense of dread and self-loathing could take root, I took a deep breath and remembered the anger hiding behind the sorrow. Mia had taken everything from me. From the magic in my veins to the love in my heart, the fae queen stole and stole until I was but a husk, empty and devoid of substance.

Shah made her way over to me, momentarily stopping to stare at Wrath—whose yellow eyes were alight with curiosity as his tail swished back and forth. When Shah leaned down, snatched up his body, and promptly set him back down on her lap, the dalistori looked too shocked to speak, tiny mouth agape to show razor sharp teeth.

If the queen noticed the hostility that slowly began to taint the air around us, she did not show it. Instead, she softly scratched Wrath in the same way I had been, shushing him sternly when he let out a soft growl. I laughed, a brief and sharp chuckle that was not enough to block out the never-ending screams of my own mind.

"You are a queen, not just by right or name, but in your very soul. Not many are brave enough to dream of something better, especially those of us who have suffered for doing the same early on. But even the brave stumble, even the brave fail. Forgive yourself so that you may save others from enduring the same fate."

With that, she stood, lifting a disgruntled yet pacified Wrath into her arms. "You are lucky that I have not feasted on that bleeding heart of yours, mortal girl."

"Oh, shut up. We are off to find cake. I tire of strategizing." Passing Henry with a soft nod, she said, "Those who are willing can travel to Eoforhild. As for the rest of the matters, send your prince back so we may further discuss."

Looking back at me once more, Shah said a goodbye in the only way someone broken by betrayal could.

"I pray to the gods that you remember who you are, Queen Asher." And then she was gone, taking Wrath with her.

Henry watched her leave, jaw tight and mind unshielded. Allowing myself a quick look, I slowly entered his mind, finding Genevieve at the forefront. My surprise was fleeting because soon the selfish desire to avoid the heavy topic Henry was about to bring up replaced it.

"So you apologized to her?" His face remained aimed at the door, but the tick of his jaw and the quick sweep of his eyes my direction made it clear he was listening. After a couple of agonizing seconds, involving me staring at the side of his freckled face and him pretending not to notice me, the pumpkin caved.

"Yes." Still, he did not face me. Not because he wished to prevent the conversation, but because he knew that discussing it meant having to fight with me. It was clear in the slump of his shoulders and the heavy sighs that repeatedly left his lips. As if I were the exhausting one of the two of us.

Well, I was—but he did not have to make it so obvious.

"Do you want to talk about it?" Tone calm, I stood, walking casually to his side. If I got close enough to the door, then I could probably—

"No. Do not change the subject, little brat." Three more steps, and I would be at the opposite side of the large table, the dark wooden furniture providing the perfect amount of space.

"I guess it is my turn then." Letting my finger slide over the last bit of table left, I looked at him and winked. His answering glare was all I needed to know he was far too serious for this early in the morning.

So I did the only reasonable thing I could when facing an uncomfortable conversation about my feelings. I ran.

"We need to talk about this, Ash!" Henry's shouts rang through the hall as I sprinted barefoot across the cold yellow floors. Twice I had run from my problems within the last twenty-four hours. A smarter fae would have learned her lesson by now, but no one had ever really classified me as smart.

Manipulative? In more ways than one.

Evil? Obviously.

Beautiful? Sure.

Smart? Rarely.

Another trait not often associated with me? Contrite.

Apologizing was not something an heir learned in Academy nor was I taught it from Mia and Xavier. In fact, I was always highly encouraged to never admit weakness by apologizing unless I was backed into a corner. Over the last few months of my time in Betovere, I had found myself practically glued into that corner, and still, I was struggling to find the words to say as I made my way to Genevieve's guest chambers.

In Henry's memory, he had walked from the room given to him—which was right beside my own despite my embarrassing self-guided tour last night—and then taken a right turn, following until he reached a green door with yellow flowers.

One set of stairs, three hallways, and an angry string of curses later, I was standing in front of the princess' chambers that she always occupied when visiting her best friend. To my eternal disbelief, the two of them were inseparable. Shah had told me little of their friendship, but she did say that Genevieve was our best chance at securing an alliance with Maliha. I truly did not expect them to ever help when I had physically assaulted their precious prince.

The foul little shit.

Still, I could make things right with her. Even if I would sooner kill her brother than allow him to breathe in my presence once more.

With clenched teeth, a racing heart, and memories of a foot slamming into my stomach, I sighed and knocked two times.

A loud groan came from the other side, followed by the creak of an old bed as someone shifted. Momentarily, I considered entering her mind, if only to see what she planned to do with the information she learned yesterday. Genevieve had the potential to not only sever any alliances between Eoforhild and the mortal kingdoms before they could be formed, but also to alert Mia and Xavier to my whereabouts. This game of chess I was beginning was dangerous, one that might involve sacrificing pawns to protect the board.

Abruptly, the door swung open, revealing a disheveled and barely awake Genevieve. Her forest green night dress was rumpled, her golden curls a mess of knots. The most interesting part of her appearance, though, was the small spot on her neck, the red mark slowly taking on a purple hue.

"Gods, it is *you.*" Acidic tone and vicious glare aside, Genevieve did not seem that upset to see me. In fact, the energy radiating off of her was strangely vibrant, as if the prospect of a conversation with me was exciting. However, that enthusiasm quickly dimmed when I attempted to smile.

Before I could say anything of substance, Genevieve was slamming the door in my face, the sound of wood meeting wood so loud that it echoed across the hallway. For a moment, I stood there in baffled silence, so surprised that I could not think beyond the rage that was slowly building inside of me.

Bitch.

This time, I did not knock. Instead, I shoved through the door, letting it smack into the wall. Genevieve's scream of shock was a glorious sound, so different from her brother's yet just as appealing. Based on the princess' horrified face, the smile I flashed her did the job. As always, that fear seemed to spark something visceral within me, the magic in my chest humming with anticipation.

"You cannot just barge into my chambers, you monster!" Cringing at the shrill tone, I walked further into the room, noting that it was nearly identical to mine. The same awful colors, as if they could not find a better shade of green or yellow—one which did not burn my eyes.

"Based on your foul attitude, I expected a far more original insult. Alas, just like your brother, you seem to be prone to disappointing me." As soon as the words slipped from my lips, I knew I had failed. My attitude had gotten out of hand in my time of freedom. Backtracking, I pasted a smile on my face and turned to face her. "That was horribly rude of me, I do apologize, I got very little sleep last night."

Genevieve huffed, crossing her arms and lifting her chin. "I am sure the demon prince did not either."

Chanting to myself that I could not kill the girl, I took four deep breaths and turned away from her once more, allowing my horribly fake smile to fall. As luck would have it, something on the bench at the end of her bed caught my eye. Something that was not green or yellow or blue. No, this was red—the deep red of Haven.

When I faced the silent mortal princess again, my smile was anything but false. "I came to apologize for my behavior last night. I should not have forced you to drink that wine, nor should I have insulted your brother. As you can likely tell, we immortals have a tendency to lean towards chaos."

Whether it was my calm voice or my specific choice of words that put Genevieve on edge, I was unsure. But whichever it was, she immediately went on defense.

"Trust me when I say that I expect no less from savage beasts such as yourselves. You are all psychotic on the best of days if your behavior last night was any indication."

I hummed in agreement, watching with glee as her eyes darted to the cloak before quickly returning to me, the panic there beneath the disdain.

"Ah yes, Henry in particular is known to be quite *savage.*" Genevieve's throat bobbed, jaw flexing. "Speaking of the carrot top, I sent him to apologize last night. Tell me, did he find you?"

What I did next was despicable, petty, and truly moronic. But watching her face as I walked to the wooden bench and sat beside the discarded red cloak, the very one Henry wore almost daily since I met him months ago, was worth any repercussions I might suffer from.

"This is a strange apology, and I do not accept. Now get out before I have you thrown out." She pointed her finger at the door, eyes burning with rage and cheeks aflame with embarrassment. Still, she made an imposing figure, even with hair rumpled from sex.

So, you shame me at a political dinner for bedding a demon, then do the exact same thing an hour later and expect no one to bat an eye? Interesting time to choose hypocrisy.

Not moving, I bore witness to the color draining from her face and a tremor shaking her hand. Fun did not begin to describe the feeling of being inside of a terrified mind. It was something that used to bring guilt to my soul. Enjoying the pain of another creature as you violated their most private thoughts was evil, and I would not dare deny that. But, in the spirit of allowing my anger to lead the way, I could not bring myself to feel that same guilt I used to drown in daily.

"I did not steal away a loved brother and child. I did not betray my fiancé by—"

"Wrong there, Gen." Her hand fell at the nickname, or perhaps it was the fact that I cut her off. No matter, the girl did not scare me in the same way she had before. Blackmail was never something I would consider months ago, but now I did not hesitate. "You are promised to the third son of King Mordicai and Queen Demis, the rulers of Heratt. Though he is too young to wed now, you both are still expected to be faithful to the coming union upon his sixteenth birthday."

And then I had her. The princess ran, the speed with which she crossed the room to dive into her bathing chamber impressive. A phantom kick to my side and grip of my neck reminded me that she was not the only quick one in her family. Nor was she the only one prone to mistakes, which was why I would not let her get away with what she had done without helping us.

Retribution came in many forms. Death. Imprisonment. Poverty. Or, in Sterling's case, threats to his sister. I heard her heave though nothing seemed to be exiting her body. More vomit had surrounded me these last few months than in my entire existence. Despite that, I walked forward slowly, making my way to the yellow door that was faintly ajar.

I rapped on it with my knuckles, rolling my eyes when Genevieve cursed and told me to leave. With my foot, I pushed the door open. She kneeled on the floor, face hanging over the basin as her body shook with the force of her gags. Someone was going to have a horrible time cleaning that out.

To my annoyance, my conscience won out, forcing me to make my way to her. Grabbing her hair with one hand, I held it up as the other hand rubbed her back. She reached up to swat me away, but I stopped rubbing her back to flick her in the head instead. To my bewilderment, the princess *laughed.*

"You know, I was actually hoping to ask you questions—on your future wedding day, I mean. I had been eager to meet you, thinking that you would bring much needed peace and hope to my brother. He has always been restless, desiring more than was given to him. Even now, I have so many questions. Too many. And I fear you will not answer any of them truthfully, just as your parents do not."

With a sigh, I leaned over and grabbed a yellow towel before sitting down beside her. Gods, my curiosity and ridiculous need to be helpful would be the end of me some day.

Dipping the towel into her already filled tub, I tried to remain calm as I dabbed the wet cloth on her forehead. Her perplexed face lessoned some of the tension, the widening of her eyes revealing flecks of green within the brown.

"First of all, they are not my parents. I was lied to my entire life, surrounded by pain and told it was bliss. Never would I do something like that to another being if I could help it. Ask me anything, and I promise to answer you truthfully." Every bit of my tone and demeanor exuded calmness, but underneath, I was full of panic at the idea of giving this girl answers she might later use against me. Like the sea just before a storm, the current of thoughts in my mind built, converging together to stir the water that was my sanity into pandemonium.

Genevieve seemed just as apprehensive, but I forced myself to remain within only my own head, affording her the peace that I often stole from others. Her gaze flicked between both of my eyes, her hands still tightly gripping the basin as I slid the wet cloth across her skin. When it became clear she was not going to speak, I huffed and slid behind her, discarding the towel on the checkered tile.

A laugh tried to fight its way to the surface when she flinched at my fingers touching her hair, but I held it back in hopes of not proving myself to be the wretched monster she thought I was. Not that I would deny what I knew to be true, but everyone enjoyed living in delusion sometimes.

Softly, I separated some of the knots, trying to restore her curls to their former glory. The coils were soft, though they had lost their silky sheen from last night. Henry deserved a pat on the back for how thoroughly he undid her, if the embarrassment and lust that leaked from the princess was any indication. Reinforcing that golden gate inside of my head, I shoved out all that she was projecting, leaving her to those thoughts.

By the time I was able to successfully untangle her hair, Genevieve still had not spoken, though her shoulders relaxed and her breathing steadied. Pushing my luck, I began braiding the strands, mimicking the way Winona had often done my hair to settle me.

"I still cannot stand you, but I respect you enough to be honest. Please, tell me what plagues your mind," I whispered, taking care not to scare her.

Her back straightened at my words, body tensing. Before I could apologize or attempt a different route, Genevieve let out a small chuckle, turning to face me for a moment. The way in which she scrutinized should have angered me, but it only reassured me that the princess was exactly who she showed herself to be—angry, smart, resilient, and determined. All traits I could understand and value.

"Something is wrong with Sterling. I can tell. He does not write often, and when he does, it is as if he is keeping secrets from us. The missives are always vague and unfeeling. I just want to know what you did to him. That is all."

Despite how infuriating the words were, her broken and sorrowful tone made me think through my answer carefully. How did one explain to a girl that her brother was a psychotic beast in mortal skin? Clearly, he was never violent or wicked with her, which likely meant it was my own refusal and dismissive nature that brought out his rage. I was not stupid. I knew that I could be difficult and hard to please, but that did not justify the abuse and mistreatment I had suffered at his hands. Even the small touches had been violating. But what would I say to Genevieve that would convince her of that truth when she so clearly was not willing to accept what her brother had become? Or worse, what he had always been just beneath her nose.

"Mia once encouraged me to imagine how it would feel to be removed from my realm and home, forced to live with beings I had never met. She said it so I could better understand your brother, though, little did she know, I would be taken weeks later and forced into the exact same situation."

The princess turned to face me, pulling her knees up to her chest and resting her chin upon them. She looked so small—so young—sitting there in that way. At twenty-eight, she was three years older than her brother, and still, that was one hundred eighty years my junior. They were quite literally children, forced to grow up too soon and push away feelings that were not royal.

For the second time that week, I realized just how similar I was to a mortal woman.

"I was not permitted to use my magic on Sterling, and I tried with all of my might to like him, but even without my abilities I could see through his façade."

Genevieve's eyes hardened, the sound of her teeth smacking together as she clenched them telling me just how angry she was growing. Time was running out to make her understand.

"Never would I dare to say that he was a bad brother, son, or prince. With that being said, Sterling was not good to me. He attacked me, breaking three of my ribs and splitting open my head. All because I did not want to speak with him—because I did not want him. I pushed first when he began insulting me, so perhaps it was my fault, but it was I who ended up broken and bloody on the floor. I can still feel his hands on my skin and his fingers around my throat." My voice was raspy, the emotions trying to fight their way to the surface, but I snuffed them out, suffocating them until they ceased their attempts. "I might have retaliated, but I did nothing to his mind."

When she stood, sneering down at me and pointing to the door, I knew my time was up. "Get out, you lying abomination. Get out before I show you how hard we mortals train to be able to tear your kind apart."

She was still as unoriginal as her brother, and just as foolish. The horrid part of me hoped she never got another letter from him. The truly evil side hoped I could drag my dagger across his throat and silence him forever. It would be a blessing to the world, really.

With the discussion so clearly over, I stood, wiping my palms on the fabric of my dress. Genevieve did not lower her finger, nor did she cease her glare as I took my time leaving. My bare feet brushed across the carpet, this one sporting a floral design, and I paused. Turning one final time, I found she was not far away, her arms crossed and her eyes narrowed.

I am sorry I could not give you the answers you wanted to hear. For what it is worth, if I succeed in taking the fae throne, I will not marry him. I will allow him to come home to you and make your family complete once more.

She jolted at the sound of my voice echoing inside of her mind, a chill racking through her body and leaving noticeable goosebumps in its wake. Her tears were quick to both come and disappear, the slight raise of her chin a sign that she was not willing to show me any more vulnerability.

I wondered what it must be like for Genevieve. She did not have power or magic, nothing that would propel her beyond the definition of female. In a world where daughters were practically sold off to eligible males, Genevieve was likely only seen as a womb and a title.

You are worthy of joy, Genevieve. Whatever makes you so angry, so bent on spewing hatred, know that you are allowed to let it go. You are not to blame for Sterling's absence, nor are you evil for enjoying the company of a willing male. Allow yourself the grace that you likely afford that brother of yours—forgive so your soul may heal.

This time, I did not turn again, making my way to the door quicker than before. There was nothing else I could do, no words that would change her mind—not even those I had spoken, so similar to Shah's that I could not begin to separate the two thoughts. All I could hope for was that she would have a change of heart and not inform anyone she saw us here. That she wouldn't tell her parents what was discussed and revealed.

"Keep Henry's cloak. If you ever need us, just pick it up, place a note in the pocket, and let it go." I paused at the doorway, my hand resting against the frame. And, though I did not know exactly why she had those thoughts at dinner, I felt it important to speak them aloud. "I know you do not want this war, that you plan to rule differently when it is your turn. I hope to one day see what Maliha can be with you atop the throne. Good luck, Genevieve."

ACT III

~ TO LEARN ~

CHAPTER TWENTY-THREE

ASHER

I was so sick of the cold.

In particular, I never wanted to experience a Gandry autumn again. Already far too chilly, the weather was made worse by our constant need to be outside. The hunt for a creature who had been wreaking havoc on the southwest kingdom for nearly eight years led us from small villages to sprawling cities.

Not noticing the horrifying difference between the quality of life in Behman and Gandry was impossible, though it did further cement our plans to aid Shah. Bellamy had agreed—rather excitedly—to my plans. In fact, his notes were a bit too enthusiastic. As if he was waiting for me to take charge in this way.

Three days after Henry, Wrath, and I left Jore, Bellamy was ready to begin portaling in mortal soldiers. To everyone's amazement, nearly three hundred Behman subjects had volunteered to go to Eoforhild. Two hundred ninety-one mortals willing to learn from the demons that they had been told their entire lives were monstrous creatures who would eat their souls.

Within hours, every single mortal had been moved to Pike, where they were clothed, fed, and prepared for what life would look like for the foreseeable future. Over a fortnight had passed since then, three full weeks since I shook Queen Shah's hand and secured our first major ally.

To say the tide had changed would be a lie, but it felt as if we had a chance to come out of this alive now. Though many disagreed, including Henry, the plan was to not fight at all. Despite that, we still searched tirelessly for the creature that was slaughtering mortals in Gandry, the goal being not only to convince it to fight for us, but also to impress the ruler of the kingdom.

Aim for the tree,

Henry's silent order was followed by him handing me a throwing dagger. I absentmindedly took it, trying to remember to lift my elbow as I released the weapon. It stuck into the tree to the left of the one I was aiming for, and only barely. But disappointment did not fill me, because I was still focused on what was to come.

Shah warned me about King Trint before we left. An arrogant and fairly young king, Trint was prone to manipulation and flirtation. However, he also had a serious problem in the form of a rogue, unknown beast that attacked any who came near.

A win-win.

Or was it win-win-win?

"What could possibly be going on in that head of yours?" Henry's voice startled me, the silence the three of us had been basking in shattering. Birds flew, screeching as they took to the skies. Wrath groaned, his signature glare flashing the demon's way. The two had still not warmed up to each other, though I found I very much enjoyed the dalistori's presence. It was always nice having someone more cynical around. The pragmatism was refreshing.

"You continue to impress me with how well you can ruin a peaceful moment." One thing I would likely never get used to was the sound of Wrath's voice. Eerie as ever, it sent chills up my spine. Henry— who refused to admit that he was terrified of the dalistori—did not flinch or balk, instead smiling down at the cat-like creature.

"Seeing as your mere presence makes my head hurt, kitty, I can safely say it is not me destroying the semblance of joy we have found." Seconds after a smirking Henry spoke, Wrath was growing, the fur on his back standing up and becoming coarse, those horrific fangs lengthening like spears. His paws tripled in size, though he still walked silently through the Vesteer forest. I pushed my hand out, stopping him when he reached my waist.

You are at least hundreds of years older. Just ignore him.

Wrath's answering hiss was both scary and humorous, though I was not exempt from his ire.

Yes, like you and the mortal princess. What a pity I was not able to witness the showdown that occurred when you found out she bedded the string bean.

Laughs that sounded similar to choking burst out of me, unable to be stifled. It was my first full laugh since we arrived in Vesteer two days ago. The first day we had spent searching the large city of brick, gleaning any information we could from the citizens who were the newest to suffer from the creature's bloodlust. Only Henry spoke the tongue of Gandry, the throaty and constantly flowing language leaving me to interpret thoughts by feel and sight rather than sound.

Henry's annoyed face and accusatory squint only made my laughing fit worse, causing me to double over. Through my cackles, I spoke to Wrath aloud.

"As a fellow lover of food-themed insults, 'string bean' is quite impressive. Though, I believe he would have to be scrawnier for it to be accurate." Wrath's shoulder seemed to lift in a shrug as we continued on, Henry's grumbles unintelligible on my left.

"I do not know. He seems quite skinny for a creature of his height. I think the dalistori is onto something."

Simultaneously, the three of us froze mid-step. Gray, green, and yellow eyes all widened, both Henry and Wrath looking to me briefly. The voice had been soft—melodic in its tune. With a nod, we all turned in the direction it had come from.

Standing there, dressed head-to-toe in a vivid shade of pink leather-like clothes, was a female with long black hair that cascaded down her back like a waterfall. Her skin, nearly as dark as Ranbir's, was practically glowing in its beauty, contrasting wonderfully with the vibrance of her outfit and the blue of her small eyes. She was enchanting.

She was also planning to kill us.

"Hello there. We did not mean to scare you." Raising my hands, I silently hoped my placating words would prevent a fight, though I was not particularly inclined to believe it would based on her graphic thoughts of ways she could dismember us.

"I am not scared of you, but I do fear that death is imminent. Quite lucky on your part, no? Life is so very dull—an infinite void of grief and sorrow."

None of us moved, the two males . at my sides likely just as perplexed as I was at the creature's words. She was slightly shorter than me, but her presence was large, as if she took up more space than the average being.

Before anyone could speak again, her form started to fade, morphing into...

"Are those bubbles?" Henry's question snapped me out of my daze, my head shaking and eyes blinking rapidly. By the time I was once more focused on the creature, she was gone. Now all that existed was a wave of small clear spheres, rainbows of color dancing off the edges when the sun shone upon them. "Not very scary."

Like the creature, they were lovely. Without thinking, I reached out for the one nearest me. "They are kind of cute."

But then my skin made contact.

I was on my knees in seconds, shrieks feeling as if they were shredding my throat in the same way the bubbles seemed to tear apart my flesh. One, five, eleven bubbles burned through my body, dissolving it like acid. Henry's screams soon followed, sending him falling to the pine needles in a heap.

Wrath shrunk in an instant, quickly maneuvering through the floating orbs and ducking at the last minute to avoid a particularly large one that seemed to follow him. When he reached my side, I was panting heavily, watching my leathers disintegrate and my flesh sizzle. The pain was blinding, worse than being burned or whipped or beaten—all things I knew intimately from my time in my low level room back home. For a moment, I thought I might faint, but Wrath pressed his head into my chest, forcing me to remain upright as he spoke.

"You must push through the hurt, Strange One. Pain is your friend, an old companion. It cannot win if you do not let it. Fight her like only you can, or we will all three die here."

Wanting to be a hero had always felt impossible yet necessary. Now, as I watched the first bubble pop against Wrath's ear, his screams were a grueling reminder that I would never win by being good. I was not born to be a golden victor bringing peace through kindness and morals. I had acknowledged it half-heartedly before, always pretending to be okay with the wickedness within but never letting go of the hope I could be— would be—better one day.

Better would leave us all lifeless on the forest floor, covered in dead leaves and staring up at a dull sky framed by bare branches. A pitiful excuse of an end for creatures as formidable as we were. What would these deaths tell the world? That even the strongest cannot win? That hope is useless?

That was the problem. We worshiped heroes as if their inability to do what was hard made them better than those deemed villains for not apologizing when they moved mountains to find their version of a happy ending. Maybe this made me more like Mia and Xavier than I wished to admit, but I was prepared to move this creature if she wanted to be a mountain blocking my way.

With gritted teeth and a vengeful heart, I pushed myself off the ground, refusing to let the weight of principles and long-dead dreams crush me. Now on my feet, I took one final heaving breath, and then I kicked open my mental gates, the golden bars shaking as they parted.

Every thought and feeling and soul within the city bombarded me at once, but unlike that time with Bellamy and his Trusted atop a mountain, I would not let them consume and break me again.

The bubbles retreated slightly, gathering together to form a silhouette of the female who once stood before us. She seemed to watch, waiting to see what I would do next. In response, I simply smiled, tasting that deeply rooted need for violence within me which roamed freely past the broken gates of my mind.

"Odd. You stand despite the bleak world that wishes you dead. One can only hope to never have such a misguided will to live." I laughed at the contrast between her serene tone and depressing words, the sound far more threatening than it was inviting. Finally, the creature seemed to realize that I was just as dangerous as she was, those bubbles of hers growing and now dripping some sort of clear liquid.

"Since you seem so convinced life is not worth the effort, allow me to spare you another moment of it." Before she could speak again— before she could so much as inhale—I dove into her mind, shredding the flimsy wall of bubbles that tried to block me out. With time being of the essence, I could not search through her head, though I did wish to better understand what and who she was.

Squeezing, I began walking forward, the creature's body blurring back together and reforming into a mortal-like shape. She stilled in agony before crumpling to the ground in a series of convulsing movements, three of my steps spanning the entire ordeal. I continued to press, wanting to feel the way her mind shattered beneath my magic and did the bidding which I placed upon it.

For a moment, my heart ached as I watched her attempt to crawl away, but then she turned. I watched as she lifted her hand, and from it poured out a stream of the bubble-like substance. A gasp left my lips as Henry's cries rang out, and then I was on top of her, the seconds in between a blur. My fists rained down on her—forcing her head to smash repeatedly into the ground—all while my magic sliced down her mind, carving out memories and thoughts and feelings. Leaving her hollow beneath me.

Blood as red as my own coated my knuckles as I beat into her again and again, my furious screams now the only thing I could hear.

It was Wrath who pulled me off, his teeth latching onto my hair and yanking me backwards. I hit the ground hard, dirt and pine needles digging into my festering wounds. All at once, the torturous shards of pain returned, obliterating every ounce of anger I had and replacing it with suffering.

"Why fight against a death that will bring you the peace you were not given in life?"

The creature's peculiar and gloomy words were the last thing I heard before my screams rang out and the world went black.

***

"What a treat."

Gods, not him again.

Padon chuckled, his cold breath tickling my cheek. It felt, as always, almost distant. Like I was absent from my body. Eyes fluttering open, I watched as a world of gray came into focus. For the second time since I left Betovere, I awoke in a bed that was not mine with a male staring at me.

Except this time, the male was entirely nude.

"Do you possess no shame?" I asked, shoving him away from me. He placed his hand atop mine, forcing it to remain on his chest.

He was broader than I had thought, his blue-tinted skin hiding none of the muscle below. In fact, I was fairly sure he was *flexing*. Males were exhausting.

"Not that I'm aware of. Definitely not with you, my love." His voice was a purr, vibrating against my palm which he still held in place. I offered him a smile, doing everything I could to shield my thoughts. When I allowed my eyes to land on his full lips, Padon's answering sigh sent a wave of his scent my way, smelling of whisky and leather. Equally as annoying, but I maintained my façade, leaning my chest forward slightly.

When the supposed emperor snaked one hand around my waist and the other behind my neck, I struck. The punch was not impressive, but it did send his head careening back. His pain gave me an opening to slip off the bed, wrapping my body in the gray quilt atop the matching gray sheets.

When I was on my feet, I scowled down at him, the blue blood leaking from his nose not enough to bring a smile to my face.

"Why am I naked?" The question was laced with disdain but little surprise. I had learned that Padon was a creature that asked for nothing and took everything. He was the opposite of Bellamy in that way.

"I can't hear your thoughts anymore. Magnificent. You learn so fast." When he stood, the sheet fell, revealing the rest of Padon's body. Because I could not help myself, I looked down, seeing that he was just as excited as he sounded. "If you keep looking at me like that, Asher, I will take you against that door you are heading for."

Pausing my slow path to the closest door, I tightened my arms around the quilt, trying to hide as much of my body as I could. "Touch me against my will, and I will kill you."

Padon's smile was patronizing, as if there was something about what I said that was particularly humorous. It made my teeth grind and my fists tighten, nails biting into my skin. Oh yes, I would kill him someday.

"Touch me, and I will never come back." Unlike the threat of death, this one stuck.

Padon froze in his pursuit, white eyes wide with what looked like genuine fear. The hesitation gave me time to take in the room around me.

Though all was gray, the multiple shades of the color gave the room dimension, highlighting the intricate carvings on the ceilings. The design was of a winged creature, its four legs and large scaled body looking so similar to the dragons Bellamy had described to me one night months ago. A five-tiered crystal chandelier hung from right above the bed, which was easily one of the largest I had ever seen. But it was not the abstract sculptures or the beautifully woven rug or even the glittering crystal glasses atop the gray dresser that caught my eye. No, it was the painting that sat above his bed. I walked to the foot of the bedframe, lips parted and gaze locked.

"Fine, then give yourself willingly." The ghost of his breath kissed my exposed shoulder, the hairs on the back of my neck rising at his sudden nearness. Padon was like the hemlock that used to flow through my system daily—invasive, corrosive, and poisonous. I knew it based on the taste of his mind and the feel of his voice.

"Never." Just as Bellamy always did, I found myself tilting my head to the side as I stepped away from Padon, further assessing the painting.

"Ugh, why?" His growled question was filled with so much annoyance that I could not help but laugh. Padon did not speak again for a moment, but I felt him come around to my side, still not wearing any clothing—to my undying frustration.

"Is that painting of me?" Asking was unnecessary because it was, without a doubt, me painted on a canvas above his bed—held within a swirling gray frame that matched my eyes. I wore a black gown made of what looked to be thousands of tiny gems, and around my neck still hung Sipho's necklace.

"Yes?" This question was full of nervous tension, as if he were waiting for me to grow angry enough to leave. For some reason, I was far more dazed than angry, especially with the hint of pain my body was beginning to feel—like a throbbing ache from head to toe.

"Why is it there?" I asked, my voice barely above a whisper. I was not sure why, but the sense of pain seemed to bring with it a bone-deep exhaustion. My eyes began to grow heavy, but I fought off the urge to sleep.

"Because you're beautiful," he said, softer than before. Could he sense my depleting energy? Would he take advantage of that weakness, just as so many before had? "Also, because you're the love of my life, and I wish to see you every day. But since you aren't ready to come to me yet, I settle for this."

Turning to face him, I looked up into the male's glowing white eyes. He had once been terrifying, the otherness of him daunting in a way not even the afriktor had managed. Now, though, he just seemed desperate, which often made for the most dangerous creatures alive.

"You do not know me, Padon." I breathed deeply, trying to pull in enough air to keep me afloat. The pain was increasing, my whole body now feeling as if tiny needles were pricking me, small holes allowing the agony to pull me under. If the emperor noticed my distress, he did not say anything about it.

"I would like to, if you'll let me. Perhaps you could tell me a story from your youth, and I can tell you one from my own." His words were so gentle, as if he were speaking to something precious. I felt him come nearer, my bare shoulder brushing his elbow.

"Put some clothes on us, and then I will."

Padon was quick to agree, snapping his fingers. I went from standing in only a quilt, to on his bed once more, this time clothed in a gray knit top that reached down to my knees, acting as a sort of dress.

Padon was wearing a strange sort of trouser, loose fitting and thick with a tie around the waist. They looked comfortable, the bagginess of them not hiding the erection he seemed more than proud to show off.

To my utter surprise, Padon reached down and covered me with the quilt, which had somehow found its way back to the bed. For a second he appeared unsure of his next move, staring into my eyes as if searching for an answer to the many questions that invaded his mind. The scene around us flickered, the strange space of nothing and everything from before trying to fight its way back. With a deep breath, Padon slouched back slightly, and the room was whole again.

I looked on, trying to understand a creature who was intimate and kind but also invasive and violent. He was a contrast to himself, switching between the two versions faster than I could comprehend. Failing at conjuring any sort of words, I merely continued to scrutinize him, his glowing white eyes doing the same to me.

"Lift your head for me." They were demanding words, full of superiority and authority, but also laced with a tenderness that calmed me. Since I was both exhausted and baffled, I did as I was told. Padon fluffed the pillow I had been resting on, then gazed at me with waiting eyes until I laid back down. When he was pleased with my comfort, he shuffled closer and laid down too, our arms the only thing touching.

Together we continued our staring contest of sorts, the tension not feeling awkward or heavy though the silence did not help the fatigue that was winning against my will.

"Speak," he demanded quietly, his head tilting closer to mine. For some reason, I knew exactly what story I would tell him. It made little sense considering recent events, but this memory felt right somehow.

"About ninety years ago, I had made the unfortunate mistake of drinking far too much wine the night before a very important council meeting. I was angry with a male that I had slept with because he was insisting that I see him again. He did not understand what it meant to be with me, just as no one ever did. He, like the rest, thought himself an exception to a fundamental rule that I made long ago. I did not see anyone more than once, did not risk someone finding out what I was doing."

Padon's body shifted closer to mine, the move feeling as if it came from interest rather than desire. His lips were set in a line, brows furrowed, his entire face contorted in concentration as he listened.

"He threatened to tell the royals about our...encounter. And, like the hot-headed creature I am, I immediately manipulated his mind. I had dug into his head and tore the memory out, convincing him he had never met me before and hurting him in the process. Taking away their memories of me was always something I did, but I was usually gentle and kind because I hated myself and my power. I did not want to be a monster. I just wanted to feel something without losing everything. My guilt did not care about justifications though. It only saw how immoral my actions were. My friend Nicola and I drank four bottles of wine between us after we left the male on the floor of his market stall, and she nearly drowned in the lake due to our idiocy."

Despite the morose nature of the memory, I still smiled slightly. Nicola had always been quick to help me, to fight for me, and to hold me. I missed her more than I allowed myself to admit. She was my best friend, and life without her was more difficult than I could have imagined. We planned for the distance, knowing that her move to the Yesterday Lands would force us apart, but it was far harder than I thought. She was my light, a wise and honest friend that could solve any problem.

"Well, the next day, I nearly got sick on the king during our council meeting. Resisting the urge had left me dizzy, which then caused me to faint. I was so sure I would be punished that I dreamed of Xavier's whip slashing through my back, but when I awoke, Mia and Xavier were on either side of my bed *smiling*.

"I immediately began apologizing, begging for the forgiveness I knew I did not deserve but selfishly wanted, and all they did was stare at me. I was horrified until Mia leaned down and placed a soothing kiss to my forehead. And when my body stopped shaking, they each climbed into my bed and held me close, cuddling up against me like I was something they loved. Like we were a family. Mia had sung to me, brushing her fingers through my tangled hair, and Xavier had told me all about his own instances of drunk or hungover mishaps. We laughed so hard that water had squirted out of my nose when I tried to drink through the giggles, which then left Xavier silently gasping for air from his own amusement.

"It is hard to explain what it feels like when someone who hurts you so badly shows you affection. It is like winning a race you were forced to run, the success of it euphoric in a way that blinds you with its brightness, preventing you from seeing the tragedy in your worn shoes and stuttering heart and teary eyes. I was desperate for their love, and even now I struggle to not hold that memory close to my heart." I paused, noting that my lips were going numb. Still, I felt the sadness, just as I sensed the prickling ache that was growing. Every bit of strength and determination faded, a ghost to me now. "I wish I could forget all of the good, because it would make the bad so much easier to hate. But the truth is that the good is too heavy to move, so I must let it remain in my mind, constantly on guard in case that love I had for them creeps back into my consciousness. I cannot afford to be weak in their presence—cannot give in to that desire to be worthy."

Convinced that any response Padon conjured would only make things worse, I sighed, focusing instead on the steadily rising pain. It was fierce now, but still not as strong as the exhaustion. It felt like floating, which was such a relief from the constant drowning I suffered from.

"Love isn't equivalent to good. Sometimes we do it in the wrong way, and sometimes it's toxic or painful. Them being unable to love you in the way you deserved doesn't make you unworthy of better."

The nonchalance with which he said the words paired with the shrug left me speechless. His tongue darted out, wetting his lips as he looked at me. When he realized that I would not say anything more, he nodded and looked up at the ceiling. I remained on my side, blinks becoming longer and harder to resist. My left hand lost feeling entirely, the pain falling victim to the cold numbness.

"I was in love once, before you. She was stunning in every way, the embodiment of life—if that makes sense. She made me laugh and never let me fall victim to sadness. The light practically followed her, shining on anyone in her proximity." The sweet taste of sadness permeated the air, the room once more seeming to flicker. "Being with her was like flying, but when I realized she didn't love me in the same way anymore, I was suddenly free-falling."

His profile was sharp, the lines and angles looking as if they were carved from marble, but his voice was not. It was deep and smooth, soft even. Padon was feeling in a way I had not seen him do so before.

Against my will, my eyes fluttered closed.

"The worst part was that I didn't just lose her but her family as well. Before she admitted that she wasn't in love with me, her father and sister went missing. They had traveled across worlds, seeking to satiate their hunger for adventure, but years passed and they never came home. It devastated her and her mother, pushing them to do foolish things in the name of remembering. Actions that pulled them from me and into an orbit of devastation. And when they too were gone, I was left with an empty palace and an empty chest, cradling a heart which had been obliterated."

With as much energy as I could conjure, I lifted my right hand and reached for Padon in an effort to console him. It was strange that the movement felt right, almost second nature. My palm met the cold skin of his cheek, his hand immediately cradling my own.

"What was her name?" I asked, my voice barely a whisper now.

I could feel some sort of tug, like I was being dragged somewhere new. For a split second, I thought that Padon was showing me something different, but when his muffled words came, it sounded as if he were a universe away.

And then I was gone, pine needles digging into my scalp and rain falling from a bruised sky.

CHAPTER TWENTY-FOUR

BELLAMY

"You fucked that mortal scum?" Noe's voice was enough to send me hurtling myself off a cliff, but Asher's unnaturally still form in front of me held me in place. She looked too much like she had in Haven, on the floor in a heap of blood.

"What was I supposed to do? I am deprived, and it is not like you are offering!" Henry, despite all of his injuries, had already recovered and gotten back to his feet. Now, he was apparently well enough to argue.

"I will kill you if you do not shut up." There was Lian, normally a calm voice of reason, pacing behind me. She would never admit it, but she had grown to love Asher—just as they all had. For all her sarcasm and casual flirting, she was far more affected than she preferred, which showed with her refusal to play into the Sun and Moon's antics.

"Oh, please. I would not get in bed with you if it would save your life." Noe got down on her knees beside me then, waving off a smirking Henry.

"I would." Cyprus raised his hand, his head tilting slightly closer to Asher's. He had insisted on lying beside her, though the way he openly hit on Henry showed that his wide-spread flirtatious nature was back in full force, rather than aimed solely at the unconscious female to his left.

"Well, you would sleep with anyone." True. Though we all knew that Luca and Cyprus would one day give into one another, the latter's sexual activities until then were many and frequent. Not that Noe—or any of us—truly judged or cared. Until recently, our little group had all been eager to put someone new beneath us nightly.

"What if it would save your life?" Henry's waggling brows and seductive grin were not enough to make Noe so much as hesitate.

"Dig my grave then."

They burst into laughter, the three of them not so much as perturbed by the abnormally unmoving Asher or the creature to our right. I brought my fingers to my temples, massaging as if I could rub away the irritation and ache.

Was it wrong to loathe your family? In this moment, I truly did. I wanted nothing more than to pick Asher up, portal her to The Royal City, and simply exist with her. If I could, I would let the world fall apart while I basked in her presence. While I worshiped her and listened to her and *held* her. We could talk about our pasts, give truths that neither of us had been willing to part with before, and dream of a future that we would never have.

Instead, I was here, listening to Noe—the hater of all males—tell Henry that his small cock and weird toes were too much of a turn off for her.

"You are all far more annoying than you are useful. Now, shut up lest you scare the Strange One into an endless sleep," Wrath hissed, his voice a haunting tenor.

Apart from Asher, none of us were fans of the dalistori. He was creepy at best but utterly devoted to Ash in the same way we were, which made him tolerable.

They were all silent now, each looking from Wrath to me, as if they were waiting for me to say something to shut up the creature. But I would not because he was saying exactly what I wanted to.

I reached down to grab Asher's hand. It was colder than normal, and I could not help but offer some of the heat that flowed through my body. The many burns across her skin were gone, healed by Ranbir—who was sure she would come to when her body and mind were ready. I touched one of her new scars, which she had made sure were always left behind.

"I want to remember," she had once said, and the Healer never forgot.

The only one not wearing the leathers I had designed for my Trusted, Ranbir was a standout amongst the group. His bright white tunic and trousers reflected the dull light of the autumn sun above, his normally shiny black hair a loose and long mess, his beard now well past his chin. He barely slept, which was made obvious by the bags under his eyes and the hunch of his shoulders. Still, he looked positive in his statement, nearly black eyes staring down at the sleeping princess with a strange mixture of sadness and love.

"I think she is awake," Ranbir said from beside Asher's head. I gasped, looking down at her closed eyes and parted lips. She did not look awake, but maybe that was my stress preventing me from seeing her as I usually did—fully and wholly.

"Oh yes, she is definitely awake." We all jumped at Asher's husky words, sounding as if she had swallowed gravel. To everyone's surprise, Lian shoved her way to Asher's side, kicking Cyprus in the stomach and causing him to let out a loud grunt of pain. The Air reached down and grabbed the princess, a hand on either cheek.

"You stupid, stupid thing. Why do you insist on trying to die?" No one spoke as a single tear ran down the Air's face, falling onto Asher's leather-clad chest. A sense of devastation seemed to bleed from Lian as the tear splashed.

Rare was not the word to explain the occurrences in which Lian showed sadness or grief. After I had brought her to Eoforhild, she had worked for years to harden herself. This small fissure in her stoic wall was by far the most pain she had shown since then, her sobs soft but jaw-dropping as she leaned down and hugged Asher.

If the princess was as baffled as the rest of us, she did not show it. Instead, she wrapped her arms around Lian and seemed to stare off into the distance, eyes flickering back and forth as if she were watching something unfold. Then, with a sad smile, she whispered into Lian's ear, "She would not want this for you."

With a gentle sort of intensity, Asher pushed Lian up slightly, forcing eye contact. Lian was now the shortest of our group since Winona was no longer here to claim that title, but she still managed to look larger, her imposing and unfaltering ruthlessness adding inches to her height. Until now, that was. As The Manipulator spoke words only Lian could hear, we all felt the heaviness of our recent losses plaguing our hearts.

Lian's tears ceased moments later, the remnants wiped away by Asher's thumbs. Slowly, Asher leaned forward and placed a gentle kiss to Lian's forehead, this time audibly whispering, "May she return to Eternity."

Tension faded when Luca reached down to offer Lian help as the two females separated, which she promptly swatted away with a sound of disgust. Amusement soon followed when Cyprus reached out his hand instead, wiggling his fingers, and Luca leaned down to lightly smack his cheek in return.

As soon as Lian was fully up, I reached for Asher, scooping her into my arms and burrowing my face in her neck. When the smell of vanilla hit my nose, I nearly broke.

"He healed me. Are they still there?" Her words were muffled against my hair, but I knew what she meant.

"He left the scars, Princess. They are still there. And *you* are still *here.*"

She was okay. She would be okay.

I did not realize how badly I was shaking until Asher's steady hand met my jaw. Relief flooded me at the simple contact. Like the rainbow after a season of rain, Asher's presence lit my world with color. In fact, I could have sworn that the sky brightened, the sun stronger and warmer than before.

"I missed you," I said into her ear, smiling at the way she shivered in response. There was nothing quite like feeling and hearing her. A box full of every note we had ever sent one another sat waiting in my small room in Pike, but no matter how many times I reread them, it would never be as beautiful as the real thing.

When she looked up, I gasped out loud, horror filling me. A violent storm of emotions raged within her eyes, cyclones and thunder of something beyond understanding. She was harder, fiercer, and angrier than the last time I had held her. I could feel it in my chest—my soul. Something about her was fundamentally different.

"I missed you, too." The hard edge to her tone—one which I knew was not meant to show anger, but was merely an example of the changes occurring within her—sent alarm bells blaring in my head. What had happened in the last couple of weeks that made her this way?

"What did you say to her?" I asked quietly.

"I told her that life and death do not conquer. We do." She shrugged, leaning up to place a gentle kiss on my lips. I desperately wished she would not pull away, but of course, she did. Suffocating on the taste of her would be better than breathing the empty air that signaled her absence.

"I love you." The words ripped free of my mouth without a second thought, and I realized how much she needed to hear them when her eyes grew glassy. She reached up again, this time offering a far more reassuring kiss. When my tongue slid across her bottom lip, she chuckled, pulling away again. But I chased her mouth with my own, securing my arms around her tighter and leaning forward. A soft breath left her mouth, and I slipped my tongue inside, taking advantage of her surprise.

She laughed into the kiss, but gave just as much as I did, locking her arms around my neck and smiling as her tongue wrapped around mine. I nearly moaned at the sensation of her, but I could still feel her strange resolve, as if she had built a wall around her, coarsening herself.

"Gross! Stop that this instant." The hiss came from near my knees, irritating, but not enough to ruin my joy at having my Asher back in my arms.

I hate that cat, you know.

Asher's answering laugh to my yelled mental words made me smile, a true moment of happiness. Those were so rare these days that I tried to memorize every blush and blink and bend of her in this moment.

I love you too, by the way.

And that, the sound of her intoxicating and demanding mental voice, I would need to remember too.

"Well, little brat, you really beat the shit out of that thing," Henry said, ruining the moment.

Cyprus laughed, leaning over to press a kiss to Asher's cheek before quickly standing and moving himself out of my reach. She was not smiling, instead staring at the bloody female who still lay unconscious a few feet away.

"What is she?" Luca asked, leaning his head forward and squinting his eyes—as if the answer to his questions were written somewhere on the female's body. Henry had told us what the creature had done, but Ranbir had been far too focused on Asher to explain anything.

Winona would have known, but it was her husband who answered.

"She is a whisp, though I have never seen one who manifested that way. I can search through...*her* research sometime soon." With that, we all quickly sobered, the amusement and joy depleting in an instant. The air was left thick and stifling, full of the stench of death and loss.

"Okay, time to go." I lifted Asher with me, holding her so tightly it might have hurt. But letting her go, losing this contact, was not an option. Not when she was suffering, and not when I was crumbling.

The silence of the fae since the battle in Grishel left us all with our hackles raised. Something sinister was brewing across the Sea of Akiva, something not even The Mist could hold back. We were preparing, training with mortals and demons and any creature willing to step up and choose a side. But we were vastly outnumbered.

Asher needed to be ready.

"Go where?" Her voice was so much higher than her normal tone that I feared she might still be hurt somehow. When she squirmed in my arms, I set her down gently, grabbing onto her face and pulling it close to mine, inspecting her for harm. "Go where, Bellamy?"

I froze, finally understanding.

"To Pike. We cannot have you looking for allies anymore. You need to train, to prepare. This will not just be hard physically but mentally as well." Henry's voice came from somewhere beside us, but all I could see was Asher—her furrowed brows and small frown and the streaks of lightning that seemed to break the storm in her eyes.

Perhaps I could ignore Pino's warning and simply tell her how limited our time was. Maybe the secrets could come to an end and we could exist together before we were ripped apart.

"I am not going to Pike. I need to find allies. I need to convince the mortals that we are worth fighting for. Why would I go to Eoforhild when I am not done yet?" She sounded genuinely confused, as if us wanting her to come back with us was a ridiculous notion.

To her, it was. She could not fathom a world in which one would think of themselves because life to her was about serving. For years, she was told that her worth was measured in success—in blood and fear and pain. She was taught to sit, be still, and speak in the same way a hound was. She did not know how to be selfish, because she was brainwashed into being self-sacrificing.

She thought herself a wicked curse, yet she refused to accept any outcome that did not result in her saving Alemthian.

And what would that make me if I forced or coerced her into following my whims? I was neither her captor nor her ruler, and she was not my servant or my possession. Asher could not—would not—be belittled in such a way again. She ached for freedom, and there was no world in which I would be the one to steal it from her once more.

"Okay, then you stay. But you will be adding one to your little gang of heathens." Asher sighed, offering a sad smile as if she were prepared to let me down gently. I smirked at her, lightly flicking her nose before portaling away.

When I landed in Farai's quarters, he did not so much as scream. After three weeks of being with us, the fae had grown used to our habits—or antics as he would call them.

"Ah, the demon prince with a penchant for abduction. How may I help you tonight?"

I chuckled at his insolence, which I greatly admired. His bright white hair was wet, the black tunic and trousers airy and light for the spring heat. He had been training with our army daily, the only thing he did more than spar was annoy Lian and ask for Asher.

"Ready to see Ash?" I asked, leaning against the wooden doorframe and crossing my arms. Farai sat up, launching himself off the small bed so quickly that it let out a loud creek in protest. When he tossed the book he was reading to the ground and rushed at me, I laughed, reaching out my hand.

To his credit, Farai did not hesitate to take it, nor did he do so much as gasp at the tearing feel of portaling. When we landed back in the small forest, the fae did buckle slightly, but he recovered quickly, his head whipping back and forth in search of his friend.

She stood near the whisp that was still unconscious on the ground, but it was Ranbir she looked at. He leaned forward, wrapping his arms around her. At first, Ash did not move, seemingly too surprised to act. But then she took a deep breath and returned the hug. Ranbir's shoulders sagged, his head falling forward. He had not confided in anyone since the loss of his wife, not so much as crying in front of us after that day.

That was the thing about Asher. She was someone that everyone wanted to like. It was difficult not to find joy in her presence, to feel the pull of her power, or to fall for her awe-inspiring desire to be better. She was brilliant and cunning and loving. So it made sense that Ranbir would finally fall apart in her arms.

My hand lifted, stopping Farai from moving towards her. "Let them have a moment."

When the two separated, Asher stared into Ranbir's eyes, so clearly communicating with her magic. A bone-chilling shake raked through Ranbir before he stepped further back, giving a small nod. Like nothing happened, he crouched down and began inspecting the female on the forest floor.

Noe beat us to her, skipping towards my princess with a smile that crinkled her eyes while her hair blew in the breeze behind her. Asher laughed as Noe reached out, the two of them quickly embracing before they began to whisper softly to one another. I could just make out my name before Cyprus walked to them and pecked Asher's forehead, Luca following not far behind and wrapping her in a tender hug.

Then, as if she could sense us, Asher turned.

One day, I would paint this scene. I would capture the beauty of friends reuniting—of a love so deep it had engraved itself into the soul. The way the two of them stared at one another, not so much as breathing, was something poets only hoped to convey through words.

Tragedy was a unique sort of lovely, like a dying flower or a shattered glass vase—broken things that held a foreboding intrigue. But the healing that comes from tragedy? That sort of magnificence could not be recreated or explained.

And so we all watched as Asher ran, crossing the distance in seconds before launching herself forward. Farai did not hesitate, opening his arms to catch her. She wrapped herself around him and sobbed onto his shoulder as he laughed, his own tears streaming freely down his cheeks.

They stayed that way for a while, just breathing the other in. I smiled, feeling as if I had finally done something right. Looking at Noe, I nodded my head. She offered a sad smile before grabbing onto Lian, Cyprus, and Luca, the four of them disappearing in a cloud of shadows. Henry watched them go then made his way to Ranbir, bending down beside him and further discussing the whisp's magic.

To my dismay, the dalistori came and sat by my feet. I groaned, wishing I could kick the damn thing and never see it again. Sadly, he was not going anywhere any time soon. Asher had told me that it believed they were meant to find one another, which apparently required the thing to never leave her side.

"That one looks odd," Wrath said, the sound of his voice making me even more uncomfortable than his horrifying yellow eyes. I stepped away, putting some distance between us. He watched me, then, with a chilling smile, closed the space once more. As if that were not enough, he began to grow, his height soaring to my chest before suddenly stopping. "Do not be scared, little fae prince. I will not bite."

I glared at him, trying to feign annoyance to hide the utter shock I felt at the fact that he knew what I was. Could he smell it on me? Did he know more than he was letting on? What if he knew how to get the magic out of me?

"Wrath, what do you know about magic being infused into someone?" My casual tone and folded arms were a terrible attempt at nonchalance, which the dalistori clearly saw through based on his amused expression.

"You wish for your veins to be clean once more, princeling." Not a question. Haughtiness filled his tone, but beneath that, there was some sort of solemnness as he stared at Asher. She had her forehead pressed against Farai's, the two of them talking in hushed excitement. "One day, those wards of yours will fail, and I do not believe much more of her can be chipped away without her becoming nothing but a shell."

"What about hers? How do we stop it? Do we even need to?" I asked, practically begging for some sort of answer to a question I have had since I met Pino at Reader River. But even he did not know—no one did. Wrath squinted his eyes, sniffing the air as if he could sample her magic.

"I do not know. She is strange, and I do not fully understand it. But she is mine, and I will not let even my god take her. I will protect her, princeling, trust that."

My smile returned in full force. I might not like the vermin, but he did care for Asher. Even if it was in his own odd way, I could count on the psycho to keep her safe.

"After a lifetime of being hated for all the wrong reasons, it is good to know she is finally loved for the right ones."

We looked to one another for a moment, both of us acknowledging our utter devotion to Asher. When we simultaneously nodded, I broke away and walked towards the still crying pair in front of us.

"—need to bring them here. It is not safe, Ash."

"It is not that simple, Fair. You should not even be here. If Mia realizes you are alive, she will be waiting for us."

OF REALMS AND CHAOS

"Exactly. That is why we must help before she can harm them." The conversation was still quiet, though it was shrouded with tension and fear. Farai reached up, cupping both sides of Asher's face. She sighed, placing hers on top of his, her eyes closed. "Please, Ash, I cannot lose him."

"Fair…"

It was clear that Asher did not want to tell him no, that she too wished to save their friends. How could we blame them? Not only were her best friend's still in Betovere, under the thumb of wicked rulers who craved revenge, but Farai's *husband* was still there. The danger was clear, and if it were Asher, I would not hesitate to slaughter an entire realm to save her.

"We will get them." The words left my lips in a rush, born of not only my need to please Asher, but also my own fears of losing her. "Leave it to me."

Farai nodded, separating from Asher and looking at me without animosity for the first time since I stole him from that battlefield. I patted his shoulder and winked before I pulled Asher into me. It seemed today was meant to be full of sad hellos and goodbyes.

Leaving her hurt worse and worse each time, like my heart was slowly being carved away. Every goodbye ended with her taking another piece of me, and I wished she knew that I would gladly give them all just to make her happy.

"I will write soon, but please, for the love of all things sacred, stay out of trouble. Okay? We will take the whisp with us, and if she chooses to not help, then we will find her a home that does not lead to the deaths of hundreds. Go to King Trint. Other than Maliha, Gandry has the largest mortal military force. He would be an excellent ally. Perhaps then we would have enough aid for you to come home to me."

Before she could respond, I leaned down and pressed my lips to hers. This time, she did not resist me when I deepened it, my tongue slipping into her mouth. I tasted her—savored her—for longer than I should have, but the kiss was still over far sooner than I wished. Farai coughed, clearing his throat after. Of course, Asher pulled away, still so unused to public displays of affection.

I groaned, gripping the side of her neck and stealing one more kiss before she laughed and stepped back. My last desperate connection of our hands had her smiling, a genuine and full upturn of her mouth that made my heartbeat stutter.

"'Enough' would mean we have an army so large that the fae pause. If we cannot do that, then innocents will be lost. I cannot—will not—rule over a realm of graves." Her voice was solemn, but that undercurrent of anger still wreaked havoc in the gray sea of her eyes. I wanted to ask, but I could feel that it was not the right time.

Farai smiled beside her, looking down with what could only be described as admiration in his eyes. It was interesting that he did not comment on our relationship, nor had he since I found him. Instead, he seemed to fall into Asher's orbit in the same way I did—in the same way we all did.

Asher was the sun, and we were merely the planets that orbited her, relying on her pull to keep us safely moving. Farai was no exception to that rule, and neither was Wrath, who had found his place at her side—once more only barely reaching her knees in height.

Turning around, I made my way to Ranbir and Henry, ready to take the Healer and the whisp back to Pike. There was too much to do, and I needed to figure out exactly how to manage it all while knowing Asher would still be away.

"Well, you could always continue to roam, but know that you might not last long if Asher finds out you are wreaking havoc on innocents." Henry was speaking to the female, who was now awake. She seemed dazed, like her mind was somewhere far away. Her long black hair was full of pine needles, streaks of dried blood covering her face. Henry had told us how badly Asher beat the whisp, so it was likely that even after being healed, she was not feeling well.

"Life is a series of joyless events and soul-breaking loss. I do not understand why you insist on prolonging it," she said, the impressively bleak words melodic and high.

A startled laugh came from my back. I turned to find Farai holding his hand over his mouth and Asher elbowing him hard enough in his side to make him grunt in pain.

"What did you do to her to make her talk like that?" I asked, the corner of my lips lifting in amusement.

Asher's eyes narrowed, her arms crossing over her chest as she jutted out her hip. "First of all, she was just as crazy when we first found her, so that is not my fault." Farai laughed again, earning a shove from Asher before she continued, "Second of all, she was going to *kill* us."

"Well, I am eager to hear about whatever heinous action you took that is making you so defensive."

She let out a soft growl before marching past me, going to the whisp's side. Henry looked back, twirling his finger in a circle near his head. Whether he was calling Asher or the whisp crazy was unclear.

"She stole my memories. Such a gift, to be free of the pain. Perhaps next you will rid me of my heart and allow me passage to The Above."

Even Ranbir looked startled by the creature's words, the entirety of our group awkwardly making eye contact with one another. What did one say to that?

"Well, you heard it, put the odd little thing out of her misery," Wrath said, sitting back and licking a paw. When his tail swished and wrapped around my ankle slightly, I made a noise of disgust and moved farther from him. His laugh echoed off the trees, putting fear into even the whisp's vacant eyes.

"Why do you wish to die so badly? Why not use that magic of yours for something good?" Asher's question was naïve in all the best ways—all the ways that she should not still be after a lifetime of suffering.

The whisp tilted her head, openly staring at Asher as if she were a confusing new discovery. "I have heard stories about you. I have followed you and listened. Torment such as yours should break you, not remake you. Why do you use your magic to help when you can kill those who wronged you instead?"

"Is that what happened? Did a mortal harm you, and now you seek revenge?" Every gaze moved to me, curious looks flashing my way. The female looked as if she were pondering my question, weighing different answers.

"Yes, a group of males did."

I did not miss the way Asher's fingers dug into the dirt below her, knuckles taking on a lighter hue from her grip. Despite every effort to not think of it, Sterling's face came to my mind. She would not talk about it, but I knew that he had touched her. Just like that, I was shaking, my body heating up.

"Killing innocents will not bring you the joy you so clearly seek. Death will not take away the pain." Wrath scoffed at Ranbir's words, still licking his paw without a care in the world. Henry watched, brows furrowed. Farai was silent as well though he had slowly begun putting space between him and the dalistori.

Asher and I looked at one another at the same time, the resolve settling between us. I squatted down, offering the whisp my hand. "Come with us. We can find you a home, even if you do not wish to fight our war."

She stared at my hand as if it were a trick, like she had once been fooled by kindness such as this. Asher reached forward, slowly bringing her fingertips to the whisp's cheek. When the female did not flinch, Asher closed the remaining space, flattening her palm out.

"Let me help you get rid of some of that pain."

CHAPTER TWENTY-FIVE

STASSI

I missed the creature in the cell.

Iniko was droning on and on about how boring life had become since I was sent away, which was probably true, but I was tired of hearing about it. Plus, it had barely been any time at all. I wanted to go back and play. I didn't wish to sit and sulk while we all waited and waited for our oh-so-glorious ruler to show his face.

Seven of us sat at the wide round table, the soft steel color of the marble reflecting back warped versions of our faces. Iniko was to my left, his skin as black as night and hair the vibrant blue of a polished sapphire, just as his magic was. He wore only a pair of cotton trousers, the loose blue fabric sitting low on his hips, every muscle straining in his body as he looked at me and winked.

To my right sat Karys, who glowed the orange of a flame as she attempted to assuage the hatred filling the room—her matching hair blowing on the breeze that creeped through an open window. She wore no clothing, covered in an array of strung jewels instead, the orange gems shining in the light of the candles around us. Briefly, she flinched, her magic flaring. I gasped, raising my hands to shield my eyes.

"A love so far away shouldn't be that powerful," Karys whispered, as crazy as she always was. Still, her magic was strong, pulsing through the room once more and demanding we submit.

As per usual, I felt weak. Sin and virtue didn't exist here as it did on Alemthian. We felt in different ways, held standards that seemed blurry in comparison to their stark contrast between good and evil. The others didn't care that we lived like this because none of them were affected in the way I was. They might differ in their strength, but it was I who was left with barely any magic at all.

"They are all doing fairly well—though I find they are unsettled by our fearless leader's aloof attitude as of late. Not to mention that new lover he has taken." Venturae's voice was louder than before, her green eyes locked on Jonah beside her. Her thin, forest green braids were nearly to the floor now, dark skin identical to one of the females I had spent a night with while on Alemthian—reminding me once more of how desperately I wanted to leave my home.

"War is on the horizon. I can feel it stirring within me. Peace has become rare, and unrest will push him to make a decision." The calmness in Jonah's voice seemed to settle the wariness that clouded the room. They all wanted war, regardless of who we were defeating. Immortality did that to a creature—made them eager for something new.

Which was why if he wasn't here in five minutes, I was going to leave. It was his mission after all; he couldn't fault me for taking it seriously. Nor could any of them blame me for wanting to feel more than stagnant comfort.

"How was it?" Druj asked from across the table. She wore a shimmering yellow gown, the shape molding to her body and cascading down her long brown figure. Her yellow hair was cut short, nearly showing her scalp, just as it had always been.

Life on Shamay never changed.

"It has been fine. I have yet to find her, but she will turn up eventually. Apparently, I caught her during her rebellious phase. She has run away from home." With a wave of my hand, I brushed off the intrigue that lit up all six of their faces. I didn't need any of them attempting to steal my mission from beneath me.

My head fell against the high-backed chair—the detailed carvings of different sins and virtues marking it as mine, just as its pink color did. The walls sported different symbols, the sky itself etched upon it—night and day. Before my eyes closed, I caught a glance of a detail upon the ceiling that reminded me of another obligation—I would need to visit Torrel before I go back to Alemthian. Her little one was likely driving her insane as he learned to fly, and I would need to make sure that Jesre— their keeper—was properly seeing to them in my absence.

"Don't go getting lost now. You wouldn't want to end up missing like Sol." That was my last straw. I looked over at Iniko, his smug smile making me want to peel the skin from his face with a dull blade. He knew what Sol meant to me, what she meant to her sister.

"I'm leaving, tell our all-powerful and imposing leader to brief me later. Whatever it is, I have more important things to do," I said, my nose tilting up as I pushed back the chair and let it scrape against the dark marble floors. Everything in here was too monochromatic. It was giving me a headache.

The others protested, all of their magic surging—electrifying the air. So heavy was the weight of it that I stumbled, my pink heels nearly snapping under the pressure. Unfortunately for them, I had maintained much of the strength I had gained on Alemthian. I whipped around, lifting my hands and forcing out as much as I could spare—adding pink to the rainbow of colors that were quickly mingling at the table.

Gasps sounded, none of them prepared for my magic to feel as potent as it was. A smile lit up my face, stretching my skin and lifting my cheeks.

"How about you all have a bit of fun while I'm gone?" And then the sin took over, each of them feeling far greater than they normally did. And as they succumbed to my magic, their own was fed as well.

Iniko's body shook under the onslaught of chaos. Kyoufu's red magic blasted out of his body as fear took hold of the others. I laughed, walking away as fast as the pink dress would allow me. The way it held my thighs together made it difficult, but soon, I was marching out of the castle, feeling the relief as I passed through the wards.

First I would go to the mountains, then to my caged creature on Alemthian.

***

"Well, you smell particularly foul," I said, leaning against the bars. I still wore my pink dress, the skin-tight fabric ripped where Milo's talons had scratched me. Torrel had scolded him little, but I wasn't bothered. They were the only two things I missed about home.

The male on the other side of the bars was slightly slumped forward, his breathing a heavy wheeze. I could hear the rattling of his lungs attempting to suck in air. They hadn't healed him this time. Interesting.

"Ah, Spice, you wound me. Since the last time you visited, I had my leg snapped in four places and my chest kicked in, so I imagine what you are smelling is the gore. Alas, two hours of torture is usually followed by alone time rather than a chance to wash off the bile and blood. But I promise that, as soon as I have access to a bubble bath, I will be sure to get squeaky clean for you." Even his playful words couldn't mask the pain that bled through his tone. He was hurt quite badly.

"Only two hours? That's a truly paltry torture session. They could use the practice."

His laugh sent him into a fit of coughs, blood pouring from his lips. "It seems I might die before I get the chance to show you just how enjoyable I can be. A pity." His charming smile wavered slightly, eyes fluttering closed.

The wicked part of me—the sinful part—was angry that he would die before I was able to have him inside of me. I was livid with myself for choosing to answer the summons home rather than stay here. What I planned to be a slow and teasing experience was now going to end before it even began.

Virtue hated early death even more than sin—when it was doled out by anyone other than me, at least. I was far too conceited a creature to believe any of my own actions were wrong. Now, that virtuous half of myself was angry at the injustice of it all. It was that half that acted, forcing me to back away from the bars. My magic seeped from me, crawling through the dungeons and up into the golden halls.

"You won't die. Not until I am ready for you to." Before he could respond, I was walking away, storming up the countless stairs. This day was proving to be heinous.

When I reached the spot where my magic had pooled, following a soul of virtue that manifested in the need to heal, I grabbed onto the female. She had short brown hair and an uninteresting face, her cream skin and thin lips not standing out as anything particularly exciting. My hand went around her throat, pink aura pulsing from me as I looked her in the eyes. They were blue, like the sea or a clear sky on this planet.

"Fix him, now." My voice echoed, tone chilling in its fury. And then I shoved my magic into her, latching onto her virtuous thoughts and igniting them, letting that desire to help run rampant in her mind. When I released her, she gagged, gripping her neck.

Only a few seconds passed before she stood up, took four deep breaths, and headed to the male dying on the stone floor below these gilded halls. I would take him with me, but it would have to be after I

298

found Asher. I needed her secure before I began making demands and stealing away foreign creatures. Evidently, I was far more like that bossy male than I realized, seeing as we both enjoyed a good abduction.

When we reached the cell on the left, the fae female pulled out a large iron key, opening the cage and walking in. She offered what sounded like genuine apologies for taking so long and then added even more as she healed him, the experience painful by the sound of his gasps and cries.

The male didn't pay much attention to her. Instead, he stared at me, his dull eyes taking on a shine that was not there before. I rolled my own eyes, but the smirk on my face could not be stopped.

When her hands ghosted across the male's chest, he was forced to stifle a scream, his body convulsing from the pain. If he didn't recover quickly, I was going to lose my patience. Luckily for everyone involved, the Healer finished. I pushed past the slightly open cell door, grabbing the female by the arm and spinning her to face me.

"Don't tell anyone that you saw me here. If you do, I will cut off your eyelids and make you watch as I slowly kill everyone you love. Understand?" She nodded, her gaze wide with fear and her lip trembling. I couldn't help but compare her to a scared fawn, her mousy brown hair and big eyes reinforcing that docile resemblance. "Now, leave before I do all of that just for the fun of it."

Shoving her away, I turned to face the now-healed male, listening halfheartedly to the rushed steps of her retreating. For the first time, the creature on the ground looked fearful. Not in the way most were when they realized just how dangerous my kind could be. No, this was an inquisitive sort of terror.

"Must you threaten someone when you can simply ask for their discretion?" I groaned at the taste of virtue that came from the words, my fingertips giving off a pink glow. It bubbled inside of me, eager to burst free. After a lifetime of straining for a semblance of the magic the others held, the overwhelming nature of having more than I could handle threatened to consume me. "Why is murder your first instinct?"

Normally, I would kill someone for having the audacity to place judgment on my character, because who were they to question me? To look down upon me? Who were they when I was closer to Eternity than I was these mortals?

But when he said it, with his eyes that now held a fragment of life and his innately curious tone, I wondered if he meant something different.

"Would you like that?" I asked, as if I couldn't help myself. As if I had to see what he would prefer.

It was strange, feeling so intrigued by something for this long. He was different. Lust and horror circled the space between us, like hawks readying for the kill, just as they always did when I found a new toy. Beyond that, however, was a new sort of experience. This male was compelled by my nature, and it seemed that outweighed everything else.

"I am no fan of death and destruction. I find myself more inclined to seek entertainment in adventure and drink." With a scoff, I walked towards him. He watched, his eyes never leaving mine—to my dismay. Slowly lowering myself to sit beside him, I leaned my head back, the grime of the cell wall quickly coating my pink locks. When I turned to look at him, the male was smiling. "Is it truly death you desire, or is it the prospect of feeling something that drives you to slaughter?"

My responding laugh was far too loud, but I could not bring myself to mask it. What an unusual thought, that we were anything more than wicked and cruel. Each of us possessed the antithesis of what made us evil, of course. I drew magic from virtue in the same way I did sin. Just as Venturae drew from both fate and chance and Kyoufu drew from fear and bravery. But that didn't make us half good. We were all unable to feel in the same way that these creatures did, and that made us more dangerous than any evil they had known.

"You seek to see redemption where there is none, handsome. But that does beg the question: If you aren't a malicious murderer, then why are you being held captive by the golden fae?"

Absentmindedly, I reached out and conjured a small pink knife, twirling it in my hand. As expected, the male seemed unbothered. Even I was unsure if this action was meant to be a threat.

"If I answer, will you explain what in the Underworld you are?" There it was. I had been waiting for him to ask, seeing as I was so clearly other.

"Prove your worth, and I will s*how* you."

He laughed, his hand brushing through his dirt-filled hair. I couldn't help but notice the cut of his jaw as he did, his neck and shoulders straining with muscle.

"How about we make a deal, Spice? You get me out of here, and I will show you exactly how worthy I am. All I need is answers and freedom."

CHAPTER TWENTY-SIX

ASHER

Farai was probably the only one other than me that Wrath tolerated. Though that was in Fair's nature. He was easy to like and difficult to hate.

We were staying at a small inconspicuous inn that rested on the border of Caless, the capital of Gandry. Despite its small size, the inn was comfortable and appealing in all the ways that the others had not been. The room was comprised of wooden floors and plaster walls, both a dark brown. The left half of the room held a large, blue sofa and two rocking chairs. A violet, circular rug sat in the center of the grouping, a too-large table atop it.

The best part of this room was that it had two beds rather than one, though they were small and had a tendency to creak when we adjusted to get comfortable at night. This would be our ninth night here—nine days worth of trying and failing to plan out a convincing appeal for the King of Gandry.

Farai sat at the top of the bed, eating an apple. I laid between his splayed legs, writing yet another horrible speech for Trint. Wrath was curled up on Farai's left, the Shifter's hand absently scratching between the dalistori's ears. Henry was on the bed to our right, making use of the empty mattress to spread out at least twelve books. Studying as he called it.

King Trint was the one we knew the least of. He was a successful monarch, his kingdom prosperous and relatively peaceful. Their military forces were large and well trained, though they had no ill will towards any of the other kingdoms it seemed. They were known for their jewels, the entire southwest portion of their lands filled with caves and mines that housed the precious gems. The maps made the area look like a network of veins, bleeding enough diamonds and rubies to sustain an entire kingdom.

Because of that, Trint need not want for anything, which was not a good thing in our case. There was little we could promise him. He was supposedly greedy and young, which made him dangerous and unpredictable. Yes, we had solved his monster problem, but would that be enough for him to risk his people in a war that would not benefit him?

As always, I had secretly considered the idea of using myself as a bargaining tool. My whole life had seen me passed around in different ways, paraded like a prize. Why not use that to my advantage?

But I knew better than to put myself at the mercy of a mortal man again. Desperation might drive me to that one day, but I was not there yet. Besides, four of the six rulers had denied a similar offer nearly two years ago when Mia and Xavier first proffered me to all the kingdoms.

There was also no use in denying that selfish desire within myself to have Bellamy at my side. Yes, there was a part of me that would have him or no one, and that was more dangerous than anything else. Self-centered thoughts or choices would doom us. So I shoved that piece of myself down, down, down until it was so deep within my mind that even I struggled to sense it. But it would lie in wait, seeking an opportunity to take over and push me towards a path that would lead to Bellamy's hand in mine as the world beyond burned.

"You have so many scars now," Farai said, startling me out of my thoughts. His finger trailed across my shoulder, which was exposed due to the oversized orange tunic I had acquired. It was odd having someone who knew me so well see all the ways in which I had changed. Did he like this version of me less? Did he think me a monster just as the rest did?

"No, I have a story." It was all too easy to shrug, dragging up the fabric to hide the jagged scars from the afriktor. Farai froze, his body going rigid behind me.

"You always had a story, Ash." His voice was firm, as if he were angry with my suggestion that I had not. Seeing as he was one of the few fae who regularly insisted I was not living before Bellamy had taken me, his animosity towards my statement surprised me. I tried to understand what it was that had upset him without allowing my eternal curiosity to take hold of my power—no, *magic*—and break his trust.

"But now it is one worth being told."

He pushed me up, his large hands grabbing onto my shoulders and forcing me to slightly face him. His bright white eyes and hair were alight from the Sun magic above us, his skin a combination of shadow and light. Despite having him with me for over a week, I still struggled to grasp the fact that he was here and safe and *whole*. His fingers met my chin, the hold tight but not painful.

"You were always deserving of a beautiful tale, no matter what they tried to convince you of. I know that two centuries worth of lies and manipulation are hard to shake, but I do not *ever* want to hear you suggest that you were any less before." When his voice broke at the word "less," I nearly let a tear slip. But I was done being a sad and broken victim. I was stronger now, and I was no captive princess patiently waiting for my next beating.

"So beautiful. Yay, friendship and all of that. Anyways, I think I found something." Henry's sarcastic tone cut through the tension, causing even Wrath to chuckle softly. A rarity, seeing as the two of them still greatly despised one another.

Leaning up, I kissed Farai's cheek and then swiftly leapt off the bed. Henry picked up an open book with one hand, using the other to shove the rest aside. I sat down in the free space, peeking over his shoulder to try and decipher the text upon the page.

It was not written in the common tongue, which was why only Henry was able to read the pages. Still, I willed myself to stare at them as I allowed my power to slither into Henry's mind, walking through the open door of light like a welcomed guest. I listened as he read for me, hoping that one day this tactic would be enough to learn the many languages of the mortals.

Though the monarchs of Gandry rule over the kingdom, it is the gods that rule over the realm. In times of strife, we look to their guidance to tell us which path to take. Their will shall be our own. Their will shall be law.

His finger traced the words as he read within his head, the excitement that pulsed from him sending my heart racing.

Above all else, we worship our gods for their glory. We ask them to steer us in the correct direction, to keep us humble and wise. Their plans are greater than our dreams, and we must vow to uphold their wishes before any law. Our gods need not a throne, for they reside in The Above, looking down in the way only they can. If any know the way, it is them.

"What is this?" I asked, an eyebrow raised. It was...fanatical. The fae did not bow for the gods—we did not let them guide or control us. In fact, other than what the demons have said of the gods, I knew very little.

Henry was smiling ear-to-ear, his body practically vibrating. The mere thought of him feeling that much joy at any time made me uncomfortable, but especially when he had a tome of religious rules on his lap.

"This is how we are going to convince Trint to help us." The enthusiastic way he waved the book in front of him garnered the attention of Farai and Wrath, who both promptly perked up.

"We are going to read to him?" I asked, my sarcastic tone not enough to affect Henry's truly horrifying smile.

Farai, on the other hand, laughed loudly. His cream-colored long-sleeve top was too tight, straining against his muscled arms and chest. The trousers he wore were form-fitting but far too long, the black fabric constantly catching under his heels. They were Henry's clothes, a result of our desire not to go into any businesses that we did not absolutely have to.

I made a mental note to insist on a trip for him.

"No, little brat. We are going to appeal to his faith."

***

"I look ridiculous."

"You look like a goddess," Farai retorted, straightening my dress. At least we had stopped and gotten him outfits that actually fit. He now wore a fitted black pair of trousers and a tunic to match, both hugging his frame without constricting him. Two birds, one stone.

Henry shoved Farai to the side, earning a huff from the Shifter. He began parting the teal fabric, showing my upper thighs. I swatted at him, but he continued his machinations, pulling the sheer gathering of fabric from my shoulders to make them hang limply against my bicep.

The black corset that forced my breasts higher and pulled in my waist was heinous, just as the dainty black heeled shoes were. Henry looked far more comfortable in his billowing teal shirt, which was split down the center to reveal his tan chest in a similar way to what Bellamy preferred—freckles creating constellations across his skin. His black trousers were identical to Farai's, both of them wearing black boots.

"Now, before you complain, come cut my hair," Henry said with a sigh, grabbing my hand and pulling me to one of the rocking chairs. On the table already sat a pair of scissors, an old and worn towel draped across the back of the chair.

Just looking at them made me want to break into a fit of sobs. I could practically hear Winona's voice as she sang while she braided my hair or hear her scolding Cyprus for refusing to let her trim his. The pain that shot through my chest seemed to make my lungs cave in, as if my body knew—just as my mind and heart did—that I was less deserving of life than she was.

Ranbir told me it was not my fault in the forest of Vesteer. I knew that he meant it, that he forgave me for that moment of hesitation which left him without vengeance or resolution. Yet, when he had pulled me close—a male who cared very little for physical affection—I thought I might never forgive myself for being the reason he lost his wife. Every morning spent trailing him as he found plants and berries and other natural medicines, each time he brought me chai, all the silent moments spent in each other's company atop our horses—it was all replaced with the agonizing reality that I had cost him the love of his life.

"Ash?" Farai's voice dragged me from the depths of my never-ending despair, the shocking pull a reminder that I was no longer going to be sad. No, I was angry. At Mia, at Xavier, at Sterling, at the world.

"I am fine." Breathing deeply, I squared my shoulders and marched over to the scissors, grabbing them. Henry was already seated, the towel wrapped around him so that his hair would not stick to his clothes. We really should have done this before he got dressed, but I had a feeling that he was putting it off until the last moment.

"Are you ready?" I asked, my voice a whispered reassurance against his round ear. He nodded, clearing his throat and sitting up straight.

Do you want me to sing her favorite?

It was a private offer of comfort and love, neither of which he would want acknowledged out loud. His head bobbed slightly, a soft nod that was paired with a quiet sniffle. And so, with my horrendous singing voice, I began the song, scissors slicing through the chin-length orange strands.

> "In times of trouble, in moments of pain,
> Remember your heart. Remember your name.
> For you are grand, your worth unmatched
> With your sparkling soul, so lovely and patched.
> As you stumble and fall, lift yourself up.
> Raise your chin. Raise your cup.
> Toast to the joy, the hope, and the grief.
> Cheers to the life, no matter how brief."

By the time I finished the lullaby, Henry was openly crying, the near-silent tears causing him to shake. I backed away, noting how horrible and uneven the trim was. Still, it would have to do. Without a razor, I could not trim his beard, though I personally liked the way it made him look more fierce and rugged.

I walked around the chair, coming to stand in front of him. Sorrow would not win, nor would fear. We would find triumph, just as Winona believed. Sadness could not claim me, nor could the darkness of grief.

"Feel it all. Let it soak into your bones and burrow into your heart. You deserve this moment of mourning. But when the tears dry, we will remember the injustice, and we will fight it." My words were meant for only Henry, but I knew that Farai, who so desperately missed his husband, would hear and internalize them. With a tenderness I rarely showed to Henry, I placed a kiss to his forehead.

"Should I be worried that the homicidal and suicidal maniac of the group is giving me emotional advice?" he asked, quickly wiping away his tears.

Flicking him on the nose, I tried to remember that I was different now. I was not sad. I was furious. I was livid. I was the monster that my enemies feared, and I would come for them.

"Ha ha. Get up. It is time to go win an army." Henry chuckled at my words, the sound snapping everyone out of their daze. "Do not forget to bow when we make our grand claims."

"I would bow for the cat if it meant Gandry's army would back us," he retorted, jabbing a thumb over his shoulder towards where Wrath laid on the bed. The dalistori glared daggers at Henry, his tail swishing back and forth as if he had caught sight of exciting new prey.

Eternity spare me.

With a sigh, I walked over to Farai, grabbed him by the hand, and hauled him towards the exit. As we passed the small standing rack, I snagged our cloaks as well as his faded brown flat cap and shoved him to the door. For a moment, he looked puzzled, but then the arguing began.

"You are lucky to be in my presence, you tainted little boy. I am crafted from the hands of the god who rules over Death and Creation! I am—"

"Annoying me," Henry muttered, cutting off Wrath.

The door shut behind us just as Wrath's growl filled the room. Farai's wide eyes and worried downturn of his lips as he put on his hat pulled giggles out of my mouth, his own laughter soon following. All the while, we walked hand-in-hand, crossing the hallway and heading down the stairs.

It felt so impossibly *right* to have Fair with me, though the missing pieces of what truly became my family over the last two centuries were far more glaringly obvious with two parts of the puzzle now reunited.

The inn was relatively empty, the dark walls and mismatched runners quaint and inviting. Each step we took made the wooden floors creak, but in a way that reminded me of a well-lived-in space. I had never been to Farai's family home, but I imagined his mother, father, and two sisters living somewhere like this. A place with warmth and love.

Of course, he had described to me in detail the small cottage he and Jas had found on Isle Shifter, which nearly rested on the border between the Multiple and Single Lands. It had vibrant blue walls and a bright white roof, as well as a small garden full of vegetables left from the previous owners. There was an extra room for the youngling they hoped to someday have, though the process of applying for a partner to carry their youngling was long and required their Warden to sign off on it. Still, the room, with its yellow walls and paintings of great Shifters from legends, had sounded beautiful—a space any youngling would be lucky to call home.

Both of us secured our cloaks around our necks, tugging our hoods up. But my mind wandered while Farai tucked away his ears, thinking of all the warmth that he could not find without his husband.

Last night, as we drifted off to sleep in each other's arms, Farai had wept, just as he had every night since Bellamy brought him to me. We talked of better times, and I listened to everything I had missed these last couple of months. I held him, promising we would find Jasper and bring him home. But, to him, this would never be home.

"Do you remember that one time Queen Mia invited Jasper and I to The Capital?" Farai asked as he pushed through the wooden door leading outside. The air was chilly, autumn in the Mortal Realm proving to be nearly as miserable as winters in Eoforhild. Above, dark clouds loomed—a mass of gray prepared to remind us all of what omens lurked in the darkness. "It was a long time ago, probably sixty or seventy years."

My head bobbed, a slight nod as I recalled the memory. Like I had told Padon, so much of my history was laced with happy moments— times that left me questioning my right to grieve or feel wronged.

"Jas and I had been so surprised. I mean, we always felt it odd that she let us be friends when the laws were so strict. But we brushed it off, thinking she just loved you so much that she could not deny you the joy of friendship."

He huffed then, a small and sarcastic laugh that forced my attention to hone in on the mood that seeped from him—a blend of anger and sorrow that seemed to taint everyone around me.

"She had let us stay a week, remember? She had the castle seamstress craft all four of us extravagant golden clothes, let us feast at her table, and did not mind when we spent three days straight hidden away in Nicola's chambers." A wistful tone settled into his words, the same that filled my mind as I thought of the kisses Mia would place on my head as she told me to enjoy myself.

Xavier had put on a little show for us one night, lighting a fire that levitated over the lake and took different forms like Shifters. Students in Academy had cheered, seeing the Element at work even from across The Capital where they resided. All four of us had gotten so drunk that we slept for an entire day—only waking up when Jasper screamed in his sleep that his father had stolen the chocolate, not him.

"I had never seen a problem with the gold and the rules and the expectations that they forced upon you. Back then, I made jokes about your clothes and hid your ear cuffs, but in the end, I thought it was just normal. You seemed distant, especially during our final year of Academy and the years immediately following, but I thought it was just the stress." He sighed, pulling off his cloak and laying it onto the dewy grass before forcing me down to sit atop it, our backs falling against the brown outer wall of the inn. When he wrapped an arm around me, I nuzzled into his side, stretching my cloak to cover him as best as I could. "We thought they loved you. Especially when they pulled us aside during Academy and warned us against telling you of the unrest. They did not want you to know how the fae felt—that they *blamed* you. Of course, back then, it was less hectic, but we still saw it as a kindness to you."

Unrest? Did he mean the anger during the public sentencings? If so, there was no hiding that from someone who could read thoughts. The mere memory of the hatred spewed my way from within their minds made me shiver.

"But then we found out about Sterling. With the king and queen allowing us to visit occasionally, we could not help ourselves. Remember when we met him? Jasper did not like him at all. Said he had the personality of a creature from the bottom of the Sea of Akiva."

We both laughed, though neither sounded genuine.

"That was when I realized there was a difference between love and loyalty. Between family and...*ownership*."

A sharp pain pinched my chest, the ache a reminder of not only what I had lost, but what was never there. Farai squeezed me tighter, a comfort and an anchor. I would not find myself lost in the desert of torment, starving and thirsty for any scrap of love offered. No. Now I had my Fair, who loved me enough to not let me drown or drift.

"You are more than a pawn, Asher. More than a means to an end. Believe me when I say that I am glad you are not in The Capital anymore. Truly. But I also fear that you have left one cage for another, that you have once more trapped yourself. Seeing you with the prince—or, more specifically, seeing you leave the prince—was a glaring display of who you are at your core."

I laughed sardonically, looking up into his white eyes. "A monster? An idiot? A traitor?"

Farai shook his head, face grim and more serious than I preferred. With a heavy release of breath, he leaned down and kissed the top of my head before whispering, "A lost soul who thinks themselves unworthy of finding their way."

CHAPTER TWENTY-SEVEN

ASHER

"Princess, it is a pleasure to make your acquaintance," King Trint said, his lips meeting the top of my hand in a lingering kiss. My smile was tight, a barely there show of gratitude.

He, unlike most of the other rulers I had met in my life, did not sport the teal and black of his kingdom's colors. Instead, the young king wore a loose cream tunic, the sleeves rolled up to expose his dark brown forearms. The olive-colored trousers were not as loose but still did not fit in the same way most males wore them. His feet were bare, as if he could care little about the cold.

Trint's hair was the only thing that looked meticulously put together. There had to be at least four dozen thick twists. Similar to braids, but without being weaved together, the chest-length groupings of black strands were perfectly positioned.

His face was round, just as his hazel eyes were, and his body showcased the active way in which he spent his time. Whether that be on the battlefield, in a training yard, or atop a bed was none of my business. Though his reputation leaned mostly towards the last option.

"The pleasure is all mine, Your Majesty. I am eternally grateful for your willingness to meet with me on such short notice." My curtsy was low, and I heard Henry shouting into his mind to not bend too far or my dress might show more skin than planned. I snorted, immediately trying to compose myself as I stood again.

Brows raised so high they threatened to reach his hairline, Trint stared openly at me, though he did not ogle in the way most males— men—might. Instead, he measured me as if I were an enemy he was preparing to battle.

Perhaps I was.

I stood on the top stair of his dais, the king's crown lazily tossed to the side of his teal throne. Trint had allowed his castle to retain its gray color, the blocks of stone not painted over to match the teal and black sigil that graced the wall behind him.

It was of a pair of black hands cupped together, a small teal book at the center. The book of gods, Henry had explained. This kingdom was believed to be blessed by the gods, and so they loved those gods above all else.

"How could I resist a fae, let alone a fae princess, that had so graciously disposed of an evil in my kingdom? I must admit that I was beginning to believe your kind to be myths, thinking perhaps the mortals trading supplies were prone to gossipping and lying. You do look eerily similar to us inferiors, after all." That raspy and quick-moving accent made even his well-versed knowledge of the common tongue sound muffled, but still, I heard and understood his words.

I startled, stepping back and nearly losing my balance. Henry was there, catching my back with a firm hand. My mind was reeling at the casually given statement, too baffled to even thank Henry for his quick thinking or attempt to capitalize on our act of kindness.

"What do you mean? Betovere contacted you all two years ago to offer my hand in marriage in exchange for aid in the coming war." If his words had left me confused, mine had left him completely bewildered. His large eyes fell slightly closed, squinting at me as if my face held answers to the questions he had not asked.

"Princess Asher, I apologize for my brashness, but I have never heard from any of your kind in the entirety of my life—nor had any of my recent ancestors. I believe if I were offered your hand I would remember, especially seeing as the stupidity it would have taken to say no would be forever branded into my brain."

Farai stifled a laugh, but I could not think beyond my racing confusion. This was impossible. Mia and Xavier had contacted all but Behman, who had a queen with no sons. They told me so. Each but Maliha had said no, too terrified of the demons to take a stand.

But no. Of course that was not true. Because, while the mortals were fearful of the rumors they heard regarding the Demon Realm, they had not directly been affected by the demons. So why lie? Why not just admit they had only asked King Lawrence?

Then it hit me.

They wanted to remind me of the threat of the demons. They wanted me angry and vengeful—prepared to kill any that got in the way of doing what I thought was right. And I believed them.

"I must be confused, I apologize. Regardless, I am so happy to meet you, King Trint."

He nodded, still looking at me with suspicious eyes. My magic begged to be set free—to decipher what was brewing in that mortal mind.

"Yes, we are eager to discuss something of great importance," Henry added, flashing a smile as bright as his Sun magic before bowing low. Trint shifted on his throne, clearing his throat in the process. Nothing could hide the heat in his eyes, nor could I miss the way his hand moved to his lap.

Well, it seemed I had not needed to wear such scandalous clothing after all.

Farai and Wrath waited at the bottom of the dais, neither bowing nor speaking. I wanted to go to them, maintain a united front that proved us to be formidable rather than weak. Instead, I smiled openly at the king, waiting.

"Unless the thing of great importance is having both of you in my bed, then I fear I have no interest. But please, do stay for dessert." With that, he stood, offering me his arm and leading me down the dais when I took it—his bare feet smacking against the stone floors.

Or maybe the clothing did have some use.

You could offer yourself as dessert.

Henry stumbled behind us, my words clearly taking him by surprise. He recovered quickly, the sound of him bouncing down the steps loud at our backs.

You know what, I will.

Before I had the chance to laugh or call his bluff, Henry was tugging my arm, pulling me out of King Trint's grasp and weaving his own arm into the mortal's. I shook my head, smiling over at Farai who watched on in astonishment with his mouth open and stare unblinking.

Wrath pranced over to me, proudly the size of a domesticated dog. We had agreed upon him coming, deciding that having an otherworldly creature with us would further cement our claims. Though Trint had looked at him with eyes far more wary than impressed when we first arrived.

Now, Trint's eyes were bouncing between Henry, who chatted animatedly with him, and me. Farai placed his arm around my shoulders, Wrath sticking to my heels. We followed the pair ahead, surrounded on all sides by guards in black and teal uniforms—the thick fabric looking so comfortable that I found myself jealous as I shivered beneath my cloak.

Exiting the throne room, we walked down a long stone hall with doors regularly popping up on either side, not stopping until we reached a set of spiraling stairs. Fear of tripping came over me because was I really expected to scale slippery winding rock like this? Henry did not hesitate to keep pace with Trint, leaning in to whisper something in his ear that made the young king throw his head back in a laugh.

Stupid demon.

"Fair, I am going to need you to hold onto me. Tightly."

Farai moved his arm from my shoulders to my waist, practically hauling me up the daunting steps. Wrath stayed behind us, likely prepared to catch me should I fall like an idiot.

Luck was on my side, though. We made it to the top of the stairs relatively quickly, my heeled shoes clicking on the landing as Farai released me. There was nothing that would be worth this annoyance and pain—nothing.

Two more hallways of stone decorated with teal and black later, and we stopped at a pair of double doors, the dark wood and brass knobs giving nothing away. The guard at the head of our party pushed the doors open, revealing an enormous set of chambers.

The king's quarters no doubt.

Where Trint's appearance lacked the love for one's kingdom that most monarchs possessed, his chambers were a different story.

Black furniture sat ceremoniously around the first room, teal rugs and drapes and accessories dutifully placed. This seemed to be a seating room, though Trint continued right past it, heading for an open archway beyond, his arm tightly around Henry's. Farai, Wrath, and I maintained a close distance from them, passing through the archway to find a long black dining table and matching chairs, both accented with teal.

Gods, he really meant it when he asked us to join him in his bed.

Henry's shouted thoughts echoed into my head, forcing me to choke back a cackle.

Trint gestured for Henry to take the seat to the left of the head, which he accepted with a smile. The king beamed, grabbing the back of the chair to the right of the head and facing me expectantly. I tried to mimic the flirtatious gaze Henry had used but imagined I looked more strained and impatient than sultry.

When we were all seated, Farai having chosen the chair beside me and Wrath shrinking slightly to curl up below me, conversation began.

"Listen, we understand why you are hesitant to help us. Gandry is peaceful and prosperous, and aiding a realm you have been told to fear is likely not a great way to gain support." Henry wasted no time letting the king process his words, aiming straight for the soft spot we all knew he had—the weakness no one but he could be blamed for. "And you do need the support, desperately."

Trint glared in response, snapping over towards a teal-clad servant who held a tray full of what I assumed was vanilla custard. The young male's skin was nearly as dark as Trint's, his eyes far smaller and build lankier. He seemed nervous though he walked with poise, softly setting a black bowl in front of each of us.

Farai did not think twice, immediately digging into the dessert. Henry looked to me, nodding. That was my cue.

"Your people fear your lack of duty to your gods. They think you disobedient and sinful, lacking the holy wisdom." Now, Trint was visibly angry, his fists clenched atop the table and body shaking. "Parties and mead and sex do not particularly scream devout ruler, do they?"

Trint turned on me, his eyes devoid of the previous lust. No, this was the real king. The one who was desperate to keep his crown—as he should be. Trint was not a bad ruler per se. He cared about his kingdom enough to ensure it still thrived, but not enough to give up what brought him joy. I did not fault him that. No, I envied him it.

"What business do you have discussing my faults, Princess Asher? Are you not a runaway child planning to take mommy and daddy's throne? Is that not why you want my armies?" I reared back, so surprised by his spot-on guess that I briefly lost my train of thought. With a swipe at my ankle, Wrath brought me back to my senses. "Did you really think you could kill one creature and I would give you every sword in my kingdom? Did you think insults would further encourage me to do so?"

"I think we can both get what we want, Your Majesty. You need proof of your holiness, and I need soldiers."

Henry nodded from across the table, and then I entered Trint's mind, the barriers blocking me nonexistent. With delicate touches, I grazed his consciousness, watching in real time as he realized something was wrong.

Well, Trint, you are currently looking at the closest thing to a god you will likely ever see.

The king yelped, pressing his palms against his ears and leaning back so far in his chair that it toppled backwards. Wrath laughed below me, a menacing sound that only made the fear in Trint's eyes morph into terror. He scrambled up, using the chair like a shield as he stared at me.

"Guards, get them! Get her! She is a witch! A demon!" He then muttered in what I assumed was the language of Gandry, likely translating his orders. They moved immediately, closing in on us with panicked expressions. "Kill her!"

When the first guard touched me, grabbing my neck as he unsheathed his sword, I stilled. Suddenly, it was Sterling's hand there, choking me, threatening me. I was vulnerable and weak again—I was nothing.

Farai drew a dagger, Henry sitting up straight but not arming himself. Wrath did not stir from below me. Because to them, I was not nothing. I was everything.

I recalled a time when Xavier once said that violence was the answer when gentleness was questioned.

319

So, with that thought fresh in my mind, I bent down, grabbed one of my heeled shoes off, and swung it into the eye of the guard holding me. He screamed, instincts driving him to release me in favor of dislodging the heel. I yanked the shoe out, stabbing him two more times in the shoulder for good measure. When it became stuck, I turned to face Trint.

Another guard ran to the screaming and injured man, pulling out all seven inches of the heel and slowly helping him to the ground, her arms struggling to bear the weight of his body. Trint watched with what could only be described as dread.

The female guard turned towards me, the horror etched on her face turning into rage. She grabbed her sword, screaming as she swung. I used this as my final chance to show Trint where my value lay.

Stop.

She froze, the sword only raised about a third of the way. Her blue eyes were wide, tan skin highlighting them beautifully. She had far more muscle than the servant, which made sense—seeing as she likely trained daily whereas he was relegated to cleanup duty.

Turn to your king and repeat after me.

She did as she was told.

A goddess walks among us, prepared to fight a wicked enemy. She is a blessing, proof that the gods shine down upon our great king. Asher Daniox is faith incarnate.

She repeated me out loud, Trint's eyes nearly popping from their sockets. The wariness was still there, but his obvious interest still won out. Just for the fun of it, I added one last thing.

"She is beautiful and wonderful and the greatest thing to happen to Alemthian since the creation of bread." The female's voice was heavily accented, making it all the more obvious that she was not normally able to speak the common tongue, her eyes staring into her king's with no emotion.

Henry burst into laughter, trying to speak between chuckles. "Of course you would go off script."

I smirked, flicking back my hair, which was now down to my hips. Unlike Henry, I was not brave enough to cut it myself yet. The normally silky curls were too often becoming tangled, parts near the base of my neck regularly needing violent brushing sessions. It would have to be soon.

Farai was shaking, his eyes flicking from me to the bloody guard. With a sigh, I ordered the female guard and the other seven nearby to help the male get to whatever medical professional they had. All nine were soon gone, leaving just our group and Trint at the table. Explaining myself to Farai—and apologizing—would have to wait.

"I can help you with your predicament, King Trint." Focus on the here, the now, the plan. Focus on the rage.

"You killed one of my guards with a shoe, and you expect me to believe you can help?" The question was more of a panicked whine, but he sat back down, his body shaking. I remained calm, straightening my skirts. Blood now stained the teal fabric.

"He will live. And he started it. Well, you started it." Trint's jaw went slack, his hands opening as if to ask "how?" Despite that, I looked to Henry. "Go get Ranbir and have him try to save the eye."

Henry nodded, winking at Trint before disappearing in a burst of light. The king nearly fell back in his chair again, but I grabbed onto his flailing hand just in time. Strange, he did not seem to be one that would panic this way.

"Are you ill?" Though my question was serious, Wrath burst into laughter, crawling out from under my chair and leaping into my lap. Trint's face took on a sickly pallor, his body swaying slightly. He ripped his hand from my grip as if I had burned him. Odd how he had gone from propositioning me to trying to have me killed.

"You tried to kill a man *with a shoe!*"

OF REALMS AND CHAOS

I laughed, my hand reaching up to scratch Wrath's neck, the dalistori looking at Trint as if he wanted to take a bite from him. Farai was nervous. I could sense it radiating from him, but I had no time to defend myself. He knew what I did at public sentencings—he knew who I was.

"Yes, well, it seems those shoes came in handy after all." It must have been my shrug that sent him over the edge of sanity, because the once flirtatious and calm demeanor turned into one of unmanageable fear. He stood once more, rushing to the other side of the table and grabbing a dinner knife.

"You are insane! You spoke to me in my mind and made my guard speak against her will! You are a monster!" When he pointed the black knife at me, I rolled my eyes, grabbing my spoon and scooping up a bite of custard.

"Wow, my compliments to the chef. This is delicious." Speaking with a mouthful of custard likely did not make me seem any more sane.

"An absolute lunatic," Trint mumbled in astonishment.

Briefly, I wondered how long it would take to kill someone with a spoon. I assessed the silverware, the light from the wall sconces bouncing off the dark edges. With Farai beside me, it was difficult not to remember how abhorrent I had once felt murder was.

"You should reconsider how you speak about my queen," Wrath warned, his yellow eyes burning holes into the mortal's face. He jumped onto the table, leaving small gray hairs all over my dress. Though the blood had already ruined it, I still huffed in annoyance.

Looking up, I found a slowly growing Wrath nearly nose to nose with a shaking Trint.

"I expected you to be...less skittish. Did you not already know what I could do?" When Trint did not respond, still visibly horrified as Wrath surpassed the height of a small youngling, I grabbed the dalistori's tail. He yelped, turning on me with wide, bewildered eyes. "Oh, please. Do not be dramatic. Sit down before he pees all over himself."

Wrath turned back to King Trint, hissing once more. Then he leapt off the table and walked away, likely searching for a bed to claim. Farai stayed put, his breathing heavy.

I know I probably scared you. We will talk later. For now, we have to focus.

His nod was small, nearly imperceptible, but after a long and deep breath, he reached over and grabbed my clean hand. My own sigh of relief was loud, just like the voices in my mind that told me he would never forgive the sins I have committed—nor would he love me when he knew I had stopped being sorry for them.

"So, how many soldiers will you be offering?" Trint's eyes were on the open archway that Wrath had exited through, his thoughts a mixture of curiosity and debilitating terror.

"What is it?" he asked instead of answering, not so much as looking my way.

"He is a dalistori—a creature that hails from the Underworld." Farai's hands tightened on my own, a squeeze likely meant to remind me that I was to be selling us as worthy allies who can encourage his subjects to accept him as king and not scaring him. But he knew what I was. The goal was not to fool him but to fool his people.

"Is that where you come from?" His voice was suddenly monotone, as if he had been stripped of all feeling. I would not be surprised. Terror had the ability to drain one of all things good—to morph them into something to be feared instead. I peeked into his head, then, and was swept away in the horror of the moment from his point of view. It reminded me of doing this very thing with Shah only weeks ago.

The difference between the two rulers' reactions was glaring. Then again, that was how it was in this world. Women suffer and climb and claw their way through merciless existences, just as the Behamn queen had. Trint, though, had always known he would be king—had never been forced to fight for that right or this rule or the luxury of it all. His fear showed that. Shah had suffered enough to not balk at the next monster that strode her way. Trint did not understand such things.

OF REALMS AND CHAOS

"Some might say so." This time, Farai kicked me under the table, the side of his boot hitting my calf hard enough to draw a gasp from my lips. I glared over at him, willing him to understand. "What, should I lie?"

The Shifter groaned, reaching his hand up to his face and roughly rubbing at his dual-toned skin. Looking back to the king, I saw he had relaxed slightly, those broad shoulders squaring once more. I felt the shift in his mood, unable to resist looking into that head of his again.

So it seems the psychopath still respects honesty to some extent. Which is more than I can say about all the many gossips and liars surrounding me who like to label and judge me too. Perhaps all in power must face the fact that no one truly knows who they are.

Well, well, the king seemed to think himself more similar to the monster before him than he liked to admit.

"What do you say?" The question took me by surprise, because when had anyone ever thought to ask me such a thing? How did I answer that? The truth was likely too dark, too damning. But to lie, to hide the fact that I am more dangerous than even the dalistori, would not do me any favors either.

Eventually, I settled on something in between. "I say that I can be whatever you need me to be in order to gain your support."

The king did not smile, did not so much as blink. He stared and stared at me, his gaze unsettling in its intensity. Though he was afraid, Trint was also smart. The king was weighing his options, assessing the pros and cons. He was deciding.

"I did not know."

The words once more caught me off-guard. The monarch had not answered a single question I asked, and yet I knew my only choice was to follow his lead. To placate him.

"Did not know what?"

"That you could control minds. We had heard rumors that you were dangerous, that you had some unheard of power, but we have only ever gotten pieces of stories. Primarily, we were told that you were deadly but leashed, that you presented no danger because your parents made sure you never harmed anyone. I was far more intrigued than scared, though I know now that I was wrong."

Before I could answer, a pencil appeared above the table, falling right in the center with a loud clatter. Trint jumped but did not scream, his eyes wide as he watched me grab the object. I undid the string, unrolling the paper from around the pencil and reading it.

A shoe, huh? Would it be insensitive of me to say that I am hard just imagining it?

A loud laugh slipped from my lips before I could purse them closed, the two males looking at me as if I were a raving lunatic. And, in the spirit of honesty, I was.

So, King Trint, when will I be making my grand debut as a goddess in the flesh to your people? I must know so I can plan what I will wear. You only get to make a first impression once, after all. I would not want them to think me a tasteless god.

The king flinched at the sound of my voice in his mind, still unsettled by my ability. Which was fair, seeing as it had been mere minutes since he discovered I could do such a thing. Now that I was there in his mind, I could hear the thoughts he was too ashamed to admit, the ones that burrowed and festered like a parasite.

King Trint was considering my offer.

I smiled, finishing off my custard as he watched warily. Farai remained silent at my side, a wall of building animosity. I squeezed his hand, reassuring both of us.

Trint's mind had been made long before the words left his mouth, but I still found myself giddy as he spoke.

"Fine, Princess Asher, you have a deal. Prove to me that you can sway my people, and Gandry will fight on your side of this war." Every ounce of my will was not enough to stop me from letting out a soft cheer, my smile lifting my cheeks so high they hurt. "But if you harm another one of my people, then the deal is off. And I need to know more about this deal with Maliha. Their army is nearly double the size of ours."

I nodded, standing up and reaching my hand out. King Trint looked at me as if I were insane, his mouth lifted on one side in a disgusted sneer. Nothing I had not experienced from the fae.

"So, where and when will I make my debut? Like I said, I would not want to look heinous." Farai stood beside me, our hands still interlocked. Wrath pranced to my side, looking far too smug. I had a feeling I would soon be dealing with a disaster.

"Have you ever seen a temple at sunset?"

CHAPTER TWENTY-EIGHT

BELLAMY

"She is depressing," Malak, one of my soldiers, whined. I groaned, leaning back in my chair and begging Stella for patience. Not that she would provide any, even if she could. The sergeant was quick to capitalize on my growing annoyance, just as everyone was lately. "And I think she tried to kill a soldier that morning. She told him that he would never find happiness and that to cease breathing would be a blessing."

Lara had proven to be more of a problem than a help, her constant need to darken every situation bringing down morale en masse. Just yesterday, she had made a young demon sob by discussing with him in detail about the way his short life would be better if he simply allowed the deep abyss of sadness to swallow him, sucking him down into a quick end. Depressing did not begin to describe her.

With a final exasperated sigh, I stood from my desk and nodded at Malak before exiting my office. Lara had been placed in a room not far from my own, the upper level hosting my Trusted the only place I deemed safe enough to let her be alone.

We had already found her tying a noose to the rafters once, which she so calmly let us know was not for herself.

The hallways still held a chill, the stone and wood structure built between and within the mountain pass not exactly a sun-filled place. I still remembered when I expanded the base, laughing as the faces of my soldiers went slack at the sight of me cracking and hollowing the mountains with my mind. The four-day nap following had been worth it, if only to impress them. In the winters, they seemed to truly thank me, as the inside of the mountain was far warmer than the outside, where snow and wind barreled into the buildings unforgivingly.

Each soldier I passed offered me a nod, mumbling my title or my rank, whichever they felt more inclined to use. Few addressed me by my first name, something I think Ash would likely hate. She enjoyed a more intimate rule, one that encouraged love over fear. But that was the difference between the hatred the demons felt for me and the kind the fae felt for her. We were both ostracized and secluded, looked at as a weapon and an enemy instead of a future ruler. Where the fear of her could be quenched with kindness and reassurance, the disgust of me could only be fought with a firm hand.

As if the dark turn to my thoughts had summoned her, I found Lara sitting with her feet dangling from an open window, the stone arch seeming to swallow her body—which she had dressed in a yellow blouse and brown trousers, looking like a sunflower saying hello to the spring air. It was far too bright for such a gloomy being.

"Lara, how are you this morning?" I asked as I approached, careful to walk slowly and nonthreateningly. She did not turn, her long black hair that swayed in the wind moving more than her entire body was. She somehow had surpassed even Wrath in her ability to unsettle those around her.

"I feel as if the days are too long, and I wish I did not need to wake up to so much light." Gods, she was something. Her tone was low, ominous. We had offered her training, quarters, clothing, food, and really anything she could think to ask for. Anything to cheer her up. However, she asked for nothing, enjoying only the act of walking around and bringing down the moods of those around her. I desperately wished I could help her, not just for our own comfort but for hers.

"Well, that is…um, unfortunate." Rubbing my temples, I groaned at my own stupidity. Unfortunate? Who says that? I walked forward, quickly swinging my legs over the edge and sitting beside her. Leave it to Lara to comfortably sit hundreds of feet in the air, by choice no less. "Listen, Lara, we are so glad to have you here. Your presence has been so…interesting. But I think—"

"That I am upsetting everyone?" She said it with little emotion, sounding detached from herself. I leaned forward slightly, noting the way she stared off blankly at the mountains, her small blue eyes unseeing. I reached my hand closer, ready to catch her if she jumped.

"No, not at all. I think we are simply unused to having someone like you around. Perhaps if you had something to do that you found fun, then you would find new ways to relate to others? I know it is hard. Life has not been fair to you, and you deserve more than forced joy. If there is anything I can do to help you acclimate, let me know."

If my words registered, she did not show it, instead continuing to stare off. My shoulders fell, the defeat sinking in. Despite knowing she had quite literally murdered innocents for vengeance, I could not help but feel sorry for her.

With the failure now heavy on my chest, I nodded and turned to get up. Before I could, she reached out and grabbed my wrist, tugging me closer. Her eyes were still vacant, but her pursed lips and the deepening of her dark cheeks made me believe that she was feeling more than she usually did.

"I like flowers. They are the only things that die when they should." Despite the horrid reasoning behind such a hobby, I smiled, eagerly nodding. Lara did not smile back, but her returned nod gave me hope.

"Luckily for you, I am incredibly adept at gardening. Tomorrow, we will pick a spot, okay?" She did not respond, opting to turn around and face the mountains once more. After a moment, she leaned forward and promptly fell off the edge.

I shouted in horror, running to grab her, but my hands had nothing to grab onto, because Lara had shifted. Now hundreds of bubbles littered the air, blowing in the breeze.

She remained too high to harm anyone, but even I could see the melancholy in the beauty of such a thing, a self-imposed isolation.

Progress was progress.

With that done, an even more daunting task lay ahead. It was time to talk to Adbeel about Malcolm. Something that I was working hard to put off, as if that would make it go away. But avoiding the truth did not change it—nothing could.

Pike was normally far too large to walk through when in a hurry, but of course, I was quite admittedly unexcited to be in a hurry, which meant I was prepared to stall in any way I could. Leisurely, almost carelessly, I made my way through the halls and down the many stairs, aiming for the training yard on the ground floor.

The stone steps were sturdy and less than a century old, but I always felt as if they were ancient. Like a worn pair of shoes, they carried a tale only those who walked them would understand. Pike's story was, to me, lovely. We started as a small military force full of demons who enlisted out of desperation or duty, none interested in doing much more than existing. And then, with an immense amount of effort and a truly heinous first few years, I expanded. Joining our ranks became something to be proud of. One did so not only for honor, but for skill and friendship.

Now, they fought for their realm, and I feared what that would do to them. Those who survived would never be the same, coming home from every battle with new scars and deeper traumas. War did that, altered one irrevocably, hardened them in the worst way.

This would be my first war, but I had seen what it did to Adbeel, to the many others who fought the last time. As much as I hated to admit it, I saw what killing did to me, too. Every time I fought the Golden Guard when trying to save a fae during a meet, all the moments of fury that led to me slaughtering those I believed deserved it, made me something new—something evil.

When I nearly slipped on a concrete step, I realized just how little attention I had been paying. So little attention that I did not notice Ray until I slammed into her as I tried to right myself, sending me stumbling once more and falling down the steps. Her body disappeared into a nearly clear puff of liquid, which soared to the bottom of the stairway and materialized once more, catching me with a loud grunt.

"Hello, Sir, I am so sorry."

I steadied myself, standing on shaky but strong legs. Ray was dusting off my arms, looking as if she might go off on a tirade if I did not stop her. Like Cyprus, Ray had deep russet skin and warm hazel eyes. They both had thinner lips and strong jaws, the only major difference being that Ray's brown hair was cut to her chin, the shorter look more convenient according to her.

"It is fine, Ray. Honestly, it was my fault. I am headed to the training yard, so I will get out of your way." Side-stepping her, I tried to make a hasty exit. Naturally, the little pest did not accept that.

"Well, Sir, I will follow you, then. Perhaps we can further discuss decorations and meal plans?"

Internally groaning, I turned and faced her, offering a tight smile and a stiff nod. Ray was not deterred, instead opting to smile widely and stick closely to my side.

"Please, Ray, you know you do not need to call me Sir."

Instead of answering right away, she pulled out paper and a pencil from her leather satchel. "Yes, Sir. Of course, Sir. Anyways, I have taken

331

the time to survey the soldiers, and they all agree that the chicken and roast, as well as the omelets, are—to be frank—disgusting. But I know you are busy, so I have made a list of other options that I think will be far more favorable!"

Ray had the ability, much like Cyprus, to talk without breathing. It was a talent that seemed to get her whatever she wanted, including a job as my so-called assistant. As we passed through the final wooden door, the two of us stepped out into the bright spring day, the sounds of sparring and running and classes filling the air. Ray's nose scrunched in disgust as she watched her brother run our way, his shirtless form drenched in sweat.

"Little sister, what could you possibly need in the training yard with those noodle arms?" Every crumb of my restraint was needed to stop me from laughing, especially when Cyprus's smirk was met with a glare from Ray. However, when she promptly stomped on his foot, twisting her heel into the toe of Cyprus' boot, I simply could not hold back.

I burst into hysterics when he yelped, grabbing his foot and bouncing up and down. Ray gave him a mischievous smile that was a mirror of his own, but I saw the way her eyes darted to me in pride. The little menace was determined to be useful, even if it was just to get me to laugh. I could not help but smile back, thankful despite my eternal annoyance with her.

"Ray, I actually could use your help with something rather important." Her tall and lanky form straightened, eyes wide as she faced me. It was rare that I gave her specific tasks, and it seemed she was prepared to take advantage of this instance. "Tomorrow, I am going to be working with Lara to craft a flower garden because she says she enjoys them. But, until then, would you mind keeping her company?"

Cyprus, who had slowly stopped hopping, froze. Before he said anything, I knew that he was angry. These moments were as rare as my need for an assistant, but they were always easy to point out. His nostrils flared, brow pinched together as he stared me down.

"She cannot watch that thing! What if she is hurt, or worse, killed? She is practically still a youngling!" His shouts drew the attention of nearby soldiers, all stopping what they were doing to look at the three of us.

"I am nearly half a century now, you cannot still call me such a thing!" When Ray stepped into Cyprus, nearly pressing her chest to his, I grabbed both of them by the shirt and dragged them away. In moments like these, I found myself thankful to be without siblings. Neither protested, though both looked at the other with quiet anger.

The moment we made it around the corner of the stone pathway that led to the open fields, I released them, lifting my hand to pinch the bridge of my nose. I was calm. I was collected. I was the sea, rolling with the tide, unaffected by the boats that sailed across the surface. I moved them, not the other way around.

"You bastard! How dare you embarrass me like that! Sir, I am so very sorry. I did not mean to cause an upset. I promise, I can do the task." I was the sea. I was the sea. I was the sea.

"No, you most definitely cannot! Lara told me she lost all of her family during the war, just like Horis." Ray flinched at his mention of another whisp who had brutally lost his family. "They left her to save our already endangered kind, and now she has no one. Do you know how dangerous someone with no one to lose is? Let alone someone who is almost half a millennia old? She is not some pet you can train. She is rabid and dangerous, Ray!"

Fuck the sea.

"Enough!" My voice was commanding, but the tremor that shook the dirt beneath our feet was what called them to attention. They both stood, looking completely without remorse. Luckily for them, I was in a time crunch. "Both of you, go see to Lara. Help her. She is struggling and alone. Like you both, she possesses immense magic, and she can aid us in this war. She needs the will and incentive to do so, which is where you two come in. I do not have the time or the puppets to explain this further."

Before either could respond, I portaled, my feet landing on the grass across the training field. With far more haste, I searched the crowd for Noe. She was supposed to be coming with me to talk with Adbeel, but I knew that she was probably out here bickering with Lian and Damon.

I found Li first, her instructions to the mortals going fairly well. The group was large, but they all listened carefully as she spoke in broken Behman, watching her with eager eyes. When she used her Air power against them, it was clear there were two distinct reactions: distrust and awe. Luckily, most looked to be a part of the latter group.

"Third position!" Her shout rang, followed by a collective grunt as everyone shifted. One man, who had found himself in first instead, was thrown to the sky on a violent gust of wind.

Oh no.

"Lian!" She turned my way. Only her pointer finger was keeping her Air power focused on the man, who was screaming so loudly that birds were taking to the sky—flapping violently to get away. I groaned as I made my way to her, feeling more like a babysitter than a prince or a general.

"What? He was not listening, and he needed to learn a lesson." Her wicked smirk did not match up with the innocent tone. She was clearly having more fun than she should be.

"You know better. These are our allies. They deserve respect and the opportunity to grow. Put him down or I will find a new swordmaster."

Lian's answering gasp was almost enough to lighten the mood, but the man screamed for help above, every mortal still standing in third position. Clearly they were used to this. "Fine, but I hope you know that you are encouraging weakness, oh benevolent General Ayad."

I did laugh then, watching as she lifted both palms and slowly lowered them, the man landing lightly on his feet. The poor thing had wet himself.

Stella save us all.

With that, I ruffled Lian's short blue hair, earning a growl of frustration before I set off looking for Noe once more. A moment later, I found her sparring with Damon, a large group of soldiers watching as they went head-to-head. Though Noe's magic was superior to Damon's, the strength and control she possessed was not enough to guarantee her win. My lieutenant general was fast, smart, and ruthless. He wielded two swords against her two whips of shadow, neither so much as stumbling as they attacked again and again.

Noe used one whip to swipe at his ankles, the other latching around his chest when he jumped to avoid the first. He grunted as she tugged, the shadows tightening around him, slowly suffocating him. He reached down and grabbed a small dagger, flicking it low and slicing into her thigh. She screamed out in pain but did not relent. Instead, the shadows spread, engulfing him for a moment, before dissipating to show him suddenly gone. Noe had portaled him.

The small crowd erupted into cheers, though I focused more on watching Noe attempt to pull out the dagger. Rushing to her, I quickly grabbed her arm and tugged her hand away. She would not heal fast enough if she hit a major artery, that much I knew from Ranbir's rants.

"Get off, Bell, I am fine!" Her eyes darted across the group, and I knew that she was likely nervous of what the others would think of her. With a quick glare at the onlookers, I scooped her into my arms, careful not to jostle her left leg too much. Everyone dispersed, looking at me with terror in their eyes.

"You need to see Ranbir, or at least one of the medics. Especially since your stupid, competitive ass is supposed to be going with me to talk to Adbeel." Her responding huff and the crossing of her arms made me smile. She had always been a brat.

Since we could not portal, I had to carry her to the infirmary. Blood poured out of her leg, leaving a trail behind us. The walk was nearly silent, the only sounds breaking the monotony being Noe's small cries of pain when the stairs left me no choice but to adjust.

"I hate you," she said between clenched teeth as I stepped onto the landing of the second floor.

I laughed, turning a corner too sharply and nearly hitting her legs on the wall. "Yeah, sure you do." My smile grew wider when she stuck her tongue out at me, acting like a youngling. Strangely enough, I missed getting to be young with her. We had so much more fun back then.

"I am serious. As payback, I am telling Ash about that time you got so drunk that you stripped naked and fell down a hill. She will love that story."

I smiled, remembering how I swore I would never drink again then woke up the next morning hungover once more.

When she failed to get a rise out of me, she contemplated in silence. It was not until we were a single hallway from the infirmary door that she finally landed on a good enough threat to speak aloud.

"I will tell her about that time you spied on her and Cyprus when they went into her room in that inn. Remember, the one in Elpis?"

Shit.

"She will not care. It is no secret that I am a jealous idiot." Even I was unconvinced, my shaky voice and heavy breathing telling Noe exactly how terrified I was of that.

Shit, shit, shit.

"We will see. Unless, that is, you do me a favor." She wiggled her brows, her smile wide despite the clear pain in her thigh that had her eyes watering slightly.

Glaring down at her, I thought for a moment. There were enough secrets between Ash and I, so perhaps telling her would be a good thing. It was no surprise that I had done something that stupid. I was a compilation of faults held together by thin threads of morality. One could not deny that Asher knew of those shortcomings. They were too obvious to ignore.

"You know what," I said with a smile as I approached the door, "tell her. I could not care less. She loves me enough to forgive me."

Noe sneered in disgust, leaning away from me as if the love I had for Asher was a sickness she was afraid would contaminate her. With Noe, it would not come as a surprise if she genuinely did believe that.

I kicked the door open, accidentally sending it into the wall with a loud smack. Every medic's head turned, looking as if they were under attack. Ranbir was the only one who seemed unaffected by our loud entrance, the hand writing something merely pausing. His dark eyes grew wide when he saw Noe in my arms, and soon, everyone was in action. They only had one other patient, who was snoring loudly on a bed in the corner. Which meant that we had our pick of beds.

The uncomfortably sterile room was larger than our dining hall, taking up the majority of the second floor. The rocky floors and wooden walls had been filled with white curtains, white rags, white bowls. Everything was so white it was jarring. Ranbir led me to one of the nearest beds, which had plain white sheets and pillows that matched his all-white ensemble. Surprise, surprise. Maybe Ray was right about redecorating.

"Noe, tell me you did not stab yourself on a dare." Ranbir's tone was completely serious, his mouth set in a thin line. A chuckle escaped me, but when he looked my way with disapproval, I quickly tried to mask it with a cough. His eye roll told me he was unimpressed.

Though Ranbir was the youngest of our group, he was definitely the oldest at heart. Lately, it seemed as if he had aged a few centuries. Winona was the one who brought him out of his shell, encouraging him to laugh and joke and enjoy life in ways he felt he could not before.

When Noe first found him, he had been the sole survivor of a mass execution, his parents and two sisters all having been beheaded in front of him. Ranbir had sucked the life out of the eight guards, but he could not heal his family in time. Noe regularly looked for any who might be unhappy, tracking Golden Guards who left post or monitoring the supposed demon attacks, so she arrived not long after the carnage. Ranbir had not hesitated to agree to go with her, whereas most discussed their possible relocation with me during a meeting she set to give them time to think.

Over twenty years had passed before he met Winona, and in that time, he had never truly recovered. But Nona's family took him in, loving the fae like he was their own. Her sisters and brothers, her parents and grandparents, they all made sure the Healer was the one being healed for once.

With her gone, I feared he would never be whole again. I could see it in his eyes as he tsked at Noe's wound. He had a hollow-like appearance to him, haunting in its lifelessness. Normally steady hands now shook, his dark brown skin constantly cast in a slightly gray hue.

"Of course not! That was Lian, and I dared her as a joke. Plus, that was years ago." Her argument did not convince Ranbir, who looked down at her with narrowed eyes. Noe must have seen that emptiness in him too, because she lifted her arms in surrender, offering Ranbir a soft smile. "I egged on Damon during a sparring session."

When he ripped out the dagger instead of responding, she screamed, forcing me to cover my ears. Ranbir shoved his hand onto the rapidly bleeding wound, muttering something about a femoral artery as he worked on healing her.

"Well, I guess I will be going to the king on my own then." Noe smacked me, her mouth wide as she pointed at her injured leg. I waved off her pain, walking away as I did. When I heard the bed creak, I ducked, barely avoiding the flying pillow. "Predictable."

Then another one smacked into the back of my head. A final laugh sounded behind me before I portaled away, holding up my middle finger at the Moon. I arrived at the border of Dunamis, allowed myself one final breath of serenity, then stepped through the wards and portaled again.

My feet met the lush blue carpet in Adbeel's office, the smell of black tea and honey permeating the air. He was there, as I knew he would be, not so much as flinching at my sudden appearance.

The office was exactly as one might expect from the king of Eoforhild. The walls were white, the floor the same bleached driftwood as the rest of the castle. Paintings of Solei, Malcolm, and Zaib hung on the wall behind me, the other walls decorated with pieces I had done for him when I was younger. His desk was a bright and shiny silver color, two sky blue chairs on the opposite side of him. I moved, taking the one on the right. They were soft—comfortable and roomy in a way that invited demons to speak with him—but still, I felt uneasy.

Adbeel looked up, black eyes meeting mine. He had secured his mahogany curls atop his head, a leather band wrapped around the thick knot. His white tunic was open down to his navel, the sleeves rolled up to his elbows. His obsidian crown glittered in the light of the sun as it lowered in the sky and shone through the windows to his back.

"Bellamy, what can I do for you today?" A formal tone was to be expected after our fight the last time we spoke. Unfortunately, I did not have the time or the will to dance around the subject. I needed to get this over with, or I would back out.

"I saw Malcolm."

Adbeel's pencil fell from his hand, clattering to the desk before rolling off the edge. He did not move to get it, instead staring at me with his hand frozen midair. We stayed that way, silent and unblinking, for what felt like hours. Waves could be heard in the distance, slamming against the side of the cliff that the castle was built upon.

Finally, he spoke.

"I apologize, but I think I misheard you. What did you just say?" The question came out as a raspy whisper, but his eyes were ablaze as they scrutinized me.

With a final deep breath, I placed my joined hands on the desk in front of me and repeated myself. "I saw Malcolm. I nearly killed Xavier Mounbetton during the battle in Grishel, but he was rescued by the traitor Noe has been searching for. It was Malcolm. He looked at me when I called his name, smiling like he was in on some sort of joke that I was not. It was him. Your son is alive."

Sadly, Adbeel did exactly as I guessed he would.

"Tell me the truth. What is it you are playing at?" The demanding words were laced with his magic, the Honey Tongue ability pressing into my mental shields and trying to force me to submit.

I stood, simultaneously letting that shield of black fire that Adbeel himself had taught me to conjure fall. His magic enveloped me, tugging on my will and encouraging me to speak the truth.

While I knew that the truth was exactly as I had said, I wanted to make sure he understood something first. "I have been around a far more formidable creature, My King. Her magic is something we could only dream of, the likes of which could crumble the world."

Adbeel followed me, standing only an inch or so shorter. As it was, we were nearly eye-to-eye, squaring off for no reason other than grief and disbelief. "She is a disease, one that will eat away at your soul until you are nothing. Whatever magic those filthy fae put into her is abhorrent, more dangerous than that which derives from the Underworld. And whatever spell she has put you under for you to so blatantly lie to me proves that!" His face grew red, deepening his tan skin.

"This is not about Ash, but while we are on the topic, I know how dangerous she is. Asher is my equal in every way, we are *both* indescribably strong, and that makes us each a different version of the same problem. If she is an abomination, then so am I. Now, instead of hurling insults, would you like to discuss your son coming back from the grave? Or should I leave?"

Neither of us moved, our faces a mere foot away from one another.

"You are mistaken; my son is dead. You may go." His words were laced with venom, spit from between clenched teeth. He was furious, but I was intimately aware of that type of fury, and I would not bow down to it.

"Did you ever see a body? Had anyone ever found him or been told he was dead? The fae never said anything other than sending you Zaib's—"

"Stop!" Magic erupted from him, sending me careening back as light blinded me. I hit the wall that held the portraits so hard they rattled, the one of Malcolm that sat in the center falling and striking my head. Despite the pain, I dove to the side, catching the enormous piece before it could be damaged.

Adbeel portaled to my side, panic in his wide eyes. I went to reassure him, to say that it had not been ruined, but Adbeel was faster. He took the painting, lightly tossed it to the side, and grabbed my shoulders. With a firm hand, he began inspecting the gash on my forehead, which was leaking blood down my temple.

"That was inexcusable. I should never lay a hand on you, let alone use my magic to harm you. I am so, so sorry." His pleading made me pause my attempt to stand. I looked at him, his sullen and worried expression so odd when paired with the problem at hand.

"It is fine. I am fine." I stood, wiping at the blood with my sleeve and staining the cream shirt crimson. He watched me, his eyes glassy. Despite how much I wished I could help him, there was no changing this situation in a way that would do so.

"Did he look...okay?" Adbeel asked, clearing his throat and walking over to the blue chairs—sitting in the one on the left. I followed, slightly dizzy, and sat in the other. What Adbeel was not asking was obvious—did he seem as if he were there against his will?

"He appeared to be healthy. Honestly, Adbeel, he seemed more than willing to be there. There was a strange feel to the air around him—a wicked and cruel chill that made me uneasy." Though he did not let the tears fall, the king had a troubled look to him, face grim and devoid of the color that signaled life. The sort of expression that I imagined only a father facing betrayal could conjure.

"Zaib used to argue with him about the fae. She would claim that they deserved a chance at peace, just as the demons did. Malcolm disagreed vehemently. His view was much like my own, destroy and eradicate them all before the war got out of hand." He paused, unease momentarily taking over his face as he admitted to a rather hateful and bigoted way of thinking. "I just cannot imagine why he would want to help them."

With a shake of my head, I tried to find the words to express what I thought. To explain that opportunities offered by an enemy were still opportunities. That to hold a broken crown and sit atop a bloody throne was just as pleasing to some as it was revolting to others. But how could I say something like that to a father who had grieved for centuries? To a father who had said goodbye, only to be forced to now raise his sword against his dead son?

"Do you think she is alive, too?" The broken and raspy question sounded more like an attempt at begging, as if he were asking the universe to let her still be breathing. Which was not possible seeing as Adbeel had received pieces of her.

It was an even more difficult question—one I could not properly answer without admitting that I had witnessed her death in the waters of a lake. That I had been shown visions of her dead body and witnessed what my mother would do after. Instead, I shook my head.

A few tears fell then, breaking through his will and running down his cheeks like water sneaking through a cracked dam. I feared what would happen when the dam broke and all of those built-up emotions came crashing through. Who would Adbeel be after?

"You remind me so much of her, you know."

With a scoff, I settled into the chair, allowing my head to lean back and my eyes to fall closed. "I believe that some might consider that an insult to her memory, so I would refrain from saying such a thing in public."

"You have this innate desire to dream, just like she did. I wonder what you could create, what you could accomplish, if given the chance." I remained silent, contemplating what he said. I had never seen myself that way, someone who could finish what Zaib started. She was a beautiful soul based on the stories I had heard. No one would ever tell stories like that about me. "You thought I would be more concerned about the painting than you. Why?"

Laughing, I opened my eyes and looked at the king, his gaze on me. Though we were both relaxed against our chairs, the conversation was anything but tranquil.

"Interesting change of subject." He did not share in my amusement, staring at me with a furrowed brow and pursed lips. Clearing my throat, I tried to say aloud what I had always believed in my heart, even if I knew it did not apply to my own situation. "I guess I know how much those three portraits mean to you. No matter what your son did or does, he is still your blood. That portrait holds thousands of memories. Seeing it ruined would be devastating, I imagine."

His frown deepened, creasing his face. I readjusted, feeling the need to move so the discomfort could not settle within me.

"I do not love Malcolm more than you, Bell. You are not my blood, but you are not any less my family than he was—is. That painting is an object. Irreplaceable in some ways, but infinitely less precious than you are." He stared, likely waiting for me to acknowledge his words, but how could I? It was far from true. I was no more precious than a lump of rock. "It will be you who sits atop the throne of Eoforhild one day."

I was not sure how one was supposed to act when finding out that their son had come back from the grave. However, there was not a single scenario in which I imagined the conversation turning to me and my future rule. I was not deserving of that throne, no matter how hard I tried to be.

"I know that is your plan, but I do not particularly desire to rule." Not alone, that was.

"That is exactly why you are the best option, why you will do so well. It is why you deserve it."

Hearing him say that brought back the memories of our last argument, the one in which he said I deserved nothing. Strange how I now agreed with the statement.

"We need to meet with the war council, Adbeel. Knowing that Malcolm is the one aiding the fae changes things. I have heard the stories of his magic, just as you are personally aware of his strength. I know this must be a lot to process, and I cannot begin to imagine what you are feeling, but taking an offensive approach has become a priority if we are going to survive this." While it had to be said, I could not prevent the guilt from consuming me at the way he flinched.

He looked more than simply hurt or scared. He looked tired. Broken.

"Okay. Schedule a meeting, and I will come." With that, he stood, making his way to the double doors behind us. I followed, so stunned by his concession that I had no words. Together, we exited his office, heading down the hallway towards his chambers. Did he want me to follow him? Was I being dense? "And after that, I want to meet my future queen."

The request stopped me in my tracks, my heart racing. I knew what he meant, yet still, I feigned ignorance. "Who might that be?"

Adbeel stopped too, his eyes red from the tears shed but clearer than they had been mere minutes ago. "Oh, please. You know exactly who I mean. The reason I tried so hard to convince you to marry Revanche was not just for the strength of unity, but also because I am ready to get this fucking crown off my head. I want to move on. I want to know peace in this realm before my soul returns to the Above—before I reunite with my Solei."

Briefly, we both stood still, absorbing what he had said. Then, without much thought, I gave the only reassurance I knew would make a difference. "She would be proud—they both would be."

His sardonic laugh echoed through the hallway, and I quickly looked around to make sure no one was listening in. Unfazed by the possibility of eavesdroppers, Adbeel walked up to one of my paintings.

The poor male had far too many to know what to do with. There were years in which I did nothing but train, eat, sleep, and paint.

This one was of The Royal City, specifically focused on the very castle we now stood in. The colors were off, duller than the real thing.

"I do not know what is worse: a dead son or a traitorous one." There was a bite to his tone, one that hinted at whatever rage was simmering within him. The king would have much to ponder, even more to accept.

"At least a traitor still breathes, still has a chance to repent." That earned me another full and sarcastic laugh, which I responded to with an eye roll as I closed the space between us. We both looked at the painting, which I now realized had shaky line work, while we spoke.

"And what does your fae princess think of the vengeance I took? Does she think repentance is in the cards for me?" Even without looking in my direction, it seemed Adbeel had correctly read the stiffening of my back and the squaring of my shoulders. I radiated tension, and he understood that for what it was. "I believe telling your lover that the male who raised you killed her parents is pretty important."

"Maybe you should be the one to tell her, to explain." A quick glance to my side showed that Adbeel was now looking at me unamusedly. "Fine. Before Pino died, he told me that you had to be there when I told Asher the truth. He said it was the only way without loss. It is hard to explain, but I have to wait. After the council, we can all three talk, I promise."

There was far too much judgment in those black eyes, but he eventually nodded, turning to walk away with a wave. I could not help the small smile that lifted the corners of my mouth, though it was more grim than joyous. If only he knew.

"Adbeel?" I asked, the questioning tone causing him to look back. "She is going to change everything. Asher is the answer."

CHAPTER TWENTY-NINE

ASHER

The temple was extraordinary. Something that looked like it did should be cherished with only the eyes, as if entering would taint it. Still, we walked forward, approaching with steady confidence.

Farai's hand was in mine, both of us marveling at the place of worship ahead. It was a towering structure, the majority of it a stunning violet color, making the small carvings in gold and black stand out. The four levels consisted of layered tiers that were shaped like pointed arches, uneven and chaotic, but beautiful all the same.

Farai, Henry, Wrath, and I had been traveling with King Trint for eleven days. Which was, to my eternal discomfort, enough time for Farai to have a complete breakdown over what had occurred at the dinner. Of course, Henry had the brilliant idea to graphically detail the many murders and instances of dismembering I had accomplished since I previously saw Farai.

My best friend who had known me for nearly two hundred years proceeded to have a panic attack. He asked what they did to me, questioned my sanity, and reminded me over and over again that I had once locked myself away for days after having to complete a public sentencing.

How could I explain to him that fighting my nature would not get us anywhere? That pretending I was not designed to dole out death was pointless? Eventually, after he teared up and told me he wanted better for me, Farai accepted that I was different. Surprisingly, I did not shed a tear during the entire conversation, instead opting to nod and apologize and promise to be better.

It was a promise I knew I would break.

Now, as we walked together and approached the Temple of the Gods, I could feel the tension radiating from him. We had all played cards and chatted idly throughout the trip, but Farai's stress remained. He regularly asked for updates on Jasper, which forced me to admit that Bellamy was still working on a plan. Henry was confident that Farai would simply be presumed dead, but my friend did not settle. No one could blame him. Jasper was his soulmate, the love of his life, his husband. Finding him was imperative. Yet, all we could do was press on, which meant entering the looming structure and winning allies.

Up close, the carvings on the outer walls were easier to decipher. The top floor had an image of a sky full of stars. The moon was depicted on one side, the sun on the other. The third floor was the beginning of a tree, the golden leaves lush and bright. But the second floor showed the tree beginning to decay, fading to black and illustrating broken and withered roots. The final floor showed skeletal figures crawling and digging their way to the surface.

It was both stunning and horrifying.

OF REALMS AND CHAOS

"Ah, I forgot how deeply the mortals of this world worship my god," Wrath said, his head grazing my hip. I looked down at him, my brows furrowed as I silently encouraged him to continue. "While the demons worship the Goddess of the Sun and Moon, the mortals worship the God of Death and Creation, as do I. This here is art crafted to symbolize him—to revere him."

Squinting my eyes, I inspected one of the crawling skeletons. "So that god manipulates life and death for the fun of bringing back those who passed on rather than allowing them to find peace in Eternity?"

Wrath scoffed, lifting both his chin and his tail to the sky as he pranced ahead of us. I took that as a yes.

I had nothing against any of the gods, but I could not find it in me to respect them when they let chaos run rampant here on Alemthian. What kind of holy beings were they if they cared not for that which they resided over?

Trint nearly jumped out of his own skin when Wrath walked up to him, the wicked little creature smiling as his tail wrapped around the king's leg. Even Henry laughed when Trint screamed in response. The king glared at us, swiping his hand across the shoulder of his tunic as if he could clean our humor from himself.

Today we all wore borrowed clothes, each of us sporting the teal and black of Gandry. While Henry and Farai matched Trint in their flowing teal trousers and tops with black sandals, I wore a robe-like teal dress. It covered every inch of my skin from my collar bones down, the sleeves so large they passed my fingertips. I had my dagger strapped to my bare thigh, the only weapon I could hide.

My hair was wild, the curls unruly now that it had grown so long, but I had no idea what to do with it anymore. I noted the way Trint looked at me, his eyes roaming over the locks with the type of scrutinization that made me grit my teeth in restraint. I could not fault him. I was the one who had said I needed to look the part after all.

We finally made it to the doors, the carvings full of runes that reminded me of those on my dagger. They did not glow in the same way, but the lines built upon one another, stacking and crossing to form symbols that looked so similar.

"You must behave," the king warned as his hands reached for the gold knobs of the doors. Before he opened them, he turned his head, eyes immediately landing on me. "No smiting people who annoy you or stabbing someone because they say something about your ears."

I gasped, my hand flying to my chest in mock outrage.

"One guard accidentally fell out of the carriage, and I stand by that statement." Trint looked at me with knowing eyes, his lids half closed and lips pursed. After about five seconds, I broke. "He said the tops looked like shriveled grapes!"

At that, Henry burst into laughter. Farai, to his credit, did not get angry or judge me. In fact, he had seemed ready to shove the man, too, after Henry translated between chuckles.

Trint was acting as if there were not skeletons crawling up the walls. They worshiped the God of *Death and Creation* for fucks sake. When Trint did not look away, staring at me like he was prepared to wait here for as long as it took, I rolled my eyes and nodded. The king flashed a brilliant smile and proceeded to pull open the doors.

The guards behind us spread out, only a handful following. It did not surprise me that they were both confident I could take on any danger and terrified I was the danger. From the corner of my eye, I saw the guard that I had ordered to jump from the carriage cringe away from me, his face still bruised.

He deserved it.

We walked through the doors, stepping into a large entryway that opened to reveal the ceiling above. From below, we could see the light of midday shining through the painted glass windows. Colors rained down from the images depicted upon the skylights, stories of what I assumed were the gods' lives stretching throughout the ceiling.

Just like the outside, the inside of the temple was a vibrant violet, bits of gold and black creating swirls and runes across the walls. I dropped

Farai's hand, letting my eyes wander greedily. It was strange going from never leaving The Capital to traveling the world. I had dreamt of this, getting to be free. Yet it did not feel like freedom. No, this felt like the final act of a book without a happy ending. Every day was another grain of sand falling in the hourglass of my life. I could feel it, that odd sense of impending doom.

"Keep up. We are running behind, and you need to get ready." Whipping my head around, I faced the pompous king, who had already begun walking down a long hallway.

With a loud groan, I sped up, reaching his side. He had gone from flirtatious to terrified to an odd animosity, but none of those things had outshone his curious nature. Entering his mind, I found that very wonder running rampant on his thoughts. Before anything else, Trint had a desire to learn.

Tell me, King Trint, does my appearance not satisfy you?

He flinched, just as he always did, glaring at me after a moment of heavy breathing. My answering smile was wide, showing enough teeth to be more of a threat than a reassurance.

Asher from months ago would have been horrified to know that I no longer cared about scaring people—that I reveled in it instead. Odd that the death of who I was did not hurt me now, like it had at first. Maybe I had unknowingly buried her, laying to rest that naïve and hopeful soul that was beaten and belittled into submission. The one who would have cowered at the thought of killing when not ordered to do so and recoiled at the use of her power.

Once, I would have been appalled by myself, and I inwardly wondered when I had decided not to be anymore.

"I wish you would stop that. I can hear perfectly fine." My laugh was not in response to his words, but to his thoughts, which strayed to me and what I could do if I sat on a throne beside him. Just as so many before him had done.

Everyone loves to imagine using me like a caged animal for their own benefit, but you all seem to forget that beasts bite when cornered. Instead of picturing what good I could do for you with your ring on my finger, you should fear how insignificant you would be if your crown was on my head.

His interest simmered into anger, the threat landing perfectly in that spot of his mind where insecurity and paranoia resided. Not only did I shut down his plotting, but I reminded him of the scheme he had already vowed to follow through with.

Bellamy had been surprised he agreed at all. The first note he sent me after Trint simply said, "That is the last time I doubt you, beautiful creature." Beyond that, Bellamy mostly used the notes to openly flirt with me. Once, he had sent a note that had suggested fairly provocative activities, but when it returned to me, Farai snatched it from the air.

"Whipped cream? Really? Does he have no shame?" the Shifter had asked, scoffing as he tossed me the paper and pencil.

To be honest, he was not wrong. Bellamy had very little shame. He would go from sending me explicit messages about licking chocolate off my breasts to discussing strategy with Henry on the same page. Like it did not matter who saw what he said—what he promised.

Trint's harsh words jerked me out of my thoughts as he said, "You look like you have not seen a comb in years, and you have circles below your eyes that are so dark it almost appears you were in a fight. You have ripped your lips to shreds, leaving them chapped and bleeding. Even worse, I have watched you wipe your hands on your robes—which were expensive—leaving sweat spots on them. At the moment, lovely princess, you are leagues away from the divine creature you are hoping to portray."

My mind was reeling with retorts as I decided if his words held merit—they did. Before I could break free of my stunned daze, Trint's hand grabbed my forearm and pulled me down a hallway to the left. There was another set of double doors at the end, looking as if it held importance in a way that only something tucked away like that could.

Instead of whisking me away to whatever lay beyond those, he quickly opened an unimpressive door to the side, practically shoving me inside of the tiny room. It was mostly empty, holding only a set of purple couches with a wooden table in the center of them. A fire roared to life on the far right wall, setting the lush golden rug stretched around the seating area aglow. The color had become easier and easier to look at the more I came across it, this particular instance not affecting me much at all. Only a short, quick tightening of my chest. So different than the panic that overtook me at the mere thought of a golden dress upon my skin.

A woman was waiting behind the smaller sofa, her face stoic as she took me in. I returned the gaze, noting her beautiful midnight skin, the brown of her eyes reminding me of liquid chocolate. She wore a thick purple dress with a white apron secured around her waist and had her graying hair in dozens of small braids. When the door finally clicked behind us, Farai, Henry, and Wrath filing in, she bent down, disappearing behind the sofa. A rustling noise sounded, followed by loud clinking that made me nervous for whatever she was planning.

It was not until she started setting products down on the wooden table that I realized what they were trying to do. "I do not need some weird makeover. Can we not simply let my magic speak for itself?"

Trint scoffed, pointing to the small couch with raised brows. Hesitating, I watched the mortal woman for a moment longer, noting the various cosmetics and lotions. What would it hurt to placate them in this?

With a heavy sigh of defeat, I made my way to her, sitting down and preparing myself. She eyed me, scrutinizing every inch of me from my head to my toes, looking horribly displeased by the end of her assessment. Trint moved to the larger sofa, plopping down ungracefully. Contrary to his title, Trint seemed to enjoy the comfort of unimportance. Producing a small flask, the king leaned his head back and closed his eyes before taking a large gulp.

"Now, you three need to leave. Find something more exciting to do, like cleaning chamber pots or licking your paw." It was a casual dismissal, the animosity not nearly as tangible in his tone or posture as it was in his words.

All three of them looked poised to argue, Wrath going so far as to grow and hiss, but I quickly cleared my throat to get their attention. "It is fine. I can handle myself. Go ask around for information on any other creatures that may be nearby."

After a moment, Henry groaned, offering Trint one final glare before he walked out. Farai's concerned frown warmed my heart, giving me the confidence to smile his way and wave my hand at him to tell him to go. He nodded, ushering Wrath out too. Then it was only Trint, the woman, and I, the king relaxing into the sofa like he had been through a great ordeal.

"I hate socks," he muttered. I almost laughed at the ridiculousness of the statement. As if he could sense my amusement, he leveled me with a glare.

The servant woman paid him no mind, dipping brushes into cosmetics and slathering my skin, going so far as to pluck some of my eyebrow hairs. I swatted her hand with a hiss, annoyed with her ministrations. More than that, I loathed the idea of being altered to fit whatever idea of beauty these people had. It reminded me of the way my eating had been restricted to please Sterling. Losing more of myself for anyone was not an option.

I was no one's but my own.

Unperturbed, she shrugged and turned to gather something else. A brush. Joy.

After what felt like years of hearing her tsk in disapproval as she ripped through my knotted curls, she finished. I thought she would braid my hair back, something to mask the now unnaturally large fluff of frizz, but she instead bent down to retrieve something from her satchel. When she stood once more, now holding a comb made of metal, suspicion crept in.

She walked away, approaching the fire. Was she going to brand me?

"Are you going to brand me?" My shouted and bewildered question startled Trint, who had begun softly snoring with the open flask held tightly against his chest. The wine spilled across the violet couch, deepening the cloth to a nearly black color.

"No, stupid girl, I am going to fix your hideous hair," she said in that throaty accent of Gandry. Surprised to hear the common tongue, it took me a moment to properly absorb what she said.

Girl? Hideous hair? Despite myself, I thought I rather liked this woman, if only for her brazenness. With that realization fresh in my mind, I settled back and begged the stupid God of Death and Creation to not take me today.

Odd, to think living was better than dying. Maybe one day I would want that for myself rather than the good of the world.

"You made me spill my wine!" Trint cut in.

"By the sound of your voice, it seems you have quite a bit of whine left in you." My mocking earned me a quiet giggle from the otherwise-stony woman as she began to drag the hot comb through my hair. The first victory of the day, excellent. Happily, I closed my eyes, relaxing into the warmth of the odd device.

"I need to get rid of you before you make my hair turn gray." Trint's grumbling was followed by sounds of panicked scrubbing and rather filthy curses. My smile grew as the comeback he had so easily offered reached the tip of my tongue.

"What does not kill you, disappoints me." A gasp sounded behind me, forcing me to open one eye and look at the king, who I imagined was as horrified as the woman. Instead of furious or appalled, King Trint looked as if he were fighting back laughter.

"You know, I do not recall us becoming friends, so please, save the flattering comments for someone else."

With that, he took another hearty sip of his wine and proceeded to stretch out on the dry portion of the sofa, once more snoring after only a minute or so. What a talent, to sleep peacefully. To not fear what might come when you close your eyes. Comfort like that was a luxury, and I doubted he realized that.

The woman spent the next hour diligently combing my hair, returning to the fireplace when it lost heat. Smelling the burning hair made my stomach churn, images of so many dead flashing before my eyes. The sorrow of lives lost and debts owed threatened to pull me down into depths I would surely drown within—how could one breathe when the air was made of despair and regret? Though I wished she would stop, I knew better than to admit that weakness. So I dutifully sat still, eyes closed and mind slowly sinking from the memories of being taught to remain silent within my pain—of the screams that accompanied burning flesh.

Turn the sorrow into anger.

I repeated that over and over again, hoping that it would be enough to prevent whatever meltdown was threatening to burst free of me.

Finally, she finished, coming around to assess me once more, ignorant of the storm raging inside my chest. Apparently, she was rather proud of her accomplishments, because she offered a smile and said something to the king in her native tongue. When he did not respond, still snoring, she groaned and stomped over to the thin door on the right wall.

This allowed me a moment to properly take in the rest of the odd space, a welcome distraction from all that I could not ignore within my mind. The window behind me was not overly large, providing just enough light for her to work. On our right was what I now knew was a closet, which the woman was pulling a purple garment from.

Beads of sweat dripped down my neck from the heat of my hair, so thick it was stifling. What had she done to it?

When the woman was once more in front of me, she held up a pool of violet, the delicate and unique structure of it reminding me of Pino. Perfect timing, I was in desperate need of more grief right about now.

I stood, reaching for the dress, but the woman smacked one of my hands. I gasped, glaring at her as I rubbed my stinging skin. She hit hard for a mortal, especially one who seemed to be at least halfway through life. Muttering something that definitely sounded like insults under her breath, she began ripping open my robe. For a second, I attempted to fight her, but then she raised her hand again. With a mumbled curse, I took the note from Bellamy out of the robe pocket, being sure to only touch it with the cloth as I shoved it into my dagger sheath.

Whether I thought it would bring me luck or comfort, I was not sure. Both, probably. But either way, I knew I needed to have that piece of him with me as I did this. Then I nodded, submitting to her ministrations.

She stripped me until I was left in only my undergarments, my necklace, and my plain black sheath. Then the lunatic tried to rip off the band securing my breasts. This time, I swatted her, and I watched as her eyes went wide. The outrage was clear, but she also radiated respect, her mind practically singing praise to me. Still, she pointed her finger to the band, then to the ground, her frown so deep it looked as if it might go full circle and become a smile.

Sighing, I pulled the cloth over my head, earning a few more tsks of disapproval when my hair got wrapped inside of it. But, soon, I was nearly fully nude, and she was forcing me to step into the purple gown. When she pulled it up past my hips and stomach, I slid my arms through the sleeves and let her adjust the neckline.

Satisfaction and pride doused the air, warming it and me further. She stepped back, clapping her hands in front of her mouth. When a single tear fell from her left eye, I shifted on my feet in discomfort. Seconds passed, and then she was composing herself once more, taking a few deep breaths before ushering me to the long, oval-shaped mirror tucked away in the far corner of the room. We made our way there, my bare feet cold on the black quartz floor.

A gasp involuntarily left my lips when I saw my reflection. She had painted my eyelids black, making the gray of my irises stand out with an eerie quality. My lips were left untouched save for healing cream, my cheeks red from the rouge. Even my under eyes, which had once been dark and sunken in, looked bright and well rested. The comb-like device had stolen the curls from my hair, leaving it straight and silky.

Even more stunning was the dress. The torso was made entirely of black and purple beads, strung together on a thick purple thread. The designer had left some areas more bare than others, exposing small sections of my tawny skin. The neckline dipped into a low V shape, offering a silent explanation for why she had refused to allow my band to stay on. Both sleeves were also beaded, the swirling patterns reaching my wrists. She tugged on a small circle of loose fabric, wrapping it over my middle finger to secure the end of the sleeve over the back of my hand.

The skirts were equally beautiful, layers upon layers of sheer purple fabric that flowed with every small movement. They split up my left thigh, stopping at a high enough point that I wondered if I would scandalize people rather than inspire them. But she did not seem concerned with the way the beads barely stayed secure on the edge of my shoulders, or the fact that the fabric threatened to show my black undergarments.

She was quick to slip a pair of black slippers on my feet, the satin glowing in the firelight. For a moment, I forgot that I was not actually a goddess, that I did not rule over the skies and bless the realms. Looking at myself now, I felt brighter than I had before. Not because I was prettier, though I wagered I was, but because something about the fierce determination and the commanding energy of my appearance made me feel so very *right*.

In that moment, I wondered if we were all once grander beings. Perhaps the gods were simply stars, existing in the ethers and united as one. Maybe life had always felt dull and tiresome because it was once so vivid. Could it be that the reason I had never felt at home in this place—in this body—was because I was once brighter than the sky itself? And if so, how does one exist in a world of darkness when they were once the light?

Breaking me from my profound musing, the woman clapped three times, finally stirring Trint from his dozing. He jolted once more, narrowly avoiding spilling his wine again. I laughed, but there was an odd feeling in my chest, one I could not shake as I looked at myself again.

"What is your name, might I ask?" She looked at me as if it was an absurd thing to say, her eyes wide and her brows raised.

"Well, Auntie Claire, do answer her so we can prepare." The woman—Trint's aunt apparently—snatched the flask as he lifted it to his mouth, the leather leaking wine. When she smacked him—her king—on the hand as he tried to take it back, I simply could not stop the surprised laugh that left me.

Somehow, the scene before me was a reminder of Xavier. There were times when I was convinced that the fae king was the funniest person alive. He always knew what to say, the right jokes to tell, the best face to give.

When my first day of Academy resulted in ten-year-old me sobbing on the floor of the castle library, Xavier was the one who cheered me up. We both sat on the floor in a dusty corner, surrounded by tomes that dated back millennia, eating cheesecake and drinking tea. It was a relief to have someone be so comfortable with me after a day full of being feared and excluded.

Academy was mostly separate, with very few interactions between the factions. I, though, was permitted to merge into them all. Mia had made that decision, telling me it was important for fae of all ages to see me for what I was, their future queen. Back then, I believed she wanted me to be seen as more than some oddity, and even now, after it all, I wondered if that were true. Yet all it had done was further outcast me. I was not allowed to befriend them, to do anything more than speak with them in classes, and they did not want me there regardless. To them, I was a horror story.

But Xavier reminded me that I was more than that. He made sure I knew that I would one day rule over all of them, not because of my strength or my power, but because of who I was to my core. We laughed as he told me stories of his mishaps with his own unfathomable Fire power. Together, we realized that the darkness did not have to win. He had ruffled my hair, and I had smacked his arm when he told me he could light the male on fire who had told me to go back to the Demon Realm where I came from.

We had been happy, had we not?

"Yes, well, it has been so wonderful to make your acquaintance, Lady Claire. Your Majesty, I think it is time for us to go, as you said." With a small curtsy, I rushed towards the door, not caring if Trint was following or where I was going.

Taking every memory I possessed of Xavier's glowing Fire power, I lit my veins ablaze. I let it burn through me, let it consume every feeling of sadness and joy.

When I threw open the door, I was no longer suffocating on the pain. I was breathing in the fury.

CHAPTER THIRTY

ASHER

" You cannot stutter. You cannot hesitate. You cannot so much as flinch. Do you understand? If you want our allegiance, if you want us to fight for you, then convince them. Not me." Despite the condescending tone, I was aware of how true Trint's words were. He was not saying this to hurt me but to prepare me. He wanted this to work as much as we did. And it had to, because this would be our biggest success to date.

"I understand." It was the most complacent and agreeable I had been with him, so it was no surprise that he stared at me with squinted eyes of suspicion. Trint was putting himself on the execution block, prepared to sacrifice everything for the slim chance that he would walk away with infinitely more. So I would give it to him.

There was no longer any other option. No world in which I would fail. I could not.

"Most of those in attendance will understand the language of the gods, as it is vital to our religious teachings. So you do not have to worry. Even those who are not fluent will be able to have someone next to them translate. Just speak as you always would." I nodded as he spoke, his hands moving in time with his words in what seemed to be a nervous tick. "Well, as you normally would but far less antagonistic."

I scoffed but could not stop the smile that tilted the corners of my lips. We continued walking, Farai and Henry on either side of me, my arms intertwined with theirs. Both had complimented my look, promising that I appeared every bit the goddess I was about to pretend I was.

Wrath, though, was far more honest. "Did we want her to look like a goddess or an offering?"

Trint had disguised his laugh with a cough, but Farai had not attempted to mask his in the slightest. Henry, of course, did his best not to laugh at anything the dalistori said out of spite, naturally.

Still, I walked on, exuding confidence and commanding the attention of every person who passed by us. "Faithfuls," Trint had called them. The people who wore the same robes I had over my dress now, the same ones I had been wearing when we arrived. Each had devoted their lives to the temple—to the gods. Each looked at me wide-eyed, one going so far as to bow as we passed. The black circlet of diamonds that rested above my brow was likely what truly convinced them, the final touch. It began at my hairline, swirling down in a twisting pattern similar to my gown until the pointed tip ended just between my eyebrows.

A crowd could be heard as we neared the colosseum, which held worship weekly for anyone in their realm to attend. It lay behind the temple, connected through a stone tunnel that took us underground, where it had been built. Trint had explained that the walls of rock helped amplify sound, but I wondered if it was more about being closer to their preferred god, whom I feared favored death far more than creation. Perhaps he resided in the Underworld rather than the Above, and this was their way of digging themselves down to him.

Either way, it was horrific to slowly descend into the earth, the tunnel lit only by torches placed incrementally on the walls. The air was stale, tasting of history and loss and obsession. I wanted out, and I could hear the projected thoughts of unrest from the two males on either side of me, both their arms tightening around mine.

It felt like every time I had been thrown into my low level room in the palace. It felt like being slowly led to an undoing. It felt like a trap.

Then the roaring grew impossibly louder, and I nearly let go of my self-proclaimed protectors to cover my ears. It hurt, in the way only fae ears could. Farai flinched beside me, and I looked to see the pained expression on his face that likely mirrored my own. Henry stopped, eyeing both of us. At Farai's side, Wrath hissed in discomfort, shrinking down until he was small enough to crawl up my body and rest on my shoulder.

"Does it not hurt your ears?" I asked Henry, finally covering my own, the jagged tops making it easier for my hands to cup around them in protection.

Henry shrugged. "It is not comfortable, but our kind were once human. We do not have the same hearing that you do."

It hit me then, the truth of his words. Suddenly, Bellamy's theory that I was injected with some sort of magic sounded like the only right answer. How had I ever questioned my parentage when I constantly peered at the portrait of my mother—one of the few items that graced the walls of the palace—growing up? Or even the smaller portrait of both my parents that hung over their shared resting place in the royal tomb. I had their dark locks, their light brown skin, and my mother's heart-shaped face. I was them in so many ways. I was the daughter of Florencia Daniox, Royal Tomorrow, strongest Reader of her time.

How had I been so horrid as to doubt such a thing?

With a deep breath and a curt nod at Trint, who tapped his foot impatiently just ahead, I urged them along, grinding my teeth at the pounding in my ears. Farai seemed to force himself forward with the same will that I had, and I dipped into his mind to watch as he thought of his husband, our sweet and loving Jasper. For him, for Nicola, for every fae, we would do this.

Softly—uncertainly—I lulled him, giving him all the peace I could not give myself. In a way, it was like living through him, feeling that assurance settle bone-deep within his chest. Light shone through a wide opening now, the end of the tunnel in sight. Somehow, that did nothing to reassure me. Instead, it lit every warning signal in my mind, bells ringing and screams sounding. As if every horrific memory was telling me that this would be a bad idea.

At the end of the tunnel, we stepped into a large open ring of dirt, which was surrounded by seating and stairs made of rock. Nearly every seat was full, reaching to the top of the large hole that held the coliseum. I had never seen so many beings in one place. My jaw dropped, my brain momentarily too stunned to register the pain of how much louder it was from here.

Farai, on the other hand, fell to the ground. His screams broke me from my trance, and suddenly, it was too much to bear. The piercing in my ears. The thoughts of hundreds of thousands of people shoving into that golden gate protecting my mind. Farai writhing on the ground as he bled from his ears, eyes, nose, and mouth.

"Henry, get him to Ranbir!" I shouted, watching as even the demon's freckled face scrunched in pain. He hesitated, eyes flicking from me to the crowd and back again. "Now!"

The king put up a hand, silencing the large crowd within seconds. Could he not have done that sooner?

Finally, Henry nodded, lunging for Farai and disappearing in a flash of white light. Gasps rang out, coming from people all around us. They had likely never witnessed such a thing. Seeing as this was their normal day of worship, it was safe to say that those in attendance were among the most devout of the mortals. Which meant they would see this as their first sign that something other—something greater—was among them.

With a deep breath, I pushed down the nausea that came from the agony in my ears and pet Wrath with my pointer finger. He nestled further into my hair, using it like a barrier.

I walked to Trint, who had made his way to the center. My feet carried me at a slow and confident pace, though the ringing in my ears had not so much as faded, leaving me unable to hear whatever Trint was saying. Had the crowd really gone quiet, or could I simply not hear them?

Behind him was a large statue of a violet throne, carvings of skulls and flowers etched into it, connected with swirling patterns and runes. Atop the throne was a male, his lengthy and thin body clothed in billowy robes. The same as my own, I realized. His black hair flowed down his body, which was left unpainted, reaching the floor and pooling along with the purple robes. His ears, I noted, were round—like a mortal's. The death god's eyes were what really stood out though, their bright golden hue startling.

Trint's arm reached out, pulling my attention away from the statue. With a smile I hoped looked genuine, I placed my hand in his, watching as he lowered his lips to my skin. Needing to know what was happening, I opened a small door within my mental shield, the gate creaking slightly as it welcomed the thoughts of those around me. My free fist clenched so tightly that my nails pierced my flesh, the skin trying to heal but failing when I did not loosen the hold. There were so many thoughts, too many.

The gods walk among us!

It must be the Goddess of the Sun and Moon, did you see the light?

King Trint has brought the gods to Gandry!

King Trint will save the world!

Bow!

Pray!

The gods! The gods! The gods! The gods!

Then there was Trint, his stoic face not betraying the calculating and eager thoughts that filled his mind.

Are you ready for the show, Asher?

I was sure that his mental voice matched the words that came from his lips, but because I could not hear, I took no chances and offered only a curt nod in return. Trint smiled, the dazzling flash of teeth like armor to a king.

Trint's mouth moved, and I forced out the other voices, focusing every ounce of my magic on him. I crafted a new gate, one that surrounded only the two of us—fighting off everyone but him. I listened through his mind as he spoke to his people.

Ladies and gentleman, I so humbly thank you for allowing this change in worship. I know the holy day is revered; therefore, I pray you understand that this alteration to schedule is not something I have done lightly.

Thoughts pelted against me, trying and only barely failing to break through my gate. Trint's words were definitely rousing them, though I was unsure if it was in a positive way or not.

Today, I beg of you to watch—to bear witness to—an extraordinary blessing. One that not even our holiest of ancestors were afforded.

Turning to face me fully, Trint's smile did not falter, did not so much as twitch. But his mind…oh, his mind told another story.

Princess, if you can hear me, make this count. Know that you will not get another chance, and neither will I.

Lying to them now was for the greater good. Not only for the demons and the fae but for them too. At least, that was what I told myself as I nodded to the king.

His warm hands met my shoulders, and as he helped me out of my robe, I shattered the gate. Bars of gold snapped in half, the barrier protecting my mind falling apart. It hit the hedges and the flowers, every ounce of protection I had built so long ago crumbling before me.

Stunned thoughts beat into me, feeling like a punch to the head in their fierceness. I nearly collapsed, my knees shaking and my vision swimming. But I did not fall. Instead, I forced my chin higher, and I readied myself for what I did best.

Let the dramatics begin.

Eyes falling closed, I slowly lifted my arms, letting my head tilt back. Wrath remained still, his claws digging into my skin. And then, with aching precision, I shoved my magic out, feeling as it grabbed hold of each mind it passed. They were like the tree roots on the outer walls of the temple, intricate and winding, but instead of broken and crumbling, these brightly lit up roots danced and sang.

The well of magic in my chest responded in kind, a conductor building their orchestra to a stunning crescendo. With every new instrument that began to play, my chest hummed louder, my magic swishing in the air to guide them all.

At the halfway mark, my fingers went numb.

At the two-thirds mark, I lost all feeling in my upper body.

At the three-quarters mark, my entire body was gone to me.

By the time my magic was crawling towards the final row of mortals, I was covered in tiny pinpricks, the tingle painful. It was like awakening after a long slumber. I felt both exhausted and revitalized, old and new. Somehow, I had simultaneously become the wave and the shore which it barreled into—like a never still, yet always steady, force of nature.

I opened my eyes, facing the crowd.

Mortals of Gandry and beyond, my name is Asher Daniox. I am the holder of minds, a goddess made flesh. I am here before you to call upon the holiest of warriors.

OF REALMS AND CHAOS

I registered the sudden shift, the edge to every mind in the coliseum. There was terror there as the low tenor of my mental voice sounded inside their heads. This was the make or break moment, when the mortals of Gandry—and elsewhere—would choose whether or not they would follow me.

Once, the beings of this world lived in unison. Beside you walked creatures with magic and power, and in the eyes of the gods, all were equal. But wickedness found its way inside Alemthian. War plagued your lands, destroyed your homes, and shredded your souls. Still, we gods see that worth in your hearts. We acknowledge your value and trust in your minds. The time has come, my children, to stand and restore the balance.

When the first mortal stood, prepared to run, I dug deeper into their minds—found purchase there.

Stay, I told them. *Listen.*

For the greater good, I thought as my stomach began to churn.

I ask you not to bow or pray but to lift your swords and fight for tomorrow. The fae king and queen seek to take up arms against the demon king. They wish to conquer and destroy. But hear me when I say, the fae are not your enemy, nor are the demons. You are one, and you must fight for that today and every day after.

I heard Xavier's voice then, the memory pulling my thoughts from the scene in front of me.

"When two of us decide to put ourselves above the realm, the realm shall fall. Therefore, it is with great sorrow that I sentence them both to death. For if not them, then all of us shall surely perish."

As those words echoed inside my head, merging with the steadily growing uproar within the coliseum, I noted that I was slowly getting my hearing back. Arms held out, as if waiting for an embrace, I caught sight of a pair of honey eyes. My own began to prick with tears as Sipho—*my Sipho*—smiled at me from the front row. His deep skin was just as youthful as the last time I saw him, his black curls a disaster. He wore a silver tunic and black trousers, with his mothers necklace around his neck—my necklace. Above the sound of the crowd, I heard his soothing and lovely voice as he spoke to me.

"You can do this, My Soul."

I let out a soft sob as he nodded my way, encouraging me to press on. So I did.

Your devout and brave king has promised his sword. Will you follow in his steps? Will you fight for your kingdom, your realm, and your world? Will you fight for your gods?

"As above, so below!" Trint shouted, a fist rising into the air.

Then they were all standing, their screamed chant of "as above, so below" bursting my ears and stealing that numbness from me. A wave of agony washed over my body, taking my breath. My vision went black, Sipho's clapping form the last thing I saw. And then I was gone.

***

"Well, it's definitely an interesting development. But this does make everything easier." A voice, sultry and deep, was speaking. That meant I could hear again, how nice.

Whisky and leather hit my nose, a smell that was not heavy or overwhelming but rather pleasant. When I opened my eyes, I was in a bed that was all too familiar. My upper body shot up, terror leaving me breathless. This time, the gray sheets felt more *real*. As if, somehow, I was here in truth, rather than just in my mind.

That frightened me more than the female and male that stood in the corner, both watching me with satisfied and eager smiles. The female, who I assumed was the one who spoke before, was ethereal. She had blonde hair, which just barely kissed her sharply pointed ears. Her skin was dark, full lips painted in a stunning shade of red. On her body she wore a cascading red dress, the silk hugging her full figure. The look in her eyes bordered on predatory, like I was an offering gifted to her.

Padon stood at her side, tall and muscular, with a far better hair cut this time around—the dark strands now more even and full. His shirt was also a sort of violent scarlet, the loose-fitting blouse looking both too large and somehow just right. His trousers were pure black, at such odds with his nearly translucent skin. Around his shoulders was a thick, black cloak. He stared at me with an excited longing, like someone who was starved of something and then finally had it within their reach.

I think I feared his expression more than hers.

"Leave us and tell no one." Padon's words proved that he likely was an emperor because the female, who looked just as formidable as him, merely gave a shallow bow and left the room. "Hello, my love."

"I am not your anything, Padon." My scolding sounded far more passive than it should have, likely because I was so startled by how soft and cold and real the silk felt on my skin. Padon did not seem to mind my chastising, looking more pleased than he ever had before. "What is different about this time?"

My words came out in a whisper, but the creature heard me, his smile growing impossibly wider. That was when I noticed his eyes, they were not white anymore. They were dark, nearly black, but I could not make out the exact color.

He made his way to me, stopping at the bed, which was tall enough to reach his waist. Leaning down, he placed his hands on the mattress, causing my body to lean towards him as it dipped. I scoffed, trying to lean away, but Padon grabbed my chin and forced me to face him.

"Everything has changed, Asher." Grip unforgiving, he reached up and slid his thumb over my bottom lip, those dark eyes tracking the movement. "I can feel you, my love. Can you feel me?"

That was when I realized that I could, in fact, feel him. Not in the same way as before, where everything had seemed oddly distant, but in a way that made my nerve endings light in warning. When Padon's lips crashed onto mine, I was so startled by the genuine sensation of his cold flesh that I did not immediately move.

His fingers gripped my hair, tugging on the strands as his tongue attempted to forcefully part my lips. Horror filled me, and then I was shoving him off, my knee jabbing upwards to connect with his groin. Padon crumpled to the ground, hissing in pain as he went down. Scrambling away, I did not realize that I was still wearing my beaded gown until it was too late.

The quick and sharp movements caused the purple thread to snap, sending beads flying across the floor as the waist split in two. I slipped, feet tangling in the loose threads, and then I went flying off the end of a bed that was at least four feet high. My head hit first, smacking hard into the marble floor before my legs went sailing over, flipping my body.

For a moment, I laid there on my stomach in stunned silence. Confusion, surprise, and pain all mingled within me, leaving me no choice but to burst into a fit of laughter.

"You kneed me!" Padon's rough voice was closer than I thought it would be, that earthy and nearly burning scent invading my senses once more. I continued to laugh, the sound slightly manic as I reached up and snagged the quilt to wrap around my body.

"You tried to shove your tongue down my throat, you pervert!" Catching my breath, I adjusted the quilt to conceal my exposed body and sat up fully. Padon was squatted down near me, his cheeks a bright blue and his elbows resting on his knees. Despite having clearly been hurt by my rejection just as much as my knee, his smile was genuine and full.

"You looked like you wanted me to," he countered with a shrug.

My mouth fell open, all humor dying out. "In what world would I ever want that?"

We scrutinized one another as my words settled between us, gazes a mixture between my scowl and his smirk.

"An ideal one." His voice sounded far too sincere to be even remotely nonchalant or joking. Which begged the question: Would he force me to help him create that world?

"Your version of ideal is my version of delusional. Let us agree not to visit there again." Forcing my face to remain stony while my mind roared with building fury and fear, I stared the creature dead in the eyes. Stay calm, get information, and run. I could do that. "Speaking of worlds, I am in yours, right? Why did you bring me here?"

Not missing a beat, Padon stood and walked away, speaking to me over his shoulder. "One day in the future, we'll look back on this fondly. Perhaps we'll even tell our younglings."

"We are never having younglings. Now, answer the question, you moron." Calm. I was calm. What did Bellamy teach me? Be a pond? Yes, I was a pond, still and peaceful.

"Why wouldn't I want you with me?" The arrogance of his tone as he grabbed a glass decanter and poured himself whisky sent me over an edge I was desperately trying to avoid. The imbecile had dropped stones in my pond, letting loose ripples of fury.

"You are a psychopath!" I screamed, standing so quickly that black dots blocked my vision. With unsteady feet, I stomped towards him.

"I'm simply a male in love." Turning to face me, Padon let his eyes roam over my quilt-clad body. Stupid, evil, foul creature.

"Send me home, now!" Like a petulant youngling, I snatched his cup and threw it against the nearest wall, the glass shattering on the floor and the whisky splattering on the wall. My chest heaved, body shaking.

I was so, so tired. Exhausted, even. Physically, mentally, emotionally.

"Eh, I don't want to."

No, I was *furious*.

"Stella save me," I muttered, walking away to the nearest set of double doors. I would find my own way out, then. Damn him to the Underworld for all I cared.

"Ah yes, those wonderful gods. You know, when you first arrived, you were projecting some interesting thoughts and memories. I distinctly recall a statue of a rather hideous god atop a throne, the ruler of flowers and decay or something like that. Truly an unimpressive lot. Rest assured, Stella has no power here. I, on the other hand, have all the power, my love. Perhaps you can pray to me instead."

With a final growl of rage, I threw open the doors and stomped down the hallway. Maybe one day I would refrain from walking semi-nude through a castle that was not mine.

CHAPTER THIRTY-ONE

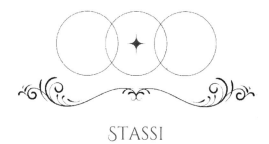

STASSI

Eoforhild was gorgeous.

The sun shone down upon the luscious greenery through little tufts of white clouds, the closest thing to perfection I'd seen since coming to Alemthian. I briefly wondered if I was going to have an even harder time leaving here than I had Betovere.

Though there I had my creature.

When had I taken to calling him that? That thought stopped me dead in my tracks, throwing my mind off course. I couldn't seem to recall when that shift had happened, but I knew that my time visiting him in his cell had resulted in a sort of obsession. I was infatuated with the male, his easy going jokes and odd habit of spewing facts I didn't ask for were charming. Though nothing was as intriguing as the way he seemed to shrink away from violence.

Not once since meeting him had I felt even an ounce of that sin. It was like he had been born without bloodlust, which was new to me, as I had yet to meet anyone without it. Similar to how he seemed unwilling to fear me.

"Hello, lovely, can I help you find anything?"

The female behind the desk was warm in every sense of the word. From her dark skin to her kind smile to her yellow skirts, she was what I imagined this world's sun would look like if it suddenly became sentient. I returned the smile, trying to remember what it was like to be so kind and not recalling a time I had been.

"Yes, actually. I'm looking for something to wear to meet a male. Do you have anything you think would suit me?" My voice was made of honey and my heart of acid—what a contrast, to be both virtuous and sinful. A startling balance that I had maintained for so long. It seemed that the more time I spent here, the more the scales tipped.

"Oh, yes! I believe I have something that will go perfectly with that stunning hair of yours!" Then she was off, running to the back end of her large clothing stall. In fact, the sheer size reminded me more of a building than a stall, but that was what all of the vendors in this market were calling their quaint stores.

Allowing myself another moment to look around, I silently thought of all the things I would need to get done today. The hardest would be finding the prince, as it seemed he was just as quick to disappear as the darling princess. We would need to break her of that when we secured her. Perhaps watching him die would make that abundantly clear.

Yes, that was likely the best route.

"What about this?" The female was back, her fingers gripping fabric that was the color of melted caramel. The dress was made for someone taller, but otherwise, I imagined she was right about how well it would work with my hair. Trading her a gold coin for the dress, I placed a soft kiss on her cheek and quickly left.

I quite liked the stunned expression she wore as I did so.

***

What sort of land had snow in the *summer?*

Stupid, disgusting mountains. Why would they choose this place? Were their soldiers not depressed? Sick? Cold? Miserable?

Maybe it was just the dress I wore, which stopped at my knees and exposed most of my back, the bunched and layered fabric wrapping around my neck the only thing keeping it up. I was freezing, which was saying something for my kind. A cloak, I should've purchased an Eternity-forsaken cloak. No matter. I'd get this done quickly.

In fact, I could hear my new little friend making his way to this very room. The padding of his footsteps was loud, an angry strut that told me I was probably about to incense him even more than I thought—which was exciting to say the least. I needed some fury to combat my boredom.

Just as he came close enough for me to hear his racing heartbeat, I felt the pull. A beacon to my magic, as if my creature were ripping on a cord secured to my chest.

I've never before had to make such a choice. This was my chance to find out once and for all where Asher was, but by the way my creature's screams seemed to echo inside of my head as he repeatedly pulled on that line of connection we now had, I would never see him alive again if I didn't leave now.

I was about to get myself into an unfortunate amount of trouble.

Before Prince Bellamy Ayad opened the door to his office, I was gone, the combination of wood and rock being replaced with the gloom of the dungeons within the golden palace. The last time I was here, the male and I talked until exhaustion stole his consciousness. Being healed by that fae had clearly been no replacement for actual rest, seeing as every time she did so he grew more and more weak. So I left him be, opting to instead search Asher's chambers for anything I could bring to him.

What I had found was a bare room that looked as if no one lived there at all. That, and the absolutely wicked little mortal boy who seemed to enjoy torturing the male in the cell. Not long after I had come into her rooms, the mortal arrived, taking his time to lay in her bed and smell the pillow. I nearly snapped his neck so he could pay for making me witness such a strange thing, but I'd chosen to simply leave instead.

Now, as he sat on top of *my* creature, I almost regretted not flaying him then.

His fists were slamming into the imprisoned male's face, beating down on him as he shouted. Hating how much it bothered me to listen, I ground my teeth and planted my feet.

"You pathetic excuse of a male! How dare you?" His voice sounded odd, those golden curls bouncing with each swing. My creature was even dirtier than usual, covered in enough blood that I could barely see his gaunt face. In fact, he looked somehow thinner than he had just days ago. "I will kill you! Do you think we need you? We do not! You are a waste of space, unloved and unwanted and unworthy of life!"

One of my feet moved forward of its own volition, my willpower crumbling before me. My magic flared, responding to the increasingly potent sin that poured from the mortal prince in the same way blood spilled when an artery was sliced through. In fact, he was about to know just how much blood he could lose.

I creeped around the corner, slowly and silently approaching the cell. I would skin him. I would tear out every little blonde eyelash one by one. I would toss him in the snow of Eoforhild then dunk him into a tub of boiling water. I would—

"Get off of him!" A burst of shadows appeared within the cell, from it walking a male wearing a tunic in a stunning shade of blue. His brown hair had a slight red tint, his face not dark per say but a hue that made me think he once had glowing brown skin. A prisoner roaming free. Interesting.

He grabbed the mortal boy by his curls, ripping him up and throwing him back into the bars. The scream that split the air nearly lit me up, the magic flooding me coming dangerously close to exposing my hiding place in the shadows. I darted back on silent feet, hoping that I wouldn't get exposed now when it was too soon for me to claim my prize.

Bending down, the new male inspected my creature's pulverized face, looking as if he couldn't care less whether or not the damage was going to cause problems. Ah, a leashed prisoner.

"Your smart mouth is doing you no favors." It was a causal statement, given with little care or compassion. Like how my creature said odd facts. It made me somehow angrier than watching him be beaten to near death.

"Well, at least one of us is smart. I dare say *Prince Sterling* could use a lesson or two on intelligence. Odd, seeing as he is rumored to be quite bookish." The glorious deep tenor of his voice brought a wicked smile to my lips. When he laughed at the growl from the mortal, I nearly let my own humor ring out. I had forgotten that one didn't have to be cruel to win. Such an oddity.

The prince in question stood, his forehead bleeding from where the bars split his skin. "One day those jokes of yours will be all you have, and that will be the moment you realize who has truly won."

With that, the golden boy left, his head held far too high for how embarrassingly stupid he sounded. Apparently, my creature thought so too.

"Here I was thinking that was already all I had left. Foolish me for forgetting my lovely home of grime and mold. Thank you, Your Highness. Please, allow me to suck that little cock of yours as a thank you. Gods know it has been neglected!"

This time, the shadow wielder laughed too, the angry mumbling of the prince fading with each chuckle. But soon the air grew tense, a feeling of foreboding filling the spaces where the humor had quickly escaped. Something was very, *very* wrong.

After a moment, I realized what it was. A clicking noise could be heard in the distance, the sharp sound making my eyes blink and my ears twitch. The male that still stood above my creature smirked, turning his head towards the hallway the prince had just left through.

"You ready for more?" Again with a tone more casual than was warranted. He was toying with the prisoner, making a show of his nonchalance. My fingertips tingled from the influx of magic as the queen, with her tangerine hair and icy eyes, came into view.

The prisoner said nothing as she approached him, his face more stoic than I'd seen it before. Maybe they would end him quickly. At least then my creature wouldn't suffer.

For some reason, the idea of his death troubled me deeply.

"Good afternoon, handsome," the queen said, her gaze locked on my creature. It was impossible to miss his small flinch, the way he seemed to recoil from her presence igniting my fury. My thoughts warred between thinking him spineless and thinking her vile. "Malcolm, can you go fetch King Xavier?"

The male—Malcolm—didn't hesitate, nodding quickly and then disappearing in a cloud of smoke-like shadows. Seeing him use that Moon magic was startling, just as it had been every time I witnessed it. It made sense of why the mortals and demons worshiped their false gods.

"Guess who we found roaming the Mortal Realm?" Her smile was wide, oddly sinister for something so beautiful. I quite liked her, despite the fact that she regularly ordered my creature to be tortured and hunted the same little fae princess that I did. She was despicable in the best way. A female hardened over time, crafted into a monster by those who raised her. I loved the potency of her, the way she so deeply burrowed herself in that sin.

My creature seemed prepared to offer a snide remark, a shaky version of his smirk on his lips, but then the cloud of shadows returned.

They disappeared to reveal Malcolm and King Xavier, the latter looking as if he might be sick.

"Eternity spare me, I do so hate portaling." His voice was strained, his pale skin taking on a green hue. The frown he wore was so deep that a single dimple appeared on his cheek, softening his pinched face.

"Pathetic," Malcolm murmured under his breath, his glare practically burning a hole into the back of the king's dark waves. Mia growled, pointing to the hallway where she had entered. For the first time, the demon hesitated, defiantly lifting his chin.

There it was, the explanation for this odd relationship. He was in love with her. Now, that was pathetic.

After a small showdown between the queen and the demon, Malcolm finally relented and disappeared, portaling to who knew where. Mia schooled her face back into neutrality, hiding some sort of eagerness that made my magic sing.

"Now that we are alone, I have some exciting news." The queen's words were enough to stop the two males from breathing, both looking at her with eyes that portrayed two very different emotions. "We found her."

Xavier's smile was bright, the pure joy on his face surprising. Did he love Asher? Could anyone love someone whom they had so thoroughly abused? "Perfect, I will go get her. Where—"

"No, you will not. You proved yourself useless when you could not kill that *thing* we call son." Venom spewed from her, the words so poisonous that I wondered how they didn't kill the foolish king.

"I fail to see why I need to be here for this little lovers' quarrel." Stupid male, why was it so hard for him to shut that luscious mouth of his?

Luckily for him, the lovers in question were too focused on one another to punish the insolence.

"Seeing as you failed to do so first, I do not see how you are any more qualified to retrieve her." His insult struck her like a slap, going so far as to make her flinch from the contact. Well, well. The king had balls after all. "While we are on the topic, perhaps we can appeal to that *thing* rather than risk her being harmed."

The stone beneath my feet began to rumble, as if the planet itself were attempting to split in two. A single rose grew from the queen's palm, thorns tearing their way through her.

"Asher will be safe, make no doubt about that." As her cold voice echoed through the room, I left, knowing the truth of her words.

Asher would be safe—until they got their claws into her.

CHAPTER THIRTY-TWO

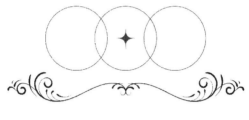

BELLAMY

Demarcus was in a wonderful mood today—which was unfortunate for me, as I was inclined to be the opposite. For the love of Stella, why was everyone not angrier? Could they not see how close we were to war—to the end?

"I believe that you are doing a wonderful job, Your Highness." Ugh, why did he have to be so nice? Why could he not simply be a prick like every other general to exist? Like me.

The forty-three-year-old mortal was determined to integrate his soldiers smoothly, not batting an eye when we started using magic in training sessions or teaching Behman soldiers how to use the fae's powers against them. In fact, as we walked to the war room, the mortal general was eagerly informing me of all that I had done right since Asher and Shah sent them here.

Was it wrong of me to wish everyone would be miserable?

With an audible sigh, I recognized that I was, in fact, wrong.

"Thank you, Demarcus. You are very kind, and I think you are also doing a good job. The war council will be quite impressed by the way your soldiers are training." Not a lie. They were far more resilient than anyone had given them credit for. Lian was, as per usual, not taking it easy on them during her private lessons. But it was the work they did when fighting beside demons that truly showed their abilities. Demarcus himself was an outstanding fighter and one of the quickest to learn how to fight against magic.

The double doors to the war room loomed ahead, my memory of the last meeting we had bringing a smile to my lips. Poor, stupid Finnick. Demarcus had begun discussing some sort of new sparring regimen, but all I could think was that Asher was traveling through Gandry, attempting to gain allies without me. I wished desperately that I could drop everything here and be with her. That I could spend every second with her before our time ran out.

With an irritated shove, I threw open the doors, watching as my captains and the four remaining war council members flinched at the sound. Even Demarcus, who was so prone to gleefully chatting, stuttered to a stop. If he had not already been sporting a head of prematurely gray hair, then I imagined he would have eventually went gray simply because of my tendency to scare him. Despite his hair, the general had flawless skin, the dark shade looking like midnight skies against his red uniform.

My own uniform was all black, small details of blue and silver stitched in swirling patterns up the arms. The others all wore uniforms as well, each sporting a beautiful silver color. Except for Damon, who instead wore the sky blue of the lieutenant general, and King Adbeel, who matched me in black.

"Ah, our fearless general, so glad you could make it." Elrial's words were laced with distaste, probably because I murdered his fellow

380

war council member in front of him. Since I knew he was right to hate me, I simply smirked at him, letting him see how little I truly cared about his thoughts. This was war, but Asher was life. Without her, we would all die.

Adbeel looked less than happy with Elrial's remarks, but I just shrugged when our eyes met. I was uninterested in arguing or attempting to prove myself to someone who would never see me as more than a pointy-eared enemy.

Demarcus and I made our way to the table that held the model of Alemthian, pulling out two of the tall wooden chairs. When we both were seated and comfortable, I began.

"We need to cut straight to the chase. It is time to take an offensive approach with the fae. As of right now, we know that their greatest asset is the demon working with them." At that, I allowed my eyes to briefly flick towards Adbeel, watching as he flinched. It was hard not to feel guilty for being the one to break him the news. "Noe?"

"I have not seen any sign of the traitor. In fact, the royals seem to be going about their days as usual. They have yet to leave the island at all. With their added security measures, I was unable to infiltrate the palace." Noe's normally sultry voice took on a commanding tone, her chin high. She had pulled her golden brown hair up, her uniform the same silver as any other soldier. Still, her kohl lined eyes and red lips gave her an evocative beauty, like the sirens of Haven.

The sirens that were nearly wiped out after the battle.

But unlike them, Noe did not call to her victims with a song. Instead, she capitalized on her beauty, letting those around her underestimate what she could do then laughing as she brutally slaughtered them. But now, as she showed that startling amount of magic, allowing shadows to leak from her skin like wisps of storm clouds, Noe did the opposite. It horrified me, knowing that whatever she was about to say, she required respect and perhaps even fear to do so.

"I visited each isle, noting the numbers at every base, and it is clear they are amassing their army. However, it was Isle Shifter that left me confused. They have double the number of soldiers than we originally thought. None looked particularly young, but I have heard rumors that they lowered the conscription age."

There it was, the thing that would spark more debate than we could afford at the moment. Letting myself sink further into my chair, I waited for the discourse to begin. It seemed Demarcus would be the first to speak.

"Conscription? You mean the fae force people—sorry, beings—to enlist in their forces? That is despicable! How young?" The disgust in the mortal general's tone was evident, as were the mixed opinions on the faces of the others around the table.

"It seems they are choosing to pull fae as young as nineteen, which is the average age that the younglings master their powers and become full-grown fae."

Demarcus seemed to let loose a breath of relief, but no one else did. No, we all understood that for what it was. When you lived to be thousands of years old, nineteen seemed so very young. But that was nearly a quarter of a mortal life. They did not know that at nineteen, a demon would not have even gone through The Almavet yet—the year-long experience of one's powers doubling and their aging beginning to slow. It was the transition out of youth, and that happened around age twenty-five—six years older than those fae who would be forced to fight.

Who we would be forced to kill.

Adbeel seemed to simmer with rage, the fury on his face turning his brown skin a shade of violent red. Tensing, I waited for the stupidity that would surely come out of someone's mouth any second.

"Good riddance. They will be easier to kill at such a young age." Ah, there it was. Wonderfully done Nrista, wonderfully done.

Her eyes darted towards Lian quickly, a look of pure disgust pinching her face. It was something Lian dealt with more often than she should from the older demons in the military, but she did nothing more than wink at the war council member.

The older female either did not care about the anger emanating from both her king and her prince, or she was unaware of it. Either way, we were now both shaking, our eyes pinned on her.

"How dare you speak of the death of those so young as if it were nothing. They are innocent in this, Nrista. Would you feel the same way if it were your daughters being forced? Even at their age, it would still be horrible to see them donning armor and wielding swords against their will, would it not?" She shot me a glare as my furious words registered, her stiff posture telling me that she understood them for the threat they were.

I wondered if she was wishing it was I on that battlefield, against her rather than beside her. Did she wish she could slaughter me, too? Many did, and I could not—would not—blame them. I was the embodiment of all they feared and hated. Prejudice had a knack for that, turning beings against one another. But those younglings, they had done nothing but be born on the opposite side. Their deaths were not fair or right.

"Enough. We are not here to fight. The purpose of this meeting is to inform you all that I have decided to take the advice of General Ayad. We are here to begin planning an offensive approach. If Tristana is right, and I cannot recall a time she was not"—at his words of recognition, Noe nodded her head in acknowledgement—"then we need to be prepared for a much larger military than we thought." At the king's declaration, everyone seemed to release a collective breath, each face going stony as we began.

Though the meeting started with a sense of unease, we quickly began concocting a plan to attack The Capital. The hardest part of this would be not harming the fae in Academy. Working through that was quickly grating on my nerves, as well as Lian's based on the look she sported. Neither of us could stand the way so many demons viewed fae life, like they were pawns to be sacrificed. Or worse, like they were lambs for slaughter.

"I agree that the fae king and queen need to be eliminated, as well as the traitor, but at the cost of our morals? Our souls? That is not worth it. We cannot be like them, murdering the young and destroying innocents." Adbeel looked impressed by my words, his small smirk and slight nod making me feel oddly proud.

Perhaps he was too. After nearly two centuries of desperately wanting revenge and death, I was finally learning.

"I agree. Noe, can you do more reconnaissance on The Capital? Maybe we can plan for a time when they will all be securely in their quarters. Or, if we can speak to them, there is a chance we can evacuate the younglings before we attack." Noe nodded, bowing when her king finished speaking. But something inside of me recoiled at the idea of her going. I needed her, now more than ever. Without her, how would I convince Asher to come home before she was finished speaking to all of the Mortal kings and queens?

"Noe needs to stay. She has an important mission. Luca can go, though. He was in and out of Betovere for the last two years. He likely knows it better than any of us." My words were firm, unwavering in their commanding tone. Marjorie huffed in annoyance, the other three council members shaking their heads with disapproval, but I did not care. Especially when Adbeel nodded, siding with me as he almost always did.

"Then let us—" Lian's words were cut off by the entrance of Henry, who burst through the door with a look of poorly masked nerves. His all-black ensemble hid the deep red shade of blood, but he reeked of it.

"I need to go," I said, not bothering to look at those around the table before I got up and made my way to the door. More than one of them muttered insults under their breath, but I ignored them in favor of offering one last comment. "Prioritize plans for attacking The Capital and ending the traitor, but if we fail, we must consider laying siege on Isle Shifter."

"Bell," Adbeel said, his voice deepening as if he were prepared to chastise me. I turned slightly, looking at his eyes that held far too much knowledge within them. "Do find time later to speak with me. I think we need to discuss the absence of a certain council member."

Shit.

With that, I left, following an uncomfortably silent Henry. His facial hair had grown, the stubble becoming an actual beard. Subconsciously, I pondered how he felt about me having my own face shaven and my hair trimmed. It was not that I wanted anyone other than Winona to cut it. Rather, I felt like I had no choice but to maintain appearances. Did he understand that? Did he hate me?

Then, of course, I remembered the look on his face, and my panic took a different turn.

Instead of speaking, he grabbed my hand and portaled us, the gray stone turning to a world of white. We were in the infirmary. "Where is she? What happened? Is that her blood?"

Without thinking, I grabbed onto the front of his tunic, nearly lifting him from the ground despite him being two inches taller. When he did not laugh or deny anything, I shoved him to the side and ran to the end of the medical area, where a set of curtains had been drawn around the last bed. Throwing them open with more force than was necessary, I tried and failed to find those stormy eyes.

White irises looked up at me, the worry so stark and raw that I nearly collapsed under the weight of all he did not say. My hands met the mattress, and I quickly shut my eyes. I could not let the panic win. No one said she was hurt. Our future was written. If I followed that path, it would be okay. *She* would be okay.

"Farai's eardrums burst from the wavelengths of the screaming crowd at the Temple of the Gods. It caused a pulmonary embolism." Ranbir's calm voice sounded from behind me, not so much as fazed by the fact that the Shifter almost died. Or it sounded like he almost did. I was not quite sure what he was talking about.

"Asher?" I asked as I faced Henry, not sparing another glance at Farai. Henry's face looked like an odd mixture of nerves and relief, as if he was unsure which to feel. I narrowed my eyes, despite knowing that there was likely nothing I could do to make my best friend—*my brother* in a way—fear me. When he cleared his throat, I relaxed slightly.

"She stayed behind with Trint to speak to the people of Gandry. She was in pain but overall okay enough to continue." My shoulders slouched, relief fizzling out the terror like water thrown on a fire. Still, I would need to go to her as soon as possible, just to make sure she was okay. Asher could take care of herself, but that did not mean I wanted her to have to. She had been alone in that for far too long. "You know, I had thought you were insinuating Asher was not fae when you accidentally let it slip that she possessed magic."

Memories of Pino repeatedly reiterating the importance of these truths being revealed in a particular order flashed through my mind. This conversation was too risky, even admitting to Henry what I had those months ago was pushing the boundaries. I went to shake my head, to tell him to drop it, but he continued on.

"The noise of the crowd hurt her. I saw the pain in her eyes and watched as she was forced to cover her ears. It was nearly as bad as Farai. Which makes me wonder if she is more like you than I thought before. Her magic, was it infused? Is she like the navalom? I watched her steal the memories from Lara, the way she seemed to rip them out with ferocious accuracy." Henry's gaze was distant, as if he were living within his head as he spoke his thoughts aloud.

Asher and Adbeel first, then I can tell him. Then I can tell all of them. These secrets were not forever. I just had to remember that.

"I think it is different." My casual tone was enough to bring his eyes back into focus, shooting me a glare that was likely twin to my own from moments ago.

"I think you know more than you are leading us to believe. In fact, I think those secrets of yours span much farther than just where Ash's magic came from. So, what was it that Pino said would happen if you told us the truth?" Henry questioned, crossing his arms and tilting his head. Behind me, Farai sat up in his bed, clearly eager to listen in. As heinous as I was for it, I wished the bastard still could not hear.

"There are only so many futures in which Eoforhild survives." Ranbir snorted from beside Farai, quickly covering it up with a cough.

The sound startled me. He had shown so little vibrance since losing Winona, and I was baffled to hear it come out now when we were talking about something so serious. It made me smirk despite how horribly the conversation was going.

"I just do not see why Pino told you anything at all when he knew it would be dangerous. Why not just say you needed to get Asher? You would have been more than willing to steal her away. There was a time when you were set on convincing Adbeel to allow us to eliminate her."

I flinched at Henry's casual tone when talking about the fact I had once wanted Ash dead. I hated myself for it. What if I had succeeded? Suddenly, I felt sick. I needed to go get her, immediately.

"I think it was important for us to love one another. I can feel it in my soul, a tug towards her. I was meant for her, and she was meant for me." Henry scoffed, rolling his eyes. I forced a smile, knowing I could never explain it. "Either way, Pino is…gone. I cannot ask him to elaborate. I can only go on and hope I am doing what is best."

"I miss him too," Henry lamented.

Ranbir abruptly stood, walking out without a word. How did you help someone who had lost everything?

Asher would feel that way one day, likely sooner rather than later. Maybe Henry was right. It probably would have been better if Pino had not told me so much. Maybe Asher would have been better off not loving me at all.

"Yeah, I miss the sound of his creepy voice," I concurred. Henry laughed softly, as if he too could hear the horrifying way Pino spoke when prophesying.

"I do not think you are supposed to call the dead creepy." Farai's voice from behind us was sobering, forcing me to straighten.

"I have to get Asher." I tried to walk away, needing to secure a map in order to make it to the temple, but Henry's arms reached out, stopping me.

"I think she will succeed. She always seems to. Now, you need to succeed too. Stay here, go back to that meeting, and figure out a way to kill that traitor. I will get Asher. Just trust me." The way he said it, the words almost came out as begging. As if he was determined to prove to me that he was on my side. I wished I could say that I knew he was, that I was proud to call him my friend. That I knew he would take care of Asher when I was gone.

But there was no time.

"I do," I whispered. Then I portaled, praying to Stella that I had a good enough memory to get me to the right place.

When I arrived outside of the temple, I nearly fell to my knees in relief. Gods, I was not sure I would make it. Walking forward, I heard the distant sound of the crowd, so loud that they could be heard even from here. This was going to hurt.

Portaling once more, I let the shadows of the moon suck me in, my feet suddenly on dirt instead of stone. Quickly, I shoved out a bubble of air, letting it create a barrier around me. I was on the edge of a sort of coliseum. Ahead, Trint, who stood alone in the center, looked around in horror.

My eyes searched for Asher, going so far as to check the front of the crowd. The panic seeped back in when I was unable to spot her. Henry should not have left her. Where was she? What happened here?

Before I consciously decided to do so, my feet were carrying me to Trint, my appearance so abrupt that I scared him. He jumped back, his hand flying to his heart. With a wave of my hand, the pocket of air grew, wrapping around him as well. The king blanched, looking around in confusion. He might not be able to see the way the air bent and thickened, but he could feel the pressure change and hear the now-muffled crowd.

"Who are you?" As soon as he asked the question, he seemed to register the murder in my eyes. If he had hurt Asher, he would learn who I was through experience. I was not above murdering a king in front of his people.

"Where is the princess? Where is Asher?" I growled out the words, barely stopping myself from yelling.

He shifted on his feet, eyes wide. "She disappeared after she convinced my people to fight for her cause. It was like nothing I have ever seen before. There was a burst of sparkling clouds around her, like a shimmering smoke. I could tell it was not her doing it because she screamed out in what sounded an awful lot like terror."

"How long?" My question was lower, almost a whisper. I knew what the answer would be.

"A minute or two. Just before you arrived." Yes, just before I arrived. Because I had wasted time talking, acting as if I had so much of it left. I was not there for her when she needed me, and now Asher was gone.

My hand gripped my chest, the painful race of my heart making my head swim. I tried to portal, feeling the discomfort of it when I normally did not. Water suddenly surrounded me, the dark abyss pulling me downwards. I let out a panicked shout at the way the icy depths seemed to consume me, stealing my vision and my hearing. Again I portaled, this time landing in a heap on the model of Alemthian in the war room.

Screams rang out, everyone present jumping back from my soaked body. Adbeel's voice came from my side, etched with worry and confusion. Shivers wracked my body, but all I could do was listen to those screams. The broken sound of them so odd.

When a hand clamped over my mouth, I realized that it was me shrieking in agony. I silenced myself, but my mind raced with thoughts of all the horrors Asher could be facing.

Adbeel grabbed me by my shoulders, using his brute strength to force me into a sitting position as he looked me over. I stared at him—through him—wondering if my death was contingent on Asher surviving. Would I live if she did not?

No world where she did not breathe was worth living in anyways.

"What happened, Bell?" Adbeel's question came out as a desperate shout while he shook me.

"Asher," I whispered, my voice meek and shattered. "Asher is gone."

ACT IV
~ TO LOSE ~

CHAPTER THIRTY-THREE

ASHER

"Leave me alone, Padon," I warned, my voice dangerously close to the deep and demanding tone of The Manipulator. His chuckle sounded behind me, an infuriating noise that left me picturing what his body would look like without a head. A wicked smile lifted my lips, the thought momentarily raising my mood along with it as I stormed through this absurd castle. My inattention nearly caused me to trip over the quilt still wrapped around my body. "Why would you make your castle gray? It looks like a storm cloud in here. Are you that determined to be utterly dull?"

Despite my cruel tone and refusal to look at him, Padon responded with an uncomfortably joyous tone. "I changed it when I first saw the color of your eyes. I dreamt of you before we met that first night on the cliff, but it was then that I got to work on the changes. You were so vulnerable to my magic, yet so remarkably strong. I couldn't help but dedicate my home to you. It was only recently finished, actually."

"Only recently? It took months to paint?" The creature had magic and probably thousands of servants. According to him, he was an emperor. How could he possibly allow it to take so long?

Not that I cared.

"Months?" he asked, the word sounding as if it were asked from between smiling lips. I hated him. No, I loathed him.

"Could you be any more cliché?" My sardonic reply was more rhetorical than genuine, and I hoped he heard it for the insult it was. Instead of leaving me alone like I asked, he continued to follow just behind me, the sound of my stomping feet drowning out his quick steps as I tugged the quilt off the ground. I found a set of stairs and quickly began descending them, trying and failing to find an exit at the bottom.

"Yes, I think I could. Would you like me to be?" I could think of many things I wanted him to be. Like dead.

"I would like you to send me home," I responded instead, voice not nearly as level as it needed to be.

"This could be your home. What's mine is yours."

I could ignore him. His arrogance was not a rock, but a feather. It could not disturb my pond.

"How do I get out of this damn castle?" Stay calm. Stay collected. Do not say words like "damn." Do not let him win.

"Through a door I imagine."

That was it.

On instinct, I reached beneath the quilt for my dagger, which had apparently not been confiscated while I slept, as it still rested in my sheath. I grabbed it, spinning around and embedding it into his chest.

Blue blood splattered my face, his scream echoing across the hall. The glass chandelier above twinkled and clinked as it shook from the force of his fury.

His knees hit the floor, and I was momentarily forced to fight back a smile as I realized that I had taken him down twice already. Then more appropriate thoughts filled my mind, like how I was going to save the wretched emperor's life when I had likely just stabbed his shriveled black heart.

I wrapped my fingers more tightly around the quilt as I bent down, trying to assess the damage, but Padon shoved my free hand away. I growled, smacking him in the head. "Let me look so I can help you, idiot!"

"You just stabbed me in the heart, but I'm the idiot?" He chuckled, clearly in shock. Could one die laughing? If so, he just might. Explaining that to his guards would be so fun.

Please, do not hang me. I promise, he liked it. He literally died laughing.

Oh yes, that sounded like a great plan. Then maybe I would fly away into the sunset. The two things were just as likely at this point.

"You were being annoying." His laugh grew louder at my defensive tone, his head moving so we were eye to eye. Up close, I could see that his irises were the color of an aubergine, dark enough to appear black.

"Well, sadly for you," he said with a smile, "I'll live."

Then he ripped my dagger out of his chest, that blue blood pouring down his front. The once-red top was now a deep shade of purple, quickly taking on the same hue as his hair. I started to contradict him, to explain that death was not evaded by simply willing it away, but he grabbed my hand and tugged me the opposite direction. He did not stumble, did not wince, as if he were not hurt at all.

While we walked, Padon inspected my dagger. Laughing, he looked at me over his shoulder, waving the blade. "Do you know what this says?"

"No, how would I?" I asked, ripping my hand free and crossing my arms over my chest to prevent the quilt from falling, my gaze on the wall as we walked. This male was insufferable.

"I didn't think so. It's an old language, one spoken by beings with extraordinary magic. They can alter time and encourage bravery and even feed on sin."

"You can read it?" I could not hide my surprise, looking up at him as I rushed to his side. His smile widened, mischief pouring into the air. So that was how he wanted to play? Lower his stupid unbreakable mental shields so he could tease me with his thoughts? Insufferable was too kind a term for him.

"Of course I can. Do you want to know what it says?"

I wanted to say no, because why give him the satisfaction of admitting that he had something I wanted? Knowledge was power, and Padon had far too much of it. Shaking my head, I faced forward once more, my arms still crossed.

After about five seconds of remaining strong, my curiosity won out.

"If you insist on showing off, then go ahead—tell me what it says." There was a bite to my words, but even I could not deny that I was very clearly interested. That I was eager to consume any information he could give me. I hated myself for it, almost as much as I hated him for throwing his stupid head back and laughing.

"It says, 'I am vengeance.'"

I am vengeance. Interesting.

"Is there a reason the runes glow when I kill with it?" If I was already playing, I might as well win. Padon's eyebrows rose, his hand softly meeting my lower back to guide me around a corner. I flinched away from him, and he let out a long-suffering sigh. As if he were the one who should be exasperated right now.

"Don't you feel the magic imbued within it?" His question was accusatory, as if I were somehow at fault for not knowing such a thing. I snatched the dagger by the hilt, slicing his palm as I did. Served him right.

How would I know anything about the runes or the dagger when I still had no idea what my own magic was? I was going to ask that, but we arrived at wherever it was Padon had been leading me. The large archway was the same gray as everything else, bordering on silver. Through it was a bunch of seats, each covered in gray velvet. Beyond, a stage loomed, gray curtains closed to block off the stunning marble floors and whatever lay beyond.

A theater?

Padon gestured to the path between the seats, which ended at the stage. I quirked a brow. If he was hoping I would sing for him, then I would gladly laugh as his stupid ears bled blue. That delicious thought propelled me forward, my feet long since frozen from the icy floors and causing my steps to be jerky. I pulled the quilt around me tighter, wishing I had anything else to wear.

We made it to the silvery stage, where Padon promptly lifted me by my hips and placed me atop it. I whipped around, ready to yell at him, and instead caught sight of him deftly jumping onto the platform as if it were mere inches instead of feet.

Show-off.

"Now, I think you could use something to wear for this." His gaze raked over me, likely imagining what hideous and provocative piece of clothing he could put on me. The worst part was that he knew I was desperate enough to wear whatever he offered. "I think I have just the thing."

With a snap of his fingers, my clothing began to wither and tear before suddenly becoming something new. The gray quilt became silver satin, forming a long and billowing dress, the purple beads turning into thin straps that sat on top of my shoulders and then layered down to my mid-bicep. There had to be at least ten of them on either arm. Warmth

OF REALMS AND CHAOS

stole my thoughts, wrapping around my feet and dragging a sigh from my throat. I looked down, seeing that he had given me soft violet slippers.

Surprisingly, the dress covered everything that might be considered private, not even showing my cleavage. His final touch renewed my annoyance though, the way his fingers lingered on my neck as he placed his black cloak around me turning my vision red. My sheath still remained, and I quickly stored my dagger before he got any ideas about confiscating it.

"Perfect, as always. Now, I'm willing to offer you a deal." He gestured to the heavy velvet curtain, parting the gray fabric to reveal a charcoal-colored pianoforte with a matching bench beneath. The keys were black and silver instead of white, the exposed strings the same color. Even the pedals sparkled silver. "Play for me. Then I'll send you both back."

Narrowing my eyes, I leveled a look of suspicion at him. A few seconds passed, and then I fully registered what he said. "Wrath, is he here too? What did you do with him? Where is he? Give him back!"

Every shouted word reverberated off the vaulted ceiling above, creating a cacophony of panic. He said both, but why was Wrath not here then? Was he holding him captive? I could not let another creature be hurt because of me. Every fucking day since Haven was a calculated compilation of moves crafted to prevent more of those I loved dying because of me.

Padon raised both hands, surrendering before the fight even began. Still, I prepared for a battle, ready to kill anyone who stood in my way of finding Wrath. He was going to insult me for at least three days once he found out I forgot about him.

"Your pet is fine. I'm surprised you didn't automatically assume he was running this place. He quite literally started ordering around my servants and insulting anyone who told him no. He's very creative." His hands remained raised as he spoke, a warm—and fine, dashing—smile lifting his lips.

I shook my head, my hair—which was far less straight and silky than it had been at the Temple of the Gods—swishing back and forth. Taking his word for it was not an option. I would need to see how badly depleted my magic was. Had they healed me fully?

I felt fine. Better than fine, really. For the first time since waking up, I acknowledged just how good I truly felt. My head was clearer than ever before, my magic a steady hum inside my chest. My limbs did not ache or crack, and my ears heard perfectly. I was more than simply healthy. This was something other, something done to me.

"I love seeing your mind work. I wonder, does whatever escape you're plotting in there take into account that I won't be leaving your side?" Padon questioned, a mocking edge to his tone. He walked forward, quickly closing the space between us. I backed up, desperate to maintain my distance. When my back hit the pianoforte, I knew I was doomed. "Play for me, Asher. That's all I ask. Let me hear you just this once."

Our chests met, and his head tilted down, a smirk masking the vulnerability that so clearly hid below. His thoughts radiated off of him like heat waves, pulsing as they met my magic. Thoughts of me playing as he and a youngling that looked nauseatingly similar to me watched on. Padon had an entire future in his mind—one he had dreamed up and was trying to force into reality.

If I did this, was I encouraging those fantasies? Was I allowing him to manipulate me?

But if I refused, would that be even more ridiculous? It would mean risking Wrath, maybe even risking myself, for what was most likely only my pride.

So, with enough rage to burn down the entire planet, I sat down. It had been some time since I played, not really having a moment to do so. But now, it seemed I had nothing but time, unless I pleased the psychotic emperor to my left. The very emperor who was now shoving me to the side to make room for him on the bench. I groaned, trying to channel my anger into the keys.

Mia had taught me that. She said that music was my chance to free everything I was not allowed to feel. Though she often scolded me for my temper, she also seemed to secretly enjoy it at times. In fact, I could recall occasions when we sat side by side on the piano bench in her chambers as I played, just like Padon and I were now. The queen would hum along to whatever ballad I crafted that day, praising me endlessly for my talent when I finished. We would sneak treats into her bed and talk about what I learned in Academy. Then, as I got older, conversations turned into talks of the council and what I thought could be changed. Sometimes, we just held each other and said nothing.

Now, all I could think was that none of it had been true. That she had never loved me at all.

The first note I played was too loud, causing Padon to flinch before he could hide it. I did not care, did not think beyond the silver and black keys in front of me. My fingers took on a life of their own, pouring out all the sorrow I would not let myself feel.

Every memory of Mia's arms around me was another note. Xavier kissing my forehead became a press of my foot on the pedals. Winona brushing my hair was a slide of my hand. The sound of Pino's laughter seemed to replace the quick-paced cluster, my fingers aching at the increased speed as the melody darkened.

I was music. I was sorrow. I was death.

Perhaps I was vengeance too.

My heart raced along with the music, tears I refused to let fall blurring my vision. When I pressed down one final time, the last note echoing off the walls, I closed my eyes and said goodbye to the pain.

"Beautiful," Padon whispered, his head resting in his hand as he leaned against the piano frame.

I growled, sniffling once before standing. Padon followed me, failing to get his arms around me before I jumped off the stage. He scrambled to catch up, my legs carrying me far faster than they normally did. Reminding me that there was something off about my body, my mind, my magic.

"Where are you going?"

"First to Wrath, then home. You promised, remember?" My eyes remained forward, not bothering to check that he was still at my back. Not even his silent feet could hide the way the hair on my arms stood on end when he was near. Though he, like Bellamy, was uncannily good at making his mind disappear.

"I said I would send you home, but I didn't say when."

I froze, stopping just before the archway. Turning slowly, I narrowed my eyes, fists clenching at my sides to avoid swinging at him. His face was calm, not betraying any of his true emotions beneath the façade.

"Liar," I hissed, wishing I could scream instead.

"No, I'll follow through with my promise. I always keep my word. Do remember that fact, Asher." It was rare that he said my name, and hearing it now was unsettling. With a deep sigh, he continued. "If you still wish to go home at the week's end, then I'll return you there, along with your bossy feline friend."

He said 'if' as though he expected I would not want to go. That alone told me just how foolish and mad he truly was.

"Take me to Wrath," was all I said, unable to express just how furious I was. If he wanted to spend a week with me, then that was a mistake on his part, which I would gladly make him regret.

Without a word, Padon walked ahead of me, forging a path to a wide door with silver swirls etched onto it. He slid it open, the door somehow disappearing within the wall. Inside was a sight to behold.

If the library in The Royal City was large, then Padon's was colossal. A set of winding glass stairs sat at the very center of the room, branching off to the many floors above. Books lined most of the walls, even more tomes residing on glass shelves that were placed intermittently to form small walkways. Gray curtains had been pulled back from the large window on the right wall, showing a sky so blue it almost looked green. The color reflected off of the room of glass, casting rainbows across the floor.

"What are we doing here?" I asked, trying and failing to tamper my awe at the sight. Padon's answering chuckle told me that I was doing a poor job of concealing that excitement. Facing him, I glared, reminding him that—no matter what beauty lay within these walls—I would still loathe him by the end of the week.

"Well, well, if it is not my Strange One. You should be embarrassed by your tardiness, but I imagine you are not."

My head whipped towards the horrifying sound of Wrath's voice, a smile tugging at my lips. The dalistori popped his head out from one of the long aisles, sporting his normal size. Nothing could have stopped me from running to him then, not even the small hiss he let out when he realized my plan. I scooped his large body into my arms, burying my head in his silky fur. He slowly shrank, turning himself into the size of a domesticated cat, and then he rubbed his small head against mine.

"Do not scare me like that again, Asher. You are mine, and I am yours. We are…" He hesitated, as if the words that were about to come out of his mouth would burn. "We are family."

"I love you too, Wrathy." I stood like that, holding him far tighter than I should and listening to his soft purr as I pet behind his ears, until Padon cleared his throat. Groaning, I turned around to see him leaning against the doorframe, a smile on his ridiculous face.

"I'll let you two have some time together. The kitty knows where your bedroom is whenever you're ready to get settled. If you need me, my door is right next to yours." With a wink and a wave, Padon left, sliding the door closed behind him.

"There is something odd about that male," Wrath murmured, his head tilted to the side. It reminded me of Bellamy, and suddenly, my mind was at work once more. We needed to find a way out of here. Eternity knows Padon would likely not send us home any time soon, no matter what he promised.

"Wrath, as much as I love cuddling you, we need to figure out a way home." The dalistori scoffed, swatting my face before jumping out of my arms. It would never get old riling up the creature, nor would it ever not amaze me to watch him grow triple his size midair, landing on paws far larger than they were mere seconds ago.

"If you tell the orange demon what I said, I will deny it." Of course he would.

Chuckling, I walked towards the closest set of shelves. How long had it been since I read? I used to pick up a book every day. Now, the mere act of running my fingers across the spines felt foreign. Was it possible to both lose and find yourself at the same time?

"What are you looking for?" Wrath asked, his head nudging my hip. In front of us, a book wrapped in black leather caught my eye. *The Story of Stella* was written on the spine in sparkling white foil. The smell of old paper and ink filled the air as I pulled the particularly large tome off the shelf.

"Research."

Neither of us spoke as I sat down, patting the floor to my right. Wrath curled up beside me, and then, with the hope that Stella was somewhere out there and rooting for me, I opened the book. It naturally opened up to a page that was—yuck—dog-eared. What sociopath would do such a thing?

Padon, probably. The fiend.

At the top of the page, in stunning script, read *The Birth of a Blessing.*

Settling further in, I began to read.

On the night when the sun was distant, hidden behind the four moons, an heir was born. Stella beheld her youngest daughter, a striking mixture of herself and the one she was soul-bonded to—the great love of her existence. Her eldest daughter, named after the sun itself, sat on her other side, their family now complete.

Behind them, standing in the corner, was a male with unfathomable magic. His veins were filled with Death and Creation, a blessing and a curse. The doler of life and loss locked eyes with Stella, and she nodded, smiling over at him. With bated breath, he made his way to the happy family, steps unsure. When he was close enough to see the baby, he gasped, watching as her body lit up, her magic brighter than any he had ever seen.

"We will name her Asta, for she is of divine strength. Asta, for she is crafted of the stars themselves. Asta, for she is love, and love shall conquer."

I smiled at the story, which had been written quite intimately for historical text. That was when I noticed another page that had been horrifically bent, and I skipped to it. This page had no title, beginning in the middle of a section.

On the seventh day of the seventh month, Asta traveled to the new and interesting world her mother had found. Tanabata had been her father's favorite holiday, just as it had been her sister's. They were gone now, and Asta would never hear their laughs or feel their embrace again. It was something she could not voice, the type of pain that left her questioning the future that had been awarded her. The destiny she was told was hers.

Asta roamed the lands of the self-proclaimed demons, their magic a mere fraction of her mother's.

A king sat inside his castle, oblivious to the magic that coursed through the beautiful creature's veins. All he could see was her startling exquisiteness. Her hair— pale as the moon—cascaded down her back in rings, flaring out and sparkling in the light of nearby Sun magic.

I thought back to Bellamy's painting of Asta, her hair dark rather than light. It seemed like such an odd discrepancy. With a shrug of my shoulders, I read on.

It is said that when Asta's eyes met Zohar's, their souls bonded, a great merging that stole their autonomy. For they were not two but one. The mortals of

Eoforhild would name the seventh day of the seventh month Star Festival, for it was the day when their queen came to them—a star from the heavens.

If Zohar had known his life would be ripped from him, would he still have gone to Asta? And if Asta had known she would be meeting the love of her life only to have him stolen from her later, would she still have come to Alemthian?

On my lap, Wrath nuzzled his head into my hand, eager for pets.

"What were you doing in here anyway?" My hand absently scratched under his chin as I looked down at him, his long tail swishing back and forth.

"Waiting for you, obviously."

CHAPTER THIRTY-FOUR

ASHER

The first five days consisted mostly of reading. I found myself skipping through books, desperately seeking any information. Nearly all the books had a sort of personal tone to them, as if they were written by those who experienced the events. It made everything sound skewed and unreliable, which proved true when I found two books that told the same story differently.

Only once did I explore, the temptation of the single door across from the library proving too much. I had made the decision to take a small peek while Wrath napped in our chambers, and I slid the door into the wall with the hopes of remaining unseen. When I had entered the room, I was graced with what almost appeared to be an office. There was glass everywhere, just as there seemed to be throughout the palace from what I had seen. A glass desk sat in front of a wall with glass shelving—books and rocks and glass symbols of the sky littering them.

The teal sun was setting, casting its bright rays upon the room and lighting it up with a haunting glow. To the left sat four enormous pillow-like spheres, the thick cushions set in a make-shift circle atop a white and black rug that depicted the night sky on one half and the light of day on the other. One was silver, one purple, one white, and one pink. A glass mug sat in front of each, clean by the looks of them. I walked over, not taking in the rest of the room as I honed in on the purple one. When I reached it, I bent my knees and brushed my fingers across what had to be velvet. Adding a bit more pressure, I found myself dipping forward.

My hand had sunk into the odd cushion, the inside beneath the velvet almost feeling like beads. Standing up, I straightened my long-sleeve cream dress before finally looking up to take in the rest of the room. There on the far wall, above a tall panel of glass that seemed to be protecting a pile of logs prepped for a fire, were four paintings. They were stunning, the portraits so life-like it almost felt as if the beings were watching me.

On the left was a male, his ebony skin standing out in stark contrast to his short gilded curls and vibrant golden eyes. He smiled brightly, a sort of wonder in his gaze that made him seem ever curious. His square jaw and high cheekbones were sharp in the way his slanted shoulders and full lips were not. He wore clothes the color of his hair, the shade of the sleek silk making my teeth grind.

To the right of that portrait was a female. Her skin was just slightly darker than mine, an earthy brown that appeared youthful despite the hardness in her siren eyes that made her look weathered. I gasped, noting that one of her irises was black while the other was white, matching the way her hair split in color down the middle with sleek black strands on the left and equally silky white locks on the right. Her face was nearly round, though the fullness of it could not stop her delicate chin from coming out to a point. She was imposing, her regal dress showing her shoulders and splitting down the center in color as well.

Next was a beautiful female with mischief in her slightly squinted bright green eyes, like perhaps she had been mid-laugh when the artist captured that stare. She had blonde hair as straight as the previous female's, though her skin was ivory in all but her rosy cheeks. Her smile flashed brilliantly white teeth framed by petal-pink lips. She wore a dress that seemed to be a more modest version of the other female's, the black on the left looking as if it had sucked the color from the white on the right at the spot where the fabric wrapped around her neck and met.

Last was a female with skin nearly identical to the first female's, her cheeks stained pink as she beamed with joy. Her boisterous curls were too full to be captured, the silver coils disappearing into the glass frame on the sides. Her heart-shaped face and full lips made way for her hypnotic silver eyes, which matched the dress that came to pointed edges on her shoulders and dipped low between her breasts. She was beautiful, and she smiled like someone who never knew sorrow.

And though I had no proof, no reason to believe such a thing, my heart lurched at the idea that this female was the exact one who would one day sire the Ayad family line.

I left the room and never looked back.

On the sixth day, I still had not discovered any information that would help me. Wrath was quite pessimistic, though he was also eating something called caviar and lounging by fires daily, so it was safe to say that the little vermin was enjoying himself. If I were being honest, I would likely have explored other rooms and taken the time to relax if I was not absolutely positive that Bellamy was surely threatening to burn the world to the ground in my absence. The male was predictable that way.

I woke up in a particularly foul mood that morning. At least, that was what Wrath said when I swatted his paw away. Sitting up in my overly extravagant four-poster bed, I threw open the gray netted curtains with unnecessary force. My night clothes so far consisted of long-sleeved tops that buttoned up the center and trousers to match. They were soft and annoyingly comfortable.

Placing my feet into the fur-lined slippers beside my bed, I quickly padded across the lush gray rug, stopping in front of a thin door. With a soft tug, the door slid open, disappearing into the wall just as most of the doors did here. Inside, a far-too-large room was filled to the brim with clothing. All *conveniently* in my size.

The first dress that caught my eye today was one in a baby pink. The layers upon layers of gauzy fabric were cinched close to the torso but had been left loose for the skirts, allowing them to flare out. The straps were thin where they connected to the bodice and gradually grew thicker as they reached the shoulder, forming a sort of upside-down triangle. But the most extraordinary part of the dress were the pink rosebuds that had been sewn onto it. It reminded me of Mia.

With a sigh, I freed it from the hanger.

As I was getting dressed to go spend yet another day drowning in books with no rhyme or reason to their shelving, I realized that the clasp for the dress was strange. It was a sort of metal that had to be pulled upwards rather than fastened together, the metal teeth on either side joining as it slid. Knowing Wrath was without opposable thumbs meant I would be forced to find help or do it myself.

During my time walking between the library and my rooms, I had yet to see another creature roaming the halls. I was convinced that Padon had made sure of that, despite explicitly saying that Wrath had been ordering around servants. When I asked the dalistori about it, he merely shrugged and said that he had not seen the servants again either. Only Padon was ever around, bringing us food and bothering me endlessly.

I would not ask him to close my dress. I just would not. So, instead, I got creative.

Reaching up, I pulled down the wire hanger that had once held the dress. Then I began bending and unwinding it, creating a sort of hook. After securing the curved end to the metal piece on my dress, I grabbed onto the opposite end and tugged upwards.

As usual, I made a mess of the situation.

The closure flew upwards, stilling the wire. Unfortunately, it was slippery, so the momentum of my hands forced them to keep moving even without the wire within my grasp. My arms swung, sending my upper half careening forward. I smacked into the shelf that I had been storing my dagger and sheath upon, hitting my elbow against the weapon. Both the sheathed dagger and I fell to the ground with a loud thud, shaking shoes loose from the other shelves. A heel landed on my cheek, stabbing into me with bruising force.

For a second, I laid there—stunned and embarrassed—but then Wrath's laughter sounded from behind me. "You have outdone yourself, Strange One. I understand why so many males are fighting for your affections. You are clearly quite the prize."

I reached back, smacking the dalistori. He did not care enough to dodge me, just continued laughing hysterically—maniacally.

Huffing, I sat up, my hand going to my wounded cheek. That would be fun to explain to the nosey emperor. Only a few shoes had lost purchase, so it took no time at all to clean them up. The last thing that remained on the ground after I straightened the final pair of shoes were my sheath and dagger, the two separated by the fall. Carelessly, I snatched the leather up first, watching in bewilderment as something fell out of it.

Not just something.

My heart galloped in my chest, the pounding beat faster than Frost racing through the Forest of Tragedies. When my fingers grazed the folded piece of paper, I nearly sobbed in relief. It was the last note I had received from Bellamy.

I opened it, laughing at the ridiculous words.

Today the sun does not shine, and I wonder if that is because you are not here. It seems you have stolen more than my heart, Princess. Please come home, I do not think I can take many more days of gloom.

Stupid, sappy demon.

Dashing out of the closet, I ran to the entirely glass vanity, slumping down into the chair. Hands shaking, I grabbed the quill out of the pot of ink, trying my best not to let it drip on the paper. It felt oddly nice using a quill again. I had mostly used them back in The Capital, only switching to pencils regularly because of Bellamy. Still, my nerves would not allow me to relish in that comfort as I wrote on the paper.

I am okay. Please do not slaughter innocents or freeze over entire villages. Trust that I will come back to you as soon as I can.
I love you.

It was all I could think to say that would not send him into a panic or have him trying to portal himself to other worlds like a lunatic. Yet I also could not help the smile that lifted my lips at the thought of him appearing in these rooms. There was so much we still needed to talk about, secrets we both kept. But he was worth every struggle and stumble.

Folding up the paper, I briefly brought it to my lips, placing a gentle kiss to it. "Please work."

Three deep breaths later, I tossed the paper into the air, watching as it fell. In my head, I chanted the same two words.

Please work. Please work. Please work. Please work.

When the paper hit the ground and remained there, a single tear crawled down my cheek, falling victim to gravity just as the note had.

And then came the rage. Head falling back, I let out a piercing scream, furious to the point that I could do nothing but let it free. The room—no, the castle itself—shook, all the many pieces of glass around me twinkling or falling to the ground. A chorus of breaking glass sounded, and then the windows shattered, raining down upon me.

Something hard smashed into me, sending me flying onto the ground. Whatever it was nearly knocked the breath from my lungs, so heavy it felt as if I might suffocate from the pressure of it.

"Dammit, Asher. You can't do things like that." So casual was the tone that, even if I did not know his voice, I would bet my life that Padon was the one on top of me. He was as aggravating as ever, but in this instance, he was unfortunately right.

Why had I done something so foolish? How had I done that?

A clicking noise sounded, mixing with the crunch of glass as someone else entered the room.

"Padon! I'm so sorry. I don't know what came over me. It was like my mind suddenly decided I was angry and—" The melodic voice abruptly cut off, a loud gasp following her apology as she probably took in the disaster.

"Don't be sorry. I felt it too. This mess isn't yours alone. You should see my office." With a wry chuckle, he looked up, facing the female. I got a brief glimpse of bright orange hair before he readjusted to cover me again. "Plus, it wasn't really our fault. Asher had a bit of an episode, and it seems that her magic took on a life of its own. It wasn't your anger at all that you felt, Kar. Can you check on everyone else within the palace? I imagine there's a lot of cleanup to do."

The female did not respond, but I still heard her heeled steps retreating and my door shutting as she left. When Padon rotated on top of me, our faces far too close for comfort, he smiled widely, as if he were proud of what I had done.

"Now, that was an interesting way of getting my attention." Prick. I shoved him off, wishing I could unsee the arrogant smirk he flashed me. A booming laugh came from him as I sat up, which I quickly silenced with an elbow to his gut. Then it was Wrath who laughed as he made his way to me from his spot under the bed.

"All I want from you is to watch you fall to a painful death. Preferably after I push you."

Was that too far?

"Asher, are you trying to tell me about a sexual kink that you have?"

Nope, not far enough.

I groaned in annoyance, tiptoeing my way around the glass and to the door that would—hopefully—take me far from him. But he grabbed my wrist, tugging my body into his.

The rise and fall of his chest felt like a battle cry, as if he were preparing for some sort of war I had no knowledge of. Wide violet eyes and pursed lips solidified that thought, and I realized that I had not once been explained what he wanted with me, despite the many times I had asked. His free hand lifted, cold knuckles grazing my flushed skin. A wave of his other hand had the room returning to its former glory. How strange, to go from feeling Bellamy's heat for months to now being forced to endure the presence of a creature that felt like ice. It was disconcerting. When his thumb rubbed against my bottom lip, I tried to lean back, needing more space before he got any ideas. His grip held firm, face going stern as he assessed me.

"Asher. Such a beautiful name. Blessed and happy. Did you know it means that?" There was a harsh and mocking edge to his words, as if a hidden meaning lay beneath them that he thought I was foolish for not understanding. "I can make you happy. I can bless you. It's your destiny, my love. I am your destiny, whether you accept it or not."

With one final pull, I wrenched myself from his grasp, stumbling backwards as I did so. Wrath was there, his fur coarse from his new height. A deep hiss emanated from him, and I smirked as Padon took a hesitant step back. Seeing as he survived a dagger to the heart, I imagined he would live to tell the tale of Wrath's, well, wrath. Still, it brought a bloodthirsty sense of glee to me as he raised his hands in submission.

"Sorry, I didn't mean to scare you, kitty cat."

Wrath shook with pent-up rage, moving around me to block my body from Padon's view. I scratched his side, leaning into his warmth.

"Do not threaten my creature," Wrath said, his eerie voice so deep it rattled my bones. I burrowed deeper into his side, trying to show just how much I appreciated his protection—his love.

"That was hardly a threat." I could hear the smile through his words, tearing another hiss of disapproval from Wrath's throat. "Fine, I won't threaten her again. Asher, will you please allow me to show you something? I think it's time you get out of this palace."

At first, Wrath did not move, opting to stare at Padon silently. I peeked around his body, catching a glimpse of the unsettled look that was on the emperor's face. Laughing with glee, despite Padon's more calculating aura, I patted Wrath's side one last time before walking around him.

"I will be okay, Wrath. If the so-called emperor tries anything funny, I will castrate him and rip out his heart." Wrath smiled at my graphic threat, but did not back down. "Thank you for taking care of me. Now, go take care of yourself. Get a snack or terrorize innocents or something."

With one last scratch under his chin and a quick kiss to his nose that he was not fast enough to dodge, I waved bye and walked to Padon, who was holding a pair of blush pink slippers out to me. I reached up and grabbed them, scoffing at the way he momentarily held them too high for me to reach. After I slipped them on, he motioned towards the door.

When he tried to grab my hand as we entered the hallway, I pulled it away and swatted his arm. Flashing him a look of disapproval, I forced myself not to laugh when the oh-so-mighty emperor feigned offense by putting his palm to his chest and gasping.

We continued forward in companionable silence for all of thirty seconds before he began speaking.

"Did you know that there are worlds where the moons bleed red and creatures sparkle different colors?" His tone was soft, almost contemplative, as if his mind had wandered. Briefly, I wondered if Padon had visited those other worlds. If he were strong enough to bring me here, then it made sense for him to be able to go other places. How enchanting, to see so much of the universe. To learn and bask in something new. A part of me would always believe that life was about the adventure—about seeing extraordinary things and becoming extraordinary because of it.

"Bellamy has told me many stories of other worlds. He told me of one where dragons roam the skies and another where gods walk among mortals. His favorite was the story of a world where magic is imbued into the land itself. Creatures are separated by mere kingdoms rather than seas, and they live in peace with one another. I loved the one about a world that is completely submerged in water, all living things breathing from gills and swimming with fins."

Padon was silent by my side, face stoic as I prattled on, my own mind taking me elsewhere. To better places with warm and strong arms around me.

"More than once, he lulled me to sleep with those stories, his voice the only thing that could bring me peace and soothe me." I sighed, smiling at the memory of him laying with me in my too-small cot when we traveled through Eoforhild. Or even the times when he would come into mine and Noe's room at one of the inns, laying on the floor and holding my hand until I fell asleep. How had I ever denied him? Denied my feelings for him? Padon scoffed, earning a glare from me. "I love him, you know."

"You love the idea of being loved. Don't mix up the two." His arms crossed as he spoke, so much vitriol in the words that I wondered if it were truly me he was speaking to.

"Yet I hate the idea of being loved by you. What does that say about you, Padon?"

He stiffened at my harsh words, his arms falling to his sides as we walked on. Suns and moons and stars were hidden within gray wall sconces and flowing curtains and even parts of the gray runners at our feet. The most covert decorations though, somehow, those designs had caught my eye time and time again over the last week. Demanding my attention.

Neither of us spoke again until we came to a stunning foyer, the gray marble stairs hugging the wall and wrapping around the nearly circular room. Two towering glass windows sat on either side of the large double doors. The glass on the left was painted with an image of the night sky, stars twinkling around the four moons. On the right, the glass was depicting what I assumed was daylight. The sky, far brighter than that in Alemthian, was a deep blue, a teal sun larger than I had ever seen taking up the center of the painting as puffs of clouds surrounded it. The true eye-catcher was the ceiling though. Above us was a painting portraying a nearly black sky with thousands of stars, constellations I could not begin to name connected by thin lines to create the universe itself. It was like seeing everything the ethers had to offer and suddenly realizing how small I was in the grand scheme of it all.

When we made it to the doors, Padon shoved them open, revealing a nearly identical scene. Their sun was teal, a vibrant and almost menacing color that cast the entirety of the sprawling town into an odd sort of glowing darkness. Structures towered beyond, most of them made of glass. Voices could be heard as they traveled to us on the wind, my magic sensing the joy and despair and love and hatred from them all. The very things that I was so used to in my own world.

I turned around, unable to resist looking up at the looming palace.

It was magnificent, made almost entirely of glass with towers reaching towards the teal stained sky as if they might puncture it. Perfectly symmetrical, there was a haunting beauty to it as it reflected the scenery of mountains and clouds and the sprawling city behind us. Despite the stunning architecture, I could practically feel the wickedness pulsing from it, as if great atrocities had been committed within those walls.

With a chill that skirted up my back and made my teeth chatter, I turned back towards the beautiful city beyond, feeling far less unsettled. I noted then that the city was taller than it was wide. An awe-inspiring bit of innovation that I had never seen before.

"Do you like it?" he asked, sounding for all the world like he was gifting me the sight before us. I nodded, my jaw hanging loose and my eyes wide as I took in the beauty of it. "Then I think you'll love this."

Padon grabbed my hand, holding firmly as we were consumed by a cloud of darkness. Whatever this was, it did not feel like portaling. There was no painful tug or pull, no sense that time and space themselves were attempting to rip us apart for defying them. No, this was quick, like taking a step and ending up in a whole new world.

"Where are we?" I asked, my voice barely audible as I stared in awe at the sweeping mountains. Snow coated the peaks, a chill floating in the air. Wind blew our way, smelling of brisk winters and fresh pine and the heat of the morning sun. There was an odd sense of familiarity to that scent, as if I had stood atop a mountain much like this and breathed in with the same relief I felt now.

I had, actually. Throughout our winter trek across Eoforhild, I found solace in few things, but the wondrous sights were always one.

"We are in the Draca Mountains." I faced him, quirking a brow. What an odd name.

Unless—

Just then, the sound of beating wings could be heard in the distance, a roar-like screech following as a shadow was cast over us. I looked up, knowing what I would see but not quite believing it until my eyes locked on the creature.

A dragon loomed above, circling us like prey. The underbelly of it was a stunning lavender, but its wings and what I could see of the rest of its body as it tilted were violet.

My head cocked to the side, eyes roaming from the dragon— which I was not nearly scared enough of—to Padon. The purple of his hair was darker, but the cloud around us had been the very same violet. A violet that matched almost the entirety of the Temple of Gods, which had been dedicated to...

"Padon," I said, caution lacing my words. He looked back down at me, smiling glumly, as if he were expecting me to be terrified. But, when his eyes met mine, his expression changed. His lips parted, gaze widening. "Tell me you are not a god. Tell me you have not been making snide comments about the deities when you are somehow in control of life and death."

Standing there, shivering in my flimsy pink dress, I felt stupid for not seeing it sooner. A nervous laugh was all he answered with before flicking his wrist my way. I looked down, watching as every single rosebud opened, flaring out to fill the dress. Then a cloak—my cloak—met my shoulders, the purple shadow-like magic disappearing in the breeze.

"I prefer Death and *Creation*. And it's not my fault they made me look heinous for that sculpture. Just seeing your projected thoughts made me feel as if I should be working on a better exercise regimen."

The dragon descended as the two of us looked at one another, landing with such force that the mountain itself shook. I moved my gaze, staring with awe at the creature. It was larger than I could have ever imagined, my head likely not even reaching its ankle. All four legs were rippling with strength, purple scales glistening in the teal sunlight. Its leathery wings still softly swayed, as if it were gaining its bearings.

Padon's arm caught my peripheral as he moved to stroke the enormous snout of the creature. It hummed in appreciation, briefly flashing razor sharp teeth that were surprisingly white. Its nostrils flared when I subconsciously stepped back, those black eyes meeting mine. A tail studded with black horns that mirrored spikes swung towards me, stopping just short of my feet.

I felt the curiosity looming beneath terror, my magic beginning to hum. I wanted to try letting it seep into the creature and see what the mind of such a thing felt like, but what if it could sense me? What if it grew angry?

Still, my thoughts raced with how interesting it would be to speak to a dragon. Frost had never spoken back, but dragons, they seemed different. Otherworldly.

Padon seemed to see the war happening in my mind, because he reached out a hand and smiled, beckoning me.

"Allow yourself to thrive, Asher. Take this first step into becoming something *more*."

Though I knew he meant allowing him to make me truly immortal with what I now knew was his life magic, I still closed the distance and placed my hand in his. The moment our skin touched, Padon visibly relaxed, but the emptiness that came with the connection made me think of Bellamy. Of the way my skin lit and sparked when it touched his. And I wondered if Padon had ever felt that, if he truly knew what love was.

Slowly, he brought our fingertips towards the dragon's nose, stilling mere inches away. It sniffed loudly, scenting me. Then it bristled, leaning away not with hatred but with clear indifference.

Was it wrong to be more offended because of that?

"Drisha, you're being rude." His tone was scolding, a father speaking to his youngling. It was startling to hear him be so gentle without any condescension or ulterior meanings. Like seeing him for the first time, the real him.

The dragon—Drisha—huffed irritably, swaying her head back and forth. But after Padon flashed her a look of warning, she sighed and pressed her nose firmly into my still outstretched hand. Her skin was slightly damp, the scales like leather under my fingers. For some reason, that feeling reassured me, pushing me to let my magic free.

Hello, beautiful. My name is Asher. It is so wonderful to meet you.

Drisha froze, her eyes going wide. She stared at me for what felt like an eternity, all three of us so still we might have passed as statues if not for our heavy and slightly panicked breathing. Then Drisha did something that I had not expected but dared to imagine. She spoke back.

Hello, Asher. I'm called Drisha. Why is it that you smell mortal but have enough magic to level an entire galaxy?

I gasped, her voice sending chills down my back. She sounded similar to Wrath, an eerie and demanding voice that made me want to cower. But I did not, instead choosing to stand straighter, to smile despite the fright coursing through me.

I think you are overestimating my ability, Drisha.

Her head tilted to the side, sniffing me again after a moment. Her breath was hot, like the heat of a scalding summer day. It knocked me back into myself, unfreezing my mind and freeing me of the daze that was seeing an actual dragon.

Fine, not an entire galaxy. But a world, for sure.

"If you're both done being rude, then we can leave," Padon drawled, leaning onto the dragon's leg and patting her scales nonchalantly.

"Leave? Like *fly*?" My voice was too uneven, raspy in a way it normally was not. I hated it, showing that I was breakable, fearful, weak. He smirked over at me, his arms crossing as if daring me. I growled, looking back at Drisha and purposefully speaking into her mind so Padon could not hear me.

Drisha, is it okay if I ride on your back? It seems I am being challenged by your friend.

A booming laugh split the air, the dragon's head falling back. I jumped, my magic subconsciously throwing down my shields to prepare for what my body thought would be a fight.

"You're odd, Asher. But yes, you may. Let me help you up, tiny." My jaw slackened, surprised to hear her speak aloud. I should not have been so astonished, seeing as Wrath spoke to me out loud. It was not unfathomable. Yet it seemed even more strange coming from her.

Drisha used her arm-length talons to pinch around my waist, lifting me up and practically tossing me onto her back. The second my body hit hers, I began to slip backwards, sliding down her scaled spine and desperately searching for purchase. Just as my hand gripped onto one of her particularly large violet scales, something firm appeared behind me.

"I don't know why I expected you to be better at this, but color me surprised." Padon's arms wrapped around me just as his voice did, his fingers tickling at my side before I smacked them. To my utter embarrassment, he and Drisha burst into laughter, the shaking of the dragon's body nearly forcing me off the side of her.

Padon's grip tightened, and then we were once more kissed by the whisky-and-leather-scented purple clouds that were portaling, but with the raw magic of a god. Perhaps that was why it merely felt like scooting forward when we went from the base of Drisha's tail to the space between her shoulder blades. My legs cramped as I attempted to adjust, the discomfort of sitting atop her like sitting on level ground that was riddled with slightly sharp rocks.

Why had I thought that dragon riders in the stories were able to sit atop a dragon with their legs hanging off the sides? It would be impossible for anyone if all dragons were this large, and yet I had never thought of the logistics.

Probably because, until today, it had not crossed my mind that I would ever see a dragon.

"Hold on tight and remember to breathe, my love." Padon's own breath warmed my ear as he spoke, but I had no time to scold him before Drisha squatted low and then shot into the air.

My scream was so loud that it hurt even my ears as her wings beat a ferocious pace, ascending so quickly it felt like the air was stolen from my lungs. If I passed out, would Padon catch me? Would he even be able to?

You're being annoying. Stop screaming.

Silencing myself, I tried to glare at her eye, which she had pinned on me, her head turned to flash her teeth. It turns out, a lack of air will make one quite dizzy.

My vision swam, body swaying as Drisha leveled out. I was going to vomit on a dragon, and then she would probably shake me off and burn me alive for my audacity. This would be a disgraceful way to die.

Before I could do so, another screech echoed across the sky, fluffy white clouds hiding the other dragon from our view. Suddenly, a looming black figure cut through them, the dragon's body corkscrewing upwards with wings tucked as it flew. I stared in awe, watching the beast dive and dip—only using its wings when it needed to. When it circled us, opting to casually fly at Drisha's side, I got the uncanny feeling that it was expecting something from me. I looked into its black eyes, trying to decipher what meaning they held as its stare bore into me.

Hello.

The dragon jolted, falling for a split second before it caught its bearings and returned to the spot beside us.

Well, I wasn't expecting that. Hello to you too. Are you our fearless emperor's new pet? You smell like a mortal snack.

Drisha's body shook below us with laughter, and I gasped.

Can you hear him?

Yes, tiny, I can. We all can hear one another. And it seems Likho has become interested in you. So make sure to actually grab on this time.

What do you mea—

And then Drisha twirled in the air, her claws grabbing me out of Padon's grasp and tossing me into a free fall. The emperor's face filled with horror, reaching out to me despite the fact that there was no chance he could catch me.

I screamed on the way down, the dizziness returning in full force. But it was the way I hit the ground—no, the dragon—that really knocked the wind out of me. My chest felt like it was caving in, my scream abruptly cutting off as I tried to fight through the pain and grab onto Likho.

His tail, thankfully free of spikes, braced my back, giving me enough aid to pull myself up and grip onto his scales. With the bruise on my cheek and the slices that now marred my palms, I must have looked like I lost a fight. It also felt like I lost a fight. Then again, I had lived two hundred years and won very few times, so this was just the standard.

You're funny. I like you.

Likho's voice was deeper and more gravely than Drisha's, making my teeth rattle as he spoke into my mind.

If nearly dying is humorous, then you have no idea just how funny I am.

Drisha laughed from above, Likho's chuckles echoing across the skies as we shot forward. I used every bit of strength I possessed to hold on, screaming in terror every time Likho jokingly twirled and dipped, his tail often the only thing keeping me astride. My cloak and hair both billowed in the wind, sometimes wrapping around to smack me in the face and leave me without sight. All the while, Likho made comments about how much fun we were having.

The one and only time I responded was to tell him that he needed to learn to speak for himself.

Padon and Drisha kept a close eye on us, his smile stretching his face into something nearly tolerable. However, I was so dizzy and disoriented that I might have been hallucinating.

When we finally began to descend, my teeth were chattering and my hair was so knotted that it hurt to move my head. While my bruised cheek barely stung anymore, the cuts on my hands were still angry and bleeding from grabbing his scales so hard.

Likho landed without mercy, hitting the ground with a deafening boom and running forward before coming to a full stop. This time, his tail did not save me. I went careening off his side, my body flipping midair and my stomach threatening to spill. Like always, Padon was ready, catching me effortlessly in his arms with a broad smile.

"Wasn't that the most fun and exhilarating thing you've ever done?" he asked, his breath coming in heavy pants and his eyes wide with excitement.

"I think I am going to be sick."

He laughed, carrying me over to a large rock, where he set me down softly. Nudging me to make room for him, he promptly flopped downwards, so ungraceful that I could do nothing but stare.

"What?" he asked, leaning back on his hands, further baffling me.

I shook my head, offering him a rare smile. It was hard not to in these moments, when he was so convincing with his easy laughs and wide grins.

"My first time riding a dragon was when I was only eight years old. Back then, my mother—Morana—was the holder of death and creation. While Stella was empress, the dragons worshiped Morana. She practically lived in the skies. As soon as she felt I was old enough, she brought me here and pushed me into the caves."

A gasp involuntarily left my lips at that. How could a mother send her son into a dragon den so carelessly? Then again, what did I know about mothers?

"She had faith that I would survive. Though if I had died, she probably would have thought I deserved it. We don't feel like you do, Asher. But she loved me in our way, and taking me here was her showing that love. She shared her passion with me, and from that, I found Drisha. When she bonded with me, it was like becoming whole." There was a wistfulness to his voice, showing how much he cherished the memory.

Vulnerability had always seemed so dangerous to me, like giving your enemies a weapon to slay you with. But as Padon gave me this honesty, letting me see a glimpse of the raw pieces of him, I recognized that there was strength in it too.

"That is beautiful, Padon."

"Perhaps Likho will bond with you, and then you can feel it too. You'll get used to riding over time, trust me. Soon, it'll be far more fun than it is scary." His smile was still full, but my own had fallen, the smell of him and the mountains and the air itself suddenly too much. The stark difference between this place and Alemthian was now painful in its blatancy.

"I leave tomorrow. That was what you promised," I whispered the words, as if saying them too loud would ignite that spark of constant fury within me. Padon stiffened, panic oozing from him.

"Please, my love, you don't really want to go back. Not when I can give you everything here. Stay another week, let me really show you what this world has to offer. I can make you happy. Just let me," he begged, reaching out to me.

I pulled away, standing up to put space between us. Behind me, the dragons stirred, truly listening in now.

"Padon, you promised. You have to send me home. I *need* to go home. You promised!" I was losing control. I felt it in the way my magic—which was so much stronger here, more volatile in its desire to command and even destroy—flared inside my chest, simmering like a pot over a fire. But my magic would not put out my anger. It would exacerbate it.

Padon dove for me, his hand wrapping around my wrist and his magic pooling around us. The heat of my rooms was painful after being cold for so long as we portaled into it, the fire sending small pinpricks across my skin—warming me. He gave me no time to acclimate, throwing me onto my bed. One of the mesh curtains got tangled around my leg, the momentum of my body tearing it down. The frame above gave out, clattering to the floor and startling Wrath awake from his spot on the gray sofa near the fireplace.

"I don't *have* to do anything, Asher. You aren't going anywhere because this is your home now. Get used to it or spend the rest of your existence pouting. Either way, you will not leave me." Padon's face was contorted into something wholly evil—the monster I had slowly convinced myself he was not. For the first time, I was genuinely terrified of him.

Wrath grew in size, running over to me and leaping onto the bed, the growl emanating from him a promise of death.

"Silence yourself, dalistori. I made you. I can just as easily unmake you," he said, his voice so sharp it mirrored a hiss.

Wrath jolted, his body shrinking back down to its normal size as he stared at the god he had been worshiping for his entire life. There was a distinct battle raging within him, as if the line between duty and love had been drawn and he feared stepping to either side.

"Do not speak to him that way!" I screamed, throwing a pillow at the god.

He laughed, his head falling back and his hands clapping together in mock amusement. "I think you don't understand, so let me explain this to you."

Padon stalked forward, coming our way. The closer he got, the more flowers on my dress—which had stayed beautiful and full thanks to Padon's magic—withered and died. I grabbed Wrath, hugging him close to my chest as I backed slowly off the bed.

OF REALMS AND CHAOS

"You are mine. Regardless of how long it takes you to see the good we can be together, you will still be mine. No matter where you are, you will still be *mine*." The deep tenor of his voice was full of violence and resolve, a threat in and of itself.

"I will never be yours! Sooner will I throw myself from the mountains than sit here and entertain your psychotic fantasies! I am *mine*!" Unable to contain it any longer, I let my mental gates open wide, my magic pouring from me in deadly waves. I felt the moment it hit Padon's shields, the force still not enough to shatter them though he stumbled back from the weight of it. Even knowing it would not work, I let my voice drop, The Manipulator free at last. *"Send. Me. Home!"*

He chuckled, a dark and malicious sound. "You want to go home so badly? Fine. Then go!"

In a blink, I was gone, my feet crashing onto a cobblestone path with more force than portaling usually consisted of. My knees gave out, Wrath and I both falling to the ground in a heap. I blinked, too exhausted to move even when a heavily accented voice cut through the silence.

"What is it?" someone asked.

"Obviously a woman," another said.

"That is no woman. Did you see how she appeared out of thin air?" The first voice again. It sounded like two men, older perhaps. The accent was familiar, but I could not quite place it.

"She is too close to the castle. Do you think she was planning something?"

Oh, great. They were panicking. I could feel it in their minds and hear it in their voices as they faltered. But at least they were speaking the common tongue.

"We should take her to the king."

"What if he blames us?"

A beat of silence, and then I felt one of my feet being lifted.

"I have an idea, grab her other foot."

With a ridiculously loud grunt, the fools began dragging me.

"Ugh, she is heavy!"

"Excuse me, who do you think you are?" My question startled them enough to drop my feet, both heels hitting the stone with bruising force. I truly could not catch a break.

426

Cracking my eyes open, I caught a brief glimpse of a navy blue uniform before a booted foot came down on my face, slamming my head into the ground. I let out a cry of pain, the piercing sting stealing my vision from me.

Disoriented and bleeding, I could not fight them as they dragged me for what felt like years, my hair snagging on rocks and my dress audibly ripping. At one point, the assholes actually yanked me up a set of stone steps.

When we finally arrived to wherever their king was waiting, they dropped my feet once more, speaking in hushed and nervous tones to someone. A moment later, hot breath hit my face, hair tickling my neck. The voice that spoke was both a relief and a nightmare.

"Hello, Asher," Genevieve said.

CHAPTER THIRTY-FIVE

BELLAMY

Gone. How was she simply *gone*?

Henry was speaking. I could see his lips moving, but I heard nothing other than the voice in my mind telling me that Asher was never coming back.

My heartbeat became a war drum, every breath a battle cry. My hands flexed and stretched, bunching into fists before repeating the cycle. I was dizzy with the fury, the anguish, the terror.

Something happened to her. Someone took her.

My head swam with the many scenarios she could be suffering from, and I knew that if I did not go, I would kill every single person on this damn base.

The wind picked up, a large boom sounding as a fissure in the ground crawled between my legs, spider webbing out. Screams came from the buildings behind me, the residents of Pike unknowingly witnessing their prince and general fall apart.

When I saw red, I portaled, landing at the base of the farthest mountain and letting free a piercing scream as my power burst out of me. My body lit, fire burning through snow and making me sink into the ground. The mountain quaked, the sound of rock exploding above like nothing I had ever heard before. Still, I screamed, lifting my arms and leaning my head back. If there were gods watching, I wanted them to know just how deeply I cursed them.

Rock and snow rained down on me, but I gladly let it, drawing a wind large enough to shove the debris forward, shattering the rest of the mountain. When my scream finally stopped, I was bleeding from the rocks that had made it past the wind and chest deep in snow.

And I was not even close to done.

***

The first week was bad. But the second week? This was torture.

Asher was one for dramatics. We all knew it, and we loved her more for it. But in my heart, I knew this time was different. Somehow, we all did. Whatever occurred in the Temple of the Gods was not Asher being Asher. There was only so much I could do, though, because the siege on Isle Shifter was quickly approaching.

"I have to be there. He will not just listen when you tell him to come. He is not a dog!" Farai was yelling at me, again. Just as he had every day since I told him that we would be securing Jasper. Now, with Asher missing, I thought I might better understand the utter panic that came from not knowing if the love of your life was safe. That did not mean he was not getting on my nerves, of course. Really, he was doing nothing but irritating me lately.

"No, he is just a large cat." My sarcastic drawl and the casual way I leaned against the wall must have been enough to set the Shifter off because then he was screaming, his hands moving with his words. I ignored him, tuning out the sound of everything save for the voice in my head as I went through the plan once more, my eyes falling shut.

First, we would sneak into the border village of the Multiple Lands. That was where Farai and Jasper's cottage was. Quaint, secluded, everything necessary for a quick and smooth rescue. After convincing him to come, I would portal him back to Pike and into Farai's waiting arms.

Second, we would find the control center for their base. Farai had drawn us an incredibly detailed map, but we would still need to navigate the building with no knowledge of guard shifts or routes. Luca had been silent for days, leaving us to not only go in ignorant but also worry about his safety. Once there, if we could fight against every set of odds against us, we would take out all leadership present.

Third, we would release pages upon pages of messages offering refuge. This was the riskiest part and the one thing that the council disagreed with me on. I firmly believed that harming innocents would make us no better than the royals who sent their soldiers to slaughter demons across our realm. But the council, and even some of my captains, wanted a bloodier approach, one that would decimate the fae army.

But all I could think of were the bodies in Haven. The hundreds of funerals we held with no one but my Trusted to bear witness and say goodbye. I thought of Asher's face as she stared out of my window in The Royal City the days following, unmoving and cradling her scarred arms. Of the way she screamed for mercy in her sleep. How she stopped speaking to those around her, losing the spark that I had witnessed flare to life on our journey through Eoforhild.

My mind stilled, hyperfixating on Asher. Her laugh, the way she wrote my name, every time she offered kindness like it was second nature. She was brilliant, strategic, commanding, and hotheaded. Asher was the most beautiful creature to ever grace our world.

And she was gone.

"Hello!" Farai yelled, waving his hands in front of my face.

I glared at him, pushing off the wall. "I understand you. I am simply choosing to ignore you."

Without another word to Farai, I portaled away to the same place I often went. My body hit the icy waters of the Ibidem Sea, the cold locking up my limbs and pulling me under just as my eye caught sight of a ship. Odd. The water here was not suitable for sailing, wild and unforgiving—the depths as dark as the stormy gray of the clouds above.

As I let myself sink, being tossed around by the waves, I thought of how closely the color matched Asher's eyes.

***

Everything was going horribly wrong. Deadly wrong.

Screams could be heard from every direction, but the worst were from those at the end of my blade. For every Shifter that fell, so fell a demon. Bodies were ripped to shreds, mauled beyond recognition. Fur-clad soldiers were hung by beams of light and wisps of shadow.

Death sang with glee, stealing lives so quickly it seemed as though the world was made of blood. I danced to the music, unable to stop the way my blade swung and my smile lifted.

I was everything I never wanted to be. Everything Asher loathed. Asher, who was still gone after three and a half weeks. Asher, who would sooner cut her own throat than do what I was doing.

Senseless death coated the air, and I breathed it in like a male suffocated.

Jasper was gone, their house empty and devoid of any signs of life. In fact, it looked as though the home had been long since deserted. Farai

OF REALMS AND CHAOS

was somewhere in this mess, his cries repeating in my head like a prayer. And perhaps they had been.

We had successfully taken out the ten fae who held high enough leadership positions to be in the command center. Yet when we had finished, Henry and I walked out into a bloodbath. The demons had, against my orders, begun seeking retribution. And when we had tried to stop them, a Shifter had come at us, tackling Henry to the ground and nearly ripping out his throat. Maybe it was the thought of losing my best friend—my *brother*—but whatever snapped inside of me then left behind an unholy wrath.

I was furious as I took down Shifter after Shifter, their biggest weakness being their fraternization laws that separated them. Still, we were not winning. No, this was an even battle, and it was only leading to bloodshed.

A flash of brown curls caught my eyes, stealing my attention.

Asher?

The blade came and went, but the pain was delayed, like my body was attempting to resist the almost-mortal reaction to having one's back sliced open. When the agony made its presence known, it did so in full force—a hot iron branding my back.

I fell to my knees, watching as the female with the long brown curls turned to face me before she shifted, morphing into a jaguar. As she stalked towards me, her gaze lethal and hungry, I wondered if maybe, just maybe, I had been the problem all along.

***

Day thirty-nine without Asher was just as miserable as the one before.

Cyprus was not himself. He stressed about Luca's absence even more than the rest of us, terrorizing new recruits—both mortal and demon. He was on edge, always tensing when I received a letter. There was only so much I could do to reassure him when I was also panicking.

Recovering after the attack on Isle Shifter was slow. Our soldiers were angry, ready for war, but they were also broken. We had not brought back any bodies, having to say goodbye to those lost without them. Burning bodies was crucial to sending a soul to the Above, which left too many devastated at the thought of those they loved being cursed to an endless existence in purgatory. It was a mournful two weeks of doing nothing but strategizing. The fae had not retaliated, despite the fact that we bathed their base in gore.

Farai sat in the corner, often not doing much else. He was convinced that his husband was in harm's way, but we did not have the means to find and rescue him. Our plan had failed in many ways, but seeing Farai's dejected expression daily was a reminder of the way absence and death haunted the present and living.

"Ash would have hated what we did," Noe said, her head hung low and her hands clasped in her lap.

"Do not speak of her like she is dead or never coming back," I seethed in return, finally looking her in the eyes. We stared off, both furious and overwhelmed and so, so scared.

"She very well might be," Lian added in a whisper, looking far sadder than I would have thought possible months ago. But that was the problem with loving someone, they irrevocably altered you, a permanent shift from who you were.

"Shut up, Lian." Henry's chastising tone left my body humming with bitter ire.

"No, you do not get to stand up for me or protect me! It is our fault that Asher is gone, our mistakes that left her alone! You sooner should have let Farai die than take your eyes off of her, and I should have gotten to her immediately! But we fucked up! So you do not get to stand up for me or make me feel better. No one does. Because I know I deserve it all!"

Everyone looked at me in horror, so baffled by my audible outburst that they were unsure of what to do. My head felt heavy on my shoulders, my entire body swaying. When had I stood up? My sweaty palms met the wooden tabletop, catching me before I fell. I was breathing too hard, too fast. Was this what dying felt like?

"I'm sorry. I should not have said that. You are not to blame for Asher being gone, and she will be back. We...we will find her." Even as I said the words, I had the feeling that was not the case.

In the corner, Farai adjusted in his chair, catching everyone's attention. Guilt burned hot as coals in my chest, the culmination of so many wrongs—wishing for Farai's death simply being the newest—boiling inside of me like a volcano ready to blow.

Every pair of eyes turned to Farai, and we all listened as he made everything infinitely more complicated and insurmountably more hopeful.

"We need Nicola. She knows things, more than just any Tomorrow. Since I've known her, she has had the uncanny ability to see the future without touch. Sometimes, I swear she is even talking about the past." When he finished speaking, his white eyes looked clearer than before, like the fog had lifted and he could now see the path ahead.

"An Oracle," Damon whispered, a collective gasp filling the room.

***

"King Trint, it is good to see you." Henry had his full charm on as he reached out and hugged Trint, clapping him on the back. Trint smirked, likely aware that Henry was being overly kind and not bothered by it.

"Henry, you as well. And, Prince Bellamy, how are you?" It was not the words themselves, nor the handshake that grated on my nerves, but the way he sounded like he were comforting a widow.

"I am great, actually. Though I imagine I will be better upon Asher's return. The very female who has your entire kingdom in an uproar. I imagine you are also eager for her return, are you not?"

The king's face fell, the regret and guilt evident in his slumped posture.

Lian's elbow met my gut, the jab hard enough to make me grunt in pain.

Damn them all.

I pasted on a horribly fake smile, clearing my throat before taking Trint's outstretched hand. He did not feign pleasantries again, instead nodding with a forlorn look.

"They call her the Goddess of Minds. Over the last month and a half she has grown a devout following, and they claim her as the goddess for the people. Faithfuls everywhere believe that she will bring a new age—that she is our salvation. They are unaware that she is—" His words cut off, eyes darting from mine to Henry's before continuing. "They do not know she is gone."

"Obviously, Trint. Come on, these creatures are older than your great great grandmother, I think they are well aware of how politics work." The man who spoke had bright blonde hair, his blue eyes nearly as light as my own. He was just as broad as Trint but shorter, his slightly weathered pale skin further contrasting him from the King of Gandry. Both men wore crowns, but Trint's casual teal robes and black sandals were the exact opposite of the other man's crisp military uniform in tan and olive green. The accent was familiar, if only from my studies and time running amuck across the world. This was the king of Heratt.

"Apologies, I did not properly introduce my good friend. This is King Mordicai of Heratt. As neighboring kingdoms, Gandry and Heratt have been close allies for centuries. King Mordicai has come with the desire to discuss a possible alliance between Eoforhild and his kingdom."

If my expression was anything like my stunned mind, then I probably looked ridiculous. Judging by Mordicai's smirk, I did. He reached out his hand, which I promptly took, his grip firmer than Trint's.

"It is a pleasure to meet you, Prince Bellamy. Or do you prefer General Ayad?" The question sounded almost sarcastic, but I still answered with as much warmth as I could muster.

"Just Bellamy is fine. It is a pleasure to meet you as well, King Mordicai." He released my hand when I used his title, that smirk becoming a full smile.

"Well, that is only because I was smart enough not to insinuate that your lover is dead. I am sure by the time these negotiations are over you will probably hate me even more than Trint over here." Henry chuckled at my side, introducing himself briefly before explaining where the soldiers would reside and discussing training methods.

I remained still, unable to move from my spot. Every ounce of my strength went towards keeping myself from portaling to the sea, to the only place where I did not feel the pain of her absence. Noe had gone to Betovere in search of both Luca and Asher. So far, she had found no sign of either, though she had noted that Asher's rooms had been left untouched and there was still talk within The Capital of her continued absence.

"We will win this war, Bellamy." Trint's voice broke me from my trance, our eyes locking. There was too much sincerity in them, as if he had convinced himself by sheer will that we would walk away from this fight. I nodded, hoping that he was right. "By the way, Shah sent word. It seems the fae have threatened her. Not surprising, seeing as I was told to stand down or watch my kingdom burn."

***

"We need to attack while they are scrambling. Do you know how easy it is for them to simply replace those they lost? We have already waited too long!" Damon was far more pushy today than he normally was, especially with both Noe and Luca being gone still. The former, at least, was sending us missives. But the continued silence from Luca had everyone ready to break. Ready to fight back.

My hesitation came only from the silence of the fae after Isle Shifter. I feared that, if they did have Asher and Luca, they would harm them to punish us. Was it entirely selfish and not in the best interest of my realm? Yes, absolutely.

As per usual, I was uninterested in pretending I was anything but selfish.

Adbeel was running his fingers along his beard, eyeing the newly redone model of Alemthian. The Capital did not just house the fae royals. On the island was a large set of four buildings arranged to make a sort of square. The fae called this Academy. There resided instructors and their families, as well as every youngling who had come into their power. Though the fae did not reproduce as easily as mortals or even demons, they had been steadily growing in their numbers. There was no telling how many young fae were there. On top of that, we had to worry about the market, the ports, the guards, and all those who resided in the castle.

Too many innocents would suffer because of us. How could we do that again?

How could *I?*

"I think that we need to be patient, there is—"

"My Prince! My Prince!" The shouts came from the other side of the war room door, getting closer as whoever it was neared. I stood from my seat, my chair sliding loudly across the floor. Making my way to the door, I threw it open, catching sight of a young soldier—his silver uniform fresh and without the stains of blood. "Please, My Prince, you must come look at this."

He was too out of breath to continue, his hands going to his knees as he gasped for air. I turned to the others in the meeting, all of them leaning in an attempt to get a better view of the commotion. I nodded to Adbeel, and he returned it, resuming the discussion as I closed the door behind me.

"Where?" I asked.

The male was so unsettled that it seemed contagious, rattling my senses. He took a deep breath, straightening his back and clearing his throat.

"The Southern border, near station eight." Without saying anything else, I grabbed his arm and portaled us, looking around to see nothing but snow. The soldier did not acknowledge the fact that there was clearly nothing to see. Instead, he walked farther south, not so much as telling me to follow.

But follow I did.

Not even five minutes later, we approached a small crowd, all facing a large golden box. I froze upon seeing it, a sense of foreboding leaving my vision hazy. What could I do but march forward, though? These were my soldiers. They did not want to follow a terror-filled general.

Making my way to it, I took a single deep breath then put my hands on the lid. It was heavy, sturdy even. Like perhaps whatever was inside weighed enough to warrant thicker packaging. My fingers gripped the edges of the lid, hands and body shaking.

"Back up, all of you. We do not know what this is." My orders were immediately followed, every soldier present taking large steps back to ensure their own safety. A part of me did it because I also did not desire them to see me shatter, if that was what loomed below the lid.

Lifting the lid reinforced that pit in my stomach, warning bells sounding in my head. I could practically hear my own voice shouting not to look at what was inside. Still, I opened it. And when the lid fell from my hands in shock, I wondered if the pain would ever end.

A shrill scream came from someone behind me, then they were all shouting. Luca's body had been hacked to pieces and shoved into the box, the smell of rotting flesh and dried blood so pungent it stung my nose. He was not clothed, stripped of that final dignity even in death. They had brutally harmed him just before ending his life, made clear by the unhealed bruises and cuts and crooked bones. Chunks of his blonde hair had been ripped out, his flesh gone on some parts of his torso. His once-bright blue eyes were open, the disgrace of it all nearly ending me there.

In one of his hands, the one missing only a single finger rather than the four the other had been separated from, sat a piece of paper. I reached in, grabbing the note from his cold grasp. A sob escaped my lips, the tears falling as I read the note.

To the false prince, this is for Isle Shifter.

I read it over and over, the tears running down my cheeks and the snow soaking my knees. Henry came, his arms around my shoulders, shaking me. Then he noticed what was in the box, and the only sound was of him vomiting. But it was when Cyprus came that I made a decision. His screams pierced something in my soul, his begging and cursing and desperate denial too much, shattering all that was left of the good within me.

Looking up at Henry, I met his bottle green eyes and said the one thing I had been convinced I never would. "It is time we destroy that fucking gilded island."

***

I stared up at the stars from the top of the mountain, my upper body bare. Tremors racked through me as the cold bit into my skin, but all I could do was look at the night sky. My eyes burned and my chest ached as I finally found my voice after nearly an hour of wordless begging.

"I cannot exist without her. In her absence, the air does not reach my lungs and my heart struggles to beat. She is *everything*. Please, give her back to me," I pleaded to the stars—to anything that would answer. They shone in the sky, twinkling like the world was still a beautiful place. But how could it be when Nona and Pino and Luca were *dead*? When Asher was *gone*? "Please."

I was met with only silence.

***

Jolting up, I let out a shout of terror, my chest rising and falling too rapidly, as it always did now. But this—it was different.

I felt it. *Her.*

OF REALMS AND CHAOS

Nearly falling after I leapt out of my bed, I stumbled my way to Henry's rooms, slamming my fist on his door repeatedly until he threw it open with a growl of frustration. With an unnecessarily hard shove, I forced my way into his rooms, pacing across the wooden floors.

"Bell, what is it?" Noe asked from the doorway. I did not look up at her, my eyes focused on the ground as I waited. After another minute or two, she let go.

With wide and crazed eyes, I looked between the both of them. My hand flew to my chest, gripping the cotton shirt as if it would slow my heart. Neither of them spoke though they both seemed to be on edge. It had only been two days since we were sent Luca's remains, so it was expected that they would fear I had lost my mind. But I had not. Yet.

"Asher. She touched one of our notes. I felt it." Disbelief colored my words red, painting them as the danger they were. Because if this was not Asher but a trap instead, then I would be risking our entire base— perhaps even the whole of the realm. They seemed to think the same thing, if their unsure gazes and the slightly judgmental purse of their lips were any indication.

"How do you know it is not a trap?" Noe finally asked, cutting through the tension with a dull stick.

"I do not know that." I thought about shrugging but could not muster the energy needed.

"Just call it back to you. We can stop any danger that comes from it." Henry, who was rarely the moderator, sounded just as tired as I felt. None of us were sleeping well, nor were we functioning during the day. We had lost so much so quickly.

I nodded, holding out my hand and beckoning the item to me. The darkness coagulated around my palm before abruptly dissipating, leaving only a gently folded note in my hand. Noe gasped, running towards me. Henry made his way closer, steps measured and full of the nerves we were all being consumed by. When I opened the note, my hand immediately covered my mouth, trying and failing to stop the tears.

I am okay. Please do not slaughter innocents or freeze over entire villages. Trust that I will come back to you as soon as I can.
I love you.

Noe, her own tears flowing, wrapped her arms around me. Her fingers massaged the back of my head, and then Henry was holding me too, all three of us crying so hard we could barely stand. Through it all, I said the same four words over and over again.

"It is her handwriting."

***

Luca's funeral was quaint, a small affair where only those closest to him came to pay their respects. Cyprus had spent most of the afternoon with his parents and Luca's dad, the four of them practically in a constant embrace.

Luca's father did separate from them eventually, walking towards me with what looked to be purpose. I wondered how long it would take him to confidently call me out for sending his only son to the enemy's territory, especially when we now knew that Asher had not been there. At least, she likely had not. Her note did not smell like Betovere, the ink slightly different than what the royals used. Which meant I had been the cause of the death of a male who had been like a brother to me.

"Bellamy," his father said, reaching out his arms to pull me into a hug. I returned the gesture, surprised by such kindness when I had a feeling the conversation would end with him cursing my existence. We stayed like that for a while, just holding one another. I listened as he sobbed, waiting for the shoe to drop. "First my wife, and now my son? The world is far crueler than I ever thought."

"I am so sorry for what I did. I never should have sent him. If I could take his place, I would. More than anything, I wish that I could somehow trade my life for his." My voice broke, fingers forming fists upon Jeremy's back. "Luca. He was better than most—better than me. You raised one of the best males I have ever met."

441

He released me then, using his hands to push me from him—those blue eyes looking so much like his son's that I felt sick. When he shook his head, gripping my arms tighter, my heart sank. I tried to apologize again, but he cut me off with a raised hand.

"I do not blame you, Bellamy. You gave my son, a creature that many feared, a chance. We wraiths are not loved, nor are we trusted, but you took him in. Despite his age and his magic, you accepted him. In fact, he used to call you all his second family, and I can see how true that is in your eyes. Please, do not blame yourself. He loved what he did. He loved you." The tears flowed faster down his face as he tugged me into him again, this time patting my back as I let the pain devour me.

"Eighty-two was too young. He deserved better. I will give those who did this to him ten times the pain. They will suffer. I promise you that, Jeremy."

He stepped away, inhaling a mouthful of air before nodding and walking back to Cyprus. I stayed alone for the remainder of the funeral, not even Noe coming up to me. One day, I would thank them for affording me space, but that would not be today.

After the pyre had been built and lit, we said our goodbyes to Luca, another unfair farewell. More that my parents had taken from me—from us. We had begun plans to obliterate The Capital, spending more time than even I cared to admit trying to decide how to save at least the younglings.

Regardless, the golden palace would fall.

***

The paint was dry.

Had I been sitting here that long?

It felt like seconds since I began the piece, Asher's eyes staring back at me as if to say, "Yes, dimwit, it has been that long."

Winona, Pino, and Luca's gazes were not much kinder.

Because I had spent an unspeakable amount of time in this room, I decided it was probably best to clean up. Last night, I had taken to smashing most of my art that resided within these four walls, which left me with ripped canvases galore.

Bending down with a sigh, my fingers only just grazed the shredded cloth when I heard the door swing open.

"Bell!" Henry's voice was startling after so many hours without any sound. I turned to see him racing towards me, waving a piece of paper around like a lunatic.

For a split second, I thought he was attempting to use Asher's note to cheer me up, which was ridiculous and also likely to work, but then I caught the look in his eyes. Whatever was in Henry's hand had him flustered and excited, a dangerous combination in times like this. When he stopped in front of me, I eagerly tried to look at the correspondence, leaning my head and snatching it from his hands. But I did not need to, because Henry was quick to summarize it for me.

"It is from Genevieve. Bell, they have Ash."

CHAPTER THIRTY-SIX

STASSI

The golden queen was flustered, something I hadn't seen from her yet. She spoke quickly, moved in jerky spurts, and even forgot to order around her many male hounds. Even more interesting was her black clothing. Never had I seen her in anything other than gold before. This was *new*, and I so loved new.

When she lifted her fingers to her mouth and began nibbling on the ends, I knew something exciting was happening. From around the corner, I watched as the dimpled king approached her from behind. So startled was she when he appeared at her side that she audibly yelped.

"Wow, I have not seen you this jumpy in centuries, Mia." Her scowl could have obliterated him in that moment. Perhaps a weaker male would have perished, but I was slowly learning that the king had a hidden backbone. "The plan will work. I do not know why you allow yourself to wallow and stress."

"Anyone with a modicum of intelligence would be thinking about every possible outcome, Xavier. The fact that you roam these halls right now without a care in the world tells me that you have still not learned anything after all these years."

Brutal.

Each venom-soaked word slammed into the king, but if they truly hurt, even I couldn't tell. All I felt within them was sin, coagulating in their chests and proclaiming itself love.

"When you bring her back, I want to be the one to speak to her." The demand fell from clenched teeth, proving that King Xavier was far more irritated than he let show. Though his leash was short, he tugged all the same.

"You will not see her until I tell you that you can. It will be me who doles out this lesson. You have failed for two centuries!" Screaming in a hallway? Tsk tsk, golden queen.

"I have loved her and taught her and molded her into what she is. You will do well to remember that! It has always been me. You are the one who sat back and did the pretty work. *I* did the hard things!" His finger was in Queen Mia's face, fire lighting his other hand aflame. Oh wonderful, perhaps they would fight to the death.

"And yet *I* am the one who is nothing without her!" The queen smacked her hands against her mouth, desperately trying to take back the truth that had been laid bare before them.

Despite the declaration of what sounded like devotion, sin still clouded her mind. That's what happens, though, when one was taught not to love but to conquer. At least she recognized it for what it was.

The king laughed and was quickly met with a slap to his face. His head tilted to the right, and they momentarily stood there, both gazing at each other in disbelief as the sound of her strike reverberated through the nearly empty golden hall. Servants could be heard not far away, their feet scurrying to take them anywhere else. Before anything more riveting could happen, Queen Mia stormed the opposite direction, leaving the king dazed in the middle of the gilded hallway.

Pity.

Taking that as my cue to move, I headed for my creature, creeping down to the now familiar dungeons until I arrived at his cell. He sat, as usual, with his back to the wall.

"Of all the times you have visited me, this has to be the most exquisite you have looked." He leaned forward, eyeing my billowing navy dress with a half-lidded gaze. If I had just met him, I would assume it was desire, but I knew now that it was his mind at work. "What is the special occasion, Spice?"

His voice was stronger today, though that wasn't anything particularly impressive. The golden-haired prince had taken to beating my creature almost daily now. The Healer had looked as if she were close to passing out that morning when she came in to check up on him. I needed to take him as soon as possible, but the stupid princess was nowhere to be found.

Every pointless visit back home, the horribly massive scolding I received for my insolence, all of it made this adventure less and less fun. But if I could bring my creature home with me, that would make it all worth it.

"Well, this is the last time I'll be visiting until it's time for us to go. Of course, me freeing you is contingent on one thing." I leaned forward, eyeing him with untamed desire. Oh, it would be sweet, winning after so long of playing the game.

Hopefully he lived up to my increasingly high expectations.

For his part, my creature simply laughed, resting his elbow on a raised knee and leaning back against the filthy wall. "Of course, there are rules. Do tell me, glorious goddess of death, what must I do for my freedom?"

Normally, I hated the gods narrative, because how absurd was the idea of such a thing? But the mere suggestion of it from his lips sounded erotic.

I was in trouble indeed.

"You agree to be mine." There was a nonchalance to my voice that did not quite match my racing heart. Before he could let the request go to his head, I added, "A pet of sorts."

"Spice, if you told me to bark, I would do it."

I laughed, my head falling back and soaking in the humor of such easily given devotion. My creature didn't respond in kind. Instead, he smiled at me, the soft lift of his pout a reminder of the fun we would have soon. "Did you know that a Multiple has, on average, about an hour to remain in any shifted form? Then they need to recuperate, though that varies in length."

More facts. Perhaps I could train that out of him. Well, Iniko would get a kick out of it if not. Actually, I would bet he might even try to steal this toy from me.

Would my creature accept such an advance? Did he even like males?

"Very interesting, creature. Anyways, tell me, have you ever been with a male?" My arms crossed as I leaned against the adjoining wall, eager to hear his answer but unwilling to let him know that. Raising his brows, he took me in with a perplexed expression, as if something I had done confused him.

"You can call me by name, you know." He stood then, walking to me on shaky legs. His ripped and worn clothes were still caked in grime, his hair matted and tangled. If I looked closely enough, I could see that there must have been at least a slight curl to it at some point. And was it truly brown, or was that the dirt?

Damn it all, that inquisitive nature was rubbing off on me.

"I don't want to."

His fingers met the bars just above where mine had been, his head leaning against them as if they were nothing more than a convenience rather than a prison. "Can I call *you* by name?"

Grunting, I pushed off the wall and brought my body to the bars as well, my face tilting up to look into his.

"Stassi. That's what my companions call me. Now, focus on what's important. Have you ever been with a male?"

"No, bossy thing, I have not. I do not have an interest in them." A shrug, a blink, and then a smile at my baffled expression was all he offered. Bossy?

"Everyone likes both—most just don't live long enough for their curiosity to take control. When you are immortal, truly so, then you grow too bored to not sample every dish available. And you learn quickly that all flavors are quite delicious. I would teach you if I wasn't so possessive." With that, I trailed my finger down a bar, watching as my magic took hold of the male beyond. "Say you'll be mine, handsome. Give in to that sin, and I'll come back for you."

Without hesitating, he leaned his face between the iron bars, smiling down at me. I had the annoying impulse to close the space between us. For some reason, the dirt didn't bother me as it normally would. How I wished that I had never met this thing.

"You wound me, Spice. You do not have to order me with that odd pink magic of yours. I will gladly be whatever you want me to be, whenever you want." A hand reached out towards me, and instead of leaning in like I might have with anyone else, I backed away slightly, not wanting to allow him to touch me for fear of what it might feel like when he let go. Sighing, he pulled away, looking me up and down with obvious interest. "You once said that you control sin and virtue, but how does your magic even begin to determine which is which?"

A laugh bubbled in my chest, freeing itself through my lips. Too much, this was too much. I could become fixated on the taste of his presence—enamored by the sound of his curiosity. And that would be the death of me. Curiosity killed even more than I did, in my experience.

"Why do you ask so many questions?" I inquired in turn, trying and failing to stay away from him. My feet moved me back towards his aura, my shoes touching the tips of his toes through the bars.

"I like to learn." The words were deliberate, just as the slow trail of his gaze from my eyes to my lips was. Groaning, I took my hand and shoved his face backwards, earning a deep chuckle from the male.

"Sin and virtue are subjective. My magic senses what you believe your deepest faults and merits are, the actions and thoughts that you deem good or evil. It even shows me them, giving me small insights into your whys. Then it capitalizes on that, intensifies it until you are so deeply within them that you can't find your way out. My magic leaves you lost in a forest of your wildest dreams and worst nightmares. And, in the end, you're left realizing that you were both the dream and the nightmare all along."

His face pinched in concentration, thinking over my words. My declaration. Because I'd just laid before him the truth of how dangerous I could be, and this was his moment to decide if my wickedness was worth his freedom.

Before I could so much as encourage him to accept my offer, a burst of magic entered the ethers, calling to me and burning through my chest. A great quake of that place where my essence existed inside of me. I bent forward, gripping my chest and holding onto one of the bars for dear life.

"Do you feel that?" I asked him, knowing that he didn't. Knowing that it was the call I had been waiting for.

His voice came out slightly panicked, his hands reaching for me as if he could help somehow. "No, what is it? Stassi, are you okay?"

All I could manage were two words, a gasped statement through pursed lips. "It's her."

And then I was gone.

CHAPTER THIRTY-SEVEN

ASHER

"I love what you have done with the place. Truly stunning work. You guys have an eye for interior design. Something about the way you paired the iron bars with the wooden bucket. My only note is that I do not think there is enough mold. I mean, look at this corner. There is practically none!" Leaning back, I gestured towards the far right corner of my cell, which was, in fact, limited in its mold.

"I see you are really leaning into your new role as a goddess. So nice to know you still have an attitude." Genevieve's voice was calm, though there was the barest hint of humor beneath her eye rolls and scowls. Dare I say she was warming up to me?

"First of all, I was always a goddess. It was just not widely recognized yet. Second of all, who knew information traveled so fast here? Your ravens must be far faster than those in the Fae Realm." My head fell back, the tangles from my dragon ride so thick that they almost acted as a cushion.

How had that just been hours ago? It felt like a lifetime.

Genevieve looked at me inquisitively, her eyes narrowed and lips pursed. My gaze wandered, uncomfortable with the turn in mood. What did I say that was so awful?

"Yes, it turns out our ravens are capable of traveling across kingdoms in two months. I do not believe it is that impressive, Princess Asher," she said, leaning her shoulder against the wall just outside of my cell.

Strangely enough, the first thing that came to my mind was a joke about mortals telling time. But then, as what she said sank in, I froze, my mouth suddenly too dry to speak.

Two months? How could it have been two months since I was taken?

"That is impossible," I whispered. Somehow, I knew that it was not, though. Maybe it was Genevieve's perplexed face as she stared at me or it could have been the snow that had found its way into my hair while I was dragged. No matter what told me that her statement was true, I still came to the same conclusion.

I had abandoned Bellamy for two months.

"Eoforhild? Shah? What has happened since I was in Gandry? Have you heard from Henry?" My questions came in rapid succession, so fast that Genevieve seemed startled by the sudden energy with which I was speaking. In fact, she did not answer for a couple of minutes, her frown deeper than before. As if she did not know how to tell me something.

"Asher, I think it is best if the prince answers those questions." Before she even finished speaking, I was up, walking towards her with newfound determination—my head shaking back and forth. I did not miss the step back she took, despite knowing I was behind bars. The princess was smart enough to fear what she could not see.

"You cannot possibly expect me to wait. Tell me whatever it is. I am not some mortal child who needs to be protected."

Though I did not use my magic on her, the princess did not hesitate a second time. Her eyes fell downwards as she spoke, more sorrow than I expected coating the air, blanketing us both in pain.

"Fine, but when that prince of yours comes, remember that you made me tell you." A deep breath, one that only further cemented how serious this would be, and then she spoke. "After you left, the demons attacked Isle Shifter. Hundreds died, and Bellamy was badly hurt."

An answering gasp of horror was all I could muster. My chest constricted as I pictured the hundreds of dead bodies, my body alight with worry that burned like flames. It required every ounce of my control not to picture Bellamy's body among them. He was safe. He had to be.

"Both Shah and Trint have received threats, giving them one final chance to stand down. Neither agreed, and Trint was able to gain the support of King Mordicai, ruler of Heratt. Soldiers have been continuously portaling into Eoforhild."

I did not speak, instead focusing solely on the still-heavy feel of her mind. She was radiating fear and sorrow. The worst part had still not been revealed. She cleared her throat, her hand running through her golden ringlets.

"The fae...they went silent for a while. Henry was fairly sure that they would outright attack, but, um, they did something else." I nodded, waving a hand for her to go on. She sighed, rubbing her hand across her face. "They killed the wraith—sent his dismembered body to Prince Bellamy in a box."

No.

No, no, no, no, no!

How had so much death befallen Alemthian in so little time? Luca, sweet and brave Luca. I had not even gotten to really know him since that first day we met on the way to my low level room. I thought of his blonde hair and young face. Of the way he radiated quiet strength, wiser than his years. Cyprus had told me stories of his best friend, the male who always kept him in check.

Bellamy, who likely had been imagining the worst happening to me, was also facing the loss of his soldiers and one of his Trusted. The beings who he considered family. Letting my back hit the wall, I slowly slid down, sitting before I fell. So much death. An unbelievable amount of loss.

"I told you it would have been better to hear it from your prince. He will be on his way soon." Genevieve, in her stunning cream gown, sat as well. We remained there in silence for a while, wallowing in the horrifying reality of what was coming. This would be the least of the blood spilled.

"You have to see how dangerous what is coming will be for you. Do you think that the fae royals will not use you all as pawns? Every mortal soldier will be placed on the front line, used as a defense while the fae fight from behind. You will be used as a shield, Genevieve. Do you not fear death, or are you all simply that ignorant?" My voice broke, choking on the final sentence. The pain tried to take hold of me, to remind me of how much easier it was to sink rather than tread water.

Winona, Pino, Haven, Luca, *me*. Each a reason to not be heartbroken but furious. My hand touched my empty sheath, remembering what my now-confiscated dagger said.

I am vengeance.

"Of course, we see that! We backed ourselves into a corner when we agreed to that stupid marriage. All I want is my brother back, and I will not have him until we follow through with our end of the bargain. We must fight, and we must win. If that means slitting Henry's throat or gutting your precious prince, then I will do it. Do not underestimate what horrors I will commit for my family." The threat in her voice as she seethed was evident.

For the first time since I arrived in Maliha, I realized that I was in Sterling's home. The grimy and wicked feeling I expected from this castle was absent, even in their dungeons. It made the entire family more real, like people rather than the villains in my imagination. That hurt more, seeing just how much they had at stake too.

"Then why is Bellamy on his way? Surely it was not your parents who told him of my presence here." If Genevieve saw my words for the trap they were, she did not show it. Her hesitant mood was long gone, replaced by a fiery need to scold and berate me.

"He is not on his way yet. I plan to tell them so they can get you out of here. You might be a useless bitch, but I would prefer not to see you hanging from the gallows. Plus, I have a feeling you would manage to kill a lot of people before you finally stopped breathing."

My laugh was heavy, like that of someone resigned to their end. And, in a way, I was. Because this had officially become the easiest plan to date.

"Genevieve, you will not be telling them anything." Her head whipped towards me, brow furrowed and mouth slightly open. She would make a great queen one day with that distrusting mind of hers. "Tell your parents that I want to speak with them."

***

My once beautiful and vibrant dress had become a torn, dirty, mess of cloth and flowers. Genevieve had offered me a rag with water and soap to clean off my skin, but nothing could save the gown. Still, I held my head high as the king and queen approached my cell.

King Lawrence's soft brown hair and pale skin were bland in comparison to Queen Paula's wild golden curls and cream complexion. She looked every bit the royal she was in a stunning white and forest green gown, the layers crossing and twisting together, while he did not make any sort of impression in his black trousers and matching green tunic. Atop their heads were crowns of gold, green and blue gems dotting them.

"Princess Asher, it is so nice to finally meet my future daughter. Though, if I am being honest, I did not expect to do so with you in my dungeons. Which is made all the more peculiar seeing as you were supposed to be in your realm. With my son." Lawrence's commanding and unfaltering voice made up for his plain appearance. He seemed to radiate power as he spoke, a force demanding attention.

"Well, then it seems we are both surprised by this turn of events. Fortunately, I do not plan to stay long. In fact, I think I am about to solve all of our problems." I tried to smile, to exude the cocky confidence that Bellamy always seemed to possess, or even my own version of that, which I had mastered over the last few months. With any other ruler I could have done so, but being in front of Sterling's parents made me want to crawl into a hole and hide. There was no surety to be found within me. The ground beneath my feet hummed, as if ready to rise and suck me in—as if to remind me that I was nothing within these walls.

"Do tell us how you plan to accomplish such a feat," Queen Paula said, the corner of her lips twitching upwards slightly before she was serious once more. Genevieve was beside her, looking nervous as her eyes bounced from me to the hall on her left. I did my best to not look in the same direction, focusing in on Lawrence and Paula. I could feel a pull towards it, as if my body itself was begging for me to peek. When I shook my head and opened my mouth to seal my fate, the reason for Genevieve's unease made itself known. Or rather, himself.

"Oh, yes, I am also quite interested in what the princess has to say." His raspy drawl was both a relief and a problem, because he would not like what I was about to offer.

No, he would hate it.

All four of our heads snapped in his direction, watching as he strutted forward. He was wearing all black save for the red cloak, his long-sleeve tunic and trousers form-fitting. Three buttons were left open at the top, revealing the magic coursing through his veins as it writhed within him, slithering up his neck like snakes on the hunt. "Especially since she so desperately did not want me to know."

Paula gasped, grabbing Genevieve by the arm and backing them both away. Lawrence placed himself in front of his wife and daughter, holding his hands forward like he could stop The Elemental with sheer will.

I shot a glare at Genevieve, who merely rolled her eyes like I was being dramatic. Soon, she would see how foolish she was for telling Bellamy.

"You know, Asher could have shattered your minds without blinking. Or, on a less deadly note, she could have just told you to let her out. Any of you would have done it too. It would seem to you like your own choice—the *only* choice. Nothing would stop you but death. So, tell me, why would a being as strong as her simply stay put? Now, that I want to know." He leaned against the wall parallel to the cells, his dimples flashing as he smiled and the blue of his eyes practically glowing against the firelight. There was no sign of the handsome and loving male I once knew. The Bellamy that looked upon us now was harder, angrier, appearing as though he were poised to burn the kingdom and bathe in the ashes.

I wanted to kiss him, to profess my endless love and unwavering loyalty to him. More than anything, I wanted to hold him. He looked so fragile beyond the mask that lay at the surface. Beneath it all, Bellamy was hurting, breaking even.

But my eyes met Genevieve's again, and I knew that she finally understood what I was about to do. The promises I would make. A gasp came out of her mouth, her hand flying up to stifle it.

Let me show you that I can be more than just a useless bitch. Trust me, Genevieve.

She twitched, not used to my voice within her head. Still, she nodded silently, further cuddling into her mother. Both king and queen looked suspiciously from Bellamy to me and back again. Their guards had not come down with them or, at least, had not come near my cage. But it seemed they were both looking for whatever help could be offered.

They would find none.

I tried and failed to get into Bellamy's mind, that wall of black flames shoving me out. White-hot fury tainted the air, burning my throat on the way down and scorching my senses. He smirked, rolling his hand towards me in a gesture to go on.

Fine.

"Well, King Lawrence, Queen Paula, I believe that I have the means to give you everything you want. If you fight for Eoforhild instead of Betovere, then you can establish a good relationship with the demons, who have an assortment of tradable goods and the ability to transfer them past The Mist. But that will not be all. Half of the mortal kingdoms have already allied with us. If you do as well, Maliha can maintain good relations with them. Beyond that, I can also vow the support and continued trade with Betovere once I become queen."

Saying it was hard to remain stoic and queen-like while behind bars and in shredded clothing would be an understatement. Even as I spoke, I watched the king and queen occasionally look me up and down, as if the words coming from my mouth paled in comparison to the heinous way I appeared. Sparing one last pleading look at Bellamy, who seemed to steam at whatever he saw on my face, I took a deep breath and gave away the rest of myself.

"And I will marry your son. He will rule at my side with a crown on his head. We can plan a rescue, bring him home to you, and then, when the war is won, I will wed him. Our children will be heirs to the fae throne, and you will be permitted access to us and them at any time." Genevieve's head fell forward, her shoulders slumping in relief.

Would it always disgust me, the way that they loved him?

"Absolutely. The. Fuck. Not." Bellamy's booming voice was closer this time, and I looked to my right to find that he had portaled into the cell. My heart raced, the closeness of him both startling and like coming home. Like the other half of myself had found me at long last.

But his words, which threatened to ruin everything, were aggravating at best. We could not fight here, could not let the king and queen know about what we had. They would never agree if they knew, and it was very clear that Genevieve had kept many secrets from her parents.

"We can talk about the logistics another time, Prince Bellamy." I turned to face the rulers of Maliha once more, hoping that they would see the sincerity in my eyes. "For now, I offer my word. My hand is his if he chooses the right side."

Bellamy grabbed my wrist, his hand so hot that I would have feared he had a fever if not for his powers. A storm was brewing within him, one that threatened to suck me in and tear apart the future I had been working so hard to craft.

If Mia and Xavier had taught me one good thing, it was that the realm comes before the self. I loved Bellamy, more than I ever knew I could love another being. And, if I could, I would have him at my side for the rest of my life. But having the forces of Maliha on our side of the battle would be enough to stop the fae, to limit the casualties. With them, we could stop the war before it began. They could help us accomplish all that I wanted.

I tried again to force my magic through his shields, noting how I still felt stronger than I did in Gandry. Whatever Padon did to me, it altered me in what felt like a very permanent way. Still, I could not get past, no matter how hard I shoved. He held firm, clearly not wanting to hear my explanations.

I pulled my wrist free, breaking eye contact and trying to remind myself of all that Bellamy would gain from this as well. He would not need to rebuild Haven, nor would he have to sneak through Betovere.

Even more was to be obtained for the fae. I could open the borders, disband the factions, create relationships across the world. There would never be another public reaping, nor would we need the fraternization law. I could merge Academy, disperse the fae council. So much good could be accomplished if I did this.

Sometimes that was what being a ruler meant. Losing so your realm could win.

My heartbeat quickened as I entered Lawrence's mind, the effort so minimal it almost made me laugh.

Free me and return my dagger.

He did as he was told, unlocking the cell before grabbing my dagger from his daughter and offering it to me. Paula gasped, Genevieve still not looking up. I made my way away from them, heading towards the mind I knew so well after having six days of only it for company. Wrath walked in, causing Paula to scream upon seeing him. In her defense, he was steadily growing, his yellow eyes nearly as large as my face and his fangs lengthening past his lips.

"Took you long enough. I cannot believe you let them drag me like that."

He laughed, saying nothing before looking back at the three mortals hunched together. I did as well, offering a final smile their way.

Bellamy was still, his face unreadable, but his mind was obviously reeling from what I said. After two months of not knowing where I was, it seemed fair that he would be struggling with knowing there was another goodbye in our future.

Eventually, though, he left the cell, glaring at Genevieve before jogging towards me. I held out my hand, stopping him mid-step. His head tilted to the side in that infuriatingly perfect way he always did. I reached into his cloak, my hand finding the pocket and pulling out a piece of paper.

"Think about my offer," I added, looking around Bellamy to see Lawrence and Paula. They were visibly frazzled, the horror seeping from them in steady waves as they held one another. Genevieve was to her mother's side, staring at me. I nodded to her, hoping that it was reassuring enough to convince her to talk her parents into agreeing. She returned the gesture, and then I broke our stare, handing Bellamy the paper. "Infuse it with your essence, please."

My Bellamy would have laughed and shook his head, but this was not necessarily my Bellamy anymore. He grabbed the paper, a muscle in his jaw ticking, and I watched as shadows crept from his palm to the white sheet, coating it before they disappeared.

When he handed it back, I steadied myself and looked back at the mortals. "Whenever you make your decision, feel free to write it on this note. The magic will do you no harm. I hope you make the right choice."

Bellamy's arm was around me the instant Lawrence grasped the paper, my free hand securing Wrath. We portaled chaotically, the scent of smoke and cinnamon engulfing me like a favorite blanket. I wished I could stay in that embrace forever, but reality had another idea.

"Go, now," Bellamy growled down to Wrath.

The dalistori laughed, practically skipping away. "I hope she kills you, idiot."

Neither of us spoke until Wrath's form faded into the distance, the silence heavy with unspoken words.

"Do you care to explain to me what the fuck you think you were doing back there?" Bellamy finally asked, his shouts echoing off the snowy mountainside. My eye caught on one mountain that had been reduced to rubble, the sight eerily beautiful.

I had never been to Pike, but if this was it, then it was stunning. I looked out, appreciating the view of the sun sitting mid-sky, kissing a far-away peak. Though its warmth did not reach us, Bellamy and I were angry enough to heat ourselves, not even the beautiful sight enough to calm me. I whipped around, finding he was right in front of me—his chest rising and falling in a rapid, furious beat.

"I think I was trying to save the fucking world, Bellamy! In all the time you have known me, I have never wavered in my desire to be a solution rather than a problem—to prevent a war that would kill thousands. Why do you act surprised when I do everything I can to make that a reality?"

As always, we ended up right against one another, my head tilted up to yell at him with everything I had left. I did not want to fight, not when I knew how much he had suffered. Not when he needed to know the truth of my disappearance. But Bellamy, he seemed almost eager to fight, as if all of his pent-up rage was boiling over. The ground beneath my feet shook, the snow seeming to pile around me.

"You do not get to simply decide that you will marry someone else because it is not just *you* anymore, Ash! Months ago, in that cave, you told me you loved me, that you chose *me*. Well, marrying someone else does not exactly scream devotion!" His hands flew up into the air, coming down to tousle his eternally disheveled black waves. My mind raced, trying to accept where I went wrong—to acknowledge and prioritize his feelings—without compromising the only stable plan I had.

"There is only so much I can do—so many I can please! I do not know what you expect." My voice was wavering, the fatigue of so much in a single day weighing me down. But I did not falter; my body did not slump.

"I expect you to please *yourself!* Stop caring about everyone else and just be selfish! For one gods damn minute, let yourself be happy!" His hands lifted to my face, shaking my head gently, as if he could force the words to find purchase in my mind.

"Fine!" Then I reached up, locked my arms around his neck, and crashed my lips into his. He did not hesitate, wrapping those large hands around my thighs and lifting me. Our tongues clashed, the lust and love and anger combining to form a storm.

I felt him portal us but did not let his mouth leave mine, both of my hands grazing his growing stubble as he walked us through a slightly dark room. He stopped at the edge of a small bed, practically throwing me onto it. I gasped, body aching from the day, but Bellamy did not so much as flinch. His hands came down to my dress, ripping the fabric to shreds as if it had committed some great offense.

Then he was splitting my undergarments, too, only being careful with the sheath and dagger, which he placed on a nearby side table. Our eyes remained locked while he reached back and tugged his shirt over his head. He slowly stripped himself bare, the tension only growing with each passing second. When he freed himself, his hardened member bouncing slightly, I groaned. The Moon magic inside of him writhed in the light of day that peeked through the window, painting his skin in ink.

As he walked to me, I saw the way the fury warred with fear on his face, felt my magic caress it in the air. He dove down before I could think of something to say, his lips on my neck and his hands on my hips.

Bellamy's touches were love made tangible, his anger not affecting the way his tongue and teeth spelled my name against my skin. Nor were his fingers anything but thoroughly doting. They danced across my thighs, tickling their way up my stomach and around my breasts. I moaned at the contact, so familiar and right and perfect.

"Tell me you will not marry him." The words were whispered against my throat, like a desperate prayer. When I did not answer right away, he bit down, the pain and pleasure drawing another moan from my lips. He soothed the mark with a kiss, taking a single finger and dragging it between my breasts, trailing slowly down my stomach. "You will marry only me, Asher. I will be your husband, and we will rule over whatever fucking kingdom you want. You will trust that I can win this war for you, without the help of that wretched family, and I will be at your side for as long as I live."

That finger continued its course, lower and lower until it slid inside of me—setting a merciless pace—followed closely by a second. When his thumb rubbed across that bundle of nerves just above, I screamed his name, my back arching up. Heat seared me, and I realized Bellamy was warming himself further—or maybe he was losing control. That thought only made the moment sweeter, the ecstasy stronger. I whimpered, tugging his hair upwards. His lips left my skin, tongue slipping into my mouth as if he could consume the sounds of my pleasure. When his other hand wrapped around my throat, ringed fingers squeezing lightly, my head spun.

"Say it, Princess. Tell me you will choose us like you promised." A third finger joined the other two, his pace barely leaving me time to breathe, let alone speak. So I nodded, eliciting a raspy groan from him. With no warning, he pulled out his fingers and shoved himself inside of me, not waiting for either of us to adjust before he set a brutal rhythm.

Lightning shot up my spine, a strange shock to my system, like something inside of me was alive—awake. Bellamy jolted, as if he felt it too, before letting his body lean forward, pressing into mine. He bent his head, tucking it near my neck to whisper into my ear.

"Can you feel how wet you are for me? How perfectly I fit inside of you? If souls can be one, then ours are, Princess. Just as surely as I am yours, you are *mine*." For the first time, I did not feel the need to correct him. Rather than losing a piece of myself, I wondered if this was just a part of becoming whole.

Sliding my fingers down his back, I nodded again, my breathing heavy as he sped up. "Drop your shield, demon. Let me in."

Without hesitation, he did, his thumb once more circling that spot between my thighs. I entered his mind with a gasp, digging my nails into his shoulder blades for purchase when my head got too close to the headboard. I saw him reach up, a single hand pressed against the shaking piece of wood as I spoke into his mind.

I love you. There is no force in this world that could stop me from doing so. Not even time and space can keep me from you. If we exist beyond this life, then I will find you every time. I am yours, and you are mine.

Letting go of the headboard, he slid the arm beneath me, securing it around my back. The other left my center and went to my neck, tightening as he placed a desperate kiss to my lips. And when his release spilled within me, I found myself tipping over that edge too, crying out against his mouth from the satisfaction. It rolled through me in waves, like the sea crashing against the shore.

As always, being with Bellamy this way was like breathing for the first time after being held beneath water. The force of oxygen entering my body was a shock that brought relief through eager inhales.

While we caught our breath, Bellamy leaned back, staring at me. Not for the first time, I watched him break before my eyes, tears running down his cheeks as his raspy voice brought us back to reality.

"I thought you were dead."

CHAPTER THIRTY-EIGHT

ASHER

We bathed before we had the serious conversation that we both knew needed to happen. Bellamy held me, working knots from my hair and massaging oils into my stiff shoulders. Our fight—if one could call it that—still hung in the air, just as my disappearance and the many losses since did. There would be no reprieve from the pain, the guilt, and the horror that had occurred in the last year.

When we finished, he dried me off and carried me back to the bed, tucking our still-naked bodies beneath the quilts. He radiated warmth, combating the chill of the Sophistes mountaintops. Slightly shaky fingers slowly tucked my hair behind my ear before sliding down my jaw and under my chin, tilting my face up as his thumb rubbed soft circles on my skin. I missed those eyes of ice, so stunning and bright—familiar. I wanted to kiss every freckle that dotted his face, if only to gently release his tension and heartache. But that was not what he wanted, and he deserved more.

"The night of the afriktor attack, I had a strange nightmare. There was this creature, fae-like but slightly other. He told me you would sooner kill me than love me, like a threat disguised as a warning. Since then, he has visited my dreams a few times, professing his devotion and love to me."

Bellamy's finger stilled, his gaze narrowing. I continued, pushing through while knowing it would only get worse.

"I was not sure what he was, and I did not know how to tell you about it. But when I was in Gandry, he portaled me, like when you call to items or clothing. Getting there was a blur, but when I awoke, he was already waiting for me. At one point, I stabbed him in the chest with my dagger."

Somehow, despite the seriousness of the story, Bellamy chuckled, motioning for me to go on as he calmed himself.

"But what I later learned was that he was..." My voice trailed off, not knowing how to put into words that I not only met a god but also that he was obsessed with me. After a few seconds passed with Bellamy just looking at me with a blank expression, I sighed and continued. "He was a god. The God of Death and Creation specifically. His name is Padon, and he is convinced that I am the love of his life. I do not know why, just that he is."

Bellamy sat up, his hands rubbing his face as he hunched forward. I followed him, letting the blanket pool around our waists as I wrapped my arms around him. There was a heartbeat of time that I feared he might push me away, but instead, he pulled me closer. Then I heard a deep inhale of air through his nose, like perhaps he was seeing if I smelled differently.

"I did not have sex with him—if that is what you are trying to figure out. Nor did he force himself on me. Or, well, that is not necessarily true. He did kiss me, both in my dreams and while I was there." A deep growl-like sound emanated from the prince, his body shaking against mine. Quickly, I tugged him closer adding, "He paid for it."

Once more, I was stuck trying to decide how to continue with this story, which likely sounded insane. Would he believe that I rode dragons and saw a teal sun and read stories of the gods within the home of one? If I told him that six days there was over two months here, would he believe it? None of it seemed real, but then again, what else would explain my disappearance?

"I tried to get back. Everyday, Wrath and I went to Padon's stupid library, looking through book after book, never finding anything. It was not until I refused him for what felt like the hundredth time that he grew angry enough to send me home. Even then, I do not think he meant to, and I fear he will take me again. While I was there, less than a week passed. But here, it has been months. If he were to steal me away, the war could break out, and I would not be here to stop it." I shook my head, wishing I could rid myself of the thought and the god.

"I cannot believe that is what your mind immediately thought. Ash, do you not see the problem with what you said? You fear not being here to save the world rather than fearing what could happen to you there. He could rape you or kill you, and all that you can think about is the war?" His voice grew harsher with each sentence, that temper of his winning out far more than usual. But loss could do that to a person, and Bellamy had suffered immensely in that regard.

"Let's not argue. Genevieve told me about what happened while I was gone. You deserve peace, Bell." I paired my words with a soft kiss to his forehead, then his chin, both cheeks, his nose, and finally his mouth— copying the very thing he did to me time and time again.

I felt more than heard his heavy exhale, his arms tightening around me, like a boat and its anchor. And I would gladly be that for him. If he needed a safe place, I wanted to be one. I would weather any storm he threw my way, because it was an honor to be his.

Even if I might not always be.

"When you disappeared, it was like pieces of me went with you—all the good ones. I was angry and scared, and it was hard not to destroy the world itself. When we were arranging to attack Isle Shifter, the plan had been to only kill those highly enough ranked that it would make a difference in the war. But the demons were angry. We have sustained a lot of attacks, only a few stopped by the army. Many lost family over the last few months. I did not take that into account."

He looked away from me, shame painting his face red. My fingers traced a line up his jaw, massaging his head when I reached his hair. A sigh escaped his lips before he continued, adjusting so our noses touched as he spoke.

"I killed a lot of innocent fae that night. They were only doing what they were told. By then, Luca had already been silent long enough for us to be worried. Even Noe could not find him. Cyprus was on edge, Henry was dealing with my unstable ass, and Lian was training the new recruits. Even after Trint brought soldiers from his kingdom as well as the king of Heratt, who later sent forces, I could not focus. So much was happening, and all I could think was that you were gone and you might never come back."

Even though I had not chosen to leave, I still felt the guilt of all that occurred in my absence. All that I could have stopped. Bellamy's hands were not the only ones coated in blood.

"Then they sent us Luca. It was…horrific. None of the cuts were clean. It looked like they used a rusted and dull knife. Ranbir said that his limbs were cut off while he was still alive. That was not the only torture they committed upon him either; he was in horrible shape. I just—I hate myself for it. He was barely in his eighth decade. He was kind and brave and strong and so funny. Luca was my brother in every way that mattered, and he died because I sent him to Betovere."

I shook my head, moving to cradle his face in my hands. He did not cry, but I could sense the excruciating agony within him.

"No, Bellamy. You cannot put that on yourself. There was nothing Luca would not have done for his home. He loved Eoforhild.

And he loved you, just as much as you love him. Do not taint his memory by tying it to this self-loathing." My voice was soft, our noses still pressed together. I knew how deeply the hatred of oneself could consume a being, and I would be damned if I let that happen to Bellamy again.

"You do not understand. I would do it all again, Ash. If it meant preventing your abduction. If it kept Luca safe. If it brought Winona and Pino back. I would do so, so much worse. To my core, I am evil and vile, and I will not change. Ever."

I jerked back, looking at him with baffled surprise.

Bellamy, the one who saved and loved and taught so many—who was prepared to rule over creatures who despised him for what he was—evil? What unjust world would ever call him evil when he was poised to save it?

Would he do the hard things, the ones that made others deem him a monster but ultimately protected us all? Yes. Did he wish he could walk away from it all without looking back? Of course. But, no matter what, he would do the right thing, in whatever way he thought that was.

Even if he did not believe that he would.

Squeezing him slightly, I forced his head to tilt up, making sure he was looking into my eyes as I spoke.

"Sometimes saving the world requires the villain, not the hero. But being the villain does not mean you are evil, it just means someone else is telling the story."

***

We stayed in bed for the remainder of the day, my stress skyrocketing as I pictured all we could get done. But Bellamy was unwavering in his request that we remain in the room. Wrath joined us eventually, complaining that I did not kill The Elemental when I had the chance.

Bellamy and I stole sweet kisses but did not come together again, even after Wrath left at nightfall—calling us disgusting beasts as he did.

It was a clear night, the sky full of so many stars that I wondered if perhaps Stella was there and smiling down at us. Or maybe nightfall was a brief glimpse of Eternity, afforded to all who cared to look. A sign that the darkness was not something to be feared because everything shined brighter within it.

Sometimes, on my optimistic days, I pictured Eternity crafting Bellamy and I, making us specifically for the other. As wishful as that thinking was, I still smiled at the thought.

"One day, we will find a way to free ourselves from this mess," Bellamy said, pulling me from my thoughts. I looked up at him, confusion pinching my brow. His eyes were already on me, the serious expression he wore making me suddenly far more alert than I had been.

"What do you mean?" Free us from what?

"There will come a day when we are free, Asher. To live, to learn, to love. We will see the world slowly, stopping to smell flowers and eat pastries and drink mead. The two of us will survive on the taste of each other and the fuel of adventure. I am going to give you everything you never let yourself dream of." Nothing could compare to the doting surety in his voice, the absolute refusal of any other outcome. Despite the unrealistic nature of those promises, I loved to simply listen to him speak of such futures.

"Queens do not abandon their realm to travel. We will not have the luxury." Even if we ended up side by side on the thrones, we still would have duties that forced our hand.

"A queen can do whatever she wants," he argued, waving a hand nonchalantly. "I think I'll take you through Betovere first. We can make it a celebration, a chance to officially meet their new queen—if you choose to rule over them, that is."

"Why would I not?" I questioned, my tone embarrassingly defensive.

"Well, you do not have to, Ash. There are others qualified. You can even pick. The rules after war are murky, especially when you will be changing so much already. We could rule in Eoforhild or not at all. I would live in a hole if you told me to."

My head fell back as my laughter split the air. He took the opportunity to bring his lips to my throat, peppering kisses from the base where my collarbones met and up.

"I will keep that in mind when you infuriate me in the future." My voice was breathy, heart beating like a hummingbird. Oh, he knew exactly what he was doing.

"As long as there is a future where we are together, then I am more than happy," he whispered, breath hitting my ear just as his fingers dipped between my legs.

"We should get up. There is a lot to do." My muttered excuse was pathetic at best, seeing as there was nothing we could do in the middle of the night. Still, I felt the need to stop before he talked me into something I normally would not agree to, especially as his mouth began to drop lower.

"Tomorrow, we can spend the day saying hello to our family and introducing you to everyone. You have a horribly depressing whisp with a penchant for saying inappropriate things to reintroduce yourself to. Plus, there are a lot of mortals eager to meet a goddess." He continued leisurely touching me, his tongue darting out to lick a small line down my stomach before biting down near my belly button. I moaned as his free hand began to palm my breast, pointer finger and thumb momentarily pinching my peaked nipple.

"I will give you one day. Then I leave." Biting down on my lip, I stifled a groan at the feel of lips on my hip. "Without Maliha, we will need every mortal kingdom on our side." Two digits slipped inside of me, slightly punishing in the speed and pressure.

"Fine. One day of joy before I have to get pissed off by a bunch of mortals," he growled. And then his tongue swiped a line up my core, causing my hips to buck up as his fingers continued to dip inside of me.

"You are not coming." He laughed against me at my word choice, but all I could do was resist the urge to cry out as he sucked my clit into his mouth. "You—you have things to do. Important things. You are needed here."

My eyes darted down and locked on his as he shook his head, face still firmly planted between my legs. We both knew I was losing, but only one of us took advantage. A third finger entered me, curving upward as his mouth consumed me. This time, I did cry out, his name leaving my lips like a prayer. Without another word, my hands went to his hair, tugging and guiding as he brought me to the brink of tears from the pleasure.

"Come, Asher. Come for me *now.*" And I did, proving that the only place where I knew how to follow instructions was the bedroom.

He swallowed the latter half of my screams, getting to me so fast that his lips were still dripping from my satisfaction. When his tongue wrapped around mine, I knew I lost. I would give him anything, and he knew it.

For my pride, I tried one final time, my words coming out as pants between gasping breaths. "You are staying here."

He pulled away, smiling down at me with those maddeningly perfect dimples. "Where you go, I go."

Before I could answer, his length filled me, the delicious pressure enough to make even me agreeable.

In one night, Bellamy reminded me of all the ways I needed him.

***

The next morning, I woke to an empty bed. I groaned, sitting up and searching the room. It was quaint, the natural rock of the mountain being met with wood to craft a livable space. A large tapestry hung on the back wall, depicting what looked like The Royal City—the towering castle upon the hill surrounded by small cottages wrapped in vines and lilies of the valley sprouting from the grass. A wave crashed into the cliffside, water splashing against the Ayad castle. The art did not look like anything I had seen of Bellamy's, somehow making it less alluring despite the lovely imagery. Small wooden tables sat on each side of the bed, which had a thick red quilt. A petite wardrobe was placed on the opposite wall from a desk that resided below the window.

Bellamy's scent of smoke and cinnamon filled the room, wrapping me in the smell of home.

I moved to get out of bed, stretching as my toes touched the floor. Then the door swung open, revealing the prince himself. His hands held wooden trays, food and beverages stacked on top. Around his hips were a pair of black cotton trousers, which hung so low they showed the V of muscle pointing downwards as well as the dusting of black hair starting at his navel and trailing south. Nothing covered his torso, the ripples of muscle looking even larger than they had been in Shah's castle. He was like a living sculpture. Even the black lines—which currently ran from his elbows to his chest and stopped at his hips—only heightened his beauty.

Hair wild and cheeks flushed, he walked forward, shutting the door with a bare foot. From his mouth hung a single flower, the muted red stem and vibrant green leaves perfectly highlighting the lively red petals. I gasped as he got closer, thinking of the first time I ever saw one.

"How did you get a Salvia Splenden? You said they only grew in Haven."

His hands deftly placed the trays at the end of the bed, not a single drop of tea or food spilling. Then, almost hesitantly, he grabbed the flower from his mouth, snapped the stem, and tucked the flower behind my ear.

Cheeks blazing, I smiled up at him, reaching to touch the flower. It was as soft as I remembered, the delicate petals smelling of fresh fruit and mint. Bellamy's face was open and full of joy, his eyes sparkling with love. I could sense the way it pulled me in, that unfaltering loyalty and commitment to me, just as clearly as I could sense the thousands of other residents within the mountain base. Even with their thoughts and feelings pressing against my mental gates, my focus did not waver from the male before me.

"You liked them; I could tell. And so did I. They were special to me. So, the last time I met with Calista, I took some. Lara has taken good care of them. Though I have twice caught her trying to convince them that they might be better off dead." His laugh was enchanting, the deep sound singing to my soul. But his words...they were a reminder of my many wrongs.

"I am so sorry for how I treated you back then. I cannot begin to explain how hard it was to live within my own head. Fighting against two hundred years of lies and manipulation, it was taxing. And I think a part of me thought that if I admitted that you were not the enemy, then it would mean I was." He watched me as I spoke, his eyes downturned and his lips pursed. "You deserved better. You still do."

His lips were on me in an instant, a claiming kiss that only broke for him to repeatedly mutter the same word. "No."

Somehow, I forgot how perfect it was to exist beside him. And now, I wondered if I would ever be able to split from him again. He sat on the edge of the bed, our lips parting. He rubbed our noses together then placed a kiss to my forehead before bending down to grab my feet. I smiled as he adjusted them on his lap, fingers massaging as he spoke.

"The trainees are excited to meet you. I have planned a few sparring sessions where they will get to experience firsthand what you can do. I want you to give it your all, magic included. Every single one of them should be covered in their own piss by the end of the day."

This time, it was my turn to chuckle. Pulling my feet away from him and moving onto my knees, I leaned forward and flicked his nose, promptly stretching over him to grab a cinnamon roll. When he smacked my backside, I let out a loud snort and nearly choked on my bite. As payback, I took the pastry and shoved it into his face, watching with more desire than amusement as he took the whole thing and my finger into his mouth. I felt his tongue circle my pointer finger before releasing it with an audible pop, my jaw slack as he chewed with a smirk on his face and a mischievous glint in his blue eyes.

Shaking my head, I snatched another from the tray, this time quickly returning to my spot near the pillows. We ate mostly in comfortable silence, only small conversations sparking here and there. The chai smelled divine, and I knew the second it hit my tongue that Ranbir had made it. Though I knew he forgave me, it was still hard to finish without thoughts of Winona—of all lost since then—swirling through my mind.

Once we finished, Bellamy took the trays and placed them on one of the tables then swiftly got up and went to his wardrobe. Black leather caught my eye, the stitching detailed enough that, even from a distance, I could see the demon sigil on it. After collecting everything he needed, the prince walked over to me, offering me his hand.

I took it, knowing exactly what he planned. Though I was aware, I still felt butterflies take flight in my stomach as he slowly slipped the top over my head, his fingers and lips meeting my skin here and there.

Before putting on my undergarments and trousers, he grabbed one of my legs and lifted it over his shoulder, mouth diving between my thighs. I jerked against his tongue, my fingers threading through his hair both for stability and as an anchor to life itself. His free hand grabbed my backside, squeezing hard and shoving me further into his face. I could not stop my head from falling back, a whimper leaving my lips as he feasted upon me.

"Gods, Ash. You taste so good," he rasped, a moan following his words. I returned the sentiment, whimpering and grinding against his face in ecstasy. "Yes, Princess, fuck my face. You are doing so good."

If his tongue had not left me teetering on the edge of oblivion, then his voice would have. I chased that high, one of my hands palming my leather-clad breast and the other holding onto Bellamy's hair for dear life.

"Now, come in my mouth. Do it for me."

With his name on my lips and his head between my legs, I did as I was told.

And then, because I enjoyed the high of control just as much as the plunge of release, I took my turn on my knees before him.

***

A short time later, after we cleaned up and he finished dressing me, it was his turn. I shamelessly watched him pull the leather on, a smug smirk on his face the entire time. Every inch of it clung to him, hiding nothing of his shape and…assets. My feet took me forward of their own accord, just as my hands mindlessly explored his body. I was only given one lingering kiss, and then he was behind me, rubbing soothing circles into my scalp and braiding my hair back.

The prince was like gravity pulling me out of space. Past the stars made up of heartbreak and despair, out of the suffocating darkness made of fury and hopelessness, and to him—my beacon of light. For the first time, I felt like maybe I was close to deserving that unconditional love.

When he finished, he went back to his wardrobe, sifting through a drawer until he found what he was looking for. He came back with a stick of kohl and an intricate set of straps. I smiled at both, knowing exactly what I was about to be practicing. But Bellamy decided to apply the kohl below my eyes first, trapping his bottom lip between his teeth as he worked—teasing me without even realizing.

"Why do you do these things for me?" I could not help but ask, so unaccustomed to the type of love that came without conditions and orders. Over time, I came to the realization that I might not ever get used to it.

"Other than getting to touch you?" he asked, winking down at me. I rolled my eyes, earning a series of chastising tsks before he continued. "It soothes me. I enjoy being the one to take care of you, and I feel like this is the only way I can do so."

"I like doing things on my own. I never got to make choices before." It was a defensive response, one that was not necessary when I knew in my heart that he did not wish for me to be different.

A sparkle of amusement lit his eyes, melting the frozen depths that always stood in stark contrast to his fiery soul and the sunshine of his mind. "Being autonomous does not require being alone, and accepting help does not equal weakness."

I had no chance to disagree before he leaned down and placed a gentle kiss to my lips, the soft pressure a thing of beauty—of perfection. He bent down once more, strapping on the throwing daggers Henry had let me borrow. When he was done, he took a step back, looking me over.

"Do I look okay?"

"You look like a warrior." He flashed a dimpled smile, offering me the stick of kohl when I held my hand out and sitting on the bed so I could properly reach. I was far worse at applying it than he was, but I had gotten enough practice over the last few months that I could manage a decent line below his lower eyelashes. Luckily for me, it did not take much for Bellamy to look like a warrior.

***

The training yard was hectic at best.

Mortals and demons were scattered about, their numbers mixed as they ran or practiced stances or sparred. Stone and grass made up the ground before us, not a single piece of padding to be seen. The mountainous area was not as cold down here. In fact, it almost felt like summer, which was a relief after nearly a year straight of fall and winter.

Bellamy was smiling ear to ear, his hand on my lower back and his head held high. There was pride in his walk, in his aura. The minds around us stirred, voices shouting into my head as I slowly let my magic loose.

The fae princess. She should not be here.
A goddess in the flesh, in our presence!
An abomination!
Perhaps we can spar together.
Will she show her magic?
She will defeat the fae!
Kill her before it is too late.

Hands grabbed my waist from behind, lifting me up. I was flipped midair before my stomach hit a rock-hard shoulder. Air escaped my lungs, leaving me momentarily stunned and gasping for breath. Until the male spoke.

"Well, little brat, I think it is safe to say you took dramatic to a whole new level."

I laughed as Henry spun, my hands trying and failing to grip his leather top. His deep chuckles were a welcome sound, one I had grown pleasantly accustomed to and unknowingly missed. Slowly, he teasingly slid me down his body, setting me back on my feet with a smirk Bellamy's way. I rolled my eyes when the prince let out a low huff and lightly smacked Henry's freckled cheek, his beard now perfectly trimmed and his hair looking far better than when I had chopped it. I silently wondered who he had trusted to do that.

"I missed you, Ash."

"I missed you too, pumpkin. The only one who desired your presence more than me was Wrath. Tell me, have you had the chance to embrace him yet?" A chill ran through Henry, his eye twitching. I beamed up at him, so happy to be with them all again. I could feel the sadness within him though, and I knew how he hid it behind winks and jokes—the only emotion he was capable of somewhat masking. "How are you doing?"

His gaze roamed to Bellamy, who stood just slightly behind me—a fading smile on his face. They seemed to have a silent conversation, as if any of Henry's thoughts were hidden from me. Both nodded, and then Bellamy engulfed me in a warm embrace before kissing my forehead.

"I am going to go get the others. They have missed you." He left without another word, patting Henry on the shoulder as he passed him. The Sun placed an arm around me, walking us towards a weapons rack.

My arm instinctively slipped around his waist as we moved, my nerves skyrocketing as the silence stretched on.

"Henry?" I asked, unable to contain my curiosity or fester in the fear any longer. He sighed, arm tightening on me before he spoke.

"None of us are okay. We have lost a lot, and recovering will be a slow process. But you already know that. Having you back is a relief, at least. Some good news after two months of loss and horror. It helps that when you feel strong, we often do too. Your magic has this aura to it, like a presence that demands attention and obedience but also exudes hope and force."

"Oh, please. They do not want to follow me. I am a walking nightmare to some of them. I can hear it, Henry." As if saying so made the voices more desperate, I felt the thoughts barrel into my head, forcing me to pull my magic back in and lock those golden gates. Still, I felt them, rattling the lock and calling my name.

"Some resist you out of fear, but those who do not will grow stronger because of it—because of *you*. Trust me, we all physically felt your absence, not just emotionally."

We arrived at the rack, and Henry grabbed two swords. They were nearly identical. Silver blade, sky blue hilt, and the demon sigil carved into the metal in black and white. I shook my head when he tried to give it to me, stepping back.

"I have not stretched yet, and I have not practiced since the last time you and I sparred."

A smirk lit his face as he shoved the weapon towards me once more.

"My room is right next to Bell's, Asher. I am confident you have done enough stretching." With a wink, he tossed the sword the remaining few inches, forcing me to catch it or let the beautiful piece fall.

Instinctively, my hand reached out and snatched it from the air. I was still not nearly as skilled as the others, but I had my magic. Never did I rely on it, but I would be damned if I ever let myself think that I was wrong to use it again. I planted my feet and swung, but Henry was there, blocking it with his sword in one hand and a smile on his face.

"Someone sounds jealous. Tell me, has Genevieve not been around lately? She seemed a bit more agreeable when I saw her, perhaps someone else has fucked that uptight attitude out of her."

After that, the fight seemed to get the slightest bit more serious.

CHAPTER THIRTY-NINE

BELLAMY

If there was one thing I could always count on Asher to do, it was make a scene.

Nearly the entire training yard was watching her and Henry spar. Their taunting had died out, replaced by grunts of force and aggravation—sometimes even hisses of pain. I watched them on the sidelines, yelling out instructions to both as they went.

"Lift your elbow, Asher!"

"Hold your mental shield, Henry!"

Again and again, they blocked and swung. Asher was fighting smart, dodging as often as she could instead of attempting to block Henry's powerful swings. She was faster than before but still not as fast as him. When he feigned left and then swung towards her right side, I thought the fight would be done, but Asher was scrappy.

Just as his blade was about to connect with her side, he froze, his face scrunching in pain. Whatever she was doing to his head gave her enough time to slam her elbow into his face, knocking him down. Henry groaned but immediately got back up, light radiating from his hands. No part of Henry would even consider holding back, and he did not as he began throwing beams of light at her. She ducked past one, barely leaning away from another before a third and fourth found their mark in her arm and shoulder. Her leathers sizzled as they burned, but my beautiful creature did not miss a beat.

Cleary aggravated, Asher finally stopped going easy on Henry. I had always told her to never hold back, and now, she did not. She ran at him, snatching one of the daggers strapped to her stomach and attacking him with both it and her sword. Henry did not laugh or brag like he normally would. Instead, he was completely silent, his moves slowing. After another couple of minutes, he stopped blocking her entirely, his body tilting to one side and his eyes rolling to the back of his head. The Sun collapsed to the ground, his body slumping without a word. The crowd fell silent, the screams and cheers that once filled the yard gone now as Asher leisurely walked towards Henry. She got down on her knees, leaning forward until her lips were inches from his ear. His eyes opened in surprise, a desperate gasp leaving his mouth as his chest filled with air.

Offering him a smile and a hand, Asher helped him to his feet, Henry leaning onto her far more than he should. I jogged over to them, pulling his other arm over my shoulder. "What did you do to him?"

"I told him to stop breathing," she said with a shrug as she smiled from ear to ear. I laughed, leaning up to smack Henry in the cheek. His eyes opened all the way for a moment, then they were half closed again, his head lulling. "He will be fine after he gets some rest. Also, we need to switch rooms."

Shaking my head at her insanity, I guided us to a set of chairs and tables, taking most of his weight as we set him down. When he was leaning back and groaning about Asher sleeping with one eye open, I crossed my arms and faced her. Dusting off her hands, she blew me a kiss and went to Noe, who had been standing beside me while Asher sparred.

Watching them run to each other, their bodies colliding and laughter splitting the air, left me wondering just how long I would have of this. Of a family to come home to. One that filled my days with laughter and annoyance and love and hope.

My hand went into the pocket of my training leathers, fingers toying with the ring that rarely left my side. Noe grabbed onto Asher's cheeks, bringing their foreheads together and whispering something to her that left them both nodding and hugging once more.

We were still working on a way to get Nicola and Jasper, who we were quite convinced were both in The Capital and being heavily guarded. But perhaps if we had both of them here too, then maybe Ash would say yes. I could see it. Farai and Jasper on either side of her, walking her down the aisle. Nicola, Noe, and Lian dressed in matching outfits near the altar. Henry, Cyprus, Damon, and Ranbir behind me. I could paint portraits of Luca and Winona, something to make our family whole again. Wrath could hold the rings, though he would probably purposefully bury them in his own shit before letting me marry her.

Adbeel could officiate, and we would write our own vows. I would cover the throne room in sage green and give her a bouquet of Salvia Splendens. Atop her head would be Solei Ayad's crown, the obsidian sparkling under the Sun magic.

And we would be happy.

"She needs to get that arm fixed," Ranbir said as he walked up beside me. I had not seen him much since the day we found Luca's body. Grieving another friend after losing his wife had not been easy, made evident by the deep circles under his eyes. His hair was knotted atop his head, beard now a couple inches off his chin. He wore white, as he always did, the clothes seeming to grow larger on him every day.

Looking back at Ash, I saw that Farai and Lian had walked up to her, the former bringing her in for a hug. His body shook with sobs as he held her, his hands disappearing in her dark curls and his head burrowing into her neck. Everyone around them watched on unabashedly, eavesdropping like pesky flies.

"If you have time to stand, then you have time to train. Get back to work!" I shouted. Every single soldier immediately started rushing away from the small group, the clanking of metal and the pounding of feet once more filling the air. "Nosy little shits."

Ranbir laughed, a half-hearted version of what once was. Without a second thought, I put my arm around him and patted his shoulder, my five or so extra inches of height making me need to adjust to the stance as we walked. But Ranbir, for all his stoic nature, slumped slightly, as if a weight had been removed rather than added—as if he suddenly felt calmer.

"Somehow, I forgot how bright she shines, even when she does not know it." Ranbir's words were soft, but I heard the way he said them, the sound of hope there. "I believe Asher heard me blame her that day we lost Winona. I did not mean it, but my thoughts got away from me. I was angry and scared, and I felt like I was dying with Nona. I do not know how to tell her that I am sorry."

I stopped, tugging him to a standstill. Placing my hands on both of his shoulders, I stared the Healer in the eye, hoping he understood every word I was about to say.

"Do not *ever* apologize for how you face loss, Ranbir. I knew Winona for over a century, and I still believe with every fiber of my being that I will never mourn her the way you do. She was brilliant and funny and beautiful and caring. But, more than that, she was your soulmate. Asher knows that. She can *feel* it. You do not need to say sorry. Just be there for her on the days she wakes up and thinks herself a monster. Remind her not only that you love her but that Winona did too."

I pulled him in, embracing a male that I had considered a brother for so long. His own wedding had been a beautiful affair, held in our home in Haven. Our safe place. And now it was rotting away, a graveyard of both loved ones and memories. Would I ever be able to say enough to someone grieving such a loss?

You did good. I can feel it within him. He loves you. We all do. Believe in that.

My eyes darted to Asher, seeking out her face upon hearing her voice in my mind. She had her back facing me as she spoke to Lian, who was none the wiser that Asher was also a nosy little shit. Ranbir sighed, pulling away and nodding before gesturing for me to walk on. Side by side we approached the group just as Lian smacked Asher on the arm.

"You rode a dragon? Oh, I hate you. I will never forgive the gods for this." Curiosity piqued, I forced myself between Asher and Noe, causing the Moon to huff at me. Ranbir smiled at Asher, offering his hand. She took it, wincing as his power flowed through her. As always, he left the scars behind. Her skin had slowly become a tapestry of art made through pain—a map from where she started to where she was now.

"You said nothing about riding a dragon," I accused, shooting her a playful glare. Ranbir patted her hand, waving goodbye to everyone as he turned. A part of me wanted to stop him, but I knew how I felt when I did not know if Asher was alive. Knowing she was gone forever would crush me. He deserved the space to mourn, no matter how long it took.

Asher threaded her hand in mine, the other firmly locked in Farai's. There was a deep sense of relief on his face as he looked down at his best friend, the gratitude of seeing her alive beside him lifting his shoulders when they had hunched for so many weeks.

"Well, I was just explaining to everyone that I not only met the God of Death and Creation, a truly psychotic male by the way, but that I also got to meet and ride a dragon. Two actually. I am surprised you all believe me. It sounds ludicrous when I hear it spoken out loud."

"Seeing as a talking cat follows you around and you can literally kill people with your mind, I think you attract ludicrous things," Noe countered, giggling when Asher's face scrunched in thought.

Sounds of sparring grew louder, Damon's shouted instructions echoing off the mountainsides. Lian groaned, waving bye to us without saying a word. I turned to see her approaching a group of mortals from Heratt, only one of them accomplishing the set of stances that Damon was ordering them to do.

"Well, that is our cue to get to work. Noe, I need you with the mortals from Gandry. Farai, go ahead and take over for Cyprus. He is with the soldiers from Behman." They both nodded, each placing a kiss on Asher's cheek before they left. She watched Farai with a contemplative gaze, her hand tightening in mine.

"You did not find Jasper." Her whispered comment was expected, but not easy. There was a blankness to her tone that made me fear for whatever was running through her mind. As strong as she was, no one could withstand the blame of every horrible thing in the world, not even her.

"We will. Plans are being set in place to retrieve both Jasper and Nicola. Farai was under the impression that Nicola would be able to find both you and Jasper—though you seemed to have found us first. Still, we will get them here safely, Asher." Each word was slightly less sure, almost strained. Lying to her was like swallowing acid, especially when I still felt Luca's cold skin, Pino's ripped clothes, and Winona's bloody hair. I feared telling Asher that her friends would be safe when I knew how easily friends were lost forever.

"They would all be safe if I had stayed home," she muttered, an indignant tone to her voice. Every time I saw her, Asher seemed to grow angrier, like she was collecting her broken pieces and slowly burying every soft and vulnerable one beneath them. But without all of those shards of herself, she would never be whole again. I wish she understood that.

"Asher," I said, turning to place both of my hands on her cheeks and forcing her to look at me. She sighed before letting those beautiful gray eyes land on mine. "I am proud and thankful, just as so many others are. You have already changed the tide of this war. You might blame yourself, but I was the one who took you, not the other way around. Selfishly, I wanted you. Because the mere sight of you makes my heart stop."

"Apparently, I make many hearts stop." It was a mumbled sentence, her eyes darting in the direction Ranbir had left.

I wanted to shake her, to explain how important she was, to remind her that she was the savior in this tale. "I see you, all of you, and I am not afraid. You are my magnificent storm of a creature, and no matter what, it has always been you." It was all I could think to say, and I hated that it was not more.

"You mean since Pino showed you our future, which you refuse to tell me anything about," she corrected, a small smile lifting her lips. I returned hers tenfold, mine lifting my cheeks and making my chest ache. Gods, she was everything.

"A part of me thought I would never deserve to be loved, but I think, even then, I knew my equal was out there—that *you* were out there. You are the beginning and the end and every moment in between, Princess. You are mine." My lips met hers, likely drawing the attention of those training. But I did not care. Let them see. Let them talk. Soon, Asher would be on that obsidian throne and they would bow. We all would.

"Equal is pushing it, but I love your ambition," she murmured against my lips.

I chuckled, pulling away slightly. Her face was flushed, those full lips swollen from the hours spent against mine. I had done exceptionally well braiding her hair, which was another thing I had Winona to thank for. Realizing Asher would be mine one day had been overwhelming at first, but when I finally saw her, I knew that I had a lot to learn. Hair alone took months to perfect.

Shrugging, I leaned down until my lips were nearly touching her ear. "You are right. I could kick your ass in a fight."

"Oh, please!" she shouted, pushing against my chest.

I stumbled back, unsure of when she had gotten quite so strong. At least I knew that Henry had been telling the truth about maintaining her daily training schedule.

"How about we get into the sparring circle and see?" Reaching forward, I quickly flicked her nose, earning a soft huff of wonderful annoyance.

"Fine." Tossing her braid over her shoulder, Asher strutted over to the nearest free ring. I followed, my eyes honed in on her swaying hips and a smirk lifting my left cheek.

Though she put up a valiant fight, I did, in fact, kick Asher's ass.

***

"You guys are more than capable of being without me for a month, and you act as if I cannot simply portal to you in a moment's notice." Damon scoffed at my words, sitting back against his seat. To my left, taking the head of the table, was Asher. She was studying the new model of Alemthian with an innocent and desperate sense of wonder. The war council members did not see it as endearing like I did. Every move she made was calculated in their eyes. They thought me a fool in love, bewitched. I could practically feel it.

Killing Finnick had been a mistake, I understood that. Not only from the numerous times Adbeel scolded me on the fact, but also because it made me seem unstable and obsessed—which I was, but the truth did not always set one free.

I could not bring myself to regret it though, especially earlier when Asher had come up behind me as I was painting. Her arms had wrapped around my neck, hands draped lazily down my chest. In my ear, she had whispered filthy things about the last time she had watched me paint, and all I could do was picture a future in which we always had that peace. A future Finnick would have stolen if given the chance.

"You are our crown prince and our general who has already taken weeks off. Gallivanting around the Mortal Realm with your stolen whore is not among your chief responsibilities!" Elrial was not one to mince his words, even if said female was currently staring at him like she wanted to roast him on a spit. Gods damn me, I wanted her to. She was smart when it came to politics, though, and more than capable of handling herself. Having as much confidence in her as I did was soothing, and I found myself placing my hands behind my head and leaning back, preparing for the show.

"Well, as the residential whore to your oh-so-glorious general, I would like to point out that there is something to be said for how incredibly moronic you must be to need a babysitter a quarter of your age. Truly, are you so incapable that you wish for your prince to lose the chance at crafting an alliance simply so you do not have to—what—breathe without him present?"

Marjorie snorted from Elrial's side, her head nodding in approval. She looked to Rakon beside her, who was drawing on a piece of paper. My newest captain was always quick to lose focus, and I watched as Vala nudged him to attention. Lian was to my right, Damon between her and Henry. My other four captains—Ilslad, Jerrinte, Quinn, and Kyrie—were all present, too. As were Nrista and Onyx, the other half of the remaining war council members. It was a large group, but still, silence hung heavy in the air, the unspoken words swinging before us like a noose.

It was Nrista who spoke first, my war council members determined to all suffer a slow and painful death. "You do not belong here, Princess Asher."

I would bet a hundred gold pieces that inside her head right now, Asher was calling Nrista unoriginal. Full pink lips tilted into a vicious smile, Asher's posture going impossibly straighter. It reminded me of the time Henry had told her she sat like she had a stick up her ass. He had not been wrong, but perhaps that was just my dirty mind at work.

"I see inside that head of yours, you know. So many secrets. They fester like sores and burn like flames. Would you like to get some of them off your chest, Nrista? I can always make you if you would like me to prove my magic worthy of your acknowledgement." The Sun's mouth opened, jaw slack and dark eyes wide. She seemed to sink back into her chair, as if she could hide from whatever threats Asher was doling out.

"Luckily for you, I do not care to do that. But please, for a moment, look inside of yourself. Peer into that shriveled abyss that you call a soul. Now, tell me, if I do not belong here, then why do you?"

Gasps of surprise and horror mingled, every set of eyes bouncing between the two females. Asher wiped her hands on her lavender skirts, a move that looked nonchalant to the others, but I knew to be a sign of her nerves. Still, her face was stoic, perhaps even a bit smug. My chuckle could not be stifled, Henry falling into a fit of laughter not long after. Soon, Lian was forcing herself to remain calm. All the while, Asher stared at Nrista, waiting for the female to concede.

"You have made your point. I think we all are very aware of what you can do and your importance in the coming war—as well as your position when the war is over." Immediately after the words left Marjorie's lips, I knew I was in for a long discussion with Asher. Seconds later, I was proven right when I felt her prodding at my mental shields, as if she were throwing water at the black flames. "Take your month, secure our allies, then come home. It is time we follow through with our plan for The Capital."

At that, Asher began pounding on that wall of fire, trying to dismantle it with brute force. Her magic stung, causing me to wince at the pressure, but she did not let up. If anything, she barreled into my mind harder, like a battering ram against a stone wall.

"Excellent. We leave for Xalie in the morning. You all will have written instructions before then, and no move is to be made against Betovere until I return." Like the coward I was, I stood and nearly bolted from the war room. Asher's chair scraped against the floor just as I made it past the door, and I almost considered portaling away from her.

"If you do it, I will go to Xalie without you. Do not test me," she seethed. I willed my feet to move faster, trying to weigh the pros and cons.

"You would have no way there!" My shouted response was immediately followed by a groan of frustration as Asher began jogging towards me, the sound of her slippers smacking against the stone floors making my heart race. Gods, she was scary when she wanted to be.

"Noe or Henry would take me! Maybe even Damon; he seems nice." Her tone was smug as she halted her steps, Henry's laughter splitting the air. I stopped, turning on my heels to face her.

Her long brown curls were loose now, small clips gifted by each of my Trusted holding them in place. They had gotten them made for her months ago for when she was ready to choose her birthday, but gave them to her this afternoon after losing her for so long. Each was silver and dotted with sapphires. Noe's was shaped like a crescent moon. Henry's was a sparkling sun. Lian's was a swirl of wind. Ranbir's was a leaf. Cyprus's was a puff of smoke. Luca's was a skull—to Asher's sorrow-filled amusement. And last was Winona's, which was shaped like a large paw. She had forced back tears as I placed them in her hair, lining them up to form a sort of crown on her head.

"You would not dare," I growled through clenched teeth. It nearly sounded like a threat, but Asher did not flinch, her smile not so much as twitching.

"Try me, Elemental."

Her arms crossed over one another, Henry chuckling from where he stood a few feet away. My hands threaded through my hair, tugging on the dark waves as I contemplated how I would tell her these plans without ruining everything.

"Fine. We can talk in our room." I held out my hand, eager to get away from the public eye. No one was there yet, but it would not stay that way. She looked back to Henry, waving before closing the distance and placing her hand in mine. We portaled straight into our room, where she promptly tucked her foot between my ankles and then wrapped her leg around my calf, pushing me off balance and throwing me to the ground.

"What do they mean by your plan for The Capital?" she hissed, her fists gripping my black tunic. I felt my cock twitch, and I had to calm myself for a moment before speaking, or else I would probably stab her with it by accident.

"They killed Luca, Asher. We cannot let it go unpunished—I cannot. He was like a little brother to me"—my voice cracked on the words, on the memory of Luca's body—"Xavier and Mia Mounbetton will pay for what they have done."

"So the innocents on the island must suffer because of their rulers?" Light as a feather, she spoke, the words falling like paper in the wind. When they settled on my heart, they were suddenly as heavy as a rock.

"We have time to plan. They are mobilizing and expect an immediate attack. We will not play into their trap. Getting all who are innocent out in time is a possibility, but the war will happen, Asher. There is no longer a way to avoid it. I would rather it be on their shores than ours."

"Theirs. Ours. That way of thinking will bury us all in a grave. Pack up; we leave tonight. I need to find Wrath. He told me earlier that he had heard of a creature roaming Xalie the last time he was there. Seems like we need all the help we can get."

With that, Asher made to stand, but paused above me on her knees. Sighing, she leaned down and kissed me. On instinct, my hand went to her neck, pulling her deeper into me. The second my tongue slid across her bottom lip, the taste of mint and the smell of vanilla encompassing me, she pulled away.

"I am so sorry for all you have lost. I would change it if I could, Bellamy. Please believe that. Yet I fail to see how killing innocent fae will bring back those lost or do anything other than tie their memory to destruction. You dedicated so much of your life to saving fae in need. Do not let that go to waste."

And then she really did leave, the sound of her fading steps matching the slow pounding of my heartbeat in my ears.

CHAPTER FORTY

ASHER

Two weeks. That was how long King Samell and Queen Prie had requested we wait to meet with them. It was a fortnight of what felt like wasted time looking for a creature we would not find and coming up with a plan for a kingdom that was notorious for their neutrality. But I could not bring myself to do anything other than press on.

Bellamy had promised to find a way to save the innocent fae in The Capital, and together, we did. The plan was not foolproof, but it was something. I would go and order everyone to leave, seeping my magic across the land and into their minds. If I could guide them slowly to a line of demons, we could portal them to safety. Not all demons had strong enough magic to do so, which meant it was a risk, but one that we would take.

It left me practicing often. For the first time in my life, I consciously existed daily with my mental gates open. At first, it was overwhelming, having my magic pull in so many thoughts and feelings and conversations. There were times when Wrath would speak to me and I would not even hear him, or others when I thought Bellamy said something, but it was really just the thoughts of someone nearby.

While I practiced, Bellamy read, diving into any and all texts we could find in Razc, the capital of Xalie. Every once in a while, he would mumble under his breath about the smell of books and the way his eyes hurt after too long, the quiet rants always bringing a smile to my face.

On the night before we were supposed to meet with Samell and Prie, Bellamy and I were sitting atop the bed, looking through historical records that dated back the last three hundred years or so, slowly fizzling out after that. Like the fae, the mortal history was lost beyond that. But even without the text, Bellamy knew of Xalie. Every king and queen passed on one important trait to their heir: rule with a neutral heart and a quick mind.

It left us with little to do other than offer everything we had. In terms of trade, Xalie was an ideal ally for Eoforhild. The former was rich in fish, with rivers running all through the kingdom. The latter could afford to trade for said fish, which would highly benefit Xalie—who had very little in terms of wealth. It was a pretty poor excuse for an alliance, which would not do much to benefit us when they had abolished their military centuries ago.

Henry had hated the mere idea of it, which was why we had not prioritized Xalie. Bellamy, on the other hand, understood my reasoning. He saw Xalie for what it was: a means to an end. If we had them, then four of the six kingdoms would have chosen to side with Eoforhild. Any chance to convince King Lazarev and Queen Nyla—the rulers of Yrassa—would be contingent on having that majority on our side. Yrassa was the top producer of salt and wine in all of Alemthian, and they also had a decent size military. The issue stemmed from their friendship with Maliha.

The two neighboring kingdoms had long been close allies. King Lawrence and Queen Paula had sent no word in the last two weeks, their silence both unsettling and relieving. In my heart, I knew that I would have a hard time taking back my word when marrying Sterling could save the world from war. Bellamy, though, would sooner see the world burn than watch me marry someone else.

Perhaps if Sterling had made me happy, then Bellamy would let me go, but now that he knew it was him I wanted...well, I was relatively sure he would never stand aside and let anyone have me.

It was that possessive love that had him watching me in my sleep, terrified that I might be taken away from him. On more than one occasion, I awoke to his eyes on me, staring as if a single blink could be the difference between me being there and then gone.

And he was right.

As my eyes grew heavy, my head lulling against Bellamy's shoulder, I thought of Padon. Was he looking for me? Or had he given up? How could I end the problem of him if he could not die? I thought of the dragons, of the glass castle, of the books. When my eyes shut fully, my hand still firmly within Bellamy's, I felt the tug. A great pull that had my mind seemingly splitting in two.

"Asher!" Padon's shout was muffled, distant even. I tried to look around, but there was nothing other than the blackness that seemed to writhe around me. "Asher, I can feel it! Something is coming—please, Asher! Wake up! Get the prince and the dalistori and get out of there!"

I shot up, heaving for air. Bellamy was at my side, finally sleeping. Wrath was nowhere to be seen, likely bothering some poor mortal for food. The sun had fully set since I fell asleep, casting our room in darkness. And though I often felt the need to do the opposite of what Padon said, there was something about his warning that made the hairs on the back of my neck stand straight. Or perhaps it was the way the darkness before me also appeared to move and sway.

Turning towards Bellamy, I pulled down the neck of his shirt, checking on the inky magic that painted his skin. It was relatively low, stopping at his shoulder blades. Nothing that would make me think it was his magic flowing into the room. My mind raced, trying to make sense of what Padon's warning meant.

With a sigh, I looked forward, coming face-to-face with a shadow-like image of myself. I screamed as it smiled—as *I* smiled. My arm was suddenly too heavy to lift, my dagger simply too far to reach. It laughed, head falling back. Everything slowly became too difficult to move, like my body was a weight that I could no longer hold. Shaking from the fear, all I could do was watch as the creature crawled towards me on the bed, a slow and jerky movement.

Bellamy did not stir, his breaths even and his body so still that it was like he could not hear or feel this at all. She approached me with that horrifying mockery of my smile, the gesture too wide and toothy.

"Asher, such a lovely name. Did you know we search for you? That he seeks you out?" Her voice was like shards of ice, splitting through my ears and into my mind. A shocking, gravelly voice that almost reminded me of Wrath's. I tried to speak, to fight, but nothing happened. I remained still, pathetic, useless.

I watched as she leaned forward, her arm nearly grazing mine when she reached over me to grab on to my dagger. A moment later, my blade kissed my arms, slowly gliding down the long scars that reminded me every day of what I was fighting for. The ones that were a visual representation of how broken I could become.

"Did death call to you? Or did you call to him?" she inquired, letting her icy finger run down the jagged flesh next. Why was she asking me if she so clearly knew I could not speak? I wanted to shout, to kick, to run, anything other than to sit here and feel her hands on me. "Sometimes, we must bleed to feel. Let me show you."

Horror and pain mingled within me as she swiped the blade horizontally across my arm, the slice crossing over the ones I had given myself. Red quickly began to coat the deep orange sheets, the cotton soaking up my blood. I felt the tear roll down my eye, but soon even my shaking stopped. When she leaned down and licked my arm, I thought I might vomit at the feel of her rough tongue on me. A hum that almost resembled a hiss emanated from her as she looked up at me, the lips she had stolen from me dripping my blood.

"Ah, I taste it in you. Would you like to taste mine?" My eyes widened as I watched her take the blade still covered in my blood and slice open her palm, thick black liquid spilling from her. It hit the bed with a loud sizzle, as if it were burning through the sheets and mattress. "Such a beautiful poison. Even a drop could kill, you know. But I am not here to kill you, sweet princess."

The dagger went flying towards the wall, the force of her throw so strong it only stopped when it reached the hilt. More tears spilled down my face as she drew closer. In the blacks of her eyes, I briefly caught sight of a small light, brighter than the sun, like the stars had found a way into her. With a blink, they were gone, and her face was mere inches from mine. Ever so softly, she placed a kiss to my lips, chuckling as my sobs could finally be heard.

"He waits for her promised doom, her Gift. And with my kiss, he shall find you. Until we meet again, tasty little princess."

Eyes rolling to the back of my head, I fell back in a heap, screaming as I landed in an all-encompassing blackness. A sea of emptiness, the darkness alive. I kicked and shouted for help, but nothing was there—no one would save me. Alone—I was alone.

Alone, alone, alone, alone.

"Ash! Asher, what is wrong? Asher, wake up!" Bellamy's voice brought me to the surface, my lungs burning as they filled with air. My eyes flew open, the light of early morning stinging as I tried to look around for the creature.

Bellamy was beside me, his face pinched and body tense, as if he did not know whether to be terrified or furious. It was Wrath, though, that caught my attention. He sat at the end of the bed, staring at me with those yellow eyes—so much understanding in them that all I could do was sit up on unsteady arms and ask.

"What was it?" Bellamy ripped his gaze from me, looking to Wrath. The dalistori appeared torn, as if the answer to my question was going to upset us somehow. Eventually, though, he answered in that haunting voice of his.

"A fetch. I can smell it on you, feel it on the bed. They are called dream walkers, and they serve…Death and Creation. Just as I do. We were all made by him, dark creatures that should not exist but do. Perhaps that is why I feel drawn to you. Maybe he has made it so." Contemplation surrounded Wrath like a cloud, raining down thoughts of Padon and me and fate. Pushing away the now-clean orange sheets, I brought my knees to my chest, my skin slick from the thin layer of sweat.

Bellamy did not move. Instead, he watched as I traced the scar on my left arm, which now bore no sign of an actual cut. If Wrath had not confirmed that I was indeed visited by the fetch, then I would have thought myself mad. Especially when the god that supposedly gave the orders had also warned me vehemently.

"Why would he warn me if he sent her?" My curious thoughts were spoken aloud with little care for the males beside me, a streak of aubergine hair flashing through my memories.

"He came to you last night before the creature?" Bellamy was moving, his hands coming to stroke my face, my shoulders, my arms, my hair, like he needed to feel every part of me to be sure I was not fading into the ethers.

"Not exactly. I heard his voice, like a faraway call. He was shouting at me, telling me to run away because he could feel it coming. I think he meant the fetch, but I do not see why he would act that way if it was him who sent it." My jaw ached with the strain of talking through the onslaught of disorder within my mind.

I tried and failed to work it out, to breathe through the disorientation of it all and find the answers that evaded me. Xavier had always done that, searched for clarity in himself first. For every piece of me that hated them, that rebelled against the two hundred years of teachings, another latched onto it. Like two halves of a different puzzle, my old self and my new self no longer fit, no matter how hard I tried to put them together.

"Wrath, how do we protect her dreams? What can we do to make sure none of them get their hands on her again?" Bellamy stood, pacing across the floor as he muttered to himself. Wrath watched, his tail swinging and body slowly shrinking.

"We do not. My god wants her, and he will come. All we can do is fight against him."

No. No more war and battle. We would not make another enemy, not find another reason to kill and plot. There were enough pieces on the board, adding more would not be acceptable. So, I did what I had been taught. I pushed all the difficult feelings down, down, down, hiding them away and promising myself I would do anything other than let myself fall apart again.

"Let him try to take me. I will not be forced anywhere ever again. Padon and his minions—sorry, Wrathy, not you—are of little importance. I am learning, and I will adapt to this. We need to focus on the task at hand, which is Xalie." With that, I threw myself off the bed, passing by a still-pacing Bellamy and grabbing the gown that I had hung on one of only two hooks.

Slipping it on, I thought of what on Alemthian we would say to the king and queen. It was not like Gandry or Behman or even Maliha. All I could offer other than trade was peace after war, death as payment for life. It was not a promising proposal.

My skin tingled where I had been cut, but as I slid my arm into the sleeve, I still noted no scar or mark. Like it had never happened. Yanking the sleeve onto my shoulder, I closed my eyes, told myself to move forward, and then walked to the mirror to inspect myself.

It was simple in comparison to what I was normally dressed in, the same deep orange as the color of the Xalie sigil. The sleeves were large and flowy down to the wrist where a ribbon cinched them tight. The

OF REALMS AND CHAOS

square neckline ended just below my collar bones, the hem of the dress tickling my ankles.

In the mirror, I noticed my dagger, still lodged into the wall. Above it, in dripping black liquid, a message was written.

A pretty name for a pretty Gift.

Whipping my head around, I found the wall bare with not a mark to be seen. I searched the room, catching sight of the dagger where it still lay atop the bedside table. Bellamy's pacing stopped, his gaze locking on me.

"Ash? What is it?" All I could do was answer with a shake of my head, turning back to the mirror. I breathed deeply, looking at my face, which was—thankfully—far less terrified than my inner turmoil warranted. In fact, I looked almost...pleased.

And then my reflection smiled back at me, jumping out of the mirror with a bone-chilling hiss. I screamed, rearing back, trying to escape its grasp. Wrath was there, his jaw growing as he latched onto the fetch's neck. She screamed in agony, writhing in his clutch as he bit down.

Bellamy grabbed onto me, forcing his body in front of mine. But she looked at me as if she could see through him, her smile—my smile— once more eerily large. With a wink, she disappeared, leaving the three of us gasping for air and frantically looking around the small room. Wrath was practically vibrating with rage, his beautiful gray fur coated in the black blood.

"Wrath, she said her blood is poison!" I shouted, trying to run to him. Bellamy did not let go of me, his arms wrapping so tightly around my waist that I felt suffocated by the security of it. "Let me go! We need to clean him! It will kill him!"

"Calm down, Strange One," Wrath ordered. "All beings crafted by our god are the same. What comes from her cannot poison me, as it is mine. Though hers seems exceptionally foul."

Bellamy released me, his large hands moving to grip my biceps as he turned me and held my head against his chest. Pressing his lips to my hair, he attempted to soothe me with his lulling voice. "It is okay. She had to be lying. That blood looked just like the afriktor's, and it did not hurt us in the forest."

"Well, the creatures within the forest are diluted versions of what was. When the fallen goddess locked them away, she ensured they would not only remain within those wards, but that their magic—their very essence that tied them to her once lover—was weakened. I myself escaped her only narrowly." Wrath was nonchalant with his words as he flicked his grime-soaked paw, a hiss following after it splashed onto his mouth.

"Wait, what do you mean that—" Bellamy had little time to speak before he was cut off by the dalistori.

"We will talk of histories forgotten another time. Go to the mortal rulers." With that, he shrunk back down to his normal size, padding his way to the bathing room. He stopped at the door, looking over at us. "Be safe and do not let her out of your sight, *princeling.*"

With a curt nod, Bellamy quickly turned me around, tying the ribbons at my back before placing a hasty kiss on my shoulder and moving to get himself ready. I watched silently, trying to calm myself enough to resume the confident air I had exuded minutes ago.

It was never going to stop. There would be no end to this madness. Even if we won this ridiculous and disgusting war, Padon would still be there, waiting for his next chance. Maybe he warned me to try to trick me into believing he wanted me safe. Or maybe he had unknowingly sent the thing. Either way, I would need to solve this problem too.

Apparently, I not only carried the world but the fucking universe as well.

"Okay, we need to go, Princess." Like a balm on a wound, Bellamy's voice tamed my tragic thoughts, offering the smallest semblance of refuge. He could help me hold the weight of it all. I had to trust that. Together, we could do this.

And maybe, just maybe, we would both live to see the world after.

I nodded, walking into his outstretched arms. His embrace was everything it had always been, warm and sunny, a sort of homecoming. When we portaled away, it did not hurt because, in his arms, I could weather anything.

I breathed him in once more, trying to memorize the smell of cinnamon and smoke that always clung to him—like a crisp autumn day beside a fire. He stiffened, as if what I had done appalled him in some way. Leaning my head back, I assessed his face, following his gaze until I caught sight of what had left him so angry.

From atop the hill, we had the perfect view of a line of guards in front of the castle walls beyond, all clad in the beige and orange of Xalie. I freed my magic, waves of it crashing into the unmoving shore of guards. Their thoughts flittered my way, like loose shells slowly being sucked out into the sea. Though I could not understand the words they said, I could make out the images clearly enough.

"They are waiting for us. Samell and Prie received a threat from Mia and Xavier. They no longer wish to see us." My voice was hollow, empty of all emotion. The guards did not feel me there, but they saw us, their thoughts ranging from terror to worship—some considering falling to their knees. A few felt as though their loyalty to the gods outweighed that of their obligations to their rulers, what was above coming before what was below.

Even those who prepared to kill us both, who thought me an abomination that needed to be eradicated, still felt the weight of what I could do, images of those thoughts bombarding me. Regardless, I knew I could make them let me in without lifting a finger. I could force the king and queen to pledge themselves to our cause. There was a part of me that wanted to because this defeat was too great. It meant we would likely lose any chance with Yrassa.

Still, I grabbed Bellamy's arm as he moved forward, a deep growl emanating from within his chest. He felt all I could not, and I wanted so badly to let him move onward, to watch as he solved this problem. But I could not, and neither could he. We both knew what it was to be forced into a fight, a *life*, that we did not ask for. We could not do the same.

Our eyes met, his pale skin flushed from the cold of winter. Snow fell lazily from above, intricate and tiny flakes of it decorating his dark waves. As always, his hair was disheveled, and I could not stop myself from reaching up to run my fingers through it. A contented hum filled the air as he closed his eyes and leaned his head into the touch.

Dread settled deep in my chest, and I combated it with memorizing the way his eyelashes brushed his lightly freckled cheeks. The dip and rise of his top lip. The cut of his strong jaw and the billowing of his familiar cloak in the wind. The way his open shirt showed the black veins below and hugged the muscles of his arms. His hands came to my cheek and neck, the cold sting of his rings further cooling my frozen skin, and I knew I would always remember that, too.

With a nod, he pulled me into him and portaled us back to our room at the inn. Wrath looked up at us from his spot on the bed, where his damp fur soaked the thick quilt. Bellamy shook his head at the dalistori before he could speak. Then he tugged me towards the bathing room, and I watched him summon water from nothing, the liquid already steaming as it poured from the skin of his palms. From his shadows appeared a glass vile, the dark liquid casting the scent of vanilla into the air as he poured it out.

As always, he came to me, untying the gown and slipping it off my shoulders. Each move was slow and methodical, never once straying into a more sexual touch. He was gentle, loving even, with the way he slipped off my shoes and pulled off my undergarments. When I was fully bare, he offered me his hand and helped me into the tub, placing a kiss to my head as I sank in.

"If you need me, let me know. I am going to contact Henry, and we will figure this out." Though I trusted him completely, I also knew that there was little to be done. Stiffly, I bobbed my head down before lying back and closing my eyes, letting the hot water cleanse me. If only I could bleed every wicked piece of myself out, let it stain the water and leave me void of the evil that I had been gifted like a prize. Perhaps then I would be a better ally to a peaceful kingdom. One worth risking so much for.

Bellamy lingered for a moment, made evident by the near silence around me. But then, with a heavy sigh, he walked away, the sound of his footsteps retreating followed only by the click of the door shutting. Then nothing.

A new silence, one full of panic rather than sorrow, enveloped me. And I let it. I settled within it, allowing it to pull me under the water, scorching my cheeks as I went. While I lay there, weightless and free of the pressure that constantly threatened to break me, I decided I would do the one thing I knew would finally make me irredeemable.

I would choose.

Tomorrow, the three of us would go back to Eoforhild. I would accept that there was nothing more that I could accomplish here, and I would do exactly what Bellamy begged of me.

I would choose myself.

ACT V
~ TO LIVE ~

CHAPTER FORTY-ONE

ASHER

I walked out of the bathing room prepared to tell Bellamy all I had decided. Ready, now, to finally stop pushing forward and simply exist in this place of stillness.

But, of course, Henry was there, waiting with the biggest smile on his face. His beard was now gone, and his tan cheeks were tinted red from the cold. He wore a light blue wool top and dark black trousers, his boots tracking mud across the gray rug below his feet. I groaned as he walked towards me, his arms open wide.

"Guess who has so graciously come to visit his favorite little brat and wallow in her failure with her?" I let him embrace me, holding my towel around my body and grumbling against his chest.

"Everyone is entitled to say stupid things sometimes, but I feel as though you are abusing my patience."

He laughed, leaning down to place a kiss to the top of my head before letting me go.

Wrath was on the bed, his body smaller than normal and curled into a ball. His eyes tracked Henry with the sort of distaste that one would afford spoiled food. I smiled, trying to remember that I agreed to free myself from the grueling task that was saving the world.

I was choosing me.

"Where is Bellamy?" I asked, my eyes darting around the rest of the room. Henry unceremoniously fell back on the bed, his head on my pillow and his feet quickly swinging to kick Wrath.

"You are quite lucky that Asher wishes for you to live, or else I would disembowel you, you ridiculous orange-haired oaf."

I laughed as Wrath swatted at Henry's exposed ankle, slicing him and earning a hiss of pain from the demon. Wrath stretched, turning to stick his tongue out at Henry before jumping down and making his way to me. He weaved between my legs while in his smaller state then headed to Bellmay's satchel and secured a black long-sleeve top in his teeth. My smile lifted as he walked back to me, growing until his mouth was level with my hand. I grabbed it, offering him a scratch beneath his chin.

"Pumpkin, focus, please. Where is Bellamy?" I asked, wrapping my towel tighter before stretching out the top and lifting it above my head. Henry tucked his hands beneath his head, facing me with a devilish smirk.

Wood creaked beyond the door, and then it swung open, revealing Bellamy carrying a tray of pastries and what smelled like coffee. My hands froze above my head, eyes flicking from Bellamy's stunned face to

Henry's smug one. Quickly, I pulled the top over my head, my towel nearly slipping when a button got stuck in my hair.

"I believe he is right there," Henry added, a chuckle following his statement.

A pair of large warm hands met my skin just above the hem of the towel, holding it in place on either side. When my head finally popped through the fabric, Bellamy was there, smiling down at me with dimples gracing his cheeks.

"How are you feeling?" The question was spoken with a soft tone coated in nerves and fear. Perhaps that stemmed from how many times I had fallen into a catatonic state right before his eyes, or maybe it was because he also felt how truly hopeless this endeavor had been. No matter which it was, I still felt the butterflies take flight within my stomach, my heart racing as I stared into his beautiful blue eyes.

Bellamy had often told me that I was the beginning, the end, and each moment in between. At first, I had not been sure what he meant by it, but now, I thought I understood. No matter what happened from here, I knew that Bellamy would always be the start and end of my life. The two hundred six years before him had been a series of tragedies that slowly left me hollow, an empty husk void of life. Nicola, Farai, Jasper, and Sipho had poured as much love as they could into me, but all that had come was just as surely taken from me by the fae royals. With Bellamy, that would never happen again.

Regardless of what the coming war brought, I would always have that—him, *us*. Bellamy had gifted me something I never thought I would have: a family that loved me.

"I am okay. Happy to be with you, here. Obviously we have nothing left to do in Xalie, but we could always use this as a chance to be a bit selfish. I know that it might seem like an inappropriate time to—"

His lips met mine, brutal and claiming and full of eager energy. I smiled into the kiss, wrapping my arms around his neck and stretching onto my toes. As if no amount of connection would ever be enough, he snaked his arms around my lower back and hoisted me up, spinning me around as I laughed against his mouth.

Wrath and Henry both let out a groan, but we ignored them, living in a unique moment of slowness and joy. Stopping mid-spin, he readjusted, gripping my thighs and pulling my legs around his waist. I gasped, feeling my still-bare lower half against him.

"Get out," he ordered Wrath and Henry before lowering his lips down my jaw. Henry grumbled, placing a hand on Wrath before the two of them disappeared in a burst of light. Teeth met the hollow of my throat, causing my head to fall back. "I love you so fucking much, Asher. Do you know that?"

Head bobbing up and down, a nearly silent moan crawled up my throat as his hands slid to my bare backside, gripping harder. My back met the wall with an audible thud, a ringed hand tracing from my hip and up my stomach, palming my breast beneath the shirt. Though I knew I could live and die happily in his touch, I also wanted to talk to him, to explain my choice.

"Bellamy," I muttered, pushing away slightly. He instantly relented, backing his head away and staring at me with lust-clouded eyes, his lids half closed and his full lips swollen from my own. We stared at one another for a moment, appreciating all that made up the one we loved more than anything else. How odd, to be loved as much as you love. To find your equal and know that they see you as such. It was a beautiful and terrifying thing, discovering the one who made your soul complete. Because once you knew life with your other half, how could you be expected to ever exist without them again? "I do not want to give up, but I think it is time I recognize when I have lost. That morning, it felt like a failure. Though it hurts, maybe it was what I needed to finally allow myself to be selfish."

Rubbing our noses together briefly, he gently set me back on the ground, a single heated hand cupping my cheek. My head automatically leaned into the touch, eyes closing at the sweet feel of what I now knew as home.

"I have always lived a selfish life, Ash. Each day was a chance for me to exist on my own terms, Adbeel made sure of it. No one allowed you that, so I understand why you desire to be someone outside of me. I desperately want to matter, to be more than a king or a general. Every fiber of my being desires to be someone. But I know that, without you, I am nothing; whereas, without me, you are still everything. I do not take for granted the fact that you are choosing me, and I hope you know that this setback does not negate all that you have accomplished. All that you are." My eyes opened in surprise, staring at him with disbelief.

"No, please do not say that. You are so much more than simply mine. That first night we met, you told me you wanted to be more than a soldier or a husband or a father. You said that, knowing who I was and what you would be to me. I may not be aware of the future to the extent that you are, and I understand why I cannot yet."

There had been a sort of silent agreement that all which could be shared with one another, would. There were secrets he could not tell me, ones that only he and a great river knew, but even those would soon be told. I could feel it, and I feared it nearly as much as the war because I knew that it would alter everything. But I had learned to love change, and I knew that I would find a way to be ready for whatever it was that he still hid from me.

Change had never been a part of my life before. Instead, I lived in a cycle, repeating the same days like a never-ending loop. An off-key melody that existed solely in the space of sorrow and duty that made up the chorus of my life's song. But Bellamy…he was the bridge, a change in the tune that allowed it to rise. He was a stunning series of notes and lyrics that coalesced and enchanted the masses. If he was not worthy of all the love in the world, then who was?

And that truth I could tell him—I *would* tell him.

"But I do know *you*. Every beautiful part of you is the embodiment of what your realm—the entire world—needs. No future exists in which you have not exceeded every expectation of yourself, and I wish you could see how worthy of your own love you are."

He shook his head, like he might rid himself of my words. To his core, Bellamy was fighting for love just as I had been. Though we grew and that deep need for acceptance manifested differently, I thought we might always be the same in the belief that any who loved us was being deceitful. That love came with a cost, one that we would pay ten times over even if it meant ruining our lives for it. That left us suspicious, unsure, and distrusting. Someone claimed us "loved," and we simply heard "useful."

"How about you and I go to that tavern nearby and, for once, have a good time? Tomorrow, we can plot and worry and fight, but today—today, let me remind you of what it is to be loved like you deserve."

A shaky laugh broke free of his chest, lifting his cheeks and crinkling his eyes before he once more brought our lips together. I opened my mouth for him, but instead of letting him lead, I took control. Tangling my fingers in his hair, I tugged his face further into mine, tasting him with the fervor of someone denied their addiction. He moaned into my mouth, the ring of his deep tenor sending chills up my back.

"Go get dressed," he muttered, his tongue only momentarily separating from mine. "If you do not, then we will never make it to that tavern."

I shook my head, biting down on his lip and eliciting a low growl from him. Fingers met my side, and I was forced to separate from him as they dug into my flesh, my uncontrollable laughter and desperate pleas ignored by his relentless tickling.

"Okay, okay! I am sorry! Stop, please!"

He chuckled right along with me, pressing my body into the wall as his teeth grazed my throat, my body shaking with each laugh.

Finally, he released me, tugging his top up my body to leave me bare, winking as he backed up. When he sat on the edge of the bed, leaning back on his hands and eying me with excitement, I rolled my eyes and flashed him my middle finger. His answered hum of satisfaction warmed my cheeks and left my chest tight with adoration. With love. With complete and utter obsession.

I slipped on undergarments and thick tights, followed by a wool dress in the same shade of green as Henry's eyes, all the while listening to whistles and murmured compliments from the male on the bed. That icy blue gaze tracked me like a predator on the hunt, and I wondered silently what it was like to be the one searching for prey.

Perhaps, for tonight, I could let go of all the inhibitions that plagued me and give it a try.

Mischief and lust tainted the air, my magic painting the male with it. His eyes widened, pupils bleeding into the blue and darkening his irises. Flashing him a wicked smile, I slowly pointed my toes as I slid my foot into my black boot, letting my fingers trace up my calf when I was done fastening the laces. Gleefully, I repeated the action with the other foot, watching his chest rise and fall more quickly with each passing second. My cloak was last, which I fastened as I cleared my throat.

I stood with a broad smile, winking at him this time. He blew out a heavy breath, shaking his head and taking the hand I outstretched. We walked that way, the skin of our palms electrified by the contact and his thumb tracing lazy circles across the back of my hand.

Henry and Wrath were at the base of the stairs, both sitting on the bottom step and spitting harsh words at one another. So, really it was no different from any other day.

"You look like a fucking hair ball, what gives you the audacity to give *me* advice?" Henry asked, the rhetorical question hissed between clenched teeth.

Wrath lifted his furry chin, as if he was above the insult. "If she has not spoken to you in three days, I think it is quite obvious that you were as unsatisfying in the bedroom as you are unappealing to look at."

I stifled a laugh, further struggling when Bellamy allowed his own to ring free. Henry turned back to us, his mouth agape and his eyes narrowed. He looked far more stricken than he had with any insult I had thrown his way recently.

Was I losing my touch?

"I hope she snaps your cock tonight." Henry followed up his oddly specific and slightly psychotic insult with a middle finger to Bellamy, then he stood and left. Wrath chuckled to himself, Bellamy doing everything he could to hold in his amusement. With a tug on his arm, I moved us forward, walking down the short hallway to the door ahead. Outside, snow still fell from above, daylight causing the puffs of white at our feet to nearly blind us. Squinting our eyes, we made our way towards Henry, who stomped ahead of us with far more anger than I thought laughter could ever ignite within him.

"Genevieve must have really done a number on him." Bellamy's muttered reply matched my own thoughts perfectly, causing me to finally let out the giggle I had been holding in. Henry turned around at the sound, staring daggers at me. Before I could so much as breathe, the Sun was in front of me, the flash of light even brighter than the snow. His hand wrapped around mine, and I was suddenly wrenched from Bellamy's grasp. We appeared within a forested area, the city still in sight.

"Henry, what on Alemth—"

"Four and a half months!" His shouted words left me speechless, trying to understand what he was referring to. My head tilted, the same thing Bellamy always did, and I knew it only further irritated Henry by the way he reached out to straighten it as he groaned. "That is how long I have been fucking Genevieve. Do you know how exhausting it is to have traded one annoying princess for another?"

Then he was pacing, his face pointed down towards the icy ground as he made quick work of unknowingly digging down to the grass.

"Immensely, I imagine."

"Exactly! So, it is not like I desire her company or even really like her. She is just something new. I have never had sex with a mortal before her, and she is far less breakable than I thought." For some reason, picturing Henry with Genevieve sent images of Sterling on top of me to my mind. I found my hands gripping my chest to keep myself from panicking in front of an already distraught Henry. This was about him. He needed me to be whole while he broke. "Okay, fine. She is incredible in bed. Still, I do not care if she ignores me for three days. She can do whatever she wants, and I truly could not care less!"

What I wanted to ask Henry was why he was explaining this to me. Every word sounded more and more like an attempt to convince himself rather than anyone else, and I found I could not just sit by and let him wallow. Or whatever it was he had decided to use as a coping mechanism.

"Henry?" No response, just more pacing. I tried his name six more times before I was finally fed up with it and slapped him across the face. A shocked gasp split the air, his hand cradling the injured cheek as he stared at me in bewilderment. Despite my annoyance with him, I found my lips tilting up slightly at the look on his face. "Calm down and help me understand."

"Why is she ignoring me? What did I do?" Freezing, I watched as his hands went to his hair, tugging violently on the orange strands. When his head fell back and he grunted in frustration, my amusement faded completely.

"Henry, do you…*like* Genevieve?"

"Oh, please. We are not younglings, Asher. I do not have a little crush." The scoff that came from him sounded far too choked to be casual. Which was why I did not joke or laugh or smack him again. Instead, I closed the space between us and wrapped my arms around his waist, my ear on his chest and my fingers interlocked at his lower back.

For a moment, he only stood there, palms pressed to his face and breathing heavily. Eventually, though, he relaxed into my embrace. His nose pressed into the top of my head, arms wound tightly over my shoulders. Our chests soon rose and fell in perfect synchronization, the silence a comfort in comparison to all the noise we were constantly surrounded by.

I did not speak. Any advice I could offer was pointless when I had no experience with that sort of thing. Telling him he deserved better would not matter, because he wanted her. Explaining that it would all be okay was ridiculous, because who knew if it would? There was no correct thing to say in that moment, so I said nothing until he did.

"Why do I care, Ash? I should not care."

"There is no blueprint, Henry. No one can determine who you should or should not care about. Your heart will choose regardless. And if it hurts you in the end, then at least you felt."

He groaned, nodding against my head. "I am so sorry it is her. I know it must be upsetting."

"No. The only thing that bothers me is seeing you hurt."

We stayed in the embrace until I felt Wrath weaving between our legs, his body nearly as small as a squirrel. Henry yelped, backing away from me. When he caught sight of Wrath, he made the most dramatic gagging sound, leaning down to wipe the bottoms of his trousers in disgust. Wrath let out a low growl before snuggling up against my ankle, and I waited patiently for Bellamy to find his way to me as well.

The smell of him arrived before his touch, cinnamon and smoke greeting me. His embrace came shortly after, and I settled into him, my head leaning back to rest on his chest. It was odd to experience the differences between Bellamy's and Henry's presences so close together. The latter felt like a blanket, comfort and warmth. But Bellamy, he felt like a storm. Like lightning crackling my nerves and thunder raging in my chest. It was like being in the center of a tornado, every emotion swarming me and sucking the air from my lungs—drowning me in love and obsession and joy and desperation. I wondered if I would ever get used to it.

If I would ever have the chance to.

With a kiss to my temple, he left me, my back suddenly ice cold at his absence. He made his way to Henry, wrapping an arm around his best friend's shoulders and walking him down the hill. They spoke in hushed tones, their conversation private—just as it should be. Wrath grew, his nose grazing my fingers and his fur now thick and scruffy. He really was horrifying in this form, his teeth so large they could probably tear me in two within seconds. I leaned down, grabbing either side of his head and placing a kiss between his wide yellow eyes.

"If I do not survive this, take care of them for me."

"Do not be melodramatic. You will live thousands of years. I am sure I will be stuck carrying a ring down an aisle at your wedding to the idiot prince and will have my fur tugged by your tiny menaces that you will force me to love."

My chuckle was stiff, sad even. I could feel how wrong he was.

Before I could wallow too much in my heavy premonitions, Wrath shoved his head into my stomach, lifting to toss me in the air. I screamed in terror, my arms and legs flailing as I fell back towards the snow. But Wrath was there, his back stopping my fall as he continued to grow until he was the size of a large horse. My smile was broad as I adjusted myself atop him. And soon, he was running forward, my hands tightly gripping the fur at the nape of his neck.

I was still a horrible rider in comparison to the others. Months atop Frost and a ride upon a dragon had not fixed my lack of coordination in that sense. Still, I held on, not falling even when Wrath leapt down the hill and caused my bottom to lift from him as we sailed. Bellamy and Henry ducked in surprise, both watching in disbelief as we charged ahead of them.

For the first time in longer than I cared to admit, I threw my head back and basked in joy.

CHAPTER FORTY-TWO

BELLAMY

She looked radiant as her face turned skyward, her long curly hair billowing in the icy breeze. My heart threatened to leap out of my chest and follow her, the beat erratic. For once there was a sense of rightness in the air, because Asher was finally choosing us.

I knew this meant taking her home to meet Adbeel, which would result in her learning about a past and a future I feared. But maybe that was what she needed to truly see how much she mattered to the world. Though, I had to admit, seeing her like this—carefree and happy—made me want to delay that inevitable conversation a little longer.

"You know, I used to think you were incapable of love." Henry's words stole my focus, my eyes hesitating on Asher's retreating form atop Wrath for a moment longer before straying to him.

"What do you mean?" The rise and fall of my shoulders was followed by a slow roll of Henry's eyes as he walked forward once more. There was silence for a few moments, as if he were collecting his thoughts to best explain. I allowed him the time—as annoying as it was.

Of course I knew how to love. Sometimes, I thought I loved too much, allowing hurt and disappointment and loss to slowly chip away at my soul. Proof could be found in the way I acted after Asher disappeared. Or after we lost Winona, Pino, and all of Haven.

"You never said it. Not to me or even to Noe or Adbeel."

My feet stilled, the accusation followed closely by memories flooding my mind. I said it. I had to have said it. They were my family. They were everything to me.

I had said I loved them, right?

"The first time I had ever heard you say you loved someone was the night you first met Asher. Do you remember that? Your hair looked ridiculous, and you were acting like a fool. I thought that you had lost your mind. And I was also terrified of what she might do to you, to our realm. But, more than anything, I was jealous of the idea that you would have someone that you cared about more than me, than our family we had built." I tried and failed to keep my face blank as he spoke, not wanting any of my feelings to distract his line of thought. But hearing him admit that left me gaping at him in disbelief. "Do not look at me like that. You know that you are bad at showing affection. Noe might assume you love her, but you have never said it to us. I truly thought you were not able to feel something like that, as if whatever they had done to you as a youngling had altered you in more ways than one."

"Of course, I love you, Henry. You are like a brother to me. No, you *are* my brother. I guess I took that for granted and never thought to explain it." We pressed on, our boots getting stuck in the snow as it deepened at the base of the hill. I tried to step into the footprints Wrath had left behind, but his leaps were too far apart. All the while, I thought about what Henry might be getting to with his statement. How had I never said that I loved them? It seemed such an odd thing not to say when so many years had passed with my Trusted at my side. "I am sorry I did not ever tell you that."

With a deep sigh, Henry draped his arm around my shoulders, weighing me down and causing the snow to sink into my boots. Gods, he could be irritating. A smirk lifted his cheeks, his freckled, tan skin slightly red from the chill.

"Saying it does not count when you are forced to, but I will still take it. I love you too, even though you are a raging lunatic. But that was not the point of what I was trying to say. I meant that I see the way you look at Ash, and I suddenly want something like that. Maybe it is jealousy, or perhaps I like the idea of copying you to steal some of the attention, just so your head does not grow too big."

We laughed, the humor nearly coming out as scoffs. Asher and Wrath had disappeared into the tavern, which remained a long distance away. Still, I slowed my gait, wanting to give Henry as much time as he needed to explain his thoughts and feelings.

"Genevieve is like Asher in a lot of ways, fiery and stubborn and a natural-born leader, but she is also vastly different. She takes more than she gives, and she is spoiled. Not just in riches either. That girl has more money and gowns and jewels than she could ever possibly have use for, but according to her, she is surrounded by an abundance of love, too. It is odd to come across someone like that. At first, she pissed me off. I hated what her brother had done to Asher, and I was sure that she was just as evil. But then I went to her, planning on apologizing, and she threatened to gut me. Suddenly, I was acutely aware of the passion that flared in her eyes, of the rise and fall of her chest as she pointed a small dagger at my stomach, of the way her curls looked like spun gold in the light of the flames. So, I kissed her, and even though I knew she would kiss me back, I had still been stunned to hear the knife clatter to the ground and feel her arms around my neck. Not a day has passed since that I have stopped thinking about that pissy princess."

There it was. The truth he had not wanted to admit. One that plagued him enough to accept that love came in many different forms, but none as strong as the love you could feel in a stranger whose heart beat in time with yours. In a future that you had not realized was possible until you looked in their eyes and understood that not even the sun could shine as bright.

"You are in love with her." Not a question, but a statement. Because neither of us would lie to one another. We never had. Until Asher, that was.

"I am." His response was quiet, a faded and pained version of his normal voice.

"And you told her," I guessed, looking at him through the corner of my eye. He winced, his arm momentarily tightening on my shoulder.

"Would you believe me if I said it was an accident?" Turning my head fully, I leveled him with a half-lidded stare, my lips pursed. He groaned, running his free hand through his hair. "Fine, I did it on purpose. But what was I supposed to do? She was on top of me, and she was making the most intoxicating noise. I swear her hair was glowing. Then she said my name, and I just could not stop the words from leaving my mouth."

"How fast did she run?" My question earned me a smack to the side of my head, pulling a snort from me before I could stop it.

"She did not run! The bitch came on my face, acted like I said nothing, then told me to leave. Do you know how many times I have got off on the memory of it? Absolutely ridiculous." His free arm flew into the air, fingers stretched wide as if the memory were before us and he was directing me towards it.

That moment would easily go down in history as one of the biggest tests of my self-control. Instead of laughing, I let out a long whistle, lifting my arm and placing it around his shoulders to match his own hold on me.

"Asher once threw a butter knife at my chest, so I think it is safe to assume that your little love story could get worse and still workout."

He groaned, mumbling something along the lines of, "Gods, please, do not let her stab me in the chest."

Slapping him right in the spot where Asher had stabbed me, I smiled. "Unfortunately for you, I do not think that Genevieve has quite as poor of aim as Ash."

By the time we walked through the door to the tavern, Asher and Wrath were both seated at a table, people all around them flashing looks of confusion and disbelief towards the dalistori. Asher had been continuously practicing leaving her shields down, so I knew she likely was being bombarded by a slew of derogatory remarks. Still, her smile did not falter, her back straight and chin high. The male beside her caught my eye, stopping me in my tracks.

He was young by the look of him, probably thirty years or so. He wore a long-sleeve top that was a blue so deep it matched the night sky. His trousers and vest were both pure black like his hair, which sat in a messy knot at the base of his neck. I could tell that he was attempting to speak to Asher, though the smile on her face could not hide the furrow of her brow that told me she did not understand much of what he was saying. Not that the dimwit seemed to care as he prattled on.

"Ah, now *this* is what I need. We can skin him alive, maybe tie his feet to Wrath and have the dalistori run for a mile. Or ten? Oh, what if we—" I cut Henry off with a raise of my hand in his direction. He groaned, knowing I was about to spoil his fun.

"As much as I would love to pull out each of his teeth and shove them into his eyes, I have to trust that Asher can take care of herself. If I always act like a jealous and possessive lover, then she will think I do not believe in her. We need her to know we have faith in her strength, especially for what is to come." Without warning, I grabbed the front of Henry's shirt and dragged him over to a secluded table in the corner, where we watched as Asher's annoyance grew.

After another few minutes, her smile faded entirely, and I saw the rage boil in her eyes when he put his arm on the back of her chair. My grip on the table threatened to snap the wood, the sound of it splintering too quiet to be heard over the voices in the crowded tavern. Apparently, this city was full of day-drinkers, and I could not blame them. Everyone knew war was coming, and that was enough to push creatures of all kinds towards paths they might not have wished to walk along before.

Fed up with sitting still, I called to my shadows, summoning the pencil and paper that I had left back at the inn. They appeared in my hand, and I quickly unrolled the paper, scribbling a quick note to Asher.

Need any help?

When the paper landed in her lap, unbeknownst to the man, I saw her shoulders sag in relief. Her hands adjusted near her knee, drawing the man's attention. As if he thought it an invitation, he smirked and grabbed her upper thigh. I shot up, Henry's hand gripping my tunic and attempting to hold me back. Wrath hissed beside her, looking as if he were prepared to tear out the man's throat.

But in the end, Asher did not need anyone's help.

She smiled wide, earning a blush from the man beside her. Her magic flooded the air, tasting like vanilla and pressing into my skin like a reckoning. Then she grabbed his wrist, smacked his palm onto the table, and shoved my pencil through his hand. He howled in agony, the pain on his face bringing a smile to my own. Asher, too, seemed pleased by the tears that streamed down his cheeks as he desperately attempted to wrestle out of her grip. But she did not let go, instead twisting the pencil further into his flesh. When she leaned forward, whispering into his ear like a lover, he silenced himself and let his head lull back.

The moment she ripped the pencil from his flesh, he slumped to the side, his body hitting the ground. All the while, no one in the tavern but Henry, Wrath, and I seemed to take notice of the scene, like they could not see or hear it. Our eyes locked then, and I laughed as she winked, tipping back the man's untouched mead—which she quickly followed with her own. Wrath's venomous chuckles could be heard from across the room, wicked delight in his yellow eyes as he stared at the man on the ground.

"Never tell her I said this, but life is so much more fun with her in it." Henry's amusement left me smiling like a fool, because all I could have asked for was my family to love her like I did. Luckily, it was hard not to. Especially as she snapped her fingers and three people stood, walking towards the stage in the far right corner where they picked up instruments and began to play. A woman walked over to Asher, handing her another mug. My love, my Princess, my future handed her a gold coin in return, whispering softly to her. The woman blushed and nodded vehemently before walking back behind the bar.

Then Asher was up, her hips swaying tantalizingly to the beat— the mead in her mug sloshing over the edge as she sped up. My eyes remained glued to her, obsessed with every minute movement. Others joined in, making their way to the center of the tavern where space had been dedicated for dancing. And dance she did. Once more, she topped off her drink, and I knew she would regret not pacing herself later. But, for now, she flashed her white teeth, those full lips perfectly framing them. Setting her mug down on a nearby table, she grabbed the woman from earlier, latching onto her waist and spinning them in a circle.

Giggles came from her as Asher tugged her into a messy dance, the two of them moving to the beat with no real rhyme or reason to the sway of their bodies. Henry stood, stealing a drink from the table in front of us before he joined in. I remained where I was, my eyes never leaving Ash. Captivating did not begin to describe her.

A barmaid offered me a drink, which I accepted with a nod despite my eyes remaining trained onto the dancing princess before us. By the time she let the woman go back to work, a shine coating her face from the heat of the bodies beside her and the constant moving, I had already consumed a cup of wine and two of mead.

We locked gazes once more, and I knew that I was in trouble by the way she pulled her bottom lip between her teeth and undid her cloak. My cock twitched in my pants when she leisurely made her way towards me, her hands roaming over her body and her hips rotating. Again, I felt the pulse of her magic, this time watching as every set of eyes looked away from us like we did not exist.

Immediately, I discovered why she was affording us privacy. Her fingers met the laces that secured the front of her dress, gently undoing them as she walked. My breathing halted—like if I so much as took in air, I would miss this moment. When the green dress was fully open, exposing the black band of fabric that supported her breasts, she let her fingers run lazily between them, tracing a teasing line down her torso.

A desperate groan left my lips as her hands tugged the fabric off her shoulders, letting the garment hang by her elbows. She continued to sway, now only ten feet away from me. Her feet stilled, and as she let her head fall back, I stood, ready to damn it all and take her on the floor.

Stay there, Elemental.

Her words were an order, though the sultry tone made the command erotic. Like always, my mental shields slipped when the temptation of her affection was nearby. Without looking forward, Asher let her dress fall, wearing only her black tights, undergarments, and boots. My moans were loud now, my hand dipping into my trousers and gripping my cock. I pumped myself to the sway of her body, a mischievous twinkle in her eyes as she watched me.

Do you want me, Bellamy?

I nodded vehemently, groaning at the memory of her on top of me. She flashed a wicked smile as one of her fingers hooked onto the fabric hiding her breasts from me.

What would you do to get what you want? Would you kill? Lie? Beg?

Again, I nodded, this time trying to fight against the order to stay where I was, my body stuck despite my efforts. So, I took a note from her words, and I begged.

Please, Asher. Please, let me have you.

Her laugh was whimsical, breathtaking in the same way her body was. I hissed out another plea, this time aloud. My hand was stroking in jerky movements now, my cock not pleased by my own touch when hers was so near.

I told you I would love you the way you deserved, and I will. But first, crawl to me, Bellamy.

And, though she did not order it with her magic, I immediately fell to my knees and crawled to her.

The moment I was within reach of her, I latched onto her ankle and summoned my shadows, portaling us back to the inn. She gasped when we appeared in our now-dark room, a snow storm growing outside and stealing the light of the day. I kissed my way up her body, stopping only when we heard a scream of fright from behind us.

I turned, shielding Asher and finding two men in our bed. No, not our bed. This room was shades of violet, with heavy winter wear scattered about. It was their room. Asher began apologizing, her slurred speech not doing much to assuage the fear in the mortal men's eyes. I, too, profusely apologized. Then I grabbed onto her tighter and willed us into the correct room. We both looked around, verifying we were where we belonged this time.

While I knew she would be embarrassed and livid in the morning, Asher only laughed as we stood there like fools. So, I kissed her, my tongue darting into her mouth with a fervor that I always seemed to have in her presence. The moment she moaned my name against my lips, I lost all control. With a growl of desperation, I separated from her and promptly stripped us until we were both completely bare.

Lifting her up, I shoved her back into the wall, lost in the addiction of the taste and feel of her. My lips and teeth and tongue consumed her neck, my fingers digging into her ass as I rubbed my now-throbbing cock against her.

"You wanted me to beg? I will beg all damn day, Asher. Please, let me fuck you. Let me worship the ground you walk on. Tell me I can have you, Princess. That is the way I want to be loved." As if my words were all it took, Asher groaned in ecstasy, her head smacking into the wall as she writhed against my cock.

"Yes," she whispered through clenched teeth, her eyes squeezing tight in preparation for what was to come. And as I took her there against the wall, watching her come undone, I knew nothing would ever be quite as stunning as Asher.

***

When our eyes were heavy and our bodies sore, I held her tightly within my arms, breathing her in and basking in the feel of her skin against mine. I found myself humming a tune, playing with the long strands of her hair. Oddly enough, it left me with the realization that Ash still did not have a birthday.

"Have you ever heard of a birthday?" I asked her, knowing the answer before she even spoke it. Her eyes fluttered open, head tilting back to look up at me. My fingers continued to massage her scalp, wishing I could exist in this moment forever.

"A birth day? Is it a day when many are born?" She rested her chin on my chest, those gray irises alight with curiosity. I smiled down at her, placing a quick kiss to her nose.

"Sort of. A birthday is one day each year when you celebrate your birth. In Eoforhild, demons remember which day they were born and throw parties and get gifts annually. It is a tradition of sorts."

A look of disbelief pinched her face, her lips turning down in a frown. "That seems horribly self-centered."

Laughing at her take, I recalled Lian and Ranbir's initial reaction to the idea of birthdays as well. They had not understood it either, but now we celebrated their chosen birthdays each year, and they eagerly counted down the days to them.

"Believe it or not, the day you were born is worth celebrating. Maybe you could pick a day? That is what Ranbir and Lian did. Me too, when I was old enough for Adbeel to explain it to me." She was silent for a few minutes, the only sound around us our synched breathing. When she did speak, there was an unexplained air of awe to her voice.

"When is Star Festival?" she asked, backing away to fully look at me. I furrowed my brow, trying to recall what day it was.

"Actually, it is in two days if my mental calendar is correct. I am surprised you even know what that is seeing as it is a holiday of the gods. Why do you ask?"

With a dazzling smile, Asher sat up and kissed my cheek. "If I am going to be selfish, then I think I better go all out."

***

The next morning, amidst planning and preparations, I offered the couple across the way an apology along with a bag full of gold coins. Asher had giggled as she listened to their thoughts of bewilderment when I went to their door to explain and then gasped in surprise when they fell to their knees upon realizing who she was. While we worked on celebrating both Asher's birthday and Star Festival, I realized just how important she had become to the world, and I smiled at the thought.

CHAPTER FORTY-THREE

ASHER

Bellamy was being ridiculous, and Noe was not helping.

The two of them were acting as if this celebration needed to be life-changing. They both were running around, yelling as they put up decorations and ordered around soldiers like slaves. Of course, Lian was having the time of her life making fun of me as I internally panicked.

"You know, they probably think you are forcing them to celebrate you," she whispered into my ear as we stood watching Noe berate a young demon recruit for misplacing a chair. Her golden brown hair had been tied in a knot atop her head, and she wore a loose teal dress that highlighted her tan skin perfectly. Despite that beauty, she was utterly horrifying to watch.

"Shut up, Lian. You know I did not want all of this." I shoved into her side, which only further lifted the corners of her mouth, the smile crinkling her almond eyes. It was unsettling to see.

"Ah, but *they* do not. I wonder how much they loathe you right now." With that, she shrugged, winked, and walked away. My hands formed fists, nails digging into my palms. From my anger, I found my magic slinking into her mind and breaking through her flimsy wall of air.

Trip.

And then she fell, her hands and knees smacking into the ground. Eyes wide, I lifted my hand to my mouth in surprise, baffled at my own audacity. Lian turned, glaring at me and flashing me her middle finger before standing. A mortal man chuckled, and before I knew it, he flew backwards from a particularly violent gust of wind. We all watched her stomp off, and I knew that someone would surely pay for what I had done in the form of a brutal training session.

"Every day you remind me why I love you so much, little brat." Henry's arm wrapped around my shoulders, his body leaning into mine enough to nearly make me stumble. Damon pushed against my other side, scoffing at Henry, his effervescent silver hair making Henry's appear particularly orange.

"You almost knocked her over." His voice was scolding as he stepped away from me, that quiet and casual presence somehow taking on an air of authority. Henry did not seem to care as he rolled his eyes Damon's way.

"Yeah, you almost knocked me over!" Shoving back at him, I groaned when he did not so much as lose his balance. Stupid little carrot.

"Oh, please. You are fine, and you just tripped poor Lian." With a wave of his hand in Lian's direction, I was put in my place. He had me there.

"Touche," I admitted, slumping under his weight. When his hand came up to ruffle my hair, I swatted at him and stepped further into Damon, who barely backed up in time to not be run over.

"By the way, I wanted to warn you that my mother is here and eager to meet you. Which spells doom for Alemthian because if the two of you end up liking each other, then I suspect world domination will not be far away." Scoffing at the mere thought of such a thing, he glared down into my eyes, preemptively loathing me for whatever crimes future Asher would supposedly commit under his mother's guidance.

"Why me? What do I even say?" Nerves found their way into my already unsteady mind, leaving me a disheveled, slightly sweaty mess as I stood beside them. She was going to hate my guts.

"Seeing as you are probably going to be her queen one day, I imagine she wants to measure you up. She appreciates a strong and independent female. That, and she quite enjoys parties." With that, he lightly smacked my cheek and walked away, heading for Bellamy. I glared, eager for whatever argument would likely stem from him bothering the prince. With everything he just dumped on me, knowing I was already stressed out and guilt-ridden, I hoped Bellamy put him on his ass.

"Luca would have liked this," Damon said from my side, pulling me out of my self-centered mindset. I looked towards him, watching as he tried to school his sorrow into stoicism. In the last month, Bellamy had gone through lapses in his joy, the pain of so much loss bleeding into the moments when he so desperately wanted to be whole and happy. I saw it then in Damon's face, too. With my mental shields down, I heard it in his mind as well. "Sorry, I should really learn to read the room."

"You are allowed to be sad, Damon. There will be those who make you think that it is wrong, that there is a time limit on grief. Some will go so far as to convince you that you are wallowing in the loss or that every moment of heartbreak is wasted time. But I want you to hear me when I say that none of that is true. I have spent months—decades really—trying to pretend that sadness and anger and grief are weaknesses, and I lost a lot because of it. Do not let anyone convince you that feeling is wrong. Do not let them steal that from you." Our eyes met, my gray locking on his brown, and I felt that silent understanding settle into us. Though I had only met Damon a couple of times now, I knew that, like all of Bellamy's family, I would one day love him dearly.

"The more you love, the more you stand to lose. Come home or watch everything you love wither before you."

Mia's words echoed through my mind, an audible reminder of all the danger and loss that threatened to come with love. Unthinking, I stepped away from Damon, creating space between us as if that would stop me from building a relationship with him.

"Thank you, Asher. I am glad that Bellamy has you. That we all do. You will make a lovely queen one day." He briefly rested his hand on my shoulder, squeezing faintly before waving and walking towards the now-arguing males before us. Bellamy held sparkling silver garland, waving it in the air as if that would better explain whatever he wanted Henry to do. For his part, Henry looked utterly dumbfounded, but also slightly pleased with the annoyance he was able to pull from Bellamy.

I smiled as I watched, the haunting threat from Mia a foreboding sound within my mind. So too was the realization that both Henry and Damon had suggested I would one day be their queen. While I had not allowed myself time to give much thought to the possibilities my future held—if I even had one—I did think about it then.

The demons would not want me there, ruling over them. I was fae, an enemy. Not to mention that Bellamy was, too. Even if they were not aware of just how fae he was, they still saw his ears and felt his power. Hostility had met us multiple times on our journey across Eoforhild those many months ago, which meant it likely festered all throughout the realm. Why would they want me ruling over them when they did not even agree that Bellamy should?

Whether it was the direction my own thoughts had taken or the way she seemed to demand focus, I did not know, but somehow, my eyes landed on Lady Odilia Nash the moment she stepped into the training yard. Like Henry, Odilia's tan skin was sprinkled with freckles, her vibrant orange locks floating in the breeze as she walked. Her trousers were a stunning shade of pink—soft, like a rose petal. They flared out as they cascaded down her long legs, nearly tricking the mind into thinking them a skirt. Her white top ended just above her navel, the off-shoulder sleeves twin to her pant legs in their billowing size.

She was not beautiful in the traditional sense; rather, she had a sharp and strong magnificence to her. Henry once told me that his mother had been the general of the military forces before Bellamy's predecessor. When she was asked to become Lady of Kratos, Odilia had nearly told Adbeel no. After quite a bit of pleading on the king's part, she said yes, but that would later put quite a bit of pressure on her future son.

In her eyes, Henry was meant to be a general, to surpass all others and exhibit the same strength and bloodlust and brilliance that she had. Despite his tendency to crack jokes and annoy everyone in the room, Henry also believed that. It would be hard not to after the training she had put him through. Like Noe's father, Henry's mother used brutal methods. At six years old, just days after his magic had manifested, Henry was forced to live in the woods for a week on his own. While Noe suffered at the hands of an unloving father and an absent mother, Henry was loved deeply by both of his parents. Though I would not pretend like I understood his mother's methods, and apparently his father was not a fan of them either, I did recognize the love she held in those green eyes as she caught sight of her son.

Every instinct told me that I should try to avoid speaking to her, so much so that I quickly slammed the golden bars of my mental shield, locking the gate. Risking her feeling me in her mind was not an option if I was going to somehow escape her attention. Silently creeping towards the mountainside entrance of the military base, I tried and failed to make myself small enough to not be seen.

Apparently, crouching down and ducking my head like a lunatic was not inconspicuous like I hoped.

"So, this is the fae princess that has left our prince smitten." Her voice was like ice, cold and unforgiving, though bits of Henry's mocking tone slipped in there as well.

I stood up straight, turning to face her. She smiled down at me, her arms crossing over her chest. I knew that parents were meant to look and sound and act like their younglings, that nature and nurture made it so, but it still unnerved me to see those similarities. Sipho and his father had been the same way. Both times I had met Jabari, I was left smiling at the little quirks they shared, so similar it was almost eerie. Maybe the only reason I had not felt uncomfortable by them was because I secretly hoped one day I would be able to join their family, that I would have the chance to tell Jabari that I loved his son.

"Tell me, Princess Asher, what makes you so special that everyone who has met you seems unbearably charmed?" She quirked a brow, eyeing me with both taunting humor and violent suspicion. If only I could portal out of this horribly unpleasant conversation. I needed to keep one of those damn demons next to me at all times.

"I think it is my sparkling personality," I said, unable to keep myself from emulating the putrid energy she was projecting.

Unimpressed, she let her smile stretch impossibly wider, those forest eyes somehow hardening in the process. "I think it is because you are a manipulative little beast." The whispered insult came through clenched teeth, a defiant tilt to her jaw as she so clearly relayed her distaste for me.

"You say that like it is a bad thing." Shrugging, I smiled back at her, unwilling to sit back and take ire from anyone. I had laid down and weathered every insult, threat, and curse my whole life. No longer. "I think you have grossly overestimated my patience, Lady Odilia. I love your son, more than I ever thought I would. He is like a brother to me, but that does not mean I will hesitate to shatter your mind where you stand."

Seconds passed in silence, neither of us breaking eye contact or daring to speak. And then, abruptly, her stiff posture melted, comfort and ease taking over.

"Excellent. I approve then." With a heavy smack on my shoulder and a rough shake of my body, she nodded, briefly flashing a much softer smile my way. I stared at her, not comprehending what just happened. "Anyways, I'm off to spar with my son. Do come watch if you are bored. He usually walks away bleeding."

And then she was gone. Henry's eyes drifted over to her as she stalked towards him, terror stretching his face. He shoved Bellamy into her path, trying to make a run for it.

His mother chuckled deeply before portaling to him, ducking her head low and shoving her shoulder into his stomach. I choked on my laughter as Odilia used her momentum to lift her son, who was at least five inches taller than her, over her shoulder and promptly throw both of their bodies backwards. Henry hit the ground first, his back audibly smacking against the rock floors. Then his mother's body slammed into his chest, air whooshing from his mouth as he grunted in pain.

It was one of the most violent displays of affection I had ever seen.

"Gods, other moms say hello, did you know that?" Even while wheezing for air, Henry still managed to say something sarcastic.

To the surprise of no one, Bellamy made his way to my side, smiling broadly as he grabbed onto my hand. It was victory painted on his face, less for the lacing of our fingers and more for the way that Odilia was mercilessly attacking Henry. I cringed when he threw his elbow into her face, sending her head snapping back. Laughter caused blood to dribble from her mouth, and then she smashed his face down into the ground.

"They will be at it for a while. Can I show you something in the meantime?" Bellamy's words fanned over my ear like a delicate breeze, his heat at my side a peaceful reminder of my vow to live for myself. This party, as ridiculous as it had become, was a new start. Like being reborn.

"I would love that," I whispered, turning my head to face him. Our lips nearly touched, his head ducking down and mine tilting up.

He smirked, rubbing the tips of our noses together before backing away slightly. "You are so obsessed with me." Swatting his arm, I tried and failed to keep the ridiculous smile from my face as he tugged me against his chest and the familiar pull of portaling stole us away in a cloud of smoke-like shadows. My eyes closed, head falling against his chest and breathing him in. "See, Princess, obsessed."

With that, he pressed his lips to mine, and I instinctively opened for him, greedily proving the idiot right. Because I was obsessed, and I thought I might only get worse as the days went on. If, by some miracle, we had the chance to live and be together when the dust settled, then I would probably continue to grow more infatuated with him as the years passed by.

A hand on my throat and one at my hip, he slowly walked me back until my legs hit the end of a bed. His bed. Our bed?

My thoughts were once more claimed by him as he pulled away, quickly backing up with the most ridiculous smile on his face. Perhaps, if I was forced to admit it, I would also call it endearing, handsome, exquisite.

But mostly ridiculous, of course.

He disappeared beneath a puff of black shadows, returning with his hands full of black fabric and red...chains?

"I made a very kind seamstress's life a nightmare the last two days trying to perfect the idea in my head for this. Keep that in mind before you say anything scathing about it, Princess."

Rolling my eyes, I stood, walking to him and the garment. When I reached my fingers out to take it, he quickly flipped one of his own hands to smack mine. I gasped, hugging my injury and glaring up at him.

"You left me desperate for the chance to touch you for months, watching as you emerged from that tent in clothes twin to mine and wishing I could have been the one to put them on you. If you think I will miss an opportunity now, then you have lost your mind." He tilted his head to the side, pursing his lips and furrowing his brow. "Which would be quite a tragic and ironic end for someone with your talents."

Groaning, I promptly lifted my arms in surrender. He chuckled, gently setting down the outfit he had apparently designed before coming back and teasingly pulling off my clothing. When he had stripped me bare of all but the thin black undergarments that he had jokingly snapped against my skin before gripping my backside, he stood and retrieved my birthday outfit.

Birthday. Such an odd creation. I thought it a bit selfish, though I would not pretend like it was not exciting to have something so special. A day that rejoiced in my birth after a lifetime of being cursed for existing was extraordinary indeed.

Bellamy came back, the smile on his face so broad that it crinkled his eyes and flashed his dimples. Without realizing it, I smiled back, so much joy filling my heart by simply being next to him.

"Black had once been my favorite color, but red felt like family in a way. Like blood—the one thing that is supposed to tie people from birth to death. I thought that by making the colors of Haven black and red, I was taking the broken and dark pieces of the refugee fae and making them whole by bringing them together—morphing us all into a sort of family. We all needed that, and it seemed fitting." He spoke as he dressed me, not once meeting my eyes. But when he paused, his voice cracking, I looked up to see he was staring down at me with a vulnerable sort of openness on his face. His eyes, so blue they appeared frozen, bore into mine with the intensity of someone who had just seen the stars for the first time.

With a tender grasp on my shoulders, he walked me over to a thin and slightly cracked mirror in the corner. Despite that, I still gasped at my reflection.

"Bellamy, it is beautiful." There was a hoarseness to my voice, the shake of it portraying all the emotions I could not speak aloud.

"Would it be cliché if I said, 'Yes, you are'?"

I laughed, looking up at him through the mirror. His smile had gone soft, a sort of melancholy taking over his features. And I knew, without a shadow of a doubt, it was because of what the dress represented.

The top was form-fitting, the sheer black fabric showing my torso and hinting at the red that hid away my breasts. Straps sat loosely at the very edge of my shoulders, leaving my arms bare. The bottom half of the dress was solid black and loose, splitting up both sides until it hit my midthigh. A cut like that would surely show my legs as I walked, but it did not seem overtly sexual. Rather, the dress was regal and beautiful—simple in the best way. Bellamy lifted a finger, rotating it. I took that as an order to turn around, so I did.

Somehow, this side of the dress managed to outshine the front. It was backless, the fabric descending my body at the very edges of my sides until it curved to meet at the base of my spine. Seven thin, red chains cascaded down the exposed flesh, connecting the split fabric and hanging lazily to form a sort of U shape. At the center of the top chain, which connected both of my straps, sat three overlapping circles—one black, one silver, and one white. Dangling in the center of the silver circle was a tiny diamond.

"The seven chains represent the seven territories of Eoforhild, and that is our sigil, but the colors—they are that of Haven." A quiet sob split the air, and I realized with horror that it was my own. For what felt like the thousandth time in the last year, I cried. For the senseless deaths of so many innocents. For all the loss that Bellamy and his Trusted had suffered. For my own pain. Even for the future, which felt as if it just might end in disaster.

"I love it," I whispered, ripping my gaze from the mirror to face the male before me. My soulmate. The most dazzling and wonderful being, who I knew was my future, no matter how short-lived. "I love *you*."

He sucked in a breath of desperate air, his eyes going glassy as he brought his forehead down to mine, his hands gripping my jaw possessively. "I love you, too, beautiful creature."

***

The festivities were even more ostentatious than I thought they would be, though it helped that we were simultaneously celebrating Star Festival. Strings of sparkling silver garland hung across the space, somehow secured between the mountain, the base, and the sparse trees. Dots of demon light glittered just above the silver, lighting the space and adding to the stars within the sky. The stars that seemed brighter than before, somehow. Tables were littered with treats—pastries, in particular, seemed to be in abundance. Once again, I was reminded just how close of attention Bellamy paid to me, and the realization brought a smile to my face.

A group of musicians sat at the center of the space, playing upbeat melodies and smiling at those dancing around them. It seemed that fashion was individual in Eoforhild; something that I had gathered based on assumption over the months but was proven correct tonight as I bore witness to the demons around me.

Colors and styles varied greatly between them all, showcasing the brilliance of autonomy and freedom. Cyprus caught my attention as he approached me, his eyes devoid of the teasing and joyous light they normally possessed. Bellamy had explained to me that Cyprus and Luca were not together, but the group always knew they would be one day. Like an inevitability—destiny. But Luca's death had torn that future from Cyprus's grasp, and the last few weeks had been a bleak and dark time for the whisp.

Now, as he made his way to my side, his blush tunic pairing beautifully with his russet skin, black trousers, and loose brown hair, I saw the sorrow that overflowed from him. My hand reached out as if I were a puppet on strings, eager to help and hold him. He took it with a smile, tugging me into his chest and swinging me around the open dance floor. Twirling us, he managed to maintain his usual swagger while still allowing a vulnerable string of thoughts to teeter into the air, freefalling my way.

I miss him, Ash. I do not know how to go on without him. Before, I thought we had time, that I could relish in the tension and avoid the possibility of ruining a friendship. But now…now, he is gone, and the time is gone with him. How do I exist now?

My breath hitched, and I found my head moving forward to rest on his chest to avoid showing him the emotions that were surely playing across my face. He did not deserve to suffer from anyone else's sadness. His was more than enough.

You do not just move on. The decades of time I spent avoiding those feelings did me no justice. Moving on was pointless, a façade to allow myself the chance to continue life. But, in the end, it broke me rather than healed me. Sipho was still dead, and I was still a shell of who I was in his presence. Being loved by him was not something I could simply forget. Do not force those shattered pieces of your heart together, because if you lose the fragments too small to see in your rush to repair the damage, then you will never be whole again.

A comfortable quiet settled between us, one of his tears hitting my upturned cheek as we swayed and spun. There was comfort in this understanding, though I still knew much of Cyprus and Ranbir's losses were my fault. If I could offer them even a semblance of relief, then I would gladly do so. There was no limit to how far I would go for my family.

Family. A term which had once been a skewed reality that I barely survived before morphing into a foreign concept that I convinced myself I would never know. Now, as Cyprus pressed a soft kiss to the top of my head and twirled me in a circle, I understood what family really was.

Family was Nicola's whispered praise and reassurance. Family was Jasper's tight embraces and words of wisdom. Family was Farai's joking tone and firm confidence in me. Family was Henry's teasing, Lian's sassy flirtation, Noe's unwavering support, Cyprus's contagious joy, and Ranbir's calming presence. It was Wrath's sarcasm and affection. Sipho's obsessive belief in me, Winona's gentle love, Luca's declaration of loyalty, and Pino's understanding of what I could be. All of this.

Dipping me at the close of the song and flashing a look of thanks, Cyprus reminded me of one final version of family. The one thing that made it complete.

Bellamy.

"Thank you, for everything. I love you, gorgeous." Cyprus's words paired with the wink of a brown eye left me giggling. Bowing, he made to leave, his direction indicating that the party would be over if he did not get some liquor in his system. Suddenly in urgent need of that dangerous honesty, I called out to him.

"Cyprus!" At my shout, he stopped, looking at me over his shoulder. Trying and failing to stop my emotions from getting the better of me, I breathed out every fear of rejection and stupidity, opening up my soul for the hurt in favor of the chance at joy.

I love you, too, little whisp. Thank you for showing me what it is to trust and love—for being my family.

His cheeks darkened, the smile he flashed a dazzling show of white teeth as he nodded and stalked off. Noe found me not long after, standing off to the side and smiling to myself as I watched the celebration grow. She was wearing a soft pink band around her breasts and a low-sitting, loose skirt that matched. Brown sandals graced her feet, similar to the red ones that I wore, though mine wrapped all the way up to my thigh. Like me, she wore a vibrant red lip and kohl on her eyes. Diamonds adorned her ears, neck, wrists, and waist, all strung on silver chains. She had let her long golden brown hair hang down her back, looking like a tamed waterfall. As always, she was stunning.

"Why are you alone? This party is for you!" She shouted the last words as the music grew louder, a flamboyant tune that made my chest flutter. It was beautiful, just as everything about this night was. I looked to her, watching her face as she fluffed my curls, enjoying the way they had all grown so comfortable with me. Enjoying the fact that I was no longer feared by them.

"No, we are celebrating Star Festival. I just thought today would be a nice one to pick since it already held something special. I read about it in—"

A loud crash cut off my sentence, and we watched in horror as a mortal boy tried and failed to get up after falling backwards in his chair and bringing down a tray full of wine, the shadows once carrying it dissipating. Running over to him, I quickly leaned down and helped to shoulder his weight. He sighed, smiling over at me momentarily before his eyes flew open in surprise.

His grip on me was hot and sweaty, slipping down my arms as I held him aloft. He began mumbling in what sounded like the dialect of

Behman, whatever he was saying clearly meant to be a plea of sorts. Unable to hold back my laughs, I gripped the boy tighter and hauled him to a nearby wooden chair beside one of the many extravagant spreads of dishes. He slumped back, eyes wide and full of what could only be described as horror.

"Let me get you some water and something to eat. Bread will soak up all that wine, and I am a firm believer that carbs can heal any wound."

For a moment, he merely stared at me, his black hair stuck to his tan face with sweat and his blue eyes darting between my own. When he finally nodded in resignation, I tried to give a comforting smile and gently tapped his shoulder with the tips of my fingers. Then I was off, searching the entirety of the decorated training yard to concoct the most epic of all dessert spreads. If the pastries did not soak up the alcohol, then at least it would not taste too foul when he vomited it back up.

Lian found me as I was piling a third scone onto the plate, tsking her disapproval. I peeked at her from the corner of my eye, stopping with my hand outstretched and whipping my head towards her in stunned amazement.

Lian had always been one of the most beautiful females I had ever seen. There was something about the blue of her hair in contrast to her dark, upturned eyes. Or maybe it was the way her flowing purple dress atop her defined and heavily honed physique made her sharper, a beauty as lethal as nightshade. Yes, that was what Lian was, a dangerous and stunning bit of nature.

"Serving food to another male? How scandalous." There was a moment where I remained stone faced, but that was quickly ruined when she leaned in and whispered, "Which of his heads do you think Bell will cut off first?"

My laugh was a combination of surprised choking and genuine amusement, which left Lian smiling far too broadly when paired with those mischievous eyes. I offered her the plate, gesturing for the boy whose head had fallen forward onto the table. Scoffing, she lifted her nose and made her way to him. From a distance, I could just make out the drool that was escaping his mouth. Poor thing. He was in for a horrible day tomorrow, and based on Lian's wicked glee that jostled my mental gates, I had a feeling she would make sure of that.

"You know, I probably would have just frozen off his cock. Nothing crazy." His voice was a caress at my back, a pair of warm lips grazing the jagged tip of my ear.

I shivered at the touch, but his words left me rolling my eyes as I turned my head to bring our lips mere inches apart. "Dramatic. Even for you, demon."

He scoffed, pinching my hip slightly and forcing a yelp free of my mouth. As if I had played right into his hands, he smirked before dipping his face and connecting our lips. Because I was a brat to my core, I reached down and pinched his already erect member through his trousers, earning a returning cry.

He backed up, mouth agape and eyebrows raised as he looked at me, the offense on his face so clear that I could do nothing but giggle and take him in. He wore a silky black top, the center split down to his navel and embroidered with red gems. His toned stomach showed every ounce of extra training he had done in my absence, the muscles flexing as he leaned back against the table. A red chain hung down his exposed skin, just like my back. Though his connected the top two corners of his shirt, the weight of them pulling the fabric further apart rather than securing them in place. He had on plain black trousers, his boots matching. Under his eyes—which practically glowed like a pool of stagnant water beneath the shine of the moon—was a thin line of kohl, his gloriously full lips slightly red from our stolen kisses. Freckles dotted his cheeks and nose, like my own personal constellation.

But it was that hair, the forever-disheveled waves that caught and held my attention. He ran a hand through it absentmindedly, looking slightly stressed if his frantic gaze and fidgety hands were any sign.

"Are you okay?" I asked, unable to ignore the behavior.

He pulled me into him, holding the back of my head with one hand as he scanned the area. I knew exactly when he found what he was looking for, because his body relaxed against mine. Before I could make any jokes about his lack of interest in me, he leaned down, delivered me one more bruising kiss, and then spun me around. Henry was heading our way, carrying what looked like a small circular cake on a ceramic plate. The edges were red, a line of white cutting it in half horizontally. Cream-colored icing seemed to drip down from the edges, and I noted a group of colorful sticks poking up from the top.

Bellamy's Trusted quickly found their positions around me as Henry approached, holding out the plate to me. Wrath and Farai also made their way over, their smiling faces bringing me more joy than I could possibly express. I looked down, noting that they had somehow written words onto the frosting.

"Happy Birthday Asher!" was written in black, the phrase so new yet so comforting. It was stupid to celebrate, but I still could not help the way my chest ached, birds taking flight in my stomach. After all this time, I could still feel Mia and Xavier within me, like a foreboding and heavy darkness that drenched my soul in constant gloom and torture.

But as Bellamy reached around my shoulder with a small black flame at the tip of his finger, lighting what I could now see were tiny candles, I felt that blackened fire somehow bathe my soul in light. I watched as the darkness fought and lost to its twin, the flames just as all-encompassing and bleak but also full of a love I had never felt in my life.

With almost all of my family around me, I smiled and forced back the tears that threatened to spill. Bellamy let his lips meet my cheek before he spoke into my ear.

"Make a wish, Princess."

What did one wish for when they had already been blessed with so many gifts?

CHAPTER FORTY-FOUR

ASHER

There was a common turn of phrase in Betovere: "Our Ending will come, and we will be ready."

It was said to understand that we would all know when we were called home to Eternity, that our Ending would feel right. I sometimes wondered about that as a youngling.

What about those that died suddenly? What about murder? War?

My parents had not been called to anything. Their lives had been stolen by demons with a cruel desire to do nothing but kill. At least, that was what I had believed then.

Death had a way of sneaking up on you. She was a cruel mistress with little time for pleasantries. Her motives began and ended with the desire to take and take until there was nothing left. Sometimes, she would bribe and barter, but in the end, the bitch would take.

"Hey, little brother. I brought you a piece of cake. It is not chocolate, but that is Ash's fault. She said she has never tried red velvet, so I was forced to show her. I hope that is okay." Bellamy slowly lowered the cake to the ground, setting it atop the grave.

On the stone, in stunning writing, read, "Luca Braviarte. Beloved son. Taken too soon, but never forgotten."

Lian bent down, setting a single Salvia Splenden at the base of the headstone. Noe followed suit, placing a kiss and mug to the top. Cyprus offered a folded piece of paper, which he forced into the dirt. I still felt the ghost of the items we had taken to Winona and Pino in my hands, but I had nothing other than my presence to offer now.

The others continued to place gifts and speak over the stone, until I was the only one left. I walked forward, not fully sure what I should say at that moment. But I knew that I needed to try despite the discomfort of feeling as though I did not belong here, as though I were intruding.

"Thank you, Luca, for being one of the first strangers to express belief in me. I want you to know that I will fight for you, for what you wanted the world to be. Even if it kills me, I will craft something better. A place worthy of your sacrifice." Then, in a far quieter voice, I leaned forward and spoke, "May you return to Eternity."

***

Bellamy was convinced that gifts were necessary. The others had each given me a pin to represent them when I first got back from wherever it was Padon nested, the psycho. They were treasured and loved, each in my hair and pairing perfectly with my dress. Henry had also gifted me with my own set of throwing daggers, the shades of blue and silver a beautiful sight. Each had a different carving that matched my pins.

The prince, though, had not offered me a pin or a weapon. Instead, he said that he was saving his gift. I had not understood or even known about birthdays then, but now, I realized tonight was what he had been so adamant about holding off for.

After we portaled back to the celebration, which had thankfully been far more dedicated to Star Festival than me, we all dispersed. When I went to find Farai and Wrath, Bellamy stopped me, pulling me in to him.

I have something for you.

Over the last few months, he had gotten exceptionally talented at speaking to me through his mind, the shouted words so loud they were impossible to ignore. I beamed up at him, for once genuinely excited about whatever it was he had planned. Never had I been averse to being given gifts. Rather, I did not enjoy forcing everyone to celebrate me when I knew it would only afford me further hostility. Being given something special by a loved one was different. Gifts were personal and considerate—intimate. Not just romantically, but in a way that left you feeling loved, even in platonic situations. Bellamy, of course, left my heart racing and my mind swimming because anything he gave me was far more. He had this ability to pour love into everything he did, and I found myself addicted to the taste and feel and sound of it. Any form of affection he offered, I would take, because I was constantly hungry for my next fix of him.

Taking my hand, his scorching skin soothing and euphoric, Bellamy led us through the crowd. We both offered smiles and hellos for all that stopped to speak to us. There were moments when I felt creatures staring at me, an avalanche of thoughts tearing through my head as the collective group's mental voices grew louder. Despite my desire to practice, I wanted to devote this moment to Bellamy. He was so rarely put first, and he deserved every second of my undivided attention that I could spare. So I shut those mental gates, noting that they were starting to take on a sort of brass hue. The gold, which once shone brighter than the sun, had lost its gleam.

Maybe this was what healing felt like.

After facing the crowd, we eventually made it to a secluded area where the mountainside caved in on itself slightly, the darkness there combated only by the gleam of the moon and stars above—which I found myself drawn to more and more these days. Dropping my hand, Bellamy fumbled around, sounding far more flustered than he normally did. Pacing my breaths, I attempted to remain calm, my nerves a menacing threat that left me fearful I might act foolish whenever he presented whatever it was.

Nearly a full minute passed before he located the item, which was small enough to be hidden away in his clenched fist. His breath fanned across my face, smelling of the sweet icing from my cake and his signature smokey cinnamon scent. I wanted to joke, to say he was taking forever or that I was experiencing secondhand embarrassment watching him open and close his mouth, but I could not bring myself to do it. Yes, serious moments like this were notorious for discomfort, but I thought then that I could manage it—would gladly suffer the awkward tension in order to have this perfect memory with him.

"Let me preface this by saying that I know how much you have been through, Asher. I cannot fathom what it was like to live the life you did, and I do not know if you have even processed all of it, let alone healed from the never-ending list of traumas. Before Pino…passed," he choked out the words, blue eyes glowing and lips turned up in a sad smile, "I told him never to put you in gold. I believed it was the most important aspect of keeping you healthy because I thought you needed separation from that if there would ever be a chance for you to recover. While I do not know if I was right then, I think now you do not need to avoid it. You need to reclaim it."

Dipping his head closer to mine, he lifted his hand, opening his fingers to reveal to me what was within. There, in his palm, sat a thin gold chain. Rubies were placed intermittently around it, the teardrop shapes dangling slightly. The clasp was two circles—one littered with diamonds so bright that they sparkled silver beneath the moon, the other boasting black gems that reflected the light from the diamonds. There was nothing but beauty there, and still, I felt my head growing too light, my breaths picking up at the thought of letting that gold touch my skin.

As always, he picked up on that inner turmoil, reaching for my hand and holding the jewelry away from me. Sometime during the last few seconds, I had begun to shake, my body succumbing to the panic the gold had brought on. Had I not just convinced myself I moved past this? That my mental gates had tarnished because I was healing? Why did the suggestion of the smallest bit of gold possibly touching my skin send me spiraling down into that darkness I had so desperately fought back against?

"I believe in you, Ash. Even if you choose not to take this, I will still have faith in your greatness. Your worth is not contingent on how fast you heal, and your strength is not determined by how unfeeling you are. There is more to life than existing for the will of others. So, if you want, we can throw this off the side of the mountain or into the Sea of Akiva. It is your gift and your choice." A nervous and reassuring smile formed on his face, his hand letting mine go to cup my cheek and jaw.

I nodded, leaning in to his hand and looking down at the gold. It was just metal. It was just a color. But, somehow, it was also a mountain of painful memories that had formed in my heart, golden and immoveable. If I wore that, would I be submitting once more to the will of Mia and Xavier—even if only somewhat?

"I—I am afraid." No, I was *terrified*.

"I know it is scary, Ash. More than that, even. I know I will never understand what it is like to be placed in a golden prison and told to be thankful. But the gold was never your captor, the fae royals were. Do not let them steal more from you. Do not allow them the satisfaction of controlling you in this way." His voice was drenched in determined sincerity, body rigid with tension as he once more held up the bracelet.

Maybe it was the logic of his words or my own desire to be more than a weak little princess. Perhaps it was simply him. Whatever the reason might have been, I found myself nodding, lifting up my arm for him. His answering smile could only be described as the sun itself. Bright and beautiful and warm—perfection incarnate.

But, instead of grabbing my wrist, he placed a bruising kiss to my mouth and then kneeled. I watched him slowly slide down my body, smirking up at me as he went.

"What, Princess, do you not trust me?" he whispered, letting his fingers drag down my legs.

I hummed in response, unable to do anything but bask in the feel of his hands on me. A finger looped through the red strap that connected to my sandal, using it to tug my foot upwards. I grabbed onto his shoulders to maintain my balance, my eyes darting down to watch as he clasped the jewelry around my ankle instead of my wrist. When he finished, he placed a kiss to the two circles.

"Our story began with a gilded princess and a bloody prince, but it ends like this, Ash. A queen of stars and a king of night, joining to secure the future. We are the clasp that holds this tale together." He paused, the air growing thick as he released my foot, with my gift now secured to my ankle. When he looked up at me once more, his face held all the love of a million hearts—stronger than any written before. "You are everything. The beginning and the end and—"

"Every moment in between," I finished, tugging him upwards and reuniting our mouths once more. Here in his arms, beneath his touch, against his lips—here I was home. Here I was *whole*.

So, I consumed him, devoured every offering I was presented. I ravished him with my mouth, my hands, my body. Our moans filled the air as he pushed me against the mountain behind us, a small giggle leaving my lips at the memory of another rocky wall he had once pressed me into. As if he understood, Bellamy's own chuckles sounded, mixing with the lust and the love—telling our story to the world around us.

Just as his hand slid between my legs, neither of us quite caring that there were others just around the corner and out of the darkness, an eerie and all-too-familiar voice cut in.

"Surely you have some modicum of shame, princeling." Wrath was quite unimpressed by our public display, sitting mere feet away with a bored and slightly disgusted look on his face.

Bellamy groaned against my mouth, squeezing my thigh before backing away. "I hope you know that we all loathe you, cat."

"Hey!" I smacked Bellamy's arm, glaring up at his smug face. "I do not hate him!"

"I think he is quite funny." Farai's voice came from around the corner, amusement filling his tone. "You are not naked, are you, Ash?"

I groaned, embarrassed and far less than satisfied. Though maybe that was for the best. Public sex was probably universally frowned upon. Patting Bellamy on the cheek, I pushed away and bent down to scratch beneath Wrath's chin. He purred, his current size that of a large dog. "You are a little shit, and I love you."

Bellamy sighed, leaning forward to place a kiss to my forehead and flicking a still-purring Wrath on the nose. He earned a horrifying growl, which only left him laughing as he patted Farai on the shoulder and left us. For his part, Farai looked at me with a knowing and devious look in his eyes. One that reminded me of who we had been before our lives were turned upside down. In moments like this, I missed those versions of us.

"Well, seeing as I successfully ruined the prince's mood, I think I will go find something sweet to eat as a reward." I watched on as Wrath allowed himself to shrink down to the size of a house cat, knowing that he used this version of himself to pull on the heartstrings of unsuspecting mortals and demons alike. "You look beautiful, Strange One."

Before I could say something kind back, Wrath darted away, leaving me grinning fondly at the place he had left. Farai came up to me, grabbing both of my cheeks and looking into my eyes. The whites of his irises bore into me, as if, like Jasper, he could see whatever aura radiated from me now.

"Ash, are you okay? Truly?" While Farai had always been the least serious of our friend group, there was a paternal tone to his voice just then, like a father checking in on his daughter. And it was those loving and concerned words that left me unable to do anything but wrap my arms around his neck and breathe him in. As always, he smelled of the woods on a warm summer day, and I relished in it. I knew that one day,

OF REALMS AND CHAOS

when our family was whole and our world was safe, I would be able to tell him the truth. Jasper and Nicola were gone though, and without them, I could not break. So I lifted my hand, cupping Faria's face just as he did mine, and I smiled.

"I am good. How are you?" I felt the flinch beneath my fingertips at the same time I saw it, his face contorting in a brief show of pain. "Tomorrow, we will discuss our next move. We will find Nicola and Jasper, and we will bring them here. They will be safe, Fair."

With a nod, he breathed deeply and leaned down to offer a soft kiss to my head. When he backed away again, he was sporting one of his enchanting smiles, those full lips rising to crinkle his nearly glowing eyes. Though I knew he was not okay, that he was hiding behind the mask of his former self, my own smile still lifted my cheeks.

Time was the most precious currency—the one thing no one could get back, no matter how wealthy or beautiful or important they were. Still, I would give him that, no matter how much I lost in the process. Farai would have as much time as he needed.

Outstretching his hand, he winked, those shoulders once more straight despite the sorrow and fear his mind radiated. "Will you dance with me, old friend?"

Laughing, I nodded back, taking his hand and allowing him to lead us to the dance floor. We were a sight to behold if those in attendance were to be believed. They stared on with open mouths and wide eyes, tracking our every movement. Farai—ever the attention seeker—lifted his chin to the sky, pulled me closer, and began.

Our first full rotation around the training yard was dedicated to Farai showing off. He lifted me in the air and dipped me to the ground and spun me until I was dizzy. I smiled like a fool the whole time, except for when we passed Henry. Resisting the urge to stick my tongue out at him was utterly impossible.

My turn next, little brat.

Nodding at Henry as we passed, I let out an embarrassing squeal when Farai lifted me above his head before letting me drop, catching me inches above the ground.

It was the second round that brought me back in time, though. First, the Shifter chose an elephant, morphing his nose into a long trunk and stretching his ears until they flopped outwards. The crowd let out a collective gasp, but I could not help letting out a snort and tilting my head back in laughter. We continued that way, dancing as he changed before my eyes.

When the song was over, he allowed his face to fade back, dipping his head to whisper in my ear, "What do you say, think they earned a grand finale?"

Not allowing me the chance to answer, he spun me one last time, my body twirling away from his. I stilled just in time to watch him spread his arms wide, morphing them into long black and white wings. His legs bent, forming a half squat, and then he launched himself up and back, flipping midair. He did not land; instead, his body shrunk and transformed, a stunning black and white eagle appearing where he once had been. The crowd remained silent, staring in awe as Farai took flight above us. Smiling, I shoved open my mental gates, letting my magic burrow into every mind in attendance and ordering them to dance—to laugh and have fun.

By the time shouts of excitement filled the space, I was walking away, searching for my pumpkin. He stood beside Damon and two females—one of them I almost immediately recognized. Her long black hair was loose, that dark and glowing skin nearly matching it.

"Lara," I said, nodding to her and trying my luck at a smile.

She stared at me like I was mad, or perhaps that was her way of assessing my will to live so that she could figure out how much effort it would take to convince me to jump off the nearest cliffside.

"You are less angry than before. That hope will only disappoint you." That voice was still melodic and high, the opposite of her attitude—

just as her periwinkle gown was, the dress tightly fitting to her body and dragging behind her.

"Charming as ever." I regretted the slight when she let her piercing blue eyes stray to the ground, and I found myself offering my hand to shake. Lara looked at it, touched my palm with one finger, and then proceeded to shamelessly stare at me in contemplation. "Good to see you again, bubbles."

Turning to face the other female, I noted that she had the exact same russet skin and deep hazel eyes as Cyprus. Even her hair, which barely passed her chin, was the soft brown of his. "You must be Ray. Cyprus has told me so much about you."

"Yes, I am. Wow, I cannot believe I am talking to you right now. You know, Lara and I planted a whole patch of vanilla in her garden just for you. I think you will really like it. I am also great at decorating! I can get you your own room if you would like space from Prince—I mean General—Bellamy. Not that he is not good to be around, which he is— not that I desire to be *with* him. I am very much so not interested. Of course, he is quite handsome, not that I look at him that way. You are handsome, too. I mean, beautiful. Not that I look at *you* that way. I do not mean to sexualize you both. I just mean that sometimes it can be nice to have space, or I can find you two a bigger room?"

Did she breathe? Ever?

"Ray, stop, you do not have to worry about offending me. Please, breathe." I laughed, watching as she bent forward and let her hands rest on her knees as she gasped for air. Her outfit consisted of brown trousers that fit tightly around her waist but slowly flared out as they went down, a thicker material than casual wear but also not nearly as thick as the fighting leathers Bellamy's Trusted favored. On her upper half, she wore a white top made of what looked almost like yarn, the string braided together in multiple rows, wrapping around her upper body and sporting no sleeves or straps.

"Would you care to dance, Asher? Perhaps give Ray a break from panic attacks for a bit?" Damon's voice was gentle as always, his outstretched hand calling attention to the navy silk top he wore which fit perfectly to his toned chest. Was it bad that I compared everyone to Bellamy? That my eyes and mind seemed to agree that no one would ever compare?

"Hey, now," Henry interjected, smacking Damon's hand away from me and quickly grabbing me by the shoulders. "I called dibs. Wait your turn."

Damon laughed, saluting as Henry guided me to the center of the dance floor. I joined in, feeling so blissful and free and, for once, calm. Henry took my hand, placing it on his shoulder before gripping my other one tightly and beginning our dance. Like most things, he was excellent at it, taking a much more technical approach than Farai had.

"My mother likes you, which possibly means that my fear of world domination held more merit than even I thought." His eyes strayed to his left, and I found my own following, catching sight of Odilia. She loomed near a table with various beverages, her gaze unabashedly glued to us as we wove through the other dancing couples. Leaning closer, he whispered, "If she did not desire a strong queen, then she likely would have forced me to court you by any means necessary."

"Ah, well, unfortunately for Lady Odilia, I am quite picky. I fear I could not get past the orange hair." Together, we laughed conspiratorially, our dance skills so evenly matched that I lost count of how many songs passed before Bellamy was there, catching me at the tail end of a rather dramatic spin. Henry released me, allowing Bellamy to wrap me in his arms and utilize the momentum to maintain time with the beat.

"It has been too long since we danced, Princess." He purred the words through a dashing smirk, all the pride of a cocky prince upon his face.

Unlike his friends, Bellamy's presence against me left my mind spinning right along with my body. The press of his hand on my waist, a position choice far more respectful than I would have expected, was like a current. It dragged my heart and my mind away from the present, carrying me towards the image of a future I longed for. Every slight graze of my chest against his stomach was a ballad, the keys of the piano pressing down to craft a song all our own. One that would exist forever in the ethers, among the stars as they danced along.

"It has, Prince." It was the only response I could muster, but I knew by the softening of his eyes that he understood what my gravelly voice meant. Once again, it was like he had magic of the mind, rather than me.

"I love you, Asher."

"And I love you, Bellamy."

Henry's bright hair came into view again, and for some reason, my eyes felt the urgent need to look his way. I watched as he jolted forward, nearly knocking over a table, as if someone had struck him. With a gasp, he looked up at us, mouthing two words before he disappeared in rays of light.

Section five.

Bellamy pulled me tighter to him, and then we portaled too, arriving in a sort of meadow. The green grass and vibrant yellow flowers were made dull in the night, giving the entire scene an eerie quality. But it was not the darkness that I feared in that moment.

Henry stood a few feet away, holding out his palm with light seeping from him. For a moment, I stared on, confused at his display of magic. Then, from the thick stream of light, Genevieve appeared.

Silence threatened to reign over us, a firm dictator prepared to steal our voices for all of eternity. But the mortal princess fought bravely against it, stuttering out a string of sentences that would drop the shoe I had been grimly waiting for.

"My parents, they—they were too scared to take your offer. I—I came to—to warn you. The fae know where you are. They know, and they are coming. Please understand I did not mean for this to happen. I just wanted my brother back!"

Henry grabbed her by the shoulders, shaking her slightly. "Where are they coming to? Pike? Haven? How many are they bringing?"

His panicked questions seemed to slam into Genevieve, like it pained her to hear them. She flinched with each syllable, her eyes shut tightly.

"Of course they know where we are. Malcolm would be aware of where nearly everything is. Not much has changed in the last three hundred years. Why now? What would your parents' information truly tell them?" Bellamy's questions were rhetorical, his words mostly spoken to himself as he thought out loud in a slightly rattled voice.

When Genevieve looked to me, desperation forming tears in her soft brown eyes, I realized it was not necessarily us in danger. I knew how Xavier thought, the ways in which he plotted and planned. He was smart, strategic, and strong. If he could hurt us indirectly, plant seeds of doubt and tear us apart from within, then he would.

"They are going to attack a mortal kingdom who sided with us. That is why they needed to know where we were. They wanted us to be away so the mortals would be unprotected." Matter of fact. That was how my words sounded. Because I knew I was right, and as Genevieve nodded solemnly, I felt how true my next words were, too. "Behman. They are going for Behman."

CHAPTER FORTY-FIVE

ASHER

In all my life, I had never thought that the sight of blood would be something I grew used to. Yet there I stood—looking on as mortals and demons fell at the hands of fae, and vice versa. Witnessing the overly green kingdom become a river of red.

My hand dug into the hilt of one of my daggers, rage clouding my vision. I caught sight of a Shifter dragging a mortal with its teeth, the man screaming for help. That was all it took for me to move. The dagger left my hand without a sound, soaring through the air and finding purchase in the bear's open mouth as it released the limp body. Gurgling roars filled the air, my dagger protruding from the back of the Shifter's throat.

Without a second glance, I moved on, using my magic as often as I could. Upon the jumbled battlefield, it was hard to distinguish between friend and foe, let alone within their minds. But I still tried, often taking the safer approach of ordering them to sleep rather than killing them.

Bodies fell like raindrops, so reminiscent of the days during which rain proceeded reapings that I nearly lost my mind to the memories. Genevieve took my left just as a fae's sword swung down towards me. She deftly blocked them, crossing both of her swords to catch the enemy blade before kicking into the fae's chest, sending her stumbling back.

Slit your throat.

The female took her blade and followed my instructions, her gushing blood staining the grass beneath her. Genevieve looked at the fallen body, grim acceptance on her face. Neither of us stood there for long, each taking a different side to protect the other's back. We fought side by side, cutting down fae as quickly as we could. Both mortals and demons were still being portaled in as quickly as they could be, but that meant fighting heavily outnumbered until reinforcements could arrive.

Shah had been furious when I saw her last, and I witnessed just how much the love for one's realm could strengthen them when she jumped on the back of a fae a head taller than her and ended his life in seconds.

Wrath, too, was proving to us why he was so feared. He towered above, ripping gold-clad soldiers in half and laughing as they screamed in terror.

Across the clearing, Henry glowed in the night, a beacon of gore and death as he slaughtered fae between portaling. Each time he came back, he brought with him groups of soldiers ready to fight for Behman.

Bellamy, Damon, and Noe had been forced to transport soldiers too, needing their strength to portal as many as they could. Ranbir stayed behind as well, healing the wounded as they were brought in. But Lian, Farai, and Cyprus were fighting alongside us, cutting down as many as they could—both air and shadow-like mist killing as often as swords.

My eye caught on Lara as she appeared beside Henry, her small blue eyes searching the crowd with the same bleak look of tragic resolution that she seemed to always sport. Then, as quickly as she had come, she was gone, her body melting into liquid before taking flight, bubbles filling the spaces between gold and silver.

More screams sounded, and I felt myself pause, hating the sound of the fae—*my fae*—begging for mercy. Because they had not chosen this. With a deep breath, I closed my eyes and begged for Eternity to guide me, to forgive me just long enough to do what needed to be done.

When I opened my eyes again, my mental gates fell.

CHAPTER FORTY-SIX

BELLAMY

Five hundred, maybe more. That was how many we needed.

I could take about twenty-five at a time without completely diminishing myself. Noe could carry around forty. Henry could take about the same as me, Damon just slightly less. Others were helping, so it would not take long.

Three trips there. Three trips back. Barely any time at all away from Ash if we could organize fast enough. She would be fine. Of course she would. There was no doubt in my mind that she would be okay.

No doubt at all.

Seconds after my hand left hers, I knew I was wrong. All the doubts in the world creeped in on me as I screamed at a group to come to

OF REALMS AND CHAOS

me, forcing them to move faster. I needed to see her. We needed to get there. She needed our help.

Gods, they were slow.

"Hurry! Move!" Ten, fifteen, twenty-one. When the twenty-fifth was followed immediately by a twenty-sixth, I growled my frustration and demanded that the murderous magic inside of my veins *for once* did what it was fucking told.

We portaled quickly, two of the mortals falling to their knees from the pain and one demon dry-heaving.

But too many were inebriated from our celebrations, so we were limited on who could come fight. I would not put it past Xavier Mounbetton to plan for this—to learn of our most sacred holiday from Malcolm and plan the attack on that very night.

For all my annoyance with Ash's self-sacrificing mindset, even I could not deny that I had been too selfish. I needed to be more alert, more prepared. Instead, I was hanging garland and sitting beside a seamstress as she sketched a dress. While I would not take those choices back, I also knew that I needed to do more than I had been.

Feet touching the hard ground at Pike, I told myself that I would be the prince that Eoforhild deserved. That we would win this battle and then win the whole damn war. For Eoforhild, for Winona, for Pino, for Luca, for Ash—for *me*.

Another group rushed me, this one moving with more purpose and quicker feet. Only twenty-three were in my vicinity before I was gone, ripping a hole through time and space and depositing them on the ground in Selkans—a secluded village in the northernmost part of Behman. Briefly, I watched Asher bend down and slice the back of a Golden Guard's knee, moving away before he even hit the ground. A wicked, gleeful smile split my face, and then I was gone once more.

Exactly twenty-five soldiers were waiting when I got back, each of them immediately gathering to portal. In the seconds it took for us to return, Asher had moved. She was back to back with Genevieve, the two of them fighting so harmoniously that it appeared they had trained together. I was momentarily stunned, so much so that I portaled back and did a fourth run. By the time I realized that I was not—in fact—planning to do that, I was already there. So I grabbed eighteen soldiers, and then I was back in the thick of it.

A Golden Guard was on me instantly, clearly ready for my return. Not even bothering to use my powers, I ducked his sword, digging my fingers into the ground below us. When I came back up, I did so with a handful of dirt and a desperate need to find Asher. I threw every grain of dirt into his face, listening with joy as he howled in pain. A foot to the chest, and then he was down.

When my eyes lifted, it was to see Asher standing just ahead of me, her eyes closed and her head slightly tilted back. Above us, thunder boomed in the sky, lightning painting the gray clouds. Just as Ash opened her eyes, I saw the reflection of the streaks light up her hair, bathing her in silver.

And then I felt her magic.

It pressed into my mind like a scalding iron, branding me with her will. My mental shields only barely held against the onslaught, legs giving out and heart racing so fast it left me dizzy. Rain plummeted down upon us, mud and blood mixing and causing my hands to sink into the ground as I moved to catch myself. The second I was steady, my eyes were forward again, teeth gritting against the pressure of her magic demanding obedience.

Her voice came not long after, the sound of it a haunting melody that echoed in my ears and my mind.

"Sleep."

Every single body in the clearing collapsed, falling to the ground where they stood. When a female nearby fell, I was not ready for her armor, my gaze fixed on Asher with enough intensity to leave me unable to move.

Heavy and dense gold hit my head with a crack, and the last thing I saw was Asher's face staring into the distance.

CHAPTER FORTY-SEVEN

ASHER

Everything hurt. Everything ached. Everything blurred.

And then she appeared.

Was I losing my mind now? Was that the consequence of such a gift? Did Eternity wish to punish me?

"You're so odd. Like a bumbling little drake." Her voice was lovely, as was her hair. So odd.

"Pink."

"It is. Want to know a secret?" She leaned in, almost conspiratorially. Her light brown skin and rosy cheeks blocked the bodies around me from view. Unbelievably long lashes framed her glowing pink eyes, her flowing navy dress sticking to her as the rain assaulted us. "He lusts only for you, that prince. Like a devoted praising their oh-so-benevolent god. That male there, he worships you."

She pointed towards Bellamy, whose head had been crushed into the mud by golden armor. I knew I needed to save him, to move, to do anything, but I felt rooted to the spot. Transfixed by the creature before me.

"Are you a goddess?" Asking that felt wrong, like it might upset her. Disgrace her. Annoy her.

"You're not one of those idiots who believe in gods, are you? Eternity is above, below, and all around. We breathe it in and speak to it in our dreams. And yet you creatures wish to pray to false gods? That's actually quite embarrassing for you."

"I have met a god," I muttered, shrugging at her. Were my knees shaking, or was it the ground beneath me? I wished it would stop.

"Sure you have. I think what you need is medical attention. Let me take you home, get you nice and cozy, introduce you to the big boss, and then all will be well. Come now, smelly." She gestured for me to come, clearly eager to go wherever she considered home.

But that was not right, was it? My home was here. With Bellamy. He was my home. And they all needed me. They would drown if I did not wake them up soon. Had any fallen upon their weapons? What would I do if they were harmed? I needed help. I could not go anywhere when my focus was so vital to this moment.

"Why are you doing that? Stop it. I'm trying to preserve my magic, and you're over here resisting your most prominent sins." Her hand gripped my wrist, tugging me away from the mass of bodies. "Color me annoyed."

"But you are pink." I looked back, my words far more absentminded than normal. Bellamy needed my help. Bellamy needed me. Bellamy was too important.

"Please tell me you're more fun when you're not disoriented, because if not, then this is going to be a long life."

A swirl of pink began to swarm us, her grip firm around my wrist and her face tight with obvious annoyance. It was then, when she lifted her free arm towards the glittering pink cloud, that I suddenly felt my control slink back into me. Groans came from behind us, and I peeked to see a bloody Bellamy being lifted by a smaller than normal Wrath.

"I think I will stay, actually." My words were calm, but my body had begun to tremble, my magic weaker than normal after exerting so much, but still there and ready to fight back with all it had.

The female sighed, turning to face me with what could only be described as a vexed expression. "Must I force you? I prefer not to, and I just know he'll use it against me if I do." She did not sound all that opposed to it.

"Who is he?" I asked, stalling for time by allowing my curiosity free rein. Her hold on my wrist tightened, her voice dropping down lower and sounding deadlier than a sword as she spoke.

"We don't have time for stupid questions. Now, come on." With one last heave, she tried to drag me into the cloud of what I assumed was magic.

"No."

"Yes."

"No!"

"Ugh, this is ridiculous! I have killed for less! How does anyone put up with you? All I want is to finish my mission, get my creature, and be done with it all. But of course, you need to be difficult!" She rambled the words, her hand moving in time as her rage and annoyance permeated the air. "I sent that fetch to make this easier, quicker even. Ha! Some joke that was."

She sent the fetch? She called me annoying, but—as per usual—I seemed to be the only one willing to answer questions around here.

"Do you know what awaits you here, Asher? Death. That's what you'll face if you don't come with me. Not just your death, but all of theirs, too." Her arms lifted, gesturing to the sea of bodies around us. When she pointed towards Bellamy, I had to do my best not to flinch. If she noticed him moving, what would she do? Would she kill him? By sheer luck, she did not let her eyes stray from mine, instead staring at me with determination. Just then, I felt the ground beneath my feet harden, a ripple of Earth power that seemed to lift every sleeping soldier out of the mud as it changed the dirt to stone. A quick glance away from the battlefield showed me that a mere foot to my right, the ground remained a mess of mud and blood. "That sexy little prince you love so much? He will die if you don't shut up, take my fucking hand, and come with me now."

"I am not going with you, and none of them will die because I will not allow it. For once, I am not afraid of my magic. It will save them. *I* will save them." While I felt the truth of what she said in my bones, I also knew that I could change it. No future was set in stone. There was always a chance to make a new one.

Did it make sense to her, that desperate need to alter the ending that had been written? Did she think me insane? Did I care if she did?

Was she glowing?

"Come with me now, or face the consequences. I won't offer a second time."

"No," I said, squaring my shoulders and lifting my chin. I felt her rage then, the taste of it sweet and foreign.

"Oh, if I could rip out your throat, I would. I hope you know that my death will stain your hands red, you little pest. When you visit my grave, because I'm sure he will gladly utilize my loss as some sort of manipulation tactic, I hope you remember this moment."

With that, she spun on her heel and walked towards the cloud of sparkling pink mist, stopping inches shy of it.

"On second thought, let me leave you with a parting gift." Over her shoulder, she looked towards Bellamy and Wrath, the white of her eyes slowly growing and every speck of pink bleeding from her irises. Her body glowed the same dusty rose color of her hair, and then she looked to me.

I felt it then, like a hammer slamming into my mind, shaking free every thought of inadequacy and each desperate need to be more than I was. I gasped, reaching for my chest.

"What do you get when you put together a female yearning for redemption and a male craving love?" The question was worded with a facetious tone, as if the entirety of our lives was a joke to her. Or perhaps she had seen something similar before and knew it would never end well. "The perfect storm."

As if on cue, thunder boomed above, rattling my jaw and making me flinch. She disappeared, the pink dissipating behind her. Bellamy's arms wrapped around me moments later, his hold on me so tight that it hurt. He clawed at my body, his mud-and-blood-soaked hands searching for injuries he would not find.

And though her magic had seemed to slowly fade from my body, it still left behind every thought and feeling that I had about my own inability to be what everyone needed. It hollowed me of all my joy and triumph and even anger, leaving me with nothing more than the need to do better.

"Are you okay? Who was that? Did she hurt you?" Each word sounded as if it were an effort to say, like he was speaking with limited air.

I shook my head, his hands finally settling on my face as he leaned down to look me directly in the eyes. Blood still dripped from a startling gash just above his eyebrow, though it seemed to be slowing as it fought to heal.

Wrath's body wove between our legs, trying to catch my undivided attention. Allowing my eyes to drift down despite my mind's inability to focus on anything but what needed to be done, I noticed the blood that coated Wrath's fur. The silky gray strands were now almost black, his sharp teeth tucked away within his mouth. Those yellow eyes bore into me—seeing what, I did not know.

All I knew was that I had failed. Spectacularly. Whatever that female and her master wanted with me, it was nothing compared to the epic ways in which we would all die if I did not fix this.

"Strange One, you do not look right. Are you sure you are okay?"

"We need to get everyone awake and start portaling back. Ranbir will be able to check you out. Once we are in Eoforhild, we can figure everything out." I pushed away from them, ignoring Bellamy's planning and stepping into the mud as I clawed at my head—willing the thoughts to leave my mind while simultaneously succumbing to them.

Bellamy's and Wrath's words became muffled, falling behind the voice within my mind that scolded me for being so selfish, that wondered why I did not do more when seeking help from Xalie or even try to convince Yrassa. Had I truly allowed myself to give up? How could I live with myself if I let that continue on?

"I need to go to Yrassa." Whatever hostile argument the two had been having was abruptly ended in favor of staring at me in disbelief. And why not? I had just promised them that I would stop trying, that I was done. While I knew that the female's magic had begun to gorge on my psyche, depleting me of any and all egocentric thoughts, I still could not stop the way it made me feel.

"What do you mean? Ash, we need to get to Dunamis. This has gone on for too long. You need to speak to Adbeel, and we need to prepare. I need for us—"

Like a bow pulled taut and held there for far too long, I snapped, the harsh arrow that was my words hitting home in Bellamy's chest.

"We have no time to waste prancing around Eoforhild and speaking to your king. Lives are at stake. The *world* is at stake! For one moment, can you please care about anything other than these stupid fantasies of us living under a rainbow and picking strawberries and having a happily ever after? That is not going to happen, especially if we do not stop this war!" I yelled, voice hoarse from the hysterical way I shoved the thoughts to the surface.

My hands flew outwards gesturing to the destruction and the death that surrounded us. A very clear show of how bad this could—and would—become. For his part, he just watched me with barely parted lips and unnaturally wide eyes.

"I was not meant to live in joy, how can you not see that? Everything I touch withers and dies—*I kill it*, Bellamy. I kill it! I cannot show you love through small kisses and pretty flowers and pregnant bellies. I was not made to be that way. But I can fight for you and I can die for you. How can you be so selfish as to not let me do so? To do everything I can to repent? To save the lives of those I have wronged? The world does not revolve around us and our self-centered desires! The world was not made for dreamers!"

Stunned, he momentarily stared at me, the great smack of my vitriol hitting him in the chest and leaving him gasping for air. But then…well, it seemed the female's magic had fed the very opposite trait of Bellamy's than it had mine. But it left him just as uncontrollably frantic.

"You want to call me selfish? Fine!" It was his turn to yell, that beautiful and raspy voice somehow sharp now, when it was so often a lulling and heavy tune. "I am selfish. I never pretended to be anything else with you, Asher. From the moment I saw your face in Reader River, I knew I would do anything, *be anything*, for you. You say you would die for me. That is the easy part. I would kill for you. I would burn the world to dust for you. I would defy the gods for you. I would become the villain, *gladly*! Do you think that I do not see how we differ in that? That I do not realize you would choose the world over me? That you would sacrifice everything for the good of the world, including us?"

Fingers threaded through his hair, tugging as he tried to speak his thoughts. Small black flames erupted near his feet, the magic in his veins writhing beneath the skin of his neck. A hiss sounded from Wrath, the dalistori looking around us with paranoia and trepidation upon his face.

Bellamy's voice caressed my heart once more, the action soothing until it was not.

"Before you, I was fighting for my realm out of obligation. Blindly attempting to save everything and everyone that would rather see me rot in the ground than sit atop a throne. I never even wanted the damn thing. I do not want to wear a crown and watch as half of me wars with the other. I barely cared to exist before you! And then I watched you walk onto that balcony in a hideous fucking gold gown, looking so clearly miserable, and I wanted nothing more than to make the world better. For you! Everything I do is for you! And if it is from my own selfish desire to be the thing that makes you happy or perhaps to feed off of that joy like a drug, then I am *selfish*. And I do not want to be anything else. Because it constantly feels like the end, and I do not regret soaking up every second when I do not know if it will be my last! But you refuse to do the same, to put me first! How do you think that makes me feel?"

I meant to speak, to apologize or argue further or maybe even laugh at the ludicrousy of such a thing because of course it was the end. We were all quickly sailing towards death, none of us prepared and each of us pretending like that was not the truth.

Before I could so much as think to conjure a response, Wrath's shouts filled the air.

"Get down!"

The hissed instructions tore my attention, and I found myself trying to dive down, Bellamy jumping towards me to cover my body. We grunted as we hit the soggy and sticky mud, the thickened substance practically grabbing hold of our limbs. Even with all of the sloshing, I still heard the cry of pain, still understood exactly what the next graphic smack into the mud was. With a shove, I got Bellamy off of me, and what I saw would live on a throne within my nightmares, just beside Winona's throat being slit.

Wrath lay in the mud, his stomach rising and falling far too quickly, his breaths coming out as pained wheezes. I screamed, unable to stop the blood-curdling sound from scratching up my throat, clawing its way to freedom and reverberating back to us as it echoed in time with a streak of lightning. Both Bellamy and I reached for him at the same time, the golden arrow wobbling as we jostled the dalistori. A small hiss of pain left Bellamy's lips as he quickly ripped his hand away, but my eyes remained on Wrath.

Cries of agony came and went—hello, goodbye; alive, dead; the beginning, the end. Not bothering to look around us, I honed in on Wrath's distressed face, his yellow eyes squinted in anguish.

"It is going to be fine, Wrath. We are going to make you better. Ranbir can help you. Please, hold on." My fingers went to his chin, rubbing just below it as I pulled back his fur to look at the arrow.

Black blood poured from his throat, soaking his body and my hands with each gurgled breath or stuttered heartbeat.

"I do not see anyone moving. Whoever shot that is either gone or hiding. Either way, we need to go, now. Places like this are too open. Wrath, can we pick you up?" Bellamy's ringed fingers appeared in my line of sight as he placed them around my forearm, but I heard the way he muttered to himself, the unsure and somewhat resigned tone to his voice.

Wrath must have too. Because he let his body relax, the tension leaving him as he looked over to me. I shook my head, not willing to hear goodbyes. No more. Please, no more.

I am proud to call you mine and to be yours, Asher.

Another arrow flew through the air, Bellamy's hand moving faster than I could fathom as he caught it just in front of his face. Both of us looked up to see a male in the distance, a large, golden bow in his hands. He stayed for but a moment, and then he was gone, disappearing in a puff of black shadows.

That was when the ground beneath us shook.

Mia was coming.

"Please, do not leave me, Wrath. I love you. I love you so much. You are my family. Please." I was begging now, the words coming out in a cracked whisper.

Kill them all for me, Strange One.

That voice, still eerie within my mind even when death—his master—knocked upon his door, was like locking the bolt. And still, I watched as his chest began to slow its pace, and his eyes fluttered closed.

And then the soldiers appeared in the distance.

Wisps of black shadows made way for golden armor, which glinted in the distance as the rain fell harder—the thunder louder than before. My fingers tightened on Wrath's unmoving body, the sound of his heart gone.

I leaned down, letting my forehead rest against his rain-and-blood-soaked side. No, I could not take this. Could not survive this.

"Please, Eternity, if you exist, bring him back to me."

Padon, help me. Help Wrath. Help your creation.

Silence kissed my cheek, death stroked my hair, and the end greeted me.

"I love you, Wrathy." My whispered affection breezed past the dalistori's unhearing ears, and suddenly, my body was vibrating with his namesake. My eyes rose, looking in the distance at the coming army.

"I cannot portal them all on my own, and if we wake them, then they will be in a daze and likely panic. We have to be the ones to fight." Bellamy's words were full of nerves, not for the fight, but for my mental state. I swore to myself then that I would not worry him, not show how broken I was, not distract him.

Nodding, I released Wrath, wiping my hand clean before grabbing onto Bellamy and squeezing his in return as he threaded our fingers together.

"Then we fight," I declared, staring into his blue eyes—into home.

"For Wrath," he whispered.

"For Luca," I returned. "For Winona and Pino."

"For you, Princess," he proclaimed, leaning in to press his lips to mine. The kiss was a promise—a vow—and though now was not the time to be thinking such things, to be dreaming at all, I saw a flash of a projected image in my mind. Something that made my soul ache and my heart cleave in two.

I watched as Bellamy showed me a vision of him down on one knee, presenting me with a ring. And I mourned all that Wrath would miss.

CHAPTER FORTY-EIGHT

ASHER

Shadows enveloped us, pulling my body apart before threading it back together. Bellamy's magic was volatile as it took us to the coming soldiers, angry and violent in its work. The second our knees landed, it shot out, black fire so hot it felt cold as it burned through the first line of soldiers. I dove, rolling to the side before standing up and forcing my own magic out.

That well of power in my chest roared at the demolishing of my mental gates, watching the faded gold bars break and charging forward upon their downfall. Minds winked into existence, thoughts swarming me as my once-barricaded magic flew forward, soaring like an eagle ready for the kill. My hands reached for the sword at my back and remaining dagger at my thigh, the one gifted to me all those months ago.

I am vengeance.

My scream marked the fall of seventy-seven mortal soldiers from Maliha, the charging force gone in the blink of an eye, dropping to the ground. For Wrath.

Never to breathe again. For Winona.

And when the fae charged on, I had no sympathy as I, too, ran. The first swing of my sword sent an arm flying, the blade slicing right through the vulnerable place where the armor connected at the elbow. For Luca.

When scorching red came for me, seeking something to burn, I gave it what it wanted. Far faster than I normally did, I found the mind of a Fire, watching with a wicked smile as they caught the flames and threw them towards a group of their own.

Bellamy was nearby, using the mud to bury soldiers alive, the rain-filled wind sweeping up bodies. The black flames had moved to form a wall at our backs, protecting all who remained unconscious. I fought to keep them that way, splitting my focus and slowing me down. Awareness pricked at my mind, a single being fighting hard against my magic—throwing up flimsy mental shields to try and allow themselves enough reprieve to awake.

I knew it was Henry, made obvious by the way the blinding Sun magic tasted of fresh citrus. But if I let him awaken I might lose control of them all, so I ordered him back into unconsciousness as I slid through the mud. Grabbing the ankle of a female who was mid shift, I shoved my elbow into her knee, which was exposed by the armor that had split during her transition. She screamed as the bone broke. I eagerly shattered her mind, moving on to the next so quickly that my wet hair whipped into my face.

The tip of my boot sunk into the mud as I stood, sticking and nearly bringing me back down. A Water made quick work of taking advantage, catching the droplets as they fell and holding them midair just long enough to look at me with sad eyes. When she lowered her arms, the movement erratic and abrupt, water barreled into me, burrowing down my throat and taking residence in my lungs—demanding my surrender.

Before my body gave in, I squeezed my dagger, heard Henry's voice telling me to picture it going straight through my target, and threw it. The blade sunk between her eyes, sending her flying to the ground and smacking into the slop at her feet. But the water had already begun to hibernate at the bottom of my lungs, comfortable in the space it did not belong. I choked and gargled, trying and failing to cough up the water. Black spots filled my vision, my head swimming and my magic still reaching out.

I tasted lilac just as my eyes closed.

But then I heard my name screamed above the battle, Bellamy's voice so loud it startled me back into consciousness, my heart slowing but arms flailing. All the water that had entered my lungs began to crawl out, climbing up my throat and leaving me gasping on the ground. I had no time to spare because Bellamy was now taking on the entire swarm of soldiers, the elements roaring around us all. I stood on shaky legs, prepared to step in. That was when I noticed that, in his distraction, he did not see the lion charging him from behind, his icy blue gaze a tunnel leading only to me.

Tears streamed down my face as I gave all that I had and let my magic do what it did best.

Kill.

They fell like dominos, the Golden Guard. Beautiful metallic dominos that slumped rather than teetered down. A wave of death crashed upon the shore that was Selkans, Bellamy's power slowly fading as he witnessed what I truly was. The damage I could do.

And I paid the price as my magic left me, the well in my chest almost completely void of that which made me special. Behind the walls of flames, creatures from both sides began to stir.

Strong arms caught me as I fell, and I managed to smile, my head tilting up in search of those annoying dimples. Instead, I found a pair of nearly black eyes and a blinding smile. Mahogany hair and brown skin sent warning bells off in my mind as he looked at me fondly, like an owner seeing their pet for the first time in too long.

The male from Haven. Malcolm, according to Bellamy.

"Hello, Asher. It is wonderful to officially meet you," he purred, a single finger tucking my bloody hair behind my ear. He grabbed the jagged top, murmuring quietly, "I remember when these had points, you know."

Without any sign of him doing so, shadows pooled beside me, from them walking Mia. Her orange hair had been soaked, her face completely bare. I had never seen her this way, without cosmetics coating her face or gold upon her body. But there she stood, wearing black of all colors, the leathers reminiscent of those that Bellamy's Trusted wore. That I now wore.

But it was her face that stunned me. There, dotting her cheeks and nose, were freckles. Seeing those paired with her eyes, so blue they looked frozen, made my heart sink. My gaze found Bellamy just as a blade of fire whizzed through the air, stopped only by the wall of mud that Mia had conjured.

"I will fucking kill you, do you hear me? I will fucking kill you!" Bellamy's words were a snarl—an oath born of hatred. He portaled to our side, his fist connecting with my captor's nose.

Mia seized my wrist, tugging me towards her just as Bellamy took the male to the ground. A branch appeared from thin air, the wood coming towards my body as if to secure me—trap me. I bent low, wrapping my arms around Mia and sending her to the ground in the same way Bellamy had the traitor.

She screamed on the way down, her foot hitting my shin as we fell. "How dare you! I cannot believe—" My head smashed into hers before she could finish, and then she was crying out, grabbing at her nose as blood fled from her presence.

Bellamy's hand found me, and we portaled a distance away, both of us heaving but unwavering as we faced off with Mia and Malcolm. They stood, mirroring us in both stance and fury.

"You are a liar, Mia. A liar and a wicked soul," I seethed. Though they were harsh words, it was grief that conjured them. Because when I found out the truth about Mia, I lost the only mother I had ever known.

She sneered, the look too eager to be hurt. "Oh, but I am not the only one, my flower. Does the male behind you not keep secrets?"

Bellamy stilled at her words, pulling my hand towards him and letting out a growl of rage. "Do not," he said, the threat of violence resting in the few feet between us and them.

"Come now, Asher. Who else do you know that has unruly dark hair and a dimple upon his cheek? Go on, think about it. I will give you a moment." She smiled as she spoke, blood coating her perfectly white teeth. Malcolm chuckled beside her, his eyes trained on Bellamy before he winked at me and disappeared beneath the magic of the moon.

Memories of Xavier's smiling face bombarded me, his left cheek showcasing a single dimple when his smile was full enough. And his hair, the dark waves he preferred to wear knotted at the base of his neck. And how similar were their half smiles? Those smirks I so often found both endearing and infuriating. But it was Mia's eyes that held the truth, her piercing irises that I had once wished nothing more than to have. Because there were many times that I wanted to be her daughter, in truth—in blood.

The rain continued to blur my vision, but I saw the victory that suddenly shone on Mia's face, and I knew that I had not felt true terror until then.

Bellamy grabbed me, pulling my body behind his as he frantically searched for Malcolm's shadows to return, but I only had eyes for Mia as she crossed her arms and nodded slowly.

"Your parents and I had planned for you to marry Baron. There was never a future in which you did not sit the throne, but I will not pretend like things were not made easier when that demon king came and stole my son as so-called retribution. Though, I do miss Florencia and Herberto." The words held little emotion, as if the death of my parents was an inconvenience at best. A tear slipped down my cheek, merging with the rain. "Lo and behold, you still found a way into the arms of my darling son."

"You are not my mother! A mother would have never let me be mutilated and tortured!" Voice breaking, his fingers tightened around mine, but all I could think was that it was simply another lie. Bellamy's discretion I could reason within my mind. I knew he wanted me to have the chance to heal. I knew Pino warned him to maintain certain secrets. I knew he loved me. But Mia and Xavier? They had allowed me to feel the guilt of being the sole survivor of a demon attack. Every day for two centuries they allowed me to wallow in the pain of something so tragic. Worse, they knew their son had been taken, and they did nothing to help him. "I could not even talk or walk. I was a youngling. I was *innocent!*"

That was when Malcolm made his reappearance, shadows forming chains as he swung towards Bellamy. My prince dodged them, sliding left and summoning his own shadows—the darkness merging with his fire. The Fire power he got from his father.

They fought, and in the distance, the drums of battle came in the form of pounding feet and furious shouts. As the two princes of Eoforhild clashed, so did the demons, the fae, and the mortals. All the while, I was left to listen as Mia casually spoke once more.

"No, Baron, you were nothing."

Losing your mind is a strange thing. Like watching all reasonable thoughts flee your consciousness. Which was exactly what happened then, the insult to Bellamy's worth the final nail in the coffin I would surely put Mia in tonight.

Running, I screamed as I ripped a sword from the hand of a dead Golden Guard. With the best swing I could muster, I aimed for Mia's neck. Her laugh came and went, cut off as I yelled with anger at the way my blade got stuck in the shield of mud she had crafted.

"Do you think that I did not train? I was a princess once, too." She laughed again, her lips forming a mockery of the soft smile I once knew and worshiped.

"Funny, because you did not train me at all. Some princess I must have been." I was inches away from landing a kick to her stomach before she stopped me with a large rock, the chunk of earth making me cry out in pain.

"You did not need to train!" she shouted, blocking every blow as if it were nothing, the mud hardening beneath my steel. "Your magic is unlike anything this world has ever seen. You do not require a sword because you *are* the sword! Do not let some male convince you otherwise!"

This time, my weapon could not be freed from the thick brown liquid, stuck in place before being yanked from my hands. Mia caught it, twirling the blade in her hand and then pointing it at my throat. I stilled, only the sound of the two separate battles at my back combating the silence.

"I promised that you would only know death until you returned home to me, and as you are well aware, I keep my promises," she hissed, her clenched teeth and lifted lips crafting a brand new smile—one that would scare even the most wicked souls in the Underworld. "Malcolm!"

Turning, I caught sight of Bellamy as he beat down Malcolm's shadows, using both magic and power to tear them apart. And though Malcolm had clearly been losing the fight, he still managed to portal away. Disappearing from Bellamy's side only to return to mine moments later with a chained male at his feet.

My scream of horror hurt even my own ears.

Diving, I was midair when a slab of rock hit me, sending my body careening in the opposite direction. My back made contact with Bellamy's chest, his shadows still dissipating from portaling, and we both crashed to the ground from the momentum. Groaning, I rolled from my back to my stomach, needing to get to them before—

"I told you, Asher. Come home or watch it all wither." She feigned sadness, the despair for what she supposedly had to do a farce I once would have blindly believed. The sword that was in my hands moments ago was now gliding through the air, drawn to the flesh it would call home. I screamed in horror as it stabbed into Jasper's stomach, his shrieks muffled by the cloth over his mouth and the chain around his throat. "You made your choice."

Malcolm let Jasper fall, his screams growing louder when he hit the ground. Somewhere in the distance, a male wailed in agony. A soulmate who felt his other half dying.

Farai's shouts of grief and loss reminded me so much of Ranbir's that my eyes clenched shut. I let myself remember it, allowing that sorrow to fill me for a moment. When I opened my eyes, I was moving for Jasper. Bellamy shouted my name, but then I heard him take off in a run too. The two of us charged forward—both without the energy to really do so, but neither willing to back down. Bellamy took Mia this time, using his Earth power against hers. The ground shook at our feet, thorned vines and boulders flying through the air. Malcolm laughed as I ran for him, not even bothering to lift his dagger.

What little magic I had left tried and failed to break past the wall of darkness that protected Malcolm's mind, his forearm blocking my swinging fist. I tried again, swinging up with my free arm, but I was too weak to do much when he stopped me again and smacked me across the face. I winced but took the opportunity of his smug inattention to grab his shoulders and lift my knee, connecting with his groin. He cried out in pain, his eyes wide with surprise as he fell to the ground. I leapt onto him, straddling his waist the same as I had Lara so long ago. Like then, I did not hold back as I rained the wrath of a million souls upon him. My fists hit and hit and hit, the male laughing when his head smacked the mud for what had to be the nineteenth time. When he reached up and caught both my wrists, I screamed. And then his head pitched forward, cracking into mine. Again, my cries of pain slipped past my lips.

I stood as fast as I could, lifting my foot and slamming it down into his face. Once, twice, thrice. He did not move, but I knew he was not dead. This, though, bought me the time I needed. I scrambled to Jasper, falling to his side and trying to see how badly he was bleeding through the rain. My fingers touched the sword, and he yelped, pale skin going green from the pain.

With little knowledge on how to fix him, I reached up and gently removed the cloth. He breathed deeply, wincing when the act moved the blade within his stomach. Tears ran down my cheeks, tickling as they mixed with the rain drops.

"You will not die, Jasper. Do you understand me? Farai is here, waiting for you. So, you will live, and you will go to him." I spoke the words between heavy breaths, my mind racing to come up with a solution I would not find.

"I am scared, Ash." We both broke down then, our sorrow and fear taking center stage. Jasper reached up, placing a hand around my neck as tears ran down his cheeks. But it was not the finale. No, we were at the penultimate chapter. Behind me, the true ending began.

Sensing him there, as I always did, my head whipped around. I watched in horror as Bellamy got up off the ground, his nose bleeding and one of his arms hanging limply at his side. Mia was not much better, her black leathers stained and her hair caked in mud. She, too, bled. Her cheek leaked red, her throat sprouting bruises where Bellamy must have choked her with something. Preparing to jump to my feet, I readied the last dregs of my magic.

As Bellamy braced himself again, Malcolm appeared at my side and grabbed me by my hair, yanking me downwards so hard that some of the strands ripped free. I screamed out, falling back and causing Jasper's grip to snag on my necklace and the silver chain to break. Bellamy's eyes locked on mine, and I watched his focus crumble. At the same moment, I heard Mia cackle, and when my eyes turned, they caught sight of a small log spearing towards the distracted prince.

My fingers went to Malcolm's eyes, my feet pushed me up, and my legs carried me forward, all of it happening so quickly that I did not quite understand what the sting was at first.

But when I looked down to find the wood sticking out of my stomach, the realization hit. Bellamy was only a couple of feet from me, his face contorted in horror at the sight of me. My hands flew to the wood, holding it still to combat the pain that would otherwise consume me.

"No!" he screamed, running towards me.

Above us, the thunder had gone quiet, the lightning absent. Even the rain had slowed to a drizzle. It allowed for everything to be seen in grim clarity. My resolve both crumpled and rebuilt itself, and I knew what needed to be done.

For the first—and likely last—time, I shattered Bellamy's mental shields, dousing his flames with every bit of magic I could call onto. My desperate determination was likely the only reason it worked. I shrieked in pain as I gave all I had to the task, my chest hollowing out and my heart racing. He reared back, stunned by the action. My focus remained on him, even as Malcolm and Mia slowly closed in.

As if to taunt us.

Stay where you are.

His feet stilled, the horror on his face also permeating the air as he looked at me in disbelief. "Ash?"

"Bell," I sobbed, my blood soaking my hands and my legs threatening to give out.

He cried out too, raising his good hand as if what was left of his magic and power could help me. Nothing could help me.

Do not move.

The betrayal on his face then would haunt me for the rest of my short life.

I am so sorry, Bell. So, so sorry that I did not love you the way you deserved.

"Asher, do not do this. Do not fucking say goodbye to me right now!" The scream was louder now that the storm had passed, allowing

OF REALMS AND CHAOS

that plea to be heard by both Mia and Malcolm—the former laughing maniacally at his request before ceasing her movements. She put a hand out to Malcolm, stilling him. Those eyes, eerily similar to Bellamy's, watched us in fascination.

Before you, I was drowning, slowly losing myself to the current. I was the daughter of a cold and unforgiving sea, more alone than I realized.

Another sob racked through him, tears streaming down his face as he fought and fought against my magic. My vision blurred, his face doubling and even tripling before going back to clarity once more.

Then you came to me, a beacon of fire and light, floating above the water like a lifeline. You led me out and gave me a new family, one full of love and warmth. You saw a lost soul, twin to your own, and taught me to dream. You took me by the hand and showed me what it was to fly. To live.

Mia remained still, her body unmoving in my peripheral. Perhaps this was her giving me a final goodbye, the last scraps of her supposed affections for me.

"Please, Ash! Please choose me! Just this one time, fucking choose *me!*" Bellamy's face filled with streaks of black as he begged, his magic as desperate as he was. My heart slowed, giving up just as I had. Broken, so broken.

I am choosing you, Bell. For once, I am. Do not let them win this. Live.

"I will not let you go! I will fight this, and I will kill them!" He thrashed, his body jerking as he attempted to throw his mental shields back up. But I would not give in, not this time.

Though I knew he would probably hate me for it, I allowed my mental voice to lower, deepening the tenor to that of The Manipulator.

"Hello, old friend," I thought as she surfaced within me.

Here is what you are going to do. You will go to the others, eliminate the remaining fae, and begin portaling them home. You will not come looking for me. You will not save me. You are going to stay in Eoforhild and strategize. You will win this war, even if that means facing off against me on the battlefield. Even if that means killing me.

Bellamy roared with fury, his eyes beginning to glaze over as my orders took hold. As his will and autonomy slipped out of his grasp.

"Asher, stop! Please! I can fix this!" he sobbed, the sound of him begging finally bringing my knees down. I crashed into the mud, feeling myself fade away.

"Take Jasper to Ranbir—to Farai. Take him home. And Wrath, too. Bury him in Haven beside Winona. She would have loved him. They can keep each other safe now."

From the corner of my eye, I saw Mia wave Malcolm forward. He stalked towards us, his eyes looking at Bellamy—who remained rooted to the spot, still valiantly trying to break my hold on him.

"I love you, Bellamy."

Now, go. Take them all and go.

With a final scream of rage, The Elemental, the heir of Eoforhild, General Ayad, the lost fae prince...the love of my life portaled to Jasper, the two disappearing a moment later.

I gasped when Malcolm's hand landed on my shoulder, his other gripping the log still protruding from my stomach. "This is going to hurt, pretty thing."

CHAPTER FORTY-NINE

STASSI

He was on edge.

Well, he was always on edge, but there was something particularly unsettling about it today. His hair was disheveled, like he'd been restlessly running his hands through it. Worse, he was *pacing*.

"I found her."

He stopped mid-step, his body stiffening. Because it was quite clear I didn't have her. Turning away from me, he faced the painting, eyeing it with what I could only assume was longing.

"Yet you didn't bring her to me." There it was, the disappointment in his scolding tone. If I didn't love him like family, if he wasn't all I had, I would surely rip his heart out.

Sol would have. She was always quick to put him in his place. And perhaps little sister would have, too. Though she'd been more tame in her desire to steady him. Until her mind drifted elsewhere, that was.

Oh, how I missed them. Desperately so.

"She didn't want to come, so I didn't force her." Making my way to his side, I hoped to better understand his desire for her, his need to have her. Beyond obsession, I feared there was no reason. His gaze remained fixed on the art, unable to look away.

"Yet you endangered her by siccing one of *my* creatures on her." His tone was curt, body tensing as he attempted to calm his fury. Refusing to apologize, I lifted my chin and squared my shoulders. I had nothing to be sorry for. Not when I did what needed to be done. Huffing, he continued, "No matter, soon she'll be at my side. I still can't leave with how precarious things are, so I need you to go get her and bring her home."

Finally, he faced me, those violet eyes alight with desperation. I'd seen them like that before, and I had lost one of my best friends because of it.

"Those sycophants want her too, and they have one of Asta's descendants helping them." They would be a problem. Just based on her bloodied and bruised appearance earlier, I knew it to be true. If they got their hands on her, it would be much easier to convince her to follow me, though. Something to consider.

"Disgusting. I still can't believe she sullied herself." Crossing his arms, he scowled at the space to my left, clearly thinking of his lost love. The one who, in the end, didn't choose him. Bitterness like his festered until it killed, and I wondered silently if he would be able to revive himself after it did.

"Is it any different than what you're doing?"

Than what I want to do with my creature?

"Yes. Asher's different. She's…special." That so-called specialness was why she was in danger, why so many wished to steal pieces of her. Something as remarkable as her magic would leave her shredded and broken, a mess of scraps. Being coveted would do that to someone.

"I don't think she wants to be here, Padon." I sighed into the words, slouching by his side. I held no love for the bratty mortal princess, but I also knew what it was like to watch someone slowly rot after dying from the suffocation of the emperor's love. Seeing that again wasn't something I desired.

"Go back and get her. We can keep her safe here. Likho misses her, and he has declared her his. They will bond, and then she can play piano and read and rule. She'll be happy, Anastasia."

We remained silent for a few minutes, staring up at the painting of Asher that sat above his bed. She was quite beautiful, but nothing extraordinary. Nothing like Asta had been.

"She'll choose me. We were meant for each other." This time, both hands went to his head, tousling his hair and rubbing at his face. Oh yes, fate so clearly was on their side.

"And if she doesn't?"

"She will."

"And if The Elemental doesn't let her?" Questions like that weren't meant to be spoken out loud, and I felt the way it racked through his body, the rage that followed strong enough to shake the ground beneath our feet. Somewhere beyond these walls, things were surely dying.

"Then I'll burn their entire miserable world to the ground! I don't know what Char was thinking when he and Sol left, but Stella breathed magic into those filthy creatures for him. For his memory. It all began with his insatiable curiosity. I won't make the same mistakes they did. I won't allow my Asher to make the same mistakes they did."

"I hope your pitch for her is better than that because you sound crazy." Despite myself, I laughed openly, trying to combat the sorrow that the thought of Stella and her family brought me.

"Oh, I have something much better than a *pitch*. Go to Jesre and tell her to ready Likho. Provide him with Asher's location once you find her. I want to give my future queen a gift."

With that, the holder of Death and Creation walked away.

CHAPTER FIFTY

HENRY

My heart raced and my head swam as I stumbled my way through the infirmary. Every step felt like walking through sludge, the hollowness in my chest like a black hole seeking energy to replace the magic I had depleted.

Still, I pushed on, seeking out those faces that would tell me my family was okay. The once-white room was drenched in dirt and blood, screams and cries echoing—reverberating death, a reminder that I fucking failed.

Asher's magic still whispered into my ear, as if I could not quite shake it from my mind. She had shattered my shields so easily, leaving me a weak and pathetic lump of flesh and bone in the mud. Stella save us all

591

when she comes in here. This loss would devastate her more than any of us, as every death did.

My eyes landed on Noe, her body hunched forward but relatively unscathed. She was taking on a slightly green hue and her head seemed to sway back and forth. We would all suffer for taking it so far. Magic was not priceless, and we were paying every coin one by one.

A medic held down Queen Shah, her writhing body forcing another demon to come and help. A gash on her cheek oozed red, the one across her stomach revealing insides that I did not know the name of. Despite the agonizing pain she had to be in, the queen still screamed demands. "Get off of me! That is my kingdom! I am a queen! I will save them or die on the soil I was born upon! Get off of me!"

Her shrill shouts drew the attention of Lian, who was not far away holding the hand of a mortal male who was quite clearly dead. Even when the Air got up and rushed towards Shah, I stared into the dead man's unseeing eyes, my heart stuttering and my stomach turning. Gods, we had led so many to their deaths.

I stumbled on, looking for Bell or Ash, needing to see them alive and well. Bellamy had portaled to the battle already far more broken and bloody than he had been when I first lost consciousness. His arm hung limp at his side, his head sporting a barely healed gash. He was so far gone that I was surprised when he grabbed a sword and started efficiently tearing down fae after fae, doing more work than five of us demons combined. Whatever had him so enraged was clearly heavy, and since I had not found Ash…well, I needed to make sure I saw her annoying smile and heard her bratty voice.

Damon was off in the far right corner, Ranbir bent forward over a male I had never seen before. His long black hair was knotted and his cream tunic was stained red over his stomach. His pale skin was gray, as if he had been long dead when Ranbir began healing him. But I saw his chest rise and fall, which meant whoever the male was lived.

BREA LAMB

Aching joints protested within my legs as I walked on, making my way to the trio. Damon caught sight of me, walking quickly towards me and reaching for my arm to sling it over his shoulder. I was at least six inches taller than him, so he was forced to bear more of my weight than normal in order to assist me, but he did not complain as he walked us forward.

Ranbir's power flowed into the male, an extraordinary sight I would likely never grow used to witnessing in real time. The gaping wound that looked like a clean jab of a sword slowly stitched together, the sides kissing one another hello. The Healer held on long after the completion of the process, bringing back the slightly pink tint of the male's skin and healing what looked like chain marks upon his wrists and neck. When his eyes opened, revealing brown irises surrounded by red, we all flinched. The male shot up, groaning from the exertion but unwilling to rest as he scanned the area desperately. As he moved, his long black hair snagged behind his ear, revealing pointed tips.

A fae. This was a fae.

I drew my remaining dagger, moving in jerky spurts that had my knees hitting the edge of the bed and nausea free climbing up my throat. But I remained on my feet, pressing the tip of the blade into the male's neck as I grabbed the sheets for balance. His already round eyes went wider, his shaking hands splaying as he lifted them in the air.

"Who are you? What is your power? Why have you come?" My questions spilled from my lips, slightly slurred from the magic depletion and the stab wound on my thigh I had not told anyone about. Ranbir's tired eyes formed slits, scanning me up and down as if he knew. His hand shot out, gripping my wrist and pulling it away from the fae. I felt his power surge through me, stinging as it traveled to the wound on my thigh and slowly spread throughout my body.

The little shit always knew.

"I am Jasper Cromwell. I mean no harm. Asher, she is my best friend. She saved me. They—they brought me, and I could not help. I—I

593

need my husband. Please, help me find him. We must leave—Ash—my Ash—please, I need to help her—I need—"

Damon's hand swung out, connecting with the fae's face and forcing it to whip left.

I smirked as Ranbir freed me, pointing his finger at Damon as if to scold him. But at least he knocked some sense into the rambling fool. A moment later, his words settled, and I realized what he was implying. I dropped my dagger, freeing my hands to grip onto the fae's tunic.

"What do you mean she saved you and you could not help? Where is Asher?" I screamed the words into his face, my vision hazy but my voice strong as I shook the male.

Ranbir began shouting for Farai, Damon's hypocritical ass trying to tug me away from Jasper, but I could do nothing other than attempt to force the answers from the idiot before me. Jasper did not fight back, instead letting tears fall down his face as he seemed to welcome my rage.

Farai's yelled pleas could suddenly be heard, begging me to let go of his husband as he ran our way. When I did not let go, a flash of pale and brown skin came barreling towards me. The Shifter's body collided with mine, sending us both to the ground. I maintained my hold on his husband, bringing him down with us. More shouting ensued, somehow louder than the shrieks of the injured and dying. I released my hold with a hiss of pain as Farai slammed his elbow into my forearm.

"Bell! Bell!" He needed to know. I needed his help. Gods above, I sounded like fucking Jasper.

Farai rolled, getting on top of me and latching his hands around my throat. His face was wild, a sense of hopelessness and fear in his eyes that I had seen when we found his home empty. Fist swinging, I connected with his jaw, trying to get him off me so I could defuse the situation I had started. My magic did not so much as stir in my chest, the remaining dregs unwilling to let go when it meant my death. So I used my hands, striking him in the side and then bringing my knee up to slide my foot between us. I kicked out, sending him flying into a wall in between two occupied beds.

Fire erupted to my left, causing screams of panic to replace our grunts of exertion. Bellamy stood not five feet away, staring forward like he saw a ghost, the dead look in his eyes telling me that Asher was truly in trouble—or worse, dead.

"Bell?" I asked, rolling to my stomach and groaning as I pushed myself up to my knees.

Bellamy did not move, his hands still lit up in red and orange flames. We all gawked as he remained still, his injuries from the battle still unhealed and his Fire power forcing smoke into the air.

That was when I smelled it. There was no mistaking the scent of burning flesh, it was never something one freed themselves of.

I lept to my feet, rushing towards the male who I had considered a brother for nearly two centuries. He did not so much as blink at my approach. With more horror in my veins than magic, I looked down at his hands to see them slowly blistering, his armor melting into his skin and the hair on his arms burning away. Despite that, Bellamy showed no sign that he could even feel the pain of it.

"Bellamy, you have to tell me what is happening right now." Silence. Even the screaming seemed to quiet down as we all waited for the prince to speak. With shaking hands, I reached up and placed my palms on his scalding pale cheeks. Gods, he was going to kill himself with that fire if he did not stop. "Little brother, I need you to let me help you."

A screech sounded to my right, and I barely ducked in time to avoid the coming raven as it flew in my direction. Someone screamed when it circled low, demons and mortals alike panicking at the sight of a mere bird. It came towards me, flapping giant black wings slowly to hover over me. I released Bellamy from my hold, catching a small piece of parchment as the bird dropped it. Before I could even read it, the bird was off, flying back to its master. Whoever that might be.

Bellamy had finally moved, his fire extinguished and his eyes trained on the parchment. Waiting. He was waiting.

Taking a fortifying breath, I slowly untied the string and unrolled the letter.

Captain Henry Nash,

First of all, if you harm Jasper or Farai again, I will seek out every single future in which you suffer a horrifying death and personally select the worst. Then I will ensure it is the only future possible for you. Do not underestimate how far I will go to keep my family safe.

Now that we have that business out of the way, tell the Healer to help Asher's prince. Then I need you to follow these instructions word for word.

I gasped at the writing upon the page, reading with renewed terror. Without a second thought, I skipped past the detailed orders the sender had written, letting my gaze roam to the perfectly scrawled signature at the bottom. Though the threat made me realize who had sent the raven, her name at the bottom still made my heart plummet into my stomach.

Nicola Salvatore

EPILOGUE

In a hallway void of light and warmth and joy, a broken princess was held up only by the arms of two males.

On her left was a traitor, one who gave up everything for a love that did not exist. His eyes of black stared forward, recalling a time it was his sister he carried to her death. Remembering the feel of her blood on his hands as she died. Though the barely conscious princess wore a thick band of leather around her neck, one with runes that glowed as they siphoned her magic from her, even she could feel the conflict that radiated from him. The regret.

On her right was a deceiver, one who gave up everything for vengeance that he would never have. His eyes of brown, eyes that were not truly his, stared down at her. His mind raced with memories of her denial, of her refusal, of her dismissal. Perhaps he understood where he went wrong, but there was no sorrow within him for the princess to sense. Only smug arrogance. For the male, with golden curls that he had only known a year, thought he had won.

Maybe he had.

As the princess's feet dragged across the stone floors, the wound on her stomach only just healed, she wondered how long it would be before death claimed her. Her mind wandered to the statue depicting the God of Death and Creation then to his true face and name. Would he doom her to the Underworld as payback for leaving him? Or had the place she had gone been the Underworld all along? It was where all wicked souls went, after all.

Try as she might, the princess feared that she was too far gone for redemption.

What the princess did not know was that her story, though tragic, had not been in vain. Whether or not she lived to see that was still to be determined.

The two males continued to pull her along, taking her deeper into the abyss that lurked beneath a gilded island. When they slowed, the Princess forced her head up, those stormy eyes locking with the warmest brown irises she had ever seen.

Behind the iron bars sat a man, his clothes torn and stained but body free of dirt and grime. It was as if he had just been afforded a bath—as if he were being prepared.

The princess let out a gasp of surprise, her mind unable to comprehend what she was seeing. Who could blame her when little sense could be made of it?

The two males opened the cage beside his, and then they shoved her, watching as she flew to the ground with enough force to tear a cry of pain from her. Still, her gaze remained fixed on the prisoner to her right, who was scrambling towards her in a panic.

"Asher! Asher, are you okay?" Terror pinched his handsome features, those full lips and that petite nose so like his sister's. In fact, there within the depths of those brown eyes were flecks of green, so similar to the bratty woman. The princess could find no words but one, the same that she had once used like a curse. As his warm pale hand met her cheek through the bars, the princess spoke.

"Sterling?"

Behind them, a Shifter loomed, his laugh wicked and vindictive in its shrillness. The princess turned, her eyes wide as she watched the male who had touched her and kissed her and threatened her morph. The thick blonde curls flattened, turning a muddy brown color. His once-pale skin deepened, taking on a shade of creamy brown. Those eyes, the ones that stared at her in her nightmares, lightened, a deep blue replacing the brown. Before her now stood a male she had not seen since Academy.

An immensely strong Multiple smiled down at the female he had long dreamed of holding. One he had wanted since he was only twelve years old. The very female who had rejected him time and time again, only to find herself at his mercy now.

"Hello, Ash." The Multiple leaned forward, wrapping his hands around the bars and leaning his head against the metal. The princess recoiled, her eyes switching between the fae in front of her and the mortal beside her. Panic began to consume her, to remind her of all that she lost and all that she would lose still. In her state, she did not notice the traitor demon disappear in a cloud of darkness, nor did she witness when he reappeared, a golden queen now at his side. "I think I did quite well. The only thing I got wrong was his height, but you did not seem to realize. Not that I blame you. The two of you only met, what, twice?"

"Once," the true prince beside her corrected with a growl.

His accent was twin to his sister's, just slightly less formal than his parents'. Despite her horror, the princess silently chastised herself for not noticing before. For not putting together the pieces of the puzzle she had been given over the last year.

Before the princess could respond, the sound of heels meeting stone sounded from down the hall, lilac flooding the air. The queen, with her icy blue eyes and her bright orange hair, strutted forward, a smile contorting her face. There was no love in that expression, but perhaps there was some in those eyes. A love that was dangerous, for it brought nothing other than violence and desperation.

"Asher, I know this is a lot to take in, but you will have time to chit chat with Theon later. It is important we get this out of the way. Vital, even. You cannot go on without learning what consequences await your disobedience." It was a tone of indifference—of finality.

"No, do not touch her!" The prince latched onto the princess's wrist, tugging her further into the bars, as if he could somehow spare her. He thought of the death angel who visited him. Stassi, she had called herself. She would save them. He knew it. As long as he kept the princess safe, then they would live.

"Malcolm, take care of that." The queen ordered with a flick of her wrist.

A deep cloud of black shadows fell upon the mortal prince. From it, the demon came. He held the mortal's hands behind his back, yanking his hair and forcing him to watch as the queen approached the princess.

"Remember, my flower, I do this because I care." From the queen's hand, a vine formed, small at first. Then it grew, finger-length thorns popping through the thick green plant. The princess watched, her eyes slowly dulling. She bent forward, bringing her knees to her chest and wrapping her arms around her legs.

The princess felt the hopelessness and resigned herself to whatever came next. At least she had saved the ones she loved, she thought. When the princess tucked her chin, shielding her face, the queen spoke one last time.

"I love you, Asher."

And then the queen lifted the vine, snapping it forward until it made contact with the princess's back. A nearly silent cry escaped the princess's lips, but before anyone could speak, the queen brought the vine down again. And again. And again. Each strike cut through the bandages that wrapped around the princess's torso, shredding the final barrier that protected her skin.

The mortal prince jerked forward, trying to fight off the demon behind him to no avail. "Asher, hold on! Please, stop! Stop hurting her! Torture me instead! Please! Asher, hold on—hold on a little longer! Please!"

The Shifter walked into the mortal's cage, covering his mouth and holding his jaw firmly in place. Tears ran down the prince's cheeks, just as they did the princess's—who remained nearly silent as her skin split and her blood flowed.

She was dying. She knew it, just as the others did. A part of her was thankful. What a heavy life it had been. Too heavy. Maybe this would be better. Death...it was a gift that she would accept. Her love—the prince of flame, water, air, and earth—would succeed. She had faith in that.

As the queen lifted her arm, poised to dole out the twentieth lashing, the princess had one final thought. Five whispered words slipped through her lips before her eyes closed and she went silent.

"May I return to Eternity."

LOVELY READER,

YOU ARE NO ONE'S BUT YOUR OWN.

ACKNOWLEDGMENTS

Another book, another section of thanking people who deserve so much more than I can begin to offer. Every single reader has my entire heart, and there is not a day that goes by that I am not grateful that you chose my world to escape into. There is no way for me to express my gratitude to each of you, but know that my love for you is endless.

With that being said, I want to first thank my mother. As always, this book would not exist if you had not fostered the passion that grew in me from a young age. You read my stories and listened to my ideas and encouraged my dreams. To you, I owe it all.

To my husband, who has believed in me and stood by my side as I fought for my aspirations to be reality, I thank you always. Every rant and rave and risk was taken in stride by your never ending support and faith in my ability. My love for you is as infinite as Asher's for Bellamy. In this life and every one after, I will choose you.

To my sons, who I hope do not ever read this, thank you for being so proud of me. Your constant praise of a book that you have not—and ideally will not—read is truly so touching. I strive to make you proud in all that I do, and I hope that you continue to look at me with wide eyes and clapping hands. More than that, I can't wait to eventually read those stories you both tell me you will write one day.

To my wonderful critique partners, Jenessa and Allie, thank you for making this story what it is. Without you, I fear I would have lost my way. I think there is something special about having two people guide you through your story, helping you navigate and perfect it. I owe you so much, but for now, know that this book would be nothing without you both.

To Lyra, who never fails to expertly dive into and dissect Asher, thank you for reminding me constantly that her story matters. Never have I had a reader, or anyone other than me, understand Ash to the extent with which you do. For you, I dedicate her, because I think there is no one more deserving.

Finally, to my beta and arc readers, your support throughout the final stages of this book was so deeply appreciated. You all have truly changed this novel and made it what it is. As Asher says, time is the most valuable currency, and it is hard to explain just how much it means to me that you chose to spend your time on my art. I am forever thankful.

About the Author

Brea has been obsessively reading for as long as she can remember, consuming any and all books she could get her hands on. Thus sparked the dream of creating something similar—a book that would make readers cry and laugh and smile and feel all those big emotions that she did. At nine-years-old, she wrote her first book. Over the years she would write many more, but it was not until Of Night and Blood that she finally felt the book she dreamed of writing had come to life.

She spends her time working with the blind and low vision community, advocating for human rights, drinking too much coffee, chasing around her toddlers, and ordering new books for her endless TBR. She lives with her spouse, their two children, and their dog.

AUTHOR'S NOTE

Asher's story contains many heavy topics. I hold her dear to my heart as she has lived through much of what I have. Most of my life I have struggled with the concept of worth and how it is measured. Like Asher, I needed to learn that I was no one's but my own, and that my worth was mine and mine alone to determine. With all of my heart I desire each and every one of you to know the same thing.

That being said, I know these themes can be hard to read, especially for those of us who have had similar life experiences to Asher. However, I truly hope that as you follow her journey, you find solace in her resilience. Just like Noe, I hope you face your evils and win.

For those who are surviving similar struggles and need aid, I encourage you to reach out to your local or national crisis hotline. If you are in the United States, visit www.988lifeline.org/chat to immediately get into contact with a crisis support specialist. You can also text or call 988.

You are not alone, and you are worthy of life. All my love.

Made in United States
Troutdale, OR
12/04/2024

25828134R10386